PUFFIN CLASSICS

Peter Pan

Once again the stars blew the window open, and that smallest star of all called out:

'Cave, Peter!'

Then Peter knew that there was not a moment to lose. 'Come,' he cried imperiously, and soared out at once into the night followed by John and Michael and Wendy.

Mr and Mrs Darling and Nana rushed into the nursery too late. The birds were flown.

J. M. BARRIE

Peter Pan

INTRODUCED BY
TONY DiTERLIZZI

PUFFIN

PUFFIN BOOKS

Published by the Penguin Group
Penguin Books Ltd, 80 Strand, London WC2R 0RL, England
Penguin Group (USA) Inc., 375 Hudson Street, New York, New York 10014, USA
Penguin Group (Canada), 90 Eglinton Avenue East, Suite 700, Toronto, Ontario, Canada M4P 2Y3
(a division of Pearson Penguin Canada Inc.)
Penguin Ireland, 25 St Stephen's Green, Dublin 2, Ireland (a division of Penguin Books Ltd)
Penguin Group (Australia), 250 Camberwell Road, Camberwell, Victoria 3124, Australia
(a division of Pearson Australia Group Pty Ltd)
Penguin Books India Pvt Ltd, 11 Community Centre, Panchsheel Park, New Delhi – 110 017, India
Penguin Group (NZ), 67 Apollo Drive, Rosedale, North Shore 0632, New Zealand
(a division of Pearson New Zealand Ltd)
Penguin Books (South Africa) (Pty) Ltd, 24 Sturdee Avenue, Rosebank, Johannesburg 2196, South Africa

Penguin Books Ltd, Registered Offices: 80 Strand, London WC2R 0RL, England

puffinbooks.com

First published by Hodder & Stoughton 1911
First published in Puffin Books 1967
Published in this edition 2010

015

Peter Pan published in support of Great Ormond Street Hospital for Children

The information on p.x constitutes an extension of this copyright page

Introduction copyright © Tony DiTerlizzi, 2008
Endnotes copyright © Penguin Books, 2008
All rights reserved

Set in Minion by Palimpsest Book Production Limited, Falkirk, Stirlingshire
Printed in Great Britain by Clays Ltd, St Ives plc

British Library Cataloguing in Publication Data
A CIP catalogue record for this book is available from the British Library

ISBN: 978-0-141-32981-9

www.greenpenguin.co.uk

MIX
Paper from
responsible sources
FSC
www.fsc.org   FSC™ C018179

Penguin Books is committed to a sustainable
future for our business, our readers and our planet.
This book is made from Forest Stewardship
Council™ certified paper.

INTRODUCTION BY
TONY DiTERLIZZI

You know, when I was younger, I never read these sorts of things – these Forewords, Introductions or Prologues. I just wanted to get into the story. I didn't want to read about how some old guy thought that this book changed his life, or some lady felt that this story changed the world. And probably Peter Pan would not have sat through this either if Wendy were reading it to him.

No, I was too eager to look at the intricate illustrations and get into the adventure. Afterwards, I'd be busy thinking of the next book I'd read, or making up stories of my own, or just playing around with my friends and family.

Sometimes I would pretend my bed was a pirate ship and I'd have to fight off my younger brother. He would have to defeat me and throw me off the bed into the hungry sea below. Sometimes I would explore the nearby woods thinking I might just find an ancient arrowhead, or the still-warm camp of reclusive Native American Indians. Other times I found myself wondering if mermaids would enjoy teasing us while we tried to see who could hold their breath longest in a friend's pool. This is why Neverland always seemed so right, so accurate, when it was first read to me. I had been there so many times and knew it inside and out, as I am sure you do.

And, like millions of other kids, I also knew Peter Pan very well. He was the one I longed to be: the crocodile tracker, the fairy's friend, the leader of the Lost Boys and, of course, the slayer of dreaded pirates. But I was just a kid who liked exploring the flora and fauna of Neverland and recording them in my own little stories, hoping that one day I may be able to capture the magic of one as gifted as J. M. Barrie.

If you are reading this tale of Peter and Neverland, or (better yet) having it read to you for the first time, then you will know exactly all the wondrous things that J. M. Barrie writes about. That's because almost all children know how to fly, know that fairies are real, and know that Peter will rescue them when they need rescuing.

Sadly, like Peter himself, most of our childhood memories begin to fade and drift off as we get older. The newspapers remind us daily of all the reasons why being a 'responsible adult' seems to be our only aspiration in life. Thankfully, stories like the one you are about to embark upon remind us of what is important. And, even if you can no longer remember how to fly to Neverland, Peter Pan will always come to rescue you if you want him to. All you have to do is believe.

Now look what I have done: I have gone on and on about how this very story changed me and could save society as a whole. You don't need to read my ramblings, you need to get on with your adventure. Go on! Get going! You already know the way – Second to the right, and straight on till morning, you can't miss it.

. . . And tell Peter 'Hi' from me – not that he'll remember.

Contents

Contents

THE PETER PAN BEQUEST

In 1929 J. M. Barrie donated all rights in *Peter Pan* to Great Ormond Street Children's Hospital. In 1987, fifty years after Barrie's death, copyright expired under UK law. However, the following year a unique Act of Parliament restored royalty income from all versions of *Peter Pan* to the hospital, which means that very sick children there will continue to benefit from J. M. Barrie's generous gift for as long as the hospital exists.

1

Peter Breaks Through

All children, except one, grow up. They soon know that they will grow up, and the way Wendy knew was this. One day when she was two years old she was playing in a garden, and she plucked another flower and ran with it to her mother. I suppose she must have looked rather delightful, for Mrs Darling put her hand to her heart and cried, 'Oh, why can't you remain like this for ever!' This was all that passed between them on the subject, but henceforth Wendy knew that she must grow up. You always know after you are two. Two is the beginning of the end.

Of course they lived at 14, and until Wendy came her mother was the chief one. She was a lovely lady, with a romantic mind and such a sweet mocking mouth. Her romantic mind was like the tiny boxes, one within the other, that come from the puzzling East, however many you discover there is always one more; and her sweet mocking mouth had one kiss on it that Wendy could never get, though there it was, perfectly conspicuous in the right-hand corner.

The way Mr Darling won her was this: the many gentlemen who had been boys when she was a girl discovered simultaneously that they loved her, and they all ran to her house to propose to her except Mr Darling, who took a cab and nipped in first, and so he got her. He got all of her, except the innermost box and the kiss. He never knew about the box, and in time he gave up trying for the kiss. Wendy thought Napoleon could have got it, but I can picture him trying, and then going off in a passion, slamming the door.

Mr Darling used to boast to Wendy that her mother not only loved him but respected him. He was one of those deep ones who know about stocks and shares. Of course no one really knows, but he quite seemed to know, and he often said stocks were up and shares were down in a way that would have made any woman respect him.

Mrs Darling was married in white, and at first she kept the books perfectly, almost gleefully, as if it were a game, not so much as a brussels sprout was missing; but by and by whole cauliflowers dropped out, and instead of them there were pictures of babies without faces. She drew them when she should have been totting up. They were Mrs Darling's guesses.

Wendy came first, then John, then Michael.

For a week or two after Wendy came it was doubtful whether they would be able to keep her, as she was another mouth to feed. Mr Darling was frightfully proud of her, but he was very honourable, and he sat on the edge of Mrs Darling's bed, holding her hand and calculating expenses, while she looked at him imploringly. She wanted to risk it, come what might, but that was not his way; his way was with a pencil and a piece of paper, and if she confused him with suggestions he had to begin at the beginning again.

'Now don't interrupt,' he would beg of her. 'I have one pound seventeen here, and two and six at the office; I can cut off my coffee at the office, say ten shillings, making two nine and six, with your eighteen and three makes three nine seven, with five naught naught in my cheque-book makes eight nine seven – who is that moving? – eight nine seven, dot and carry seven – don't speak, my own – and the pound you lent to that man who came to the door – quiet, child – dot and carry child – there, you've done it! – did I say nine nine seven? yes, I said nine nine seven; the question is, can we try it for a year on nine nine seven?'

'Of course we can, George,' she cried. But she was prejudiced in Wendy's favour, and he was really the grander character of the two.

'Remember mumps,' he warned her almost threateningly and off he went again. 'Mumps one pound, that is what I have put down, but I dare say it will be more like thirty shillings – don't speak – measles one five, German measles half a guinea, makes two fifteen six – don't waggle your finger – whooping-cough, say fifteen shillings' – and so on it went, and it added up differently each time; but at last Wendy just got through, with mumps reduced to twelve six, and the two kinds of measles treated as one.

There was the same excitement over John, and Michael had even a narrower squeak; but both were kept, and soon you might have seen the three of them going in a row to Miss Fulsom's Kindergarten school, accompanied by their nurse.

Mrs Darling loved to have everything just so, and Mr Darling had a passion for being exactly like his neighbours; so, of course, they had a nurse. As they were poor, owing to the amount of milk the children drank, this nurse was a prim Newfoundland dog, called Nana, who had belonged to no one in particular until the Darlings engaged her. She had always thought children important, however, and the Darlings had become acquainted with her in Kensington Gardens, where she spent most of her spare time peeping into perambulators, and was much hated by careless nursemaids, whom she followed to their homes and complained of to their mistresses. She proved to be quite a treasure of a nurse. How thorough she was at bath-time; and up at any moment of the night if one of her charges made the slightest cry. Of course her kennel was in the nursery. She had a genius for knowing when a cough is a thing to have no patience with and when it needs stocking round your throat. She believed to her last day in old-fashioned remedies like rhubarb leaf, and made sounds of contempt over all this new-fangled talk about germs, and so on. It was a lesson in propriety to see her escorting the children to school, walking sedately by their side when they were well behaved, and butting them back into line if they strayed. On John's footer days she never once forgot his sweater, and she usually carried an umbrella in her mouth in case of rain. There is a room in the basement of Miss Fulsom's school where the nurses wait. They sat on forms, while Nana lay on the floor, but that was the only difference. They affected to ignore her as of an inferior social status to themselves, and she despised their light talk. She resented visits to the nursery from Mrs Darling's friends, but if they did come she first whipped off Michael's pinafore and put him into the one with blue braiding, and smoothed out Wendy and made a dash at John's hair.

No nursery could possibly have been conducted more correctly, and Mr Darling knew it, yet he sometimes wondered uneasily whether the neighbours talked.

He had his position in the city to consider.

Nana also troubled him in another way. He had sometimes a feeling that she did not admire him. 'I know she admires you tremendously, George,' Mrs Darling would assure him, and then she would sign to the children to be specially nice to father. Lovely dances followed, in which the only other servant, Liza, was sometimes allowed to join. Such a midget she looked in her long skirt and maid's cap, though she had sworn, when engaged, that she would never see ten again. The gaiety of those romps! And gayest of all was Mrs Darling, who would pirouette so wildly that all you could see of her was the kiss, and then if you had dashed at her you might have got it. There never was a simpler, happier family until the coming of Peter Pan.

Mrs Darling first heard of Peter when she was tidying up her children's minds. It is the nightly custom of every good mother after her children are asleep to rummage in their minds and put things straight for next morning, repacking into their proper places the many articles that have wandered during the day. If you could keep awake (but of course you can't) you would see your own mother doing this, and you would find it very interesting to watch her. It is quite like tidying up drawers. You would see her on her knees, I expect, lingering humorously over some of your contents, wondering where on earth you had picked this thing up, making discoveries sweet and not so sweet, pressing this to her cheek as if it were as nice as a kitten, and hurriedly stowing that out of sight. When you wake in the morning, the naughtiness and evil passions with which you went to bed have been folded up small and placed at the bottom of your mind; and on the top, beautifully aired, are spread out your prettier thoughts, ready for you to put on.

I don't know whether you have ever seen a map of a person's mind. Doctors sometimes draw maps of other parts of you, and your own map can become intensely interesting, but catch them trying to draw a map of a child's mind, which is not only confused, but keeps going round all the time. There are zigzag lines on it, just like your temperature on a card, and these are probably roads in the island; for the Neverland is always more or less an island, with astonishing splashes of colour here and there, and coral reefs and rakish-looking craft in the offing, and savages and lonely lairs, and gnomes who are mostly tailors, and caves through which a river runs, and princes with six elder brothers, and a hut fast going to decay, and one very small old lady with a hooked nose. It would be an easy map if that were all; but there is also first day at school, religion, fathers, the round pond, needlework, murders, hangings, verbs that take the dative, chocolate-pudding day, getting into braces, say ninety-nine, threepence for pulling out your tooth yourself, and so on; and either these are part of the island or they are another map showing through, and it is all rather confusing, especially as nothing will stand still.

Of course the Neverlands vary a good deal. John's, for instance, had a lagoon with flamingoes flying over it at which John was shooting, while Michael, who was very small, had a flamingo with lagoons flying over it. John lived in a boat turned upside down on the sands, Michael in a wigwam, Wendy in a house of leaves deftly sewn

7

together. John had no friends, Michael had friends at night, Wendy had a pet wolf forsaken by its parents; but on the whole the Neverlands have a family resemblance, and if they stood still in a row you could say of them that they have each other's nose, and so forth. On these magic shores children at play are for ever beaching their coracles. We too have been there; we can still hear the sound of the surf, though we shall land no more.

Of all delectable islands the Neverland is the snuggest and most compact; not large and sprawly, you know, with tedious distances between one adventure and another, but nicely crammed. When you play at it by day with the chairs and table-cloth, it is not in the least alarming but in the two minutes before you go to sleep it becomes very nearly real. That is why there are night-lights.

Occasionally in her travels through her children's minds Mrs Darling found things she could not understand, and of these quite the most perplexing was the word Peter. She knew of no Peter, and yet he was here and there in John and Michael's minds, while Wendy's began to be scrawled all over with him. The name stood out in bolder letters than any of the other words, and as Mrs Darling gazed she felt that it had an oddly cocky appearance.

'Yes, he is rather cocky,' Wendy admitted with regret. Her mother had been questioning her.

'But who is he, my pet?'

'He is Peter Pan, you know, mother.'

At first Mrs Darling did not know, but after thinking back into her childhood she just remembered a Peter Pan who was said to live with the fairies. There were odd stories about him; as that when children died he went part of the way with them, so that they should not be frightened. She had believed in him at the time, but now that she was married and full of sense she quite doubted whether there was any such person.

'Besides,' she said to Wendy, 'he would be grown up by this time.'

'Oh no, he isn't grown up,' Wendy assured her confidently, 'and he is just my size.' She meant that he was her size in both mind and body; she didn't know how she knew it, she just knew it.

Mrs Darling consulted Mr Darling, but he smiled pooh-pooh. 'Mark my words,' he said, 'it is some nonsense Nana has been putting into their heads; just the sort of idea a dog would have. Leave it alone, and it will blow over.'

But it would not blow over; and soon the troublesome boy gave Mrs Darling quite a shock.

Children have the strangest adventures without being troubled by them. For instance, they may remember to mention, a week after the event happened, that when they were in the wood they met their dead father and had a game with him. It was in this casual way that Wendy one morning made a disquieting revelation. Some leaves of a tree had been found on the nursery floor, which certainly were not there when the children went to bed, and Mrs Darling was puzzling over them when Wendy said with a tolerant smile:

'I do believe it is that Peter again!'

'Whatever do you mean, Wendy?'

'It is so naughty of him not to wipe,' Wendy said, sighing. She was a tidy child.

She explained in quite a matter-of-fact way that she thought Peter sometimes came to the nursery in the night and sat on the foot of her bed and played on his pipes to her. Unfortunately she never woke, so she didn't know how she knew, she just knew.

'What nonsense you talk, precious. No one can get into the house without knocking.'

'I think he comes in by the window,' she said.

'My love, it is three floors up.'

'Were not the leaves at the foot of the window, mother?'

It was quite true; the leaves had been found very near the window.

Mrs Darling did not know what to think, for it all seemed so natural to Wendy that you could not dismiss it by saying she had been dreaming.

'My child,' the mother cried, 'why did you not tell me of this before?'

'I forgot,' said Wendy lightly. She was in a hurry to get her breakfast.

Oh, surely she must have been dreaming.

But, on the other hand, there were the leaves. Mrs Darling examined them carefully; they were skeleton leaves, but she was sure they did not come from any tree that grew in England. She crawled about the floor, peering at it with a candle for marks of a strange foot. She rattled the poker up the chimney and tapped the walls. She let down a tape from the window to the pavement, and it was a sheer drop of thirty feet, without so much as a spout to climb up by.

Certainly Wendy had been dreaming.

But Wendy had not been dreaming, as the very next night showed, the night on which the extraordinary adventures of these children may be said to have begun.

On the night we speak of all the children were once more in bed. It happened to be Nana's evening off, and Mrs Darling had bathed and sung to them till one by one they had let go her hand and slid away into the land of sleep.

All were looking so safe and cosy that she smiled at her fears now and sat down tranquilly by the fire to sew.

It was something for Michael, who on his birthday was getting into shirts. The fire was warm, however, and the nursery dimly lit by three night-lights and presently the sewing lay on Mrs Darling's lap. Then her head nodded, oh, so gracefully. She was asleep. Look at the four of them, Wendy and Michael over there, John here, and Mrs Darling by the fire. There should have been a fourth night-light.

11

While she slept she had a dream. She dreamt that the Neverland had come too near and that a strange boy had broken through from it. He did not alarm her, for she thought she had seen him before in the faces of many women who have no children. Perhaps he is to be found in the faces of some mothers also. But in her dream he had rent the film that obscures the Neverland, and she saw Wendy and John and Michael peeping through the gap.

The dream by itself would have been a trifle, but while she was dreaming the window of the nursery blew open, and a boy did drop on the floor. He was accompanied by a strange light, no bigger than your fist, which darted about the room like a living thing; and I think it must have been this light that wakened Mrs Darling.

She started up with a cry, and saw the boy, and somehow she knew at once that he was Peter Pan. If you or I or Wendy had been there we should have seen that he was very like Mrs Darling's kiss. He was a lovely boy, clad in skeleton leaves and the juices that ooze out of trees; but the most entrancing thing about him was that he had all his first teeth. When he saw she was a grown-up, he gnashed the little pearls at her.

2

The Shadow

Mrs Darling screamed, and, as if in answer to a bell, the door opened, and Nana entered, returned from her evening out. She growled and sprang at the boy, who leapt lightly through the window. Again Mrs Darling screamed, this time in distress for him, for she thought he was killed, and she ran down into the street to look for his little body, but it was not there; and she looked up, and in the black night she could see nothing but what she thought was a shooting star.

She returned to the nursery, and found Nana with something in her mouth, which proved to be the boy's shadow. As he leapt at the window Nana had closed it quickly, too late to catch him, but his shadow had not had time to get out; slam went the window and snapped it off.

You may be sure Mrs Darling examined the shadow carefully, but it was quite the ordinary kind.

Nana had no doubt of what was the best thing to do with this shadow. She hung it out at the window, meaning

'He is sure to come back for it; let us put it where he can get it easily without disturbing the children.'

But unfortunately Mrs Darling could not leave it hanging out at the window; it looked so like the washing and lowered the whole tone of the house. She thought of showing it to Mr Darling, but he was totting up winter great-coats for John and Michael, with a wet towel round his head to keep his brain clear, and it seemed a shame to trouble him; besides, she knew exactly what he would say: 'It all comes of having a dog for a nurse.'

She decided to roll the shadow up and put it away carefully in a drawer, until a fitting opportunity came for telling her husband. Ah me!

The opportunity came a week later, on that never-to-be-forgotten Friday. Of course it was a Friday.

'I ought to have been specially careful on a Friday,' she used to say afterwards to her husband, while perhaps Nana was on the other side of her, holding her hand.

'No, no,' Mr Darling always said, 'I am responsible for it all. I, George Darling, did it. *Mea culpa, mea culpa.*' He had had a classical education.

They sat thus night after night recalling that fatal Friday, till every detail of it was stamped on their brains and came through on the other side like the faces on a bad coinage.

'If only I had not accepted that invitation to dine at 27,' Mrs Darling said.

'If only I had not poured my medicine into Nana's bowl,' said Mr Darling.

'If only I had pretended to like the medicine,' was what Nana's wet eyes said.

'My liking for parties, George,'

'My fatal gift of humour, dearest.'

'My touchiness about trifles, dear master and mistress.'

Then one or more of them would break down altogether; Nana at the thought, 'It's true, it's true, they ought not to have had a dog for a nurse.' Many a time it was Mr Darling who put the handkerchief to Nana's eyes.

'That fiend!' Mr Darling would cry, and Nana's bark was the echo of it, but Mrs Darling never upbraided Peter; there was something in the right-hand corner of her mouth that wanted her not to call Peter names.

They would sit there in the empty nursery, recalling fondly every smallest detail of that dreadful evening. It had begun so uneventfully, so precisely like a hundred other evenings, with Nana putting on the water for Michael's bath and carrying him to it on her back.

'I won't go to bed,' he had shouted, like one who still believed that he had the last word on the subject. 'I won't, I won't. Nana, it isn't six o'clock yet. Oh dear, oh dear, I shan't love you any more, Nana. I tell you I won't be bathed, I won't, I won't!'

Then Mrs Darling had come in, wearing her white

evening-gown. She had dressed early because Wendy so loved to see her in her evening-gown, with the necklace George had given her. She was wearing Wendy's bracelet on her arm; she had asked for the loan of it. Wendy so loved to lend her bracelet to her mother.

She had found her two older children playing at being herself and father on the occasion of Wendy's birth, and John was saying:

'I am happy to inform you, Mrs Darling, that you are now a mother,' in just such a tone as Mr Darling himself may have used on the real occasion.

Wendy had danced with joy, just as the real Mrs Darling must have done.

Then John was born, with the extra pomp that he conceived due to the birth of a male, and Michael came from his bath to ask to be born also, but John said brutally that they did not want any more.

Michael had nearly cried. 'Nobody wants me,' he said, and of course the lady in evening-dress could not stand that.

'I do,' she said. 'I so want a third child.'

'Boy or girl?' asked Michael, not too hopefully.

'Boy.'

Then he had leapt into her arms. Such a little thing for Mr and Mrs Darling and Nana to recall now, but not so little if that was to be Michael's last night in that nursery.

They go on with their recollections.

'It was then that I rushed in like a tornado, wasn't it?' Mr Darling would say, scorning himself; and indeed he had been like a tornado.

Perhaps there was some excuse for him. He, too, had been dressing for the party, and all had gone well with him until he came to his tie. It is an astounding thing to have to tell, but this man, though he knew about stocks and shares, had no real mastery of his tie. Sometimes the thing yielded to him without a contest, but there were occasions when it would have been better for the house if he had swallowed his pride and used a made-up tie!

This was such an occasion. He came rushing into the nursery with the crumpled little brute of a tie in his hand.

'Why, what is the matter, father, dear?'

'Matter!' he yelled; he really yelled. 'This tie, it will not tie.' He became dangerously sarcastic. 'Not round my neck! Round the bedpost! Oh yes, twenty times have I made it up round the bedpost, but round my neck, no! Oh dear no! begs to be excused!'

He thought Mrs Darling was not sufficiently impressed, and he went on sternly, 'I warn you of this, mother, that unless this tie is round my neck we don't go out to dinner tonight, and if I don't go out to dinner tonight, I never go to the office again, and if I don't go to the office again, you and I starve, and our children will be flung into the streets.'

Even then Mrs Darling was placid. 'Let me try, dear,' she said, and indeed that was what he had come to ask her to do; and with her nice cool hands she tied his tie for him, while the children stood around to see their fate decided. Some men would have resented her being able to do it so easily, but Mr Darling was far too fine a nature for that; he thanked her carelessly, at once forgot his rage, and in another moment was dancing around the room with Michael on his back.

'How wildly we romped!' said Mrs Darling now, recalling it.

'Our last romp!' Mr Darling groaned.

'O George, do you remember Michael suddenly said to me, "How did you get to know me, mother?"'

'I remember!'

'They were rather sweet, don't you think, George?'

'And they were ours, ours, and now they are gone.'

The romp had ended with the appearance of Nana, and most unluckily Mr Darling collided against her, covering his trousers with hairs. They were not only new trousers but they were the first he had ever had with braid on them, and he had to bite his lip to prevent the tears coming. Of course Mrs Darling brushed him, but he began to talk again about its being a mistake to have a dog for a nurse.

'George, Nana is a treasure.'

'No doubt, but I have an uneasy feeling at times that she looks upon the children as puppies.'

'Oh no, dear one, I feel sure she knows they have souls.'

'I wonder,' Mr Darling said thoughtfully, 'I wonder.' It was an opportunity, his wife felt, for telling him about the boy. At first he pooh-poohed the story, but he became thoughtful when she showed him the shadow.

'It is nobody I know,' he said, examining it carefully, 'but he does look a scoundrel.'

'We were still discussing it, you remember,' says Mr Darling, 'when Nana came in with Michael's medicine. You will never carry the bottle in your mouth again, Nana, and it is all my fault.'

Strong man though he was, there is no doubt that he had behaved rather foolishly over the medicine. If he had a weakness, it was for thinking that all his life he had taken medicine boldly; and so now, when Michael dodged the spoon in Nana's mouth, he had said reprovingly, 'Be a man, Michael.'

'Won't; won't,' Michael cried naughtily. Mrs Darling left the room to get a chocolate for him, and Mr Darling thought this showed want of firmness.

'Mother, don't pamper him,' he called after her. 'Michael, when I was your age I took medicine without a murmur. I said "Thank you, kind parents, for giving me bottles to make me well."'

He really thought this was true, and Wendy, who was now in her night-gown, believed it also, and she said, to encourage Michael, 'That medicine you sometimes take, father, is much nastier, isn't it?'

'Ever so much nastier,' Mr Darling said bravely, 'and I would take it now as an example to you, Michael, if I hadn't lost the bottle.'

He had not exactly lost it; he had climbed in the dead of night to the top of the wardrobe and hidden it there. What he did not know was that the faithful Liza had found it, and put it back on his wash-stand.

'I know where it is, father,' Wendy cried, always glad to be of service. 'I'll bring it,' and she was off before he could stop her. Immediately his spirits sank in the strangest way.

'John,' he said, shuddering, 'it's most beastly stuff. It's that nasty, sticky, sweet kind.'

'It will soon be over, father,' John said cheerily, and then in rushed Wendy with the medicine in a glass.

'I have been as quick as I could,' she panted.

'You have been wonderfully quick,' her father retorted, with a vindictive politeness that was quite thrown away upon her. 'Michael first,' he said doggedly.

'Father first,' said Michael, who was of a suspicious nature.

'I shall be sick, you know,' Mr Darling said threateningly.

'Come on, father,' said John.

'Hold your tongue, John,' his father rapped out.

Wendy was quite puzzled. 'I thought you took it quite easily, father.'

'That is not the point,' he retorted. 'The point is, that there is more in my glass than in Michael's spoon.' His proud heart was nearly bursting. 'And it isn't fair; I would say it though it were with my last breath – it isn't fair.'

'Father, I am waiting,' said Michael coldly.

'It's all very well to say you are waiting; so am I waiting.'

'Father's a cowardy custard.'

'So are you a cowardy custard.'

'I'm not frightened.'

'Neither am I frightened.'

'Well, then, take it.'

'Well, then, you take it.'

Wendy had a splendid idea. 'Why not both take it at the same time?'

'Certainly,' said Mr Darling. 'Are you ready, Michael?'

Wendy gave the words, one, two, three, and Michael took his medicine, but Mr Darling slipped his behind his back.

There was a yell of rage from Michael, and 'O father!' Wendy exclaimed.

'What do you mean by "O father"?' Mr Darling demanded. 'Stop that row, Michael. I meant to take mine, but I – I missed it.'

It was dreadful the way all the three were looking at

him, just as if they did not admire him. 'Look here, all of you,' he said entreatingly, as soon as Nana had gone into the bathroom. 'I have just thought of a splendid joke. I shall pour my medicine into Nana's bowl, and she will drink it, thinking it is milk!'

It was the colour of milk; but the children did not have their father's sense of humour, and they looked at him reproachfully as he poured the medicine into Nana's bowl. 'What fun,' he said doubtfully, and they did not dare expose him when Mrs Darling and Nana returned.

'Nana, good dog,' he said, patting her, 'I have put a little milk into your bowl, Nana.'

Nana wagged her tail, ran to the medicine, and began lapping it. Then she gave Mr Darling such a look, not an angry look: she showed him the great red tear that makes us so sorry for noble dogs, and crept into her kennel.

Mr Darling was frightfully ashamed of himself, but he would not give in. In a horrid silence Mrs Darling smelt the bowl. 'O George,' she said, 'it's your medicine!'

'It was only a joke,' he roared, while she comforted her boys, and Wendy hugged Nana. 'Much good,' he said bitterly, 'my wearing myself to the bone trying to be funny in this house.'

And still Wendy hugged Nana. 'That's right,' he shouted. 'Coddle her! Nobody coddles me. Oh dear no! I am only the breadwinner, why should I be coddled, why, why, why!'

'George,' Mrs Darling entreated him, 'not so loud; the servants will hear you.' Somehow they had got into the way of calling Liza the servants.

'Let them,' he answered recklessly. 'Bring in the whole world. But I refuse to allow that dog to lord it in my nursery for an hour longer.'

The children wept, and Nana ran to him beseechingly, but he waved her back. He felt he was a strong man again. 'In vain, in vain,' he cried; 'the proper place for you is the yard, and there you go to be tied up this instant.'

'George, George,' Mrs Darling whispered, 'remember what I told you about that boy.'

Alas, he would not listen. He was determined to show who was master in that house, and when commands would not draw Nana from the kennel, he lured her out of it with honeyed words, and seizing her roughly, dragged her from the nursery. He was ashamed of himself, and yet he did it. It was all owing to his too affectionate nature, which craved for admiration. When he had tied her up in the backyard, the wretched father went and sat in the passage, with his knuckles to his eyes.

In the meantime Mrs Darling had put the children to bed in unwonted silence and lit their night-lights. They could hear Nana barking, and John whimpered, 'It is because he is chaining her up in the yard,' but Wendy was wiser.

'That is not Nana's unhappy bark,' she said, little

guessing what was about to happen; 'that is her bark when she smells danger.'

Danger!

'Are you sure, Wendy?'

'Oh yes.'

Mrs Darling quivered and went to the window. It was securely fastened. She looked out, and the night was peppered with stars. They were crowding round the house, as if curious to see what was to take place there, but she did not notice this, nor that one or two of the smaller ones winked at her. Yet a nameless fear clutched at her heart and made her cry, 'Oh, how I wish that I wasn't going to a party tonight!'

Even Michael, already half asleep, knew that she was perturbed, and he asked, 'Can anything harm us, mother, after the night-lights are lit?'

'Nothing, precious,' she said; 'they are the eyes a mother leaves behind her to guard her children.'

She went from bed to bed singing enchantments over them, and little Michael flung his arms round her. 'Mother,' he cried, 'I'm glad of you.' They were the last words she was to hear from him for a long time.

No. 27 was only a few yards distant, but there had been a slight fall of snow, and Father and Mother Darling picked their way over it deftly not to soil their shoes. They were already the only persons in the street, and all the stars were watching them. Stars are beautiful, but they may not take an active part in anything, they must just look on for ever. It is a punishment put on them for something they did so long ago that no star now knows what it was. So the older ones have become glassy-eyed and seldom speak (winking is the star language), but the little ones still wonder. They are not really friendly to Peter, who has a mischievous way of stealing up behind them and trying to blow them out; but they are so fond of fun that they were on his side tonight, and anxious to get the grown-ups out of the way. So as soon as the door of 27 closed on Mr and Mrs Darling there was a commotion in the firmament, and the smallest of all the stars in the Milky Way screamed out:

'Now, Peter!'

3

Come Away, Come Away!

For a moment after Mr and Mrs Darling left the house the night-lights by the beds of the three children continued to burn clearly. They were awfully nice little night-lights, and one cannot help wishing that they could have kept awake to see Peter; but Wendy's light blinked and gave such a yawn that the other two yawned also, and before they could close their mouths all the three went out.

There was another light in the room now, a thousand times brighter than the night-lights, and in the time we have taken to say this, it has been in all the drawers in the nursery, looking for Peter's shadow, rummaged the wardrobe and turned every pocket inside out. It was not really a light; it made this light by flashing about so quickly, but when it came to rest for a second you saw it was a fairy, no longer than your hand, but still growing. It was a girl called Tinker Bell, exquisitely gowned in a skeleton leaf, cut low and square, through which her figure could be seen to the best advantage. She was slightly inclined to *embonpoint.*

A moment after the fairy's entrance the window was blown open by the breathing of the little stars, and Peter dropped in. He had carried Tinker Bell part of the way, and his hand was still messy with the fairy dust.

'Tinker Bell,' he called softly, after making sure that the children were asleep. 'Tink, where are you?' She was in a jug for the moment, and liking it extremely; she had never been in a jug before.

'Oh, do come out of that jug, and tell me, do you know where they put my shadow?'

The loveliest tinkle as of golden bells answered him. It is the fairy language. You ordinary children can never hear it, but if you were to hear it you would know that you had heard it once before.

Tink said that the shadow was in the big box. She meant the chest of drawers, and Peter jumped at the drawers, scattering their contents to the floor with both hands, as kings toss ha'pence to the crowd. In a moment he had recovered his shadow, and in his delight he forgot that he had shut Tinker Bell up in the drawer.

If he thought at all, but I don't believe he ever thought, it was that he and his shadow, when brought near each other, would join like drops of water; and when they did not he was appalled. He tried to stick it on with soap from the bathroom, but that also failed. A shudder passed through Peter, and he sat on the floor and cried.

His sobs woke Wendy, and she sat up in bed. She was

not alarmed to see a stranger crying on the nursery floor; she was only pleasantly interested.

'Boy,' she said courteously, 'why are you crying?'

Peter could be exceedingly polite also, having learned the grand manner at fairy ceremonies, and he rose and bowed to her beautifully. She was much pleased, and bowed beautifully to him from the bed.

'What's your name?' he asked.

'Wendy Moira Angela Darling,' she replied with some satisfaction. 'What is your name?'

'Peter Pan.'

She was already sure that he must be Peter, but it did seem a comparatively short name.

'Is that all?'

'Yes,' he said rather sharply. He felt for the first time that it was a shortish name.

'I'm so sorry,' said Wendy Moira Angela.

'It doesn't matter,' Peter gulped.

She asked where he lived.

'Second to the right,' said Peter, 'and then straight on till morning.'

'What a funny address!'

Peter had a sinking. For the first time he felt that perhaps it was a funny address.

'No, it isn't,' he said.

'I mean,' Wendy said nicely, remembering that she was hostess, 'is that what they put on the letters?'

He wished she had not mentioned letters.

'Don't get any letters,' he said contemptuously.

'But your mother gets letters?'

'Don't have a mother,' he said. Not only had he no mother, but he had not the slightest desire to have one. He thought them very over-rated persons. Wendy, however, felt at once that she was in the presence of a tragedy.

'O Peter, no wonder you were crying,' she said, and got out of bed and ran to him.

'I wasn't crying about mothers,' he said rather indignantly. 'I was crying because I can't get my shadow to stick on. Besides, I wasn't crying.'

'It has come off?'

'Yes.'

Then Wendy saw the shadow on the floor, looking so draggled, and she was frightfully sorry for Peter. 'How awful!' she said, but she could not help smiling when she saw that he had been trying to stick it on with soap. How exactly like a boy!

Fortunately she knew at once what to do. 'It must be sewn on,' she said, just a little patronizingly.

'What's sewn?' he asked.

'You're dreadfully ignorant.'

'No, I'm not.'

But she was exulting in his ignorance. 'I shall sew it on for you, my little man,' she said, though he was as tall as herself; and she got out her housewife, and sewed the shadow on to Peter's foot.

'I dare say it will hurt a little,' she warned him.

'Oh, I shan't cry,' said Peter, who was already of opinion that he had never cried in his life. And he clenched his teeth and did not cry; and soon his shadow was behaving properly, though still a little creased.

'Perhaps I should have ironed it,' Wendy said thoughtfully; but Peter, boylike, was indifferent to appearances, and he was now jumping about in the wildest glee. Alas, he had already forgotten that he owed his bliss to Wendy. He thought he had attached the shadow himself. 'How clever I am,' he crowed rapturously, 'oh, the cleverness of me!'

It is humiliating to have to confess that this conceit of Peter was one of his most fascinating qualities. To put it with brutal frankness, there never was a cockier boy.

But for the moment Wendy was shocked. 'Your conceit,' she exclaimed with frightful sarcasm; 'of course I did nothing!'

'You did a little,' Peter said carelessly, and continued to dance.

'A little!' she replied with hauteur; 'if I am no use I can at least withdraw'; and she sprang in the most dignified way into bed and covered her face with the blankets.

To induce her to look up he pretended to be going away, and when this failed he sat on the end of the bed and tapped her gently with his foot. 'Wendy,' he said, 'don't withdraw. I can't help crowing, Wendy, when I'm pleased with myself.' Still she would not look up, though she was listening eagerly. 'Wendy,' he continued in a voice that no woman has ever yet been able to resist, 'Wendy, one girl is more use than twenty boys.'

Now Wendy was every inch a woman, though there were not very many inches, and she peeped out of the bedclothes.

'Do you really think so, Peter?'

'Yes, I do.'

'I think it's perfectly sweet of you,' she declared, 'and I'll get up again'; and she sat with him on the side of the bed. She also said she would give him a kiss if he liked, but Peter did not know what she meant, and he held out his hand expectantly.

'Surely you know what a kiss is?' she asked, aghast.

'I shall know when you give it to me,' he replied stiffly; and not to hurt his feelings she gave him a thimble.

'Now,' said he, 'shall I give you a kiss?' and she replied with a slight primness, 'If you please.' She made herself rather cheap by inclining her face towards him, but he merely dropped an acorn button into her hand; so she slowly returned her face to where it had been before, and said nicely that she would wear his kiss on the chain round her neck. It was lucky that she did put it on that chain, for it was afterwards to save her life.

When people in our set are introduced, it is customary

for them to ask each other's age, and so Wendy, who always liked to do the correct thing, asked Peter how old he was. It was not really a happy question to ask him; it was like an examination paper that asks grammar, when what you want to be asked is Kings of England.

'I don't know,' he replied uneasily, 'but I am quite young.' He really knew nothing about it; he had merely suspicions, but he said at a venture, 'Wendy, I ran away the day I was born.'

Wendy was quite surprised, but interested; and she indicated in the charming drawing-room manner, by a touch on her night-gown, that he could sit nearer her.

'It was because I heard father and mother,' he explained in a low voice, 'talking about what I was to be when I became a man.' He was extraordinarily agitated now. 'I don't want ever to be a man,' he said with passion. 'I want always to be a little boy and to have fun. So I ran away to Kensington Gardens and lived a long long time among the fairies.'

She gave him a look of the most intense admiration, and he thought it was because he had run away, but it was really because he knew fairies. Wendy had lived such a home life that to know fairies struck her as quite delightful. She poured out questions about them, to his surprise, for they were rather a nuisance to him, getting in his way and so on, and indeed he sometimes had to give them a hiding. Still, he liked them on the whole, and he told her about the beginning of fairies.

'You see, Wendy, when the first baby laughed for the first time, its laugh broke into a thousand pieces, and they all went skipping about, and that was the beginning of fairies.'

Tedious talk this, but being a stay-at-home she liked it.

'And so,' he went on good-naturedly, 'there ought to be one fairy for every boy and girl.'

'Ought to be? Isn't there?'

'No. You see, children know such a lot now, they soon don't believe in fairies, and every time a child says, "I don't believe in fairies," there is a fairy somewhere that falls down dead.'

Really, he thought they had now talked enough about fairies, and it struck him that Tinker Bell was keeping very quiet. 'I can't think where she has gone to,' he said, rising, and he called Tink by name. Wendy's heart went flutter with a sudden thrill.

'Peter,' she cried, clutching him, 'you don't mean to tell me that there is a fairy in this room!'

'She was here just now,' he said a little impatiently. 'You don't hear her, do you?' and they both listened.

'The only sound I hear,' said Wendy, 'is like a tinkle of bells.'

'Well, that's Tink, that's the fairy language. I think I hear her too.'

The sound came from the chest of drawers, and Peter

made a merry face. No one could ever look quite so merry as Peter, and the loveliest of gurgles was his laugh. He had his first laugh still.

'Wendy,' he whispered gleefully, 'I do believe I shut her up in the drawer!'

He let poor Tink out of the drawer, and she flew about the nursery screaming with fury. 'You shouldn't say such things,' Peter retorted. 'Of course I'm very sorry, but how could I know you were in the drawer?'

Wendy was not listening to him. 'O Peter,' she cried, 'if she would only stand still and let me see her!'

'They hardly ever stand still,' he said, but for one moment Wendy saw the romantic figure come to rest on the cuckoo clock. 'O the lovely!' she cried, though Tink's face was still distorted with passion.

'Tink,' said Peter amiably, 'this lady says she wishes you were her fairy.'

Tinker Bell answered insolently.

'What does she say, Peter?'

He had to translate. 'She is not very polite. She says you are a great ugly girl, and that she is my fairy.'

He tried to argue with Tink. 'You know you can't be my fairy, Tink, because I am a gentleman and you are a lady.'

To this Tink replied in these words, 'You silly ass,' and disappeared into the bathroom. 'She is quite a common fairy,' Peter explained apologetically; 'she is called Tinker Bell because she mends the pots and kettles.'

They were together in the arm-chair by this time, and Wendy plied him with more questions.

'If you don't live in Kensington Gardens now –'

'Sometimes I do still.'

'But where do you live mostly now?'

'With the lost boys.'

'Who are they?'

'They are the children who fall out of their perambulators when the nurse is looking the other way. If they are not claimed in seven days they are sent far away to the Neverland to defray expenses. I'm captain.'

'What fun it must be!'

'Yes,' said cunning Peter, 'but we are rather lonely. You see we have no female companionship.'

'Are none of the others girls?'

'Oh no; girls, you know, are much too clever to fall out of their prams.'

This flattered Wendy immensely. 'I think,' she said, 'it is perfectly lovely the way you talk about girls; John there just despises us.'

For reply Peter rose and kicked John out of bed, blankets and all; one kick. This seemed to Wendy rather forward for a first meeting, and she told him with spirit that he was not captain in her house. However, John continued to sleep so placidly on the floor that she allowed him to remain there. 'And I know you meant to be kind,' she said, relenting, 'so you may give me a kiss.'

For a moment she had forgotten his ignorance about kisses. 'I thought you would want it back,' he said a little bitterly, and offered to return her the thimble.

'Oh dear,' said the nice Wendy, 'I don't mean a kiss, I mean a thimble.'

'What's that?'

'It's like this.' She kissed him.

'Funny!' said Peter gravely. 'Now shall I give you a thimble?'

'If you wish to,' said Wendy, keeping her head erect this time.

Peter thimbled her, and almost immediately she screeched. 'What is it, Wendy?'

'It was exactly as if someone were pulling my hair.'

'That must have been Tink. I never knew her so naughty before.'

And indeed Tink was darting about again, using offensive language.

'She says she will do that to you, Wendy, every time I give you a thimble.'

'But why?'

'Why, Tink?'

Again Tink replied, 'You silly ass.' Peter could not understand why, but Wendy understood; and she was just slightly disappointed when he admitted that he came to the nursery window not to see her but to listen to stories.

'You see I don't know any stories. None of the lost boys know any stories.'

'How perfectly awful,' Wendy said.

'Do you know,' Peter asked, 'why swallows build in the eaves of houses? It is to listen to the stories. O Wendy, your mother was telling you such a lovely story.'

'Which story was it?'

'About the prince who couldn't find the lady who wore the glass slipper.'

'Peter,' said Wendy excitedly, 'that was Cinderella, and he found her, and they lived happy ever after.'

Peter was so glad that he rose from the floor, where they had been sitting, and hurried to the window. 'Where are you going?' she cried with misgiving.

'To tell the other boys.'

'Don't go, Peter,' she entreated, 'I know such lots of stories.'

Those were her precise words, so there can be no denying that it was she who first tempted him.

He came back, and there was a greedy look in his eyes now which ought to have alarmed her, but did not.

'Oh, the stories I could tell to the boys!' she cried, and then Peter gripped her and began to draw her towards the window.

'Let me go!' she ordered him.

'Wendy, do come with me and tell the other boys.'

Of course she was very pleased to be asked, but she

said, 'Oh dear, I can't. Think of mummy! Besides, I can't
fly.'

'I'll teach you.'

'Oh, how lovely to fly.'

'I'll teach you how to jump on the wind's back, and
then away we go.'

'Oo!' she exclaimed rapturously.

'Wendy, Wendy, when you are sleeping in your silly bed
you might be flying about with me saying funny things
to the stars.'

'Oo!'

'And, Wendy, there are mermaids.'

'Mermaids! With tails?'

'Such long tails.'

'Oh,' cried Wendy, 'to see a mermaid!'

He had become frightfully cunning. 'Wendy,' he said,
'how we should all respect you.'

She was wriggling her body in distress. It was quite as
if she were trying to remain on the nursery floor.

But he had no pity for her.

'Wendy,' he said, the sly one, 'you could tuck us in at
night.'

'Oo!'

'None of us has ever been tucked in at night.'

'Oo,' and her arms went out to him.

'And you could darn our clothes, and make pockets for
us. None of us has any pockets.'

How could she resist? 'Of course it's awfully fascinating!' she cried. 'Peter, would you teach John and Michael to fly too?'

'If you like,' he said indifferently; and she ran to John and Michael and shook them. 'Wake up,' she cried, 'Peter Pan has come and he is to teach us to fly.'

John rubbed his eyes. 'Then I shall get up,' he said. Of course he was on the floor already. 'Hallo,' he said, 'I am up!'

Michael was up by this time also, looking as sharp as a knife with six blades and a saw, but Peter suddenly signed silence. Their faces assumed the awful craftiness of children listening for sounds from the grown-up world. All was as still as salt. Then everything was right. No, stop! Everything was wrong. Nana, who had been barking distressfully all the evening, was quiet now. It was her silence they had heard.

'Out with the light! Hide! Quick!' cried John, taking command for the only time throughout the whole adventure. And thus when Liza entered, holding Nana, the nursery seemed quite its old self, very dark; and you could have sworn you heard its three wicked inmates breathing angelically as they slept. They were really doing it artfully from behind the window curtains.

Liza was in a bad temper, for she was mixing the Christmas puddings in the kitchen, and had been drawn away from them, with a raisin still on her cheek, by Nana's absurd suspicions. She thought the best way of getting a little quiet was to take Nana to the nursery for a moment, but in custody of course.

'There, you suspicious brute,' she said, not sorry that Nana was in disgrace, 'they are perfectly safe, aren't they? Every one of the little angels sound asleep in bed. Listen to their gentle breathing.'

Here Michael, encouraged by his success, breathed so loudly that they were nearly detected. Nana knew that kind of breathing, and she tried to drag herself out of Liza's clutches.

But Liza was dense. 'No more of it, Nana,' she said sternly, pulling her out of the room. 'I warn you if you bark again I shall go straight for master and missus and bring them home from the party, and then, oh, won't master whip you, just.'

She tied the unhappy dog up again, but do you think Nana ceased to bark? Bring master and missus home from the party! Why, that was just what she wanted. Do you think she cared whether she was whipped so long as her charges were safe? Unfortunately Liza returned to her puddings, and Nana, seeing that no help would come from her, strained and strained at the chain until at last she broke it. In another moment she had burst into the dining room of 27 and flung up her paws to heaven, her most expressive way of making a communication. Mr and Mrs Darling knew at once that something terrible was happening in their nursery, and without a good-bye to their hostess they rushed into the street.

But it was now ten minutes since three scoundrels had been breathing behind the curtains; and Peter Pan can do a great deal in ten minutes.

We now return to the nursery.

'It's all right,' John announced, emerging from his hiding-place. 'I say, Peter, can you really fly?'

Instead of troubling to answer him Peter flew round the room, taking in the mantelpiece on the way.

'How topping!' said John and Michael.

'How sweet!' cried Wendy.

'Yes, I'm sweet, oh, I am sweet!' said Peter, forgetting his manners again.

It looked delightfully easy, and they tried it first from the floor and then from the beds, but they always went down instead of up.

'I say, how do you do it?' asked John, rubbing his knee. He was quite a practical boy.

'You just think lovely wonderful thoughts,' Peter explained, 'and they lift you up in the air.'

He showed them again.

'You're so nippy at it,' John said; 'couldn't you do it very slowly once?'

Peter did it both slowly and quickly. 'I've got it now, Wendy!' cried John, but soon he found he had not. Not one of them could fly an inch, though even Michael was in words of two syllables, and Peter did not know A from Z.

Of course Peter had been trifling with them, for no one can fly unless the fairy dust has been blown on him. Fortunately, as we have mentioned, one of his hands was messy with it, and he blew some on each of them, with the most superb results.

'Now just wriggle your shoulders this way,' he said, 'and let go.'

They were all on their beds, and gallant Michael let go first. He did not quite mean to let go, but he did it, and immediately he was borne across the room.

'I flewed!' he screamed while still in mid-air.

John let go and met Wendy near the bathroom.

'Oh, lovely!'

'Oh, ripping!'

'Look at me!'

'Look at me!'

'Look at me!'

They were not nearly so elegant as Peter, they could not help kicking a little, but their heads were bobbing against the ceiling, and there is almost nothing so delicious as that. Peter gave Wendy a hand at first, but had to desist, Tink was so indignant.

Up and down they went, and round and round. Heavenly was Wendy's word.

'I say,' cried John, 'why shouldn't we all go out!'

Of course it was to this that Peter had been luring them.

Michael was ready: he wanted to see how long it took him to do a billion miles. But Wendy hesitated.

'Mermaids!' said Peter again.

'Oo!'

'And there are pirates.'

'Pirates,' cried John, seizing his Sunday hat, 'let us go at once.'

It was just at this moment that Mr and Mrs Darling hurried with Nana out of 27. They ran into the middle of the street to look up at the nursery window; and, yes, it was still shut, but the room was ablaze with light, and most heart-gripping sight of all, they could see in shadow on the curtain three little figures in night attire circling round and round, not on the floor but in the air.

Not three figures, four!

In a tremble they opened the street door. Mr Darling would have rushed upstairs, but Mrs Darling signed to him to go softly. She even tried to make her heart go softly.

Will they reach the nursery in time? If so, how delightful for them, and we shall all breathe a sigh of relief, but there will be no story. On the other hand, if they are not in time, I solemnly promise that it will all come right in the end.

They would have reached the nursery in time had it not been that the little stars were watching them. Once again the stars blew the window open, and that smallest star of all called out:

'Cave, Peter!'

Then Peter knew that there was not a moment to lose. 'Come,' he cried imperiously, and soared out at once into the night followed by John and Michael and Wendy.

Mr and Mrs Darling and Nana rushed into the nursery too late. The birds were flown.

4

The Flight

'Second to the right, and straight on till morning.'

That, Peter had told Wendy, was the way to the Neverland; but even birds, carrying maps and consulting them at windy corners, could not have sighted it with these instructions. Peter, you see, just said anything that came into his head.

At first his companions trusted him implicitly, and so great were the delights of flying that they wasted time circling round church spires or any other tall objects on the way that took their fancy.

John and Michael raced, Michael getting a start.

They recalled with contempt that not so long ago they had thought themselves fine fellows for being able to fly round a room.

Not so long ago. But how long ago? They were flying over the sea before this thought began to disturb Wendy seriously. John thought it was their second sea and their third night.

Sometimes it was dark and sometimes light, and now

they were very cold and again too warm. Did they really feel hungry at times, or were they merely pretending because Peter had such a jolly new way of feeding them? His way was to pursue birds who had food in their mouths suitable for humans and snatch it from them; then the birds would follow and snatch it back; and they would all go chasing each other gaily for miles, parting at last with mutual expressions of good-will. But Wendy noticed with gentle concern that Peter did not seem to know that this was rather an odd way of getting your bread and butter, nor even that there are other ways.

Certainly they did not pretend to be sleepy, they were sleepy; and that was a danger, for the moment they popped off, down they fell. The awful thing was that Peter thought this funny.

'There he goes again!' he would cry gleefully, as Michael suddenly dropped like a stone.

'Save him, save him!' cried Wendy, looking with horror at the cruel sea far below. Eventually Peter would dive through the air, and catch Michael just before he could strike the sea, and it was lovely the way he did it; but he always waited till the last moment, and you felt it was his cleverness that interested him and not the saving of human life. Also he was fond of variety, and the sport that engrossed him one moment would suddenly cease to engage him, so there was always the possibility that the next time you fell he would let you go.

He could sleep in the air without falling, by merely lying on his back and floating, but this was, partly at least, because he was so light that if you got behind him and blew he went faster.

'Do be more polite to him,' Wendy whispered to John, when they were playing 'Follow my Leader'.

'Then tell him to stop showing off,' said John.

When playing Follow my Leader, Peter would fly close to the water and touch each shark's tail in passing, just as in the street you may run your finger along an iron railing. They could not follow him in this with much success, so perhaps it was rather like showing off, especially as he kept looking behind to see how many tails they missed.

'You must be nice to him,' Wendy impressed on her brothers. 'What would we do if he were to leave us?'

'We could go back,' Michael said.

'How could we ever find our way back without him?'

'Well, then, we could go on,' said John.

'That is the awful thing, John. We should have to go on, for we don't know how to stop.'

This was true; Peter had forgotten to show them how to stop.

John said that if the worst came to the worst, all they had to do was to go straight on, for the world was round, and so in time they must come back to their own window.

'And who is to get food for us, John?'

'I nipped a bit out of that eagle's mouth pretty neatly, Wendy.'

'After the twentieth try,' Wendy reminded him. 'And even though we became good at picking up food, see how we bump against clouds and things if he is not near to give us a hand.'

Indeed they were constantly bumping. They could now fly strongly, though they still kicked far too much; but if they saw a cloud in front of them, the more they tried to avoid it, the more certainly did they bump into it. If Nana had been with them she would have had a bandage round Michael's forehead by this time.

Peter was not with them for the moment, and they felt rather lonely up there by themselves. He could go so much faster than they that he would suddenly shoot out of sight, to have some adventure in which they had no share. He would come down laughing over something fearfully funny he had been saying to a star, but he had already forgotten what it was, or he would come up with mermaid scales still sticking to him, and yet not be able to say for certain what had been happening. It was really rather irritating to children who had never seen a mermaid.

'And if he forgets them so quickly,' Wendy argued, 'how can we expect that he will go on remembering us?'

Indeed, sometimes when he returned he did not remember them, at least not well. Wendy was sure of it.

She saw recognition come into his eyes as he was about to pass them the time of day and go on; once even she had to tell him her name.

'I'm Wendy,' she said agitatedly.

He was very sorry. 'I say, Wendy,' he whispered to her, 'always if you see me forgetting you, just keep on saying "I'm Wendy", and then I'll remember.'

Of course this was rather unsatisfactory. However, to make amends he showed them how to lie out flat on a strong wind that was going their way, and this was such a pleasant change that they tried it several times and found they could sleep thus with security. Indeed they would have slept longer, but Peter tired quickly of sleeping, and soon he would cry in his captain voice, 'We get off here.' So with occasional tiffs, but on the whole rollicking, they drew near the Neverland; for after many moons they did reach it, and, what is more, they had been going pretty straight all the time, not perhaps so much owing to the guidance of Peter or Tink as because the island was out looking for them. It is only thus that anyone may sight those magic shores.

'There it is,' said Peter calmly.

'Where, where?'

'Where all the arrows are pointing.'

Indeed a million golden arrows were pointing out the island to the children, all directed by their friend the sun, who wanted them to be sure of their way before leaving them for the night.

Wendy and John and Michael stood on tiptoe in the air to get their first sight of the island. Strange to say, they all recognized it at once, and until fear fell upon them they hailed it, not as something long dreamt of and seen at last, but as a familiar friend to whom they were returning home for the holidays.

'John, there's the lagoon.'

'Wendy, look at the turtles burying their eggs in the sand.'

'I say, John, I see your flamingo with the broken leg.'

'Look, Michael, there's your cave.'

'John, what's that in the brushwood?'

'It's a wolf with her whelps. Wendy, I do believe that's your little whelp.'

'There's my boat, John, with her sides stove in.'

'No, it isn't. Why, we burned your boat.'

'That's her, at any rate. I say, John, I see the smoke of the redskin camp.'

'Where? Show me, and I'll tell you by the way the smoke curls whether they are on the war-path.'

'There, just across the Mysterious River.'

'I see now. Yes, they are on the war-path right enough.'

Peter was a little annoyed with them for knowing so much; but if he wanted to lord it over them his triumph was at hand, for have I not told you that anon fear fell upon them?

It came as the arrows went, leaving the island in gloom.

In the old days at home the Neverland had always begun to look a little dark and threatening by bedtime. Then unexplored patches arose in it and spread; black shadows moved about in them; the roar of the beasts of prey was quite different now, and above all, you lost the certainty that you would win. You were quite glad that the night-lights were on. You even liked Nana to say that this was just the mantelpiece over here, and that the Neverland was all make-believe.

Of course the Neverland had been make-believe in those days; but it was real now, and there were no night-lights, and it was getting darker every moment, and where was Nana?

They had been flying apart, but they huddled close to Peter now. His careless manner had gone at last, his eyes were sparkling, a tingle went through them every time they touched his body. They were now over the fearsome island, flying so low that sometimes a tree grazed their face. Nothing horrid was visible in the air, yet their progress had become slow and laboured, exactly as if they were pushing their way through hostile forces. Sometimes they hung in the air until Peter had beaten on it with his fists.

'They don't want us to land,' he explained.

'Who are they?' Wendy whispered, shuddering.

But he could not or would not say. Tinker Bell had been asleep on his shoulder, but now he wakened her and sent her on in front.

Sometimes he poised himself in the air, listening intently with his hand to his ear, and again he would stare down with eyes so bright that they seemed to bore two holes to earth. Having done these things, he went on again.

His courage was almost appalling. 'Do you want an adventure now,' he said casually to John, 'or would you like to have your tea first?'

Wendy said 'tea first' quickly, and Michael pressed her hand in gratitude, but the braver John hesitated.

'What kind of adventure?' he asked cautiously.

'There's a pirate asleep in the pampas just beneath us,' Peter told him. 'If you like, we'll go down and kill him.'

'I don't see him,' John said after a long pause.

'I do.'

'Suppose,' John said a little huskily, 'he were to wake up.'

Peter spoke indignantly. 'You don't think I would kill him while he was sleeping! I would wake him first, and then kill him. That's the way I always do.'

'I say! Do you kill many?'

'Tons.'

John said 'how ripping', but decided to have tea first. He asked if there were many pirates on the island just now, and Peter said he had never known so many.

'Who is captain now?'

'Hook,' answered Peter; and his face became very stern as he said that hated word.

'Jas. Hook?'

'Aye.'

Then indeed Michael began to cry, and even John could speak in gulps only, for they knew Hook's reputation.

'He was Blackbeard's bo'sun,' John whispered huskily. 'He is the worst of them all. He is the only man of whom Barbecue was afraid.'

'That's him,' said Peter.

'What is he like? Is he big?'

'He is not so big as he was.'

'How do you mean?'

'I cut off a bit of him.'

'You!'

'Yes, me,' said Peter sharply.

'I wasn't meaning to be disrespectful.'

'Oh, all right.'

'But, I say, what bit?'

'His right hand.'

'Then he can't fight now?'

'Oh, can't he just!'

'Left-hander?'

'He has an iron hook instead of a right hand, and he claws with it.'

'Claws!'

'I say, John,' said Peter.

'Yes.'

'Say, "Aye, aye, sir."'

'Aye, aye, sir.'

'There is one thing,' Peter continued, 'that every boy who serves under me has to promise, and so must you.'

John paled.

'It is this, if we meet Hook in open fight, you must leave him to me.'

'I promise,' John said loyally.

For the moment they were feeling less eerie, because Tink was flying with them, and in her light they could distinguish each other. Unfortunately she could not fly so slowly as they, and so she had to go round and round them in a circle in which they moved as in a halo. Wendy quite liked it, until Peter pointed out the drawback.

'She tells me,' he said, 'that the pirates sighted us before the darkness came, and got Long Tom out.'

'The big gun?'

'Yes. And of course they must see her light, and if they guess we are near it they are sure to let fly.'

'Wendy!'

'John!'

'Michael!'

'Tell her to go away at once, Peter,' the three cried simultaneously, but he refused.

'She thinks we have lost the way,' he replied stiffly, 'and she is rather frightened. You don't think I would send her away all by herself when she is frightened!'

For a moment the circle of light was broken, and something gave Peter a loving little pinch.

'Then tell her,' Wendy begged, 'to put out her light.'

'She can't put it out. That is about the only thing fairies can't do. It just goes out of itself when she falls asleep, same as the stars.'

'Then tell her to sleep at once,' John almost ordered.

'She can't sleep except when she's sleepy. It is the only other thing fairies can't do.'

'Seems to me,' growled John, 'these are the only two things worth doing.'

Here he got a pinch, but not a loving one.

'If only one of us had a pocket,' Peter said, 'we could carry her in it.' However, they had set off in such a hurry that there was not a pocket between the four of them.

He had a happy idea. John's hat!

Tink agreed to travel by hat if it was carried in the hand. John carried it, though she had hoped to be carried by Peter. Presently Wendy took the hat, because John said it struck against his knee as he flew; and this, as we shall see, led to mischief, for Tinker Bell hated to be under an obligation to Wendy.

In the black topper the light was completely hidden, and they flew on in silence. It was the stillest silence they had ever known, broken once by a distant lapping, which Peter explained was the wild beasts drinking at the ford, and again by a rasping sound that might have been the branches of trees rubbing together, but he said it was the redskins sharpening their knives.

Even these noises ceased. To Michael the loneliness was dreadful. 'If only something would make a sound!' he cried.

As if in answer to his request, the air was rent by the most tremendous crash he had ever heard. The pirates had fired Long Tom at them.

The roar of it echoed through the mountains, and the echoes seemed to cry savagely, 'Where are they, where are they, where are they?'

Thus sharply did the terrified three learn the difference between an island of make-believe and the same island come true.

When at last the heavens were steady again, John and Michael found themselves alone in the darkness. John was treading the air mechanically, and Michael without knowing how to float was floating.

'Are you shot?' John whispered tremulously.

'I haven't tried yet,' Michael whispered back.

We know now that no one had been hit. Peter, however, had been carried by the wind of the shot far out to sea, while Wendy was blown upwards with no companion but Tinker Bell.

It would have been well for Wendy if at that moment she had dropped the hat.

I don't know whether the idea came suddenly to Tink, or whether she had planned it on the way, but she at once popped out of the hat and began to lure Wendy to her destruction.

Tink was not all bad: or, rather, she was all bad just now, but, on the other hand, sometimes she was all good. Fairies have to be one thing or the other, because being so small they unfortunately have room for one feeling only at a time. They are, however, allowed to change, only it must be a complete change. At present she was full of jealousy of Wendy. What she said in her lovely tinkle Wendy could not of course understand, and I believe some of it was bad words, but it sounded kind, and she flew back and forward, plainly meaning 'Follow me, and all will be well.'

What else could poor Wendy do? She called to Peter and John and Michael, and got only mocking echoes in reply. She did not yet know that Tink hated her with the fierce hatred of a very woman. And so, bewildered, and now staggering in her flight, she followed Tink to her doom.

5

The Island Come True

Feeling that Peter was on his way back, the Neverland had again woke into life. We ought to use the pluperfect and say wakened, but woke is better and was always used by Peter.

In his absence things are usually quiet on the island. The fairies take an hour longer in the morning, the beasts attend to their young, the redskins feed heavily for six days and nights, and when pirates and lost boys meet they merely bite their thumbs at each other. But with the coming of Peter, who hates lethargy, they are all under way again: if you put your ear to the ground now, you would hear the whole island seething with life.

On this evening the chief forces of the island were disposed as follows. The lost boys were out looking for Peter, the pirates were out looking for the lost boys, the redskins were out looking for the pirates, and the beasts were out looking for the redskins. They were going round and round the island, but they did not meet because all were going at the same rate.

All wanted blood except the boys, who liked it as a rule, but tonight were out to greet their captain. The boys on the island vary, of course, in numbers, according as they get killed and so on; and when they seem to be growing up, which is against the rules, Peter thins them out; but at this time there were six of them, counting the Twins as two. Let us pretend to lie here among the sugar-cane and watch them as they steal by in single file, each with his hand on his dagger.

They are forbidden by Peter to look in the least like him, and they wear the skins of bears slain by themselves, in which they are so round and furry that when they fall they roll. They have therefore become very sure-footed.

The first to pass is Tootles, not the least brave but the most unfortunate of all that gallant band. He had been in fewer adventures than any of them, because the big things constantly happened just when he had stepped round the corner; all would be quiet, he would take the opportunity of going off to gather a few sticks for firewood, and then when he returned the others would be sweeping up the blood. The ill luck had given a gentle melancholy to his countenance, but instead of souring his nature had sweetened it, so that he was quite the humblest of the boys. Poor kind Tootles, there is danger in the air for you tonight. Take care lest an adventure is now offered you, which, if accepted, will plunge you in deepest woe. Tootles, the fairy Tink, who is bent on mischief this night, is looking for a tool, and she thinks you the most easily tricked of the boys. 'Ware Tinker Bell.

Would that he could hear us, but we are not really on the island, and he passes by, biting his knuckles.

Next comes Nibs, the gay and debonair, followed by Slightly, who cuts whistles out of the trees and dances ecstatically to his own tunes. Slightly is the most conceited of the boys. He thinks he remembers the days before he was lost, with their manners and customs, and this has given his nose an offensive tilt. Curly is fourth; he is a pickle, and so often has he had to deliver up his person when Peter said sternly, 'Stand forth the one who did this thing,' that now at the command he stands forth automatically whether he has done it or not. Last come the Twins, who cannot be described because we should be sure to be describing the wrong one. Peter never quite knew what twins were, and his band were not allowed to know anything he did not know, so these two were always vague about themselves, and did their best to give satisfaction by keeping close together in an apologetic sort of way.

The boys vanish in the gloom, and after a pause, but not a long pause, for things go briskly on the island, come the pirates on their track. We hear them before they are seen, and it is always the same dreadful song:

'Avast belay, yo ho, heave to,
A-pirating we go,
And if we're parted by a shot
We're sure to meet below!'

A more villainous-looking lot never hung in a row on Execution dock. Here, a little in advance, ever and again with his head to the ground listening, his great arms bare, pieces of eight in his ears as ornaments, is the handsome Italian Cecco, who cut his name in letters of blood on the back of the governor of the prison at Goa. That gigantic black behind him has had many names since he dropped the one with which dusky mothers still terrify their children on the banks of the Guidjo-mo. Here is Bill Jukes, every inch of him tattooed, the same Bill Jukes who got six dozen on the *Walrus* from Flint before he would drop the bag of moidores; and Cookson, said to be Black Murphy's brother (but this was never proved); and Gentleman Starkey, once an usher in a public school and still dainty in his ways of killing; and Skylights (Morgan's Skylights); and the Irish bo'sun Smee, an oddly genial man who stabbed, so to speak, without offence, and was the only Nonconformist in Hook's crew; and Noodler, whose hands were fixed on backwards; and Robt. Mullins and Alf Mason and many another ruffian long known and feared on the Spanish Main.

In the midst of them, the blackest and largest jewel in

that dark setting, reclined James Hook, or, as he wrote himself, Jas. Hook, of whom it is said he was the only man that the Sea-Cook feared. He lay at his ease in a rough chariot drawn and propelled by his men, and instead of a right hand he had the iron hook with which ever and anon he encouraged them to increase their pace. As dogs this terrible man treated and addressed them, and as dogs they obeyed him. In person he was cadaverous and blackavised, and his hair was dressed in long curls, which at a little distance looked like black candles, and gave a singularly threatening expression to his handsome countenance. His eyes were of the blue of the forget-me-not, and of a profound melancholy, save when he was plunging his hook into you, at which time two red spots appeared in them and lit them up horribly. In manner, something of the grand seigneur still clung to him, so that he even ripped you up with an air, and I have been told that he was a *raconteur* of repute. He was never more sinister than when he was most polite, which is probably the truest test of breeding; and the elegance of his diction, even when he was swearing, no less than the distinction of his demeanour, showed him one of a different caste from his crew. A man of indomitable courage, it was said of him that the only thing he shied at was the sight of his own blood, which was thick and of an unusual colour. In dress he somewhat aped the attire associated with the name of Charles II, having heard it said in some earlier period of his career that he bore a strange resemblance to the ill-fated Stuarts; and in his mouth he had a holder of his own contrivance which enabled him to smoke two cigars at once. But undoubtedly the grimmest part of him was his iron claw.

Let us now kill a pirate, to show Hook's method. Skylights will do. As they pass, Skylights lurches clumsily against him, ruffling his lace collar; the hook shoots forth, there is a tearing sound and one screech, then the body is kicked aside, and the pirates pass on. He has not even taken the cigars from his mouth.

Such is the terrible man against whom Peter Pan is pitted. Which will win?

On the trail of the pirates, stealing noiselessly down the war-path, which is not visible to inexperienced eyes, come the redskins, every one of them with his eyes peeled. They carry tomahawks and knives, and their naked bodies gleam with paint and oil. Strung around them are scalps, of boys as well as of pirates, for these are the Piccaninny tribe, and not to be confused with the softer-hearted Delawares or the Hurons. In the van, on all fours, is Great Big Little Panther, a brave of so many scalps that in his present position they somewhat impede his progress. Bringing up the rear, the place of greatest danger, comes Tiger Lily, proudly erect, a princess in her own right. She is the most beautiful of dusky Dianas and the belle of the Piccaninnies, coquettish, cold and amorous by turns; there is not a brave who would not have the wayward thing to wife, but she staves off the altar with a hatchet. Observe how they pass over fallen twigs without making the slightest noise. The only sound to be heard is their somewhat heavy breathing. The fact is that they are all a little fat just now after the heavy gorging, but in time they will work this off. For the moment, however, it constitutes their chief danger.

The redskins disappear as they have come, like shadows, and soon their place is taken by the beasts, a great and motley procession: lions, tigers, bears, and the innumerable smaller savage things that flee from them, for every kind of beast, and, more particularly, all the man-eaters, live cheek by jowl on the favoured island. Their tongues are hanging out, they are hungry tonight.

When they have passed, comes the last figure of all, a gigantic crocodile. We shall see for whom she is looking presently.

The crocodile passes, but soon the boys appear again, for the procession must continue indefinitely until one of the parties stops or changes its pace. Then quickly they will be on top of each other.

All are keeping a sharp look out in front, but none suspects that the danger may be creeping up from behind. This shows how real the island was.

The first to fall out of the moving circle was the boys. They flung themselves down on the sward, close to their underground home.

'I do wish Peter would come back,' every one of them said nervously, though in height and still more in breadth they were all larger than their captain.

'I am the only one who is not afraid of the pirates,' Slightly said in the tone that prevented his being a general favourite; but perhaps some distant sound disturbed him, for he added hastily, 'but I wish he would come back, and tell us whether he has heard anything more about Cinderella.'

They talked of Cinderella, and Tootles was confident that his mother must have been very like her.

It was only in Peter's absence that they could speak of mothers, the subject being forbidden by him as silly.

'All I remember about my mother,' Nibs told them, 'is that she often said to father, "Oh, how I wish I had a cheque-book of my own." I don't know what a cheque-book is, but I should just love to give my mother one.'

While they talked they heard a distant sound. You or I, not being wild things of the woods, would have heard nothing, but they heard it, and it was the grim song:

> *'Yo ho, yo ho, the pirate life,*
> *The flag o' skull and bones,*
> *A merry hour, a hempen rope,*
> *And hey for Davy Jones.'*

At once the lost boys – but where are they? They are no longer there. Rabbits could not have disappeared more quickly.

I will tell you where they are. With the exception of Nibs, who has darted away to reconnoitre, they are already in their home under the ground, a very delightful residence of which we shall see a good deal presently. But how have they reached it? for there is no entrance to be seen, not so much as a pile of brushwood which, if removed, would disclose the mouth of a cave. Look closely, however, and you may note that there are here seven large trees, each having in its hollow trunk a hole as large as a boy. These are the seven entrances to the home under the ground, for which Hook has been searching in vain these many moons. Will he find it tonight?

As the pirates advanced, the quick eye of Starkey sighted Nibs disappearing through the wood, and at once his pistol flashed out. But an iron claw gripped his shoulder.

'Captain, let go,' he cried, writhing.

Now for the first time we hear the voice of Hook. It was a black voice. 'Put back that pistol first,' it said threateningly.

'It was one of those boys you hate. I could have shot him dead.'

'Aye, and the sound would have brought Tiger Lily's redskins upon us. Do you want to lose your scalp?'

'Shall I after him, captain,' asked pathetic Smee, 'and tickle him with Johnny Corkscrew?' Smee had pleasant names for everything, and his cutlass was Johnny Corkscrew, because he wriggled it in the wound. One could mention many lovable traits in Smee. For instance, after killing, it was his spectacles he wiped instead of his weapon.

'Johnny's a silent fellow,' he reminded Hook.

'Not now, Smee,' Hook said darkly. 'He is only one, and I want to mischief all the seven. Scatter and look for them.'

The pirates disappeared among the trees, and in a moment their captain and Smee were alone. Hook heaved a heavy sigh; and I know not why it was, perhaps it was because of the soft beauty of the evening, but there came over him a desire to confide to his faithful bo'sun the story of his life. He spoke long and earnestly, but what it was all about Smee, who was rather stupid, did not know in the least.

Anon he caught the word Peter.

'Most of all,' Hook was saying passionately, 'I want their captain, Peter Pan. 'Twas he cut off my arm.' He brandished the hook threateningly. 'I've waited long to shake his hand with this. Oh, I'll tear him.'

'And yet,' said Smee, 'I have often heard you say that hook was worth a score of hands, for combing the hair and other homely uses.'

'Aye,' the captain answered, 'if I was a mother I would pray to have my children born with this instead of that,' and he cast a look of pride upon his iron hand and one of scorn upon the other. Then again he frowned.

'Peter flung my arm,' he said, wincing, 'to a crocodile that happened to be passing by.'

'I have often,' said Smee, 'noticed your strange dread of crocodiles.'

'Not of crocodiles,' Hook corrected him, 'but of that one crocodile.' He lowered his voice. 'It liked my arm so much, Smee, that it has followed me ever since, from sea to sea and from land to land, licking its lips for the rest of me.'

'In a way,' said Smee, 'it's a sort of compliment.'

'I want no such compliments,' Hook barked petulantly. 'I want Peter Pan, who first gave the brute its taste for me.'

He sat down on a large mushroom, and now there was a quiver in his voice. 'Smee,' he said huskily, 'that crocodile would have had me before this, but by a lucky chance it swallowed a clock which goes tick tick inside it, and so before it can reach me I hear the tick and bolt.' He laughed, but in a hollow way.

'Some day,' said Smee, 'the clock will run down, and then he'll get you.'

Hook wetted his dry lips. 'Aye,' he said, 'that's the fear that haunts me.'

Since sitting down he had felt curiously warm. 'Smee,' he said, 'this seat is hot.' He jumped up. 'Odds bobs, hammer and tongs, I'm burning.'

They examined the mushroom, which was of a size and solidity unknown on the mainland; they tried to pull it up, and it came away at once in their hands, for it had no root. Stranger still, smoke began at once to ascend. The pirates looked at each other. 'A chimney!' they both exclaimed.

They had indeed discovered the chimney of the home under the ground. It was the custom of the boys to stop it with a mushroom when enemies were in the neighbourhood.

Not only smoke came out of it. There came also children's voices, for so safe did the boys feel in their hiding-place that they were gaily chattering. The pirates listened grimly, and then replaced the mushroom. They looked around them and noted the holes in the seven trees.

'Did you hear them say Peter Pan's from home?' Smee whispered, fidgeting with Johnny Corkscrew.

Hook nodded. He stood for a long time lost in thought, and at last a curdling smile lit up his swarthy face. Smee had been waiting for it. 'Unrip your plan, captain,' he cried eagerly.

'To return to the ship,' Hook replied slowly through his teeth, 'and cook a large rich cake of a jolly thickness with green sugar on it. There can be but one room below, for there is but one chimney. The silly moles had not the sense to see that they did not need a door apiece. That shows they have no mother. We will leave the cake on the shore of the mermaids' lagoon. These boys are always swimming about there, playing with the mermaids. They will find the cake and they will gobble it up, because, having no mother, they don't know how dangerous 'tis to eat rich damp cake.' He burst into laughter, not hollow laughter now, but honest laughter. 'Aha, they will die.'

Smee had listened with growing admiration.

'It's the wickedest, prettiest policy ever I heard of,' he cried, and in their exultation they danced and sang:

'Avast, belay, when I appear,
By fear they're overtook;
Naught's left upon your bones when you
Have shaken claws with Hook.'

They began the verse, but they never finished it, for another sound broke in and stilled them. It was at first such a tiny sound that a leaf might have fallen on it and smothered it, but as it came nearer it was more distinct.

Tick tick tick tick.

Hook stood shuddering, one foot in the air.

'The crocodile,' he gasped, and bounded away, followed by his bo'sun.

It was indeed the crocodile. It had passed the redskins,

who were now on the trail of the other pirates. It oozed on after Hook.

Once more the boys emerged into the open; but the dangers of the night were not yet over, for presently Nibs rushed breathless into their midst, pursued by a pack of wolves. The tongues of the pursuers were hanging out; the baying of them was horrible.

'Save me, save me!' cried Nibs, falling on the ground.

'But what can we do, what can we do?'

It was a high compliment to Peter that at that dire moment their thoughts turned to him.

'What would Peter do?' they cried simultaneously.

Almost in the same breath they added, 'Peter would look at them through his legs.'

And then, 'Let us do what Peter would do.'

It is quite the most successful way of defying wolves, and as one boy they bent and looked through their legs.

The next moment is the long one; but victory came quickly, for as the boys advanced upon them in this terrible attitude, the wolves dropped their tails and fled.

Now Nibs rose from the ground, and the others thought that his staring eyes still saw the wolves. But it was not wolves he saw.

'I have seen a wonderfuller thing,' he cried as they gathered round him eagerly. 'A great white bird. It is flying this way.'

'What kind of a bird, do you think?'

'I don't know,' Nibs said, awestruck, 'but it looks so weary, and as it flies it moans, "Poor Wendy".'

'Poor Wendy?'

'I remember,' said Slightly instantly, 'there are birds called Wendies.'

'See, it comes,' cried Curly, pointing to Wendy in the heavens.

Wendy was now almost overhead, and they could hear her plaintive cry. But more distinct came the shrill voice of Tinker Bell. The jealous fairy had now cast off all disguise of friendship, and was darting at her victim from every direction, pinching savagely each time she touched.

'Hallo, Tink,' cried the wondering boys.

Tink's reply rang out: 'Peter wants you to shoot the Wendy.'

It was not in their nature to question when Peter ordered. 'Let us do what Peter wishes,' cried the simple boys. 'Quick, bows and arrows.'

All but Tootles popped down their trees. He had a bow and arrow with him, and Tink noted it, and rubbed her little hands.

'Quick, Tootles, quick,' she screamed. 'Peter will be so pleased.'

Tootles excitedly fitted the arrow to his bow. 'Out of the way, Tink,' he shouted; and then he fired, and Wendy fluttered to the ground with an arrow in her breast.

6

The Little House

Foolish Tootles was standing like a conqueror over Wendy's body when the other boys sprang, armed, from their trees.

'You are too late,' he cried proudly, 'I have shot the Wendy, Peter will be so pleased with me.'

Overhead Tinker Bell shouted, 'Silly ass!' and darted into hiding. The others did not hear her. They had crowded round Wendy, and as they looked a terrible silence fell upon the wood. If Wendy's heart had been beating they would all have heard it.

Slightly was the first to speak. 'This is no bird,' he said in a scared voice. 'I think it must be a lady.'

'A lady?' said Tootles, and fell a-trembling.

'And we have killed her,' Nibs said hoarsely.

They all whipped off their caps.

'Now I see,' Curly said; 'Peter was bringing her to us.' He threw himself sorrowfully on the ground.

'A lady to take care of us at last,' said one of the twins, 'and you have killed her.'

They were sorry for him, but sorrier for themselves, and when he took a step nearer them they turned from him.

Tootles' face was very white, but there was a dignity about him now that had never been there before.

'I did it,' he said, reflecting. 'When ladies used to come to me in dreams, I said, "Pretty mother, pretty mother." But when at last she really came, I shot her.'

He moved slowly away.

'Don't go,' they called in pity.

'I must,' he answered, shaking; 'I am so afraid of Peter.'

It was at this tragic moment that they heard a sound which made the heart of every one of them rise to his mouth. They heard Peter crow.

'Peter!' they cried, for it was always thus that he signalled his return.

'Hide her,' they whispered, and gathered hastily around Wendy. But Tootles stood aloof.

Again came that ringing crow, and Peter dropped in front of them. 'Greetings, boys,' he cried, and mechanically they saluted, and then again was silence.

He frowned.

'I am back,' he said hotly, 'why do you not cheer?'

They opened their mouths, but the cheers would not come. He overlooked it in his haste to tell the glorious tidings.

'Great news, boys,' he cried. 'I have brought at last a mother for you all.'

Still no sound, except a little thud from Tootles as he dropped on his knees.

'Have you not seen her?' asked Peter, becoming troubled. 'She flew this way.'

'Ah me,' one voice said, and another said, 'Oh, mournful day.'

Tootles rose. 'Peter,' he said quietly, 'I will show her to you'; and when the others would still have hidden her he said, 'Back, twins, let Peter see.'

So they all stood back, and let him see, and after he had looked for a little time he did not know what to do next.

'She is dead,' he said uncomfortably. 'Perhaps she is frightened at being dead.'

He thought of hopping off in a comic sort of way till he was out of sight of her, and then never going near the spot any more. They would all have been glad to follow if he had done this.

But there was the arrow. He took it from her heart and faced his band.

'Whose arrow?' he demanded sternly.

'Mine, Peter,' said Tootles on his knees.

'Oh, dastard hand,' Peter said, and he raised the arrow to use it as a dagger.

Tootles did not flinch. He bared his breast. 'Strike, Peter,' he said firmly, 'strike true.'

Twice did Peter raise the arrow, and twice did his hand fall. 'I cannot strike,' he said with awe, 'there is something stays my hand.'

All looked at him in wonder, save Nibs, who fortunately looked at Wendy.

'It is she,' he cried, 'the Wendy lady; see, her arm.'

Wonderful to relate, Wendy had raised her arm. Nibs bent over her and listened reverently. 'I think she said "Poor Tootles",' he whispered.

'She lives,' Peter said briefly.

Slightly cried instantly, 'The Wendy lady lives.'

Then Peter knelt beside her and found his button. You remember she had put it on a chain that she wore round her neck.

'See,' he said, 'the arrow struck against this. It is the kiss I gave her. It has saved her life.'

'I remember kisses,' Slightly interposed quickly, 'let me see it. Aye, that's a kiss.'

Peter did not hear him. He was begging Wendy to get better quickly, so that he could show her the mermaids. Of course she could not answer yet, being still in a frightful faint; but from overhead came a wailing note.

'Listen to Tink,' said Curly, 'she is crying because the Wendy lives.'

Then they had to tell Peter of Tink's crime, and almost never had they seen him look so stern.

'Listen, Tinker Bell,' he cried; 'I am your friend no more. Begone from me for ever.'

She flew on to his shoulder and pleaded, but he brushed her off. Not until Wendy again raised her arm did he relent sufficiently to say, 'Well, not for ever, but for a whole week.'

Do you think Tinker Bell was grateful to Wendy for raising her arm? Oh dear no, never wanted to pinch her so much. Fairies indeed are strange, and Peter, who understood them best, often cuffed them.

But what to do with Wendy in her present delicate state of health?

'Let us carry her down into the house,' Curly suggested.

'Aye,' said Slightly, 'that is what one does with ladies.'

'No, no,' Peter said, 'you must not touch her. It would not be sufficiently respectful.'

'That,' said Slightly, 'is what I was thinking.'

'But if she lies there,' Tootles said, 'she will die.'

'Aye, she will die,' Slightly admitted, 'but there is no way out.'

'Yes, there is,' cried Peter. 'Let us build a little house round her.'

They were all delighted. 'Quick,' he ordered them, 'bring me each of you the best of what we have. Gut our house. Be sharp.'

In a moment they were as busy as tailors the night before a wedding. They skurried this way and that, down for bedding, up for firewood, and while they were at it, who should appear but John and Michael. As they dragged along the ground they fell asleep standing, stopped, woke up, moved another step and slept again.

'John, John,' Michael would cry, 'wake up. Where is Nana, John, and mother?'

And then John would rub his eyes and mutter, 'It is true, we did fly.'

You may be sure they were very relieved to find Peter.

'Hallo, Peter,' they said.

'Hallo,' replied Peter amicably, though he had quite forgotten them. He was very busy at the moment measuring Wendy with his feet to see how large a house she would need. Of course he meant to leave room for chairs and a table. John and Michael watched him.

'Is Wendy asleep?' they asked.

'Yes.'

'John,' Michael proposed, 'let us wake her and get her to make supper for us'; but as he said it some of the other boys rushed on carrying branches for the building of the house. 'Look at them!' he cried.

'Curly,' said Peter in his most captainy voice, 'see that these boys help in the building of the house.'

'Aye, aye, sir.'

'Build a house?' exclaimed John.

'For the Wendy,' said Curly.

'For Wendy?' John said aghast. 'Why, she is only a girl.'

'That,' explained Curly, 'is why we are her servants.'

'You? Wendy's servants!'

'Yes,' said Peter, 'and you also. Away with them.'

The astounded brothers were dragged away to hack and hew and carry. 'Chairs and a fender first,' Peter ordered. 'Then we shall build the house round them.'

'Aye,' said Slightly, 'that is how a house is built; it all comes back to me.'

Peter thought of everything. 'Slightly,' he ordered, 'fetch a doctor.'

'Aye, aye,' said Slightly at once, and disappeared, scratching his head. But he knew Peter must be obeyed, and he returned in a moment, wearing John's hat and looking solemn.

'Please, sir,' said Peter, going to him, 'are you a doctor?'

The difference between him and the other boys at such a time was that they knew it was make-believe, while to him make-believe and true were exactly the same thing. This sometimes troubled them, as when they had to make-believe that they had had their dinners.

If they broke down in their make-believe he rapped them on the knuckles.

'Yes, my little man,' anxiously replied Slightly, who had chapped knuckles.

'Please, sir,' Peter explained, 'a lady lies very ill.'

She was lying at their feet, but Slightly had the sense not to see her.

'Tut, tut, tut,' he said, 'where does she lie?'

'In yonder glade.'

'I will put a glass thing in her mouth,' said Slightly; and he made-believe to do it, while Peter waited. It was an anxious moment when the glass thing was withdrawn.

'How is she?' inquired Peter.

'Tut, tut, tut,' said Slightly, 'this has cured her.'

'I am glad,' Peter cried.

'I will call again in the evening,' Slightly said; 'give her beef tea out of a cup with a spout to it'; but after he had returned the hat to John he blew big breaths, which was his habit on escaping from a difficulty.

In the meantime the wood had been alive with the sound of axes; almost everything needed for a cosy dwelling already lay at Wendy's feet.

'If only we knew,' said one, 'the kind of house she likes best.'

'Peter,' shouted another, 'she is moving in her sleep.'

'Her mouth opens,' cried a third, looking respectfully into it. 'Oh, lovely!'

'Perhaps she is going to sing in her sleep,' said Peter. 'Wendy, sing the kind of house you would like to have.'

Immediately, without opening her eyes, Wendy began to sing:

'I wish I had a pretty house,
The littlest ever seen,
With funny little red walls
And roof of mossy green.'

They gurgled with joy at this, for by the greatest good luck the branches they had brought were sticky with red sap, and all the ground was carpeted with moss. As they rattled up the little house they broke into song themselves:

'We've built the little walls and roof
And made a lovely door,
So tell us, mother Wendy,
What are you wanting more?'

To this she answered rather greedily:

'Oh, really, next I think I'll have
Gay windows all about,
With roses peeping in, you know,
And babies peeping out.'

With a blow of their fists they made windows, and large yellow leaves were the blinds. But roses –?

'Roses,' cried Peter sternly.

Quickly they made-believe to grow the loveliest roses up the walls.

Babies?

To prevent Peter ordering babies they hurried into song again:

> 'We've made the roses peeping out,
> The babies are at the door,
> We cannot make ourselves, you know,
> 'Cos we've been made before.'

Peter, seeing this to be a good idea, at once pretended that it was his own. The house was quite beautiful, and no doubt Wendy was very cosy within, though, of course, they could no longer see her. Peter strode up and down, ordering finishing touches. Nothing escaped his eagle eye. Just when it seemed absolutely finished:

'There's no knocker on the door,' he said.

They were very ashamed, but Tootles gave the sole of his shoe, and it made an excellent knocker.

Absolutely finished now, they thought.

Not a bit of it. 'There's no chimney,' Peter said; 'we must have a chimney.'

'It certainly does need a chimney,' said John importantly. This gave Peter an idea. He snatched the hat off John's head, knocked out the bottom, and put the hat on the roof. The little house was so pleased to have such a capital chimney that, as if to say thank you, smoke immediately began to come out of the hat.

Now really and truly it was finished. Nothing remained to do but to knock.

'All look your best,' Peter warned them; 'first impressions are awfully important.'

He was glad no one asked him what first impressions are; they were all too busy looking their best.

He knocked politely; and now the wood was as still as the children, not a sound to be heard except from Tinker Bell, who was watching from a branch and openly sneering.

What the boys were wondering was, would anyone answer the knock? If a lady, what would she be like?

The door opened and a lady came out. It was Wendy. They all whipped off their hats.

She looked properly surprised, and this was just how they had hoped she would look.

'Where am I?' she said.

Of course Slightly was the first to get his word in. 'Wendy lady,' he said rapidly, 'for you we built this house.'

'Oh, say you're pleased,' cried Nibs.

'Lovely, darling house,' Wendy said, and they were the very words they had hoped she would say.

'And we are your children,' cried the twins.

Then all went on their knees, and holding out their arms cried, 'O Wendy lady, be our mother.'

'Ought I?' Wendy said, all shining. 'Of course it's frightfully fascinating, but you see I am only a little girl. I have no real experience.'

'That doesn't matter,' said Peter, as if he were the only person present who knew all about it, though he was really the one who knew least. 'What we need is just a nice motherly person.'

'Oh dear!' Wendy said, 'you see I feel that is exactly what I am.'

'It is, it is,' they all cried; 'we saw it at once.'

'Very well,' she said, 'I will do my best. Come inside at once, you naughty children; I am sure your feet are damp. And before I put you to bed I have just time to finish the story of Cinderella.'

In they went; I don't know how there was room for them, but you can squeeze very tight in the Neverland. And that was the first of the many joyous evenings they had with Wendy. By and by she tucked them up in the great bed in the home under the trees, but she herself slept that night in the little house, and Peter kept watch outside with drawn sword, for the pirates could be heard carousing far away and the wolves were on the prowl. The little house looked so cosy and safe in the darkness with a bright light showing through its blinds, and the chimney smoking beautifully, and Peter standing on guard.

After a time he fell asleep, and some unsteady fairies had to climb over him on their way home from an orgy. And of the other boys obstructing the fairy path at night they would have mischiefed, but they just tweaked Peter's nose and passed on.

7

The Home Under the Ground

One of the first things Peter did next day was to measure Wendy and John and Michael for hollow trees. Hook, you remember, had sneered at the boys for thinking they needed a tree apiece, but this was ignorance, for unless your tree fitted you it was difficult to go up and down, and no two of the boys were quite the same size. Once you fitted, you drew in your breath at the top, and down you went at exactly the right speed, while to ascend you drew in and let out alternately, and so wriggled up. Of course, when you have mastered the action you are able to do these things without thinking of them, and then nothing can be more graceful.

But you simply must fit, and Peter measures you for your tree as carefully as for a suit of clothes: the only difference being that the clothes are made to fit you, while you have to be made to fit the tree. Usually it is done quite easily, as by your wearing too many garments or too few; but if you are bumpy in awkward places or the only available tree is an odd shape, Peter does some things to you, and after that you fit. Once you fit, great care must be taken to go on fitting, and this, as Wendy was to discover to her delight, keeps a whole family in perfect condition.

Wendy and Michael fitted their trees at the first try, but John had to be altered a little.

After a few days' practice they could go up and down as gaily as buckets in a well. And how ardently they grew to love their home under the ground; especially Wendy. It consisted of one large room, as all houses should do, with a floor in which you could dig if you wanted to go fishing, and in this floor grew stout mushrooms of a charming colour, which were used as stools. A Never tree tried hard to grow in the centre of the room, but every morning they sawed the trunk through, level with the floor. By tea-time it was always about two feet high, and then they put a door on top of it, the whole thus becoming a table; as soon as they cleared away, they sawed off the trunk again, and thus there was more room to play. There was an enormous fire-place which was in almost any part of the room where you cared to light it, and across this Wendy stretched strings, made of fibre, from which she suspended her washing. The bed was tilted against the wall by day, and let down at 6.30, when it filled nearly half the room; and all the boys except Michael slept in it, lying like sardines in a tin. There was a strict rule against turning round until one gave the signal, when all turned at once. Michael should have used it also; but Wendy would have a baby, and he was the littlest, and you know what women are, and the short and the long of it is that he was hung up in a basket.

It was rough and simple, and not unlike what baby bears would have made of an underground house in the same circumstances. But there was one recess in the wall, no larger than a bird-cage, which was the private apartment of Tinker Bell. It could be shut off from the rest of the home by a tiny curtain, which Tink, who was most fastidious, always kept drawn when dressing or undressing. No woman, however large, could have had a more exquisite boudoir and bedchamber combined. The couch, as she always called it, was a genuine Queen Mab, with club legs; and she varied the bedspreads according to what fruit-blossom was in season. Her mirror was a Puss-in-boots, of which there are now only three, unchipped, known to the fairy dealers; the wash-stand was Pie-crust and revers-ible, the chest of drawers an authentic Charming the Sixth, and the carpet and rugs of the best (the early) period of Margery and Robin. There was a chandelier from Tiddlywinks for the look of the thing, but of course she lit the residence herself. Tink was very contemptuous of the rest of the house, as indeed was perhaps inevitable; and her chamber, though beautiful, looked rather conceited, having the appearance of a nose permanently turned up.

I suppose it was all especially entrancing to Wendy,

because those rampagious boys of hers gave her so much to do. Really there were whole weeks when, except perhaps with a stocking in the evening, she was never above ground. The cooking, I can tell you, kept her nose to the pot. Their chief food was roasted bread-fruit, yams, coconuts, baked pig, mammee-apples, tappa rolls and bananas, washed down with calabashes of poe-poe; but you never exactly knew whether there would be a real meal or just a make-believe, it all depended upon Peter's whim. He could eat, really eat, if it was part of a game, but he could not stodge just to feel stodgy, which is what most children like better than anything else; the next best thing being to talk about it. Make-believe was so real to him that during a meal of it you could see him getting rounder. Of course it was trying, but you simply had to follow his lead, and if you could prove to him that you were getting loose for your tree he let you stodge.

Wendy's favourite time for sewing and darning was after they had all gone to bed. Then, as she expressed it, she had a breathing time for herself; and she occupied it in making new things for them, and putting double pieces on the knees, for they were all most frightfully hard on their knees.

When she sat down to a basketful of their stockings, every heel with a hole in it, she would fling up her arms and exclaim, 'Oh dear, I am sure I sometimes think spinsters are to be envied.'

Her face beamed when she exclaimed this.

You remember about her pet wolf. Well, it very soon discovered that she had come to the island and it found her out, and they just ran into each other's arms. After that it followed her about everywhere.

As time wore on did she think much about the beloved parents she had left behind her? This is a difficult question, because it is quite impossible to say how time does wear on in the Neverland, where it is calculated by moons and suns, and there are ever so many more of them than on the mainland. But I am afraid that Wendy did not really worry about her father and mother; she was absolutely confident that they would always keep the window open for her to fly back by, and this gave her complete ease of mind. What did disturb her at times was that John remembered his parents vaguely only, as people he had once known, while Michael was quite willing to believe that she was really his mother. These things scared her a little, and nobly anxious to do her duty, she tried to fix the old life in their minds by setting them examination papers on it, as like as possible to the ones she used to do at school. The other boys thought this awfully interesting and insisted on joining, and they made slates for themselves, and sat round the table, writing and thinking hard about the questions she had written on another slate and passed round. They were the most ordinary questions – 'What was the colour of Mother's eyes? Which was taller, Father or Mother? Was Mother blonde or brunette? Answer all three questions if possible.' '(A) Write an essay of not less than 40 words on How I spent my last Holidays, or The Characters of Father and Mother compared. Only one of these to be attempted.' Or '(1) Describe Mother's laugh; (2) Describe Father's laugh; (3) Describe Mother's Party Dress; (4) Describe the Kennel and its Inmate.'

They were just everyday questions like these, and when you could not answer them you were told to make a cross and it was really dreadful what a number of crosses even John made. Of course the only boy who replied to every question was Slightly, and no one could have been more hopeful of coming out first, but his answers were perfectly ridiculous, and he really came out last: a melancholy thing.

Peter did not compete. For one thing he despised all mothers except Wendy, and for another he was the only boy on the island who could neither write nor spell; not the smallest word. He was above all that sort of thing.

By the way, the questions were all written in the past tense. What was the colour of Mother's eyes, and so on. Wendy, you see, had been forgetting too.

Adventures, of course, as we shall see, were of daily occurrence; but about this time Peter invented, with Wendy's help, a new game that fascinated him enormously, until he suddenly had no more interest in it, which, as you have been told, was what always happened with his games. It consisted in pretending not to have adventures, in doing the sort of thing John and Michael had been doing all their lives: sitting on stools flinging balls in the air, pushing each other, going out for walks and coming back without having killed so much as a grizzly. To see Peter doing nothing on a stool was a great sight; he could not help looking solemn at such times, to sit still seemed to him such a comic thing to do. He boasted that he had gone a walk for the good of his health. For several suns these were the most novel of all adventures to him; and John and Michael had to pretend to be delighted also; otherwise he would have treated them severely.

He often went out alone, and when he came back you were never absolutely certain whether he had had an adventure or not. He might have forgotten it so completely that he said nothing about it; and then when you went out you found the body; and, on the other hand, he might say a great deal about it, and yet you could not find the body. Sometimes he came home with his head bandaged, and then Wendy cooed over him and bathed it in lukewarm water, while he told a dazzling tale. But she was never quite sure, you know. There were, however, many adventures which she knew to be true because she was in them herself, and there were still more that were at least partly true, for the other boys were in them and said they were wholly true. To describe them all would require a book as large as an English–Latin, Latin–English Dictionary, and the most we can do is to give one as a specimen of an average hour on the island. The difficulty is which one to choose. Should we take the brush with the redskins at Slightly Gulch? It was a sanguinary affair, and especially interesting as showing one of Peter's peculiarities, which was that in the middle of a fight he would suddenly change sides. At the Gulch, when victory was still in the balance, sometimes leaning this way and sometimes that, he called out, 'I'm redskin today; what are you, Tootles?' And Tootles answered, 'Redskin; what are you, Nibs?' and Nibs said, 'Redskin; what are you, Twin?' and so on; and they were all redskin; and of course this would have ended the fight had not the real redskins, fascinated by Peter's methods, agreed to be lost boys for that once, and so at it they all went again, more fiercely than ever.

The extraordinary upshot of this adventure was – but we have not decided yet that this is the adventure we are to narrate. Perhaps a better one would be the night attack by the redskins on the house under the ground, when several of them stuck in the hollow trees and had to be pulled out like corks. Or we might tell how Peter saved Tiger Lily's life in the Mermaids' Lagoon, and so made her his ally.

Or we could tell of that cake the pirates cooked so that the boys might eat it and perish; and how they placed it in one cunning spot after another; but always Wendy snatched it from the hands of her children, so that in time it lost its succulence, and became as hard as a stone, and was used as a missile, and Hook fell over it in the dark.

Or suppose we tell of the birds that were Peter's friends, particularly of the Never bird that built in a tree overhanging the lagoon, and how the nest fell into the water, and still the bird sat on her eggs, and Peter gave orders that she was not to be disturbed. That is a pretty story, and the end shows how grateful a bird can be; but if we tell it we must also tell the whole adventure of the lagoon, which would of course be telling two adventures rather than just one. A shorter adventure, and quite as exciting, was Tinker Bell's attempt, with the help of some street fairies, to have the sleeping Wendy conveyed on a great floating leaf to the mainland. Fortunately the leaf gave way and Wendy woke, thinking it was bath-time, and swam back. Or again, we might choose Peter's defiance of the lions, when he drew a circle round him on the ground with an arrow and defied them to cross it; and though he waited for hours, with the other boys and Wendy looking on breathlessly from trees, not one of them dared to accept his challenge.

Which of these adventures shall we choose? The best way will be to toss for it.

I have tossed, and the lagoon has won. This almost makes one wish that the gulch or the cake or Tink's leaf had won. Of course I could do it again, and make it best out of three; however, perhaps fairest to stick to the lagoon.

8

The Mermaids' Lagoon

If you shut your eyes and are a lucky one, you may see
at times a shapeless pool of lovely pale colours suspended
in the darkness; then if you squeeze your eyes tighter, the
pool begins to take shape, and the colours become so
vivid that with another squeeze they must go on fire. But
just before they go on fire you see the lagoon. This is the
nearest you ever get to it on the mainland, just one heavenly moment; if there could be two moments you might
see the surf and hear the mermaids singing.

The children often spent long summer days on this
lagoon, swimming or floating most of the time, playing
the mermaid games in the water and so forth. You must
not think from this that the mermaids were on friendly
terms with them; on the contrary, it was among Wendy's
lasting regrets that all the time she was on the island she
never had a civil word from one of them. When she stole
softly to the edge of the lagoon she might see them by
the score, especially on the Marooners' Rock, where they
loved to bask, combing out their hair in a lazy way that

quite irritated her; or she might even swim, on tiptoe as it were, to within a yard of them, but then they saw her and dived, probably splashing her with their tails, not by accident, but intentionally.

They treated all the boys in the same way, except of course Peter, who chatted with them on Marooners' Rock by the hour, and sat on their tails when they got cheeky. He gave Wendy one of their combs.

The most haunting time at which to see them is at the turn of the moon, when they utter strange wailing cries; but the lagoon is dangerous for mortals then, and until the evening of which we have now to tell, Wendy had never seen the lagoon by moonlight, less from fear, for of course Peter would have accompanied her, than because she had strict rules about every one being in bed by seven. She was often at the lagoon, however, on sunny days after rain, when the mermaids come up in extraordinary numbers to play with their bubbles. The bubbles of many colours made in rainbow water they treat as balls, hitting them gaily from one to another with their tails, and trying to keep them in the rainbow till they burst. The goals are at each end of the rainbow, and the keepers only are allowed to use their hands. Sometimes hundreds of mermaids will be playing in the lagoon at a time, and it is quite a pretty sight.

But the moment the children tried to join in they had to play by themselves, for the mermaids immediately disappeared. Nevertheless we have proof that they secretly

95

watched the interlopers, and were not above taking an idea from them; for John introduced a new way of hitting the bubble, with the head instead of the hand, and the mermaid goal-keepers adopted it. This is the one mark that John has left on the Neverland.

It must also have been rather pretty to see the children resting on a rock for half an hour after their midday meal. Wendy insisted on their doing this, and it had to be a real rest even though the meal was make-believe. So they lay there in the sun, and their bodies glistened in it, while she sat beside them and looked important.

It was one such day, and they were all on Marooners' Rock. The rock was not much larger than their great bed, but of course they all knew how not to take up much room, and they were dozing, or at least lying with their eyes shut, and pinching occasionally when they thought Wendy was not looking. She was very busy, stitching.

While she stitched a change came to the lagoon. Little shivers ran over it, and the sun went away and shadows stole across the water, turning it cold. Wendy could no longer see to thread her needle, and when she looked up, the lagoon that had always hitherto been such a laughing place seemed formidable and unfriendly.

It was not, she knew, that night had come, but something as dark as night had come. No, worse than that. It had not come, but it had sent that shiver through the sea to say that it was coming. What was it?

There crowded upon her all the stories she had been told of Marooners' Rock, so called because evil captains put sailors on it and leave them there to drown. They drown when the tide rises, for then it is submerged.

Of course she should have roused the children at once; not merely because of the unknown that was stalking towards them, but because it was no longer good for them to sleep on a rock grown chilly. But she was a young mother and she did not know this; she thought you simply must stick to your rule about half an hour after the midday meal. So, though fear was upon her, and she longed to hear male voices, she would not waken them. Even when she heard the sound of muffled oars, though her heart was in her mouth, she did not waken them. She stood over them to let them have their sleep out. Was it not brave of Wendy?

It was well for those boys then that there was one among them who could sniff danger even in his sleep. Peter sprang erect, as wide awake at once as a dog, and with one warning cry he roused the others.

He stood motionless, one hand to his ear.

'Pirates!' he cried. The others came closer to him. A strange smile was playing about his face, and Wendy saw it and shuddered. While that smile was on his face no one dared address him; all they could do was to stand ready to obey. The order came sharply and incisive.

'Dive!'

There was a gleam of legs, and instantly the lagoon seemed deserted. Marooners' Rock stood alone in the forbidding waters, as if it were itself marooned.

The boat drew nearer. It was the pirate dinghy, with three figures in her, Smee and Starkey, and the third a captive, no other than Tiger Lily. Her hands and ankles were tied, and she knew what was to be her fate. She was to be left on the rock to perish, an end to one of her race more terrible than death by fire or torture, for is it not written in the book of the tribe that there is no path through water to the happy hunting-ground? Yet her face was impassive; she was the daughter of a chief, she must die as a chief's daughter, it is enough.

They had caught her boarding the pirate ship with a knife in her mouth. No watch was kept on the ship, it being Hook's boast that the wind of his name guarded the ship for a mile around. Now her fate would help to guard it also. One more wail would go the round in that wind by night.

In the gloom that they brought with them the two pirates did not see the rock till they crashed into it.

'Luff, you lubber,' cried an Irish voice that was Smee's; 'here's the rock. Now, then, what we have to do is to hoist the redskin on to it, and leave her there to drown.'

It was the work of one brutal moment to land the beautiful girl on the rock; she was too proud to offer a vain resistance.

Quite near the rock, but out of sight, two heads were bobbing up and down, Peter's and Wendy's. Wendy was crying, for it was the first tragedy she had seen. Peter had seen many tragedies, but he had forgotten them all. He was less sorry than Wendy for Tiger Lily; it was two against one that angered him, and he meant to save her. An easy way would have been to wait until the pirates had gone, but he was never one to choose the easy way.

There was almost nothing he could not do, and he now imitated the voice of Hook.

'Ahoy there, you lubbers,' he called. It was a marvellous imitation.

'The captain,' said the pirates, staring at each other in surprise.

'He must be swimming out to us,' Starkey said, when they had looked for him in vain.

'We are putting the redskin on the rock,' Smee called out.

'Set her free,' came the astonishing answer.

'Free!'

'Yes, cut her bonds and let her go.'

'But, captain –'

'At once, d'ye hear,' cried Peter, 'or I'll plunge my hook in you.'

'This is queer,' Smee gasped.

'Better do what the captain orders,' said Starkey nervously.

'Aye, aye,' Smee said, and he cut Tiger Lily's cords. At once like an eel she slid between Starkey's legs into the water.

Of course Wendy was very elated over Peter's cleverness; but she knew that he would be elated also and very likely crow and thus betray himself, so at once her hand went out to cover his mouth. But it was stayed even in the act, for 'Boat ahoy!' rang over the lagoon in Hook's voice, and this time it was not Peter who had spoken.

Peter may have been about to crow, but his face puckered in a whistle of surprise instead.

'Boat ahoy!' again came the cry.

Now Wendy understood. The real Hook was also in the water.

He was swimming to the boat, and as his men showed a light to guide him he had soon reached them. In the light of the lantern Wendy saw his hook grip the boat's side; she saw his evil swarthy face as he rose dripping from the water, and, quaking, she would have liked to swim away, but Peter would not budge. He was tingling with life and also top-heavy with conceit. 'Am I not a wonder, oh, I am a wonder!' he whispered to her; and though she thought so also, she was really glad for the sake of his reputation that no one heard him except herself.

He signed to her to listen.

The two pirates were very curious to know what had brought their captain to them, but he sat with his head on his hook in a position of profound melancholy.

'Captain, is all well?' they asked timidly, but he answered with a hollow moan.

'He sighs,' said Smee.

'He sighs again,' said Starkey.

'And yet a third time he sighs,' said Smee.

'What's up, captain?'

Then at last he spoke passionately.

'The game's up,' he cried; 'those boys have found a mother.'

Affrighted though she was, Wendy swelled with pride.

'O evil day,' cried Starkey.

'What's a mother?' asked the ignorant Smee.

Wendy was so shocked that she exclaimed, 'He doesn't know!' and always after this she felt that if you could have a pet pirate Smee would be her one.

Peter pulled her beneath the water, for Hook had started up, crying, 'What was that?'

'I heard nothing,' said Starkey, raising the lantern over the waters, and as the pirates looked they saw a strange sight. It was the nest I have told you of, floating on the lagoon, and the Never bird was sitting on it.

'See,' said Hook in answer to Smee's question, 'that is a mother. What a lesson! The nest must have fallen into the water, but would the mother desert her eggs? No.'

There was a break in his voice, as if for a moment he recalled innocent days when – but he brushed away his weakness with his hook.

Smee, much impressed, gazed at the bird as the nest was borne past, but the more suspicious Starkey said, 'If she is a mother, perhaps she is hanging about here to help Peter.'

Hook winced. 'Aye,' he said, 'that is the fear that haunts me.'

He was roused from this dejection by Smee's eager voice.

'Captain,' said Smee, 'could we not kidnap these boys' mother and make her our mother?'

'It is a princely scheme,' cried Hook, and at once it took practical shape in his great brain. 'We will seize the children and carry them to the boat: the boys we will make walk the plank, and Wendy shall be our mother.'

Again Wendy forgot herself.

'Never!' she cried, and bobbed.

'What was that?'

But they could see nothing. They thought it must have been but a leaf in the wind. 'Do you agree, my bullies?' asked Hook.

'There is my hand on it,' they both said.

'And there is my hook. Swear.'

They all swore. By this time they were on the rock and suddenly Hook remembered Tiger Lily.

'Where is the redskin?' he demanded abruptly.

He had a playful humour at moments, and they thought this was one of the moments.

'That is all right, captain,' Smee answered complacently, 'we let her go.'

'Let her go!' cried Hook.

''Twas your own orders,' the bos'un faltered.

'You called over the water to us to let her go,' said Starkey.

'Brimstone and gall,' thundered Hook, 'what cozening is here?' His face had gone black with rage, but he saw that they believed their words, and he was startled. 'Lads,' he said, shaking a little, 'I gave no such order.'

'It is passing queer,' Smee said, and they all fidgeted uncomfortably. Hook raised his voice, but there was a quiver in it.

'Spirit that haunts this dark lagoon tonight,' he cried, 'dost hear me?'

Of course Peter should have kept quiet, but of course he did not. He immediately answered in Hook's voice:

'Odds, bobs, hammer and tongs, I hear you.'

In that supreme moment Hook did not blanch, even at the gills, but Smee and Starkey clung to each other in terror.

'Who are you, stranger, speak?' Hook demanded.

'I am James Hook,' replied the voice, 'captain of the *Jolly Roger*.'

'You are not; you are not,' Hook cried hoarsely.

'Brimstone and gall,' the voice retorted, 'say that again, and I'll cast anchor in you.'

Hook tried a more ingratiating manner. 'If you are Hook,' he said almost humbly, 'come, tell me, who am I?'

'A codfish,' replied the voice, 'only a codfish.'

'A codfish!' Hook echoed blankly; and it was then, but not till then, that his proud spirit broke. He saw his men draw back from him.

'Have we been captained all this time by a codfish?' they muttered. 'It is lowering to our pride.'

They were his dogs snapping at him, but, tragic figure though he had become, he scarcely heeded them. Against such fearful evidence it was not their belief in him that he needed, it was his own. He felt his ego slipping from him. 'Don't desert me, bully,' he whispered hoarsely to it.

In the dark nature there was a touch of the feminine, as in all the great pirates, and it sometimes gave him intuitions. Suddenly he tried the guessing game.

'Hook,' he called, 'have you another voice?'

Now Peter could never resist a game, and he answered blithely in his own voice, 'I have.'

'And another name?'

'Aye, aye.'

'Vegetable?' asked Hook.

'No.'

'Mineral?'

'No.'

'Animal?'

'Yes.'

'Man?'

'No!' This answer rang out scornfully.

'Boy?'

'Yes.'

'Ordinary boy?'

'No!'

'Wonderful boy?'

To Wendy's pain the answer that rang out this time was 'Yes.'

'Are you in England?'

'No.'

'Are you here?'

'Yes.'

Hook was completely puzzled. 'You ask him some questions,' he said to the others, wiping his damp brow.

Smee reflected. 'I can't think of a thing,' he said regretfully.

'Can't guess, can't guess,' crowed Peter. 'Do you give it up?'

Of course in his pride he was carrying the game too far, and the miscreants saw their chance.

'Yes, yes,' they answered eagerly.

'Well, then,' he cried, 'I am Peter Pan.'

Pan!

In a moment Hook was himself again, and Smee and Starkey were his faithful henchmen.

'Now we have him,' Hook shouted. 'Into the water, Smee. Starkey, mind the boat. Take him dead or alive.'

He leaped as he spoke, and simultaneously came the gay voice of Peter.

'Are you ready, boys?'

'Aye, aye,' from various parts of the lagoon.

'Then lam into the pirates.'

The fight was short and sharp. First to draw blood was John, who gallantly climbed into the boat and held Starkey. There was a fierce struggle, in which the cutlass was torn from the pirate's grasp. He wriggled overboard and John leapt after him. The dinghy drifted away.

Here and there a head bobbed up in the water, and there was a flash of steel, followed by a cry or a whoop. In the confusion some struck at their own side. The corkscrew of Smee got Tootles in the fourth rib, but he was himself pinked in turn by Curly. Farther from the rock Starkey was pressing Slightly and the twins hard.

Where all this time was Peter? He was seeking bigger game.

The others were all brave boys, and they must not be blamed for backing from the pirate captain. His iron claw made a circle of dead water round him, from which they fled like affrighted fishes.

But there was one who did not fear him: there was one prepared to enter that circle.

Strangely, it was not in the water that they met. Hook

rose to the rock to breathe, and at the same moment Peter scaled it on the opposite side. The rock was slippery as a ball, and they had to crawl rather than climb. Neither knew that the other was coming. Each feeling for a grip met the other's arm: in surprise they raised their heads; their faces were almost touching; so they met.

Some of the greatest heroes have confessed that just before they fell to they had a sinking. Had it been so with Peter at that moment I would admit it. After all, this was the only man that the Sea-Cook had feared. But Peter had no sinking, he had one feeling only, gladness; and he gnashed his pretty teeth with joy. Quick as thought he snatched a knife from Hook's belt and was about to drive it home, when he saw that he was higher up the rock than his foe. It would not have been fighting fair. He gave the pirate a hand to help him up.

It was then that Hook bit him.

Not the pain of this but its unfairness was what dazed Peter. It made him quite helpless. He could only stare, horrified. Every child is affected thus the first time he is treated unfairly. All he thinks he has a right to when he comes to you to be yours is fairness. After you have been unfair to him he will love you again, but he will never afterwards be quite the same boy. No one ever gets over the first unfairness; no one except Peter. He often met it, but he always forgot it. I suppose that was the real differ-ence between him and all the rest.

So when he met it now it was like the first time; and he could just stare, helpless. Twice the iron hand clawed him.

A few minutes afterwards the other boys saw Hook in the water striking wildly for the ship; no elation on his pestilent face now, only white fear, for the crocodile was in dogged pursuit of him. On ordinary occasions the boys would have swum alongside cheering; but now they were uneasy, for they had lost both Peter and Wendy; and were scouring the lagoon for them, calling them by name. They found the dinghy and went home in it, shouting, 'Peter, Wendy,' as they went, but no answer came save mocking laughter from the mermaids. 'They must be swimming back or flying,' the boys concluded. They were not very anxious, they had such faith in Peter. They chuckled, boylike, because they would be late for bed; and it was all Mother Wendy's fault!

When their voices died away there came cold silence over the lagoon, and then a feeble cry.

'Help, help!'

Two small figures were beating against the rock; the girl had fainted and lay on the boy's arm. With a last effort Peter pulled her up the rock and then lay down beside her. Even as he also fainted he saw that the water was rising. He knew that they would soon be drowned, but he could do no more.

As they lay side by side a mermaid caught Wendy by the

feet, and began pulling her softly into the water. Peter, feeling her slip from him, woke with a start, and was just in time to draw her back. But he had to tell her the truth.

'We are on the rock, Wendy,' he said, 'but it is growing smaller. Soon the water will be over it.'

She did not understand even now.

'We must go,' she said almost brightly.

'Yes,' he answered faintly.

'Shall we swim or fly, Peter?'

He had to tell her.

'Do you think you could swim or fly as far as the island, Wendy, without my help?'

She had to admit that she was too tired.

He moaned.

'What is it?' she asked, anxious about him at once.

'I can't help you, Wendy. Hook wounded me. I can neither fly nor swim.'

'Do you mean we shall both be drowned?'

'Look how the water is rising.'

They put their hands over their eyes to shut out the sight. They thought they would soon be no more. As they sat thus something brushed against Peter as light as a kiss, and stayed there, as if saying timidly, 'Can I be of any use?'

It was the tail of a kite, which Michael had made some days before. It had torn itself out of his hand and floated away.

'Michael's kite,' Peter said without interest, but next moment he had seized the tail, and was pulling the kite towards him.

'It lifted Michael off the ground,' he cried; 'why should it not carry you?'

'Both of us!'

'It can't lift two; Michael and Curly tried.'

'Let us draw lots,' Wendy said bravely.

'And you a lady; never.' Already he had tied the tail round her. She clung to him; she refused to go without him; but with a 'Good-bye, Wendy,' he pushed her from the rock; and in a few minutes she was borne out of his sight. Peter was alone on the lagoon.

The rock was very small now; soon it would be submerged. Pale rays of light tiptoed across the waters; and by and by there was to be heard a sound at once the most musical and the most melancholy in the world; the mermaids calling to the moon.

Peter was not quite like other boys; but he was afraid at last. A tremor ran through him, like a shudder passing over the sea; but on the sea one shudder follows another till there are hundreds of them, and Peter felt just the one. Next moment he was standing erect on the rock again, with that smile on his face and a drum beating within him. It was saying, 'To die will be an awfully big adventure.'

9

The Never Bird

The last sounds Peter heard before he was quite alone were the mermaids retiring one by one to their bedchambers under the sea. He was too far away to hear their doors shut; but every door in the coral caves where they live rings a tiny bell when it opens or closes (as in all the nicest houses on the mainland), and he heard the bells.

Steadily the waters rose till they were nibbling at his feet; and to pass the time until they made their final gulp, he watched the only thing moving on the lagoon. He thought it was a piece of floating paper, perhaps part of the kite, and wondered idly how long it would take to drift ashore.

Presently he noticed as an odd thing that it was undoubtedly out upon the lagoon with some definite purpose, for it was fighting the tide, and sometimes winning; and when it won, Peter, always sympathetic to the weaker side, could not help clapping; it was such a gallant piece of paper.

It was not really a piece of paper; it was the Never bird, making desperate efforts to reach Peter on her nest.

By working her wings, in a way she had learned since the nest fell into the water, she was able to some extent to guide her strange craft, but by the time Peter recognized her she was very exhausted. She had come to save him, to give him her nest, though there were eggs in it. I rather wonder at the bird, for though he had been nice to her, he had also sometimes tormented her. I can suppose only that, like Mrs Darling and the rest of them, she was melted because he had all his first teeth.

She called out to him what she had come for, and he called out to her what was she doing there; but of course neither of them understood the other's language. In fanciful stories people can talk to the birds freely, and I wish for the moment I could pretend that this was such a story, and say that Peter replied intelligently to the Never bird; but truth is best, and I want to tell only what really happened. Well, not only could they not understand each other, but they forgot their manners.

'I – want – you – to – get – into – the – nest,' the bird called, speaking as slowly and distinctly as possible, 'and – then – you – can – drift – ashore, but – I – am – too – tired – to – bring – it – any – nearer – so – you – must – try – to – swim – to – it.'

'What are you quacking about?' Peter answered. 'Why don't you let the nest drift as usual?'

'I – want – you –' the bird said, and repeated it all over.

Then Peter tried slow and distinct.

'What – are – you – quacking – about?' and so on.

The Never bird became irritated; they have very short tempers.

'You dunderheaded little jay,' she screamed, 'why don't you do as I tell you?'

Peter felt that she was calling him names, and at a venture he retorted hotly:

'So are you!'

Then rather curiously they both snapped out the same remark:

'Shut up!'

'Shut up!'

Nevertheless the bird was determined to save him if she could, and by one last mighty effort she propelled the nest against the rock. Then up she flew; deserting her eggs, so as to make her meaning clear.

Then at last he understood, and clutched the nest and waved his thanks to the bird as she fluttered overhead. It was not to receive his thanks, however, that she hung there in the sky; it was not even to watch him get into the nest; it was to see what he did with her eggs.

There were two large white eggs, and Peter lifted them up and reflected. The bird covered her face with her wings, so as not to see the last of her eggs; but she could not help peeping between the feathers.

I forget whether I have told you that there was a stave

on the rock, driven into it by some buccaneers of long ago to mark the site of buried treasure. The children had discovered the glittering hoard, and when in mischievous mood used to fling showers of moidores, diamonds, pearls and pieces of eight to the gulls, who pounced upon them for food, and then flew away, raging at the scurvy trick that had been played upon them. The stave was still there, and on it Starkey had hung his hat, a deep tarpaulin, watertight, with a broad brim. Peter put the eggs into this hat and set it on the lagoon. It floated beautifully.

The Never bird saw at once what he was up to, and screamed her admiration of him; and, alas, Peter crowed his agreement with her. Then he got into the nest, reared the stave in it as a mast, and hung up his shirt for a sail. At the same moment the bird fluttered down upon the hat and once more sat snugly on her eggs. She drifted in one direction, and he was borne off in another, both cheering.

Of course when Peter landed he beached his barque in a place where the bird would easily find it; but the hat was such a great success that she abandoned the nest. It drifted about till it went to pieces, and often Starkey came to the shore of the lagoon, and with many bitter feelings, watched the bird sitting on his hat. As we shall not see her again, it may be worth mentioning here that all Never birds now build in that shape of nest, with a broad brim on which the youngsters take an airing.

Great were the rejoicings when Peter reached the home under the ground almost as soon as Wendy, who had been carried hither and thither by the kite. Every boy had adventures to tell; but perhaps the biggest adventure of all was that they were several hours late for bed. This so inflated them that they did various dodgy things to get staying up still longer, such as demanding bandages; but Wendy, though glorying in having them all home again safe and sound, was scandalized by the lateness of the hour, and cried, 'To bed, to bed,' in a voice that had to be obeyed. Next day, however, she was awfully tender, and gave out bandages to every one; and they played till bedtime at limping about and carrying their arms in slings.

10

The Happy Home

One important result of the brush on the lagoon was that it made the redskins their friends. Peter had saved Tiger Lily from a dreadful fate, and now there was nothing she and her braves would not do for him. All night they sat above, keeping watch over the home under the ground and awaiting the big attack by the pirates which obviously could not be much longer delayed. Even by day they hung about, smoking the pipe of peace, and looking almost as if they wanted tit-bits to eat.

They called Peter the Great White Father, prostrating themselves before him; and he liked this tremendously, so that it was not really good for him.

'The Great White Father,' he would say to them in a very lordly manner, as they grovelled at his feet, 'is glad to see the Piccaninny warriors protecting his wigwam from the pirates.'

'Me Tiger Lily,' that lovely creature would reply. 'Peter Pan save me, me his velly nice friend. Me not let pirates hurt him.'

She was far too pretty to cringe in this way, but Peter thought it his due, and he would answer condescendingly, 'It is good. Peter Pan has spoken.'

Always when he said 'Peter Pan has spoken', it meant that they must now shut up, and they accepted it humbly in that spirit; but they were by no means so respectful to the other boys, whom they looked upon as just ordinary braves. They said 'How-do?' to them, and things like that; and what annoyed the boys was that Peter seemed to think this all right.

Secretly Wendy sympathized with them a little, but she was far too loyal a housewife to listen to any complaints against father. 'Father knows best,' she always said, whatever her private opinion might be. Her private opinion was that the redskins should not call her squaw.

We have now reached the evening that was to be known among them as the Night of Nights, because of its adventures and their upshot. The day, as if quietly gathering its forces, had been almost uneventful, and now the redskins in their blankets were at their posts above, while, below, the children were having their evening meal; all except Peter, who had gone out to get the time. The way you got the time on the island was to find the crocodile, and then stay near him till the clock struck.

This meal happened to be a make-believe tea, and they sat round the board, guzzling in their greed; and really, what with their chatter and recriminations, the noise, as

Wendy said, was positively deafening. To be sure, she did not mind noise, but she simply would not have them grabbing things, and then excusing themselves by saying that Tootles had pushed their elbow. There was a fixed rule that they must never hit back at meals, but should refer the matter of dispute to Wendy by raising the right arm politely and saying, 'I complain of So-and-so'; but what usually happened was that they forgot to do this or did it too much.

'Silence,' cried Wendy when for the twentieth time she had told them that they were not all to speak at once. 'Is your calabash empty, Slightly, darling?'

'Not quite empty, Mummy,' Slightly said, after looking into an imaginary mug.

'He hasn't even begun to drink his milk,' Nibs interposed.

This was telling, and Slightly seized his chance.

'I complain of Nibs,' he cried promptly.

John, however, had held up his hand first.

'Well, John?'

'May I sit in Peter's chair, as he is not here?'

'Sit in father's chair, John!' Wendy was scandalized. 'Certainly not.'

'He is not really our father,' John answered. 'He didn't even know how a father does till I showed him.'

This was grumbling. 'We complain of John,' cried the twins.

Tootles held up his hand. He was so much the humblest of them, indeed he was the only humble one, that Wendy was specially gentle with him.

'I don't suppose,' Tootles said diffidently, 'that I could be father.'

'No, Tootles.'

Once Tootles began, which was not very often, he had a silly way of going on.

'As I can't be father,' he said heavily, 'I don't suppose, Michael, you would let me be baby?'

'No, I won't,' Michael rapped out. He was already in his basket.

'As I can't be baby,' Tootles said, getting heavier and heavier, 'do you think I could be a twin?'

'No, indeed,' replied the twins; 'it's awfully difficult to be a twin.'

'As I can't be anything important,' said Tootles, 'would any of you like to see me do a trick?'

'No,' they all replied.

Then at last he stopped. 'I hadn't really any hope,' he said.

The hateful telling broke out again.

'Slightly is coughing on the table.'

'The twins began with mammee-apples.'

'Curly is taking both tappa rolls and yams.'

'Nibs is speaking with his mouth full.'

'I complain of the twins.'

'I complain of Curly.'

'I complain of Nibs.'

'Oh dear, oh dear,' cried Wendy, 'I'm sure I sometimes think that children are more trouble than they are worth.'

She told them to clear away, and sat down to her work-basket: a heavy load of stockings and every knee with a hole in it as usual.

'Wendy,' remonstrated Michael, 'I'm too big for a cradle.'

'I must have somebody in a cradle,' she said almost tartly, 'and you are the littlest. A cradle is such a nice homely thing to have about a house.'

While she sewed they played around her; such a group of happy faces and dancing limbs lit up by that romantic fire. It had become a very familiar scene this in the home under the ground, but we are looking on it for the last time.

There was a step above, and Wendy, you may be sure, was the first to recognize it.

'Children, I hear your father's step. He likes you to meet him at the door.'

Above, the redskins crouched before Peter.

'Watch well, braves, I have spoken.'

And then, as so often before, the gay children dragged him from his tree. As so often before, but never again.

He had brought nuts for the boys as well as the correct time for Wendy.

'Peter, you just spoil them, you know,' Wendy simpered.

'Aye, old lady,' said Peter, hanging up his gun.

'It was me told him mothers are called old lady,' Michael whispered to Curly.

'I complain of Michael,' said Curly instantly.

The first twin came to Peter. 'Father, we want to dance.'

'Dance away, my little man,' said Peter, who was in high good humour.

'But we want you to dance.'

Peter was really the best dancer among them, but he pretended to be scandalized.

'Me! My old bones would rattle.'

'And mummy too.'

'What,' cried Wendy, 'the mother of such an armful, dance!'

'But on a Saturday night,' Slightly insinuated.

It was not really Saturday night, at least it may have been, for they had long lost count of the days; but always if they wanted to do anything special they said this was Saturday night, and then they did it.

'Of course it is Saturday night, Peter,' Wendy said, relenting.

'People of our figure, Wendy.'

'But it is only among our own progeny.'

'True, true.'

So they were told they could dance, but they must put on their nighties first.

'Ah, old lady,' Peter said aside to Wendy, warming himself by the fire and looking down at her as she sat turning a heel, 'there is nothing more pleasant of an evening for you and me when the day's toil is over than to rest by the fire with the little ones near by.'

'It is sweet, Peter, isn't it?' Wendy said, frightfully gratified. 'Peter, I think Curly has your nose.'

'Michael takes after you.'

She went to him and put her hand on his shoulder.

'Dear Peter,' she said, 'with such a large family, of course, I have now passed my best, but you don't want to change me, do you?'

'No, Wendy.'

Certainly he did not want a change, but he looked at her uncomfortably; blinking, you know, like one not sure whether he was awake or asleep.

'Peter, what is it?'

'I was just thinking,' he said, a little scared. 'It is only make-believe, isn't it, that I am their father?'

'Oh yes,' Wendy said primly.

'You see,' he continued apologetically, 'it would make me seem so old to be their real father.'

'But they are ours, Peter, yours and mine.'

'But not really, Wendy?' he asked anxiously.

'Not if you don't wish it,' she replied; and she

distinctly heard his sigh of relief. 'Peter,' she asked, trying to speak firmly, 'what are your exact feelings for me?'

'Those of a devoted son, Wendy.'

'I thought so,' she said, and went and sat by herself at the extreme end of the room.

'You are so queer,' he said, frankly puzzled, 'and Tiger Lily is just the same. There is something she wants to be to me, but she says it is not my mother.'

'No, indeed, it is not,' Wendy replied with frightful emphasis. Now we know why she was prejudiced against the redskins.

'Then, what is it?'

'It isn't for a lady to tell.'

'Oh, very well,' Peter said, a little nettled. 'Perhaps Tinker Bell will tell me.'

'Oh yes, Tinker Bell will tell you,' Wendy retorted scornfully. 'She is an abandoned little creature.'

Here Tink, who was in her boudoir, eavesdropping, squeaked out something impudent.

'She says she glories in being abandoned,' Peter interpreted.

He had a sudden idea. 'Perhaps Tink wants to be my mother?'

'You silly ass!' cried Tinker Bell in a passion.

She had said it so often that Wendy needed no translation.

'I almost agree with her,' Wendy snapped. Fancy Wendy snapping. But she had been much tried, and she little knew what was to happen before the night was out. If she had known she would not have snapped.

None of them knew. Perhaps it was best not to know. Their ignorance gave them one more glad hour; and as it was to be their last hour on the island, let us rejoice that there were sixty minutes in it. They sang and danced in their night-gowns. Such a deliciously creepy song it was, in which they pretended to be frightened at their own shadows; little witting that so soon shadows would close in upon them, from whom they would shrink in real fear. So uproariously gay was the dance, and how they buffeted each other on the bed and out of it! It was a pillow fight rather than a dance, and when it was finished, the pillows insisted on one bout more, like partners who know that they may never meet again. The stories they told, before it was time for Wendy's good-night story! Even Slightly tried to tell a story that night, but the beginning was so fearfully dull that it appalled even himself, and he said gloomily:

'Yes, it is a dull beginning. I say, let us pretend that it is the end.'

And then at last they all got into bed for Wendy's story, the story they loved best, the story Peter hated. Usually when she began to tell this story he left the room or put his hands over his ears; and possibly if he had done either of those things this time they might all still be on the island. But tonight he remained on his stool; and we shall see what happened.

11

Wendy's Story

'Listen, then,' said Wendy, settling down to her story, with Michael at her feet and seven boys in the bed. 'There was once a gentleman –'

'I had rather he had been a lady,' Curly said.

'I wish he had been a white rat,' said Nibs.

'Quiet,' their mother admonished them. 'There was a lady also, and –'

'O Mummy,' cried the first twin, 'you mean that there is a lady also, don't you? She is not dead, is she?'

'Oh, no.'

'I am awfully glad she isn't dead,' said Tootles. 'Are you glad, John?'

'Of course I am.'

'Are you glad, Nibs?'

'Rather.'

'Are you glad, Twins?'

'We are just glad.'

'Oh dear,' sighed Wendy.

'Little less noise there,' Peter called out, determined that she should have fair play, however beastly a story it might be in his opinion.

'The gentleman's name,' Wendy continued, 'was Mr Darling, and her name was Mrs Darling.'

'I knew them,' John said, to annoy the others.

'I think I knew them,' said Michael rather doubtfully.

'They were married, you know,' explained Wendy, 'and what do you think they had?'

'White rats,' cried Nibs, inspired.

'No.'

'It's awfully puzzling,' said Tootles, who knew the story by heart.

'Quiet, Tootles. They had three descendants.'

'What is descendants?'

'Well, you are one, Twin.'

'Do you hear that, John? I am a descendant.'

'Descendants are only children,' said John.

'Oh dear, oh dear,' sighed Wendy. 'Now, these three children had a faithful nurse called Nana; but Mr Darling was angry with her and chained her up in the yard; and so all the children flew away.'

'It's an awfully good story,' said Nibs.

'They flew away,' Wendy continued, 'to the Neverland, where the lost children are.'

'I just thought they did,' Curly broke in excitedly. 'I don't know how it is, but I just thought they did.'

'O Wendy,' cried Tootles, 'was one of the lost children called Tootles?'

'Yes, he was.'

'I am in a story. Hurrah, I am in a story, Nibs.'

'Hush. Now, I want you to consider the feelings of the unhappy parents with all their children flown away.'

'Oo!' they all moaned, though they were not really considering the feelings of the unhappy parents one jot.

'Think of the empty beds!'

'Oo!'

'It's awfully sad,' the first twin said cheerfully

'I don't see how it can have a happy ending,' said the second twin. 'Do you, Nibs?'

'I'm frightfully anxious.'

'If you knew how great is a mother's love,' Wendy told them triumphantly, 'you would have no fear.' She had now come to the part that Peter hated.

'I do like a mother's love,' said Tootles, hitting Nibs with a pillow. 'Do you like a mother's love, Nibs?'

'I do just,' said Nibs, hitting back.

'You see,' Wendy said complacently, 'our heroine knew that the mother would always leave the window open for her children to fly back by; so they stayed away for years and had a lovely time.'

'Did they ever go back?'

'Let us now,' said Wendy, bracing herself for her finest effort, 'take a peep into the future'; and they all gave themselves the twist that makes peeps into the future easier. 'Years have rolled by; and who is this elegant lady of uncertain age alighting at London Station?'

'O Wendy, who is she?' cried Nibs, every bit as excited as if he didn't know.

'Can it be – yes – no – it is – the fair Wendy!'

'Oh!'

'And who are the two noble portly figures accompanying her, now grown to man's estate? Can they be John and Michael? They are!'

'Oh!'

'"See, dear brothers," says Wendy, pointing upwards, "there is the window still standing open. Ah, now we are rewarded for our sublime faith in a mother's love." So up they flew to their mummy and daddy; and pen cannot describe the happy scene, over which we draw a veil.'

That was a story, and they were as pleased with it as the fair narrator herself. Everything just as it should be, you see. Off we skip like the most heartless things in the world, which is what children are, but so attractive; and we have an entirely selfish time; and then when we have need of special attention we nobly return for it, confident that we shall be embraced instead of smacked.

So great indeed was their faith in a mother's love that they felt they could afford to be callous for a bit longer.

But there was one there who knew better; and when Wendy finished he uttered a hollow groan.

'What is it, Peter?' she cried, running to him, thinking he was ill. She felt him solicitously, lower down than his chest. 'Where is it, Peter?'

'It isn't that kind of pain,' Peter replied darkly.

'Then what kind is it?'

'Wendy, you are wrong about mothers.'

They all gathered round him in affright, so alarming was his agitation; and with a fine candour he told them what he had hitherto concealed.

'Long ago,' he said, 'I thought like you that my mother would always keep the window open for me; so I stayed away for moons and moons and moons, and then flew back; but the window was barred, for mother had forgotten all about me, and there was another little boy sleeping in my bed.'

I am not sure that this was true, but Peter thought it was true; and it scared them.

'Are you sure mothers are like that?'

'Yes.'

So this was the truth about mothers. The toads!

Still it is best to be careful; and no one knows so quickly as a child when he should give in. 'Wendy, let us go home,' cried John and Michael together.

'Yes,' she said, clutching them.

'Not tonight?' asked the lost boys bewildered. They knew in what they called their hearts that one can get on quite well without a mother, and that it is only the mothers who think you can't.

'At once,' Wendy replied resolutely, for the horrible thought had come to her: 'Perhaps mother is in half-mourning by this time.'

This dread made her forgetful of what must be Peter's feelings, and she said to him rather sharply, 'Peter, will you make the necessary arrangements?'

'If you wish it,' he replied as coolly as if she had asked him to pass the nuts.

Not so much as a sorry-to-lose-you between them! If she did not mind the parting, he was going to show her, was Peter, that neither did he.

But of course he cared very much; and he was so full of wrath against grown-ups, who, as usual, were spoiling everything, that as soon as he got inside his tree he breathed intentionally quick short breaths at the rate of about five to a second. He did this because there is a saying in the Neverland that every time you breathe, a grown-up dies; and Peter was killing them off vindictively as fast as possible.

Then having given the necessary instructions to the redskins he returned to the home, where an unworthy scene had been enacted in his absence. Panic-stricken at the thought of losing Wendy, the lost boys had advanced upon her threateningly.

'It will be worse than before she came,' they cried.

'We shan't let her go.'

'Let's keep her prisoner.'

'Aye, chain her up.'

In her extremity an instinct told her to which of them to turn.

'Tootles,' she cried, 'I appeal to you.'

Was it not strange? She appealed to Tootles, quite the silliest one.

Grandly, however, did Tootles respond. For that one moment he dropped his silliness and spoke with dignity.

'I am just Tootles,' he said, 'and nobody minds me. But the first who does not behave to Wendy like an English gentleman I will blood him severely.'

He drew his hanger; and for that instant his sun was at noon. The others held back uneasily. Then Peter returned, and they saw at once that they would get no support from him. He would keep no girl in the Neverland against her will.

'Wendy,' he said, striding up and down, 'I have asked the redskins to guide you through the wood, as flying tires you so.'

'Thank you, Peter.'

'Then,' he continued in the short sharp voice of one accustomed to be obeyed, 'Tinker Bell will take you across the sea. Wake her, Nibs.'

Nibs had to knock twice before he got an answer, though Tink had really been sitting up in bed listening for some time.

'Who are you? How dare you? Go away,' she cried.

'You are to get up, Tink,' Nibs called, 'and take Wendy on a journey.'

Of course Tink had been delighted to hear that Wendy was going; but she was jolly well determined not to be her courier, and she said so in still more offensive language. Then she pretended to be asleep again.

'She says she won't,' Nibs exclaimed, aghast at such insubordination, whereupon Peter went sternly towards the young lady's chamber.

'Tink,' he rapped out, 'if you don't get up and dress at once I will open the curtains, and then we shall all see you in your *négligé*.'

This made her leap to the floor. 'Who said I wasn't getting up?' she cried.

In the meantime the boys were gazing very forlornly at Wendy, now equipped with John and Michael for the journey. By this time they were dejected, not merely because they were about to lose her, but also because they felt that she was going off to something nice to which they had not been invited. Novelty was beckoning to them as usual.

Crediting them with a nobler feeling, Wendy melted.

'Dear ones,' she said, 'if you will all come with me I feel almost sure I can get my father and mother to adopt you.'

The invitation was meant specially for Peter; but each

of the boys was thinking exclusively of himself, and at once they jumped with joy.

'But won't they think us rather a handful?' Nibs asked in the middle of his jump.

'Oh, no,' said Wendy, rapidly thinking it out, 'it will only mean having a few beds in the drawing-room; they can be hidden behind screens on first Thursdays.'

'Peter, can we go?' they all cried imploringly. They took it for granted that if they went he would go also, but really they scarcely cared. Thus children are ever ready, when novelty knocks, to desert their dearest ones.

'All right,' Peter replied with a bitter smile; and immediately they rushed to get their things.

'And now, Peter,' Wendy said, thinking she had put everything right, 'I am going to give you your medicine before you go.' She loved to give them medicine, and undoubtedly gave them too much. Of course it was only water, but it was out of a calabash, and she always shook the calabash and counted the drops, which gave it a certain medicinal quality. On this occasion, however, she did not give Peter this draught, for just as she had prepared it, she saw a look on his face that made her heart sink.

'Get your things, Peter,' she cried, shaking.

'No,' he answered, pretending indifference, 'I am not going with you, Wendy.'

'Yes, Peter.'

'No.'

To show that her departure would leave him unmoved, he skipped up and down the room, playing gaily on his heartless pipes. She had to run about after him, though it was rather undignified.

'To find your mother,' she coaxed.

Now, if Peter had ever quite had a mother, he no longer missed her. He could do very well without one. He had thought them out, and remembered only their bad points.

'No, no,' he told Wendy decisively; 'perhaps she would say I was old, and I just want always to be a little boy and to have fun.'

'But, Peter –'

'No.'

And so the others had to be told.

'Peter isn't coming.'

Peter not coming! They gazed blankly at him, their sticks over their backs, and on each stick a bundle. Their first thought was that if Peter was not going he had probably changed his mind about letting them go.

But he was far too proud for that. 'If you find your mothers,' he said darkly, 'I hope you will like them.'

The awful cynicism of this made an uncomfortable impression, and most of them began to look rather doubtful. After all, their faces said, were they not noodles to want to go?

'Now then,' cried Peter, 'no fuss, no blubbering; goodbye,

Wendy'; and he held out his hand cheerily, quite as if they must really go now, for he had something important to do.

She had to take his hand, as there was no indication that he would prefer a thimble.

'You will remember about changing your flannels, Peter?' she said, lingering over him. She was always so particular about their flannels.

'Yes.'

'And you will take your medicine?'

'Yes.'

That seemed to be everything; and an awkward pause followed. Peter, however, was not the kind that breaks down before people. 'Are you ready, Tinker Bell?' he called out.

'Aye, aye.'

'Then lead the way.'

Tink darted up the nearest tree; but no one followed her, for it was at this moment that the pirates made their dreadful attack upon the redskins. Above, where all had been so still, the air was rent with shrieks and the clash of steel. Below, there was dead silence. Mouths opened and remained open. Wendy fell on her knees, but her arms were extended towards Peter. All arms were extended to him, as if suddenly blown in his direction; they were beseeching him mutely not to desert them. As for Peter, he seized his sword, the same he thought he had slain Barbecue with; and the lust of battle was in his eye.

12

The Children are Carried Off

The pirate attack had been a complete surprise; a sure proof that the unscrupulous Hook had conducted it improperly, for to surprise redskins fairly is beyond the wit of the white man.

By all the unwritten laws of savage warfare it is always the redskin who attacks, and with the wiliness of his race he does it just before the dawn, at which time he knows the courage of the whites to be at its lowest ebb. The white men have in the meantime made a rude stockade on the summit of yonder undulating ground, at the foot of which a stream runs; for it is destruction to be too far from water. There they await the onslaught, the inexperienced ones clutching their revolvers and treading on twigs, but the old hands sleeping tranquilly until just before the dawn. Through the long black night the savage scouts wriggle, snake-like, among the grass without stirring a blade. The brushwood closes behind them as silently as sand into which a mole has dived. Not a sound is to be heard, save when they give vent to a wonderful imitation of the lonely call of the coyote. The cry is answered by other braves; and some of them do it even better than the coyotes, who are not very good at it. So the chill hours wear on, and the long suspense is horribly trying to the paleface who has to live through it for the first time; but to the trained hand those ghastly calls and still ghastlier silences are but an intimation of how the night is marching.

That this was the usual procedure was so well known to Hook that in disregarding it he cannot be excused on the pleas of ignorance.

The Piccaninnies, on their part, trusted implicitly to his honour, and their whole action of the night stands out in marked contrast to his. They left nothing undone that was consistent with the reputation of their tribe. With that alertness of the senses which is at once the marvel and despair of civilized peoples, they knew that the pirates were on the island from the moment one of them trod on a dry stick; and in an incredibly short space of time the coyote cries began. Every foot of ground between the spot where Hook had landed his forces and the home under the trees was stealthily examined by braves wearing their moccasins with the heels in front. They found only one hillock with a stream at its base, so that Hook had no choice; here he must establish himself and wait for just before the dawn. Everything being thus mapped out with almost diabolical cunning, the main body of the redskins folded their blankets around them, and in the phlegmatic manner that is to them the pearl of manhood squatted above the children's home, awaiting the cold moment when they should deal pale death.

Here dreaming, though wide awake, of the exquisite tortures to which they were to put him at break of day, those confiding savages were found by the treacherous Hook. From the accounts afterwards supplied by such of the scouts as escaped the carnage, he does not seem even to have paused at the rising ground, though it is certain that in that grey light he must have seen it: no thought of waiting to be attacked appears from first to last to have visited his subtle mind; he would not even hold off till the night was nearly spent; on he pounded with no policy but to fall to. What could the bewildered scouts do, masters as they were of every warlike artifice save this one, but trot helplessly after him, exposing themselves fatally to view, the while they gave pathetic utterance to the coyote cry.

Around the brave Tiger Lily were a dozen of her stoutest warriors, and they suddenly saw the perfidious pirates bearing down upon them. Fell from their eyes then the film through which they had looked at victory. No more would they torture at the stake. For them the happy hunting-grounds now. They knew it; but as their fathers' sons they acquitted themselves. Even then they had time to gather in a phalanx that would have been hard to break had they risen quickly, but this they were forbidden to do by the traditions of their race. It is written that the noble savage must never express surprise in the presence of the white. Thus terrible as the sudden appearance of the pirates must have been to them, they remained stationary for a moment, not a muscle moving; as if the foe had come by invitation. Then, indeed, the tradition gallantly upheld, they seized their weapons, and the air was torn with the war-cry; but it was now too late.

It is no part of ours to describe what was a massacre rather than a fight. Thus perished many of the flower of the Piccaninny tribe. Not all unavenged did they die, for with Lean Wolf fell Alf Mason, to disturb the Spanish Main no more; and among others who bit the dust were Geo. Scourie, Chas. Turley, and the Alsatian Foggerty. Turley fell to the tomahawk of the terrible Panther, who ultimately cut a way through the pirates with Tiger Lily and a small remnant of the tribe.

To what extent Hook is to blame for his tactics on this occasion is for the historian to decide. Had he waited on the rising ground till the proper hour he and his men would probably have been butchered; and in judging him it is only fair to take this into account. What he should perhaps have done was to acquaint his opponents that he proposed to follow a new method. On the other hand this, as destroying the element of surprise, would have made his strategy of no avail, so that the whole question is beset with difficulties. One cannot at least withhold a reluctant admiration for the wit that had conceived so bold a scheme, and the fell genius with which it was carried out.

What were his own feelings about himself at that triumphant moment? Fain would his dogs have known, as breathing heavily and wiping their cutlasses, they gathered at a discreet distance from his hook, and squinted through their ferret eyes at this extraordinary man. Elation must have been in his heart, but his face did not reflect it: ever a dark and solitary enigma, he stood aloof from his followers in spirit as in substance.

The night's work was not yet over, for it was not the redskins he had come out to destroy; they were but the bees to be smoked, so that he should get at the honey. It was Pan he wanted, Pan and Wendy and their band, but chiefly Pan.

Peter was such a small boy that one tends to wonder at the man's hatred of him. True, he had flung Hook's arm to the crocodile; but even this and the increased insecurity of life to which it led, owing to the crocodile's pertinacity, hardly account for a vindictiveness so relentless and malignant. The truth is that there was a something about Peter which goaded the pirate captain to frenzy. It was not his courage, it was not his engaging appearance, it was not –. There is no beating about the bush, for we know quite well what it was, and have got to tell. It was Peter's cockiness.

This had got on Hook's nerves; it made his iron claw twitch, and at night it disturbed him like an insect. While Peter lived, the tortured man felt that he was a lion in a cage into which a sparrow had come.

The question now was how to get down the trees, or how to get his dogs down. He ran his greedy eyes over them, searching for the thinnest ones. They wriggled uncomfortably, for they knew that he would not scruple to ram them down with poles.

In the meantime, what of the boys? We have seen them at the first clang of weapons, turned as it were into stone figures, open-mouthed, all appealing with outstretched arms to Peter; and we return to them as their mouths close, and their arms fall to their sides. The pandemonium above has ceased almost as suddenly as it arose, passed like a fierce gust of wind; but they know that in the passing it has determined their fate.

Which side had won?

The pirates, listening avidly at the mouths of the trees, heard the question put by every boy, and alas! they also heard Peter's answer.

'If the redskins have won,' he said, 'they will beat the tom-tom; it is always their sign of victory.'

Now Smee had found the tom-tom, and was at that moment sitting on it. 'You will never hear the tom-tom again,' he muttered, but inaudibly of course, for strict silence had been enjoined. To his amazement Hook signed to him to beat the tom-tom; and slowly there came to Smee an understanding of the dreadful wickedness of the order. Never, probably, had this simple man admired Hook so much.

Twice Smee beat upon the instrument, and then stopped to listen gleefully.

'The tom-tom,' the miscreants heard Peter cry; 'an Indian victory!'

The doomed children answered with a cheer that was music to the black hearts above, and almost immediately they repeated their good-byes to Peter. This puzzled the pirates, but all their other feelings were swallowed by a base delight that the enemy were about to come up the trees. They smirked at each other and rubbed their hands. Rapidly and silently Hook gave his orders: one man to each tree, and the others to arrange themselves in a line two yards apart.

13

Do You Believe in Fairies?

The more quickly this horror is disposed of the better. The first to emerge from his tree was Curly. He rose out of it into the arms of Cecco, who flung him to Smee, who flung him to Starkey, who flung him to Bill Jukes, who flung him to Noodler, and so he was tossed from one to another till he fell at the feet of the black pirate. All the boys were plucked from their trees in this ruthless manner; and several of them were in the air at a time, like bales of goods flung from hand to hand.

A different treatment was accorded to Wendy, who came last. With ironical politeness Hook raised his hat to her, and, offering her his arm, escorted her to the spot where the others were being gagged. He did it with such an air, he was so frightfully *distingué*, that she was too fascinated to cry out. She was only a little girl.

Perhaps it is tell-tale to divulge that for a moment Hook entranced her, and we tell on her only because her slip led to strange results. Had she haughtily unhanded him (and we should have loved to write it of her), she would have been hurled through the air like the others, and then Hook would probably not have been present at the tying of the children; and had he not been at the tying he would not have discovered Slightly's secret, and without the secret he could not presently have made his foul attempt on Peter's life.

They were tied to prevent their flying away, doubled up with their knees close to their ears; and for the trussing of them the black pirate had cut a rope into nine equal pieces. All went well until Slightly's turn came, when he was found to be like those irritating parcels that use up all the string in going round and leave no tags with which to tie a knot. The pirates kicked him in their rage, just as you kick the parcel (though in fairness you should kick the string); and strange to say it was Hook who told them to belay their violence. His lip was curled with malicious triumph. While his dogs were merely sweating because every time they tried to pack the unhappy lad tight in one part he bulged out in another, Hook's master mind had gone far beneath Slightly's surface, probing not for effects but for causes; and his exultation showed that he had found them. Slightly, white to the gills, knew that Hook had surprised his secret, which was this, that no boy so blown out would use a tree wherein an average man need stick. Poor Slightly, most wretched of all the children now, for he was in a panic about Peter, bitterly regretted what he had done. Madly addicted to the drinking of water when he was hot, he had swelled in consequence to his present girth, and instead of reducing himself to fit his tree had, unknown to the others, whittled his tree to make it fit him.

Sufficient of this Hook guessed to persuade him that Peter at last lay at his mercy; but no word of the dark design that now formed in the subterranean caverns of his mind crossed his lips; he merely signed that the captives were to be conveyed to the ship, and that he would be alone.

How to convey them? Hunched up in their ropes they might indeed be rolled downhill like barrels, but most of the way lay through a morass. Again Hook's genius surmounted difficulties. He indicated that the little house must be used as a conveyance. The children were flung into it, four stout pirates raised it on their shoulders, the others fell in behind, and singing the hateful pirate chorus the strange procession set off through the wood. I don't know whether any of the children were crying; if so, the singing drowned the sound; but as the little house disappeared in the forest, a brave though tiny jet of smoke issued from its chimney as if defying Hook.

Hook saw it, and it did Peter a bad service. It dried up any trickle of pity for him that may have remained in the pirate's infuriated breast.

The first thing he did on finding himself alone in the

fast-falling night was to tiptoe to Slightly's tree, and make sure that it provided him with a passage. Then for long he remained brooding; his hat of ill omen on the sward, so that a gentle breeze which had arisen might play refreshingly through his hair. Dark as were his thoughts his blue eyes were as soft as the periwinkle. Intently he listened for any sound from the nether world, but all was as silent below as above; the house under the ground seemed to be but one more empty tenement in the void. Was that boy asleep, or did he stand waiting at the foot of Slightly's tree, with his dagger in his hand?

There was no way of knowing, save by going down. Hook let his cloak slip softly to the ground, and then biting his lip till a lewd blood stood on them, he stepped into the tree. He was a brave man; but for a moment he had to stop there and wipe his brow, which was dripping like a candle. Then silently he let himself go into the unknown.

He arrived unmolested at the foot of the shaft, and stood still again, biting at his breath, which had almost left him. As his eyes became accustomed to the dim light various objects in the home under the trees took shape; but the only one on which his greedy gaze rested, long sought for and found at last, was the great bed. On the bed lay Peter fast asleep.

Unaware of the tragedy being enacted above, Peter had continued, for a little time after the children left, to play gaily on his pipes: no doubt rather a forlorn attempt to prove to himself that he did not care. Then he decided not to take his medicine, so as to grieve Wendy. Then he lay down on the bed outside the coverlet, to vex her still more; for she had always tucked them inside it, because you never know that you may not grow chilly at the turn of the night. Then he nearly cried; but it struck him how indignant she would be if he laughed instead; so he laughed a haughty laugh and fell asleep in the middle of it.

Sometimes, though not often, he had dreams, and they were more painful than the dreams of other boys. For hours he could not be separated from these dreams, though he wailed piteously in them. They had to do, I think, with the riddle of his existence. At such times it had been Wendy's custom to take him out of bed and sit with him on her lap, soothing him in dear ways of her own invention, and when he grew calmer to put him back to bed before he quite woke up, so that he should not know of the indignity to which she had subjected him. But on this occasion he had fallen at once into a dreamless sleep. One arm dropped over the edge of the bed, one leg was arched, and the unfinished part of his laugh was stranded on his mouth, which was open, showing the little pearls.

Thus defenceless, Hook found him. He stood silent at the foot of the tree looking across the chamber at his enemy. Did no feeling of compassion disturb his sombre breast? The man was not wholly evil; he loved flowers (I have been told) and sweet music (he was himself no mean performer on the harpsichord); and let it be frankly admitted, the idyllic nature of the scene stirred him profoundly. Mastered by his better self, he would have returned reluctantly up the tree but for one thing.

What stayed him was Peter's impertinent appearance as he slept. The open mouth, the drooping arm, the arched knee: they were such a personification of cockiness as, taken together, will never again, one may hope, be presented to eyes so sensitive to their offensiveness. They steeled Hook's heart. If his rage had broken him into a hundred pieces every one of them would have disregarded the incident, and leapt at the sleeper.

Though a light from the one lamp shone dimly on the bed Hook stood in darkness himself, and at the first stealthy step forward he discovered an obstacle, the door of Slightly's tree. It did not entirely fill the aperture, and he had been looking over it. Feeling for the catch, he found to his fury that it was low down, beyond his reach. To his disordered brain it seemed then that the irritating quality in Peter's face and figure visibly increased, and he rattled the door and flung himself against it. Was his enemy to escape him after all?

But what was that? The red in his eye had caught sight of Peter's medicine standing on a ledge within easy reach.

He fathomed what it was straightaway, and immediately he knew that the sleeper was in his power.

Lest he should be taken alive, Hook always carried about his person a dreadful drug, blended by himself of all the death-dealing rings that had come into his possession. These he had boiled down into a yellow liquid quite unknown to science, which was probably the most virulent poison in existence.

Five drops of this he now added to Peter's cup. His hand shook, but it was in exultation rather than in shame. As he did it he avoided glancing at the sleeper, but not lest pity should unnerve him; merely to avoid spilling. Then one long gloating look he cast upon his victim, and turning, wormed his way with difficulty up the tree. As he emerged at the top he looked the very spirit of evil breaking from its hole. Donning his hat at its most rakish angle, he wound his cloak around him, holding one end in front as if to conceal his person from the night, of which it was the blackest part, and muttering strangely to himself stole away through the trees.

Peter slept on. The light guttered and went out, leaving the tenement in darkness; but still he slept. It must have been not less than ten o'clock by the crocodile, when he suddenly sat up in his bed, wakened by he knew not what. It was a soft cautious tapping on the door of his tree.

Soft and cautious, but in that stillness it was sinister. Peter felt for his dagger till his hand gripped it. Then he spoke.

'Who is that?'

For long there was no answer: then again the knock.

'Who are you?'

No answer.

He was thrilled, and he loved being thrilled. In two strides he reached his door. Unlike Slightly's door it filled the aperture, so that he could not see beyond it, nor could the one knocking see him.

'I won't open unless you speak,' Peter cried.

Then at last the visitor spoke, in a lovely bell-like voice.

'Let me in, Peter.'

It was Tink, and quickly he unbarred to her. She flew in excitedly, her face flushed and her dress stained with mud.

'What is it?'

'Oh, you could never guess,' she cried, and offered him three guesses. 'Out with it!' he shouted; and in one ungrammatical sentence, as long as the ribbons conjurers pull from their mouths, she told of the capture of Wendy and the boys.

Peter's heart bobbed up and down as he listened. Wendy bound, and on the pirate ship; she who loved everything to be just so!

'I'll rescue her,' he cried, leaping at his weapons. As he leapt he thought of something he could do to please her. He could take his medicine.

His hand closed on the fatal draught.

'No!' shrieked Tinker Bell, who had heard Hook muttering about his deed as he sped through the forest.

'Why not?'

'It is poisoned.'

'Poisoned? Who could have poisoned it?'

'Hook.'

'Don't be silly. How could Hook have got down here?'

Alas! Tinker Bell could not explain this, for even she did not know the dark secret of Slightly's tree. Nevertheless Hook's words had left no room for doubt. The cup was poisoned.

'Besides,' said Peter, quite believing himself, 'I never fell asleep.'

He raised the cup. No time for words now; time for deeds; and with one of her lightning movements Tink got between his lips and the draught, and drained it to the dregs.

'Why, Tink, how dare you drink my medicine?'

But she did not answer. Already she was reeling in the air.

'What is the matter with you?' cried Peter, suddenly afraid.

'It was poisoned, Peter,' she told him softly; 'and now I am going to be dead.'

'O Tink, did you drink it to save me?'

'Yes.'

'But why, Tink?'

Her wings would scarcely carry her now, but in reply she alighted on his shoulder and gave his chin a loving bite. She whispered in his ear, 'You silly ass'; and then, tottering to her chamber, lay down on the bed.

His head almost filled the fourth wall of her little room as he knelt near her in distress. Every moment her light was growing fainter; and he knew that if it went out she would be no more. She liked his tears so much that she put out her beautiful finger and let them run over it.

Her voice was so low that at first he could not make out what she said. Then he made it out. She was saying that she thought she could get well again if children believed in fairies.

Peter flung out his arms. There were no children there, and it was night-time; but he addressed all who might be dreaming of the Neverland, and who were therefore nearer to him than you think; boys and girls in their nighties, and naked papooses in their baskets hung from trees.

'Do you believe?' he cried.

Tink sat up in bed almost briskly to listen to her fate.

She fancied she heard answers in the affirmative, and then again she wasn't sure.

'What do you think?' she asked Peter.

'If you believe,' he shouted to them, 'clap your hands; don't let Tink die.'

Many clapped.

Some didn't.

A few little beasts hissed.

The clapping stopped suddenly, as if countless mothers had rushed to their nurseries to see what on earth was happening; but already Tink was saved. First her voice grew strong; then she popped out of bed; then she was flashing through the room more merry and impudent than ever. She never thought of thanking those who believed, but she would have liked to get at the ones who had hissed.

'And now to rescue Wendy.'

The moon was riding in a cloudy heaven when Peter rose from his tree, begirt with weapons and wearing little else, to set out upon his perilous quest. It was not such a night as he would have chosen. He had hoped to fly, keeping not far from the ground so that nothing unwonted should escape his eyes; but in that fitful light to have flown low would have meant trailing his shadow through the trees, thus disturbing the birds and acquainting a watchful foe that he was astir.

He regretted now that he had given the birds of the island such strange names that they are very wild and difficult of approach.

There was no other course but to press forward in redskin fashion, at which happily he was an adept. But in what direction, for he could not be sure that the children had been taken to the ship? A slight fall of snow had obliterated all footmarks; and a deathly silence pervaded the island, as if for a space Nature stood still in horror of the recent carnage. He had taught the children something of the forest lore that he had himself learned from Tiger Lily and Tinker Bell, and knew that in their dire hour they were not likely to forget it. Slightly, if he had an opportunity, would blaze the trees, for instance, Curly would drop seeds, and Wendy would leave her handkerchief at some important place. But morning was needed to search for such guidance, and he could not wait. The upper world had called him, but would give no help.

The crocodile passed him, but not another living thing, not a sound, not a movement; and yet he knew well that sudden death might be at the next tree, or stalking him from behind.

He swore this terrible oath: 'Hook or me this time.'

Now he crawled forward like a snake; and again, erect, he darted across a space on which the moonlight played: one finger on his lip and his dagger at the ready. He was frightfully happy.

14

The Pirate Ship

One green light squinting over Kidd's Creek, which is near the mouth of the pirate river, marked where the brig, the *Jolly Roger*, lay, low in the water; a rakish-looking craft foul to the hull, every beam in her detestable, like ground strewn with mangled feathers. She was the cannibal of the seas, and scarce needed that watchful eye, for she floated immune in the horror of her name.

She was wrapped in the blanket of night, through which no sound from her could have reached the shore. There was little sound, and none agreeable save the whir of the ship's sewing machine at which Smee sat, ever industrious and obliging, the essence of the commonplace, pathetic Smee. I know not why he was so infinitely pathetic, unless it were because he was so pathetically unaware of it; but even strong men had to turn hastily from looking at him, and more than once on summer evenings he had touched the fount of Hook's tears and made it flow. Of this, as of almost everything else, Smee was quite unconscious.

A few of the pirates leant over the bulwarks drinking

in the miasma of the night; others sprawled by barrels over games of dice and cards; and the exhausted four who had carried the little house lay prone on the deck, where even in their sleep they rolled skilfully to this side or that out of Hook's reach, lest he should claw them mechanically in passing.

Hook trod the deck in thought. O man unfathomable. It was his hour of triumph. Peter had been removed for ever from his path, and all the other boys were on the brig, about to walk the plank. It was his grimmest deed since the days when he had brought Barbecue to heel; and knowing as we do how vain a tabernacle is man, could we be surprised had he now paced the deck unsteadily, bellied out by the winds of his success?

But there was no elation in his gait, which kept pace with the action of his sombre mind. Hook was profoundly dejected.

He was often thus when communing with himself on board ship in the quietude of the night. It was because he was so terribly alone. This inscrutable man never felt more alone than when surrounded by his dogs. They were socially so inferior to him.

Hook was not his true name. To reveal who he really was would even at this date set the country in a blaze; but as those who read between the lines must already have guessed, he had been at a famous public school; and its traditions still clung to him like garments, with which indeed they are largely concerned. Thus it was offensive to him even now to board a ship in the same dress in which he grappled her; and he still adhered in his walk to the school's distinguished slouch. But above all he retained the passion for good form.

Good form! However much he may have degenerated, he still knew that this is all that really matters.

From far within him he heard a creaking as of rusty portals, and through them came a stern tap-tap-tap, like hammering in the night when one cannot sleep. 'Have you been good form today?' was their eternal question.

'Fame, fame, that glittering bauble, it is mine,' he cried.

'Is it quite good form to be distinguished at anything?' the tap-tap from his school replied.

'I am the only man whom Barbecue feared,' he urged; 'and Flint himself feared Barbecue.'

'Barbecue, Flint – what house?' came the cutting retort.

Most disquieting reflection of all, was it not bad form to think about good form?

His vitals were tortured by this problem. It was a claw within him sharper than the iron one; and as it tore him, the perspiration dripped down his sallow countenance and streaked his doublet. Oft-times he drew his sleeve across his face, but there was no damming that trickle.

Ah, envy not Hook.

There came to him a presentiment of his early dissolution. It was as if Peter's terrible oath had boarded the ship. Hook felt a gloomy desire to make his dying speech, lest presently there should be no time for it.

'Better for Hook,' he cried, 'if he had had less ambition.' It was in his darkest hours only that he referred to himself in the third person.

'No little children love me.'

Strange that he should think of this, which had never troubled him before; perhaps the sewing machine brought it to his mind. For long he muttered to himself, staring at Smee, who was hemming placidly, under the conviction that all children feared him.

Feared him! Feared Smee! There was not a child on board the brig that night who did not already love him. He had said horrid things to them and hit them with the palm of his hand, because he could not hit with his fist; but they had only clung to him the more. Michael had tried on his spectacles.

To tell poor Smee that they thought him lovable! Hook itched to do it, but it seemed too brutal. Instead, he revolved this mystery in his mind: why do they find Smee lovable? He pursued the problem like the sleuth-hound that he was. If Smee was lovable, what was it that made him so? A terrible answer suddenly presented itself: 'Good form?'

Had the bo'sun good form without knowing it, which is the best form of all?

He remembered that you have to prove you don't know you have it before you are eligible for Pop.

With a cry of rage he raised his iron hand over Smee's head; but he did not tear. What arrested him was this reflection:

'To claw a man because he is good form, what would that be?'

'Bad form!'

The unhappy Hook was as impotent as he was damp, and he fell forward like a cut flower.

His dogs thinking him out of the way for a time, discipline instantly relaxed; and they broke into a bacchanalian dance, which brought him to his feet at once; all traces of human weakness gone, as if a bucket of water had passed over him.

'Quiet, you scugs,' he cried, 'or I'll cast anchor in you': and at once the din was hushed. 'Are all the children chained, so they cannot fly away?'

'Aye, aye.'

'Then hoist them up.'

The wretched prisoners were dragged from the hold, all except Wendy, and ranged in line in front of him. For a time he seemed unconscious of their presence. He lolled at his ease, humming, not unmelodiously, snatches of a rude song, and fingering a pack of cards. Ever and anon the light from his cigar gave a touch of colour to his face.

'Now then, bullies,' he said briskly, 'six of you walk the plank tonight, but I have room for two cabin boys. Which of you is it to be?'

'Don't irritate him unnecessarily,' had been Wendy's instructions in the hold; so Tootles stepped forward politely. Tootles hated the idea of signing under such a man, but an instinct told him that it would be prudent to lay responsibility on an absent person; and though a somewhat silly boy, he knew that mothers alone are always willing to be the buffer. All children know this about mothers, and despise them for it, but make constant use of it.

So Tootles explained prudently, 'You see, sir, I don't think my mother would like me to be a pirate. Would your mother like you to be a pirate, Slightly?'

He winked at Slightly, who said mournfully, 'I don't think so,' as if he wished things had been otherwise. 'Would your mother like you to be a pirate, Twin?'

'I don't think so,' said the first twin, as clever as the others. 'Nibs, would –?'

'Stow this gab,' roared Hook, and the spokesmen were dragged back. 'You, boy,' he said, addressing John, 'you look as if you had a little pluck in you. Didst never want to be a pirate, my hearty?'

Now John had sometimes experienced this hankering at maths. prep.; and he was struck by Hook's picking him out.

'I once thought of calling myself Red-handed Jack,' he said diffidently.

'And a good name too. We'll call you that here, bully, if you join.'

'What do you think, Michael?' asked John.

'What would you call me if I join?' Michael demanded.

'Blackbeard Joe.'

Michael was naturally impressed. 'What do you think, John?' He wanted John to decide, and John wanted him to decide.

'Shall we still be respectful subjects of the King?' John inquired.

Through Hook's teeth came the answer: 'You would have to swear, "Down with the King."'

Perhaps John had not behaved very well so far, but he shone out now.

'Then I refuse,' he cried, banging the barrel in front of Hook.

'And I refuse,' cried Michael.

'Rule Britannia!' squeaked Curly.

The infuriated pirates buffeted them in the mouth; and Hook roared out, 'That seals your doom. Bring up their mother. Get the plank ready.'

They were only boys, and they went white as they saw Jukes and Cecco preparing the fatal plank. But they tried to look brave when Wendy was brought up.

No words of mine can tell you how Wendy despised those pirates. To the boys there was at least some glamour in the pirate calling, but all that she saw was that the ship had not been scrubbed for years. There was not a porthole on the grimy glass of which you might not have written with your finger, 'Dirty pig'; and she had already written it on several. But as the boys gathered round her she had no thought, of course, save for them.

'So, my beauty,' said Hook, as if he spoke in syrup, 'you are to see your children walk the plank.'

Fine gentleman though he was, the intensity of his communings had soiled his ruff, and suddenly he knew that she was gazing at it. With a hasty gesture he tried to hide it, but he was too late.

'Are they to die?' asked Wendy, with a look of such frightful contempt that he nearly fainted.

'They are,' he snarled. 'Silence all,' he called gloatingly, 'for a mother's last words to her children.'

At this moment Wendy was grand. 'These are my last words, dear boys,' she said firmly. 'I feel that I have a message to you from your real mothers, and it is this: "We hope our sons will die like English gentlemen."'

Even the pirates were awed; and Tootles cried out hysterically, 'I am going to do what my mother hopes. What are you to do, Nibs?'

'What my mother hopes. What are you to do, Twin?'

'What my mother hopes. John, what are –?'

163

But Hook had found his voice again.

'Tie her up,' he shouted.

It was Smee who tied her to the mast. 'See here, honey,' he whispered, 'I'll save you if you promise to be my mother.'

But not even for Smee would she make such a promise. 'I would almost rather have no children at all,' she said disdainfully.

It is sad to know that not a boy was looking at her as Smee tied her to the mast; the eyes of all were on the plank; that last little walk they were about to take. They were no longer able to hope that they would walk it manfully, for the capacity to think had gone from them; they could stare and shiver only.

Hook smiled on them with his teeth closed, and took a step towards Wendy. His intention was to turn her face so that she should see the boys walking the plank one by one. But he never reached her, he never heard the cry of anguish he hoped to wring from her. He heard something else instead.

It was the terrible tick-tick of the crocodile.

They all heard it – pirates, boys, Wendy; and immediately every head was blown in one direction; not to the water whence the sound proceeded, but towards Hook. All knew that what was about to happen concerned him alone, and that from being actors they were suddenly become spectators.

Very frightful was it to see the change that came over him. It was as if he had been clipped at every joint. He fell in a little heap.

The sound came steadily nearer; and in advance of it came this ghastly thought, 'The crocodile is about to board the ship.'

Even the iron claw hung inactive; as if knowing that it was no intrinsic part of what the attacking force wanted. Left so fearfully alone, any other man would have lain with his eyes shut where he fell: but the gigantic brain of Hook was still working, and under its guidance he crawled on his knees along the deck as far from the sound as he could go. The pirates respectfully cleared a passage for him, and it was only when he brought up against the bulwarks that he spoke.

'Hide me,' he cried hoarsely.

They gathered round him; all eyes averted from the thing that was coming aboard. They had no thought of fighting it. It was Fate.

Only when Hook was hidden from them did curiosity loosen the limbs of the boys so that they could rush to the ship's side to see the crocodile climbing it. Then they got the strangest surprise of this Night of Nights; for it was no crocodile that was coming to their aid. It was Peter.

He signed to them not to give vent to any cry of admiration that might rouse suspicion. Then he went on ticking.

15

'Hook or Me this Time'

Odd things happen to all of us on our way through life without our noticing for a time that they have happened. Thus, to take an instance, we suddenly discover that we have been deaf in one ear for we don't know how long, but, say, half an hour. Now such an experience had come that night to Peter. When last we saw him he was stealing across the island with one finger to his lips and his dagger at the ready. He had seen the crocodile pass by without noticing anything peculiar about it, but by and by he remembered that it had not been ticking. At first he thought this eerie, but soon he concluded rightly that the clock had run down.

Without giving a thought to what might be the feelings of a fellow-creature thus abruptly deprived of its closest companion, Peter at once considered how he could turn the catastrophe to his own use; and he decided to tick, so that wild beasts should believe he was the crocodile and let him pass unmolested. He ticked superbly, but with one unforeseen result. The crocodile was among those who heard the sound, and it followed him, though whether with the purpose of regaining what it had lost, or merely as a friend under the belief that it was again ticking itself, will never be certainly known, for, like all slaves to a fixed idea, it was a stupid beast.

Peter reached the shore without mishap, and went straight on; his legs encountering the water as if quite unaware that they had entered a new element. Thus many animals pass from land to water, but no other human of whom I know. As he swam he had but one thought: 'Hook or me this time.' He had ticked so long that he now went on ticking without knowing that he was doing it. Had he known he would have stopped, for to board the brig by the help of the tick, though an ingenious idea, had not occurred to him.

On the contrary, he thought he had scaled her side as noiseless as a mouse; and he was amazed to see the pirates cowering from him, with Hook in their midst as abject as if he had heard the crocodile.

The crocodile! No sooner did Peter remember it than he heard the ticking. At first he thought the sound did come from the crocodile, and he looked behind him swiftly. Then he realized that he was doing it himself, and in a flash he understood the situation. 'How clever of me,' he thought at once, and signed to the boys not to burst into applause.

It was at this moment that Ed Teynte the quartermaster emerged from the forecastle and came along the deck.

Now, reader, time what happened by your watch. Peter struck true and deep. John clapped his hands on the ill-fated pirate's mouth to stifle the dying groan. He fell forward. Four boys caught him to prevent the thud. Peter gave the signal, and the carrion was cast overboard. There was a splash, and then silence. How long has it taken?

'One!' (Slightly had begun to count.)

None too soon, Peter, every inch of him on tiptoe, vanished into the cabin; for more than one pirate was screwing up his courage to look round. They could hear each other's distressed breathing now, which showed them that the more terrible sound had passed.

'It's gone, captain,' Smee said, wiping his spectacles. 'All's still again.'

Slowly Hook let his head emerge from his ruff, and listened so intently that he could have caught the echo of the tick. There was not a sound, and he drew himself up firmly to his full height.

'Then here's to Johnny Plank,' he cried brazenly, hating the boys more than ever because they had seen him unbend. He broke into the villainous ditty:

'Yo ho, yo ho, the frisky plank,
You walks along it so,
Till it goes down and you goes down
To Davy Jones below!'

To terrorize the prisoners the more, though with a certain loss of dignity, he danced along an imaginary plank, grimacing at them as he sang; and when he finished he cried, 'Do you want a touch of the cat before you walk the plank?'

At that they fell on their knees. 'No, no,' they cried so piteously that every pirate smiled.

'Fetch the cat, Jukes,' said Hook; 'it's in the cabin.'

The cabin! Peter was in the cabin! The children gazed at each other.

'Aye, aye,' said Jukes blithely, and he strode into the cabin. They followed him with their eyes; they scarce knew that Hook had resumed his song, his dogs joining in with him:

> *'Yo ho, yo ho, the scratching cat,*
> *Its tails are nine, you know,*
> *And when they're writ upon your back –'*

What was the last line will never be known, for of a sudden the song was stayed by a dreadful screech from the cabin. It wailed through the ship, and died away. Then was heard a crowing sound which was well understood by the boys, but to the pirates was almost more eerie than the screech.

'What was that?' cried Hook.

'Two,' said Slightly solemnly.

The Italian Cecco hesitated for a moment and then swung into the cabin. He tottered out, haggard.

'What's the matter with Bill Jukes, you dog?' hissed Hook, towering over him.

'The matter wi' him is he's dead, stabbed,' replied Cecco in a hollow voice.

'Bill Jukes dead!' cried the startled pirates.

'The cabin's as black as a pit,' Cecco said, almost gibbering, 'but there is something terrible in there: the thing you heard crowing.'

The exultation of the boys, the lowering looks of the pirates, both were seen by Hook.

'Cecco,' he said in his most steely voice, 'go back and fetch me out that doodle-doo.'

Cecco, bravest of the brave, cowered before his captain, crying, 'No, no': but Hook was purring to his claw.

'Did you say you would go, Cecco?' he said musingly.

Cecco went, first flinging up his arms despairingly. There was no more singing, all listened now; and again came a death-screech and again a crow.

No one spoke except Slightly. 'Three,' he said.

Hook rallied his dogs with a gesture. ''Sdeath and odds fish,' he thundered, 'who is to bring me that doodle-doo?'

'Wait till Cecco comes out,' growled Starkey, and the others took up the cry.

'I think I heard you volunteer, Starkey,' said Hook, purring again.

'No, by thunder!' Starkey cried.

'My hook thinks you did,' said Hook, crossing to him. 'I wonder if it would not be advisable, Starkey, to humour the hook?'

'I'll swing before I go in there,' replied Starkey doggedly, and again he had the support of the crew.

'Is it mutiny?' asked Hook more pleasantly than ever. 'Starkey's ring-leader.'

'Captain, mercy,' Starkey whimpered, all of a tremble now.

'Shake hands, Starkey,' said Hook, proffering his claw.

Starkey looked round for help, but all deserted him. As he backed Hook advanced, and now the red spark was in his eye. With a despairing scream the pirate leapt upon Long Tom and precipitated himself into the sea.

'Four,' said Slightly.

'And now,' Hook asked courteously, 'did any other gentleman say mutiny?' Seizing a lantern and raising his claw with a menacing gesture, 'I'll bring out that doodle-doo myself,' he said, and sped into the cabin.

'Five.' How Slightly longed to say it. He wetted his lips to be ready, but Hook came staggering out, without his lantern.

'Something blew out the light,' he said a little unsteadily.

'Something!' echoed Mullins.

'What of Cecco?' demanded Noodler.

'He's as dead as Jukes,' said Hook shortly.

His reluctance to return to the cabin impressed them all unfavourably, and the mutinous sounds again broke forth. All pirates are superstitious; and Cookson cried, 'They do say the surest sign of a ship's accurst is when there's one on board more than can be accounted for.'

'I've heard,' muttered Mullins, 'he always boards the pirate craft at last. Had he a tail, captain?'

'They say,' said another, looking viciously at Hook, 'that when he comes it's in the likeness of the wickedest man aboard.'

'Had he a hook, captain?' asked Cookson insolently; and one after another took up the cry, 'The ship's doomed.' At this the children could not resist raising a cheer. Hook had wellnigh forgotten his prisoners, but as he swung round on them now his face lit up again.

'Lads,' he cried to his crew, 'here's a notion. Open the cabin door and drive them in. Let them fight the doodle-doo for their lives. If they kill him, we're so much the better; if he kills them we're none the worse.'

For the last time his dogs admired Hook, and devotedly they did his bidding. The boys, pretending to struggle, were pushed into the cabin and the door was closed on them.

'Now, listen,' cried Hook, and all listened. But not one dared to face the door. Yes, one, Wendy, who all this time had been bound to the mast. It was for neither a scream nor a crow that she was watching; it was for the reappearance of Peter.

She had not long to wait. In the cabin he had found the thing for which he had gone in search: the key that would free the children of their manacles; and now they all stole forth, armed with such weapons as they could find. First signing to them to hide, Peter cut Wendy's bonds, and then nothing could have been easier for them all to fly off together; but one thing barred the way, an oath, 'Hook or me this time.' So when he had freed Wendy, he whispered to her to conceal herself with the others and himself took her place by the mast, her cloak around him so that he should pass for her. Then he took a great breath and crowed.

To the pirates it was a voice crying that all the boys lay slain in the cabin; and they were panic-stricken. Hook tried to hearten them; but like the dogs he had made them they showed him their fangs, and he knew that if he took his eyes off them now they would leap at him.

'Lads,' he said, ready to cajole or strike as need be, but never quailing for an instant, 'I've thought it out. There's a Jonah aboard.'

'Aye,' they snarled, 'a man wi' a hook.'

'No, lads, no, it's the girl. Never was luck on a pirate ship wi' a woman on board. We'll right the ship when she's gone.'

Some of them remembered that this had been a saying of Flint's. 'It's worth trying,' they said doubtfully.

'Fling the girl overboard,' cried Hook; and they made a rush at the figure in the cloak.

'There's none can save you now, missy,' Mullins hissed jeeringly.

'There's one,' replied the figure.

'Who's that?'

'Peter Pan the avenger!' came the terrible answer; and as he spoke Peter flung off his cloak. Then they all knew who 'twas that had been undoing them in the cabin, and twice Hook essayed to speak and twice he failed. In that frightful moment I think his fierce heart broke.

At last he cried, 'Cleave him to the brisket,' but without conviction.

'Down, boys, and at them,' Peter's voice rang out; and in another moment the clash of arms was resounding through the ship. Had the pirates kept together it is certain that they would have won; but the onset came when they were all unstrung, and they ran hither and thither, striking wildly, each thinking himself the last survivor of the crew. Man to man they were the stronger; but they fought on the defensive only, which enabled the boys to hunt in pairs and choose their quarry. Some of the miscreants leapt into the sea; others hid in dark recesses, where they were found by Slightly, who did not fight, but ran about with a lantern which he flashed in their faces, so that they were half blinded and fell an easy prey to the reeking swords of the other boys. There was little sound to be heard but the clang of weapons, an occasional screech or splash, and Slightly monotonously counting – five – six – seven – eight – nine – ten – eleven.

I think all were gone when a group of savage boys surrounded Hook, who seemed to have a charmed life, as he kept them at bay in that circle of fire. They had done for his dogs, but this man alone seemed to be a match for them all. Again and again they closed upon him, and again and again he hewed a clear space. He had lifted up one boy with his hook, and was using him as buckler, when another, who had just passed his sword through Mullins, sprang into the fray.

'Put up your swords, boys,' cried the newcomer, 'this man is mine.'

Thus suddenly Hook found himself face to face with Peter. The others drew back and formed a ring round them.

For long the two enemies looked at one another; Hook shuddering slightly, and Peter with the strange smile upon his face.

'So, Pan,' said Hook at last, 'this is all your doing.'

'Aye, James Hook,' came the stern answer, 'it is all my doing.'

'Proud and insolent youth,' said Hook, 'prepare to meet thy doom.'

'Dark and sinister man,' Peter answered, 'have at thee.'

Without more words they fell to, and for a space there was no advantage to either blade. Peter was a superb swordsman, and parried with dazzling rapidity; ever and anon he followed up a feint with a lunge that got past his foe's defence, but his shorter reach stood him in ill stead, and he could not drive the steel home. Hook, scarcely his inferior in brilliancy, but not quite so nimble in wrist play, forced him back by the weight of his onset, hoping suddenly to end all with a favourite thrust, taught him long ago by Barbecue at Rio; but to his astonishment he found this thrust turned aside again and again. Then he sought to close and give the quietus with his iron hook, which all this time had been pawing the air; but Peter doubled under it and, lunging fiercely, pierced him in the ribs. At sight of his own blood, whose peculiar colour, you remember, was offensive to him, the sword fell from Hook's hand, and he was at Peter's mercy.

'Now!' cried all the boys; but with a magnificent gesture Peter invited his opponent to pick up his sword. Hook did so instantly, but with a tragic feeling that Peter was showing good form.

Hitherto he had thought it was some fiend fighting him, but darker suspicions assailed him now.

'Pan, who and what art thou?' he cried huskily.

'I'm youth, I'm joy,' Peter answered at a venture, 'I'm a little bird that has broken out of the egg.'

This, of course, was nonsense; but it was proof to the

unhappy Hook that Peter did not know in the least who or what he was, which is the very pinnacle of good form.

'To't again,' he cried despairingly.

He fought now like a human flail, and every sweep of that terrible sword would have severed in twain any man or boy who obstructed it; but Peter fluttered round him as if the very wind it made blew him out of the danger zone. And again and again he darted in and pricked.

Hook was fighting now without hope. That passionate breast no longer asked for life; but for one boon it craved: to see Peter bad form before it was cold for ever.

Abandoning the fight he rushed into the powder magazine and fired it.

'In two minutes,' he cried, 'the ship will be blown to pieces.'

Now, now, he thought, true form will show.

But Peter issued from the powder magazine with the shell in his hands, and calmly flung it overboard.

What sort of form was Hook himself showing? Misguided man though he was, we may be glad, without sympathizing with him, that in the end he was true to the traditions of his race. The other boys were flying around him now, flouting, scornful; and as he staggered about the deck striking up at them impotently, his mind was no longer with them; it was slouching in the playing fields of long ago, or being sent up for good, or watching the wall-game from a famous wall. And his shoes were right, and his waistcoat was right, and his tie was right, and his socks were right.

James Hook, thou not wholly unheroic figure, farewell.

For we have come to his last moment.

Seeing Peter slowly advancing upon him through the air with dagger poised, he sprang upon the bulwarks to cast himself into the sea. He did not know that the crocodile was waiting for him; for we purposely stopped the clock that this knowledge might be spared him: a little mark of respect from us at the end.

He had one last triumph, which I think we need not grudge him. As he stood on the bulwark looking over his shoulder at Peter gliding through the air, he invited him with a gesture to use his foot. It made Peter kick instead of stab.

At last Hook had got the boon for which he craved.

'Bad form,' he cried jeeringly, and went content to the crocodile.

Thus perished James Hook.

'Seventeen,' Slightly sang out; but he was not quite correct in his figures. Fifteen paid the penalty for their crimes that night; but two reached the shore; Starkey to be captured by the redskins, who made him nurse for all their papooses, a melancholy come-down for a pirate, and Smee, who henceforth wandered about the world in his spectacles, making a precarious living by saying he was the only man that James Hook had feared.

Wendy, of course, had stood by taking no part in the fight, though watching Peter with glistening eyes; but now that all was over she became prominent again. She praised them equally, and shuddered delightfully when Michael showed her the place where he had killed one; and then she took them into Hook's cabin and pointed to his watch which was hanging on a nail. It said, 'half past one'!

The lateness of the hour was almost the biggest thing of all. She got them to bed in the pirates' bunks pretty quickly, you may be sure; all but Peter, who strutted up and down on deck, until at last he fell asleep by the side of Long Tom. He had one of his dreams that night, and cried in his sleep for a long time, and Wendy held him tight.

16

The Return Home

By two bells that morning they were all stirring their stumps; for there was a big sea running; and Tootles, the bo'sun, was among them, with a rope's end in his hand and chewing tobacco. They all donned pirate clothes cut off at the knee, shaved smartly, and tumbled up, with the true nautical roll and hitching their trousers.

It need not be said who was the captain. Nibs and John were first and second mate. There was a woman aboard. The rest were tars before the mast, and lived in the fo'c'sle. Peter had already lashed himself to the wheel; but he piped all hands and delivered a short address to them; said he hoped that they would do their duty like gallant hearties, but that he knew they were the scum of Rio and the Gold Coast, and if they snapped at him he would tear them. His bluff strident words struck the note sailors understand, and they cheered him lustily. Then a few sharp orders were given, and they turned the ship round, and nosed her for the mainland.

Captain Pan calculated, after consulting the ship's chart,

that if this weather lasted they should strike the Azores about the 21st of June, after which it would save time to fly.

Some of them wanted it to be an honest ship and others were in favour of keeping it a pirate; but the captain treated them as dogs, and they dared not express their wishes to him even in a round robin. Instant obedience was the only safe thing. Slightly got a dozen for looking perplexed when told to take soundings. The general feeling was that Peter was honest just now to lull Wendy's suspicions, but that there might be a change when the new suit was ready, which, against her will, she was making for him out of some of Hook's wickedest garments. It was afterwards whispered among them that on the first night he wore this suit he sat long in the cabin with Hook's cigar-holder in his mouth and one hand clenched, all but the forefinger, which he bent and held threateningly aloft like a hook.

Instead of watching the ship, however, we must now return to that desolate home from which three of our characters had taken heartless flight so long ago. It seems a shame to have neglected No. 14 all this time; and yet we may be sure that Mrs Darling does not blame us. If we had returned sooner to look with sorrowful sympathy at her, she would probably have cried, 'Don't be silly; what do I matter? Do go back and keep an eye on the children.' So long as mothers are like this children will take advantage of them; and they may lay to that.

Even now we venture into that familiar nursery only because its lawful occupants are on their way home; we are merely hurrying on in advance of them to see that their beds are properly aired and that Mr and Mrs Darling do not go out for the evening. We are no more than servants. Why on earth should their beds be properly aired, seeing that they left them in such a thankless hurry? Would it not serve them jolly well right if they came back and found that their parents were spending the weekend in the country? It would be the moral lesson they have been in need of ever since we met them; but if we contrived things in this way Mrs Darling would never forgive us.

One thing I should like to do immensely, and that is to tell her, in the way authors have, that the children are coming back, that indeed they will be here on Thursday week. This would spoil so completely the surprise to which Wendy and John and Michael are looking forward. They have been planning it out on the ship: mother's rapture, father's shout of joy, Nana's leap through the air to embrace them first, when what they ought to be preparing for is a good hiding. How delicious to spoil it all by breaking the news in advance; so that when they enter grandly Mrs Darling may not even offer Wendy her mouth, and Mr Darling may exclaim pettishly, 'Dash it all, here are those boys again.' However, we should get no thanks even for this. We are beginning to know Mrs Darling by this time and may be sure that she would upbraid us for depriving the children of their little pleasure.

'But, my dear madam, it is ten days till Thursday week; so that by telling you what's what, we can save you ten days of unhappiness.'

'Yes, but at what a cost! By depriving the children of ten minutes of delight.'

'Oh, if you look at it in that way.'

'What other way is there in which to look at it?'

You see, the woman had no proper spirit. I had meant to say extraordinary nice things about her; but I despise her, and not one of them will I say now. She does not really need to be told to have things ready, for they are ready. All the beds are aired, and she never leaves the house, and observe, the window is open. For all the use we are to her, we might go back to the ship. However, as we are here we may as well stay and look on. That is all we are, lookers-on. Nobody really wants us. So let us watch and say jaggy things, in the hope that some of them will hurt.

The only change to be seen in the night-nursery is that between nine and six the kennel is no longer there. When the children flew away, Mr Darling felt in his bones that all the blame was his for having chained Nana up, and that from first to last she had been wiser than he. Of course, as we have seen, he was quite a simple man; indeed he might have passed for a boy again if he had been able to take his baldness off; but he had also a noble sense of justice and a lion courage to do what seemed right to him; and having thought the matter out with anxious care after the flight of the children, he went down on all fours and crawled into the kennel. To all Mrs Darling's dear invitations to him to come out he replied sadly but firmly:

'No, my own one, this is the place for me.'

In the bitterness of his remorse he swore that he would never leave the kennel until his children came back. Of course this was a pity; but whatever Mr Darling did he had to do in excess; otherwise he soon gave up doing it. And there never was a more humble man than the once proud George Darling, as he sat in the kennel of an evening talking with his wife of their children and all their pretty ways.

Very touching was his deference to Nana. He would not let her come into the kennel, but on all other matters he followed her wishes implicitly.

Every morning the kennel was carried with Mr Darling in it to a cab, which conveyed him to his office, and he returned home in the same way at six. Something of the strength of character of the man will be seen if we remember how sensitive he was to the opinion of neighbours: this man whose every movement now attracted surprised attention. Inwardly he must have suffered torture; but he preserved a calm exterior even when the young criticized his little home, and he always lifted his hat courteously to any lady who looked inside.

It may have been quixotic, but it was magnificent. Soon the inward meaning of it leaked out, and the great heart of the public was touched. Crowds followed the cab, cheering it lustily; charming girls scaled it to get his autograph; interviews appeared in the better class of papers, and society invited him to dinner and added, 'Do come in the kennel.'

On that eventful Thursday week Mrs Darling was in the night-nursery awaiting George's return home: a very sad-eyed woman. Now that we look at her closely and remember the gaiety of her in the old days, all gone now just because she has lost her babes, I find I won't be able to say nasty things about her after all. If she was too fond of her rubbishy children she couldn't help it. Look at her in her chair, where she has fallen asleep. The corner of her mouth, where one looks first, is almost withered up. Her head moves restlessly on her breast as if she had a pain there. Some like Peter best and some like Wendy best, but I like her best. Suppose, to make her happy, we whisper to her in her sleep that the brats are coming back.

They are really within two miles of the window now, and flying strong, but all we need whisper is that they are on the way. Let's.

It is a pity we did it, for she had started up, calling their names; and there is no one in the room but Nana.

'O Nana, I dreamt my dear ones had come back.'

Nana had filmy eyes, but all she could do was to put her paw gently on her mistress's lap; and they were sitting together thus when the kennel was brought back. As Mr Darling puts his head out of it to kiss his wife, we see that his face is more worn than of yore, but has a softer expression.

He gave his hat to Liza, who took it scornfully; for she had no imagination, and was quite incapable of understanding the motives of such a man. Outside, the crowd who had accompanied the cab home were still cheering, and he was naturally not unmoved.

'Listen to them,' he said; 'it is very gratifying.'

'Lot of little boys,' sneered Liza.

'There were several adults today,' he assured her with a faint flush; but when she tossed her head he had not a word of reproof for her. Social success had not spoilt him; it had made him sweeter. For some time he sat half out of the kennel, talking with Mrs Darling of this success, and pressing her hand reassuringly when she said she hoped his head would not be turned by it.

'But if I had been a weak man,' he said. 'Good heavens, if I had been a weak man!'

'And, George,' she said timidly, 'you are as full of remorse as ever, aren't you?'

'Full of remorse as ever, dearest! See my punishment: living in a kennel.'

'But it is punishment, isn't it, George? You are sure you are not enjoying it?'

'My love!'

You may be sure she begged his pardon; and then, feeling drowsy, he curled round in the kennel.

'Won't you play me to sleep,' he asked, 'on the nursery piano?' and as she was crossing to the day-nursery he added thoughtlessly, 'And shut that window. I feel a draught.'

'O George, never ask me to do that. The window must always be left open for them, always, always.'

Now it was his turn to beg her pardon; and she went into the day-nursery and played, and soon he was asleep; and while he slept, Wendy and John and Michael flew into the room.

Oh no. We have written it so, because that was the charming arrangement planned by them before we left the ship; but something must have happened since then, for it is not they who have flown in, it is Peter and Tinker Bell.

Peter's first words tell all.

'Quick, Tink,' he whispered, 'close the window; bar it. That's right. Now you and I must get away by the door; and when Wendy comes she will think her mother has barred her out; and she will have to go back with me.'

Now I understand what had hitherto puzzled me, why when Peter had exterminated the pirates he did not return to the island and leave Tink to escort the children to the mainland. This trick had been in his head all the time.

Instead of feeling that he was behaving badly he danced with glee; then he peeped into the day-nursery to see who was playing. He whispered to Tink, 'It's Wendy's mother. She is a pretty lady, but not so pretty as my mother. Her mouth is full of thimbles, but not so full as my mother's was.'

Of course he knew nothing whatever about his mother; but he sometimes bragged about her.

He did not know the tune, which was 'Home, Sweet Home', but he knew it was saying, 'Come back, Wendy, Wendy, Wendy'; and he cried exultantly, 'You will never see Wendy again, lady, for the window is barred.'

He peeped in again to see why the music had stopped; and now he saw that Mrs Darling had laid her head on the box, and that two tears were sitting on her eyes.

'She wants me to unbar the window,' thought Peter, 'but I won't, not I.'

He peeped again, and the tears were still there, or another two had taken their place.

'She's awfully fond of Wendy,' he said to himself. He was angry with her now for not seeing why she could not have Wendy.

The reason was so simple: 'I'm fond of her too. We can't both have her, lady.'

But the lady would not make the best of it, and he was

unhappy. He ceased to look at her, but even then she would not let go of him. He skipped about and made funny faces, but when he stopped it was just as if she were inside him, knocking.

'Oh, all right,' he said at last, and gulped. Then he unbarred the window. 'Come on, Tink,' he cried, with a frightful sneer at the laws of nature; 'we don't want any silly mothers'; and he flew away.

Thus Wendy and John and Michael found the window open for them after all, which of course was more than they deserved. They alighted on the floor, quite unashamed of themselves; and the youngest one had already forgotten his home.

'John,' he said, looking around him doubtfully, 'I think I have been here before.'

'Of course you have, you silly. There is your old bed.'

'So it is,' Michael said, but not with much conviction.

'I say,' cried John, 'the kennel!' and he dashed across to look into it.

'Perhaps Nana is inside it,' Wendy said.

But John whistled. 'Hallo,' he said, 'there's a man inside it.'

'It's father!' exclaimed Wendy.

'Let me see father,' Michael begged eagerly, and he took a good look. 'He is not so big as the pirate I killed,' he said with such frank disappointment that I am glad Mr Darling was asleep; it would have been sad if those had been the first words he heard his little Michael say.

Wendy and John had been taken aback somewhat at finding their father in the kennel.

'Surely,' said John, like one who has lost faith in his memory, 'he used not to sleep in the kennel?'

'John,' Wendy said falteringly, 'perhaps we don't remember the old life as well as we thought we did.'

A chill fell upon them; and serve them right.

'It is very careless of mother,' said that young scoundrel John, 'not to be here when we come back.'

It was then that Mrs Darling began playing again.

'It's mother!' cried Wendy, peeping.

'So it is!' said John.

'Then you are not really our mother, Wendy?' asked Michael, who was surely sleepy.

'Oh dear!' exclaimed Wendy, with her first real twinge of remorse, 'it is quite time we came back.'

'Let us creep in,' John suggested, 'and put our hands over her eyes.'

But Wendy, who saw that they must break the joyous news more gently, had a better plan.

'Let us all slip into our beds, and be there when she comes in, just as if we had never been away.'

And so when Mrs Darling went back to the night-nursery to see if her husband was asleep, all the beds were occupied. The children waited for her cry of joy, but it did not come. She saw them, but she did not believe they were there. You see, she saw them in their beds so often in her dreams that she thought this was just the dream hanging around her still.

She sat down in the chair by the fire, where in the old days she had nursed them.

They could not understand this, and a cold fear fell upon all the three of them.

'Mother!' Wendy cried.

'That's Wendy,' she said, but still she was sure it was the dream.

'Mother!'

'That's John,' she said.

'Mother!' cried Michael. He knew her now.

'That's Michael,' she said, and she stretched out her arms for the three little selfish children they would never envelop again. Yes, they did, they went round Wendy and John and Michael, who had slipped out of bed and run to her.

'George, George,' she cried when she could speak; and Mr Darling woke to share her bliss, and Nana came rushing in. There could not have been a lovelier sight; but there was none to see it except a strange boy who was staring in at the window. He had ecstasies innumerable that other children can never know; but he was looking through the window at the one joy from which he must be for ever barred.

17

When Wendy Grew Up

I hope you want to know what became of the other boys. They were waiting below to give Wendy time to explain about them; and when they had counted five hundred they went up. They went up by the stair, because they thought this would make a better impression. They stood in a row in front of Mrs Darling, with their hats off, and wishing they were not wearing their pirate clothes. They said nothing, but their eyes asked her to have them. They ought to have looked at Mr Darling also, but they forgot about him.

Of course Mrs Darling said at once that she would have them; but Mr Darling was curiously depressed, and they saw that he considered six a rather large number.

'I must say,' he said to Wendy, 'that you don't do things by halves,' a grudging remark which the twins thought was pointed at them.

The first twin was the proud one, and he asked, flushing, 'Do you think we should be too much of a handful, sir? Because if so we can go away.'

'Father!' Wendy cried, shocked; but still the cloud was

on him. He knew he was behaving unworthily, but he could not help it.

'We could lie doubled up,' said Nibs.

'I always cut their hair myself,' said Wendy.

'George!' Mrs Darling exclaimed, pained to see her dear one showing himself in such an unfavourable light.

Then he burst into tears, and the truth came out. He was as glad to have them as she was, he said, but he thought they should have asked his consent as well as hers, instead of treating him as a cypher in his own house.

'I don't think he is a cypher,' Tootles cried instantly. 'Do you think he is a cypher, Curly?'

'No, I don't. Do you think he is a cypher, Slightly?'

'Rather not. Twin, what do you think?'

It turned out that not one of them thought him a cypher; and he was absurdly gratified, and said he would find space for them all in the drawing-room if they fitted in.

'We'll fit in, sir,' they assured him.

'Then follow the leader,' he cried gaily. 'Mind you, I am not sure that we have a drawing-room, but we pretend we have, and it's all the same. Hoop la!'

He went off dancing through the house, and they all cried 'Hoop la!' and danced after him, searching for the drawing-room; and I forget whether they found it, but at any rate they found corners, and they all fitted in.

As for Peter, he saw Wendy once again before he flew away. He did not exactly come to the window, but he brushed against it in passing, so that she could open it if she liked and call to him. That was what she did.

'Hallo, Wendy, good-bye,' he said.

'Oh dear, are you going away?'

'Yes.'

'You don't feel, Peter,' she said falteringly, 'that you would like to say anything to my parents about a very sweet subject.'

'No.'

'About me, Peter?'

'No.'

Mrs Darling came to the window, for at present she was keeping a sharp eye on Wendy. She told Peter that she had adopted all the other boys, and would like to adopt him also.

'Would you send me to school?' he inquired craftily.

'Yes.'

'And then to an office?'

'I suppose so.'

'Soon I should be a man?'

'Very soon.'

'I don't want to go to school and learn solemn things,' he told her passionately. 'I don't want to be a man. O Wendy's mother, if I was to wake up and feel there was a beard!'

'Peter!' said Wendy the comforter, 'I should love you in

a beard'; and Mrs Darling stretched out her arms to him, but he repulsed her.

'Keep back, lady, no one is going to catch me and make me a man.'

'But where are you going to live?'

'With Tink in the house we built for Wendy. The fairies are to put it high up among the tree-tops where they sleep at nights.'

'How lovely,' cried Wendy so longingly that Mrs Darling tightened her grip.

'I thought all the fairies were dead,' Mrs Darling said.

'There are always a lot of young ones,' explained Wendy, who was now quite an authority, 'because you see when a new baby laughs for the first time a new fairy is born, and as there are always new babies there are always new fairies. They live in nests on the tops of trees; and the mauve ones are boys and the white ones are girls, and the blue ones are just little sillies who are not sure what they are.'

'I shall have such fun,' said Peter, with one eye on Wendy.

'It will be rather lonely in the evening,' she said, 'sitting by the fire.'

'I shall have Tink.'

'Tink can't go a twentieth part of the way round,' she reminded him a little tartly.

'Sneaky tell-tale!' Tink called out from somewhere round the corner.

'It doesn't matter,' Peter said.

'O Peter, you know it matters.'

'Well then, come with me to the little house.'

'May I, Mummy?'

'Certainly not. I have got you home again, and I mean to keep you.'

'But he does so need a mother.'

'So do you, my love.'

'Oh, all right,' Peter said, as if he had asked her from politeness merely; but Mrs Darling saw his mouth twitch, and she made this handsome offer: to let Wendy go to him for a week every year to do his spring cleaning. Wendy would have preferred a more permanent arrangement; and it seemed to her that spring would be long in coming; but this promise sent Peter away quite gay again. He had no sense of time, and was so full of adventures that all I have told you about him is only a halfpenny-worth of them. I suppose it was because Wendy knew this that her last words to him were these rather plaintive ones:

'You won't forget me, Peter, will you, before spring-cleaning time comes?'

Of course Peter promised; and then he flew away. He took Mrs Darling's kiss with him. The kiss that had been for no one else Peter took quite easily. Funny. But she seemed satisfied.

Of course all the boys went to school; and most of them got into Class III but Slightly was put first into Class

IV and then into Class V. Class I is the top class. Before they had attended school a week they saw what goats they had been not to remain on the island; but it was too late now, and soon they settled down to being as ordinary as you or me or Jenkins minor. It is sad to have to say that the power to fly gradually left them. At first Nana tied their feet to the bedposts so that they should not fly away in the night; and one of their diversions by day was to pretend to fall off buses; but by and by they ceased to tug at their bonds in bed, and found that they hurt themselves when they let go of the bus. In time they could not even fly after their hats. Want of practice, they called it; but what it really meant was that they no longer believed.

Michael believed longer than the other boys, though they jeered at him; so he was with Wendy when Peter came for her at the end of the first year. She flew away with Peter in the frock she had woven from leaves and berries in the Neverland, and her one fear was that he might notice how short it had become; but he never noticed, he had so much to say about himself.

She had looked forward to thrilling talks with him about old times, but new adventures had crowded the old ones from his mind.

'Who is Captain Hook?' he asked with interest when she spoke of the arch enemy.

'Don't you remember,' she asked, amazed, 'how you killed him and saved all our lives?'

'I forget them after I kill them,' he replied carelessly.

When she expressed a doubtful hope that Tinker Bell would be glad to see her he said, 'Who is Tinker Bell?'

'O Peter,' she said, shocked; but even when she explained he could not remember.

'There are such a lot of them,' he said. 'I expect she is no more.'

I expect he was right, for fairies don't live long, but they are so little that a short time seems a good while to them.

Wendy was pained too to find that the past year was but as yesterday to Peter; it had seemed such a long year of waiting to her. But he was exactly as fascinating as ever, and they had a lovely spring cleaning in the little house on the tree-tops.

Next year he did not come to her. She waited in a new frock because the old one simply would not meet; but he never came.

'Perhaps he is ill,' Michael said.

'You know he is never ill.'

Michael came close to her and whispered, with a shiver, 'Perhaps there is no such person, Wendy!' and then Wendy would have cried if Michael had not been crying.

Peter came next spring cleaning; and the strange thing was that he never knew he had missed a year.

That was the last time the girl Wendy ever saw him. For a little longer she tried for his sake not to have growing pains; and she felt she was untrue to him when she got a prize for general knowledge. But the years came and went without bringing the careless boy; and when they met again Wendy was a married woman, and Peter was no more to her than a little dust in the box in which she had kept her toys. Wendy was grown up. You need not be sorry for her. She was one of the kind that likes to grow up. In the end she grew up of her own free will a day quicker than other girls.

All the boys were grown up and done for by this time; so it is scarcely worth while saying anything more about them. You may see the twins and Nibs and Curly any day going to an office, each carrying a little bag and an umbrella. Michael is an engine-driver. Slightly married a lady of title, and so he became a lord. You see that judge in a wig coming out at the iron door? That used to be Tootles. The bearded man who doesn't know any story to tell his children was once John.

Wendy was married in white with a pink sash. It is strange to think that Peter did not alight in the church and forbid the banns.

Years rolled on again, and Wendy had a daughter. This ought not be written in ink but in a golden splash.

She was called Jane, and always had an odd inquiring look, as if from the moment she arrived on the mainland she wanted to ask questions. When she was old enough to ask them they were mostly about Peter Pan. She loved to hear of Peter, and Wendy told her all she could remember in the very nursery from which the famous flight had taken place. It was Jane's nursery now, for her father had bought it at the three per cents from Wendy's father, who was no longer fond of stairs. Mrs Darling was now dead and forgotten.

There were only two beds in the nursery now, Jane's and her nurse's; and there was no kennel, for Nana also had passed away. She died of old age, and at the end she had been rather difficult to get on with; being very firmly convinced that no one knew how to look after children except herself.

Once a week Jane's nurse had her evening off; and then it was Wendy's part to put Jane to bed. That was the time for stories. It was Jane's invention to raise the sheet over her mother's head and her own, thus making a tent and in the awful darkness to whisper:

'What do we see now?'

'I don't think I see anything tonight,' says Wendy, with a feeling that if Nana were here she would object to further conversation.

'Yes, you do,' says Jane, 'you see when you were a little girl.'

'That is a long time ago, sweetheart,' said Wendy. 'Ah me, how time flies!'

'Does it fly,' asks the artful child, 'the way you flew when you were a little girl?'

'The way I flew! Do you know, Jane, I sometimes wonder whether I ever did really fly.'

'Yes, you did.'

'The dear old days when I could fly!'

'Why can't you fly now, mother?'

'Because I am grown up, dearest. When people grow up they forget the way.'

'Why do they forget the way?'

'Because they are no longer gay and innocent and heartless. It is only the gay and innocent and heartless who can fly.'

'What is the gay and innocent and heartless? I do wish I was gay and innocent and heartless.'

Or perhaps Wendy admits that she does see something. 'I do believe,' she says, 'that it is this nursery.'

'I do believe it is,' says Jane. 'Go on.'

They are now embarked on the great adventure of the night when Peter flew in looking for his shadow.

'The foolish fellow,' says Wendy, 'tried to stick it on with soap, and when he could not he cried, and that woke me, and I sewed it on for him.'

'You have missed a bit,' interrupts Jane, who now knows the story better than her mother. 'When you saw him sitting on the floor crying, what did you say?'

'I sat up in bed and I said, "Boy, why are you crying?"'

'Yes, that was it,' says Jane, with a big breath.

'And then he flew us all away to the Neverland and the

fairies and the pirates and the redskins and the mermaids' lagoon, and the home under the ground, and the little house.'

'Yes! Which did you like best of all?'

'I think I liked the home under the ground best of all.'

'Yes, so do I. What was the last thing Peter ever said to you?'

'The last thing he ever said to me was, "Just always be waiting for me, and then some night you will hear me crowing."'

'Yes.'

'But, alas! he forgot all about me.' Wendy said it with a smile. She was as grown up as that.

'What did his crow sound like?' Jane asked one evening.

'It was like this,' Wendy said, trying to imitate Peter's crow.

'No, it wasn't,' Jane said gravely, 'it was like this', and she did it ever so much better than her mother.

Wendy was a little startled. 'My darling, how can you know?'

'I often hear it when I am sleeping,' Jane said.

'Ah yes, many girls hear it when they are sleeping, but I was the only one who heard it awake.'

'Lucky you,' said Jane.

And then one night came the tragedy. It was the spring

of the year, and the story had been told for the night, and Jane was now asleep in her bed. Wendy was sitting on the floor, very close to the fire, so as to see to darn, for there was no other light in the nursery; and while she sat darning she heard a crow. Then the window blew open as of old, and Peter dropped on the floor.

He was exactly the same as ever, and Wendy saw at once that he still had all his first teeth.

He was a little boy, and she was grown up. She huddled by the fire not daring to move, helpless and guilty, a big woman.

'Hallo, Wendy,' he said, not noticing any difference, for he was thinking chiefly of himself; and in the dim light her white dress might have been the night-gown in which he had seen her first.

'Hallo, Peter,' she replied faintly, squeezing herself as small as possible. Something inside her was crying, 'Woman, woman, let go of me.'

'Hallo, where is John?' he asked, suddenly missing the third bed.

'John is not here now,' she gasped.

'Is Michael asleep?' he asked, with a careless glance at Jane.

'Yes,' she answered; and now she felt that she was untrue to Jane as well as to Peter.

'That is not Michael,' she said quickly, lest a judgement should fall on her.

Peter looked. 'Hallo, is it a new one?'

'Yes.'

'Boy or girl?'

'Girl.'

Now surely he would understand; but not a bit of it.

'Peter,' she said, faltering, 'are you expecting me to fly away with you?'

'Of course, that is why I have come.' He added a little sternly, 'Have you forgotten that this is spring-cleaning time?'

She knew it was useless to say that he had let many spring-cleaning times pass.

'I can't come,' she said apologetically, 'I have forgotten how to fly.'

'I'll soon teach you again.'

'O Peter, don't waste the fairy dust on me.'

She had risen; and now at last a fear assailed him. 'What is it?' he cried, shrinking.

'I will turn up the light,' she said, 'and then you can see for yourself.'

For almost the only time in his life that I know of, Peter was afraid. 'Don't turn up the light,' he cried.

She let her hands play in the hair of the tragic boy. She was not a little girl heart-broken about him; she was a grown woman smiling at it all, but they were wet smiles.

Then she turned up the light, and Peter saw. He gave

a cry of pain; and when the tall beautiful creature stooped to lift him in her arms he drew back sharply.

'What is it?' he cried again.

'I am old, Peter. I am ever so much more than twenty. I grew up long ago.'

'You promised not to!'

'I couldn't help it. I am a married woman, Peter.'

'No, you're not.'

'Yes, and the little girl in the bed is my baby.'

'No, she's not.'

But he supposed she was; and he took a step towards the sleeping child with his dagger upraised. Of course he did not strike. He sat down on the floor instead and sobbed; and Wendy did not know how to comfort him, though she could have done it so easily once. She was only a woman now, and she ran out of the room to try to think.

Peter continued to cry, and soon his sobs woke Jane. She sat up in bed and was interested at once.

'Boy,' she said, 'why are you crying?'

Peter rose and bowed to her, and she bowed to him from the bed.

'Hallo,' he said.

'Hallo,' said Jane.

'My name is Peter Pan,' he told her.

'Yes, I know.'

'I came back for my mother,' he explained, 'to take her to the Neverland.'

'Yes, I know,' Jane said, 'I've been waiting for you.'

When Wendy returned diffidently she found Peter sitting on the bedpost crowing gloriously, while Jane in her nighty was flying round the room in solemn ecstasy.

'She is my mother,' Peter explained; and Jane descended and stood by his side, with the look on her face that he liked to see on ladies when they gazed at him.

'He does so need a mother,' Jane said.

'Yes, I know,' Wendy admitted rather forlornly; 'no one knows it so well as I.'

'Good-bye,' said Peter to Wendy; and he rose in the air, and the shameless Jane rose with him; it was already her easiest way of moving about.

Wendy rushed to the window.

'No, no,' she cried.

'It is just for spring-cleaning time,' Jane said; 'he wants me always to do his spring cleaning.'

'If only I could go with you,' Wendy sighed.

'You see you can't fly,' said Jane.

Of course in the end Wendy let them fly away together. Our last glimpse of her shows her at the window, watching them receding into the sky until they were as small as stars.

As you look at Wendy you may see her hair becoming white, and her figure little again, for all this happened long ago. Jane is now a common grown-up with a daughter called Margaret; and every spring-cleaning time, except when he forgets, Peter comes for Margaret and takes her to the Neverland, where she tells him stories about himself, to which he listens eagerly. When Margaret grows up she will have a daughter, who is to be Peter's mother in turn; and thus it will go on, so long as children are gay and innocent and heartless.

THE END

PUFFIN 🐧 CLASSICS

Peter Pan

**With Puffin Classics, the adventure isn't
over when you reach the final page.
Want to discover more about your favourite
characters, their creators and their worlds?
Read on . . .**

CONTENTS

NAME: James Matthew Barrie, nicknamed Jamie
BORN: 9 May 1860 in Kirriemuir, Scotland
DIED: 19 June 1937 in London, England
NATIONALITY: Scottish
LIVED: mainly in London
MARRIED: to Mary Ansell in 1894, divorced 1909
CHILDREN: five adopted sons: George, Jack, Peter, Michael and Nico Llewelyn Davies

What was he like?

J. M. Barrie was a man who half wished he hadn't grown up. Kind and funny, but also short (he was only one and a half metres (or five feet) tall), timid, often ill, and hopeless at grown-up relationships with women – he just wasn't very good at being an adult.

Where did he grow up?

He was born in Kirriemuir, Scotland, and later also lived in Glasgow, Forfar and Dumfries. When he was seven, his older brother David was killed while ice-skating. Jamie always felt that his mother had loved David best of all her ten children, and he was deeply affected by her sadness.

What did he do apart from writing books?

When Barrie wasn't writing books, he was writing plays, smoking his pipe or walking his St Bernard dog, Porthos, in the park. It was while walking Porthos that he met George and Jack

Llewelyn Davies with their nurse. Soon, he had become a friend of the family, and when the boys' parents died, Barrie adopted George, Jack and their three brothers and raised them as his own.

Where did he get the idea for Peter Pan?

J. M. Barrie told the Llewelyn Davies boys – the original Lost Boys – lots of stories, and these tales are where Neverland and Peter Pan came from. He came up with the name 'Peter Pan' by putting together the name of one of the boys and the Greek god of nature and shepherds, Pan – a lively and very naughty god with the legs and horns of a goat who is, of course, forever young.

What did people think of Peter Pan *when it was first published?*

Peter Pan (which was first published in 1911 with the title *Peter and Wendy*) was a bestseller when it came out, probably because it had been a very successful play before Barrie adapted it into a book.

If it wasn't for the play of *Peter Pan*, the book might have been very different. When he first wrote the play, Captain Hook and his crew weren't in it. He only added them because the theatre needed a scene played in front of a closed curtain towards the end, so that the scenery could be changed from Neverland back to London. The great battle on the pirate ship was born, and so was the story of Captain Hook.

What other books did he write?
J. M. Barrie wrote over eighty books, plays and film scripts, mainly for adults. They were very successful during his lifetime, but today *Peter Pan* is by far the most famous of all his works.

Some books Barrie *didn't* write are any of the prequels or sequels to *Peter Pan*.

Peter Pan – according to Peter, he ran away from home the day he was born because he didn't want ever to grow up. Peter doesn't know how old he is, but he is 'quite young' and smaller than any of the Lost Boys. Charming and cocky, brave and selfish, merry and heartless, he quickly forgets people and events, and is always on the lookout for the next adventure. He hates mothers, but also secretly longs for one – as long as she never makes him grow up!

Wendy Moira Angela Darling – a practical, motherly little girl, Wendy is persuaded by Peter to come to Neverland and be a mother to him and the Lost Boys. Wendy is the only person in the book capable of standing up to Peter.

John and Michael Darling – Wendy's younger brothers. Although Peter's not too bothered about them, Wendy insists on involving John and Michael in the adventure.

Mrs Darling – Wendy, John and Michael's mother, whose wonderful bedtime stories are what attracts Peter to their house in the first place.

Mr (George) Darling – Wendy, John and Michael's father. A little foolish and proud, Mr Darling isn't nearly such a good parent as Mrs Darling.

Nana – the Darlings' nurse (actually a large Newfoundland dog, because they can't afford a human nurse).

Liza – the Darlings' maid-of-all-work.

Tootles, Nibs, Slightly, Curly and the Twins – The Lost Boys living in Neverland with Peter at the time of the story. Peter tells Wendy that the Lost Boys are boys who fell out of their prams while their nurses weren't looking. Whereas Peter is pretty much a permanent resident of Neverland, the Lost Boys are only temporary lodgers – if they seem to be growing up, Peter sends them home.

Tinker Bell – a small, rude, female fairy, a friend of Peter's. Desperately jealous of Wendy, she hates her with a passion and nearly causes her death. She is named Tinker Bell because her special magic is mending pots and pans – in J. M. Barrie's time a person who did this for a living was called a tinker.

Captain Hook (James or Jas. Hook) – cunning, ruthless and inwardly tortured pirate captain, with a hook instead of a hand. Hook's two great weaknesses are his fear of his own blood, and his fear of the island's resident crocodile, which got a taste for Hook's flesh when it ate his severed hand.

Cecco, Bill Jukes, Cookson, Gentleman Starkey, Skylights, Smee, Noodler, Robt. (Robert) Mullins, Alf Mason, Geo. (George) Scourie, Chas. (Charles) Turley, Foggerty, Ed Teynte – members of Captain Hook's dastardly and occasionally mutinous crew.

Tiger Lily – beautiful Native American princess of the 'Piccaninny' tribe, saved by Peter from drowning. (However, in reality there was never any such tribe.)

Lean Wolf and Great Big Little Panther – braves of the 'Piccaninny' tribe. There are also many more members of the tribe in Neverland.

Jane – Wendy's daughter.

Margaret – Wendy's granddaughter.

What do you think of the character of Peter? What are his good and bad qualities?

What does Peter sacrifice in order to stay a boy for ever?

What are the differences between Wendy and the boys in *Peter Pan*? Do you think this is a fair representation of the differences between boys and girls?

People often tell each other stories in *Peter Pan*. What examples can you think of? Why do you think that storytelling is so important in the book?

Is Neverland nothing but fun, or does it have a darker side?

Is Mr and Mrs Darling's grown-up world more sensible and orderly than Neverland?

Many things about Neverland aren't really explained, or are just hinted at, in the book. For example, who are 'they' who don't want the children to land at the beginning? Why do you think J. M. Barrie wrote the novel in this way?

Draw a map of your own Neverland.

Pick one of the adventures that J. M. Barrie tells us happened on the island, but doesn't actually give us the full story of (for example, Tinker Bell's attempt to send Wendy back to the mainland on a floating leaf). Write your own full-length version!

There are many film and TV adaptations of *Peter Pan* (including a famous Disney film). Watch one of them and compare it to the book. Which do you like better, and why?

Find a copy of the play of *Peter Pan*, and act out a scene from it.

You are the set designer for a new theatre production of *Peter Pan*. Draw detailed diagrams, or even make models, of your sets. How would you manage the scene changes?

Imagine that Captain Hook kept a diary or ship's log, found by the children after his death. Write some of the entries Hook might have made.

About Fairies

✷ Think that all fairies are pretty, innocent little creatures with wings? Think again. Fairies come in all different shapes and sizes. And whilst fairy magic can be friendly and helpful, it can also be mischievous, malicious or downright bad.

✷ Fairies used to be blamed for many things that went wrong around a house or farm, such as animals dying, milk going sour or tangles in the hair of a person who'd just woken up.

✷ Never trust a payment from a fairy. Fairy gold is usually nothing of the sort, but a worthless substance enchanted to look like gold.

✷ Fairies are well known for kidnapping babies or children and taking them to live in fairyland. One of the dangers of this is that time passes differently in fairyland – one day there might be one hundred years here.

✷ Some things you can do to protect yourself against malicious fairies are using iron, running water or four-leaf clovers, and wearing your clothes inside out. Avoid paths that fairies are known to use, and never dig in or enter a fairy mound (a grass-covered mound, often said today to be a human burial mound).

★ Modern fairies are technologically advanced beings. The fairies in Eoin Colfer's *Artemis Fowl* series of books, for example, have equipment such as neutrino blasters.

ABOUT PIRATES

★ As long as there have been ships, there have been pirates! Piracy was a big problem for ancient civilizations such as the Egyptians, Greeks and Romans.

★ The best time and place in history to be a pirate was probably in the Caribbean (known then as the 'Spanish Main') from about 1560 to 1730. It's from that period that we get most of our modern ideas about how pirates dress, speak and behave.

★ *Peter Pan* (along with many other pirate films and books) shows pirates making their victims walk the plank. However, this probably happened very rarely, if at all – guns, swords or simply throwing people overboard would have been much more efficient.

★ When the famous pirate Blackbeard was killed in 1718, five out of the eighteen members of his crew were black. Black people may have been treated more equally on pirate ships than they were in 'civilized' European and American society at that time, and it's possible that up to 30 per cent of pirates in the Caribbean were black. If pirates attacked slave ships, they might liberate the slaves.

* Some of the pirates mentioned in *Peter Pan*, such as Blackbeard, were real people. Some others, such as Flint, come from the famous pirate novel *Treasure Island*, written by J. M. Barrie's friend Robert Louis Stevenson (and also available in Puffin Classics).

* Pirates still exist today in areas such as South-east Asia, the Red Sea and off the coast of South America. Nowadays they are more likely to have balaclavas and machine guns than bandannas and cutlasses.

About 'Redskins'

* In *Peter Pan*, 'redskins' means Native Americans, i.e. the descendants of the peoples who lived in North America before the arrival of Europeans. If someone used that word to describe a Native American today, many people would find it offensive.

* No one really knows how many people were living in North America when Europeans first arrived (around the year 1500), but the population was probably in the millions. The people had many different beliefs, languages and ways of life, and they were often at war with one another.

* The arrival of Europeans was a disaster – in some areas, more than 80 per cent of the population died. Some were killed in battle, some were enslaved and worked to death,

some died because they became refugees. Most lethal
of all, though, were European diseases to which Native
Americans had no inherited immunity, such as smallpox.

★ There were many stories told by white people about Native
American tribes, most of which weren't very accurate.
Sometimes, Native Americans were brutal, barely human
monsters. Sometimes they were noble savages, living at
peace with the land. J. M. Barrie created the 'redskins' in
Peter Pan from these stories, rather than trying to paint a
realistic picture of Native Americans.

★ One thing in *Peter Pan* that does have some basis in fact
is the scalps the tribe carry around with them. To 'scalp'
someone means to slice the skin and hair off the top of
their head as a battle trophy. During the centuries of
conflict over land between Native Americans and settlers,
both sides sometimes scalped their enemies.

★ Today, the US government recognizes over 500 tribal
governments as independent, self-governing entities with
the right to make many of their own laws.

About Mermaids

★ The first recorded story about a mermaid is around 3,000
years old! Cultures all over the world have stories about
mermaids.

★ Some mermaids are dangerous temptresses. They sing so sweetly that sailors jump overboard to try and reach them, only to drown.

★ Mermaids can also be a portent of doom for sailors. If you see a mermaid combing her long golden hair whilst sitting on the rocks, beware!

★ One mermaid was made into a saint. Irish legends tell of Liban, a girl who nearly drowned but was transformed into a mermaid. Three hundred years passed before a messenger to Rome heard Liban singing beneath the waves. She asked him to arrange a meeting with St Comgall a year hence. St Comgall baptized Liban, and she was taken up to heaven.

★ In Japan, mermaids are called ningyo. By eating the flesh of one of them, supposedly you can become immortal.

★ A distant cousin of the mermaid is the Orkney selkie. These are creatures that can transform themselves from seals to humans by casting off their selkie skin. However, if the skin is lost or stolen they can't turn back into a seal.

If you have enjoyed *Peter Pan* you may like to read
The Wizard of Oz in which Dorothy finds herself
in the magical world of Oz and meets the Scarecrow,
the Tin Woodman and the Cowardly Lion on her
journey along the yellow brick road:

The Deadly Poppy Field

Our little party of travellers awakened next morning refreshed and full of hope, and Dorothy breakfasted like a princess off peaches and plums from the trees beside the river.

Behind them was the dark forest they had passed safely through, although they had suffered many discouragements; but before them was a lovely, sunny country that seemed to beckon them on to the Emerald City.

To be sure, the broad river now cut them off from this beautiful land; but the raft was nearly done, and after the Tin Woodman had cut a few more logs and fastened them together with wooden pins, they were ready to start. Dorothy sat down in the middle of the raft and held Toto in her arms. When the Cowardly Lion stepped upon the raft it tipped badly, for he was big and heavy; but the Scarecrow and the Tin Woodman stood upon the other end to steady it, and they had long poles in their hands to push the raft through the water.

They got along quite well at first, but when they reached the middle of the river the swift current swept the raft down stream, farther and farther away from the road of yellow brick; and the water grew so deep that the long poles would not touch the bottom.

'This is bad,' said the Tin Woodman, 'for if we cannot get to the land we shall be carried into the country of the wicked Witch of the West, and she will enchant us and make us her slaves.'

'And then I should get no brains,' said the Scarecrow.

'And I should get no courage,' said the Cowardly Lion.

'And I should get no heart,' said the Tin Woodman.

'And I should never get back to Kansas,' said Dorothy.

'We must certainly get to the Emerald City if we can,' the Scarecrow continued, and he pushed so hard on his long pole that it stuck fast in the mud at the bottom of the river, and before he could pull it out again, or let go, the raft was swept away and the poor Scarecrow left clinging to the pole in the middle of the river.

'Good bye!' he called after them, and they were very sorry to leave him; indeed, the Tin Woodman began to cry, but fortunately remembered that he might rust, and so dried his tears on Dorothy's apron.

Of course this was a bad thing for the Scarecrow.

'I am now worse off than when I first met Dorothy,' he thought. 'Then, I was stuck on a pole in a cornfield, where I could make believe scare the crows, at any rate; but surely there is no use for a Scarecrow stuck on a pole in the middle of a river. I am afraid I shall never have any brains, after all!'

Down the stream the raft floated, and the poor Scarecrow was left far behind. Then the Lion said:

'Something must be done to save us. I think I can swim to the shore and pull the raft after me, if you will only hold fast to the tip of my tail.'

So he sprang into the water and the Tin Woodman caught fast hold of his tail, when the Lion began to swim with all his might toward the shore. It was hard work, although he was so big; but by and by they were drawn out of the current, and then Dorothy took the Tin Woodman's long pole and helped push the raft to the land.

They were all tired out when they reached the shore at last and stepped off upon the pretty green grass, and they also knew that the stream had carried them a long way past the road of yellow brick that led to the Emerald City.

'What shall we do now?' asked the Tin Woodman, as the Lion lay down on the grass to let the sun dry him.

'We must get back to the road, in some way,' said Dorothy.

'The best plan will be to walk along the river bank until we come to the road again,' remarked the Lion.

So, when they were rested, Dorothy picked up her basket and they started along the grassy bank, back to the road from which the river had carried them. It was a lovely country, with plenty of flowers and fruit trees and sunshine to cheer them, and had they not felt so sorry for the poor Scarecrow they could have been very happy.

They walked along as fast as they could, Dorothy only stopping once to pick a beautiful flower; and after a time the Tin Woodman cried out,

'Look!'

Then they all looked at the river and saw the Scarecrow perched upon his pole in the middle of the water, looking very lonely and sad.

'What can we do to save him?' asked Dorothy.

The Lion and the Woodman both shook their heads, for they did not know. So they sat down upon the bank and gazed wistfully at the Scarecrow until a Stork flew by, which, seeing them, stopped to rest at the water's edge.

'Who are you, and where are you going?' asked the Stork.

'I am Dorothy,' answered the girl; 'and these are my friends, the Tin Woodman and the Cowardly Lion; and we are going to the Emerald City.'

'This isn't the road,' said the Stork, as she twisted her long neck and looked sharply at the queer party.

'I know it,' returned Dorothy, 'but we have lost the Scarecrow, and are wondering how we shall get him again.'

'Where is he?' asked the Stork.

'Over there in the river,' answered the girl.

'If he wasn't so big and heavy I would get him for you,' remarked the Stork.

'He isn't heavy a bit,' said Dorothy, eagerly, 'for he is stuffed with straw; and if you will bring him back to us we shall thank you ever and ever so much.'

'Well, I'll try,' said the Stork; 'but if I find he is too heavy to carry I shall have to drop him in the river again.'

So the big bird flew into the air and over the water till she came to where the Scarecrow was perched upon his pole. Then the Stork with her great claws grabbed the Scarecrow by the arm and carried him up into the air and back to the bank, where Dorothy and the Lion and the Tin Woodman and Toto were sitting.

When the Scarecrow found himself among his friends again he was so happy that he hugged them all, even the Lion and Toto; and as they walked along he sang 'Tol-de-ri-de-oh!' at every step, he felt so gay.

'I was afraid I should have to stay in the river forever,' he said, 'but the kind Stork saved me, and if I ever get any brains I shall find the Stork again and do it some kindness in return.'

'That's all right,' said the Stork, who was flying along beside them. 'I always like to help anyone in trouble. But I must go now, for my babies are waiting in the nest for me. I hope you will find the Emerald City and that Oz will help you.'

The Wizard of Oz is available in Puffin Classics

The Oxford Library of Italian Classics

GENERAL EDITOR : ARCHIBALD COLQUHOUN

THE DIARY

OF ONE OF

GARIBALDI'S THOUSAND

THE DIARY
of one of
GARIBALDI'S THOUSAND

GIUSEPPE CESARE ABBA

Translated with an Introduction by
E. R. VINCENT

LONDON
OXFORD UNIVERSITY PRESS
NEW YORK   TORONTO
1962

Oxford University Press, Amen House, London E.C.4

GLASGOW NEW YORK TORONTO MELBOURNE WELLINGTON
BOMBAY CALCUTTA MADRAS KARACHI LAHORE DACCA
CAPE TOWN SALISBURY NAIROBI IBADAN ACCRA
KUALA LUMPUR HONG KONG

Printed in Great Britain by Richard Clay and Company, Ltd.,
Bungay, Suffolk

CONTENTS

MAPS

Italy, 1860. The route of the Expedition

INTRODUCTION

GIUSEPPE CESARE ABBA, an unknown young man of twenty-two, started on his great adventure as one of Garibaldi's volunteers in 1860, with two ambitions; to strike a blow for the new Italy and to write the epic poem of the Sicilian expedition. His material equipment was not large: an old musket, a bayonet, and twenty cartridges for Italy, and a little pocket-book for the poem. He relied on his youth, his brave spirit, and his romantic imagination to help him play the Tyrtaeus.

It is the notebook, in which he jotted down his impressions in intervals between the marches and skirmishes of irregular warfare, that forms the basis of the present book. The poem was eventually written (*Arrigo, Da Quarto al Volturno*, 1866), but it was not a very good poem and few have read it. The prose amplification of the little notebook has, however, become a precious possession of the Italian people, who treasure it as an authentic reflection of the spirit that inspired the best of those who made Italy. It has often been re-published in its original language, but never before in English.

The *Noterelle*, as its author modestly called the book, is not only an historical document which has proved a useful source of first-hand information for later writers, it is also a conscious work of literature. For twenty years after the events he describes Abba worked on the bare bones of his notes, enriching them from his unfading memories of the epic occasion in which he had played a part. The book is therefore a combination of present observation and later recollection. One of the translator's difficulties has been to follow the swing of Abba's verbs to and fro between the now and the then.

History is the record of what happened, and also of how we think, on incomplete evidence, it did happen. History tells us that on a certain day in 1860 Garibaldi sailed from Genoa with a small body of men in two ships, touched at Talamone, landed at Marsala, clashed with the Bourbon troops at

Calatafimi, and deceived his enemy by feints at Palermo while circling the city, which he entered by the Termini Gate. After bluffing a greatly superior garrison into capitulation he marched to Messina after assuring his flank by overcoming the Bourbon garrison of Milazzo. With greatly increased numbers he crossed the Straits; traversed Calabria; entered Naples; fought a pitched battle on the River Volturno after junction with Piedmontese regular troops; met Victor Emmanuel; handed over his power to the King, and gracefully retired to Caprera. That is what happened and nothing can change it now, but it might have happened quite differently. He might not have gone first to Sicily, but followed the advice of his Mazzinian friends and advanced from Talamone to attack Rome. Had he succeeded in landing in Sicily he might easily have been turned back from Calatafimi and retired to the mountains to organize the Sicilian insurgents, as many expected him to do. He might have played a waiting game. He might not have wished to invade the mainland. He might have met the Piedmontese troops as enemies rather than friends. He might have been rude to the King. These are the things that did not happen; they are not history. A diary written when events are unfolding, and before it is known how they will unfold, reflects all the uncertainties of the actual moment. Abba's *Noterelle* is, in part, such a book and in his pages we are able to experience the doubts, fears, and hopes that filled the minds of those who participated in the hazards of an enterprise now congealed into the set form of history. At the end we share with him the disillusion of the soldier when the battle is won and the politicians come in.

At the start all is confusion. Where is Garibaldi? What are his intentions? They say 30,000 insurgents are besieging Palermo. Surely Garibaldi must respond to such a situation. But is it true? There are no beds to be had in Genoa. The place is swarming with exuberant chattering young men. The inns are packed with excited customers, eating, drinking, and for ever talking. 'It's absolutely disgraceful,' says the elderly gentleman, 'whatever right have these turbulent people to go

invading the country of His Majesty the King of Naples? Whatever is the world coming to?' And off he goes. What is that song that young Doctor Bandini is singing:

> *Eran trecento, eran giovani e forti*
> *E sono morti.*

Yes, Pisacane tried the same thing three years before and failed, and where are his young men? *E sono morti.* They are all dead!

Then before you properly know what is happening you're on board a small steamship packed with strangers, mostly young men, but also old men of seventy and little boys of twelve. All is confusion and only a few have any arms at all, and nearly all are unknown to one another. What an extraordinary way to start an invasion! But after all you're not going to Sicily; your ship and its consort approach the Tuscan shore and cast anchor. You land with the rest and while the others strip and bathe you enter the small, cool, dark, church. How will all this end? You feel disturbed and not at all heroic and you write home to tell your parents what you have done and where you are. Then someone says Sicily is off, the aim is Rome; and when the orders come to re-embark, quite a few refuse and Zambianchi, cursing the priests, leaves with a small band to attack the Papal states on his own. The Thousand are now less than a thousand, but you have a rusty old rifle and wonder where the splendid new carbines are that were promised earlier. But Garibaldi has got some artillery from the fortress and, with twenty cartridges each, who knows what cannot be done.

Bixio is always cursing, he finds two or three men dressed in red shirts. 'Take those things off at once!' he shouts. 'What do you think you are, Turks?' He, or you, or they, little know that you will all wear red shirts in the history books. Long, boring hours pass as you sail over a smooth sea to an unknown fate.

Then on the far horizon a looming appearance that is not sea. It is Sicily, the 'Sant'isola'. All the Sicilians aboard crowd the bows, for they are coming home after exile. A small

ship flying the English flag comes from the direction of land. Bixio puts his hands to his mouth and shouts: 'Tell them at Genoa that General Garibaldi landed at one o'clock this afternoon at Marsala.' So history anticipates the event it chronicles. At least you know where you have landed! It seems doubtful, however, if you will land, for in the offing there are the dim forms of warships. But you do land under the shells of the Bourbon ships and here you are sitting on a warm stone writing in your pocket-diary. Now many seem to be wearing red shirts. The General has seen the propaganda value of red shirts. Off you go among the vineyards and then across barren desolate country on the first of many weary marches to unknown destinations. Nobody tells you anything. At the first halt you have some news: 'Garibaldi has assumed the dictatorship of the island in the name of Italy and Victor Emmanuel.' You think that is all right but many do not, for this is not what they have learnt from Mazzini. If the King wanted Sicily why did he not come and liberate it himself? It pours with rain and you are soaked to the skin and your rusty rifle gets still rustier. At last you see the enemy. The mountain opposite is swarming with little ant-like figures. The clash is coming. If you survive, it will be good, years hence, to read what you are scribbling in your pocket-diary. The bullets start whining overhead. The order comes to charge downhill into the ranks of the Neapolitans as they advance in open order. Then the difficult ascent of the opposite hill, terrace by terrace, sweating and panting, while the enemy pours down a rain of bullets and rocks from above. The hillside is covered with dead and dying. Bixio is everywhere, impossibly mounted on a horse. The terrific final struggle on the hilltop. The dazed numb feeling when the fight is won.

So the Diary continues chronicling the heat, the cold, the night marches, the bewilderment of the common soldier, who rarely knows why or where or how, the charge through the Termini Gate into the heart of Palermo and eventually the fight before Capua. It is an individual, not a historical view of events.

To understand Abba's point of view, political and literary, we have to go back to his school-days in the small Piedmontese township of Cárcare and see him as a quiet little boy drinking in the words of a very remarkable master, Father Athanasius Canata of the teaching order founded by San Giuseppe Calasanzio. In his teaching, Father Athanasius combined deep religious conviction with an ardent love for the cause of emergent Italy. The fact that he made his pupils learn by heart the patriotic odes of Manzoni and read aloud Colletta's history of the recent events in Naples and at the same time instilled in them a love of Christian virtues and a feeling for the poetic nature of the pastoral scene of Biblical Galilee (which with Abba persisted in spite of his later Mazzinian anticlericalism), illustrates that he was a worthy exponent of the Italian romantic movement. No less than four of his pupils were with Garibaldi in 1860. The seed certainly fell on fruitful ground in Abba's case, for he was a romantic by nature. He was a very modest young man of comparatively humble birth and few pretensions. He regarded those above him—social superiors, schoolmasters, officers, the strong, the brave, and the handsome—with unassuming admiration, but it was only in Garibaldi that he found a supreme hero worthy of all his aspirations.

It is a feature of Abba's romanticism that he is constantly feeding on past memories; of childhood and home, of school-days, of the experiences of his brief period under arms in 1859. Physically tough and courageous, as irregular warfare proved him to be, yet he is as sensitive as a girl. With feminine sympathy he is always imagining what others must be thinking, feeling, or suffering. Sometimes this tendency becomes morbid as when he identifies himself with Tuköry's corpse in its coffin.

Abba's literary background may be deduced from the pages of this book. Apart from the stock Latin classics known to all young Italians, the authors whose influence we can most plainly recognize are Dante, Byron, Foscolo, and Manzoni, together with the Bible. A patriotic, romantic, sentimental, heroic mixture!

Byron, the true romantic prototype of the heroic adventurer, is with him from the moment he lifts his eyes to the Genoese villa from which the poet set out for Greece on an earlier liberating mission. A youth is seen at the bows of the *Lombardo* burning tarry tow as a signal flare and Abba compares him to Byron's Corsair. Bixio, in his impetuous rages, is Byronic, 'Lara, a real Lara'; Garibaldi is compared to Conrad, the hero of *Tho Corsair.* On a difficult night march Abba is stirred to the depths as a companion recites aloud the verses of Foscolo's *Sepolcri*, '*cibo leonino*', he says, food for lions. Thus the literary Abba in his more heroic mood; the softer, more sentimental side of his nature is in tune with what he has read in the Bible, in Manzoni and (one guesses, only because it had been translated into Italian by Foscolo), in Laurence Sterne's *Sentimental Journey.* It is Abba's extreme sensibility which sometimes topples him over into sentimentality and this is invariably so whenever he sees a young girl's eyes looking at him from a nun's hood. The fine-drawn flirtatious scenes between nuns and soldiers are pure Sterne.

I Promessi Sposi is a more natural text for such a one as Abba, and we are not surprised to find that it is the sack of the Milanese bakeries which comes immediately to his mind when he stands guard over a bread-shop of Palermo; nor that, caught up in crowds, he remembers Manzoni's great crowd descriptions, nor that he quotes the famous chorus from the *Carmagnola.*

Men sleeping in the open, moving over great plains, climbing mountain paths, consorting with a pastoral people with their sheep and goats, watering at their wells, resting under their olive trees, are living the life described in the Bible. Time after time, Biblical images come naturally into Abba's descriptions; he drinks from a young girl's earthen pot and thinks of Rebecca; the troops are piloted through the night by fires and he refers to the column of fire that guided the Israelites through the desert; the name Gibilrossa reminds him of Gilboa and he wishes he had a Bible in his knapsack so that he could read of David and his curse on those mountains. Perhaps

the most typical—because the most romantic—of the many Biblical allusions in this book is the following description of the waters of the Messina straits that separated the invaders from the mainland: 'At this noon-day hour the sea has an air of infinite benevolence, perhaps enjoying the sun that penetrates its very depths. I almost dare say that one could walk over it, dry-shod. Gazing at it, I am overcome by the exquisite sweetness of things learnt long ago in childhood, about the skies, the lakes, and the good people of the land of Galilee.'

Possibly enough has been said to give some idea of the kind of literary influences which made Abba the author he was. It is the kind of background that could—and probably would—have produced a very commonplace sentimental book, had the author relied only on literature and remained to write at his desk in a remote Piedmontese village. But it was not so, for he was plunged into most vigorous action and his, possibly undue, intellectualism suffered a most salutary shock treatment. Moved by a very fine spirit of idealistic patriotism, Abba had volunteered in 1859 as a private in the Aosta cavalry. He saw no action in that short-lived campaign, and immediately left for Genoa when he heard that Garibaldi was preparing an expedition for the liberation of the South.

What did Sicily mean to a young northerner in 1860 and what did he think about it when he got there? First of all—something unknown, strange, and mysterious! '*A nominarla, sento un mondo nell' antichità*'—a world lost in the mists of antiquity. Its very name evokes an image of classical myth and he thinks of the Greeks, of stories read in Plutarch, of school lessons about the Normans, of childhood memories of certain enormous almonds which came from a distant land, far, far away, from Sicily. 'And what is Sicily?' the child asked. 'A land burning in the midst of the sea.' If the distant prospect of Sicily was strange, the experience was stranger still. The world, physical and social, so well mirrored in *Il Gattopardo* was something undreamed of by a young man from Piedmont. The vast bare deserts—without vines or olives, just an occasional patch of beans, then nothing. The sun strikes fiercely

down on an endless undulating plain of parched grass; no drop of water, no sign of habitation—'We might as well be in the Pampas,' said one of the volunteers who had been in South America. Abba heard an officer say: 'You would think we had come to Sicily to liberate their land from sloth.'

Then the terrible slum villages; houses piled in squalor one above the other on steep hillsides. As for the people—'They always answer that they don't know, they shrug their shoulders, or reply by gestures or grimaces; to understand them is a real feat.' As individuals Abba couldn't make head or tail of the Sicilians and their political reactions were equally incomprehensible. One village they enter is full of barred windows and scowling faces, the next welcomes them with a brass band and wine. Abba is completely mystified. 'The inhabitants of Misilmeri who greeted us with illuminations when we were only a small company now show us the cold shoulder. But what have we done? They don't say and we can't guess. They chat and smile gaily but they signal behind our backs with hardly perceptible signs. They seem to have several personalities in the same body. Yet how civilized they are!' ('*Certe gentilezze s'hanno nel sangue*'.)

The underlying fact of Sicilian life then, and as Danilo Dolci describes it now, was the devastating poverty. Listen to Abba's conversation with a liberal Carmelite friar in the village of Parco.

'. . . I have spoken with many of your comrades and the only thing they could say to me was that you wish to unite Italy.'

'Certainly we do, to make one great people.'

'You mean one territory; as far as the people are concerned, one or many, they are bound to suffer and they go on suffering and I have not heard that you want to make them happy.'

'Of course! The people will have liberty and education——'

'Is that all?' broke in the friar. 'Liberty is not bread, nor is education. Perhaps these things suffice for you Piedmontese but not for us here.'

'Well. What do you want then?'

'War! We want war, not war against the Bourbons only but against all oppressors, great and small, who are not only to be found at Court but in every city, every hamlet.'

"Well, then, war also against you friars, for wherever I go I see you have convents and properties, houses and fields.'

'Yes, indeed. Also against us, first of all against us. But with the Bible in your hand and the cross before you—then I should join you; your aims now are too limited. . . .'

We may imagine that hearing ideas so much more complicated than the simple concept of a 'United Italy', seeing a way of life so different, and meeting people so strange to them, made a deep impression on the young northerners who formed the great majority of the Thousand. Abba's descriptions of Sicilian scenes, Sicilian types, Sicilian strangeness, are a memorable part of his book. The eternal Italian problem of North and South is forced on the reader more vividly than in the history books.

An equally striking feature of the *Noterelle* is the character drawing of individuals. Garibaldi and what he meant to his followers and the impression he made on the Sicilians has nowhere been better described. Reading historical accounts we understand the distrust and reserve of the politicians towards Garibaldi, reading the *Noterelle* we understand the enthusiasm he invariably evoked in simple people. We first catch a glimpse of him as he strides down to the sea from the Villa Spinola at Genoa. Abba sees him again at Talamone, that halt on the Tuscan shore when the whole fate of the expedition was in jeopardy, calm and quiet with a smile on his face: '*lento e sorridente*.' After the landing at Marsala, the troops start off inland, a little band of amateurs to confront a regular army. It was then, if ever, that the cheering presence of an apparently confident leader was necessary. 'Finally came Garibaldi with his General Staff, smiling and confident (*sorridente e colla buona novella in fronte*) he rode by on a bay horse fit for a Vizier with magnificent saddle and decorated stirrups. He wore a red shirt and grey trousers, with a Hungarian-style hat on his head and a silk handkerchief round his neck. . . . We gave him a

B

great shout of affectionate greeting. He looked at us with a paternal air as he pressed on to the head of the column. Then the trumpets sounded and we set off again on the march.'

Garibaldi's great gift was to appear both splendid and modest. The man, mounted like a Pasha on the march, was to be seen at the first halt sitting under an olive tree eating bread and cheese with his own clasp knife. '*Io lo guardo*', says Abba, '*ed ho il senso della grandezza antica.*' It was a natural primitive simplicity that endeared him to his men. On one occasion he was seen by Abba instructing a sentry how to tell the time by the position of certain stars '*con la semplicità d'un re pastore*'—like a shepherd king.

The Sicilians with their propensity for hagiolatry seemed to adopt Garibaldi into their family of Saints. The peasant women took his name as Sinibaldo, the father of Santa Rosalìa, and knelt to him in the streets holding out their infants for him to touch. Who knows what mystic confusion was in their minds as they saw this gently smiling, blond-bearded figure pass through their streets. The Sicilian beatification and Abba's own hero-worship is nowhere better fused and concentrated than in the description of Garibaldi as a *Gesù guerriero*. It was indeed as a Warrior-Christ that he appeared to simple men. On their way to the firing line at Calatafimi the troops look up and see their leader above them silhouetted against the sky like a Saint in glory: '*Garibaldi ad una svolta della via, veduto dal basso, grandeggiava sul suo cavallo nel cielo; in un cielo di gloria da cui pioveva una luce calda; che insieme al profumo della vallata ci inebriava.*' When Garibaldi speaks to the people from the balcony of Palazzo Pretorio in Palermo the enthusiasm knows no bounds: '*l'anima di quel popolo pareva tutta trasfusa in lui.*'

The devotion inspired by Garibaldi is strange, perhaps, in its excesses, but understandable. No one, however, could take Nino Bixio for a Saint. He it was who put the ramrod of discipline into the motley volunteer troops. As commander of the steamer *Lombardo* he strides up and down the bridge, bare to the waist, glaring at the men under his command like a tiger.

A corporal mumbles some sullen words and Bixio in a flash smashes a plate in his face. 'Listen to me all of you,' he shouts, 'I'm thirty-seven years old; I'm young, I've been round the world, I've been shipwrecked, I've been a prisoner; but here I am and here I command. Here I'm everything, Czar, Sultan, Pope, I'm Nino Bixio. You've all got to obey me, woe to the man who dares shrug his shoulders, woe to the man who thinks he can mutiny. I shall come down in my uniform, with my sabre, with my medals and I'll kill the lot of you. The General has ordered me to land you in Sicily and get you to Sicily I shall. Once there you can string me up on the first tree, but I give you my word, we *shall* land in Sicily.'

Once on land the sea-captain becomes *condottiere* and is constantly seen spurring by on a fiery horse and Abba compares him to Giovanni dei Medici (Giovanni delle Bande Nere). Abba later wrote a biography of Bixio and there too he compares him to the sixteenth-century captain, and d'Annunzio borrowed the comparison:

> Il grifagno
> Bixio, il risorto Giovanni delle Bande
> Nere, temprato animato metallo. . . .

Bixio is always typically himself, typically violent whether he stands guard over a well to stop the parched soldiers from drinking to their hurt; whether, with sabre raised, he spurs his horse against a peasant who is robbing the dead; whether he is blowing out his horse's brains to stop him neighing on a night march and thus revealing their position to the enemy. In battle he is always where the mêlée is fiercest. He treats the men under him with an unbelievable harshness and though they say he is insufferable they will serve under no one else. His brigade becomes the best, the most disciplined, and the bravest of the patriot army.

In little scenes interspersed in his main narrative Abba gives us the authentic characters of many of the Thousand, both captains and men. He is a master of the vignette. He has also given us unforgettable scenes of action. His vision of the crisis

of the fight at Calatafimi remains in the reader's mind, as it remained in his mind, like an unforgettable piece of sculpture. 'The supreme clash came when the Valparaiso banner, which had passed from hand to hand and finally to Schiaffino, was seen wavering for some instants in a furious bloody tussle and then go down. But Giovanni Maria Damiani of the Scouts snatched it up by one of its streamers. He and his rearing horse formed a group such as Michelangelo might have carved in stone against a confused tumult of fighting men, friend and foe.'

Take another scene, less importantly dramatic but no less real. When one thinks of the Red-shirts one does not immediately consider how unsuitably they were dressed for meeting the bulls which roamed the Sicilian plains. It is, however, just as unpleasant to be killed by a bull as by a Bourbon. 'Cattle grazing in meadows along our way snuffed the air and gazed, startled, at our endless column of red-clad soldiers. A couple of our men who had fallen out of the ranks, perhaps in search of water, were charged by a bull. We saw them rushing up the slope of a hill with the infuriated animal's formidable horns right at their backs. One managed to clamber into a tree while the other continued running along a bank where the bull would have got him, had not a mounted herdsman come at full gallop, bending so low that his face was hidden in his horse's mane. He thrust his pole at the bull's flank like a lancer and the animal fled bellowing, kicking up the turf and furiously lashing his tail.'

The *Noterelle*, as the reader soon discovers, is a personal view of war seen through the eyes of a most sympathetic character. It was Abba's goodness and modesty that endeared him to his fellow countrymen. After he had relapsed into the unassuming life of a village school-master, the publication of the *Noterelle* in 1880 brought him fame, which his other literary works—novels, poems, sketches, and school books—never achieved and possibly did not deserve. After the success of the *Noterelle*, Abba became an almost symbolic figure for the next generation of Italians and no commemoration or patriotic

occasion was complete without his always modest presence. In 1910, the jubilee year of the 1860 Expedition, he visited Sicily once more and then, as though his life had come full circle, suddenly died.

In the end what mattered for Abba, as for all who have had similar experiences in any war at any time, was the memory of close comradeship between young men facing danger and death. The feeling is summed up in the following paragraph written after he had rejoined his comrades in Naples after a temporary absence:

'I have found my brigade once more. Nothing, there is absolutely nothing in the world to compare with the sensation of feeling oneself absorbed into the life of a great body of youth, love, and valour.'

Corpus Christi College
Cambridge   E. R. VINCENT

TRANSLATOR'S NOTE

A limited number of footnotes have been included at appropriate places, not with any idea of supplying an exhaustive commentary, but merely to clarify passages in the text which might puzzle or impede the English reader.

Those interested in the political and military background of the 1860 Expedition should consult Professor G. M. Trevelyan's works: *Garibaldi and the Thousand*, 1909; *Garibaldi and the Making of Italy*, 1911. Both have been reprinted many times since the first editions.

Information about Abba himself may be found in the following: Domenico Bulferetti, *G. C. Abba; Versi e Prose*, Paravia; Luigi Russo, *Da Quarto al Volturno*; Introduction, Vallecchi, 1925; Gaetano Mariani, *Giuseppe Cesare Abba*; Carlo Marzorata, Milano; this last study contains a useful bibliography of further works on the subject.

The *Dizionario Biografico Degli Italiani* (1960) contains an excellent article on Abba, also by Gaetano Mariani.

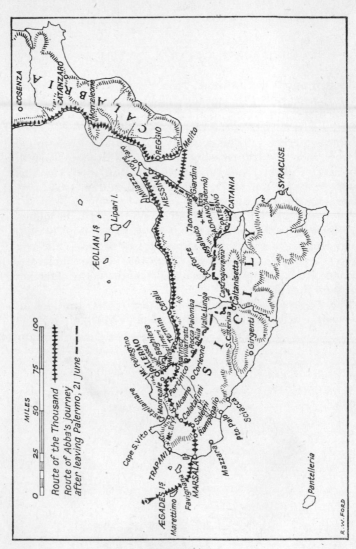

Sicily. Abba's journey after leaving Palermo, 21 June

May 1860

At last there will be an end to rumours! We have heard so many and some that even sounded like accusations. All Sicily in armed revolt! Piedmont incapable of action! What will Garibaldi do? Thirty thousand insurgents surrounding Palermo, only waiting for a leader! Garibaldi! But wherever is he? Some say he is shut away on the island of Caprera, others that he is in Genoa. If that's so, what hinders him? 'Ah,' say some, 'he is sore about the cession of Nice to France.'[1] The more charitably minded think he'll go all the same, even though heart-broken; he won't fail Sicily.

It is the more generous who have guessed aright. Garibaldi is going and I am to be one of the fortunate few who will go with him.

I have just been discussing this business with Petitbon, the lawyer. He it was who last year in the barracks of the Aosta cavalry regiment agreed with us in wanting revolution in the Papal States or the Kingdom of Naples, seeing that the armistice of Villafranca had cut short the war in Lombardy. Now the poor man can't join us as his mother is ill. We parted with a promise to meet the next day and he went slowly down Via dei Genovesi, looking miserable. While I stood watching him, I could hear from afar the sound of axes and hammers ringing through the night. I hear them still as I write. The citizens will not complain at the disturbance, for there is need for urgent haste. They have to work day and night to put up flagpoles, erect stands, and make triumphal arches for the coming of King Victor. So now this King will come acclaimed, among

---

[1] Garibaldi was born at Nice when it was part of the Piedmontese State. The town was included in the territory ceded to France in compensation for her help in the 1859 war against Austria. Garibaldi naturally resented this.

the people who, six years ago, witnessed the assassination of their Duke Charles III, stabbed in the street. I was a fourteen-year old schoolboy at the time and I remember the account of this horrible affair given us by our master, a Scolopian.[2] Rare friar that he was, he blamed the assassin, but did not praise the victim. I wonder whether Charles III was the Duke who served in Piedmont, as a cavalry officer, before '48? If so he had a poor reputation. I was told that in Turin one night two waggish fellow officers of noble birth, friends of his, as a joke, accosted him as he was on his way to visit a lady friend. It appears he was so terrified that they had to reveal their identity to prevent him dying of fright. He then threatened them with dire penalties if ever they set foot in his Duchy. 'If we ever have occasion to pass that way,' said one of them, 'we'll spur our horses and jump clear over your Duchy without touching it.'

Poor Duke! Now King Victor takes possession of your Duchy. The latter certainly is fortunate! Anyone who wishes to do something for Italy, even if no friend to kings must be prepared to add to his glory. Parma will give him an enthusiastic welcome; but we shall be on our way.

Parma, 4 May. At the station

I've counted them! Seventeen in all, mostly students, a few workmen, three doctors. Of the latter, Soncini is pretty old, he saw service at the time of the Roman Republic of '49. They say that in the Romagna train we shall find plenty of comrades, first-rate people. They will be pouring in from all sides. There is a great mystification about our departure. To hear some talk, not even the air must know about it. They have given us a serious security talk, although everybody knows Garibaldi is at Genoa and that he's going to Sicily. Passing through the city of Parma, people came up and shook our hands and heartily wished us well.

[2] This is the first of many references to Abba's school-master Father Canata (v. Introduction p. xi).

4 May. In the train

Some unexplained mishap has brought our train to a halt. We are near Montebello where the battle was. What smiling hills, what a profusion of villas on the green slopes! I look carefully at the whole extent of this landscape and yet there is no vestige of what happened here barely a year ago. The sun is setting. At the end of the long furrows a peasant is talking to his yoked oxen. On they go, dragging the plough after them. Perhaps he saw the fighting and knows where the main clash occurred. I can call up a vision of horses, riders, lances, sabres drawn from three hundred scabbards, and a shrill trumpet call, just as was described by that poor cavalry corporal of the Novara regiment, who returned from the front only two days after the battle. We all pressed round him as he stood there in the barracks with his sabre on his arm, his cloak slung round him, his uniform torn and dirty, looking proud but not at all arrogant.

'Well, what of the Novara cavalry?'

'Our lovely regiment is no more. We've been cut to pieces!'

He then told us of Morelli di Popolo, colonel of the Montferrato cavalry, dead; of Scassi, dead; of Gerone, dead; and of so many others; a long mournful tale.

'And the French?'

'Courageous people,' he replied, 'but you should have heard how their officers spoke of us Italians.'

He spoke out so well, I could have embraced him. A poor fellow from the provinces who had fought in the Crimean war and had been called up for this one. At home he had wife, children, and poverty. He had no fondness for the volunteers; his view was that if they had stopped at home in Lombardy, he would not have had to risk his skin once more, father of a family as he was and thirty years old. He made no pretence of understanding things; what was good for his superiors was good for him, God save the King and *pazienza*. I only wish we could have two or three hundred men like him when we reach Sicily, good horsemen and good fighters!

In the railway station of Novi

You can recognize them by their looks. They are not every-day travellers. They look gay, but at the same time thoughtful. One understands; they have all left someone they love and many regret they have had to leave by stealth.

Well, our party is growing larger and better. On the platform there are some infantry soldiers waiting for a train. A second-lieutenant comes over to me and says: 'Would you send me a wire from Genoa telling me when you are to sail?' I hesitated and didn't answer. What was I to say after our security warning? The officer looked me in the eyes and understood. 'Ah well,' he said smiling, 'keep your secret, but believe me I have no bad intentions in asking.' After he had moved away I wanted to call him back, as I was somewhat mortified by his gentle air of reproof. A fine young man, hardly out of a military college I should think, by his accent a Piedmontese. I don't know his name and I shan't ask it. Nevertheless, I shall the better cherish his memory.

Genoa, 5 May. Morning

I have seen Genoa again for the first time since I was left there on my own five years ago. I shall always remember the panic that seized me as night fell. When I saw the street lamps being lit my heart broke. I stopped a man who was hurrying past and asked him if one could reach Cairo di Montenotte, my home, before dawn if one galloped all night on a good horse. He told me angrily that it was out of the question. That night was long and painful. And now how can I sleep peacefully, far from my people and on such an adventure?

Last night we arrived late and it was impossible to get into any hotel, all crowded with young men who had come into the city. By pure chance under the dark porticos of Sottoripa we were approached by a young man who, guessing who we were, led us without more ado to the hotel where we now are. The principal room was packed with people, eating, drinking, and chattering in all the dialects of Italy. One could recognize,

however, that most of the young men were Lombards. Some of
them were dressed quite elegantly, others in original fashions of
their own, and some very oddly indeed. Daring resolute faces;
sturdy bodies made for the fatigues of war; or slender youths
who will perhaps break down on their first march. That's what
I saw at a glance. In we went and I soon learnt that the young
man who had guided us was called Cariolati, born at Vicenza,
but an exile from home for ten years; he had fought at Rome
in '49 and in Lombardy last year. Most of the others seemed
to me to be experienced men.

Later

The first thing I did this morning was to call on C. to whom
I will introduce the Parma doctors whom, as a medical
student, he will be glad to meet. If only he could come with us!

'You're going to Sicily?' he exclaimed directly he saw me.

'Thank you for the compliment, you couldn't have said
better.'

'Well, you are lucky,' he added, thoughtfully.

After we had had a good talk he took charge of the letter I had
written to my parents. He will deliver it only when he knows
we have landed in Sicily. If things go amiss I do not want the
family to know how I died. They will await my return and as
they grow old they will never abandon hope of seeing me again.

I have just run into Signor Senatore who knew me as a boy.
He informed me that a band of factious persons had assembled
in Genoa with the intention of setting sail one of these days to
wage war against His Majesty the King of Naples. 'One
simply doesn't know what the world is coming to!' he exclaimed, 'and if the government here doesn't lay hands on
these insolent ne'er-do-wells—well, well, there is still hope.'
He gave vent to his rage in this way. All of a sudden he stopped
short and asked me if, by any chance, I was one of them. I
made no reply, so he knew he had guessed right and began to
express his amazement and then proceeded to exhortations.
However was it possible? Had the world gone so topsy-turvy
that a well brought up young man from a remote valley,

educated by friars, the son of peaceable folk, adored by his mother. . . . ? Then he went on to threaten. He would write, he would get help from people from my village who might be in Genoa, he would confront me as I embarked and hold me back. . . . All this time I said nothing. As a last attempt, almost weeping, with hands clasped, he came out with: 'But whatever has the King of Naples done to you, who don't know him, that you must go to war with him? Brigands, that's what you are!' He doesn't know that one of his own sons is coming with us!

*　　　*　　　*

Four of us dined together. We were rather thoughtful as we sat at table, each with his own thoughts far away. We weren't exactly sad, but we were hardly gay. All of a sudden Dr. Bandini sitting opposite me sprang up with his eyes fixed on the wall above my head. There was a portrait there. Pisacane.[3] I read aloud the verses of the poem *The Girl Gleaner of Sapri* printed beneath. Dr. Bandini chimed in with his powerful voice as I read the refrain:

> They were three hundred, young and strong,
> And now they're dead, all dead!

We fell silent once more. I thought of the gloom that fell on the Kingdom of the Two Sicilies after the Sapri massacre. How any further revolt must have seemed hopeless to those poor people! The exiles faced the prospect of death far from home and the whole kingdom was a prison.

Quarto, near Villa Spinola. One a.m. 5 May

Well, here we go! We leave this evening. What a strange coincidence of dates. I wonder how many of us realize that today is the anniversary of the death of Napoleon?

[3] Carlo Pisacane with a small band of patriots attempted to start an insurrection after landing in Southern Italy in June 1857. The attempt failed and Pisacane and many others were killed at Sapri. Luigi Mercantini wrote a well-known poem on the subject *La Spigolatrice di Sapri* of which Abba quotes the refrain. Pisacane was considered their precursor by the Thousand. See pp. 8, 90.

At sea. On board the steamship Lombardo.
The morning of 6 May

We're sailing in convoy with the *Piemonte*. Those on board
that ship are luckier than we, for they are with Garibaldi. So
two ships with the names of two free provinces, Piedmont and
Lombardy, are sailing to bring liberty to two slave provinces.

We are a large company on the *Lombardo*; if there are as
many on the *Piemonte*, we must be nearly a thousand. I wonder
what each of us as individuals thinks about our expedition and
about Sicily. To me the very name Sicily suggests an antique
land. That story of how the Syracusans liberated the prisoners
captured from the army of Nicias, simply on hearing them
chant Greek choruses, has always struck me as one of the most
civilized actions ever recorded. What the island is like today I
simply don't know. I imagine it down there in the south, solitary and profoundly mysterious. And Trapani? I shall never
forget, and I well remember at this moment, the words of that
Crimean veteran: 'We anchored off Trapani and saw it
huddled on a squalid spit of land, a city brimming over with
wretched poverty. Some poor ragged people came out in
boats to sell fruit, rowing round our ship and staring up in
astonishment.

' "What are you?" they called out.

' "Piedmontese."

' "Where are you bound?"

' "To Crimea, to the war."

' "To the war in Crimea!" they repeated, casting down
their eyes in sign of compassion as they rowed away.'

Shall we really see Palermo? Shall we see the Square where
Fra' Romualdo and Suor Gertrude were burnt alive by the
Inquisitors? Father Canata read us the account of it out of
Colletta's History when I was at school. As he read it he
seemed to be dealing out blows to populace and Grandees
alike, those who banqueted as they watched the scene.

Another pleasanter memory! My father told us that in
1811, a year of famine, our people were fed on enormous

almonds, as big as your thumb, that had come from far, far away . . . from Sicily. 'And what is Sicily?' we children asked, and his answer was: 'A land burning in the midst of the sea.'

In 1857, the year of Orsini, Agesilao, and Pisacane,[4] I read chalked up on the columns of Via Po in Turin 'Sicily has revolted. To arms, brothers!' Who knows who wrote those words? If a Sicilian exile, how happy he will be now if he is one of our number!

*　　　*　　　*

At the critical moment Genoa was admirable. No noisy demonstrations; an absorbed silence and complete accord. At the Pila gate there were simple women of the people who wept as we passed. At the foot of the hill of Albaro I looked up to see the villa again where Byron passed his last days before leaving for Greece, and Childe Harold's invocation to Rome came to my mind. If he were alive today he would be there on board the *Piemonte* to inspire Garibaldi.

'Is this the village of Quarto?' 'Yes.' 'And Villa Spinola?' 'Farther on.'

On I went and all of a sudden there was the villa.

Beyond a high railing there was a small building glimmering white through a dark plantation. I could see the figures of men moving busily to and fro along the paths. In front, on the road above the sea, there was a great whispering crowd and a surge of emotion filled my heart. The crowd swayed. 'There he is!' No, not yet! Instead of Garibaldi someone else came out and disappeared down the road towards Genoa. Towards ten o'clock the crowd made way in great excitement and there was a hush. It was he. He crossed the road and, through a gap in the wall opposite the railings, followed by only a few com-

---

[4] Felice Orsini attempted to assassinate Napoleon III (actually in January 1858); Agesilao Milano, a Calabrian soldier attempted to stab Ferdinand II of Naples during a review of troops (actually in December 1856). Pisacane's invasion was of June 1857. Abba's point is that all these indications of unrest happened within a short period.

panions, he went swinging down the cliff. Then everyone
started saying 'good-bye', and I, who had no one to bid me
farewell, had tears in my eyes. As I took the path down to the
sea I ran into Dapino, my school-fellow of six years ago. He
had a rifle on his shoulder. I was just going to greet him when I
saw his father and brother were with him, and I felt I couldn't.
I was afraid of intruding on a painful scene, for I thought the
father, whom I knew to be deeply attached to his son, might
have come to hold him back. The boats were just below and a
silent crowd were coming down like ghosts. I was quite wrong,
here are the father and brother embracing my friend and . . .
oh well, I feel a gulp in my throat!

Nearby I hear some young men talking about a youth I
don't know. They are Venetians, good-looking and polite.

'Do you know that Luzzatto's mother has come to look for
him?'

'From Udine?'

'Either from there or from Milan, I really don't know. She
has run all over the place from Genoa to Foce, from Foce to
Quarto inquiring, imploring, until finally she found him!'

'And he?'

'He begged her not to tell him to go back, because he would
go just the same and with the remorse of having disobeyed
her.'

'And the mother?'

'She left by herself.'

*   *   *

Now we are out of sight of land. The boat in which I happened to embark last night was so overladen that it rocked. In
order to keep it from capsizing the boatmen told us to keep our
eyes on certain green and red lights shining through the night
from Genoa. About eleven o'clock, from a boat already out in
the open sea we heard a beautiful clear voice hailing: 'La
Masa.' Then another voice in reply: 'General.' Then we heard
no more.

Meanwhile time passed and, rocked by the motion of the

C

waters, I fell asleep. I was roused at dawn and saw two stately
ships lying before us. All the boats were rowing towards them.
I looked back; Genoa and the coast could be seen indistinctly
in a misty haze, but beyond, my native mountains reared up
proudly in lofty purity, dominating the scene. A little breeze
ruffled the surface of the sea. On board the ships there was a
great deal of shouting, repeated hailing, remonstrances, and
curses that seemed to fly through the air like arrows. There
was half an hour of turmoil, all trying to be the first to scramble
on board. At last I managed to seize a rope and climb up. I
still have before my eyes the picture of a young man flinging
himself about convulsively in the bottom of one of the boats,
scarcely restrained by three others. Had he thought better of
it? Or had sea-sickness reduced him to such a state?

*   *   *

One hears all the various dialects of north Italy, but it
seems that the Genoese and Milanese predominate. By their
looks, manners, and speech the greater number seem to be
cultivated people. Some of them are wearing uniform. On the
whole bright faces, dark or fair hair, youth and vigour. There
are a few grey-haired and five or six as bald as coots. This
morning I noticed some disabled; certainly old patriots who
have taken part in all the revolutionary movements of the last
thirty years.

'So you're here too!' someone exclaimed as he embraced a
friend: 'Weren't you in Paris?'

'I got here last night.'

'Just in time to come with us then.'

'And would you have considered going without me?'

It sounded like inappropriate boasting, but the elegant
young man had such a straightforward, assured air. I never ask
who anyone is and then I regret it. The only one I know of the
newcomers is Airenta. As I write he is stretched out at my feet
asleep with his head on his knapsack. He is pure gold. We
struck up a friendship yesterday ashore, we are both in the
same ship and we've promised to stick together. When his

tutors at the Archiepiscopal Seminary of Genoa learn the step
he has taken!

Hullo! Man overboard!

*   *   *

A quarter of an hour of great anxiety. 'Reverse engines!'
yelled the captain and the vessel came to a stop, puffing. The
man, however, was already far behind. Now we could see him,
now not, and he seemed to be struggling. A boat was quickly
launched. We all urged it on with eyes, gestures, and prayers.
The man was over-hauled, seized, and saved. They say he is a
Genoese.

*   *   *

I had the idea that this captain of the *Lombardo* must be a
Frenchman. His bearing, behaviour, and tone of command
prove him a man worth ten. He stands up there on the bridge,
stripped to the waist, bare-headed, irascible, just as though he
were at the enemy already. His eye blazes as he takes everything in. It's plain he could do anything single-handed. If he
were alone on the ship in the midst of the ocean, he would
contrive to escape from such a predicament. He has a profile
as sharp as a sabre-cut; if he frowns, everyone tries to look as
small and inoffensive as possible; full face, none can withstand
his glance. Sometimes, however, he has a look of real amiabil-
ity. What a funny thing it was to give him the name of Nino!
Bixio, his surname, suits him excellently. It produces the effect
of a flash of lightning.

Night falls. The *Piemonte* is steaming ahead faster than we.
This is the hour when at home they are lighting the lamp,
my father comes in, supper is set on the table, steaming
hot, but they are waiting . . . one member of the family is
missing.

At sea. 7 May

We are told to stop talking. The whole ship is silent while a
powerful voice reads aloud from a paper in trumpet tones. We

are once more to be called the *Cacciatori delle Alpi* ('Sharp-shooters of the Alps') and certain expressions in this Order of the Day strike straight to the heart. No personal ambitions, no selfish greed; Italy above all and a spirit of good will and sacrifice.

I know another Order of the Day that was read, I don't quite remember whether in 1849 at the retreat from Rome or last year when the volunteers passed the Ticino. One recognizes the same spirit. In that too the General said that he offered neither rank nor honour, but toil, peril, battle, and then—the sky for tent, the earth for bed, and God above as witness.

Talamone, 7 May

We could see a village in the distance, a slender, graceful tower soaring to the sky and on it a flag streaming in the wind, an Italian flag. It was a Tuscan village called Talamone on the Maremma coast. When we came in close to shore, a boat approached as fast as oars could row, bearing the commander of this poor little fortress. The good gentleman was half-buried under two enormous epaulettes and he had a cocked hat on his head covered with gold lace.

What a poverty-stricken place! Just charcoal-burners and fishermen. Our landing has quite cheered them up.

'What's the name of that mountain facing us?'

'Monte Argentaro.'

'And those white houses almost in the sea?'

'Porto San Stefano.'

'With a view like this you must lead a very pleasant life here.'

'Ah yes, if we could eat with our eyes!—but it's not so bad, as long as one makes do.'

These were the words of a young charcoal burner and, chatting, he wanted to know who we are and where we're bound. I absolutely hung on his lips, drinking in the sweetness of his Tuscan speech while comparing it to the harshness of my native dialect.

*   *   *

I saw him as he landed. Slow and smiling he went up the shelving beach. He was dressed in the uniform of a general of the Piedmontese army and his long hair and full beard accorded ill with such clothes. Captain Montanari, who seems to be a close friend, walked beside him jesting and I heard him say: 'Dressed like that you look like a lion in a cage.' Garibaldi smiled.

* * *

I felt I wanted to go into the church. A little, plain, tranquil church just right for prayer and nothing else. I sat down among the benches in order to enjoy the coolness of the place, but a great sadness came over me. Directly I came out I wrote home admitting where I was and in what company and whither bound.

* * *

I plunged into the sea with indescribable pleasure. The water was tepid. Along the whole beach there was a light-hearted throng of bathers and on the dunes whole companies of our men were stretched out on the grass enjoying the coolness. Along the road to Orbetello there was a great coming and going.

But whatever are we doing here? What are we waiting for? We shall sleep ashore tonight and our ships will be at anchor. They say that they were taken from Genoa by stealth. What a blow it would be if a warship appeared to take them off. It would be far better to be on our way. But perhaps the General is waiting for news, or more men, or arms? In fact up to the present we have got no arms! Only a few have carbines that they cherish like brides and always keep slung over their shoulders. They are certain Genoese who are crack shots and they have trained for this moment with faithful devotion. The grey-haired man yonder, not yet old, but no longer young, is a Professor of literature, a friend of Mazzini's, only out of prison last year. He had been condemned for his part in the Genoa affair of 1856. His name is Savi. I have heard that when

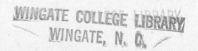

the National Society was founded and Garibaldi was one of the first to join, Savi remonstrated with him for identifying himself with a monarchical movement—he, the military head of the Roman republican party. But now for the sake of our country he too is with us. He keeps aloof, modest, and taciturn, although it is obvious that he is much revered and sought after. Even those who don't know who he is salute him respectfully as they pass.

*   *   *

Four of us have mustered what we could of our book-learning. One said that the Gallic spearmen on their way to attack Rome armed with lances, must have been encamped somewhere here in the plain towards Orbetello when they were taken by surprise by the Romans, who had landed on returning from the island of Sardinia. Here too Marius came ashore secretly after his African exile, with his heart full of a hatred bred from the marshes of Minturno, and embittered by the honours given to Sulla. It was here, towards the end of last century, that the Neapolitan troops of Count Damas had their first sight of the banners of the French republicans. Perhaps posterity will now add that Garibaldi and his men landed here, sailing against Sicily.

Talamone, 8 May

We have been formed into companies, eight in all. I and my friends are in the sixth. Giacinto Carini, a Sicilian of about thirty-six years old, is our company commander. They say that in '48 he was a cavalry colonel who fought to the end and the final collapse of the republic, and that he has lived in France since that time, writing and hoping. We are glad to serve under a Sicilian with such a reputation, and then he is such a fine type of soldier, affable, courteous; when he speaks he wins your devotion. Most of the other officers of our company are Sicilians too, except one who is a Modenese, who knows his job and must be a daring, resolute man.

Bixio, La Masa, Anfossi, Cairoli, and others with names

renowned in Italian history, each have the command of a company. All the officers have some feat of valour on record, several have served in the South American wars, there are three who have each lost an arm. The General's senior Aide-de-camp is the Hungarian, Colonel Türr; Sirtori is Chief of Staff. The son of Daniele Manin is with us and I have heard that there is a poet in our ranks and that he will write the epic of our battles. His name is Ippolito Nievo.[5]

All the Genoese who have rifles, about forty of them, are being formed into a corps of Sharpshooters. If you saw the head of their captain, Antonio Mosto, in a portrait, you would think it was that of an ancient philosopher. He looks austere and behaves austerely, and it seems as though he had performed penance up to today in order to hasten the resurrection of Italy. He is known to be extremely brave, and how could it be otherwise if these young men accept him as leader?

*   *   *

I've seen the two gentlemen who travelled with me from Parma to Genoa. They're here too! Soldiers in No. 1 company. The name of the younger, a Piedmontese, is Giovanni Pittaluga. He is a regular volcano! When he saw some French soldiers strolling about near the station at Piacenza, he jerked his head back into the carriage and shouted out to ask whether those foreigners were never going to clear out. The elder, Spangaro by name, a Venetian of some importance to judge by the respect shown to him here, announced very sensibly that we shall be lucky if we can get rid of them peaceably. The other fretted and fumed. Now they will have ample time to continue their argument as to the efficacy of the forcible methods the younger would like to adopt in order to finish once and for all with the enemies of Italy. There is something

[5] This is the first mention of Ippolito Nievo (but see pp. 47 and 87) to whom Abba looks up with admiration as already known in the literary world. Abba himself went to war with literary ambitions and a lesser man might have shown some jealous feeling in speaking of Nievo.

of a Saint-Just in his looks. I should be sorry for the unfortunate priest or friar who fell into his clutches.

* * *

Poor Sartori was sitting on the very edge of the cliff with a sheer drop to the sea below. He was muttering to himself, but stopped when he heard my footsteps. I asked him what was the matter. He told me he was on the point of throwing himself over as he had been grossly insulted by a captain who had ordered him to take off the officer's kepi that he had previously worn in the army of Emilia. There must have been a furious argument about it. Sartori obeyed, but he has sworn to vindicate himself.

* * *

One of our chaps, bursting with merriment, rides up the slope, bareback on a little donkey, while his friends roar with laughter. The poor beast falls and the young man tumbles off and hurts himself. He is put to bed in the inn and who knows for how long? Poor fellow, if we go off without him!

* * *

A group of our people are going to be detached from the main body. They are going to cross the border of the Roman State under the leadership of Zambianchi,[6] a bloodthirsty anti-clerical. I'm so sorry for the three Parma doctors who have to follow him. Different destinies, although the goal is the same. We never said farewell.

I heard that some, I don't know how many, have left us, or are going to do so, as they are no longer prepared to follow Garibaldi because he has associated the name of King Victor Emmanuel with our battle cry. The matter is discussed and variously judged, but I have not heard any ill-disposed criticism.

[6] Zambianchi, see p. 112.

9 May. From the Lombardo *off San Stefano*

Last evening we embarked, as the sea seemed to be working up for a storm. The inhabitants of Talamone waved to us from the shore, sending us off with compassionate good wishes.

Three *Bersaglieri* who deserted from Orbetello are on board the *Lombardo*. There was already one with us from Genoa, Pilade Tagliapietre of Treviso. Whatever would Lamarmora have said (the man who created this regiment and led them, always victoriously, from Goito to the Crimea) if it had been predicted that one day four young men in his uniform would be gazing from the deck of a ship towards Sicily in revolt? What a swelling of his heart he would have felt and what words would he have stammered out! Oh, that old Sicily of the time of Vittorio Amedeo. [7]

There must be urgent need to depart, for Bixio is shouting to the boatmen who come and go bringing water: 'Twenty francs for every barrel you bring me before eleven o'clock!' They simply make the boats fly!

While we wait for the water, we are served out with arms. My share has been a rusty old gun (what a thing!), a belt like a policeman's, a bayonet, a cartridge pouch and twenty cartridges. But, didn't they tell us at Genoa that we should have brand new carbines? This is not the worst! Colonel Türr went to Orbetello yesterday and came back with three cannon, great long old culverins, things that must date from the time when this strip of coast was known as the Stato dei Presidii. What shall we do in Sicily so ill equipped?

Well, the water is all shipped and the anchor weighed. Santo Stefano, good-bye! Once we round that cape we shall be on the open sea again and may God be with us!

---

[7] Duke Vittorio Amedeo II of Savoy was created King of Sicily by the Treaty of Utrecht (1713). This is one of the few direct connexions between Piedmont and Sicily and Abba frequently mentions it.

9 May. Evening

Not a sail on the horizon. Once past the islet of Giglio a delicious little breeze got up which did us all good. The sky is absolutely clear. Not a cloud, not even a single one of the mob of sea-birds that at first followed the ship, hovering above, and then diving down like lightning to plunge into the water as though to entertain us. We saw lots of dolphins leaping gaily through the water as they followed in our wake for quite a while.

Soon it will be night. A strong tuneful voice from the poop is singing a song that should be heard by our comrades on the *Piemonte*. It is the flight of a soul to his belovèd. Now the single voice gives way to a rousing chorus:

Si vola d'un salto nel mondo di là.

Oh dear, oh dear, what if we were to be captured on the high sea!

10 May

From dawn until now it has been simply wonderful. We sailed triumphantly on and on without anything to disturb us. We had a calm sea and a clear sky all to ourselves. But there was one anxious moment. Someone threw himself overboard and they say it was the same man as before. So on the previous occasion it can have been no accident. As the ship stopped, we could see his head in the distance and we anxiously measured the space between the drowning man and the boat that sped to the rescue. They got him! Once aboard, Bixio cursed him heartily, then he relented and had him put in a cabin where he is under guard. They've stripped him of his soaking clothes and dressed him in an officer's tunic. He's lying down now, glaring around like a maniac.

*   *   *

The *Piemonte* is several miles ahead. She sails proudly as though she were conscious of her destiny and of the man she

carries. We can just see her as a black dot on the far horizon; now hardly more than her smoke is visible, trailing behind her like the tail of a comet. Oh, if she should run into the Neapolitan squadron! Now we have come into enemy waters orders are stricter. A few have put on red shirts. Bixio rebukes them, calls them Turks and orders them to keep out of sight. No sail on the horizon. We are the only living thing as far as the eye can see.

*   *   *

Corporal Plona gave vent to some grouse or other and Bixio was on him in a flash and smashed a plate in his face. There was some confusion, but Bixio was up on the bridge like a rocket, shouting at the top of his voice 'All on the after-deck! All on the after-deck!' And there we were packed together, staring up at him as he stood above looking as though he were about to pulverize the lot of us. Then he spoke: 'I'm young, I'm thirty-seven years old, I've been round the world. I've been shipwrecked; I've been a prisoner; but here I am and here I command! Here I'm everything, Czar, Sultan, Pope. I'm Nino Bixio! You've all got to obey me, all of you! Woe to the man who dares to shrug his shoulders, woe to the man who thinks he can mutiny. I shall come out in my uniform, with my sabre, with my medals, and I'll kill the lot of you. Garibaldi has left me with the order to land you in Sicily. I shall do it! Once there, you can string me up on the first tree, but'—and he took us all in with a slow stare—'but we shall, I give you my word, we *shall* land in Sicily.'

'Three cheers for Nino Bixio! Hurrah, hurrah, hurrah!'

Hundreds of arms were stretched out towards him, as he stood proudly there for a little. Then he went pale, his eyes flashed, and he turned his back on us. From high up on the rigging the seamen cheered too. Then from our midst a rather feeble voice was heard coming from a man who had got up on a barrel and had started to harangue us, waving his arms about and praising Garibaldi and Bixio to the skies. He was not young nor did he seem robust, but he had a refined gentle

face set off by hair and beard of a wishy-washy blond colour. It remains to be seen, I thought, if Bixio doesn't shoot him down with his pistol! I turned round, really fearing that this would happen, but Bixio had left the bridge. The orator went on a little, but he had to climb down without having made any tangible effect. No one paid any attention to him because they had all been stirred by Bixio's words that had swept over them like wind over the waves. They were all greatly excited and not one of them but would have given his life for Bixio. I inquired the name of the orator with the gentle Christ-like face and they told me it was La Masa.

On board the Lombardo *11 May, morning*

After sunset yesterday the sailors up on the yards could still see the *Piemonte* like a distant shadow. A youth at the bows was lighting bundles of tarry tow and throwing them overboard, always in the same direction. Could they be signals? He looked born for high adventure. His face was lit up in the ruddy glow that gave a curious oblique tilt to his countenance, set off by fair curls. As I took note of his well-shaped hands, his broad chest, his fine sturdy neck in its silk scarf falling back over his shoulders, I thought of the seas of the Orient and of Byron's *Corsair*.

I curled up in a corner and, with my mind in a whirl, fell dead asleep.

'Get up! Get up!' exclaimed Airenta, shaking me violently. I didn't know what the time was but up I leapt. All those on deck were crouching down on their knees with faces turned to the left. Only whispers could be heard. Their fixed bayonets glittered.

'Whatever is it?' said I, and Airenta replied, 'A ship is making straight for us at full speed.'

Can it be a Bourbon ship? It has sounded its bell and, at Bixio's order, we make no reply.

The ship was coming straight at us and we could hear the angry threshing of its paddle-wheels. It seemed to spit flame as it advanced. Bixio was staring hard from up on the bridge.

He was certainly contemplating some desperate action, perhaps blowing us up, both us and the ship almost now alongside. I hardly took in what happened next owing to some agitation that broke out near me, I only heard Bixio's great cry of *'Generale!'* Then joy broke out.

It was the *Piemonte*. The General ahead of us had sighted the Bourbon patrol and had turned back to find us. Now we had met, he discussed matters with Bixio and we started off again on a new tack. I believe we're closer to Africa than to Sicily.

*   *   *

Now we're steering once more for Sicily. At the stern the Lombards among us are singing songs of their native lakes. They are not sad, like the songs of my own mountains; they do not echo the sorrows of generations of men born to suffer under the shadow of those castle keeps, now but inglorious ruins crowning the hills above the valley hamlets. But there is something pathetic about them and they are deeply touching.

Near me is a Hungarian whom I spotted yesterday. He can't say anything in Italian except for a coarse Venetian jest. He looks at me with his little green eyes all puckered up. His hair straggles over a narrow brow and he has the nose of a Hun. He lies stretched out, thoughtful and gloomy, sun-bathing. Perhaps he is thinking of his own country as he goes to die for mine.

*   *   *

A lovely view of little islands! They seem just risen from the sea. There is green of all shades, there is dazzling cliff, and everything enshrined in an atmosphere of blue. The islands have a silvery fringe at their feet. They tell me that there are dreadful prisons there. The King of Naples keep his political prisoners in that place, and families who have some member there say: 'Better dead!'

*   *   *

Sicily! Sicily! Down there in the blue distance between sea and sky something misty appears. It is the sacred island! On our left are the Ægades and far ahead is Mount Eryx with its summit in the clouds. A Sicilian who was with me on deck told me about the adventures of Eryx, son of Venus, buried by Hercules on those heights. Delightful people the ancients, but not more so than my friend who can now find it in him to talk of mythology! He told me that there is a village on the mountain called San Giuliano where the most beautiful women in Sicily are to be found.

*   *   *

How easy it is to recognize the Sicilian exiles among us! There they are, all crowding at the bows. They seem to concentrate their whole being in their eyes. There are about twenty of them, of all ages. It will be a miracle if Colonel Carini gets ashore alive, seeing that his heart is bursting with joy.

*   *   *

Doctor Marchetti, who always laughs when he sees me writing, has no idea that I am now writing about his son! The boy was in exile with him and now, at his father's wish, is on this expedition. He is perhaps only about twelve years old, yet he has such a bold look. Lucky boy to have such a splendid morning to his life! If death does not catch him, he will be a man risen early for his journey through the world. What's up now? Everybody is looking aft.

*   *   *

There are two ships in sight astern. A wind has got up behind us. All sails are set and the seamen at work aloft look like birds. Bixio gives his orders and the men are smart about it. He shouted out that any man aloft who blunders will be hanged on the mainmast! We simply fly through the water.

*   *   *

A small ship came from land. It was flying the English flag.
Bixio took a sheet of paper; wrote something on it; cut open a
loaf of bread and inserted the paper. Then, when the ship was
passing close alongside he threw the loaf, but it fell into the
sea. So, making a trumpet of his hands he shouted: 'Tell them
at Genoa that General Garibaldi landed at Marsala at one
p.m. today.'

Cheers rose from the little vessel; they gesticulated, waved
their handkerchiefs, and clapped. Hurrah! Hurrah! Hurrah!

*   *   *

There's Marsala! Its walls, its white houses, its green
gardens, and the lovely slope on which it lies. In the port, little
shipping. There is an English warship at the entrance dressed
over all.

'Ready boys,' shouts Bixio, 'neck or nothing!' If he had the
strength he would throw us all ashore in one heave! But we
are now certain to be able to land, although the two ships
pursuing us have gained a good deal. Their funnels send up
clouds of smoke as they come on.

Marsala, 11 May

I am sitting on a stone in front of the piled arms of my company in this squalid, solitary, rather frightening little square.
Captain Ciaccio of Palermo is weeping like a child from pure
happiness. I pretend not to see him. The company is dispersed
here and there, half of them in search of something to eat.
But at the first note of the bugle they will all be back. There
are bursts of cannon-fire from the port, directed at the city.
Many of the houses are flying foreign flags, most of them
English.[8] Whatever does this mean?

The *Lombardo* is almost under water. The *Piemonte* still floats
in majesty. The frigates that chased us arrived within range
when we were nearly all ashore. The earth rocked under our
feet so that we could hardly stand upright. The city had not

[8] There was a considerable British colony in Marsala engaged in the wine
trade.

yet woken up to what was happening, but a mob of little urchins had put in an appearance. Some white-robed friars took off their great hats to us; they proffered enormous snuff-boxes, shook us by the hand and inquired if we were returned exiles, immigrants, Swiss?

Some naval officers in white ducks appeared from the city gates and went down to the port in the direction of the English ship, talking among themselves in an excited way. Meanwhile we were getting into some order. All of a sudden there was a cannon shot. What's that? 'Only a salute,' said Colonel Carini, smiling. He was dressed in a red tunic with a great broad-brimmed hat on his head, with a feather stuck in it. A second explosion and, with a roar, a large cannon ball came bouncing between us and the seventh company, throwing up the sand as it went. The street-urchins throw themselves to the ground, the friars bolt—as well as they can with their gross bodies, waddling along in the ditches. A third ball crumples up the roof of the near-by guard-house. A shell falls into the middle of our company and lies smoking ready to explode. Beffagna, the Paduan, rushes to it and draws the fuse. Bravo! But he neither hears nor cares.

Then came salvo after salvo, more than I could count. What fury! But now the city was ours. We ran from the port to the walls under fire from the flank. No one was hurt. The people cheered us in the streets; friars of every order split their throats with shouting; women and girls looked admiringly down from the balconies. 'Beddi! Beddi! Bless you, bless you!' arose from all sides. I drank from the amphora of a young girl of the people who was returning from the well. Rebecca!

And that arch of the gate through which we came into the city, how it comes back to me as I write! It seemed to be the entrance to an Arab town, and at the same time I thought I was at the gate of my own village that has a similar arch. I paused to cast a glance towards the port. The last detachments of our men were running uphill; the two Bourbon ships were wrapped in smoke as their cannonade still flashed forth; our *Lombardo*, which had heeled over, filled me with compassion.

They say that Bixio insisted on sinking it. That man leaves his mark wherever he passes.

*   *   *

On guard over the ancient port of Marsala. Evening

Those of us on this side can't see what is happening on the other where we landed; the sound of quick-firing certainly comes from the Genoese Sharpshooters. Perhaps the ships are attempting to put landing parties ashore. I only hope they don't continue to do so at night and catch our people still in the city unawares, or worse. There is a certain treacherous wine here and our men have been so long without! But our leaders have thought of everything and almost all companies are now out of the city. Mine is here complete. We have before us a great curve of beach and on the horizon a dark promontory, perhaps Trapani. Those little boats that are putting off over there and taking to the open sea are loaded with fugitives.

Meanwhile the firing from the ships goes on.

Marsala, 12 May, 3 a.m.

Last night at ten o'clock Corporal Plona put me on guard at the foot of a cliff, the last sentinel of our line, and left me here for five hours. I composed verses to the stars. It was my vigil of arms.

Wednesday. During the principal halt of the day

At break of day a man on a horse came and spoke with the captain; we picked up our rifles and re-entered the city. Along a sleepy street, skirting certain hovels where poverty-stricken people were astir in the foul half-open ground-floor rooms, we gained the open country on the other side. There we found all our people lined up ready: there was a feeling of whole-hearted healthy happiness which encouraged one. Far out at sea, the two Neapolitan ships were sailing away, towing the *Piemonte* behind them. A fine consolation for them! The

D

Lombardo still lay stranded. When the sun got up, part of her keel that was out of the water shone as though on fire, as though indeed to bid us farewell and wish us luck.

There was a delicious scent in the air. Nevertheless that field beyond the walls of Marsala with its blackish boulders strewn here and there, with those yellow flowers in patches, began to give me a kind of feeling of things dead.

Bixio came by on horseback. As haughty as on the bridge of the *Lombardo*, he gave a scowl towards that poor ship, made an abrupt gesture towards her as though to say 'That's that!' and went off at a trot. After him came some of the Scouts who had been in the *Piemonte*; fine horses, fine riders, dressed in the smart uniforms they had worn last year in Lombardy. Nullo came prancing along, sitting loose to his mount. A bizarre figure with a torso like a Perseus and an aquiline face, the handsomest man of the expedition. He might be one of the thirteen champions who jousted at Barletta.[9] The Milanese Missori is dressed in a short red tunic that adds to his aristocratic appearance, on his head he wears a smart gold-frogged red cap. He is in command of the Scouts. A charming, gentle face, but full of spirit. He and Nullo are like the Trojan friends Eurialus and Nisus. The Scout over there, a simple ranker, with a sulky look on his open face, is the oldest of the contingent. He's about forty. He is Nuvolari from Mantua, a rich countryman who has both conspired and fought, a plain steadfast Cromwellian type. The others are in the flower of their youth; a certain Manci from Trent has the charm of an innocent girl, he might be Grossi's heroine Fiorina.

A smile on his face, radiating confidence, Garibaldi, with his General Staff, brought up the rear. He rode a bay horse fit for a Vizier. The saddle was magnificent, the stirrups decorated with filigree work. He wore a red shirt and grey trousers,

[9] This is the first of several references to an historic combat of 1503 when thirteen Italians beat an equal number of French. It was adopted as an encouraging symbol of Italian prowess throughout the *risorgimento* period and was popularized, in particular by D'Azeglio in his novel *Ettore Fieramosca*.

with a Hungarian-style hat on his head and a silk handkerchief round his neck, which he pulled up to shade his face when the sun was high. An affectionate cheer broke out and he looked at us with a paternal air as he pressed on to the head of the column. Then the trumpets sounded and we set off again on the march.

After we had gone a good way along the main road we took to the open country along a difficult little path winding between the vineyards. Our guns followed with difficulty, mounted on carts painted with sacred scenes and drawn by spirited stallions, whose bells tinkled out merrily. We halted at the farmstead where I now write, a white house and a well in an olive grove. How pleasant it is to enjoy a little shade and relish a ration of bread! The General, seated at the foot of an olive tree, eats his bread and cheese, slicing it with his own knife and chatting simply with those around. I look at him and have a feeling of the greatness of bygone days.

Evening. Written from the Fief of Rampagallo

After a good hour's rest we started again, making our way through a vast stretch of open country. No more vineyards or olive gardens, but every now and again a little patch of beans, then no more cultivation. The sun poured down on us like a liquid as we passed through endless undulating wastes, where the grass grows and dies as in a cemetery. And never a spring of water, not even a runnel, never a glimpse of a village on the horizon. 'Why, are we in the Pampas?' exclaimed Pagani, who had been in South America as a youth.

Those solitudes, farther than the eye could reach, were barely relieved at rare intervals by some shepherd's hut or by a herd of horses running free in their wild liberty. Some, on catching sight of us, were startled and galloped far away; some stopped short, prancing gaily. In the afternoon we came on an old shepherd by the side of the track. He was dressed in goat-skins and on his unkempt, almost savage head he wore an enormous woollen hat. His hands rested on the shoulders of a young lad of about fifteen, who was silently staring at us as we

passed. When my company reached the spot where he was standing, he addressed our captain in loud, resolute tones, crying out in patois: 'Oh, Prince Carini, start the revolt in the Capital!' As he spoke he thrust the lad into our ranks. Then he dried his eyes, and turning his back, made off through the desert land. Far, far away on the horizon we could see a hut, perhaps his.

'Is our captain a prince?' I asked Lieutenant Bracco, who comes from Palermo himself. 'No . . . but there is a Prince Carini, a Bourbon supporter, who would like to poison the very air we breathe.'

This great frowning edifice is an ancient fief. We arrived as the sun was setting and we threw ourselves down on a slope, full length on the rank grass. I was dispatched to draw water. Some of our senior officers were standing in a group on a little mound near the building. In passing I heard one of them say: 'Did you take note of that desert today? You might say we've come here to help the Sicilians liberate their country from sloth!'

No word of the enemy.

13 May. Salemi. From a convent balcony, facing the glory of the sun

As reveillé sounded, Bixio appeared, already in the saddle, from goodness knows where. If, instead of an infantry uniform, he wore a sixteenth-century costume he could be the *Condottiere,* Giovanni delle Bande Nere.[10]

During the night, bands of Sicilian insurgents arrived, armed with double-barrelled sporting guns and strange pikes. Some wear sheepskins over their clothes. They all seem resolute men and they have cast in their lot with us.

When we left the camp at Rampagallo, we were all benumbed from having slept just as we arrived, without blankets or tents under the heavy dew that falls during these nights. But we threw off the chill very quickly and after half an hour's march

[10] The famous commander Giovanni de Medici (1498–1526). Abba compares him to Bixio elsewhere.

we were already longing for water. We passed close to several
springs, but we drank with our eyes only for Bixio was there
on guard, inexorable, and wouldn't even let us wet our lips.
He was quite right. One of our men, who managed to have a
drink, fell half-way up the great climb to this place. I saw him
writhing in great pain surrounded by anxious friends. A doctor
felt his pulse and shook his head. Let's hope he isn't dead.

That confounded climb nearly burst our lungs, but '*Pazienza!*' On arrival we were welcomed by a crowd of men,
women, and shrieking children; we could hardly hear the
band playing in our honour.

A woman, with a black cloth lowered over her face, stretched
out her hand, muttering something.

'What is it?' I asked.

'I am dying of hunger, Excellency.'

'Are you making fun of us up here?' I exclaimed. Then a
man gave the woman a shove and offered me a drink from a
great earthen pitcher. I nearly smashed it in his face, but I
put my lips to it out of politeness; then I left him and tried to
catch up with the woman. I failed to find her. But then a
young girl with big gentle eyes, but ill, wasted, offered me a
lemon with her right hand, and held out the left saying, 'Young
Gentleman!' A rag of a skirt flapped against her shins and her
feet were bare. I put a little money into her hand, the small
thin local coins like butterflies, and away she fled. I see her yet,
running away in satisfaction or shame, with her dirty, ragged,
brief garment flapping against her skinny legs.

When the General arrived, there was an outbreak of de-
lirious enthusiasm. A band played madly. All that could be
seen were raised arms and brandished rifles. Some swore
fealty, some fell on their knees, and some uttered blessings.
The square, the streets, the by-ways were thronged. It was
only with great difficulty that some room could be made for
his passage. Patient and pleased he saluted on all sides and
paused, smiling.

There is an officer here dressed in Piedmontese uniform, who
seems to be the man I met at Novi. I shall try to get to speak

to him and if it really is the man, I shall ask his pardon for not having told him what he asked me. They say that he is a deserter from the regular army and that his name is De Amicis and that he is from Novara.

*   *   *

I have taken a turn through the city. They built it up here in such a way that one house is on the top of another and all seem about to collapse at any moment. Even had the Saracens wished to land off Salemi the city would have been safe. Vast, over-crowded, filthy, its streets seem to be drains. One can hardly keep one's feet. One goes in search of an inn and finds a den. But the friars, oh yes, the friars have the most beautiful convents and this one where my company is billeted is absolutely spotless. The friars have made themselves scarce.

The inhabitants are not impolite, but, if we ask them questions they seem embarrassed. They don't know anything. They shrug their shoulders or reply by gestures or grimaces. If one can understand what they mean, one is certainly clever. Weary, I went into a tavern four or five steps below the level of the street. There I found a whole party of my friends who were gaily eating macaroni out of certain wooden vessels that . . . ah well! Despite the filth I set to and ate. And so we drank and chattered and we had almost forgotten what we were here for when Bruzzesi of the Scouts came in and told us that a great body of Neapolitan troops was only a few miles away. All the better, exclaimed Gatti, now we shall see what kind of a welcome they are preparing for us.

Salemi, 14 May

The General has ridden through the city on horseback. When the populace sees him they take fire. There is a magic in his look and in his name. It is only Garibaldi they want.

The General has assumed the dictatorship of Sicily in the name of Italy and Victor Emmanuel. There is a good deal of talk about this and not everyone is satisfied. But such will be our battle-cry. At the street corners one can read the proclamation

issued by the new dictator. He addresses the *buoni preti*, the good priests, of Sicily. A purist among us has said that it would have been better Italian style if he'd written *preti buoni*.

The Sicilian insurgents come in from all sides by the hundred, some on horseback, some on foot. There is a tremendous confusion and they have bands which play terribly badly. I have seen mountaineers armed to the teeth, some with rascally faces and eyes that menace one like the muzzles of pistols. All these people are led by gentlemen whom they obey devotedly.

It's now pelting with rain. We have various contradictory reports about the enemy. They say there are 4,000, no— 10,000, with horses and guns. On certain mountains they are digging themselves in! No—somewhere else! They are advancing! They are retiring! Tonight we shall stay here and meanwhile they will finish getting the carts ready to transport our artillery.

* * *

I have heard a pretty tale. The day before yesterday, directly we had landed, some of our men occupied the telegraph office. Before the official had run away, he left a sheet of paper on which was written 'Two Sardinian steamers are dis-embarking men.' It was the copy of a dispatch sent to the military commander of Trapani. And from Trapani came the question, 'How many are there, what do they want?' Then our men answered, 'Excuse me, I have made a mistake, the ships are unloading sulphur.' From Trapani came one dry word 'Imbecile'. Then our people cut the telegraph wire and all was silence.

Salemi, 15 May, 5 a.m.

I have just flung wide the windows of this monkish cell where I am billeted and given a glance at the countryside, still sleepy under the wisps of vapour rising from the valleys below. Who knows what road we are to take and at what point in the vast sweep of country within my sight we shall be confronted by

the Neapolitans? Who knows along what roads they are now marching towards us, or in what ravine they are lying in wait? Margarita and Bozzani are stretched out on a green rug, still asleep. I don't know where they got it from. Raccuglia, the good little old Palermitan who never opens his mouth, is doing up his gaiters by the light of my candle. He's coming back from abroad in our company just as though he were a medieval exile returning to his city. 'Sergeant Raccuglia, what sort of weather shall we have today?' 'You'll know when you see the General's face, but it'll turn out fine because, just look, Gatti is combing his hair! He's always neat and dandified.'

Outside the gate, two Milanese are discussing our situation. One of them is more knowing than the other and argues that things are very serious from all points of view. A numerous enemy provided with everything, we with our poor arms and insufficient ammunition, only fifteen cartridges per man and the Sicilian insurgents worse-armed than we are. 'What's all that,' thundered a great voice from the corridor, 'did you come to Sicily to tot up such accounts?' The two fell silent. A bugle-call sounds. And Simonetta comes to tell us that we are off.

Simonetta is a great young man. He cares nothing for himself, he only lives for others. Is there guard duty to be done? Simonetta volunteers. A difficult job? There he is, slender of build and gentle of mien. Bread is being distributed? He is the last to come forward to collect his own. At Milan he has left a widowed father alone.

*   *   *

We're off in a few minutes. The enemy is really nine miles away. For two days and nights we have rested on this height with this poor uncivilized population. Who knows where we shall sleep tonight? The carts for the guns are ready. The long muzzle of the culverin protrudes from one of them. An artillery section has been formed. The gunners are almost all engineers.

15 May, 11 a.m. On the hills of Pianto Romano

One last thought for those at home and then we're all ready. Our guns are up above us, on the main road to the left. The enemy is over there; the mountain opposite is swarming with them. They must be about 5,000. Our companies are in echelon. From a point above us the General is observing the enemy movements. Between our positions and theirs is a fairly small barren plain. At the highest point in our centre our banner waves in the breeze. The lieutenant who carries it sent me on a message to the General and the General sent me back to him with the command, 'Tell him to carry it to the highest point and let it be seen waving by all'. Oh God, with what a voice he uttered these words!

Colonel Carini's horse reared and he fell. No damage done. Here he is once more in the saddle. A short time ago I saw La Masa fall off too and I think he hurt himself. I felt as though I had knocked my own head against the stones. The Neapolitan riflemen are coming down from the heights. How calm they seem. What certainty there is in their movements. Before long—— But their trumpets have a lugubrious sound.

16 May. From the Convent of San Vito above Calatafimi

If I survive it will be nice to read, several years hence, what I am now scribbling in my notebook. If only I had time I could have written a hundred pages since yesterday morning.

All Salemi was out to wave us good-bye. 'Bless you! bless you!' they shouted. And when I turned from the foot of the descent to look back at them I stretched out my arms to the city and its inhabitants and I should like to have been able to embrace them all. Our companies came down at a brisk pace, singing. At a bend in the road Garibaldi on his horse loomed grandly up above us against the sky. It was a sky of glory from which a warm light poured down which, blending with the perfumes of the valley, intoxicated us all. Accompanying us down from the mountain came the bands of Sicilian

insurgents. It was a procession which I myself didn't wait to see finish, as my company was sent off through the open country, which became more beautiful as we advanced. When we came to the village of Vita we met some Scouts who were coming back at a half-trot. They had discovered the enemy. We only had to climb the nearby hill and we should have had them before us.

Meanwhile the inhabitants of Vita were fleeing, carrying their household goods with them, dragging their old folk and children behind them. It was a miserable sight. Saddened, we went through the village and those unfortunates looked at us and made gestures of compassion and said to us, 'Poor souls'.

After a little we halted. And then I saw our lovely banner. It was carried at the centre of the 7th Company, formed by some hundred and fifty young men almost all from the University of Pavia, the very flower of Lombardy and Venetia, the most numerous and the best-equipped company of the lot. I could read these words embroidered in large golden characters on one side of the banner, 'To Giuseppe Garibaldi, from the Italian residents in Valparaiso, 1855'. On the other side was Italy as the august figure of a woman with broken chains at her feet, standing over a trophy of cannons and rifles, worked in gold and silver. As I gazed at the banner, I thought that in those distant lands where it was made, among those patriots who had presented it, lives one of my uncles. Meanwhile there was a great running to and fro of officers and Scouts. Then the General appeared, the trumpets sounded, we left the main-road and set off through the fields over a barren hillside, one company treading on the heels of the next. From the top we could see the enemy. The hill before us was flashing with arms. It appeared to be covered by at least 10,000 soldiers.

'What? They are wearing red trousers, the Neapolitans have already got the French to back them up,' exclaimed some indignantly as they saw the red among the hostile ranks. But Sicilians among us who overheard them quietened them,

informing them that the Neapolitan officers also wear red trousers.

We lay down when it was just on eleven o'clock. We seemed to have been watching the Royalist troops for only a matter of minutes, yet the first shot was not fired until 1.30 p.m. The Neapolitan Sharpshooters, who had gradually come down through the rows of prickly-pear bushes were the first to fire. Garibaldi, surrounded by many other officers, including Türr, Tuköry, and Sirtori, had kept them under observation for a long time from the high point where he had taken his station. I believe that at this first encounter he half-hoped . . . in something which, however, the Neapolitans failed to realize. And yet our Italian flag was flying up there in the full light of day!

'Don't fire! Don't reply to their fire!' shouted our commanders; but the bullets passed over us with such a provocative whine that we couldn't restrain ourselves. One shot after another was heard, then the General's own trumpeter sounded the call to arms, then the charge.

We got to our feet, closed up and rushed like a flash down to the plain below. There we came under a perfect hail of bullets, while from the smoke-wreathed mountain two guns began a furious cannonade against us.

The plain was quickly crossed and the first enemy line was broken but when we came to the slopes of the opposite hill it was not pleasant to look upwards. I saw Garibaldi there on foot with his sheathed sword over his right shoulder, walking slowly forward, keeping the whole action in view. Our men were falling all round him and it seemed that those who wore the red shirt were the most numerous victims. Bixio came up at a gallop to offer some shelter with his horse, and he pulled the General behind his animal calling out, 'General! Is this the way you wish to die?' 'And how could I die better than for my country?' replied the General, and, freeing himself from Bixio's restraining hand he went forward with a frown. Bixio followed respectfully.

Goro da Montebenichi and Ferruccio at the battle of Gavinana, I thought to myself, and I was pleased that I remem-

bered the episode;[11] but the mood quickly passed and I began to fear, and even to guess, that the General thought it impossible that we could win this fight and that he was therefore seeking death on the battlefield.

At that moment one of our guns thundered from the road above. A cry of joy from all greeted the shot because it seemed as though we were getting the aid of a thousand strong arms. 'Forward! Forward! Forward!' was the cry heard on all sides and the trumpet that had continuously sounded the charge now pealed out with a kind of anguish as though it were the voice of our country in danger.

The first, second, and third terraces up the hillside were attacked at the point of the bayonet and passed, but it was terrible to see the dead and wounded. Little by little, as they yielded ground, the Royalist battalions retreated higher up. They concentrated and thus grew stronger. At last it seemed impossible that we could face them. They were all on the top of the hill and we were around the brow, tired, at the end of our tether, and reduced in numbers. There was a moment of pause; it was difficult to recognize the two opposing sides, they up there and we all flat on the ground. One could hear rifle fire and the Royalist troops started rolling down boulders, and hurling stones, and it was said that even Garibaldi was hit by one of these.

Already we had lost a great many of our men and I heard friends bewailing their comrades. Near by, among the prickly-pear bushes, I saw a fine young man fatally wounded, propped up by two of his comrades. He seemed to want to continue to charge, but I heard him ask his two friends to be merciful to the Royalist soldiers because they too were Italians. Tears came into my eyes.

[11] Another notable episode of Italian history (*cf.* note 9, p. 26) was the battle of Gavinana (1530) and the heroism of Francesco Ferruccio was known to all nineteenth-century Italians from Guerazzi's novel *L'Assedio di Firenze*. During the battle Goro da Montebenichi tried to shield Ferruccio with his body as Bixio did Garibaldi and with the same result. Abba is constantly seeing life in terms of literature.

The whole hillside was covered with fallen, but I heard no complaints. Quite close to me was Missori, commander of the Scouts, who, with his left eye all bloody and bruised, seemed to be listening to the noises floating down to us from the hill-top. We could hear the heavy tramp of the Royalist battalions up there and thousands of voices like waves of an angry sea, shouting from time to time, 'Long live the King!'

Meanwhile new re-inforcements came up on our side and we felt stronger. Our commanders moved about among us encouraging us. Sirtori and Bixio had come up the whole way on horseback. Sirtori, dressed in black with a little bit of red shirt showing from beneath his lapel, had many rents in his clothes made by bullets, but he was unwounded. Impassive, riding whip in hand, he seemed hardly present in all that confusion. Yet on his pale, thin face I could read something as though he felt a passionate desire to die for us all.

Bixio was to be seen on all sides as though he were one man divided into a hundred; the right hand of Garibaldi. I saw them up there for a moment together. 'Take a rest lads, take another short rest,' said the General, 'one more effort and the job's done.' And Bixio followed him through our ranks.

Lieutenant Bandi stood up to salute him, but he was on the point of falling, at the end of his tether. He could do no more. He had been wounded several times, but the last bullet had struck his left breast and blood was pouring out. He will be dead in another half-hour, I thought, but when the companies charged on a last assault at that hedge of glittering bayonets pointed so menacingly at us, I turned and saw that officer in the leading rank. Someone, who must be a friend of his, called out, 'How many lives have you got?' And he smiled happily.

The supreme clash came when the Valparaiso banner, which had passed from hand to hand and finally to Schiaffino, was seen wavering for some instants in a furious bloody tussle and then go down. But Giovan Maria Damiani of the Scouts snatched it up by one of its streamers. He and his rearing horse formed a group such as Michelangelo might have carved in stone against a confused tumult of fighting men, friend and foe.

As long as I live I shall never forget that scene.

At that moment the royalists fired their last salvo and a certain Sacchi from Pavia was blown to pieces. Then there was a shout of joy because the gun was captured. A rumour went round that the General was dead, and Menotti, wounded in his right arm, was running round asking for him. Elia lay wounded to death; Schiaffino, the Dante da Castiglione[12] of this battle, was dead and I saw his tall body lying on the bloody ground.

Almost on the hilltop, near the hut, I recognized, by his clothes more than his face, the body of poor Sartori. Certainly he must have been killed instantaneously because only five minutes before I had seen him climbing up the hill and he had greeted me by name. He lay on his left side, all huddled up with clenched fists. He had been wounded in the chest. I fell on him, kissed him, and bade him farewell. Poor Sartori, in his staring eyes and drawn features, something still remained of his longing for yet one more breath of that heroic air. All those who knew Eugenio Sartori from Sacile will for long speak of him. Like a hero, he had kept the promise he made at Talamone.

The dead Neapolitans were a piteous sight. Many of them had been killed by the bayonet. Those who lay on the brow of the hill had nearly all been wounded in the head. Yonder I could see a little dwarfish monster, who seemed by his clothes to be a local peasant, ferociously stabbing one of the dead Neapolitans. 'Kill the brute!' yelled Bixio and spurred against him with raised sabre, but the savage creature slid away among the rocks and disappeared; more brute than man.

As details of the great picture I can see those Franciscan friars who fought on our side. One of them was cramming a muzzle-loader with handfuls of bullets and stones, then he climbed up and let loose a hailstorm from his ancient piece. Short, thin, filthy dirty, as we saw him from below tearing his bare shins against the prickly bushes which gave out a nauseat-

---

[12] Another hero (of large stature) celebrated by Guerazzi in the novel *L'Assedio di Firenze*.

ing cemetery stink, he was an object for laughter and applause. How brave those monks were! I saw one of them, who had been wounded in his thigh, pull out the bullet from the flesh and return to fire against the enemy. During the battle we could see crowds of peasants intently watching the fierce spectacle from the high crags around us. From time to time they uttered yells which must have terrified our common enemy.

When the Neapolitans began to retreat under cover of their riflemen I saw the General again watching them with a look of exultation. We pursued them for some way and then they disappeared into a fold of the ground. When they emerged they were out of range on the opposite mountainside, followed by some hundreds of their cavalry, who had been under cover up to that moment and now rejoined them at full speed. From the battlefield we could see their long column climbing up to Calatafimi, which appeared as a grey mass halfway up the grey mountain, until finally they were swallowed up in the town. It seemed a miracle that we had conquered. A chill wind began to blow. We lay down on the ground. There was a melancholy silence. Night came all at once and Airenta and Bozzani and I went to sleep in a little cornfield, caressed by the ears of corn bending over us.

It was scarcely dawn this morning when reveillé sounded, but already larks were singing on high. I thought that perhaps we should have to march against Calatafimi, as last night I heard the General discuss it with Bixio. But during the night people had come from Calatafimi to inform us that the Royalist troops had left in the direction of Palermo. It occurred to me then to take a stroll over the battlefield.

I found Sartori there where he had fallen. No one had touched him, but he seemed to have been dead for three days. His cheeks had lost all colour, his hair was stiff, his skin had turned yellow, so that he was a horrible sight. I was so shaken I had not the courage to give him a last kiss. He would have done it for me; he would have buried me with his own hands.

Now I can see the hill, tranquil and deserted. Yesterday,

even the stones seemed alive and on our side. Up on those slopes lie our dead, more than thirty of them. I still have them all before my eyes as they were two days ago, bold, confident, gay. But one of them fills me with disquiet, that officer I saw at Novi and again at Salemi, and whom I shall never see again. For De Amicis, too, is dead and lies there in his glory with a name not his own.

The dead are less to be pitied than the poor wounded, lying together in that miserable village of Vita. They suffer God knows what pangs, alone, without attention, and with no other defence than their own helplessness. But what if a column of those savage Neapolitan soldiers should arrive? They have had orders to give no quarter.

The sun is setting. Down in the city the air is full of the sound of music from the local bands. They tell me that they have organized a ceremony for blessing the Dictator, presided over by a friar who has followed us all the way from Salemi. I shall not go down from this height. I cannot tear myself away from this lovely view until night comes. Among the many little woods down below I can see Alcamo; from here to there it is as lovely as the vale of Tempe. The scene is closed by the bay of Castellamare which seems to blend with the sky. And the sky is open to one's questing thoughts and swallows them up. Those distant waters have a smile of promise and one loses oneself in the depths as in the eyes of one's beloved. I catch a little glimpse of shore, only a glimpse, but I think that when we get there we shall hear some news of ourselves and of the world that has by now passed judgement on us.

Tonight I have to read out to our company Garibaldi's Order of the Day that I copied out in the municipal offices of Calatafimi where I found Captain Cenni in a furious temper about something or other. This is what I shall read.

'Soldiers of Italian liberty! With comrades such as you I can attempt everything!' What a shout there will be when the company hears this further passage: 'Your mothers, your sweethearts, when they come out on to the street, proud of you, their brows radiant etc. etc.'

Here comes Colonel Carini up the hill on horseback and he seems delighted. Can it be that we are off?

Alcamo, 17 May. On the threshold of a little church almost on the seashore.

We had a happy march from Calatafimi here, through a fertile countryside. But on all sides, there were traces of the defeat we had inflicted on the Royalists: knapsacks, caps, bloody bandages scattered along the road. When we left at dawn we were all singing, but later, what with the sight of this debris and what with the sun which was enough to overwhelm us, we grew silent and proceeded like so many ghosts. Towards ten o'clock we came across some splendid carriages out to meet us, as though we were important people. Alcamo was close. In the carriages there were spruce gentlemen who paid their respects and welcomed the General, and where the footpaths ran down into the road there were crowds of peasant women, confident and quite without fear of us. Some of them devoutly made the sign of the cross. I saw one with two children in her arms fall to her knees as the General passed, and one of our men recalled how in Rome, eleven years before, the women from across the Tiber called him 'The Nazarene'.

At eleven o'clock we made our way into Alcamo. It is a lovely city, though sad. In its shadowed streets one seems to breathe a Moorish atmosphere. Lofty palm trees grow along the walls of its gardens. Every house looks like a monastery. A pair of eyes flash from a lofty balcony; you stop, look, and the vision disappears.

We were told that, before our arrival, numerous Royal troops in a great fury had landed at Castellamare, but soon retreated and re-embarked. Nothing further is said of this manoeuvre, but out at sea one can see two ships. They could be warships.

*   *   *

Five of us were guests of a gentleman who absolutely insisted upon having us to his house, and there we supped. What

E

humanity there is in this remote island, but what ingenuous ignorance of Italian affairs! He did not conceal his daughters, but they looked anxious, although they talked to us as if to old friends.

'Where do you come from?' the father asked Delucchi.

'I'm a Genoese.'

'And you?' turning to Castellani.

'I come from Milan.'

'And I from Como,' replies Rienti, without waiting to be asked. He has a head like one of those curly-haired, chubby angels that one sees with their wings spread, carved above the altars of churches.

'What wonderful places you come from, but why are you so poorly dressed, just like peasants? Come along now, tell the truth, you're really Piedmontese soldiers. No? Well, how have you managed to beat so many Neapolitans? They passed through here in such a plight, not half of them will reach Palermo.'

Then the talk fell on the war of last year. That good gentleman seemed born yesterday. He hardly believed that there was such a person in the world as Victor Emmanuel. Meanwhile we'd all had our share of wine and somebody mentioned Ciullo d'Alcamo and his lovely poem, and then we talked of Bari, of Puglia, and of the challenge that led to the joust of Barletta.[13] Our host was amazed to hear us speak of such things. He could hardly be prevailed on to let us go; when we could in decency depart, his daughters gave us their hands, which we kissed respectfully and timidly and came away with something of a flutter in our hearts.

*   *   *

There was a hollow growl of thunder from over the mountains; all crowded down to the shore, thinking it was gunfire. 'Palermo has risen! On to Palermo!' But then over the moun-

[13] Ciullo (or Cielo) d'Alcamo, an early Sicilian poet known for his *contrasto* in Dialogue form 'Rosa fresca aulentissima', mentioned here because he came from Alcamo. For the Barletta challenge see note 9, p. 26.

tains we could see certain dark clouds, sign of a thunderstorm that was passing away.

* * *

A mysterious rumour is going round that the General has lost all hope of succeeding against the 30,000 troops the Bourbons have in Sicily, that our expedition will be called off, that each of us will be given permission to escape as well as he can from this predicament. Everyone was in the depths of gloom at this. But the rumour turned out to be entirely false—perhaps a trick played by the enemy.

* * *

The friar who followed us from Salemi wants to spread an aura of religiosity over us. A short time ago I saw him on a horse on his way back to Calatafimi. 'Colonel Carini,' he said, passing my Commander, 'tomorrow I shall celebrate Mass at a tricolour altar. After that I shall be with you again.'

* * *

A few who had been left behind, having been slightly wounded at Calatafimi, have now rejoined us here. They tell us of the sufferings of our comrades in hospital at Vita. It is not known why, but wounds seem to become gangrenous. The doctors do their best for the sufferers, but death snatches them from their hands. Francesco Montanari from Mirandola, that friend of the General who was joking with him at Talamone, was one of the first to die.

And if it be true, I can understand the words that friar uttered when he was leaving for Calatafimi an hour ago. Our dead, I was told, are still lying unburied on the hills of Pianto Romano.

* * *

18 May, Between Partinico and Burgeto

We'd have done better to cross the mountain and avoid Partinico, even at the cost of burst lungs.

We ascended the slope on which the village stands and the slight breeze that freshened the air bore with it waves of unbearable stink. Hardly had we reached the top than we came in sight of the village, almost burnt out, and still smoking from its ruins. The column of troops we had beaten at Calatafimi had engaged the really heroic insurgents of Partinico. Having burnt the village, the Bourbon troops massacred the women and the helpless of all ages. There were corpses of soldiers and peasants with butchered horses and dogs among them. When we arrived, all the bells were ringing, I don't know whether in fury or triumph; the houses were still smoking and the people were in a frenzy among the ruins, priests and friars shrieking frantic cries of welcome. There were women wringing their hands in desperation and young girls, holding hands and singing, as though they were out of their minds, dancing in a ring around seven or eight already swollen and smouldering corpses. The corpses were those of Bourbon soldiers. The General spurred away from this scene with his hat over his eyes. And we all followed him deafened and disgusted. Now we are far away, but we still hear the bells ringing. It is 4.30 and I wish we could camp here tonight among these olive groves, so as not to lose the view of the Bay of Castellamare which, at sunset, must be a miracle of colour.

* * *

19 May. Passo di Renna

Yesterday Burgeto looked like a place of ambush. From out of their frowning houses, half-concealed among gigantic olive trees, peasants peered at us silently as though at a procession of ghosts. I have noticed that if one population welcomes us with joy the next we come across is cold and hostile.

We went on.

Along a road dug in the arid mountainside we passed through a gorge. A cold evening wind was blowing through it, which seemed to threaten us with a poor night's camp. It was very late when we halted on this mountain in a perfect amphitheatre. When we stopped we were completely worn out. From

Alcamo to this place, called Passo di Renna, are very many weary miles. But we hardly noticed them until we got to Partinico where all our gaiety was quenched and we sang no more.

Not since leaving school have I slept as I did tonight. My head on my haversack and my haversack on a stone, my body stretched along the roadside. But this morning, what joy; at daybreak, some village band or other came to wake us playing an air from *I Vespri Siciliani*. I jumped up and ran to the highest point where I am now writing, and my eye travels over the vast plain of Palermo, the Conca d'Oro. There lies the city, a vague shape between sea and mist. I can see ships out in the roadstead; so many that it seems if all the fleets of Europe have come by appointment to look on when, one day, we shall suddenly attack the city. Oh wonderful Cacciatori dell'Alpi!

Down below everybody is swarming round a great cistern, washing their clothes and their persons. It looks like a scene from the Bible in the valleys of Judea.

*   *   *

I forgot to say that about ten o'clock last night, as soon as we had camped and lit our fires, some Palermitan gentlemen appeared, after passing through who knows what dangers. I watched them as they met their old friend Colonel Carini who, after ten years of exile, is coming home with arms in his hand. Their affectionate embraces spoke more than words. Afterwards I learnt from them that everything is prepared in Palermo and directly we reach the gates of the city the people will pour out of their houses and overcome the garrison of 20,000 troops. They further told us that the police are trying to make the people believe that we sack houses, violate women, are the wrath of God, as they say in these parts. They went on to speak of the secret police. Ah, the Palermitan police spies must be terrible indeed. According to these gentlemen the police boast that one of these fine days they will massacre all the patriots, and make cushions for their wives out of the tresses of the Palermitan ladies.

Calatafimi is known to have made a very deep impression on the Neapolitan troops but, although stunned, they are still faithful to their King. About us, and the mainland of Italy, and of what they are saying about our operations and about our victory beyond the island, not a word. Before leaving, these gentlemen embraced us and arranged to meet us in Palermo in their own houses. Benedini, the doctor, pulled out his notebook and wanted to write their addresses by the light of the fire.

'Whatever are you doing?' exclaimed one of them, seizing his hand. 'Such things must be memorized.'

Sicilians are old hands at conspiracies, one can see. None of us would have imagined it was dangerous to have an address on one's person. Well, we shall remember the addresses given us by these gentlemen and we'll try to seek them out, always provided that they don't fall into the hands of Royalists on their way home.

*   *   *

Lieutenant Colonel Tuköry is riding up and down the road exercising a black horse which hardly touches the ground, it is so fresh. Extremely young for his rank, this officer seems to me the personification of Hungary, our sister nation in servitude. His face is darkly pale and he has refined features lit up by a pair of flashing, melancholy eyes. He had fought in the battles of ten years ago, battles with such strange names that they frightened me as a child when I heard them. He had seen Italian regiments in the service of Austria giving the *coup-de-grace* to his own country. But affection for Italy survived in the heart of that generous nation. The only thing is that we do not yet know how far the war we won last year may not be fatal for Hungary. That country has two worthy representatives with us, Tuköry and Türr, and in addition there are two rankers; that uncouth man whom I saw on board ship and Sergeant Goldberg of my own company. He is an old soldier, taciturn, touchy, but trustworthy and brave. We saw how he behaved at Calatafimi!

*   *   *

I have found out that Tuköry was aide-de-camp to General Bem and that he is a real military genius. Since '49 he has been in exile at Constantinople and we ought to honour him as much as we honour the exiles of '21, that sacred springtime of Italy's first awakening.

*   *   *

Soon we shall have rain. 'Lucky man who can get a seat down there in the Ministry of War,' said Giusti, that humorist from Asti, always joking as though the wine of his own hills ran in his veins. The 'Ministry of War' is a broken-down old carriage that follows behind us on the road with our secretariat and military treasure, which amounts to only thirty thousand francs as I have heard. But there are two real treasures in that old carriage, Acerbi's heart and Ippolito Nievo's mind. Nievo is a Venetian poet who at twenty-eight years of age has written novels, ballads, and tragedies. He will be the soldier-poet of our expedition. I saw him curled up in the corner of that carriage; a fine-cut profile, gentle eye, and genius flashing from his brow. With his robust physique he makes a fine soldier.

*   *   *

I can see five great casks of wine, basketfuls of cigars, and a pile of cloaks, sent up by some town council or other to help keep us warm. What generosity!

20 May. Passo di Renna

It poured with rain all night. We huddled round a great fire and took what shelter we could, while listening to the tales of Sicilians about this place, which has a very evil reputation. A murderous spot! The traveller about to enter this Pass from either end makes the sign of the cross and thinks sadly of home before he ventures further. A highwayman could easily appear among these steep rocks, or between the leaves of the prickly-pears and level a rifle at you. These evil-doers sometimes form a gang and lay up in this place and woe betide the traveller on

the road at such a time. Money won't buy them off; they're after blood.

Colonel Carini, who is a most eloquent speaker, told us tales of more chivalrous highwaymen who used to lurk in this neighbourhood. Although I could hardly keep my eyes open, I made a great effort to stay awake, but most of the others fell asleep. When he noticed this, Carini pulled his cloak over his head and said, smiling: 'Just like Mazeppa in the last verse of Byron's poem.'[14]

*　　　*　　　*

I have heard a rumour that on a certain mountain, whose name I can't at the moment recollect, there are thousands of Sicilians concentrating under the command of La Masa. Would it were true, because up to the present we are a small enough number and we feel the lack of those we lost at Calatafimi.

21 May. Above the village of Pioppo

There was tremendous excitement last evening towards sunset. All of a sudden they ordered us to strike camp and it was whispered that we were going to Palermo. As we came down the road that twists and turns to where the plain of the Conca d'Oro begins, we had the jolliest march in the world. This is what we had been waiting for, a night of adventure. All of a sudden we were halted.

'What's the matter?'

'Nothing, this is where we sleep.'

'What's the name of this little hamlet?'

[14] The last lines of Byron's *Mazeppa* are as follows:

> With leafy couch already made,
> A bed nor comfortless nor new
> To him, who took his rest whene'er
> The hour arrived, no matter where:
> His eyes the hastening slumbers steep.
> And if ye marvel Charles forgot
> To thank his tale, *he* wondered not—
> The king had been an hour asleep.

'Pioppo.'

'And continuing down this road, where do we go from here?'

'First to Monreale, then Palermo.'

'Well, we might as well have stopped at the Passo di Renna,' mumbled Gaffini, who has always got something to complain about. But in he went, together with the rest of us, through a great gateway and we were shut in like a flock of sheep. We lay down and kept quiet.

Before sunrise we were already up, our rifles on our shoulders. The dawn was so lovely, what with the colours in the sky above and fragrant scents rising from the earth below, that one longed to be able to transfuse one's whole being into such beauty. To our left and ahead towards Monreale, on the hills of San Martino, we could hear volleys of musketry growing louder and coming nearer. Then we saw smoke and our men retreating along the steep cliffs, firing as they came. The Bourbon troops, who had come out from Monreale, had attacked them and were trying to turn our left flank and force us back into the mountains by the Passo di Renna. Had they succeeded, they would have annihilated us. What if today we are going to have the worst of it, we thought? A handful of Scouts passed at a gallop coming back from the Monreale direction. What's the trouble, now? Nothing! The General with his staff passed us at a half-trot and the musketry on the hills continued. The men retreating, slowly and obstinately, along the heights, were the Genoese Sharpshooters. But beyond the hill where they were putting up such a stubborn resistance, there was also fighting going on. Who was over there? One of our companies who had got cut off? Or some band of Sicilian insurgents? One couldn't make head or tail of it.

Meanwhile the sun had risen high and was burning hot and we were ordered, now forward, now back, halted, marched forward again and, always before our eyes, we could see a train of slow-moving mules bearing stretchers for the wounded. So it went on for an hour until once more we came back to the entrance to the Passo di Renna without anybody interfering with

us. We can hear no more gunfire. Two of our guns are planted up there on the brow of the hill keeping watch over Pioppo and the camp that the Royalist troops have pitched down below in the orchards. It is a large, well-laid-out camp. From where I am now I can see Palermo and the enormous green mass of Monte Pellegrino. Those white lines that look as though they were sketched in on the mountain slopes must be little walls to prevent landslides or paths leading to the summit. There is such peace in all the world below us here, such profound silence in all that life that one imagines must be there. Certainly they are waiting for us.

*   *   *

The friar who left for Alcamo to celebrate Mass on the battlefield of Calatafimi is now back with us. He rides an old mare, sitting firmly in the saddle as though under his robe he wore a soldier's uniform. He is gay and young and is called Friar Pantaleo from Castelvetrano. Well, a friar too is part of the picture! He provides a contrast against the background of our little encampment. Salvator Rosa would have given anything to have seen those seven friars who fought at Calatafimi. Perhaps they are still with us now, having cast aside their habits.

*   *   *

A short time ago, while I was going down the road singing a hunting song, carrying an order from my captain, I came across an armed Sicilian who stopped me, exclaiming, 'So here you sing, while up there they die.' He told me that in the fighting of some hours back Rosolino Pilo had been killed. He pointed to the hills above Monreale. Killed by a bullet in the head while he was scribbling a note to Garibaldi. That poor little Sicilian volunteer wept as he told me this, and when he understood from my speech that I was not a Sicilian he asked pardon for having stopped me. He begged me for a few cartridges, but I could not give him any from the eleven that I still have in my pouch, and I left him perplexed and mortified.

21 May. Parco

While my clothes are drying by the fire, I take up my pencil to write, my head still ringing with the great strain of last night's march. The woman of the house, a good little old thing, who welcomed us like a mother, is cooking us a dish of macaroni, for we are nearly famished.

All yesterday up to the evening it was wonderful weather, clear and serene, but when we took up our arms once more, the sky became overcast. The sun had gone down and we were off. This time really to Palermo! No, we're going to San Giuseppe! And where is this San Giuseppe? Here on the right some miles on beyond the mountains.

Having gone some little way along the military road, we arrived at a dark, tumble-down little house standing all by itself, a real highwaymen's haunt. As we came up to this place they ordered us to leave the road and we followed one another down a narrow, stony, path. In front of the house two men worked as hard as they could to distribute loaves out of great baskets; each of us had three as we went past. It was as though we received three stabs in the heart, for we realized that we had to spend three days in these lonely mountains. How were we to carry these loaves? We fixed bayonets and spiked them one on top of the other. Our rifles, thrown out of balance in this way, pressed heavy on our shoulders.

It was then that I had the anguish of seeing Delucchi from Genoa seated on a stone, hugging his knees, racked by pain that robbed him of all his strength. 'Go back to our waggons,' I said to him, 'they will take you somewhere or other. You'll do nothing here; we can't take you with us and in half an hour we shall all have passed. Night will come and you will be here all alone.' I helped him to rise and he slowly made off towards the tail of the column, looking at us as though we were carrying away his last hope. And to think that he might have fallen into the hands of the Royalist troops; but I hope that he will be able to gain the waggons and be safe. As it grew dark, rain began to pour violently down in heavy drops; they were like

hailstones and hurt our cheeks. The wind blew cold and, ahead of us, there was a deep cold gorge and it seemed as though we were entering a wolf's den. Nevertheless, Lieutenant Rovighi rode his horse at breakneck speed. But all of a sudden we heard a rifle shot, fired accidentally by one of my company, and saw Rovighi roll to the ground. He had barely touched it when, like a cat, he leapt up and stood there without saying a word. He was unhurt. But his poor animal had a broken leg. We marched on, leaving Rovighi to bewail his horse, who was threshing about in the dark. We advanced as best as we could tapping the ground before us with our rifle butts like a procession of blind men. The darkness could not have been more complete. The path petered out. We had been walking for two hours and we had barely covered a mile. Not one of us could say he had not fallen over in the rough scree. 'Courage, up you go, show your mettle!' These encouragements were whispered to us as we got to a point where a group of men were busy with ropes and levers. They were trying to extricate that unfortunate old culverin that we've dragged with us from Orbetello and was now bogged. 'Oh, leave it lying there for good, for if we ever succeed in firing it, it will blow up and kill the half of us.' I was about to call out some such joking remark but the words died in my throat, for in the group I saw Garibaldi, Orsini, and Castiglia, all busy getting our artillery shifted as best they could. I heard the General charge Castiglia to see to its transport and to do it at whatever cost; then the group broke up and off we went again, marching on in the dark.

Turning back to look, we could see our camp fires at Renna still blazing away as though we were still there to enjoy the warmth. Down to our left, in the depths below, we could see lines of fires burning. It was the enemy camp near Pioppo. Away ahead, a great stationary light, like a supernatural eye watching us, was burning brightly, perhaps lit to give us our bearings.

The rain never stopped. We were soaked to the skin and the wind bore back the neighing of a horse that seemed to mock us. Towards midnight we heard a shot that shook us all. 'Ah,

so now it's come!' exclaimed somebody, imagining that the vanguard had run into the enemy. It would indeed have been a misfortune in that darkness and in the state we were in. But nothing more was heard of this and on we trudged; sometimes we fell, then we picked ourselves up, but nobody grumbled. What did that shot mean? We found a horse lying dead by the side of the path and they said it was Bixio's, who had been enraged because its neighing could have revealed our presence to the enemy and had blown its brains out with his own pistol. Byron, always Byron! Lara would have done the same.[15]

Towards dawn we passed close to that circle of light and found it was the mouth of a kiln or furnace. In front of it stood a tall dark figure watching us. Perhaps it was only an ignorant charcoal-burner but I like to think that he was placed there on purpose to keep the flame going like the column of fire that guided the Israelites through the desert.

At the first light the rain stopped. We could see Palermo before us and Monreale not far off, about as far as the Conca d'Oro is wide. We now saw each other and we looked like ghosts; our clothes were torn and muddy; many had almost bare feet. Tired, worn out as we were if a detachment of the enemy had fallen on us we should have been defeated.

We went down to this little village named Parco.

The indefatigable Genoese Sharpshooters keep watch in the orchards so that we can rest in peace. There are so many fires burning in the broad square that it looks like an inferno. Everybody is drying their clothes standing half naked in front of the flames. There's not a window open. We don't know where Garibaldi is, but we know he watches over us all.

[15] Lara, the romantic hero of Byron's poem of that name.

> . . . 'all that gave
> Promise of gladness, peril of a grave,
> In turn he tried
>
> (stanza 8).

22 May. Still at Parco

I have made a friend. He is twenty-seven years old, although he looks as though he were forty. He is a monk called Fra' Carmelo. We've been sitting half-way up the hill on which there is a Calvary with three crosses, near the cemetery above this village. Before us stretched Monreale in its wealth of gardens. The atmosphere was gloomy and we discussed the revolution. Fra' Carmelo was deeply moved.

He would like to join us and share our adventures, great soul that he is, but something holds him back.

'Why don't you come with us, we should all love it.'

'I can't.'

'Perhaps because you are a friar? We've already got one and still others fought side by side with us without fear of blood.'

'I should have come, if I were only sure that you were on some great mission, but I have spoken with many of your comrades and the only thing they could say to me was that you wish to unite Italy.'

'Certainly we do, to make one great people.'

'You mean, one territory; as far as the people are concerned, one or many, they are bound to suffer and they go on suffering and I have not heard that you want to make them happy.'

'Of course! The people will have liberty and education——'

'Is that all?' broke in the friar. 'Liberty is not bread, nor is education. Perhaps these things suffice for you Piedmontese but not for us here.'

'Well. What do you want then?'

'War! We want war, not war against the Bourbons only, but against all oppressors, great and small, who are not only to be found at court but in every city, in every hamlet.'

'Well, then, war also against you friars, for wherever I go I see you have convents and properties, houses and fields.'

'Yes, indeed. Also against us, first of all against us. But with the Bible in your hand and the cross before you—then I

should join you; your aims now are too limited. If I were Garibaldi I shouldn't find myself at this stage of the proceedings still supported almost only by you people who came with him.'

'What about the insurgent bands?'

'And who told you they don't expect something more than you're after?'

I really didn't know how to reply so I got up. He embraced me and, clinging to my hands, told me not to laugh at him, that he prayed to God for me, and that on the following morning he would say a Mass on my account. I felt a great surge of emotion in my heart and should like to have stayed with him, but he moved off, climbed the hill, turned once more to look back at me from above, and then disappeared.

*   *   *

It is evening now and it does not appear that the enemy knows what has become of us. There must have been a great confusion in the Bourbon camp, they've lost touch with us and nobody informs them where we've gone. This people deserves high praise; not one single informer has been found among them.

23 May. Above Parco. Afternoon

At last the enemy has discovered where we are, and during the night the Bourbon troops have drawn nearer. At dawn we were ordered to set off in all haste and we have clambered up here. From where we are, a good thrower could toss a stone on to the roofs of Parco. Half-way down the hill below us, we have the Calvary and the cemetery. I can see the stones on which Fra' Carmelo and I were sitting yesterday. That monk has disturbed me. I should like to see him again. We shall stop in camp here all today and perhaps also tomorrow. What are we waiting for? What does this circling round Palermo mean, as though we were moths round a lamp? The crags to the right and at the back of us are magnificent, the view in front indescribable. Whoever is born here cannot complain of being

poor, for even on a handful of greenstuff you can live well enough here, if you have eyes to see and a heart to feel.

* * *

A young gentleman has reached us from Palermo and from his appearance I should think he might be Colonel Carini's brother. Tall, blond, robust, just as the latter. His name is Narciso Cozzo. He came well-armed to join us, and has been enrolled in my company. He too speaks of a city impatient and ready to rise. If all the youths of Palermo feel as he does there is no doubt we shall triumph.

* * *

With the telescope you can pick out great detachments of soldiers camped outside the walls of Palermo. While watching them manoeuvre in that great silence below somebody said, 'But one day or the other won't they come up here and attack us?'

* * *

A column of Royal troops is cautiously advancing across the plain up to the first slopes of the mountain that lies to our right. It is separated from us only by the dry bed of a little torrent. From the topmost peak we could hear a piercing shriek of alarm and a great cloud of smoke rose black from the summit into the pure, warm air of sunset. We picked up our rifles. Far below at the edge of the plain we could hear firing.

A band of insurgents hidden among the rocks was opposing the Royalist troops who were attempting to reach the first slopes of the mountain. Garibaldi stood there for a short time watching, then he ordered Bixio with his company to go down as far as the cemetery below us, and ordered Carini to occupy the top of this hill which, he said, would be the centre of much fighting. We were all ready. The skirmish down below grew livelier. On the crag behind us that column of smoke still rose, but white and thin now.

All of a sudden the rifle fire died away and the column of

troops trying to dislodge the insurgents retreated through the fields. Then it disappeared into the thick groves of oranges and olives stretching as far as Palermo.

*   *   *

Night falls. On every peak of this immense semi-circle fires are blazing as far as Monte Pellegrino; so many indeed that it looks as though we are celebrating Midsummer Eve. And Palermo sees them and perhaps hopes that tonight is the last of its servitude.

24 May. Piana dei Greci

Here I am sitting at the gate of a convent like a beggar. The town looks as though it has been devastated by a plague. A few ragged people wander along the streets and beg for alms. Our camp is beyond the walls, but not in such a pleasant place as on previous occasions. I woke up this morning while everyone was getting up and, in that dawn light, it looked like the resurrection of the dead.

On the far horizon one could see a calm leaden sea. Palermo could hardly be made out against the dark mass of Monte Pellegrino. In front of us there was a white mist which stretched all the way from Palermo to Pioppo. When the sun rose at our backs it threw long shadows down the slope from our persons and everything seemed to palpitate and we exchanged our 'Good mornings'. After the fog had lifted, we could see a column of soldiers coming out from Monreale; a confident body of men who took the road to Pioppo. It occupied the whole length of the road and even when the vanguard had entered the woods to approach Parco the rest of the dark mass of men was still coming on.

This time they really will come for us, we said, and meanwhile our gunners began to construct emplacements, with all speed. Our companies were drawn up on the road. We waited in silence and seemed to hear the heavy tramp of that long column of men far away out of earshot. From below Parco we heard a burst of rifle fire. The Genoese Sharpshooters are

F

taking the first shock, but although everything seemed ready for us to stand fast in the place where we now are, after the General had swept by, accompanied by his staff and mounted Scouts, a whirlwind of galloping figures, we were ordered to follow them at the double.

For some way we ran as hard as we could, then slowed down and then ran on again. I saw many throw themselves to the ground, utterly blown, others sobbing with pain. Somebody said that the Bourbons had burnt Parco, beaten the Genoese Sharpshooters, and were after us with cavalry as fast as they could, and that they would soon be on us. It was also said that most of those troops were Bavarian mercenaries, drunken types who would stick at nothing. It was a sad retreat on our part, almost a rout.

The road from Parco here to the Piana dei Greci winds between steep mountains. We rushed along as quick as we could, to the point where the road no longer ascends but levels out and reveals the latter town in the bosom of the valley. Panting, hungry, scorched by the sun, we let our eyes rest in this peaceful valley, but at a certain point we saw three mounted Scouts blocking the road. When we got there they made us turn to the right up the gloomy mountainside before us. Other Scouts stationed on the heights shouted to spur us on that the General was in danger. We climbed as fast as possible towards the peak from whence we could hear a trumpet anxiously sounding the call to arms. We reached the top in fives and tens as well as we could. The General had been up there for some time. In front of us, on the top of another mountain, the one which overlooked our camp of yesterday, we could see lines of Neapolitan Sharpshooters firing against us and their bullets hissed round us like snakes. A few Genoese marksmen returned their fire, but our rifles were quite useless at such a range and we merely stood looking on. That game lasted perhaps for an hour, then the Neapolitans began to retire and they disappeared over the top of the mountain. We too then retreated by the same way we had come up, heartily wishing that Monte Campanaro would sink into the bowels of the earth as far as it rises high

and haughty into the air. It is said that the enemy general had
had the idea of crossing the two mountains hoping to occupy
Piana dei Greci before we arrived, so as to throw us back and
chase us all the way to Palermo. But Garibaldi forestalled him
with wonderful foresight. Now we think that he has given up
this idea and will follow us along the military road, the one
that we had taken in our precipitate retreat. I have heard that
some of our men were taken prisoner at Parco, among them
Carlo Mosto, brother of the Sharpshooters' commander. It
seems that he was also wounded, and we are afraid that all
prisoners will be shot.

Marineo, 25 May

The Piana dei Greci friars were most polite. They gave us
bread, cheese, wine, and cigars, as much as we wanted. And
they showed us round the convent and the chambers where
their dead are piled up along the walls, like people asleep or
praying, immersed in thoughts of another life. It was in those
gloomy surroundings that we heard the 'fall in' sounded and
we rushed back to camp. The companies were already drawn
up with artillery in the van. There were whispers in the ranks:
'The Royalists are coming, about 10,000 of them.' Evidently
our retreat had to continue. But where will it all end? Perhaps
at Corleone, where the road taken by the artillery eventually
leads. Discussing the possibilities, we started on the march as
the sun went down.

It was already almost night when, having left the military
road, we set off along narrow paths through woodland, silent,
subdued, full of melancholy thoughts. About ten o'clock we
were halted and ordered to lie down where we were. It was
forbidden to smoke, say a word, or move. I stretched out next
to Airenta, watching a great fire burning far off in the mountains, and the sight aroused memories of those fires that are lit
along my valleys on the eve of Saints' Days. Full of sweet
thoughts of home I fell asleep.

When I woke it was dawn. Companies were quietly falling
in. I learnt that during the night the Royalists, who are

pursuing us, passed along the military road quite near, watched by our sentries. They are going boldly ahead, quite certain of catching us, but in fact have us on their flank. Now we begin to understand yesterday's retreat and our spirits rise. I had the good fortune to get a billeting ticket. When I presented it the little old woman, who had to be my hostess, was trembling like a poplar leaf. In order not to scare her I retired resignedly. Then she grew sorry for me and, almost in tears, begged me to come into a miserable little room with only one chair and a bed fit for a dog. On the other side of a wooden partition I could hear a pig grunt.

'What are you trembling about?'

'Young gentleman, I have a little daughter.'

'Well, what of it, I have a mother and sisters too.'

'You have a mother and sisters, and where are they?'

'Oh, hundreds of miles away.'

'Poor souls!'

And she regained confidence and chattered away so much that I had to ask her to leave me alone. Just as I was about to throw myself on the pallet I heard a subdued whispering. I went to the door, curious to see the young girl. She was barely more than a child and I exclaimed resolutely to the mother, 'I'm certainly not going to sleep in that room.' So without another word I took my rifle and knapsack and cleared out.

*   *   *

Half naked and half clad in skins like a savage, pale, famished-looking, a poor lad stood and watched us with yearning eyes as we lined up outside the town. He was simply longing to come with us.

'What's your name?'

'Cicio.'

'What're you doing here?'

'I've come with you from Piana dei Greci.'

'Where are you going?'

'With you.'

'In this sorry state, and barefoot?'

Down he sat and made no reply. We found him something
to put on his feet and to cover himself. And so clothed he came
with us. He was so happy that he seemed another boy. And of
course he wanted a rifle! In half an hour he knew the whole
company by name.

'We'll teach you to read and write.'

'Oh! young sir, I'm not worthy.'

25 May. On the mountains of Gibilrossa

The name of Gibilrossa reminds me of Gilboa and casts a
veil of tragedy over all I see around me. I wish I had a Bible
so that I could read that passage where they pray that dew
may never more bathe the hills, the cursed hills, of Gilboa.

These gloomy thoughts are quite out of place, because our
fortunes are turning for the better and we should really bless
these heights. Nevertheless, it would be prudent not to linger
too long. We should either be all dried up by the sun or driven
mad. Our heads seem wrapped in bonnets of fire. Wherever
has the cool breeze of last night gone to? All of a sudden at
6 o'clock we left Marineo. The voices of shepherds could be
heard gathering their flocks up the mountainside.

We were outside the town waiting for the order to march.
When the General went by on horseback Captain Ciaccio
gave the order to present arms. The General made a gesture of
annoyance as though to show that this was no time for ceremony. We took the road down from Marineo into a deep
valley, moving slowly and quietly. A few of us were singing in
a subdued way. Only a man from Friuli, from the midst of the
7th Company, sang out loud, with a voice of silver, four verses
from a sorrowful, charming air that went straight to the heart:

> *La rosade da la sere*
> *Bagna el flor del sentiment,*
> *La rosade da Mattine*
> *Bagna el flor del pentiment.*[16]

[16] The dew of eve bathes the flower of sentiment, the dew of morn the
flower of repentance (literal translation).

I broke ranks and went ahead to try to find the singer,
thinking that it must be a certain Osterman from Gemona, a
friend of mine from last year. It was, however, a mathematics
student called Bertossi from Pordenone.

'Bertossi! Was he at San Martino in a Piedmontese regiment?'

'Yes,' replied the friend from whom I was inquiring.

'Well, he must be the man who was promoted officer on the
battlefield.'

'That's he. But say nothing about it, because if he knew he
would resent it.'

'And why?'

'Why? Because he's made that way.'

I looked at the young man, who is only twenty but looks
thirty on account of his dark full beard. I could hardly believe
that he was the singer he had such a severe look, but the verses
he had sung were not unworthy of him. What marvellous
young men there are in that 7th Company.

All of a sudden, some time after dark, the column halted.
We were at the lowest point of the valley and it was whispered
among us that the vanguard had met the enemy, but fortunately this was untrue, for if it had been so we should have been
annihilated. Once more on the march, we soon came out of the
tortuous windings of that fearful terrain and saw thousands of
lights before us on the heights. It was Missilmeri, all lit up at
that late hour to do us honour. We got there at midnight.
Every window of every house had a lamp shining in it, but very
few people were out in the streets. We had news of La Masa
and the force he had raised in these parts and it seemed that
we should have a quiet night. At dawn we had to fall in and
were told that in an hour's time we should have to take to the
mountains to reach the camp where we now are. I went in to
a miserable little hovel to drink a cup of coffee and there I
found Bixio in such a black mood that at the sight of him I
retreated. I went to the square where there was a water-seller
who went along swinging his little cask as though it were a
bell and selling drinks to our men who swarmed round his

barrel. He watched those who were drinking with such a look and with a laugh that seemed to suggest he would like to put poison in their glasses. I went off and met the youth that we brought with us from Marineo, who triumphantly offered me a bowl of milk. He offered it to me with trembling hands, so pleased he was to have found me again.

A trumpet call brought all our men running out from the houses from all directions. We started off on the march and arrived here. On our right I can see a great concourse of men swarming like ants; La Masa's bands. Looking round the landscape I can make out all the places we have been to since leaving the Passo di Renna. It looks nothing, but has cost us such labour! Over there is Marineo and its crag, which seen from here, seems more formidable than from near to. If it broke off from the mountain it would roll down on the town like a monster and disembowel it.

*　　　*　　　*

At last we learn that there is a world outside. For a fortnight we have been in a limbo and a little news is a god-send. Well, well, well; so the Government of Naples calls us filibusters! Their papers have reported that we were defeated at Calatafimi, that one of our leaders has been killed, that we have been scattered and are now pursued so that we cannot turn highwaymen and haunt the roads to murder travellers. We have learnt this news from some officers from the American and English ships anchored in the port of Palermo. A friendly visit that has done us all good! They first spoke with the General and then they wandered through our camp. What handshakes, so friendly and brotherly! One of these officers, a very young man with light blue eyes and the pink hands of a girl, rapidly sketched three or four of our men, including Colonel Carini. In his sketch-book I recognized the portrait of one of the insurgent leaders from Partinico, a figure suitable to sit as a model for Spartacus. The others mingled with us, exchanging news. They were obviously pleased to find us civil, educated people.

We loaded them with letters and notes, scribbled in pencil

on scraps of paper; greetings from the heart! These will be for-
warded by them to our families by the first boat out of Palermo.
They stayed an hour, and told us the city is like a barracks,
crammed with soldiers; but they have given us good hopes of
success. It is known they have brought the General a plan of
Palermo marked with the Royalist positions and the barricades. Now they've gone and the General is in consultation
with the Company Commanders.

*   *   *

We are no longer to wait at Castrogiovanni for reinforce-
ments from the mainland. In half an hour, just as we are, many
or few, we're off to Palermo. Bixio has told us: 'It's Palermo or
Hell now!'

Colonel Carini has addressed our company. He said that the
sun will rise tomorrow on our day of glory but he told us to
stand firm if charged by cavalry. Meanwhile all the other companies had gathered round their own captains. They broke up
with loud shouts of exultation.

*   *   *

31 May. In the Convent of San Nicola

The violent tempest we let loose on Palermo lasted three
days—more than three days! Those who missed the fight must
feel nearly mad with disappointment. We who were to go, left
Gibilrossa as happy as though we were off to a fair!

From the Porta Sant'Antonino I have looked back and seen
the mountain from which we descended on the night of the
26th and could more or less identify the spot where we halted
to wait for dark. It was a solemn pause. Gaiety had changed
to a mood of seriousness, as though a spirit from above had
breathed over us. I had lain down between two rocks still holding the great heat of the day, and felt a delicious warmth stealing through all my limbs. Stretched out in that kind of tomb
with my face turned to where the sun had set, I was seized with
a melancholy desire for death itself. Then, recalling that the

next day was Pentecost, I was filled with a childlike happiness
and a confused memory from my school-days came that the
Normans[17] had attacked Palermo on the eve of that very day.
I imagined them as gigantic figures in armour, gleaming
through the murk of antiquity, ready for the fray, a small
faithful band under good leaders just as we were.

A delicious half-hour of dreaming!

It was, I think, about seven in the evening when we set off
again. After nightfall we found ourselves clambering down in
single file from crag to crag, by a scarcely perceptible track.
Shortly before we had shouted 'Hell or Palermo!' and this
seemed the road all right! The sky was clear and all was quiet.
We were forbidden to utter a word. We felt hungry and at the
same time drowsy. If somebody stumbled he fell on the man
below and he on another, until there were eight or ten in a
heap. Luckily no one was hurt by our weapons. After midnight
we were down on the plain, only a few miles from the city.
Dogs barked at us from scattered hamlets and to the right we
could hear the sound of the sea. A few lights, fishermen's lamps
perhaps, were shining beyond dense groves of ancient olive
trees whose contorted boughs seemed to be writhing under
torture. To our left, on the heights of Monreale, fires were
burning. In the darkness ahead I could hear the heavy tramp
of the preceding company. 'Who will be in front?' we asked
each other, and we prayed they would be our best, most experienced men, so that they could fall on the enemy positions
and overwhelm them.

All of a sudden there was turmoil in ranks near me and a
shout of 'Cavalry!' and we heard the thud of hooves on gravel.
In spite of the warning given as we left camp some of us
panicked and in a flash we broke ranks and dashed into the
fields as best we could, some clambering over walls lining the
path, others sitting astride them. In the confusion shots were
fired at a white horse coming at us like a phantom. But it was
only Captain Bori's mount, poor beast, and the captain identified himself by shouting. The hubbub died down and we felt

[17] In 1071 the Normans under Roger I invaded Sicily.

ashamed at Colonel Carini's severe silence and blamed each other for, perhaps, having given ourselves away to the enemy.

The shooting increased the dogs' barking; there seemed no end of them, near and far.

We passed close to an enormous building, but the inmates were all asleep or it had been evacuated. A few steps farther and we reached the main road to Palermo. The air was growing chill at the approach of dawn.

Groups of houses were now more frequent and we could see scared-looking people peeping at us as we went by. We were ordered to split up into fours and keep to the right of the road, close to garden walls; then we quickened our pace. From the head of the column came a shot, then a desperate cry 'to arms!' A terrible yell, a sudden fusillade, a rush:

'Charge! Charge!' and we were in the fight.

We collided with a crowd of Sicilian insurgents, the so-called 'picciotti'. Some we bowled over into the gardens and some we carried along with us. One of them, a gentleman, their leader perhaps, was upbraiding them furiously, as he moved away shaking his sword; but at that instant he was hit, spun round, called out 'God!', took three or four steps like a drunken man and fell into the ditch at the foot of two tall poplars alongside a dead Neapolitan soldier, perhaps the first sentry surprised by our men. I see him yet. Just as I can still hear a Genoese who cried out in his dialect when the fire was hottest, 'How can we pass here?' He was answered by a bullet square in the forehead that toppled him over with a split skull.

We gained ground rapidly, but at the Ponte dell' Ammiraglio came up against almost savage resistance. On the road, on the arches, beneath them and in the surrounding gardens there was bloody bayonet fighting. Dawn broke and we saw that we all had something fierce in our looks. Once in possession of the bridge itself we were held up by heavy point-blank fire from behind a wall manned by a long line of infantry, whose crossed belts showed up white. I could see a wounded Neapolitan soldier dashing his head against the bridge wall to brain himself, but Airenta shot him out of pity and then with

that unshakeable calm of his, went on firing against the enemy line. Suddenly this vanished, enfiladed perhaps, while some cavalry charged our men on the left flank but were repulsed and fled into open country. Faustino Tanara, that pale, handsome, bold *Bersagliere* officer, came storming along from there with a handful of his men and we joined up with them, shoving forward and being shoved from behind, until we came to the cross-roads of the Termini Gate, swept by bursts of fire from a warship as well as from a barricade ahead of us. Some of the most daring had already got across in a wild rush under the eyes of Garibaldi, whom I saw on a horse, wonderfully cool and collected. Türr was next to him. Tuköry had fallen wounded shortly before, and I heard him say gently to two who wanted to carry him under cover 'On, on, on you go and see the enemy doesn't come to capture me here.' Nullo was already in the city with a handful of his Bergamasks, having leaped his powerful horse over the barricade among fleeing Royalists. The assault was also successful at Porta Sant'Antonino, but we were luckier, for with one dash we gained the Fieravecchia. Suddenly a bell began to peal hailed by our cries of joy, for it seemed like a promise fulfilled.

'But whatever are the Palermitans doing?' I asked a working man who popped out of a doorway armed with a dagger.

'Ah, young sir, three or four times the police let off guns and made an uproar in early morning hours with shouts of *Long live Italy! Long live Garibaldi!* Those who came out prepared were seized without mercy.'

'I see,' I said, 'the citizens fear another trick.'

In the company of this man we went through the narrow streets as far as Via Maqueda. There no one was to be seen, except a youth busy trampling underfoot the Royal arms torn down from the gateway of a palace. Gun-fire came from one end of the street, perhaps aimed at him. We entered another alley and what a sight met our eyes!

Three lovely girls in white, their lily hands clutching the grill of a broad low window above a gloomy arch, were gazing silently at us.

We stopped to stare in admiration.

'Who are you?'

'Italians. And you?'

'Nuns.'

'Poor things!'

'*Viva Santa Rosalìa!*'

'*Viva l'Italia!*'

And they too started crying '*Viva l'Italia!*' in sweet psalm-singing tones and then they wished us success in the battle. I shall always remember them as they were at that moment, like Fra Angelico angels. One of these days, if peace returns, I shall re-visit the convent and seek them out.

We reached Piazza Bologni and found it already occupied by about a hundred of our men. On the steps of a palace the General was interrogating a couple of prisoners, who were weeping like children.

'Do you want to go back to your own side? You can if you want to,' he said, and one of them started off, but the other stayed. The former hesitated a little and then, he too, decided to remain. They were young Calabrians, who seemed amazed that we had not torn them to pieces.

Hardly had Garibaldi seated himself in the entrance hall of the palace when a pistol shot rang out from within.

'They've assassinated him!' we yelled from the Piazza and crowded into the door. It was nothing! A pistol he carries at his belt had gone off and the ball had pierced the trousers above his ankle. We calmed down, and at that moment Bixio arrived.

I had seen him a short time before hurl himself at a man who, seeing him wounded, had begged him to retreat. Lucky for him that he found a door through which to save himself! Bixio was scarlet in the face; he grasped what was left of a broken sabre and planted himself in front of us: 'Now then!' he said, 'I want twenty volunteers, good ones—in half an hour we shall be dead, we're going to storm the Royal Palace.' He told off the twenty and they were already moving away when he was recalled by the General; he obeyed and entered the hall for

consultations. Inside there were already some Palermitan gentlemen and a priest.

The city was beginning to stir and one could hear a subdued clamour. All of a sudden there was an explosion from Castellamare and the first shell came roaring through the air and fell. The sky seemed filled with the sound of curses.

From that moment all the bells of the city began to peal. Shellfire continued at intervals of five minutes. The pauses were cruel and fraught with anxiety. About three in the afternoon citizens began pouring out into the streets, and we, who had been somewhat disheartened earlier, became more cheerful. Barricades now rose, as men and women worked with a will. A shell would fall and all threw themselves down, but once it had burst all started work again with a '*Viva Santa Rosalìa!*' So night came and the castle ceased fire. The Royalists were in occupation of the high quarters of the city and we of the rest. The General had his headquarters in the Palazzo Pretorio and municipal beadles in their scarlet liveries, young and old, busily ran errands for him. Meanwhile new bands of insurgents were entering the city all night through the Termini Gate. As for us, we prayed for the night to be long that we could get some rest and prepare for what was to come.

31 May. Continuation

Dawn came and the night hours had passed so quickly that they seemed minutes. The Royalist shells from Castellamare sounded our reveillé. They were systematically aimed at the Palazzo Pretorio in the hope, no doubt, of smashing General Headquarters. The shells, however, fell on the Convent of Saint Catharine at one corner of the square. The General stood at the foot of one of the statues of the large fountain facing the palace. There he received messages from the fighting fronts and from there he issued orders. Every now and then we caught a glimpse of him as we sped through the Piazza from one quarter of the city to the other, wherever needed.

At one such moment as Bozzani and I were crossing a little square we longed for a drink. 'Let's see if they'll give us a sip

of water in this house here,' I said, and knocked on a great door on which were written the words 'English House'. The door opened a crack and in the courtyard we saw a crowd of frightened people. We went in and a gentleman approached in doubt as to how to receive us. However, on hearing us speak, he immediately became polite, drew us in among the others and had water and wine brought us. We drank, thanked him, and made to go. But the whole crowd thronged round us, including ladies, old and young; they took us by the hand, they begged us to stop and protect them. Some wept with compassion for us. They wanted to know our names and we wrote them on scraps of paper. They marvelled that soldiers were able to write. They bombarded us with questions. 'What's happening in the city? Who's firing? How long will it last? *Santa Rosalìa*, how frightening it all is!'

'Please forgive my initial hesitation,' said the gentleman who had let us in, 'they told us you were all ferocious monsters, who drank babies' blood and cut old peoples throats . . . but you're civilized!'

At that we started to laugh. The women then asked us: 'Where is Garibaldi? Is he young? Is he handsome? How is he dressed?'

We answered in the midst of all that amiable hubbub while the lads handled our rifles and talked among themselves. Their faces lit up as they looked at us with envy. The old man, however, restrained them with a glance.

Out we went, promising to return. Hardly had we got outside when we saw a crowd at the door of a baker's shop. 'Why, it is the baker of *I Promessi Sposi*,'[18] I said to Bozzani. 'We'd better hurry before they sack it.' On reaching it, however, we saw there was no rioting; people were taking their loaves, paying for them, and making way for others. A gentleman told us that his family had eaten nothing since the previous day as they had been caught by the revolution without provisions in the house.

[18] The bread riots in Milan of 1628 were described by Manzoni in chapters XI–XIII of his novel *I Promessi Sposi* (The Betrothed).

He added: 'You arrived so suddenly!'

'Well, are you pleased?' I asked him.

'I should just think so; you are our liberators.'

Off we went, making for the Benedictine Monastery where our company was. We came across Captain Bori's horse lying dead under an arch-way, the same poor beast which had nearly been shot as we came down from Gibilrossa.

'Here's the horse, perhaps that's his master,' said Bozzani, approaching a corpse lying a little farther on. 'Oh, just look, it's the poor lad who was pushed into our midst by that old man on our first march out of Marsala.'

Yes, it must really have been the same boy. I had not seen him since that first day and felt indescribable horror on finding him lying there. I should like to have been transported to the old man's hut, conjured up by me at that moment far away in its peaceful solitude, and know if he had any sad presentiment.

'What's that?' said Bozzani, listening, and we went off at the double towards a sound of shrieking women. 'Spy! Spy! After the rat!' they were yelling. We arrived too late! Ten or twelve furies had torn an unfortunate policeman to pieces. They had been on the watch for him since the previous day and he had finally risked coming out, dressed as a woman. But they recognized him, seized him, and reduced him to a terrible condition that passes description.

We fled horrified, but were cheered immediately afterwards by having to escort some nuns from a blazing convent.

Terrified by the general upheaval and possibly too by the armed Sicilian insurgents, who were going about in a threatening manner, they were being escorted by a handful of our men to another convent. Walking in single file they pressed close to us confidingly and invested us with an odour of chastity. They kept expressing their thanks so warmly that they seemed to be treating us like old friends. One of them, a very pretty young creature, gave me a filigree reliquary containing a fragment of bone, gazing at me with soft tear-filled eyes, and telling me it was Saint Rosalìa's and urging me to wear it round my neck

as it would save me from death. I hadn't the heart to laugh at her faith in its powers of protection and put on the reliquary. Among the nuns were two ancient ladies who might have been made of parchment. They were quite fearless and looked at us disdainfully as they let themselves be carried like inanimate objects by a couple of Bergamask soldiers.

'Who are those two?' I asked of the little nun who had given me the reliquary.

'Two sisters, duchesses, who bully us the whole year long.' So we reached the convent.

In the confusion of getting the nuns into their refuge I got detached from Bozzani and went off by myself to the Benedictine monastery. In an attic above the church, lit by a little window facing the garden, I found a section of my company taking turns to fire through the opening. I joined the queue and fired my shot on getting to the window. When I looked out to see the enemy below Cavallini impatiently pulled me away in order to fire himself, but hardly had he taken aim when a bullet grazed the wall plaster and hit him in the right temple; he fell headlong without a groan, dead. He had embarked on the *Lombardo* at Porto Santo Stefano and was enrolled in my company. On the evening of 25 May at Missilmeri he told me how happy he was. A humble man of the people, he felt deeply the honour of taking part in our expedition. We covered his face with a cloth. For him everything was over, happiness, fatherland, all else, even our pity, for we were soon concentrating on footsteps heard on the roof over our heads. It might be Royalists, we thought, but it was only some Genoese Sharpshooters who had got up there to fire from a better position. Some swung down from the roof to the cornices of the façade and we heard them chatting gaily as they fired.

So the hours passed and night came, the second night! By command of the Dictator lights were lit in every window of every house, rich or poor.

In the streets it was as light as day. We were cheered by news spreading about the city from mouth to mouth: the Royalists,

it was said, had been pushed back at all points. The barricades that had sprung up in every street made it impossible for them to break back into the city. On the gutters of houses and on balconies were piles of stones, tiles, and household stuff of all kinds. The enemy could either burn down the city or else leave it free to us.

* * *

They say that on the morning of the 29th the Consular Corps had protested and that warships out in the Roads threatened to blow up Castellamare unless the barbarous bombardment of the city ceased. Just rumour! The castle continued to fire worse than ever and hundreds of houses were destroyed and innumerable inhabitants buried in the ruins. There will be much weeping after these feverish days. The Royalists have done things fit for savages. Towards eleven a.m. that day Margarita and I, in an alley leading to the Piazzetta della Nutrice, found the corpse of a fifteen-year-old girl. She was beautiful even in death, and never have I been so moved as by the sight of that corpse. She had been violated and her tender body wounded in many parts until a bayonet thrust through the neck must have freed her from her torments. We wonder if we could carry the body to safety, for her mother might be searching for her. We had just lifted her when yells from the enemy pouring from a breach in a neighbouring house and a burst of fire only thirty paces off forced us to retreat. They were many and we were only two. We fell back on Porta Montalto where Colonel Carini was on guard. That bastion had been taken by assault by Sirtori with a small detachment from the 6th and 7th Companies. There were so many enemy corpses lying round that I still wonder who it was that despatched them.

Carini sent me to the Palazzo Pretorio to fetch ammunition. There I found Sirtori. Ammunition must be short, for he ordered me to tell Carini that the bastion must be defended with the bayonet. There seemed an air of discouragement in the Palazzo Pretorio. I wondered what the news was. Yet the

G

city was now in full revolt and resolved for anything rather than see the enemy in possession again. I went back to Carini with empty hands, he understood and said nothing. Later he sent me back again. In Piazza Pretorio there was such a dense crowd that, in Manzoni's words, a grain of millet couldn't have fallen to the ground. From a balcony on the left, almost at the corner of Via Macqueda, the Dictator was just finishing a harangue, of which I caught the final words . . . 'The enemy has made me proposals that I have considered insulting to you all, People of Palermo, and as I know you to be ready to die, buried in the ruins of your city, I have refused them!'

I can find no words to describe the crowd's reaction to this. At the terrifying yell that broke out from the Piazza my hair stood on end and my skin went all goose-flesh. People kissed each other, embraced, almost suffocated in their passion. Women, even more than men, demonstrated their desperate readiness to face all dangers. 'Thank you, thank you!' they cried, stretching out their hands towards the General. From the end of the Piazza I, too, blew him a kiss. Such a radiant face had never, I believe, been seen before as on that balcony at that moment. The very soul of the people seemed transfused in him. But about ten that evening I saw him under the statue where he spent the night, and he looked gloomy and worried. Lieutenant Rovighi had called me up to carry a message. With his own hands the General placed a paper between barrel and ram-rod of my rifle and ordered me to have it read by all commanders I could find as far as Porta Montalto and, once there, deliver it to Colonel Carini. I set off feeling upset. Vigo Pelizzari was the first section-commander I found and I handed him the note. He read it, looked somewhat worried and gave it back to me, but he said nothing to his men crowding round him. On I went, burning to know what was in the note, but although there was nothing to stop me, I dared not read it. Finally when I delivered it to Colonel Carini he told me the contents—'800 Austrians are said to have landed, the tyrant's last hope. In case of attack by superior numbers retire

to the Palazzo Pretorio.' Carini did not look at all put out by
this news, but sent me back with an acknowledgement for the
order received. I retraced my steps, thinking that a handful
of foreigners could alter the fate both of the city and of ourselves. But on getting back to the Palazzo Pretorio I found the
General in a better mood. He was talking to Rovighi and saying he hoped to settle things by next day and that the Royalists
in the Palace were short of provisions and their communications cut with Castle and fleet.

I was overjoyed and, dead tired as I was, lay down not far
off with the picket-guard.

Yesterday about noon we at last got the order at Porta
Montalto to cease fire. I ran at once to the Palazzo Pretorio
where I learnt that an armistice of twenty-four hours had been
concluded, for the dead to be buried. It had only just been
signed when a priest arrived, I think the one who had joined
us in Piazza Bologni as long ago as the morning of the 27th.
He was shouting out 'treachery' and saying the Bavarians
were coming in by the Termini Gate: 'What Bavarians?' we
cried. 'Why, Bosco's men, returned from Corleone!'

Off we all rushed helter-skelter and reached the Termini
Gate just as they had surmounted a barricade. They stopped
on seeing someone coming to parley and firing ceased, but one
of their last shots hit Colonel Carini in the left arm near the
shoulder. He fell and was carried to the Palazzo Pretorio as
though in triumph.

Down at the end of the street in the midst of all those grim
foreign faces I caught sight of Colonel Bosco, angrily pacing
to and fro like a scorpion in a ring of fire. Oh if only he had
arrived half an hour earlier! He could have got straight in and
surprised us at Palazzo Pretorio with those troops of his,
maddened at pursuing will-of-the-wisps by forced marches
all the way to Corleone.

Luck has eluded this brilliant, bold, young Sicilian officer!

On the way back to Porta Montalto I went with Erba, by
way of Piazzetta della Nutrice, to see if we could find that
poor dead girl of the day before yesterday. She was no longer

there. While I was talking about her to Erba a pigeon settled on a gutter above our heads and fluffed out its feathers.

'Shall I have a shot?'

'Go on!'

Amazingly the pigeon fell like a rag—decapitated. 'Bravo!' we heard someone cry and saw five Neapolitan officers approaching us. 'Well, you are a good shot,' they said, shaking hands with Erba then with me, who was rather mortified by that lucky shot. But Erba said:

'Oh that's nothing, we shoot them on the wing!'

'In flight?' exclaimed the officers; 'then you really are Piedmontese *Bersaglieri*, are you?'

'What *Bersaglieri*?' we replied and, still under a hail of questions, let ourselves be led on by the five of them as far as the palace square. There we saw thousands of soldiers encamped. They were eating greenstuff like sheep by the handful and looked at us as though they would like to murder us. Had we not been so well escorted, not more than an ear apiece would have been left of us I believe. We went up to where a group of officers was standing among them. An old colonel received us courteously. He had a beard like cotton-wool glued to his chin, but was a fine figure of a man, ruddy and bronzed. He too tried to make us confess that we were Victor Emmanuel's regulars.

'Eh', said he, 'your king would be better advised to look to his own affairs. He won't always have the French to help him as last year.'

'If you'd been with us it would have been quite different,' said Erba quickly, 'we'd have driven the Austrians out of Venice too.'

'What's that?—Venice—Austrians?' exclaimed the Colonel, looking round, trying to conceal his annoyance but getting quite hot.

'And if we have another go at Austria as allies one year, you'll see——' The Colonel looked like a man losing his footing and searching round for something to hold on to.

'You'll see—you'll see you'll all be dead tomorrow,' he

broke off abruptly, 'you deserve a better fate, but you've forced your way into Palermo and Palermo will see you crushed.'

'So far though, we can only be pleased with Palermo.'

'Very well, go on being pleased.' Then seeing soldiers crowding round, and perhaps fearing for our safety, he made a move and had us escorted back.

31 May

Noon today was a solemn moment. We were ready. But the armistice was prolonged. Until dawn on 3 June we can rest, work, and make ready, and if we fail then, the city will have written a page of history to thrill the world which will be for the good of Italy.

*   *   *

The General has made a tour of the city, wherever a horse can go. People knelt in the streets, touched his stirrups, kissed his hands. I saw children held up towards him as before a Saint. He is well pleased. He has seen barricades as high as the first floor of houses; there are eight or ten of these every hundred metres. Now we can really say the whole population is on our side. An infinite multitude honours us, heeds us, and we feel warmed by their affection.

There is no longer any doubt! Simonetta is dead. We came across a *picciotto* wearing a red and white check shirt. 'Where did you get that shirt?' 'I took it off a corpse.' 'Where?' 'At the Benedictine Monastery.' 'Come with us.' A hole in the shirt proved that our poor friend had been shot through the heart. That splendid young man had died without one of us there to whom he could give his dying message.

We ran to the monastery and searched but found nothing. We could not even find out where he had been buried.

Many are missing from all companies and we don't know if they are dead or lying wounded in some house. Giuseppe Naccari, that tall young man with a face any artist would have loved to paint, the joy of my section on the march, fought to

the last without visiting his family here in Palermo. And they had been waiting so long for his return from exile! The day before yesterday he was struck by a bullet from below while firing from a belfry. It entered his side, passed behind his chest and came through a shoulder. He will die they say, and he has fallen at the very threshold of his home.

June 1860

Many of the Bavarian troops brought back into the city by Bosco have passed our way. They say that, on their march of 24 May, they were convinced of catching and finishing us off. On learning they had left us behind and we had entered Palermo, Bosco nearly went mad. He drove them here by forced marches, promising them they could fire and sack the city, paying no heed to those who fell exhausted by the way. 'Oh,' they say, 'if only we'd arrived in time!' and screw up their faces like cats licking their chops at sight of a dainty morsel. An ugly looking lot, these mercenaries! They are known as Bavarians, but are Swiss, Austrians, even Italians. They promise to fight against their comrades. Revolting boasters!

3 June, morning

Great joy! The ruined houses, the hundreds of citizens buried in debris are all forgotten! The Royal troops are evacuating; capitulation is as good as signed! We hug ourselves and stare about. Can we really have done so much? I seem to hear something like a pæan of triumph in the air, as when the waters of the Red Sea divided.

*   *   *

I have been back to that convent and got the nun who gave me the reliquary to come to the parlour-grating. On seeing me she seemed made of alabaster with an inner flame. She cried out and gave thanks to Santa Rosalìa. I made so bold as to lift my hand to the grille, our fingers touched, she cast down her eyes and we were both silent.

6 June

The ratings of the English Squadron here seem much friendlier than our own men from the Piedmontese ships *Governolo* and *Maria Adelaide*. When we go out boating in the evenings we come across French, Austrians, Spaniards, Russians, even Turks, who all stare at us dumbly with curiosity. But the English hail us, invite us to climb aboard and, when we do, welcome us like admirals. There's no bottle they don't open to share with us, no knick-knack they don't offer us, no corner of their ships they refuse to show us. We pass whole hours with them; whether we're good-looking or ill-looking they want to make pencil sketches of us, and before we leave we all have to sign our autographs. An idea comes to me; Sicily is lovely, rich, a world on its own. By our united efforts we have now detached it, or nearly so, from the mainland kingdom—if we don't succeed in making a united Italy, I wouldn't mind betting that it would be the English who would take possession of the island. Isn't their flag-ship here in port called *Hannibal*?

7 June

We were a merry party dining in the large room of the Hotel Trinacria to celebrate the arrival of a group of patriots who had come by fishing-boat from Malta. They landed at Scoglietti and by dint of hard riding and hard cash had come straight to Palermo. Champagne flowed and joy was unconfined. Joy on your account, gallant Lombard spirits!

9 June

Well, we watched them go! An endless column, horse, foot, baggage-wagons, filed before us down to the sea for embarkation. To us it seemed a dream, but what can it have seemed to them? Some were downcast, others haughty. The infantry of the 8th Battalion that was in action at Calatafimi and here in Palermo, where they had losses all over the city,

came proudly by. They must have been commanded by some brave man.

Off they go and may we meet again as friends. But it is a long road to Naples!

10 June

Tuköry is dead. Not out in the open, not in battle where we could see him. His soul has passed, but not to shouts of victory. He has died by inches, in bed. Death that he so often rode to meet at the gallop with sword in hand has crept to seek him. They had amputated a leg smashed by a bullet at Ponte dell' Ammiraglio. We might yet have had him on his horse with us, but gangrene set in and killed him. Goldberg, my old Hungarian sergeant, now lying in bed with two wounds received on the morning of the 27th, when told of Tuköry's death drew the sheet over his face and said no word. His *Loyos*, he used to call him. Thus sheeted, he too seemed a corpse. Perhaps he was thinking that when the Magyar exiles return to Hungary it will be without the fine wise cavalier who gave so much of himself on his way through the world. Or maybe he pictured him when serving with the Sultan's Arabs against the rebel Druse, galloping across Armenia. Or maybe he regretted his sword was ever drawn on the side of a tyrant. But whatever his regrets, he washed them away in Russian blood when, from the bastions of Kars, he could wreak his hatred against a people who had joined with Austria to ruin his country. . . .

11 June

By the same route as we followed from Marsala to Pioppo and then direct, sixty young men under command of Carmelo Agnetta have reached Palermo. They made the voyage from Genoa to Marsala in a nut-shell called the *Utile*, crammed like negro slaves. What a relief it must have been for them to land at Marsala after such an agonizing journey! What a sensation to pass the field of Calatafimi! They must have thought of our fallen and felt sad at not having known them in life. And on

getting here and seeing Palermo half in ruins, they must have felt their anger rise and gesticulated towards the foe and sworn to get even. . . .

They have brought us some two thousand rifles, good and bad, ammunition, and their own brave hearts. Among them is my friend Odoardo Fenoglio from Oderzo in Venetia, a resplendent officer of the Pavia Brigade whom I met and embraced at the cross-roads in the centre of Palermo; there is Cavalieri, there is Frigerio, brave, civilized men come in time to pay their respects to the remains of Tuköry, who is to be buried today.

* * *

We were all there, all of us, even such of the wounded who could leave their houses and hospitals. At the head of the cortège of mourners came Türr, an ironside, not made to show sorrow but so dejected that he seemed on his way to his own death. Flowers were thrown from windows on to the bier and on to us. From them and from laurel wreaths came a sweet odour of death. This impression was heightened by the silence of the crowd and the attitude of weeping women, dressed in white, kneeling on balconies. Everything, the very stones even, seemed to share a sense of consternation. I saw some of our men, tough, experienced types, pace forward with pale scared faces. Rodi and Bori, two scarred veterans, seemed to be walking in their sleep. Maestri, who lost an arm at Novara and from there hastened to Rome where a French shell-splinter shattered the stump, my poor Maestri from Spotorno, simple and brave like all from our Ligurian shore, he too was weeping. And so was I. At one moment of intense emotion I prayed with a bitter longing, never before experienced, to be enclosed in that coffin, side by side with the corpse. Oh to be there on the bier, yet be aware of this slow procession, of streets, of windows thronged with people, following the cortège as far as possible with their eyes and then pursuing it in thoughts! The crowd divides; voices are heard now—what do they say?—things fall—flowers?

The funeral march now sounds loud and must penetrate
the coffin. Shrill notes of trumpets and wailing of flutes seem
to turn to tears. Down, down, it goes into darkness, into the
earth, to the sound of human weeping transformed into music.
And as soil covers the newly dead, soil itself but dust of those
who died before, one is aware of the *lacrimae rerum*.

A bare week ago Adolfo Azzi died too. How boldly he stood
there on the *Lombardo* as we approached land, his powerful
arms on the tiller, his eyes fixed on Bixio whose ardent gaze
now took in Marsala close at hand, now the dark shapes of the
ships pursuing us like lionesses over the desert. I see him yet
and I shall see him as long as I live, with his calm face and
challenging air, with his broad shoulders, standing erect
stripped to the waist, a chest fit to receive a hero's wound.
Yet death came by a bullet through his thigh, a splintered ball,
and within five days poor Azzi was dead.

Night

Not during the restless nights of battle, but now when we
have a measure of tranquillity, as I think over scenes at the
barricades sadness overcomes me. I remember one March
evening of my childhood when we little ones were listening to
our mother telling stories as we clustered round the fire
crackling merrily as though itself one of the family. Suddenly
a bell tolled from the belfry; the *De Profundis*. Mother made us
pray for the departed. But single tolls now changed to double,
which in our parts mean that former dead of earlier years are
to be commemorated on the morrow. Mother raised her
beautiful eyes as though in thought, striving to remember who
was to be commemorated; we kept quiet, waiting for the
story to begin again. Suddenly father came in and sat down
sadly by the fire.

'What's the matter?' asked mother.

'Nothing.'

'But they've just tolled the bell; who for?'

'For those who died at the barricades of Milan.'

I trembled as I looked at my father. *Dead, Barricades, Milan;*

three words from another world that struck chill into my heart.
I was only nine years old. That night I couldn't sleep. Ever
since, I have treasured a store of sadness in my heart, a draught
which, as I grew older, I sometimes quaffed, this I could
never find words to express until I found it echoed in Giusti's
poem, *Sant' Ambrogio*, in those words: *Sgomento di lontano
esiglio* . . .[1]

12 June

I had said to Airenta: 'My dear Jerry, one of these fine
nights you will be found murdered in some alley.'

Jerry blushed to the roots of his hair and nearly grew angry.
Gradually, however, he opened up and told me that on our
first morning in Palermo when we lost each other in the
Fieravecchia he and a man of Cairoli company had been
ordered by Bixio to enter a house and get those inside to throw
things down to others below making a road-block.

'They must have been suddenly wakened by our shouts,'
said Jerry, 'for they were rushing about like madmen, weeping
and crying out: "Take what you want! Only spare our lives!
Who are you?" "Garibaldi's men." Then they all started to
help us, men and women alike, and they threw out everything
that came to hand; they would have thrown themselves down
as well as their goods! We entered a room where there were
two young girls. In a flash we seized the mattresses, hardly
noticing they were still warm, the girls having just scrambled
out. We paid them scant attention and they hardly troubled
to cover themselves, but started to help us fling the stuff out,
crying *Santa Rosalìa!* and *Viva L'Italia!* I pulled my comrade
downstairs, but when I got to the street looked up. There they
were, hanging out of the window, clapping their hands for the
revolution, quite transfigured by hair flying loose over bare

---

[1] A reference to a well-known poem by the Tuscan poet Giuseppe Giusti
in which his customary humour is blended with compassion for his fellow
men, even for the Croat mercenaries in the service of Austria. The words
quoted 'Fear of distant exile' express homesickness and, in the context of
the poem, childhood memories.

shoulders. . . . I took note of the house . . . I've been back; they remembered me . . .'

Poor Jerry! I too have seen the girls and he's in love with one of them. Though I've said nothing, if I were he I'd take back this sixteen-year-old daughter-in-law to that saintly mother of his, about whom he talked so often in our nightly bivouacs that I could imagine her in her lonely country house with its towers, half-buried in green woods beyond Genoa. And to tease my bride I would often ask her later if she had not been scared that particular morning. She would blush and lay her head on my shoulder then and I would kiss her hair and bless the memory of our first chaste, heroic, meeting.

In the Convent of the Trinity. 13 June

By the witches of Macbeth whatever have I seen! Crossing the portico of this building in the semi-dark, I tripped over something; startled, I groped with my arms to keep my balance and all but smashed my head against the wall. Then I spun round and saw a hand, a horrid black hand, protruding from the earth. It seemed to be moving in a threatening way. I called for help and we began to excavate. Three Neapolitan infantry-men, still half dressed in blue uniforms, had been bundled into a shallow grave. . . . So far I have put up with everything, but when the face of one of those corpses was revealed I fled. It is well to cover the faces of the recent dead.

On the way back from Monreale. 14 June

How superb life must have been when the Saracens, the Normans, and then those other high venturers who bore the Swabian eagle on their wrists came here to graft the native Sicilian stock.[2]

Let your imagination run free, go back in time and adopt what rôle you please—warrior, poet, or churchman and come on to the stage. Here before us is the famous cathedral. But

---

[2] A brief indication of the three great Epochs of Sicilian history, the Saracen (or Arab) in the 9th and 10th, the Norman in the 11th and 12th, and the Swabian (or Hohenstaufen) in the 13th centuries.

with the best will in the world we can't attune ourselves to the
spirit of such a place of worship as this. One of us said: 'Here
we should really remove our shoes.' He was expressing his
awe. Another, after gazing for some time at the columns and
great mosaic in the apse, fell on his knees and, still staring up
at the vaulting, clasped his hands with arms raised to form an
arch above his head. The gesture was a prayer.

One leaves, apparently inspired. But no! The tip of the
devil's tail must intrude, as the saying goes! Hardly had we
come out when we nearly started a brawl.

Our doctor, Benedini from Mantua, had been grumbling
all the way about coming to Monreale, at a rumour he'd
heard that we wanted to appropriate Sicily for ourselves and
that the bells should be rung to rouse the people against us.

We told him to keep quiet and it was just a joke, not dreaming what he was hatching. In church, however, he had become
angrier and angrier, and, when we came out, went up to the
first man he saw whose appearance he didn't fancy and
shouted out: 'So you're the one who wants to start another
Sicilian Vespers, are you?'

The man, who though no simpleton, only half understood
the question, seemed about to answer 'yes'. So Benedini
started hitting him. What a business! Had a priest not inter-
vened in time, there'd have been trouble!

We pitched into Benedini as we came away, but he was now
calm, as one who had done his duty.

Convent of the Trinity. 15 June

I have paid a visit to Colonel Carini in his little room high
up in the Hotel Trinacria. Whatever has happened to that
robust physique? He held my hand and inquired after Garibaldi, the Company, and his friends. Then suddenly: 'Were
you present at Tuköry's funeral?' 'Yes, Colonel.' He looked
round and held my hand tight. His two boys never leave his
side. They are the image of their father, especially in eyes, now
bright with suppressed tears as they heard him ask me if I had
been at Tuköry's funeral. When he went into exile in '49

these sons of his can hardly have been more than babies. They came from Messina aching to embrace him and share his triumph, and have found him incapacitated by that accursed Bavarian bullet.

A lady, marked by suffering, moves slowly and sadly through the room. When her eyes meet her husband's she stifles a sob lest he notice it. Obviously he is very down. What tragedies, what mourning, what bereavements there are on every hand.

I left, much affected. As a contrast, up dashed that little grig of a boy, Ragusa's son, who is always running after us as merry and lively as can be. The father, who runs the hotel on the grand scale, kept open house for us during the bombardment. Any of us who wanted could go in for refreshment. There were, however, other things to do, and few could avail themselves of the opportunity. Some did, though, and I know one who gormandized like Margutte in Pulci's *Morgante*.[3]

*   *   *

Gusmaroli, an old Mantuan priest, is a small, thick-set, stooping figure who walks like a sailor. He has flowing white locks and copies the cut of Garibaldi's beard. He gives one an idea of what Garibaldi himself will look like in twenty years' time. I've studied him and it really is so. He is aware of the slight resemblance and revels in it; during the three days' battle he went round playing the part, and when he appeared at the barricades the Sicilian volunteers cheered for Garibaldi and fought and died willingly beneath his eyes.

16 June

Ippolito Nievo always walks by himself, looking into the distance, as though to broaden the horizon before him. Those who know him catch the notion of looking too, to see if they can capture some shape or glimpse of the landscape of his imagination. His usual companions are from the Scouts:

[3] Margutte was a huge glutton in Luigi Pulci's poem *Il Morgante*. Pulci was a Florentine (1432–1484).

Missori, Nullo, Zasio, Tranquillini. Today I saw him with Manci, whose eyes are as blue as the lakes of his native Tyrol. When I come across any of these Scouts, now in smart Hungarian-style uniforms, already rendered illustrious in '49 at Rome by Masina's cavalry, I feel like saying: 'Would any of you take me pillion when you charge across the battlefield?' I should like to feel my heart beat in unison with, I think, Manci, a hero not yet celebrated in any poem. He is neither Virgil's Eurialus nor Ariosto's Medoro, nor do I see him as a modern; he has some knightly quality of days to come. If one were a woman one would fall in love with him and were love unreturned, die for him.

I often see him with Damiani whom, if I were a sculptor, I'd like to cast in bronze, he and his horse together, rearing over a confused mass of heads and arms as I saw him when he snatched up our banner at Calatafimi. During the second day of the bombardment of Palermo, I caught sight of him leaning against a side pillar of the main gate of the Serra di Falco Palace in Piazza Pretorio, perhaps as Garibaldi's orderly, for his saddled horse was stamping beneath the portico. He had the same expression I saw at Calatafimi. He was talking to himself as I passed. He seemed to be watching, first the palace where Garibaldi was, then St. Catherine's Convent where shells were falling and which was ablaze through the roof. Perhaps he was wondering how to save Garibaldi should one of those monsters pitch a little nearer.

17 June

Every day I have been to visit that divine little nun in her tomb-like fortress of piety. 'When will you come again?' she always repeats in her musical voice. For some time the old nun chaperoning our interviews must have guessed me to be no relation, but she said nothing and seemed to enjoy the situation.

Today I went on purpose to say good-bye, but couldn't do it. Poor Sister! . . . She must have guessed this was farewell from the expression in my eyes, for she looked at me in such a

way that my arms throbbed with longing to seize the bars
and smash them so that I could say to that poor soul: 'Oh
leave this gloom and live!' She drew near, her face was close
to the grille; I kissed the cold metal, we both kissed it and I
drank in her breath.

Away I came and as I marched on in the dust under the
burning sun to unknown destinations, my fancy conjured up a
vision of a red shirt and white veils. And meanwhile she is
shut in there waiting for me to come tomorrow, tomorrow,
and tomorrow!

*   *   *

Patriots, patriots
We conquer or die!
Fire, fire, fire!

Singing such popular songs and strumming instruments, the
Palermitans, rich and poor, are thronging with wild enthusiasm to throw down the walls of Castellamare. Some wield
huge iron bars, and ladies of the high nobility carry little
hammers for pulverising lumps of mortar. After several days
and nights of work the castle is now demolished.

It lies flat like a giant of a heroi-comic poem, its belly split
open for all dogs that pass to sniff at and cock their legs
against.

*   *   *

What a card Giusti is, that volunteer from Asti. While we
were all snoozing during the noon-day heat in he marched
with his mask-like face, stood in the middle of our dormitory
of forty beds, and cried out, 'Boys!' Up we all sat, thinking it
was the Colonel. 'I've just had news from Piedmont! Victor
Emmanuel has founded the Order of Disembarkation and
has made you all *Cavalieri*.' A burst of laughter followed. He
went on: 'Silence! Each of us is to be given one of those estates
we saw on our march. . . . I can't promise to accept mine, but
His Majesty's intention is not displeasing to me. Bye-bye.'

H

He fled, flapping his feet like a clown, pursued by a storm of yells, and was still guffawing in the street.

But Giusti is no fool, and I wouldn't mind betting he meant to touch one or other of us on the raw.

Palermo, 17 June

I've not yet seen them, but I know that some days ago six or seven of Pisacane's men, who had escaped the Sapri massacre, arrived here from Favignana. When we sailed past the Ægades, those islands which seemed to spring up from the sea to welcome us, they were there in dungeons below water level. What a quiver of joy they must have felt, if, by one of those mysterious premonitions that sometimes come like flashes from somewhere beyond human experience, they guessed that out beyond the surges beating and foaming at their prison bars, Garibaldi and Liberty were sailing by.

Oh precursors, what tears we shed, what things we imagined after your disaster! Sapri, a name lovelier, more renowned, than our own Marsala. Only three years ago! It seems an age! Far away in the Alps we cast our thoughts longingly southwards. This land of the Two Sicilies called to us with the magic of its name, its seas, its skies, and the verses of the girl-gleaner who in the poem followed the corn-coloured hair and blue eyes of the hero Pisacane. The Bandiera brothers, Conradin, Manfred, and then Pisacane, yet another blond hero of courteous aspect. And now here is Garibaldi, as fair and as fine as any of them, but the only one of them all favoured by fortune.[4]

Dark Sicilian girls, ignorant of all beyond their island and of the world opened to them by Garibaldi, worship him. I'm told

[4] Abba here lists those who came to a tragic end in southern Italy, both ancient and modern. First Pisacane (see note 3, p. 6), then the Bandiera Brothers who invaded Calabria unsuccessfully in the year 1844; Conradin, son of the Emperor Conrad IV, who was defeated by Charles of Anjou (1269) and executed; Manfred, son of the Emperor Frederic II, who was killed in battle at Benevento (1266). Influenced by Dante (*Purgatorio* III, v. 102–144), where Manfred is described as: '*Biondo . . . e bello e di gentile aspetto.*' Abba tells us that all these were of fair complexion, as indeed was Garibaldi.

they whispered together in groups after he had ridden through the city, their eyes flashing in adoration like so many Saint Theresas.

*   *   *

Antonio Semenza says that they have found among the papers of the Royal Palace a fleet order issued in Naples, with instructions as to what to do if they intercepted us. 'Send them to the bottom, saving appearances.' Can it be true?

We certainly should have been too many for gallows or prisons! But were there in the Neapolitan navy men prepared to obey such an order, men ready to wipe us out?

18 June

There is a certain man I have noticed admiringly ever since Marsala. He has a wrinkled hatchet face, fresh complexion, and eyes and gestures of a hawk. With his mixture of brown and grey hair, he might be any age. Whoever can he be? How old is he, with his athlete's frame and spare body? Maybe, I thought, someone like Nullo's uncle or elder brother. But today I inquired. I record it so as not to forget; he is Alessandro Fasola from Novara and is over sixty. He has spent the forty years since 1821, working, hoping, and fighting. Always ready for the call, from Santorre Santarosa[5] or from Garibaldi, ever youthful, bold, and dependable.

*   *   *

The Genoese Sharpshooters have come out in new uniforms. How smart they are in their light blue tunics and caps of the same colour setting off their refined faces! I'm not sure if the general effect is added to or diminished by this tan from the burning Sicilian suns.

Everyone would like to join the Sharpshooters, but not all are Genoese. Well, it's understandable! There exists a certain

[5] Santorre Santarosa (1783–1825); one of the leaders of the Piedmontese revolution of 1821. He later came to England and died at Sfacteria fighting for Greek independence.

aristocracy of courage and these men rightly appreciate the the fact and wish to be on their own. Have I not myself heard one of my own company, and not one of the best, say that Garibaldi should keep apart those who landed at Marsala and send us on and on and on, as long as one man was left alive?

19 June

We are off, and not under Garibaldi's command! Of course everything depends on him, the revolution, the war, and much more—including the demagogues—so he must stay here.

To help him he has Francesco Crispi, a little man who puts me in mind of the powerful Pier delle Vigne.[6] But even though far from Garibaldi we shall still be with him. 'Go in good spirits, boys,' he said. 'I've given you Türr. If I need you he'll bring you flying back.' Then he began talking Genoese dialect with some of us from Liguria, seeming to take a childish pleasure in the language of Bixio and the Sharpshooters.

21 June

Medici has arrived with a regiment already organized and equipped. They came in by Porta Nuova under a rain of flowers. The vanguard was composed of forty officers in the uniform of the Piedmontese army.

My brigade, led by Türr, has left for the interior of the island. We of the original expedition are lost in the flood of newcomers, but treasure the memory of the twenty-five days when we toiled and fought in faith, alone. Now we are to go through the island, recruiting men and passing like pilgrims from place to place, until the enemy stops us and we come to blows and blood once more or unite for the honour of Italy.

[6] Francesco Crispi, the statesman (for whom see Trevelyan, *Garibaldi and the Thousand, passim*) is compared to Frederick II's great chancellor Pier delle Vigne immortalized by Dante (*Inferno* XIII).

From Palermo to Missilmeri, 22 June

Romeo Turola, who is dozing, and I, who am writing in my diary, are riding in a princely carriage drawn by two powerful greys which would look well under a couple of dragoons. Once again I have seen Porta Sant'Antonino and the Convent and that wall which, at dawn on 27 May, thundered and lightninged like a storm cloud as we advanced. The two tall poplars, at the foot of one of which I had seen that first dead Neapolitan soldier, rustled all their leaves with an almost conscious whisper of happiness.

As we passed beneath them I thought with horror of the dead man and of some poor peasant mother from the mountains of Calabria or Abruzzi standing at the door of her cottage, filled with anxiety at the thought of war and of her soldier son whom she still perhaps believes fighting. And the thought occurred to me of the Bourbon princes, of whom not one has so far drawn his sword.

I turn to look back. Palermo is far below, just as we saw it from Gibilrossa, from Parco, and from the Passo di Renna but now free in its glory, rejoicing day and night amid its ruined houses. As we left I heard that certain intriguers had arrived in the city to try and upset things. Perhaps they had been there soon after the capitulation? What can have been on, for instance, that night when we were hurriedly assembled and kept under arms for hours in Via Macqueda? Rovighi told me that a popular rising was planned to set up La Masa, snatch power from Garibaldi and replace him by the Sicilian. It was calumny, but why?

Missilmeri, 22 June

The population here, who had illuminated the village in our honour on the night of 20 May when we were few and had little hope of success, now turn their backs on us. Whatever have we done to offend them? They won't say, and we can't guess. They smile as they speak, are gay, converse with us, but they communicate with each other by scarcely

perceptible signs. They seem to have several souls in their bodies.

* * *

Fra' Pantaleo has put his finger on it. They are hostile because of the conscription decreed by Garibaldi as Dictator.

'What do you expect?' said the friar in church. 'Conscription is necessary, but it's something easily avoided. Fathers and mothers, get your sons to go as volunteers for the nation's sake and they won't be conscripted. And if you don't want to deprive the aged of support, or wives of husbands—here's another way: enrol as National Guards! No more talk of conscription then!' Down from the pulpit came the wonder-worker, made a great sign of the cross with a sweep of his arm, and the people, now satisfied, showered blessings on his head.

* * *

Now we are really beginning to look like soldiers. The group of officers I have just seen in the square would do honour to the finest army in the world. All in the prime of life, between twenty and thirty, robustly built, with frank open faces and courage in their looks. They are doctors, engineers, lawyers, artists. Suppose they'd all been like Daniele Piccinini? What a wrench it must have been when he left his father. I can imagine the austere old man at the gate of his Pradalunga, staring after his son who has turned away and is striding down towards Bergamo with the gait of a Greek mountaineer. Unspoilt by vice or idleness, he bears the story of his youth on his brow. His only recreation has been climbing and hunting in the mountains. During the battle of Calatafimi he was seen to cover Garibaldi with his cloak so that the General's red shirt should not form a mark for the enemy's rifle-fire. At a doubtful moment of the battle he encouraged those around with inspired words.

Missilmeri, 23 June

General Türr's wound has opened again and he has spat blood. Ever since we entered Palermo this man has worn him-

self to a shadow. His Brigade is very sad because they fear that he will have to leave us. I saw him for an instant, pale, his eyes blue-ringed, his lips bloodless, his chest sunken. Can he really be that second-lieutenant of the Hungarian company who passed through my village in '49 after the battle of Novara? I remember them as though I had them before my eyes now. There were about a hundred tall young men with a great tricolour flag. They were half hidden in the dust that rose from the road, hot under the March sun. '*Elien! Elien!*' they cried when they got to the bridge, as people came out to meet them. The second-lieutenant seemed happy in the midst of his men, but I felt a pang as I heard my father say: 'They are Hungarians, and suffer under the Austrians!'

Villafrati, 24 June

They rode proudly past, mounted on black stallions with glittering eyes and flowing manes. They hardly gave us a glance, but held their heads high. Guns were slung over their shoulders, they had pistols and daggers at their belts and ribbons on their hats and harness. I seemed to have seen their leader somewhere before. The villagers chatting with us seemed uncertain whether to greet or ignore them, but I noticed one gave them a wink, another exchanged signs with them; a flexion of the brow, cheek, chin—devilment that serves for their secret communications. 'Who are those seven men?' I asked a gentleman standing by. 'Oh, patriots, sir, didn't you notice, their tricolour favours?' Another glanced at him with a quick frown. Meanwhile the seven horsemen had reached the edge of the village and set off at a steady trot.

Suddenly a lieutenant came out from General Türr's headquarters and spurred to overtake them. He soon brought them back. We noticed their mocking, self-possessed, haughty, air. The lieutenant had put his pistol to their leader's temple ready to shoot if they disobeyed. . . .

We crowded into the house where there was great hubbub. We could hear General Türr's voice raised in anger as he uttered the name 'Santo Mele'. 'Santo Mele?' I said. 'Why,

he's the brigand we had in irons at the Passo di Renna and who managed to escape. He's a blood-thirsty murderer and thief!'

At this the gentleman who had spoken up for the seven slid off without so much as a 'by your leave'.

We heard whispering. A summary Council of War! Major Spangano appeared and is to preside over the Council. He is an elderly man with hair and beard already grizzled; he served as an officer during the defence of Venice.

Villafrati, 26 June

Bassini's battalion has gone off in a hurry. They are hastening to Prizzi, a village near at hand, where people have started to murder and rob as though there were no authority left. Fra' Carmelo knew what he was talking about when he spoke to us at Parco.

'Down in the plain', he said, 'there are great riches, but enjoyed by few and badly distributed; but these poor people up here have to beg for bread. Bread, bread, they cry and I have never heard the like.'

Bassini has marched off, but not so willingly as when he scents danger. This gay grumbler, tough, without frills, has a kind heart that shows in his good-humoured crusty countenance. He's always wagging his cropped grey head, nobbly as a club to beat the enemy with. He must be at least fifty, yet he's younger than any of us, and at Calatafimi held his company together as though at a party. His officers, all Lombard gentlemen, look up to him as to a father. If he finds, on getting to Prizzi that he needs to evoke the law, he has qualified lawyers by the dozen in his battalion; if he needs to make a speech, he can call on plenty of men-of-letters to help him: but he's sharp and to the point, he'll do the talking with his sword! Anyone guilty there had better look out!

Villafrati, 26 June

Not one person has been found willing to tell the truth. The evidence given before the Council of War that told most against Santo Mele was his own.

'I a brigand, Your Excellency? I have simply been fighting against those on the Bourbon side, burnt down the houses of Royalists, executed spies and police. Since early April I have served the revolution. Here are my testimonials!'

Saying this he threw down a bundle of documents, all stamped by the municipal authorities of the places where he had been. They praise him to the skies as though he were a Garibaldi. But the Council did not set him free. His murderous reputation is well-known and when he is taken to Palermo someone will see that he gets a bullet in his skull.[7]

Villafrati, 27 June

Colonel Eber has arrived. He looks half soldier, half poet. They say that he is Hungarian and he came out of Palermo on 26 May to see Garibaldi, then insisted on accompanying us back on that glorious, terrible, day of the 27th. He is a famous traveller and has visited all parts of Asia as *Times* correspondent. Now he is to be our commander, as Türr is at the end of his tether and is leaving as an invalid.

Rocca Palomba, 28 June

What a delicious place for a vigil it is at the foot of this fairy castle. Tired out after an eight-hour march, the men lay sleeping in the fields, so silent that I seemed to be alone.

How is it that this countryside is so deserted? We go for hours without seeing a house. As for peasants, there aren't any! Those who till the fields live in villages as large as our towns. Their houses are dens piled one on another and they sleep there together with their donkeys and other less respectable animals. What a stench and what depravity! At dawn they trudge off to their remote fields and there is hardly time to set to work before they have to return. Poor people! What a life!

Rocca Palomba is similar to all the other villages, but seen from a distance it looks much more promising as it nestles on

[7] Santo Mele, the brigand, later came before another court in Palermo and was executed.

the mountainside, half hidden in almond orchards, with its gently graded road winding upwards. We found the inhabitants *en fête*. They had sent out a party of horsemen to meet us who advanced waving flags, shouting and calling out 'Welcome, brothers!' They looked like people from the Middle Ages preserved for this very purpose of greeting us. These gentlemen did the honours of the place with such polish that they hardly seemed like people used to a secluded life. But civilized manners are innate. Its always the same story, however; if one village welcomes us, the next seems resentful, the one after that friendly. Here we found priests and town authorities at the gate; the band played, bonfires blazed on the heights and the gentry competed in entertaining our officers, while the soldiers had bread, cheese, wine, kisses, anything they wanted.

Somehow or other I always get billeted on priests! This one wanted me to touch the Bible, but I opened it instead, read a couple of verses and translated them straight from the Latin. Thereupon the priest threw his arms around my neck and called in all the household to meet the great Christian he had in his house. I supped with them. There were women, girls, children, old men, youths, a whole tribe. It was like Christmas and I could hardly get away to my room. What a charming little room it is, with its bed as white as lilies. And I, poor sinner, do I dare get into the purity of these sheets?

Bassini has joined us with his battalion; he, his officers, and men are quite ashamed, for at Prizzi they had a princely welcome. There were illuminations, banquets, dances, and pretty girls who greeted them from afar with cries of 'Bless you! Bless you!'

Alia, 29 June

It was only a short march from Rocca Palomba to Alia, through a fertile countryside that stretches from the plain up to the hills all golden with corn, which seemed to bow in the wind as though in homage to our red-clad column.

30 June, 4 a.m.

We're off again and this time have a long march before us and the day promises to be scorching hot. Up and down the dirty streets go the soldiers, but only a few of the citizens are to be seen at the windows, half dressed and quite indifferent to what is going on. Two priests go past on their way to church and they bid us farewell. Ah, the trumpet call! I wonder who composed that fine call to arms of the Piedmontese *Bersaglieri*. Certainly a musician with a gay, bold, nature, for it strikes such a bracing note. Perhaps it was written by Colonel Lamarmora himself. It shakes off sleep and sloth and sets one's nerves a-tingle for action. The Austrians have often heard it, and the Russians in the Crimea, and now we have brought it to the old island of Victor Amedeus [8] where street boys sing it as their own.

Valle Lunga, 30 June, p.m.

Some friends from Palermo have reached us and they report that men from the ports of Liguria and Tuscany are arriving every day. There has been some trouble owing to the haste with which the Palermitans have been urged to unite with Piedmont; but the Dictator has everything under control.

I am writing in a tiny room and feel like a cricket in a cage. If I look out of the window, however, I can see the whole length of the High Street, filled with a gay concourse of red-clad soldiers. Officers are sitting smoking and drinking in front of company headquarters. How quickly one catches the manners of the local gentry, who spend the whole year laughing and playing cards in an effort to make time pass and escape boredom. As long as the earth brings forth its fruits they can write idylls and tragedies for the ladies. I have listened to wonderful popular rhymed histories of love, of bitter jealousy, or dire revenge. Ordinary people here are all poets.

[8] Vittorio Amadeo, see note 7, p. 17.

July 1860

Eber knows how to move troops without tiring them. He divides the march into two parts; we go off in the evening and camp after a considerable distance has been covered. Then we take the road again before dawn and reach our destination some time in the morning before the sun has become too hot. Last night we rested in the fields round Cascina Postale. The weather was fine and the sky so clear that I seemed to see much farther into the heavens than ever before.

By sunrise this morning we had already been on the road for a couple of hours. The companies were singing Lombard and Tuscan folk songs, while Sicilians competed with one of their arias which was deeply touching: *La palombella bianca—Si mangia la racina.* But from time to time the song broke into expressions of hate for the Bourbons and scorn for Queen Sophia.

At the head of the column Genoese were singing Mameli's inspired verses.[1] All of a sudden the song broke off and all stopped singing on arriving at a certain spot. I understood why when I got there. It was the first view of Etna, far, far away, dark and enormous, casting its shadow over half Sicily and the sea beyond, looming gigantic to eye and imagination.

*   *   *

In the Piazza of Santa Caterina are pitched two tents, over the finer of which hangs the French flag. As I passed I caught sight of a woman within, a lovely girl with sparkling eyes as far as I could see. Stretched out on a gaily coloured rug beside her

---

[1] Goffredo Mameli (1827–1849), the young soldier poet, who composed the most sung poem of the risorgimento, *Fratelli d'Italia.*

was Alexandre Dumas.[2] My heart gave a leap! How wonderful to live like that in a desert with the young nun of Palermo,
gazing through a tent door at vast horizons, palm trees, a
distant caravan of camels; smiling together in the unbroken
silence.

So the Three Musketeers played out their adventures under
that creole-like mane of hair! They tell me Dumas has a
schooner in the Port of Palermo called *Emma*, after the young
woman whom I saw. He's come to Sicily with the idea of
avenging his father's imprisonment by the old Bourbons when,
as a French general, the latter was driven by a storm to the
coast of Apulia on returning ill from the Egyptian campaign.
They say he is a close friend of Garibaldi and of Colonel Eber
whom he met in Asia. He guards his woman most jealously.
He only has one servant, dressed as a sailor. Tonight he is dining with the officers and it would be wonderful to be able to
listen to him—he has seen and imagined so much!

*   *   *

Poor Major Bassini has to leave again, as he has been picked
to execute justice at a village called Resotano, where some
malefactors are intimidating the population. I've learnt con-
fidentially that tonight we have to move on to Caltanisetta
where our welcome could easily be gunfire.

Alexandre Dumas has struck his tents and is returning to
Palermo. They say he is leaving, after a disagreement with
some of our people who cut him short when he spoke of
Italians with scant respect.

Caltanisetta, 2 July

These villages and towns slander each other as though they
enjoyed it. From what was told us, we should have been met
by gunfire in this place. Quite the contrary! We found decora-

---

[2] Alexandre Dumas (père), the French novelist, an enthusiastic supporter of the Italian liberation movement, had come to Sicily in search of
romance and material for the book he published in 1861, *Les Garibaldiens*.
He later edited Garibaldi's Memoirs in French.

tions, flags and greenery put out for us. We had to pass under a triumphal arch, together with the town authorities and the National Guard, who had come to meet us. The boys did their best to be allowed to carry our soldiers' rifles, to relieve them for the last stretch of the way, but this kindly thought was *not* welcomed by the men. Perhaps some of them remembered the early days after we'd landed, when we slept in the open hugging our rifles between our legs, and some even tied them to their bodies for fear of waking up disarmed.

Quite right! There were peasants at that time who, to lay hands on a rifle, were bold enough to steal one from our bivouacs.

3 July

Could that festive welcome of yesterday have been all a pretence? Today the town is quite silent, as though we had ceased to exist. The people go about their business and seem to infer: 'We've done what was expected of us and that's enough.'

*   *   *

Bassini's men are back, worn out by a long march over fearful roads. They say that they arrived at Resotano around midnight and found the population under arms, determined to prevent their entry. Bassini, quite prepared to get in at the point of the bayonet, acted with circumspection and managed to lay hands on eleven scoundrels, guilty of endless aggressions and murders. One managed to break away, but a Sicilian was after him like a demon, caught him up, and killed him.

5 July

On mustering we find that about fifty of the Sicilians who came with us from Palermo have deserted, some even taking their rifles with them. They are peasants who blaze up like straw and then lose interest. The Council of War condemns them to death. Notices containing death-sentences are stuck up

at all street corners like washing, but they leave the deserters alone, provided they clear right off. The good ones are townsmen and the Palermitans themselves. They are civilized, well-intentioned, respectful young men. Some of the officers, however, who look like clerics, are not much thought of. When the companies go out for drill they march along carrying their swords as though they were tapers. Then they stand on one side as if their presence was sufficient and learning how to drill and handle arms was beneath them. If only they could have been in Piedmont last year! Some of the most aristocratic young men of Italy put up with the roughest usage at the hands of grey-haired corporals who had served at Goito, Novara, and the Crimea, and who shouted stinging insults as they instructed them. Well, they put up with everything in order to learn! I recall a Venetian count loading a cart with stable litter. Corporal Ragni came by carrying a mess-tin.

'Are they all such idiots where you come from? Where did you learn to handle a pitch-fork?' The count replied something in good Italian and smiled.

'Ah, so you're a volunteer? D'you know what this is?'

'A mess-tin.'

'This is what we're fighting for!' jeered the corporal, rapping the tin with his knuckles. The count still smiled.

And the corporal: 'This evening pack up and go on smiling in the cells.'

'Yes, sir!'

Caltanisetta, 7 July

A real festival in fairyland! Garden paths seemed to be all alight, the green of trees and espaliers to shine with a metallic sheen. The women of Caltanisetta, walking together with husbands, brothers, or with us, seemed to form one great family rejoicing over some fortunate event. There were enough refreshments—wine and cakes—to last all the poor in the town for a week. There was dancing and chatting and discussions about liberty and love. And, indeed, some of the Lombards among us are handsome as demi-gods.

Castrogiovanni, 10 July

Why must we march across mountains by tracks such that only by a miracle no one broke his neck? At any rate we have seen a lush countryside looking like a great golden cup. Cattle grazing in the meadows along our way snuffed the air and gazed, startled, at our endless column of red-clad soldiers. A couple of our men who had fallen out of the ranks, perhaps in search of water, were charged by a bull. We saw them rushing up a slope with the infuriated animal's formidable horns right at their backs. One managed to clamber into a tree, the other continued running along a bank where the bull would have got him, had not a herdsman come up at full gallop, bending so low over his horse that his head was right down on the mane. He thrust his pole at the bull's flank like a lancer and the animal fled bellowing, kicking up the turf and furiously lashing his tail.

*   *   *

I have been thinking that when we were at Gibilrossa six weeks ago, two possibilities were open to us; we could either have attacked Palermo, or retreated to these heights and organized revolution, gathered strength and then carried on the war. Almost all our leaders were for the latter plan, but not so Garibaldi. He wanted Palermo. Perhaps he guessed that once we had retreated up here we should have gradually lost vigour; the revolution would have collapsed and we with it.

*   *   *

While we were waiting in the street in order to direct the companies to billets, the Venetian blinds of a convent opposite were broken and fragments flew through the air. Young nuns clapped from the barred windows and cried out the name of Garibaldi, or rather Sinibaldo. The name, that I have heard mispronounced in a thousand different ways ever since we landed at Marsala, has now changed to Sinibaldo, the father

of Santa Rosalia who once lived in a hermitage on Mount Pellegrino! Who knows what fantastical notions were in the minds of those ingenuous creatures who looked like the groups of angels our artists paint amid golden clouds, bearing the Virgin Mary up to Heaven. Perhaps they think Garibaldi is really the King, father of the Saint, reborn! Among these imaginative islanders any fantasy can pass for truth. A lady asked me in Palermo, quite seriously, if I had ever seen the angel whose wings shelter Garibaldi against bullets. I replied that I hadn't. I felt like saying, 'But I see her now and should like to kiss her.' It was a piece of gallantry I simply couldn't utter, for the question had been asked with such devotion and the lady was in such a state of exaltation.

Some old Sisters put up a pretence of pulling the young white-clad nuns away from the windows, but they too were enjoying watching us as we stood below, dusty and lusty. Dear, oh dear! What a thing life is, what sweet longings in the human heart! An idea flashed through my mind. In every town there is a monastery for men and a convent for women. Senses swoon under these burning suns. Amid the age-long gloom of these buildings ancient as Faith itself, buildings that give a feeling of things of no beginning and no end, set in the voluptuous rankness of their gardens where trees spread and entwine as if tormented by their own exuberance, desire creeps through every one of a man's senses and overwhelms his spirit, so that, calling on God's mercy, he concedes the flesh its triumph.

When we have gone, liberty will sweep away this medieval residue, but meanwhile, why have priests and friars not come out to fight to the death for those wonderful places where they live? Perhaps the times are now ripe.

* * *

I am writing at the foot of a castle that once dominated the town. It is now a prison where a sergeant of Agesilao Milano's[3] company was incarcerated. He was freed by the revolution, but came out white-haired, bowed, finished, without strength

[3] Agesilao Milano, see note 4, p. 8.

I

enough even to rejoice at what was happening to his country. So I was told and so I jot it down. I also record that I can see Lake Pergusa about five miles away. It looks like a piece of sky fallen into the midst of flowery meadows. *Circa Lacus lucique sunt plurimi et laetissimi flores omni tempore anni*, says Cicero speaking of Enna, the ancient city, now Castrogiovanni. I read this passage in the *Verrine* about six years ago. Who would have told me then that I was to see those places with my own eyes?

*   *   *

Opposite Castrogiovanni stands Calascibetta, secure and sombre on its mountain rent by ravines as though by lightning and apparently made of basalt. Down in the valley is the Misericordia entrepôt,[4] an ominous name that suggests the blades of highwaymen's daggers shining in the night.

I can see our artillery below, waggons, sentries, and a swarm of red soldiers. There can't be a breath of air down there, while here we have a light breeze that caresses our cheeks so sweetly it might be a breath from those young nuns of this morning.

*   *   *

News of Bixio! He is leading his brigade through the island to our right. He has seen Parco, Piana de' Greci, Corleone once again and is proceeding in the direction of Girgenti. Our comrades will see the ruins of the temples Byron loved, there in the wastes that cover the bones of a great people. Herdsmen pay little heed to those rows of silent columns and seafarers bow to them from afar.

Leonforte, 11 July

Captain Faustino Tanara, standing solitary on a hilltop, scans the wide horizon with his little eyes like an eaglet studying the best way to launch out on his first flight. His bold, open nature shines in his face, but he never seems completely

---

[4] This place the 'Misericordia' sounds ominous to Abba as the lay fraternity of that name in Italy attends the sick and dying and bury the dead.

happy. Yet he should be cheered by observing how fond we
all are of him. What a sweet nature he has! He shows affection
for the meanest of us, even for Mangiaracina, a Sicilian from
some village on Etna, a blockhead with tousled hair like a bear
and two eyes that peep out from sunken pits like footpads in
ambush. One day I saw Tanara really angry with Mangiaracina, who throws his legs about like a hippopotamus and
can't keep step with the company. 'Why have you joined up
with us? Surely we can unite Italy without your great carcass!'
Mangiaracina's eyes filled with tears and, looking at his officer
as though at a saint, he replied humbly and quietly: 'I have
feelings too, Captain!' Tanara shook him by the hand.

Mangiaracina is about thirty years old. In battle he is
another man. He darts and jumps and tears about as quick as
lightning. Then we all admire him and we fear for his safety.
Afterwards he creeps glumly into some corner and you can't
get a word out of him.

San Filippo D'Argina, 12 July

We left Leonforte in the cool, at two in the morning, and
marched slowly until sunrise. Then we all shook ourselves, just
as birds do, and our thoughts flew over the great expanses of
the island. The usual views; groves of almond trees just as we
have chestnuts; land that should produce abundance; every
now and then groups of peasants watching us with indifference,
and thinking who knows what about us.

San Filippo is a gay little town, and they tell us that from
here to the sea the most beautiful part of Sicily is to be found.
We arrived just as a procession was entering the church, after
having made a round to pray for rain. We saw the tail-end as it
slowly went by chanting; nearly all priests in stole and surplice,
too many! How do these poor Sicilians provide for them all?

There is a rumour that a column of Royalist troops has come
out from Syracuse and is waiting for us near Catania. It must
be true because we shall be leaving shortly. Shall we join battle
where the Athenians of Nicias fought? Or maybe beneath
Mount Etna, where so many dramatic events took place during

the servite wars? And Garibaldi is not with us! If only Bixio could arrive from Girgenti in the thick of the battle like the hurricane he is!

Regalbuto, 13 July

We have been entertained at table, willingly so it appeared, by some thirty Augustinian monks. They did the honours of their monastery dressed in black cassocks, sleek and greasy. The monastery is secluded, a tranquil backwater, a place to grow fat in. The monks are like trees in a garden whose soil drains all the good from the rest of the village.

Doctor Zen, who wasn't in laughing mood today, sat in the pulpit at the end of the refectory and read passages from the lives of the saints. Such gloomy stuff, all mortification and fasting! While we ate and chatted quietly with the monks, the Prior kept his eye on the novices in case they should be led astray and he wake up next morning to find the garden littered with discarded cassocks! But they were courteous to the end and gave us an ancient wine that might have been made when Vittorio Amedeo was king of Sicily. Little by little things warmed up and heads began to spin, and all of us, monks too, began saying so many unseemly things that Zen left the pulpit and went out.

We all left and in the square I saw Nuvolari, an officer of the Scouts, looking glummer than usual. He watched us in silence and perhaps secretly blamed us.

Adernò, 14 July. Afternoon

For the whole march I have been with Telesforo Catoni, whom I have wanted for a friend ever since Marsala. He was in the Cairoli company and used to study law at Pavia. There is something about him that makes one sad; one doesn't know why but feels sorry for him. He has a mane of black hair, large, eloquent, piercing eyes, and a head that should have topped an athlete's body. And, instead, he has slender limbs and a frame that a breath of air would blow away. Yet he has never fallen a yard behind! You can read in his face his essential

purity; no vulgar word ever passes his lips. He is nearly always on his own. He adores the poet Foscolo and knows the *Sepolcri* [5] by heart and seems to draw spiritual nourishment from it as from a food for lions. Walking next to me, he recited the verses about Marathon and, coming from him in the midst of the column marching through the night, they struck me as the most beautiful and most virile poetry written since the age of Dante.

Catoni is very Foscolian and if his portrait were prefixed to *Ortis* everyone would think that Jacopo must have looked like that. He is nineteen, with a head full of literary projects; he is religious and prays, but hates priests. Nevertheless he too kept guard over friars that the Palermitans wanted to ill-treat. He's a Mantuan like Nuvolari, Gatti, and Boldrini, all courageous men with a touch of eccentricity, rather like Sordello.

As I was walking with Catoni I saw a beautiful woman gazing from the balcony of a superior-looking house. In the blazing heat of the early afternoon her eyes were fixed on some distant cherished prospect. Of what was she dreaming? Perhaps of us. She seemed unhappy.

'Look up there,' I said, 'Pia de' Tolomei.' [6] Catoni looked and his eyes flashed at that vision of divine beauty, but he turned his head away, saying: 'Don't look, we are in a country where a woman is dearer than life, dearer than liberty.'

When we came out into the open countryside towards Catania, it seemed we were no longer in Sicily, or that what we had thitherto seen, except perhaps for the Conca d'Oro, was not the real Sicily. Gone was that almost savage exuberance of growth and in its place was a regular cultivation. One would almost imagine oneself to be in the fair land of Tuscany,

[5] Ugo Foscolo (1778–1827) wrote much that inspired later Italian patriots. Here his famous blank-verse poem *Dei Sepolcri* and his romantic epistolary novel *Le Ultime Lettere Di Jacopo Ortis* are mentioned. Foscolo spent the last eleven years of his life in England.

[6] Pia de Tolomei, mentioned by Dante (*Purgatorio* V, vv. 124–136) as an innocent wife left to pine. She was finally killed by her husband.

were it not for the huge ox-horns fixed to chimneys, copings, and even straw-stacks, as protection against the powers of evil.

Paternò, 14 July

From Adernò to Paternò we marched in full view of Mount Etna and we never once lost it from sight after reaching Santa Caterina. Along the lower slopes, that seem to rise up to infinite distances, are majestic woods of dark green. Thence the great mountain rears up, bare and arid as far as the snow-covered peak, topped by a plume of smoke rising sluggishly from the crater as though it could climb no higher. The giant sleeps and marks the passing years by his own furious eruptions and the peoples he has destroyed. There have been many of these and what annals have been theirs! And yet there are still numerous villages up there in the scrub and, from afar, one senses the inhabitants are prosperous.

Catania, 15 July

I thought I was entering a city of the Cyclops, but once past its menacing gate, built of massive blocks, one finds a broad street stretching all the way to the sea. It was as clean and sweet as though awaiting a Corpus Christi day procession. We were a small vanguard in front of the brigade and so were pelted with the first flowers. In the Piazza dell' Elefante, a sentry called out the guard and ten or a dozen youths tumbled out and presented arms, looking fierce. They are men from the district around, recruited by Nicola Fabrizi.

*   *   *

The brigade marched in. Eber rode at the head and the companies strode out well with a rhythmic step and their rifles were sloped in good order as though they were veterans. It was a pleasure to see them.

We shall rest here for some days. The Bourbon troops have not stirred from Syracuse and Augusta, but we have to be on our guard because we are between them and those at Messina.

17 July

I understand now that, for us, this period of inaction is a
Capuan idyll of indolence. There are certain scents in Catania
that lull you to sleep. The town lies like Venus in a shell,
swooning in sky, landscape, and ocean that seem to blend into
one living entity for its delight. One feels a sweet breath of
Anacreontic air; bring wine, bring roses! As women come out
of the churches like so many Goddesses, their eyes sparkle and
hips sway under white dresses, while black silk mantillas ripple
down over their shoulders from coiled hair. We gaze at them,
drinking in the enchantment, lost in admiration.

20 July

Before dawn this morning we were down on the sea-shore.
I was very upset. Two men had to be executed; one a Sicilian
volunteer who had murdered a comrade out of jealousy, the
other a villain who had strangled his old mother and children
to clear his hovel for another wife. The latter howled all the
way from prison to place of execution, the former smoked with
a smile on his arrogant face. In the pale dawn light, while
land and sea seemed to arise from their nocturnal embrace,
twelve shots rang out and two men were launched into the
next world.

*   *   *

The Benedictines of Catania, some of the highest born
gentlemen of Sicily, seem to live in the antechamber to
Paradise itself. I said this in joke to one of them, and he
opened wide his arms, cast up his eyes and sighed: 'As befits
poor monks.' Can he have said this in mockery? Ah! the
parable of the camel and the needle's eye!

We enjoyed peaches from the monastery gardens, steeped in
sherry wine. The watchful monks wouldn't let us drink this
wine, 'spoiled' as they called it, but poured out fresh, limpid
as amber and richly scented.

22 July

Now for a curious tale! Among the Sicilians who joined up with us as we passed through the island several young women have been discovered. They were wearing red shirts in the most self-possessed way and nobody knew anything about them, except their particular gallants. They have been taken away with all respect and will be sent back home. Who knows what welcome they will receive when they get there, these gypsies of love!

*   *   *

I have just met Pittaluga in Via Etnea. I had not come across him since Talamone, nor did I know he was one of the sixty men sent into the Papal States under Zambianchi.[7] He tells an extraordinary story! The first evening they camped on the frontier. A man is missing, Stoppani from Terracina. Where can he be? About eleven o'clock a sentry hears galloping in the dark.

'Halt! Who goes there?'

'Don't make a row, it's me!' And Stoppani leaps from a horse and comes in with a grin on his face.

'What's happened?' And Stoppani:

'I knew the Papal dragoons had fine horses, so I've laid out the owner of this one; he's dead or dying.'

Three or four of us ran to look for the wounded man, but only found bloodstains. Perhaps the dragoon had managed to drag himself away or his comrades had rescued him. Next day, however, a squadron of them attacked us without warning, but our men, who were caught in the streets of Grotte, fought well and got away. But there is a sad tale to tell—that Zambianchi! And to think that he had first-class people under him —Guerzoni, Leardi, Soncini, Bandini, Fochi, Ferrari, Ughi, Pittaluga! Did you ever hear the like?

[7] Callimaco Zambianchi was put in charge of a party detached at Talamone to invade the Papal States. The so-called 'diversion' is considered as one of Garibaldi's mistakes, both from a political and military point of view. Zambianchi himself was unworthy of command, as Abba infers here.

Victor Emmanuel's grenadiers arrived after that and took the whole company prisoner. They were escorted to Genoa where they at once took ship with Clemente Corte. Next they were captured at sea by Bourbon ships and held a month at Gaeta. Liberated, they were shipped back to Genoa instead of to Sicily—a long Odyssey! Yet they never gave up. They were determined to come, and by one way or another, have all joined up with us.

*   *   *

Where is the place? What is Milazzo?[8] I've gone to look at the map. There it is between Cefalù and the lighthouse, a thin tongue of land sticking out into the sea like a flickering flame.

From today I shall never imagine that strip of dark land with its castle, as they describe it, without a vision of lines of red-clad soldiers percolating like streams of blood through the green of prickly pears, cane-brakes and dry beds of torrents, as far as the blazing white sea-shore. I seem to see the austere faces of Medici, Cosenz, and Fabrizi as they hurry to and fro; I don't know them, but I know what heroes look like, and the kind of men Garibaldi moulds. Then I see a party of Neapolitan horse galloping like madmen through our men. Where are they going? Whom are they seeking? They form a ring around Garibaldi, who is on foot. He is surrounded by threatening swords and lances. A ferocious yell of triumph from Royalist throats echoes to the farthest corners of the field. Ah! This is the moment when Queen Sophia's crown can be saved for her. But Missori and Statella appreciate that this is the rôle they are destined to play in the great epic. Death spits from the Lombard's pistol and sweeps out from the sword wielded by the paladin from Syracuse. The miracle happens! Fly, ye lancers! Your captain, as he led you out from Messina promised you the Lion's head, but now you will see that captain no more. He has fallen from his horse transfixed by the

[8] Abba himself did not take part in the battle of Milazzo and the following imaginative description is based on hear-say and appears to be material for poetry—obviously no part of a diary.

Dictator's sword. He lies in the dust! Now Garibaldi, with his seaman's instinct, has boarded the *Veloce* and taken to the waves, and thunders from her deck his new contribution to the battle.

The poem ends with the tale of the old castle; with the fugitives seeking safety there; with Bosco, unavailing hero, leaving under truce, with his horse and sword granted by Garibaldi. The *Veloce* that had come to our aid as though inspired by the spirit of the dead Magyar hero who fell at the Termini Gate, will be re-named *Tuköry*.

Catania, 24 July

The foreign *Wolf* company[9] is leaving. It moves off towards Taormina led by Captain Giulio Adamoli, a young Lombard, courteous and dashing. They go to see if Bourbon troops have left Messina to challenge us. The brigade leaves tomorrow.

27 July

In they came, dusty but radiant, with their band in front playing martial music. Bixio was riding a glossy coal-black stallion that danced under him as light as a swallow. His dark face, framed by a white hood, gave him the appearance of an Emir returning from some mysterious desert foray. He wheeled gracefully round with the officers behind him and came to a halt in front of the stone elephant that seems to drowse in the square. He rapped out a command and ranks divided, battalions turned smartly about and came to a halt in perfect column order. They carried out the movement like one man. This really is a regiment to win veterans' respect. I have spoken with friends and they tell me that Bixio gave them no rest as they crossed the island. More than once the soldiers were on the point of mutiny, in protest at the forced marches. But who would dare be the first to oppose this man, who never eats, sleeps, or stops?

[9] The *Wolf* company was formed from foreign deserters from the Royalist army. It was named after its Bavarian commander.

I don't know why but, as he rode into Catania, Bixio
looked ill-content. His habitual frown seemed deeper than
usual. It may be that he is not in accord with the captain
riding beside him, who must be his chief-of-staff. This officer
rides with dangling legs, but he has a back like a ramrod. He
has wispy hair as pale as his complexion, and looks as though
he were about to fall asleep. Under his ragged, drooping,
moustache his lips always have a mocking smile. He seems
listening to mysterious sounds from far away. They tell me
that he is a brilliant man, originally of the Piedmontese army.
He was a second-lieutenant of *Bersaglieri* since 1848, but when
the Milan riots of '53 occurred, resigned for patriotic reasons.
I notice that everyone seems to hold aloof from him. A good
man in action, but so satirical that his words can scorch and
wound. He would even mock Garibaldi himself. His name is
Giovanni Turbiglio and I call him Mephistopheles in a red
shirt.

Giardini, 28 July

Acireale, Giarre, Giardini, are three little towns for which
the sea and the volcano seem to compete. Etna drags
them to her foot like three slaves. However far one goes the
mountain is always there with constantly changing aspect. As
we march under the blazing sun on roads yellow with lava
dust that shimmers like a fiery curtain before us with almost
palpable heat, our eyes seek the relief of foothills lying in cool
shade.

To our right as far as the eye can reach is blue sea, quite
unlike the waters of Liguria or those of Marsala. It is the same
lovely sea, but here it has a deep remote transparency, as
though there were deeps on deeps, one beyond the other, like
Dante's successive heavens. Perhaps the sea experiences a sense
of pleasure as the sun penetrates its depths, for in this noon-day
hour it has an air of infinite benevolence. I almost dare say that
you could walk over it dry-shod. As I gaze I am overcome
with the exquisite sweetness of childhood memories, of things
heard about the skies, the lakes, and the good people of Galilee.

Far away, beyond the ultimate horizon that, seen from elsewhere, seems in fancy to end in a fearful precipice, one can guess at other lands like Sicily, yet more beautiful. Greece must be yonder; it could be nowhere else! On the air, over the waters, comes a waft of antiquity, and a music sweet today as when Virgil sang of the love of Alphaeus and Arethusa.

*   *   *

Sant' Alessio is a little fort, built in ancient days to give the Barbary pirates something to laugh about. No guard is kept now, but an old cannon sticking out of its loop-hole seemed to wink at us. As we passed under the fort, Raveggi said to me:

'There's my dream! To be at least forty years old and posted there with four decrepit old soldiers. I'd lie stretched out, first on one glacis then on another, staring at the sea with close attention. There I should grow old little by little, sipping my life, sipping wine, and enjoying fantastical conceits of my own invention.'

*   *   *

On the sea-shore

I can begin to make out quite clearly the cape of Spartivento. When, as boys, we used to recite the verses *Dall' Alpe a Spartivento* I could imagine these blue waters. I seemed to conjure them up as though breathing their very atmosphere. But now I should hesitate to try to describe the variation of blues; nuances of tint as numerous as the little headlands from here to Messina. Those lines beyond the Straits that look like quivers in the air, can they be the mountains of fabled Calabria, land where death has always met any armed invader who set foot on its shore?

To and fro through the Straits pass the Neapolitan ships of war. Silent, solemn, puffing smoke, they look gloomy. That's our problem, to get over to the opposite shore! But Garibaldi lives!

Messina, 28 July

On the plain of Terranova, between town and citadel, are
two sentry-beats, ours and the enemy's. Between the lines is
neutral ground, a bare twenty paces wide. Sentries watch each
other, start chatting, continue the discussion, and then one of
two things happens; either the Bourbon soldier turns sulky, or
suddenly throws off cap, equipment, and everything else,
shouts *Viva l'Italia!* and makes a dash for our lines. There the
deserter is heartily embraced by a mob of women fruitsellers
and fish-hawkers. But sometimes our men tempt in vain and
rude things are said. Some of the Bourbon soldiers then let
fly with their rifles and our men reply. General alarm! Drums
roll and bugles blow, both on our side and in the citadel.
Gunners' heads pop up on the bastions and one can see their
fuses smoking. Then a staff officer runs up from our side and a
Bourbon of similar rank appears from the citadel. They meet,
speak, shake hands, turn about and the incident is closed.
Little comedies that raise a laugh, but which can be serious
enough for someone or other! This morning the citadel even
fired a cannon-shot! The enormous ball passed clean through a
customs shed and went rolling far down the quay. Our men
came running up from all sides furious, and I even saw a young
man without a leg leaping along with his wooden one as fast as
anyone. He was brandishing a rifle with bayonet fixed and
yelling that it was time to attack the citadel.

Messina. Returning from Torre del Faro, 28 July

It's a delicious walk to the Torre del Faro. First, one finds
very neat little villages, then a sandy plain all the way to
where a white tower leaps to the eye above a cluster of miserable hovels. There is little vegetation round about, but sea
shimmers in the background and, beyond, are distances only
to be penetrated by the imagination, if one has any.

In front of the Torre del Faro, on the other side of the Straits,
the eye is caught by a strip of dark green at the foot of the
mountains. The mountains themselves seem straining forward

to topple over and fill up the watery gulf between the two shores. Here and there the green is broken by villages shining white in the sun. Men are moving along the beach. Up and down a road that must lead to Reggio one can see the glint of arms from marching troops. Out at sea the patrolling warships keep watch on what is going on on our side, namely digging and shovelling, to prepare gun-emplacements. And what guns! Among the scrap iron I recognized the culverin we brought away from Orbetello. There she sits in the battery, sticking out her green neck most flirtatiously from her emplacement-coop. One fine day we shall see her wheeling round in display like a turkey. She could tell a tale! If the gunners who now guard and polish her only knew the things we said about her as we marched from Marsala to Piana de' Greci, they'd throw her into the sea.

*   *   *

Garibaldi is shut up in a miserable little room in the tower roof, while all round Genoese Sharpshooters are camped. These are no longer the forty men of Calatafimi, a company unbeaten for daring, devotion to duty, and all military virtues, but they have formed the nucleus of the battalion that stormed ahead at Milazzo and held all the ground they captured. Now they are not even all Ligurians, as their ranks have been opened to admit young men from all parts of Italy. Five or six survivors from the Sapri massacre who volunteered to wear uniform again no sooner liberated from the dens of Favignana, have been incorporated into the battalion and brought with them something of Pisacane's great inspiration.

August 1860

Last night, after complete darkness had fallen, twenty boats left the Torre del Faro shore, steering for Calabria. Each carried ten or twelve armed men and, standing up in the last boat, was Garibaldi. They went away into the silent Straits and were soon lost to view. Bourbon warships had been cruising up and down opposite till evening. Then some of them had stationed themselves behind the Sicilian promontory in that vaporous shadow where, when I saw it from here by day, it reminded me of my peaceful childhood dreams. Two of them, however, had remained in mid-channel. Our men, crowded on the shore, waited in trepidation, expecting to hear at any moment the cries of our drowning comrades and perhaps see flashes from the enemy ships out in the Straits. But towards eleven o'clock the fort at Scilla flashed out and the rumble of a cannon shot roused all the camps along both shores. Then we could hear rifle-fire from out of the dark distance. And then silence, as when the lid of a tomb is lowered.

*   *   *

Now we know what happened. When the boats had got halfway across, Garibaldi, having assured himself that there was no danger from warships, let them proceed, one rigged with a lateen sail as pilot-boat. Then he returned here. In the boats were Alberto Mario, Missori, Nullo, Curzio, and Salomone, the flower of our people, with two hundred picked volunteers under the command of Captain Racchetti of Sacchi's brigade. Leader of the expedition was Mussolino from Pizzo.

Two of the boatmen who were with them told me the tale and trembled as they told it. On realizing what a risky enterprise was afoot they stopped rowing. But forced to go on, proceeded with those dare-devils, weeping and crying on Mary

and the Saints to protect them. Some boats got detached in the dark and went off course towards Scilla. The Neapolitans, on spotting them from the fort, fired that cursed shot, precisely when the main body was reaching the agreed spot near another fort, that of Torre Cavallo, and was disembarking ladders, ropes, and all sorts of gear to help them clamber up. There was some confusion and the boats stood off quickly, leaving our men on a hostile shore, in darkness, without a guide and engaged with the Neapolitan patrols from the fort.

*　　*　　*

Our brigade came here to be ferried across to Calabria, had last night's operation been successful. We are encamped in the shingly bed of a dried-up torrent at the mouth of a well-cultivated, little valley. No one has moved a stone to make himself more comfortable in camp by those little improvements which soldiers contrive when they know they will be making a stay. We all consider ourselves birds on the bough, ready to fly off.

Fiumara della Guardia, 10 August

Between us and three hundred of our men are sea, warships, and Bourbon troops on the opposite shore.

There they are yonder, somewhere in that pale green patch high on the mountainside above Villa San Giovanni, but farther along. We see smoke rising, spreading, thickening; we hear muffled rifle shots. One can guess that our men are defending themselves against attacks and must be proud to be fighting, only three hundred, in view of every regiment encamped on this shore from Messina to the Faro.

*　　*　　*

I had a sudden flash of intuition. This longing for Sicily that has fascinated me for so long, filling my imagination with delight and my heart with strange pangs; this certainty that here, in this island, I should meet a friend I had long loved, although whom I had no idea; all this came from having read,

years ago, the novel *Dottor' Antonio*[1] by Giovanni Ruffini. I have just realized this on hearing someone mention the book which once so kindled my imagination that I seemed lifted up on wings for days after I had read it. I all but went down on my knees in the sand to offer up thanks with clasped hands to the author who, from England, revealed to Italy this island and this people, no matter whether as it is or as it will be.

11 August

A parade of officers! That stocky Colonel who jerks his head up and down, walking as though he were threatening someone in front of him, is an Englishman. His name is Peard and he is a crack shot. He has no command but sticks close to the unit that is nearest to the enemy. He carries his fifty years as we do our twenty. He wages war as though he loved it and, in action, shoots as though out for tigers. He loves Italy. There is another who rather resembles him, a Major Speech, artist and soldier. He has shed blood whenever men have been fighting for liberty, in Italy and elsewhere. He has never been under fire without being wounded, the last time at Milazzo. Garibaldi loves him like a brother. They've been together all over the world, ever since the days of the Roman republic, their eyes ever fixed in hope on the goddess Liberty.[2]

The man with the full beard who walks somewhat bowed, dressed in black, is De Flotte. He was marching beside Speech and they were chatting like old friends. De Flotte is one of those people whose air of serene sadness, permeating his whole being, leads one to guess at his history. In imagination one sees the cross under whose weight he walks. When the *coup d'état* took place in Paris he was a people's deputy and he remained there as long as resistance lasted, then he went into

[1] Giovanni Ruffini (1807–1881) wrote the novel *Doctor Antonio* in English, while an exile in England. The protagonist of the book is himself a Sicilian exile and there is much about Sicily in it.

[2] For the English fighting with Garibaldi see Professor Trevelyan's books and in particular for Peard, his 'War-Journals of Garibaldi's Englishmen', *Cornhill Magazine*, June, 1908.

K

exile. I think he was a naval officer. Here he is only an individual who wishes us well, who has answered the call of
Italy, like the Poles, Hungarians, and all the generous spirits
of other nationalities who have brought us the aid of their
glorious swords.

I saw Nicola Fabrizi, who looks like a Biblical warrior.
Should this man appear at a congress of kings to demand
justice for Italy, the kings would rise to their feet out of respect
for the people who could produce such a worthy representative.
Simple in manners, never put out, he seems to spread an aura
of benevolence around him. If he goes by, one longs to follow,
sure of going towards some worthy goal. If, at a desperate
moment with his very life at stake, some child should clasp his
legs, Fabrizi would bend down to caress him. He has per-
severed ever since the days of Ciro Menotti.[3] His faith has
grown day by day. He has never looked back, age has not
disillusioned him; he has always felt certain of witnessing
Italy's great moment. Now one begins to understand how
Garibaldi could undertake this enterprise. It is known that
Fabrizi from Malta, Crispi and Bixio in Genoa, all three impressed on him that Italy must be made this very year, or
perhaps never.

*　　　*　　　*

I have come across Major Vincenzo Statella again. His
natural look of fierceness has been increased by a cut across his
nose. A Hungarian officer was trotting along from the Torre
del Faro, bearing orders from Garibaldi. At one point he
stopped below a battery and asked something of Statella, who
was up there. Statella either paid no attention or did not
understand. The Hungarian began to shout and Statella to
get angry. Before you could say Jack Robinson a duel had
been arranged on the spot and sabre strokes were exchanged.
Statella was wounded and the Hungarian went on about his
business.

When Garibaldi reached Palermo, this Statella, scion of a

[3] Ciro Menotti, a Modenese patriot who was executed in 1831.

family of princes, whose father was one of the oldest and most
faithful generals in the Bourbon army, rushed to embrace the
man who had come to liberate Sicily and had been his
captain in '49. Who would have guessed it? He is a Syracusan.
His high lineage is written in his face, and as for his valour—
ask the Bourbon lancers who got away from him and Missori at
Milazzo!

15 August

The *Veloce*, in '48 a warship of the Sicilian revolutionaries,
later captured by the Bourbons, has now been brought back to
the side of the revolution by a certain Anguissola and renamed
Tuköry. She did yeoman service at Milazzo, and the other
night Piola, an officer of the Sardinian navy, took her on an
adventure that, had it only succeeded . . . ! The plan was to
go as far as Castellamare, capture an eighty-gun Bourbon ship
called the *Monarca*, tow her over and make use of her at the
Faro as a floating fort. The *Tuköry* reached Castellamare without opposition. It was midnight and the *Monarca* towered up
like a giant, a black bulk over the sea. The thing seemed
done! Some of our *Bersaglieri* from Bonnet's battalion got into
boats to cut the *Monarca*'s cables, others were boarding her,
when all of a sudden the alarm was given, there were bugle
calls, drums, and the entire garrison of Castellamare opened
fire with shot and shell. The attempt had to be abandoned.
The *Tuköry*'s commander thought it better not to risk being hit,
and retreated, but in his own good time like Ajax, leaving the
Neapolitans firing into the darkness.

*   *   *

There is an air of mystery about, emanating presumably
from some cave or other. Garibaldi has not been seen for several days. Some say he has gone away, and some that he is shut up
in the Torre del Faro. He is just like Conrad of Byron's *Corsair*,
or he would be, if there were a Gulnara! Talking of Gulnara, I
observed an officer of Scouts walking with rapid steps along
the beach, without a sabre, obviously a woman, hips, bust, and

all. She was a handsome creature, and had adopted an innocent air, but kept on casting snaky glances behind her from the
tail of her eye. The brigade officers were discussing her, and
Colonel Bassini grumbled in her wake, shaking his head and
switching his whip. She's a Piedmontese countess who's come
adventuring. They say she scatters the balm of charity around
her like a sister of mercy. On the other hand, old Doctor
Ripari had her chased out of the Barcellona hospital where she
was playing the angel with the wounded from Milazzo.

* * *

I've just made a quick trip to Giardini. I treasure such
pleasant memories of that coast and its little towns. *En route*
I came across lots of friends from Bixio's brigade. They've
all caught something of him in their manner, their speech,
even in the way they look at you. This general seems made to
fit the times and ourselves. He takes men and moulds them as
he wants them. With him, it is either do as he says or be flung
aside. A look or a word is not enough with him, he is quite
prepared to strike out with his sabre, and this is the sole defect
in his character. They all grumble; from time to time his
volunteers want to leave him. He's violent, insupportable! 'All
right, whom do you want to serve under?' 'What do you say?
Well if that's the way of it, under Bixio!' Indeed there are not
thirty like him in the whole of Italy. If he were struck down by
a bullet, it would be as though our strength had suddenly been
halved. If the Bourbons had an officer like Bixio, perhaps . . .
But no! stifle the thought! They say Bosco is of equal value.
Heresy!

Bixio in a few days has raged like a tiger through the villages
of Etna, where terrible rioting had broken out. He was seen
in one place after another as an apparition of terror. At Bronte
there had been division of property, arson, vendettas, fearful
orgies, and, to cap all, cheers for Garibaldi! Bixio takes a
couple of battalions and transports them up there on horseback, in carriages, in carts, by every means, to reach the place.
As they go they keep meeting people who had escaped from

the massacres. They stretch out their arms, supplicating him and his officers, some trying to dissuade them from going to be massacred too. For two days Bixio presses on and the road is strewn with exhausted men who can't stand the pace. At last he arrives with a small party. A most horrible sight meets their eyes and they feel like plucking them out so as not to see. Houses burnt down with the occupants inside; people with throats cut lying in the streets; pupils in seminaries massacred in the presence of their old Rector! One of the savage crew is tearing with his teeth at the breast of a dead girl. 'Charge with the bayonet!' The inhuman villains are taken and bound, but in such numbers that it is hard to pick out the worst of them, about a hundred. Bixio then issues a furiously indignant proclamation:

'Bronte is guilty of crimes against humanity and declared to be in a state of siege. All arms are to be given up on pain of death. The Town Council, the National Guard, and all other organized bodies are dismissed! Until order be restored a war tax to be levied.'

The guilty are to be judged by a Council of War. Six of them are to be executed, shot in the back together with the lawyer Lombardi, an old man of sixty, who had been the leader of the horrid outburst. Among those who carried out the sentence were cultured, gentle, young men in red shirts; doctors, artists, and the like. What a tragedy! Bixio was present with eyes full of tears.

After Bronte; Randazzo, Castiglione, Regalbuto, Centorbi, and other villages; all felt the weight of Bixio's powerful hand. They called him a savage brute, but they dared not do more. However far the fortunes of war take us away, the terror of witnessing this man's tempestuous wrath will suffice to keep the population of Etna quiet. If not, this is what he has written: 'We don't waste words; either you keep orderly and quiet or, in the name of Justice and Country, we'll destroy you as enemies of humanity.'

There are people yet living who remember a rising in those hill villages forty years ago. A General Costa went there with

three thousand soldiers and four guns, but had to leave without achieving anything.

At the end of the last century the title of Duke of Bronte was conferred on Nelson. And what title shall we give to Bixio? Not the one that belonged to the man who murdered Caracciolo![4]

Messina, 18 August

Garibaldi is no longer at the Torre del Faro, neither in Messina, nor in Sicily! Everyone feels there is something missing in the air, in nature, in us. No one, however, dares to speak of it, nor inquire what has happened to him. We fear, it seems, a shattering reply from the General himself: 'What is it *you* want to know?'

Meanwhile one hears startling rumours. They speak of the French Emperor and of Victor Emmanuel and of a certain letter written by the latter ordering Garibaldi to desist from all further action against the King of Naples. 'Camouflage to keep Europe guessing,' says one; 'Let people write and read what they please,' says another, 'one of these fine nights we shall cross the Straits.'

But those who would prefer to act sooner even say that Vittorio would do better to send Persano with the *Governolo* and the *Maria Adelaide* to take station in mid-channel and clear the way for our crossing.

20 August, morning

Gunfire from the sea down towards Capo dell' Armi. What poetical names! But what anxiety in thinking that every shot may snuff out many men's lives and, among them, friends we

[4] Italians have never forgotten an episode in Nelson's history when in 1799 he was, through his connexion with the Bourbon King and Queen associated with the reprisals taken against those who had organized the shortlived *Repubblica Partenopea*. In particular they consider him guilty of the execution of Admiral Caracciolo. Abba remembers here the account given in Colletta's *Storia del Reame di Napoli* he had studied at school. See also p. 132.

shall see no more. People arriving here from Catania say that two ships sailed into Giardini during the night and that all Bixio's men have embarked; but they know nothing further.

Bixio is in Calabria, Bixio! And Garibaldi too! Once again this man has appeared unexpectedly on an enemy coast. Sometimes he seems more than a living being or is he an archangel who spreads his wings and whirls his sword like a sunray? Marsala and Melito, two place-names, two landings; Garibaldi and Bixio twice covered with glory! And here are we left behind and would willingly throw ourselves into the sea and reach them by swimming. Never before have I felt so strongly the aching longing which Virgil expressed when describing the spirits in his sixth Canto:

> *Stabant orantes primi transmittere cursum*
> *tendebant manus ripae ulterioris amore.*

The romanticism that Garibaldi has introduced into the art of war has not caused me to forget the classical charm of Virgil, so that on thinking of the effect produced on the Neapolitan Court at the news that Garibaldi was in Calabria and that the din of arms was growing louder, I caught a solemn echo from the passage in the *Aeneid* where all the palace is described as in dire distress. To think of Queen Sophia! What anguish for her! One can understand how the gallant, handsome, General Bosco was captivated by her plight and that, after Milazzo, he has dedicated himself to her service. But Garibaldi, as though he had foreseen it all, has bound him by the terms of his surrender to remain out of the field for six months. And Francis II? Why doesn't he mount his horse and make a stand at the Monteleone Pass? That is what he should do! Perish there, or hurl us back to drown in these waters that we now so long to cross.

22 August. At the Faro

At the moment I think I can feel most deeply and completely the sentiment expressed by Manzoni in the verses:

Eternal regret for him who, sighing, says, 'I was not there'.[5] It is a kind of suffering, an exquisite pain, like no other. Our men are over on the other side, they have been in action—and we were not with them!

Oh my old school-master,[6] Oh Calasanziano friar, I wonder what you are doing at this instant there in your cell, from which, in the great explosion of '48 that we boys scarcely felt, your poet's soul burst forth with patriotic fervour. You nearly died of grief, when on that terrible day of 1849 you informed your scholars from the dais: 'We have been beaten at Novara.'

The elder boys told us that as our teacher said this he fell in a faint. We used to see him as he strode rapidly along the school corridors in his usual agitated way, with his lofty brow, his white locks flying loose, and his eyes fixed on some world which he alone could see. We felt quite overcome and thought of the figure of Sordello,[7] whose humanity, strength, and righteous indignation he had impressed on us as he read us Dante.

He it was, worthy friar, who recited to us in school, in the year 1853, the ode: *Halted on the arid river bank.* He did not tell us who wrote it, but promised to send the boy who guessed the name of the author to the top of the class. But we all guessed right! Had we not already read the chorus from *Carmagnola*?

The last verses of that ode and the tone with which our teacher read them, come back to me now: *Dovrà dir sospirando: io non v'era*—I was not there! Seven or eight of his old pupils, who are now here, perhaps turn their thoughts to him. It may be that he remembers how he made us furious with indignation when he read us, in Colletta's history, the account of the death of Caracciolo and about the Neapolitan massacres of

[5] A quotation from Manzoni's ode *Marzo 1821* expressing a not dissimilar feeling to that in the verses of Virgil quoted above. The opening verse 'Halted on the arid river bank' is quoted below.

[6] For Abba's school-master see *Introduction*, p. xi.

[7] Sordello in Dante (*Purgatorio* VI and VII) is depicted as one who loved his country and countrymen and gives rise to a diatribe against Dante's unworthy contemporaries. Sordello was a Mantuan who distinguished himself as a poet in the Provençal language.

1799. Perhaps he claims that it is he who prepared us to fight in this Sicilian war!

25 August. On the shore by the Faro

On the opposite shore, at Bagnara in Calabria there has been a sad incident. When Cosenz's men were disembarking under fire from the Neapolitan troops of General Briganti, De Flotte, in the red shirt as one of Garibaldi's colonels, fell dead. They say that as he was getting into the boat at the Faro, Major Speech wanted to give him a revolver, but he, smiling and thanking, refused to accept it. Directly he fired a shot, he said, someone else would kill him. So he wanted to face the foe like that old hero in the *Henriade*, who charged into the thick of the fray, ready to be killed, but not to kill. De Flotte has died, but Garibaldi has immortalized him for the glory of France and of humanity, in an Order of the Day with words worth more than any life.

De Flotte will sleep in the poetic land of Calabria which now belongs to him rather than to us. His name will be heard as long as the war lasts, for they say that the company of two hundred and fifty Frenchmen, who have come to lend us the aid of their valour, will be known by his name.

26 August. By the sign of a star

The dispositions as follows: General Briganti's brigade is in the low-lying ground and along the shore, while our men are on the heights like spectators on the stepped terraces of an ancient theatre. If the Neapolitans don't capitulate, all our forces will charge down on them and thrust them into the sea to perish. Everyone is waiting. It is night. Garibaldi, who wants to finish it before dawn, is at an advance post.

'Lieutenant, have you a watch?'

'No, General.'

'No matter, lie down here, like this, look at that star, the brightest one over there: and look at this tree. When the star is hidden by the top of the tree it will be two o'clock. Then rouse up and call the men to arms.'

So with the simplicity of a shepherd king, or shall we say with the elegance of a hero from the pages of Xenophon, or perhaps better still—like himself, when young, in the virgin forests of Rio Grande, Garibaldi set the hour by a star.

But, after all, there was no need for an assault. It is said that General Briganti had an interview with Garibaldi and they agreed on a cease-fire. I have had the meeting described to me. What a sight it must have been, the whole brigade reduced to impotence and all those soldiers disbanded. I did not see them myself, but I rejoice. It must have been a heart-breaking business.

27 August

More news! This is like the month of March when ice is breaking up and currents carry it away in huge pieces. General Melendez and his brigade have been encircled by our men and he has gone off after disbanding his troops. The Bourbon commanders are washing their hands of all responsibility, one after the other, according to the rumours that come in thick and fast; there's no discipline, everything is disintegrating. The fact is that the Royal Palace is full of cravens and the revolution has put the army in an impossible position.

*   *   *

I hear that the day before yesterday General Briganti was making his way all alone on horseback towards some unknown destination, to do who knows what, when he ran into the 15th Neapolitan regiment encamped at Mileto. There were cries of 'Down with the traitor!' So he dismounted and walked into the midst of the soldiers. They were held by his senile dignity and the calmness in his face, but a drum-major rushed at him with his staff and the point went right through and killed him. Others say he was killed by a shot at point blank range.

When we, in our turn, traverse that tragic neighbourhood, I shall feel the air still shuddering at that foul deed. Tragedy haunts these Calabrian mountain crags. Near that spot the Romeos were killed, and not far away is the Angitola Pass

where Mussolino's men and the Calabrians fell in '48. And then
there is the whole story of the French followers of King Joseph
and King Joachim . . . and surely Joachim's tragic ghost must
haunt the castle of Pizzo down there.[8]

I can't get that unfortunate General Briganti out of my
mind. I have heard that when Garibaldi entered Palermo by
the Termini Gate he was in command of the Castellamare fort
and he could hardly bring himself to order the city to be bombarded. The rumour goes that there was a son of his among the
officers, but of a quite different temper. What mysteries lie
hidden under a soldier's uniform when tyrants rule and,
between throne and army, a country groans.

30 August

About a hundred of us are sailing in the *Carmel*, a French
packet steamer hailing from Syrian ports. We were picked up
at Messina, nearly all wounded or sick, going home on leave.
Among us is Medici from Bergamo, half mad with homesickness, who threatens to kill the captain because the ship
doesn't go as fast as he would like. On the quarter-deck are
ladies, who create a sweet atmosphere of spring. Two lovely
girls from Catania are dreams.

They all seem happy except a tall handsome grey-haired
Frenchwoman, about fifty. According to a French infantry
captain, she has come from Syria, as he has, where she went to
visit the grave of her son, a second lieutenant who died there.
The captain speaks of the Lebanon Christians and of the
French forces in those parts. He seems almost to resent our
own war because it deflects attention from that lovely poetical
part of the Near East. But aren't the Calabrians, indeed all in
the kingdom of the two Sicilies, Christians too, and suffering
there worse than under the Turks?

[8] Giandomenico and Gianandrea Romeo led an ill fated rebellion in
1847; Benedetto Mussolino was the leader of the Calabrians who attempted
to support the anti-Bourbon forces in 1848 and 1849. Joseph Bonaparte and
Joachim Murat, who succeeded him as King of Naples, relied on the liberals,
who were bitterly persecuted after the collapse of French power. Abba is
conjuring up the tragic scenes of half a century.

In the Port of Naples, 31 August

The sky, the bay, the island, Vesuvius standing proudly in the burning blue sky, the countryside in its dress of delicate colours that fade away till they blend with the air itself—is all this indifferent to what is happening? At any rate the sprawling city itself, almost frightening to contemplate, must be boiling with passion, easily to be imagined. There's the Royal Palace! It was from those balconies that Ferdinand II pointed out prisoners in jail to his children, telling them that their chains were the first things young princes should learn about.

In the distance one can see an endless column of soldiers marching down a street leading to the sea. Who knows what will be their fate in a few days from now? I gaze at the sea around the ships. Perhaps where the *Carmel* now lies is the very spot where the corpse of Caracciolo floated up to the surface, seventy years ago.[9] Among these old boatmen rowing round our ship there may be some who saw it. Yet to us the episode seems to belong to the dark days of long ago. Police boats go the rounds, but some Neapolitans have managed to come aboard and not minded being seen chatting with us. All they can talk about is Garibaldi and how they long for his coming. When will he come?

One of our fellow passengers, who has taken a turn through the city, tells us that there is talk of a great event in Calabria. Garibaldi has made 15,000 men under General Ghio surrender at Soveria Manelli. Whatever will the King of Naples do? Really one can hardly restrain a certain pity for him.

[9] Caracciolo, see note 4, p. 126.

September 1860

Captain Lavarello, an old sea-dog from Leghorn, called us aside and suggested a splendid plan.

'Look yonder! That Papal warship is the *Immacolata*. What do you say to a little bit of piracy? All of you? All right, hold hard for a bit, then tell all those red-shirts to pay attention to me. We'll pounce on the captain of the *Carmel* and his men and stow 'em below without hurting a hair of their heads, but they'd better look out if they interfere! A few of you lower yourselves over the side down a hawser and make a surprise attack on the Papal schooner, push the few lads aboard into the holds, then make fast a rope. I'll take command of the *Carmel* and tow the *Immacolata* away full steam ahead. When they've got her engines running, I'll go aboard, we'll let the *Carmel* go where she likes and we'll sail off to Calabria and make a present of the schooner to Garibaldi.'

The thing seemed as good as done and we were already relishing the adventure. It was like something out of Byron. One could imagine the shrieks of the ladies and the amazement of the French captain with us and of a French sentry on the edge of the quay! And then the flight over the sea! What perils! What unknown hazards! But, all of a sudden, the *Carmel* hoisted her anchor and farewell to all that! As we sail away I gaze at the mountains of Latium. It was on these very waters that Garibaldi, as a youth, first thought of Rome.

2 September

A mother's heart! That fair French lady has been staring for three days with shining eyes at one of our men wounded at Milazzo. A fine looking lad who makes me think of Pulci's Baldovino, because he knows his father acted as a spy for the

Austrians.[1] I noticed it from the first day out and hoped no one else did, for I should not have wished to see the lady, who bears such a load of sorrow, laughed at. But it is only too easy to think ill of people and as I write I have tears in my eyes. A short while ago the lady approached me and said:

'Do you know that soldier with his arm in a sling? Would you ask him to have a word with me?' I could read the rest in her eyes and I asked her if her dead son was very like him.

'Yes, indeed!' she replied. 'For three whole days I seem to have seen him once again, but my poor son is really yonder, buried in sacred Lebanon earth. How did you know, though?'

I didn't stop to tell her that the French captain had told me and ran to the bows to fetch the soldier. I spoke to him and he stared hard at me. Then he said: 'Let's go!' So the young man and the lady met in public without paying any heed to the curious eyes watching them. Over their heads the clear blue sky seemed to rest lightly on the mountain tops of Argentaro and Elba. I left them and went aside to think. A curious memory comes back to me at this juncture. I once heard a mother in my village at home say to her son who had returned from the Crimean war: 'I'd have sought you out had you been ill, or wounded, or killed.' 'And what if I'd been buried?'— he replied, and she said: 'I'd have recognized your very bones!'

Well, I take back what I have just been saying! Human nature isn't so bad as it seems! When the lady embraced and kissed the young man as though she had gone out of her mind there wasn't a snigger; they all understood and some wept. But the younger of the two Catanian girls stared as though her eyes would drop out of her head. If one were only a king of ancient days and could take her by the hand and lead her to that fine, strong, young man and clasp it in his and say to them: 'Go and get married, I ennoble you with the title of Count or Duke. Love each other and make your own Paradise.'

[1] In Luigi Pulci's poem *Il Morgante* (see note 3, p. 87) the traitor Gano's son Baldovino is a loyal follower of Orlando.

Naples, 14 September

Ten or twelve days ago when I saw Naples from the harbour, I should have liked to throw myself overboard in order to get there by swimming. Now that I'm here I don't feel the same about it . . . perhaps I am dazed by it all. Vast, splendid, heterogeneous; one loses one's way in it; it is a city magnificent even in its squalor. Never have I seen such an open display of filth. I've made a tour of the slums. One's brain reels, it is as though one traversed a swamp. People swarm, so that you have to squeeze yourself small to get through and end by being deafened. But on all these faces there is an air of lively expectancy. What do they want? What do they hope? Who can say? If one night they should rise in wrath, shouting out the name of one or other of their Saints, what would become of us, of Garibaldi? Yet he is quite unruffled in the Angri palace. It is we puny ones of little faith who feel dubious. He has enough to move mountains and feels the spirit of the people strong within him. Has he not done all he set out to do? What could we, a few thousand men, have done if he had not been our leader? Could all the Generals of Italy rolled into one, with all their skill, have done what he has done? There was need of a heart like his, perhaps of a head like his, and that face that makes one think of Moses, of Charlemagne, of some Warrior–Christ! You only had to see him to be won over.

14 September. In the Barns at Naples

I have rejoined my brigade. There is nothing, absolutely nothing, to compare with this feeling of being absorbed into the life of a great body of youth, love, and valour. I've imagined all the places they've been through: Catanzaro, Tiriolo, Soveria, Rogliano, Cosenza; Eber's brigade marched all that way through Calabria, 'The sky their tent, the earth their bed', but without firing a shot. Daniele Piccinini, the best captain in the brigade, told me the whole story.

Nearly all our Divisions, coincided at Cosenza, as though by pre-arrangement. Had Bixio intended this to be so? They were

drawn up on the spot where, sixteen years before, the Bandiera brothers had been shot.[2] It was a commemorative parade for the fallen heroes. Bixio pronounced a stirring address: 'Soldiers of the Italian revolution, soldiers of the European revolution; we who pay respect to God alone now bow in reverence before the grave of the Bandieras. Here are our Saints.' The Divisions listened in silence to his speech, which was brief and eloquent, and as stormy as the sea on which he had spent half his life. Piccinini says that if they had been asked whether they would change places with the dead, everyone of them would have replied 'yes'. For Bixio spoke of them in such a way that they passed before us living and triumphant so that their death seemed better than our own victories. For sure, martyrdom is more divine than triumph!

While this ceremony was taking place at Vallo di Crati, Garibaldi was entering the city of Naples almost alone, saluted by the troops left behind by Francis II, and acclaimed by the populace, which must have looked like the people of Jerusalem on the first Palm Sunday. Things to turn a man's head, to make him stretch out for a crown . . . but Garibaldi passed on smiling, and did not even give a glance at the Royal Palace.

Naples, 15 September

Off we go for Caserta as hard as we can! Yesterday the Royalists came out from Capua, and who knows their objective? It is no distance, they say, from Capua here and there's practically nothing to stop them, save a handful of red-shirts. How terrible their sudden return would be! Ruffo, Fra' Diavolo, and the orgies of 1799![3]

[2] The brothers Attilio and Emilio Bandiera made an unsuccessful attempt to start a rebellion after landing in southern Italy in 1844. They were executed near Cosenza (see note 4, p. 90).

[3] Colletta's account of the cruelties of the reactionaries in 1799 made a deep impression on Abba. Here he refers to the anti-liberal Cardinal Ruffo, leader of the so-called *Sanfedisti* and Michele Pezza, called Fra' Diavolo, who committed many atrocities on the Bourbon side.

Caserta, 15 September

Yesterday's sortie was only a reconnaissance, though in strength. The Hungarian legionaries can't be driven from their chosen positions. The Neapolitan cavalry charged and charged again, but they broke against the Hungarian positions like waves against the rocks. Their infantry then advanced, but Tanara's and Corrao's *Bersaglieri* charged them with the bayonet and made them retreat, helter-skelter, and pursued them right to the walls of the citadel. They had a bad time going back, for the fortress artillery fired point-blank at them.

*　　　*　　　*

General Türr is most capable and, at the same time, mild! You wouldn't think so from his fierce looks. He has spilled little blood in quelling re-action. No one was executed at Avellino, none at Ariano; and to the latter place he went almost alone, yet pacified it. The day before yesterday he dispatched Major Cattabene to Marcianise, a large place not far from here, where the people had risen to the old Bourbon war-cry of '*Viva Maria!*' When he had quietened everything down, Cattabene returned, having executed only two out of the fourteen condemned to death. The people of Marcianise vociferated that they wanted the other twelve executed too, and sent a deputation to Türr to beg for this satisfaction. 'No! no!' says Türr, 'pardon, oblivion, reconciliation; we're not here to carry out your petty vendettas.'

16 September

No one's to know! Don't breathe it! Garibaldi is going to Sicily for some undisclosed reason. But what could happen if the Bourbon troops in Capua got to know he is no longer here?

L

20 September

Yesterday we made a great demonstration against Capua. They say this was to enable other forces of ours to capture Caiazzo, a large place on the farther side of the Volturno. They also say it was to test the enemy, once and for all, and discover how many of them remain loyal to their fugitive king. Much blood was shed. Too much ardour, in both officers and men.

The action began on the extreme left, then hell was let loose down the whole front. We of Eber's, on the Sant' Angelo road, had the least opposition. We did, indeed, see riflemen, infantry, and artillery preparing to come against us, but a detachment of our troops with two guns opened up against them. Their fire was so accurate and heavy that the enemy column retreated. It was then pursued, and our guns were taken right up to the fortress. They carried on firing as long as one gunner was left standing, defying forty pieces firing at them. Then, as it was seen that a sortie was in preparation to capture the guns, the *Bersaglieri* of the Milan brigade rushed up and dragged them to safety.

It was precisely at that moment that we could hear shouting on our right—'He's here! He's coming! The General! Garibaldi!' And from the direction of Sant' Angelo came Garibaldi, radiant. Under his eyes we were ordered to move to the left to throw back a new attack from the Bourbon troops who had once more come out from Capua. We fell on the flank of their column and it disappeared. It seemed to be over in a flash, but we had casualties. Captain Marani from Adria lay with the others, his arm shattered, a fair, handsome man; who knows what mutilation he will suffer.

Let me now celebrate the fallen. I did not know Colonel Puppi who was disembowelled by shrapnel almost at the gates of Capua. I feel sad at never having seen him, almost as though I were at fault.

Then what of poor Captain Blanc from Belluno? He had sacrificed his rank of Grenadier officer and now he has lost a

leg here. And Cozzo, Narciso Cozzo, the Palermitan baron
who looked like a gentleman of the Altavilla stock, preserved
alive as a specimen of the race. Well, he was laid low by a bullet
that found him among the Genoese Sharpshooters, that splendid élite that has sworn always to be first.

28 September

Every morning now for five days we have been stood to and
have remained under arms for hours at a time. That's the way
to test one's nerve! It is a hard ordeal, this preparing to die
and then learning that the time is not yet, and then wondering
if tomorrow is the day. But some tremendous event is about to
happen. There is a hint of approaching storm in the air, of
tragic happenings. The bulletin of some evenings ago spoke
vaguely of heavy attacks and contained some '*in the eventuality
of*'s which made one tremble. Not out of fear, no, but out of
anxiety for our country's cause. '*In the eventuality of ... we
should try to fall back on Maddaloni.*' And what then? It means,
of course, that all would be lost and that at Maddaloni we
should all die.

*   *   *

Well, we can put up with it, but in Caserta there are innocent people who suffer, the wives and daughters of Bourbon
officers besieged in Capua. There can hardly have been a more
tragic spectacle in time of war. At night many of these women,
who are starving, beg from our men. And, it must be admitted,
not all have the decency and courtesy to give and turn away.
The next day some of these men may be at the front, perhaps
fighting against the husbands and fathers of the women whose
misfortune they have not respected. So to hunger and the results of hunger is added a third horror—blood!

30 September. Evening; in quarters at Falciano, near Caserta

All the afternoon the guns of Capua have thundered; now,
as the evening bell tolls, all is silent. There is no doubt now;

the Neapolitans are coming out, and in strength! Their patrols are probing here and there along the whole Volturno front and this morning they tried to cross the river at the Triflisco ferry. But Spangaro's men repulsed them.

I know that Garibaldi has visited Bixio at the Maddaloni Pass, down our way, and that solemn words were spoken and that Bixio has been inspired to act the part of a Leonidas. 'As long as I am alive, no one shall get through here,' he said, and he will keep his word.

October 1860

After one's heart gives a jump comes a feeling of great sadness! A sound of galloping and up comes a Scout on a horse: Colonel Bassini! Colonel Cossovich! Then trumpets blow. How raucous is the note from the picket guard and how ill-omened! But the reveillé that trills forth like a mountain lark from our courtyard would awaken the dead. This is the trumpeter Viscovo and he pours his whole soul into it. When he puts his instrument to his mouth he seems to lose his identity and float away in music. He seems to say 'Oh to die! Oh to die like this!' Poor little waif, picked up somewhere in Sicily as we marched along the great road that leads to a united Italy, he came to us with that frail body of his, and only sixteen! What is he searching for? Nothing more than death! Virgil must have imagined Misenus, son of Aelus, like this, him who surpassed all others in inspiring heroes with his trumpet.

1 October, Caserta, in the Courtyard of the Royal Palace

Here we are, nearly the entire Türr division, in reserve. The battle is raging on a wide perimeter that would need a complete sweep of one's arm to indicate it. Well, none of us are dying, but we suffer like souls in Limbo. I look at the faces around me; some are deadly pale; some are gay; others are thoughtful; still others, vacant. Who knows what mine's like?

In one corner of the courtyard there is a battalion of the Savoia regiment, now known as the King's Brigade. The soldiers are in tents and officers stand around, fearing perhaps that some of their men may nip out and join us. They watch us, though, and envy us, for, unlike them, we are waiting for our call at any moment. But why shouldn't they be called? What have they come here for? I see a Captain, a typical Savoyard,

certainly one of those of '48. He gazes at us with his frank eyes, in which I seem to see the thoughts of all his compatriots who have been lost to France.[1] Perhaps he is sad, for they were of the best. Now when in war the cry goes up, *Savoia!* Savoy cannot answer.

*   *   *

Here's another captain in Victor Emmanuel's army! He's as young as I am and a captain already. I thought he was one of ours who, out of vanity, get themselves a uniform. But I saw that he was closely followed by some gunners, regulars from Piedmont, some of them with the Crimean medal. They have come from Naples, looking for Garibaldi, with whom they wish to enrol, they and their captain together. He is a Piedmontese nobleman called Savio.

'Well, what are they coming for now?' asked one of our officers. 'Afterwards they'll claim to have done the whole job themselves and get the honour and all the rest of it.'

'Ah, my friend, let's provide them with the guns and let them get on with it—you'll see Garibaldi won't adopt your attitude.'

Here comes a carriage from Santa Maria with a woman in it. Flushed face, vigorous gestures, who ever is she? An angel, a fury, or what? She's talking with a Hungarian colonel, who must be telling her frightful things, for she clasps her head in her hands. What is it? Perhaps that the dead and wounded are already to be numbered in hundreds, or that disaster is about to erupt on us from Capua? Oh dear! Why isn't she an Italian? Her name was Miss White[2] and she is now the wife of Mario, one of our best. Perhaps I have seen the loveliest head that could be shattered today by a miserable bullet fired by some soldier, oblivious of what he had done.

*   *   *

[1] A reference to the cession of Savoy to France (see note 1, p. 1).

[2] Jessie White (1832–1906) married Alberto Mario the close friend and follower of Mazzini. She wrote several works in favour of the Italian movement, including a biography of Mazzini.

Now comes one of the Scouts from Maddaloni at full gallop. 'Where's General Türr? Where is he? Bixio is asking for help.' Gracious, Bixio imploring help! Things must be desperate. Oh sun, that has witnessed so many terrible things on this earth. Oh God, do not let Italy perish here, today. . . .'

*   *   *

Number one Battalion, first two companies, shoulder arms, right turn, march! It's our turn now! Such as we are, a mere handful, we're going to support Bixio, wrens to help a vulture!

1 October, 2 p.m.

We climbed the mountain, turning about apprehensively to look at Caserta behind us and, in the distance, Santa Maria and the open country, all smoke and confusion. From beyond Mont Tifata we could hear gunfire, sounding like echoes, but really coming from another battle. Very soon, on the opposite slope from that we are now climbing, we shall come on Bixio's camp. By the sound of the gunfire it seems as though he is retreating. But, once we are up at the top, what a sight meets our eyes! All the way down the slopes to the left, on the great aqueduct,[3] and beyond, is a swarm of red-clad men and cries as though from a hundred thousand throats. Lower still, black dots retreating, beaten Bourbon troops taking the bitter way of flight. On the main road, beyond the range of our most advanced troops, there is a dense mass of cavalry. Two guns are still firing their shells here and there from a distance; Parthian shots!

Bixio comes back and there is victory in his look! 'Who are you people?' he asks Captain Novaria—'Eber's men'—'Go down that way to Valle as fast as you can and put yourselves under the orders of Colonel Dezza.'

[3] The aqueduct (otherwise called the Bridge, or the Arches of the Valley) was a lofty three-tiered structure pierced by arches built by the architect Vanvitelli to carry water across a valley to Caserta palace.

1 October, 3 p.m.

Far away here, on the steeps of Monte Calvo, I have been reminded of my own lovely countryside, Le Langhe, almost unknown to the rest of Italy. For a moment I have felt, seen, and enjoyed the hills of home.

I was making my way across those lofty scrub-covered heights along a track where only those born to suffer and sweat and pray to God for his aid, that is to say poor peasants, had gone before, when suddenly an officer seemed to leap up from under the ground. His face was bleeding, his shirt was all torn and he had the stump of a sabre gripped in his hand. He called out: 'Where are you off to?' 'To my company above Valle.'—'And where have you come from?' 'From General Headquarters.'—'And Bixio?' 'Victorious!' On exchanging these few words, I realized I was talking to one from my own part of the country. 'Who are you?' I said and I already began to taste the happiness of having met a compatriot in a red shirt. 'I am Sclavo from Lezegno.'—'And I am so and so.' Then we fell on each other's necks. I have never felt the close ties of my native place so strongly as at that moment. Our rivers, the many-channelled Bormida and the Tanaro, all those fair mountains, our towns and villages, the home of such excellent people, good, modest, simple, and content with little! He then told me how he came to be here in such poor shape. Only a few hours before, in one of the last advances, he had fallen into the hands of Bavarians, who had dragged him away, loading him with indignities. But he had managed to escape and was on his way back when he ran into me, one from his own home district! It probably never occurred to him that I can sing his praises through our valleys.

Towards evening

News begins to trickle in, but still vague. Gunfire has died away. We have been victorious at Santa Maria, Sant' Angelo, all along the line, after a battle that went on for ten hours. Here, on the left flank, among the Castelmorone gorges, the

Pass was held by Major Bronzetti and half a battalion against
Bourbon troops, six times as numerous. He died, many died,
but the enemy couldn't get through. What must the men feel,
who now lie down to rest after such an achievement? And what
has become of the souls of those who have fallen? One simply
cannot believe that they have ceased to exist and that nothing
of them remains. On the battlefield death seems hardly death!
Here it is a mere transition.

Above Valle, 2 October, morning

Who should be honoured in the words of Sallust? 'The
battle over, then you should consider the great daring, the
strong spirit shown. . . .' There were the Bavarians who
climbed up to find their death on the peak of Monte Caro,
held by our men; there were red-shirts who rushed so impetu-
ously in pursuit of the foe almost to the outskirts of Valle, and
fell there. Bavarians lying dead in their grey uniforms look
fierce still, stout, thick-set fellows, no longer young and some
with wrinkles. If you investigate their flasks you will find them
still half-full of brandy. They must have eaten and drunk well
a few hours before fighting against our men who had little
enough with which to fill their bellies. One of them had found
a small enclosure of dry-stone walling, right on the top of
Monte Caro, made by shepherd boys, perhaps in idle sport.
He occupied it and couldn't be dislodged, not even when his
comrades had fled and he was alone. They had to finish him
off like a mad beast, as he kept lunging out fiercely with his
bayonet. In his pocket-book it was found his name was Stolz,
from some Bavarian village. Who knows? Perhaps on that
mountain peak, he thought he was saving the throne for fair
Sophia, daughter of German kings, come from his own country to rule in the sweet land of Italy. Now he lies quiet as one
who has done his duty. He is stretched out on his left side and
seems to be asleep; or is he peeping and listening? Our men
come up, one after another, to look at him. Well, it is good to
end so, rather than of old age in a bed, or perhaps on straw
after causing many others to suffer too. It is nice that all look

at him with respect, only regretting that such valour was wasted.

Tonight, on sentry-duty close to the corpse, a young Sicilian from Bivona, a nobleman of sorts and still almost a boy, kept calling out to the corporal. His voice seemed to come from the pit of all woes. The corporal ran to him: 'What's the matter?' —'Nothing.' But at last the corporal understood, for the youth was trembling and staring at the corpse only a few yards away.

'Ah, you're scared of that?'

'Yes, corporal!'

'Imagination!'

* * *

I paid a visit, yesterday, to all the small plateaux in turn, that descend the mountain like steps. Here it was that a hundred and fifty of Boldrini's men held up a couple of battalions of Bavarians, attacking from Valle. They held them sufficiently to let a few re-inforcements from Menotti's command come up, but it was not enough. Boldrini was wounded, and many of his officers were killed or wounded and it looked as though this strong position was to be lost. Menotti and Taddei went to Colonel Dezza:

'Colonel, it will be disastrous if the enemy turns this wing! He'll get between Villa Gualtieri and Caserta and in an hour he'll be down in the plain and the whole Terra del Lavoro will be roused in support of Bourbon re-action. Our people fighting on the River Volturno will have hostile forces in their rear, and who knows what will happen in Naples, just waiting for such an opportunity—Italy may be lost again today.'

That was the moment when the *Picciotti*, the Sicilian volunteers, covered themselves with glory. Two months before, they were riotous on embarking for the continent; it appeared they had no notion of any Italy besides their own three-cornered island. Marching through Calabria, however, they have become new men and they have won our respect here. They charged like veterans.

Down on the small plateaux, among the few poor trees that

cannot flourish in the stony ground, there are, ah! so many red-shirts lying who will never move again! I counted some twenty here and there, some of them recognizable by their swarthy, almost moorish, hue, as volunteers from the Vallo di Mazzara, where Bixio raised men. But there are fair, northern, almost girlish heads among them. I passed by one who could not have been older than sixteen and, speaking for myself and for him, I uttered words that, had I been able to transcribe them, would have been a masterpiece of poetry. A piece of biscuit was poking out of his haversack. Had I known who he was, I would have carried that morsel back to the girl who must have loved him and told her to treasure it all her life through.

I hear that many are missing and that more than twenty officers are either dead or wounded. And this only in our small section and out of so few men! So what are the losses all down the line, at Villa Gualtieri, at the Aqueduct, at the Mill and down on our left? It is a long front on such a strange curve that Maddaloni, on the extreme right, was at the back of those fighting on the Volturno! When the full losses are known there will be much mourning.

2 October, about 11 a.m.

We can see a large party of Bourbon soldiers, perhaps those who tried to get past Bronzetti yesterday, twisting and turning up and down the steeps of Caserta Vecchia, as though they did not know which way to fly. On all sides we can see the red shirts of our men who are encircling them. Seen from this vantage point of Monte Caro, it is like a Royal hunt. The Bourbon soldiers are now concentrating as though to stand and defend themselves among the tumbled ruins that lend the landscape its sad tone of past grandeur and melancholy. What is the meaning of those rifle-shots? Very shortly Bixio will be there. We can see from here the long line of men climbing the mountain and its head is almost at the plateau. When Bixio started he said to his men: 'You won't eat till all those have been captured!' It looks as if the Royalists have recognized

him; there is some confusion—a horseman gallops out from their midst and then returns.

Now their retreat is cut off from the rear. They set off in the direction of Sant' Angelo, then come back. They go down towards Caserta Nuova—no, they climb up again. . . . A white flag! What an impression one gets from the yell of triumph that fills the air over there. The earth seems to shake, everything is in motion, our men run in from all sides a great stillness—they have surrendered.

3 October

However long we waited, those we beat the day before yesterday did not return. If only we had had cavalry to pursue their flying tails! It would not have been cruelty, for they were all foreign mercenaries. But those captured yesterday at Caserta Vecchia were Italians and they were indeed from the column which came to grips with Bronzetti at Castelmorone and couldn't get past him. It would have been bad for us had they succeeded!

4 October

Yesterday, Telesforo, who seems to drink in everything he sees with such passion (perhaps because he feels he is not long for this world), came to visit me from Santa Maria and told me to come with him. 'Where to?' I said. He replied: 'To see what there is to be seen (quoting Dante) "*At the end of the bridge near Benevento*".'[4]

'Let's go!'

It was almost night. Once down from Monte Caro we passed through the hamlet of Valle, ten hovels looking like ragged old crones. The day before yesterday, as the Royalists went through on their way to the battle, the women in those houses leant out of the windows shrieking like furies: 'Long live the

---

[4] Abba is here again looking for literature in life. All Italians know of the presumed fate of Manfred at the battle of Benevento (see note 4, p. 90) because of Dante's sympathetic references to it (*Purgatorio* III, 112–145).

King and Death to . . .', yes—to us! They say they were heard
half-way up the mountain and that they created more effect
than the advancing battalions!

On and on we trudged along the big road. But wherever is
this bridge? Like children, we always imagine things to be
nearer than they are; but Benevento was a long way farther
on. We met no living soul, but, every now and again, in the
fields by the roadside, there were corpses, perhaps soldiers who
had been wounded the day before yesterday, died on the way
and been thrown out of carts.

We couldn't find the bridge!

'Yet,' said Telesforo, 'if we keep going, sooner or later we
should hear water—I should like to see it running in starlight,
I'd like to hear the bridge echo under our feet, I should like to
drop a stone from the parapet and imagine myself an Angevin
soldier and that Manfred lay below. Antiquity, that which is
no more, is everything for me. What lives is nothing. I feel myself to be nothing. I would never have followed Garibaldi had
I not felt he belonged to antiquity.'

So spake Telesforo and made me sad to hear him.

At that moment we heard horses trotting from the Volturno
direction. This is it! They must be Bourbon Scouts! Down into
the fields! Three horsemen went swiftly by and I too felt a waft
of antiquity. I thought of the riders sent by Charles of Anjou
on the track of Manfred who was thought to have fled from the
battle. The living riders, however, were some of our own Scouts,
bold, even reckless, young men. We could hear them talking
gaily in the Lombard dialect. So back we got to the road and
trudged on for quite a while, pursuing our fantasies.

'Manfred? Charles of Anjou?' continued Telesforo. 'The
modern king is a coward. The day before yesterday Francis
was in the midst of his 30,000 soldiers; he could have put himself at the head of a thousand horsemen, tried a point in our
front, broken through, and galloped all the way to Naples in
triumph! Either that, or be killed, pierced to the heart by one
of our champions, by Nullo for instance. He couldn't do either,
so he's finished. As for Charles of Anjou, let's say Victor

Emmanuel. There's a gap of 600 years between them, and instead of a Pope to present him with the southern kingdom, we have Garibaldi to invite him down! How I should like to see the meeting between those two—the King and Garibaldi!'

We took our way back and, as we went, we talked away like a couple of friars, but every now and then Telesforo coughed and said he was cold. He huddled his old cloak about him and clutched the hems to cover his chest. Dawn seemed near when we reached our sentries. Some small fires were dying down on the slopes of Monte Caro and of Villa Gualtieri. The red shirts of our troops stood out in bold relief against the grey screes and among the greeny-grey of the olive trees. They lent life and a kind of emotion to the scene. Ranks of red-clad soldiers were going quietly over the Vanvitelli Aqueduct, on their way perhaps to relieve others on guard. But it was up there that at a certain moment in the battle our men met the Bavarians and some had fallen from that height. God! it's terrible to think of. And to think that at this time on the day before yesterday my dear Traverso woke up full of sturdy confidence, as indeed did the other Traverso and Stella too (all three of them landed at Marsala), and yet before midday they were dead for ever, as much part of 'antiquity' as those who had died in ages past.

Caserta, 7 October

I told my friend Sclavo that what he had witnessed at the Aqueduct he must record here in my notebook. He wrote as follows: 'Three or four days before the battle, Garibaldi came to Bixio and said: "I have complete faith in you; this is our Thermopylae." Such was our task and we all knew we had to stand or die. We waited.

'On the morning of 1 October Von Mechel's Division, eight or nine thousand men, advanced from Ducenta by way of Maddaloni, with the Aqueduct Pass as their objective. At the head of the column was a squadron of dragoons with helmets and red lapels; two guns and a battalion of Sharpshooters followed. When they got to the village of Valle the head of the column opened out with the Sharpshooters to the right and

they began to probe the high ground where I was with my company. They started firing systematically with their excellent rifles at five hundred yards, but it was too far out of range for us to reply. Meanwhile the main column marched on towards the Aqueduct, the centre of our front.

'I immediately dispatched a certain Calogero, a man from Messina, who was attached to me as a scout, with a note to Major Boldrini to say we were under attack. The reply came that I was not to be taken in by any feint movement. It fell out badly, because that battalion of Sharpshooters was already pouring into a wood on our left and was beginning to surround us, keeping up a steady fire on us all the time.

'At this point Major Boldrini flew to our aid with two companies and, without delay, charged forward in the direction of thick trees where flashes of rifle fire revealed the enemy's position. "Cold steel," he shouted, "*Viva l'Italia!*"

'I've not yet told you that a bullet had already penetrated his chest and come out by the shoulder blade. I tried to support him and drag him away as the enemy was now charging from the wood and we had to retreat. But he would not have it and, pushing me away, said, "Leave me, I'm a useless man now." So he stayed where he had fallen. We fell back overwhelmed, but after being reinforced by some fifty of Menotti's *Bersaglieri* we came back again. I looked in vain for poor Major Boldrini. I learnt later that the Bavarians had lugged him, head and feet, down over the crags to Valle where they abandoned him and where he was found in a dying condition by our people after the victory.

'Many of our men fell dead or wounded in our counter-attack, among others the Genoese Evangelisti and Carbone, who had both been with you at the Marsala landing. But this was nothing, we had hardly begun yet! You know how time flies. The attacks went on. Towards eleven, or shortly after, the Bavarians were up to Menotti's position and they began to encircle the hill called Siepe, a bastion of Monte Caro. Here Bedeschini's and Meneghetti's companies received them with rifle-fire and the bayonet and repulsed them. Dezza, Menotti,

and other officers directed and also took an active part in the fighting.

'Meanwhile other Bavarians appeared on the top of Monte Calvo, dug in, and tried to position two mountain guns there so as to spray us below with shells and shrapnel. From that point they could perhaps push out columns against Bixio's rear. It would have needed only a few men to cut his communications with the Caserta Headquarters and to set all the Terra di Lavoro ablaze with Bourbon reaction. It was a moment of the greatest anxiety. Even the least expert of us could guess the great danger threatening. But, all of a sudden, a battalion could be seen up on the mountain. Is it ours? Yes, it is! Quite unexpectedly it was marching straight to the summit of Monte Calvo. It was a marvellous sight! The Commander could be seen in front with his hat on the point of his sword and one seemed to hear him shouting. The others pressed hard behind him with long strides in a compact body up the slope.

'It was Taddei.

'Their bold effrontery impressed the Bavarians who wavered but defended themselves and continued to resist and to cause casualties. But they broke and fled in rout, abandoning their dead and wounded together with the position.

'Those of us fighting down below watched the action above lost in admiration for the victors. At the same time we could watch the great dense Bourbon column making their attack in the centre at the Aqueduct, where Bixio was stationed with his *picciotti*. The situation was terrifying! If they break, we said, if they pass over Bixio's dead body, they will be in Naples this evening and there will be a repetition of the orgies of 1799.

'We could see them as they skirted the mountain slopes between the plain and the dry stone walls of the road parallel with the Aqueduct. Behind those walls we could see the red shirts of our men as they crouched, waiting as though spellbound, without firing a shot. We really suffered; we trembled; I even heard someone curse and cry out: "But what are they doing?" When the Bourbon troops, however, came almost up to the line of walls, those red-shirts seemed to explode; a tor-

rent, a hurricane of men, poured over into the head of the column and there were ferocious yells and bayonet thrusts. We went hot and cold by turns.

'The Bourbon troops had no opportunity, or room, to spread out, so they took to flight, one section on the heels of another; away they went in complete disorder, and the whole column in confusion fled towards Valle as best they could.

'We dominated the spectacle from where we were and we understood that all that heroic mass of *picciotti* had been inspired by the spirit of Bixio. There were two heroes that day: Bixio and Taddei.

'In the evening we counted our fallen. But it was my battalion that suffered the heaviest losses. Innocente Stella was hit in the head by a bullet and died; Herter was wounded; both he and Stella were with us at Marsala. So were Rambosio and Rugerone. The latter, poor fellow, was hit in the stomach by a shell-splinter that came out at his back. They found him in a ravine in the evening and brought him down to Villa Gualtieri, where he lingered in pain for eighteen hours till death liberated him. Antonio Traverso of my own company met his death in a little wood near Menotti's battalion, one doesn't know how he got there. I found him next day with a bullet through his chest and a bloody white handkerchief clapped to his mouth. Of Boldrini's three companies, only some twenty men under Lieutenant Baroni of Lovere, wounded in his head, joined up that evening with Menotti's men and formed a nucleus when the broken battalion was re-formed.' That is what my friend wrote.

Caserta, 8 October

I wouldn't record their names, even if I knew them, and I have no intention of asking. All those who were present when they were read out by Garibaldi, in that tremendous voice of his, can never forget them, however much they might like to.

In the first courtyard to the left, as one enters the Royal Palace precincts, the battalions commanded by Taddei, Piva, Spinazzi, Menotti, Boldrini, with the remnant of Bixio's

M

division, were waiting for Garibaldi, who was to congratulate them on their victory at Maddaloni. They were drawn up on the four sides of the courtyard, facing the centre.

'Microscopic Division, about turn!' shouted Bixio to the troops, and he is not a man to have said so in joke. They called those battalions a Division before the action, perhaps to make them sound bigger, but they were hardly a brigade then, now you could call them companies.

Garibaldi then entered the courtyard with his Hungarian-style hat in his hand and, directly he was in the middle of the square, he addressed the men as follows: 'Heroes of the 18th Division, I thank you in the name of all Italy!' His speech was short, in his typical style, and he finished by reading out the names of those who had particularly distinguished themselves in action. The very air seemed shining with glory. Then Garibaldi's face darkened and his voice was raised in anger:

'Now the brave have had their reward, I have to punish the cowards.'

There was a shudder as three officers, called by name into the centre of the square, came forth from the ranks. I don't know how they found the strength to take the few necessary steps forward and not fall struck down by shame. Under the General's eyes they were then stripped of their badges of rank by a Major acting as adjutant. And yet they did not die! After that painful scene Garibaldi continued to speak to them as if he were saying farewell to the dead: 'Go, fall on your knees before your Commandant and beg him to give you a rifle, and when next you confront the enemy, see that you die.'

In the Convent of Santa Lucia, 9 October

You're going to Naples? There are too many busy-bodies there! Don't go there to have all the romance rubbed off! Stay here, oh Filibuster! These monkish cells are the place for us: what more do you need?

I pay great heed to Captain Piccinini, although he is only eight or nine years older than I am. Indeed I look up to him as

though he were the great Niccolò in person.[5] The day before yesterday I found him under an olive tree, so radiantly happy that I could almost see the vision he had before his eyes. He was reading a letter *sotto voce* and, directly he saw me, came forward saying: 'My father now knows his son has been promoted captain and is so exultant that all my native mountains rejoice!'

His voice then fell and his eyes filled with tears and he embraced me and I felt puny indeed against his great heart. But to be such as he, straightforward and courageous, one must be born with such a heart. And then his modesty! How trying certain situations must be for him! At Caserta yesterday he was with Garibaldi when some American naval officers came to visit the 'Washington of Italy'. Here's the pattern of my officers, he said, pointing out Piccinini to them. Surely one would give anything to have half such words spoken by him about oneself. Yet Piccinini almost went out in mortification. But there it is; he has no idea that of all officers he is the one who most closely resembles Garibaldi. He has the same simplicity, the same good looks, the same goodness, and the same proud courage. He too could live in a wilderness, create his own world and forget the one made by men. I seem to see him, when all is over, going straight back to his Alpine home, to the solitude of Pradalunga. And if they ask him: 'What was it like?' he will reply as though he had just been for a stroll. But to that father of his he will tell all.

13 October

Nullo, Zasio, Mario, Caldesi with a dozen Scouts under the command of our Candiani, left yesterday at the head of a battalion for some distant objective; somewhere beyond the Volturno, who knows how much farther, where Samnium is, famous Samnium. Nullo the strength, Zasio the beauty, Mario the mind, Caldesi the goodness! Everything is represented! But what are they going to do? Some say to meet Victor

[5] Niccolò Piccinini of Perugia (1375–1444) was a famous captain of mercenaries. There is no connexion with Daniele Piccinini except the name.

Emmanuel; others, to subdue a revolt. They seem to me like men going forth into the unknown.

14 October

Today I am really happy. I have seen the man who is even more wedded to the simple life than Garibaldi himself. A youthful face, although he is seventy, a sturdy figure unbowed by toil, hardships, and disasters of all kinds; dressed in rusty black—cap, overcoat, trousers—not in the least in military style—so I saw General Avezzana. Perhaps the Vicar of Wakefield was like this. He is of the race of men who advance with his gaze fixed on some distant goal, unseen by the world. Yet for them, that remote ideal springs from a living reality within them. As for his present outward appearance he looks like the Son of Man who had nowhere to lay His head. Such men will obtain food for the morrow, for even the birds of the air are provided for. To do good is sufficient for the day.

Men must have been like Avezzana when the parables of Jesus were heard along the shores of the lakes of Galilee. It is something to see him carelessly gird on his sword of honour, the weapon presented to him for one or other of his glorious feats in South America. They say he got back from those parts just in time to reach Caserta hot-foot, to meet with Garibaldi at the crisis of the Volturno battle, greet him and enter the fray. To have explored continents and oceans, have been a homeless wanderer from youth to old age, have loved and been faithful to Italy and have sworn to see her independent before his death; to have arrived to greet his friend on a battle-field such as the Volturno, he who was once Minister for War at the time of the Roman Republic and the other, who was then his subordinate and is now Dictator here! Don't talk to me of the chivalry of ages past! This is a classic tale, a lay of ancient Rome! . . .

15 October

There was a great event this morning. For the first time Victor Emmanuel's soldiers really fought side by side with Garibaldi's volunteers. I say 'really', because already on 2 October that battalion of the King's Brigade, which we left waiting in the Royal Palace courtyard, was used, together with a few *Bersaglieri*, to round up the Bourbon column from Caserta Vecchia. But that was an uninspiring feat of arms. Today, however, the Bourbon troops came boldly out from Capua and set off towards Sant' Angelo where they came up against *Bersaglieri* and regular infantry who blew them away like chaff. Colonel Corte's volunteers competed with them, to see who could do best. The Bourbon troops may wish to leave Capua again, but it is doubtful if they will ever dare to do so.

20 October

Let no dew nor rain ever fall on the villages of Pettorano, Carpinone, and Isernia as long as the memory of our poor fellows lasts, those who were tricked and hunted and slain in your fields and woods.

What remains of Nullo's column is coming in and their account is horrifying. Their tale is one of death and nothing but death. They still have before their eyes the bestial ferocity of peasants, soldiers, and friars killing and killing to the cry of '*Viva Francesco II! Viva Maria!*'

Poor Bettoni! His Soresina will see him no more. He was at the rear of the column, lying wounded in a carriage, with Lavagnolo and Moro riding by his side. They hoped to get him to safety at Boiano and then to gallop back as hard as they could to where Nullo was fighting and our men were falling, singly or in small groups, with their ears ringing with the savage yells of the furious village harridans; intimidated more by those unleashed bitches than by the great numbers of armed men who had attacked them. Alas for those poor cavalrymen! Lieutenant Candiani found them next day lying in the road

stripped naked and outraged. Ah! Samnium, dire Samnium! I feel a chill breath of air blowing across my brow as I did when that expedition set forth. From that day the name of the Caudine Forks rings in my head.[6]

25 October

Some curious influence must have passed over this neighbourhood. The inhabitants, as a trick of speech, either magnify or belittle things. The *Volturnus Celer* resounds today as in the verses of Lucan; one sees a majestic rush of green water racing clamorously to the sea. Yet one of its fords is known by the name of Scafa di Formicola (the Little Ant's Ferry). When we crossed, we laughed at the strange little name. Garibaldi had got Colonel Bordone to make a bridge of boats there, and over we got, though it was frightening to feel it rocking and the ill-connected planks opening and closing under our feet. We were men of Eber's, Bixio's, and Medici's divisions together with the Milan brigade. With us were the English Legion, fine-looking men, dressed as we were in red shirts and green uniforms, though of a superfine cloth and with belts as highly polished as though they had just come back from India.[7]

Today has been unfortunate. General Bixio's horse fell and the hero cracked his skull and broke a leg. He allowed himself to be carried to Naples and as he went he looked back at us enviously. He is only one man, but without him, there is a feeling of loss in the air.

*   *   *

We are camped on the edge of such a wood as the fleeing Angelica might have ridden through, although it is called Caianiello as though it were a clump of small shoots grown for a Christmas crib.

[6] The so-called 'Caudine Forks' (narrow mountain passes) was the scene of a Roman defeat by the people of Samnium in 321 B.C.

[7] The English contingent arrived too late to take part in any important action.

Meanwhile what are we here for? Capua is over there. We have found the Calabrians here and they tell us that the Bourbon troops occasionally appear in the low-lying land below. Far away to the right is Gaeta. Those must be the mountains old Colombo told me about when he described how he took part in Massena's siege operations in '85. While I am thinking of the man who was a soldier with Garibaldi's Legion in South America, he may be talking to my father about this very place and my father will question him, with who knows what emotion in his heart.

Oh, how I'd like to be that hawk and hurl myself across the sky, calling, calling through the darkening air. Now a bell is tolling . . .! Where is the sound coming from? *'Era già l'ora che volge il desio.'* [8]

*   *   *

Some say we're here to fight one last battle and that, while we're engaged against the 50,000 Bourbon troops who are still faithful to Francis II, Victor Emmanuel's soldiers, with himself in person at their head, are coming down through the Abruzzi by way of Venafro. Others reply that we might get jars of good wine from Venafro, that ancient wine beloved of Horace, but as far as set battles are concerned they are over and done with since the day of 1 October. Perhaps then we shall march to meet the King!

26 October

Should I live a thousand years, I shall never forget, but I could never set it down precisely and clearly, what flashed into my mind, rambling through the countryside beyond Maddaloni with Catoni. The idea came to him first. Six hundred years ago Charles of Anjou came here from Rome with the Pope's blessing and picked up Manfred's crown from among

---

[8] A verse from Dante (*Purgatorio* VIII, 1) describing the evening hour when thoughts are nostalgic. Gray and Byron both drew inspiration from the passage in which the verse occurs.

the slain at Benevento. The Pope had promised it to him if only he could come and take it. Today a man of the people as brave as—ah well, comparisons are unnecessary—a man of the people as generous as none can ever be again, as simple as Curius Dentatus, as tactful and ingenious as Sertorius, as proudly disdainful as Scipio, in the name of the people snatches that crown from the King of Naples and says to Victor Emmanuel: 'It's yours!'

* * *

My head is in a whirl. I'm still full of what I have seen, and I write. . . .

A white house at a cross-roads, horsemen in red and horsemen in black mingled together, Garibaldi on foot; poplar trees shedding their pale dead leaves over the heads of regulars marching towards Teano. With my eyes I see the living soldiers, but in my imagination the great dead Romans of the second civil war, Sulla and Sertorius, who met at this very spot. Their figures loom gigantic as the mountains of Samnium in the distance, but perhaps they were really no bigger than the living men I see before me. What elements are lacking to bring about another civil war?[9]

All of a sudden, quite near, there is a roll of drums and the royal fanfare of Piedmont. All leap on their horses. At that moment a peasant, but half-clothed in skins, turned towards the Venafro mountains and, shading his eyes with his hand, stared hard, perhaps to read the time from some shadow cast by distant crags. Then, a cloud of dust swirled up, there was galloping and shouted commands and then: 'Viva! Viva! The King! The King!'

Everything went black for an instant and I could hardly see Garibaldi and Victor Emmanuel clasp hands or hear the immortal greeting: 'Hail, to the King of Italy!' It was midmorning, Garibaldi talked with bare head, while the King stroked the neck of his handsome grey horse who arched her

[9] Here Abba hints at the possibility of civil war between the modern monarchists and republicans.

neck under his caresses like an Arab princess. Perhaps Garibaldi felt sad, for he looked sad as Victor Emmanuel spurred
his horse and rode away with himself on the King's left. Behind them followed a very large mixed cavalcade. Garibaldi's
charger, Saïd, perhaps felt his master less masterful in the
saddle, for he snorted and pulled to the side as though he
wanted to carry him away into the desert, away to the Pampas, far away from this procession of Great Ones.

*   *   *

Sparanise, 27 October

If rumour is right everything is understandable. Was King
Victor cold in his attitude when he met Garibaldi? True it is
that Francis II is his cousin and that he had invited him to
join in his great war against the enemies of Italy and that he
had admonished him. Also there exists a certain letter!
Francis wouldn't or couldn't heed and it was fortunate for
Italy that he refused.[10] He was as obstinate and impotent as his
father and he now pays the price for both of them.

Perhaps then a certain aloof dignity of Victor Emmanuel's
when he met Garibaldi was due to delicate reserve? Or are
those right who think he was meditating on the strange fate of
kings? However, all this is only gossip, which will pass as the
wind passes without trace. Up to now one hears nothing but
of the greatness of Garibaldi and knows nothing of those
watching for the sun that is yet to rise.

*   *   *

Yesterday Garibaldi did not go to breakfast with the King.
He said he'd breakfasted already, but later he ate bread and
cheese in a church porch surrounded by his friends, sad, reserved, resigned. But resigned to what? Now we shall go back
over the Volturno, back to our camps or to who knows where.

[10] Victor Emmanuel wrote a leter to his 'dear cousin' of Naples on 15
April 1860 offering an alliance on the principle of Italian national freedom.
The offer was refused.

We shall no longer be a vanguard; they will put us at the rear. They say the General spoke in this vein to Mario. What afflicts him most is that he wanted to present a million armed men to the nation yet all that Italy gave him was twenty thousand volunteers.

November 1860

We can hear guns thundering in the distance. They are bombarding Capua and we are out of it. Victor Emmanuel's gunners will not have much to do, because the garrison is only waiting for a decent excuse to give themselves up. Griziotti, our colonel, predicted it.

'General,' he said, 'let me fire a couple of shells at the citadel and they'll give in.'

But Garibaldi replied: 'No! If a child, a woman, or an old man should die because of a shell fired from our camp I should never forgive myself!'

Then Griziotti: 'But our young men are dying of fever at this siege; they pine away and are dying daily.' And Garibaldi:

'We came here to die!'

'Well, General, the Piedmontese will arrive and they won't be squeamish. They will make the city surrender by firing a few shells and then they'll say that everything we've done up to the present, before they came, counts for nothing.'

'Let them talk,' said Garibaldi, 'we didn't come here for glory . . .'

All Saints day, All Souls day, and now the day when they present medals, a third celebration in this sad season.

In front of the Royal Palace, where all signs show that no Bourbon will ever set foot again, the San Francesco di Paola Square was decorated with flags. In the centre there was a chair, ladies, generals, and bigwigs surrounding Garibaldi, who was wearing the same hat he wore at Marsala. I saw Carini who is now a general, rejuvenated, his arm in a sling

and, by his looks, happy. The Hungarian Legion provided the Guard of Honour and the Piedmontese Grenadiers too. We waited with our backs to the Palace. At a certain moment Garibaldi rose and approached us, saying in his loud, clear voice: 'Soldiers of Italian independence. Veterans, although still young, of the army of liberation, I consign to you the medals given by special decree by the municipality of Palermo. Let us begin with the fallen, our fallen. . . .'

Then an officer began to read out the names of the dead, and there was a response in our hearts as we conjured up the image of each one of them in turn. But when today has gone, will there be no more solemn commemorations for them? A hundred names, humble or illustrious, were read out and at each one a thrill ran through our ranks. Were it better to be dead or alive? A feeling of gloom spread among us, masked as enthusiasm.

When our turn came, we were called up, one by one, to the dais where a young girl, standing on tiptoe, pinned a medal to one's chest and as she did so, peeped up at one with large smiling eyes. I don't know who she was and didn't inquire. Names mean nothing. I heard the General say, turning to a lady standing near him, 'I know all those faces, and I shall see them as long as I live.'

In the meantime the bands were playing and the Grenadiers' band seemed to say: 'That's enough, that's enough now, be off with you.'

Caserta, 9 November. Evening

Today the great Palace looked down the long avenue stretching far away in front as though wanting to reach Naples; it could see ranks of red-shirted battalions drawn up under the quiet trees, which looked gloomy under a lowering sky. The King was to come to review the whole of Garibaldi's army, some 12,000 men, who stood in parade order with rifles grounded. We waited. The King was due to come about two o'clock and a cannon-shot would announce his arrival. We

chatted in our places, and odd rumours, quips, and sarcasms
spread along the ranks, material for poems or comedies. There
were crude things said too, but there was little gaiety. Clouds
came down over us and seemed to bring a chill with them, and
as time passed we grew tired. Some Venetians of my battalion
were whispering that when the King went by it would be a
fine thing to surround him and take him up to the mountains
and force him to declare war, with Rome and Venice as our
objectives. Were they serious? Some certainly were, but most
of them were only talking for talking's sake. In the middle of
these discussions trumpets were heard on the right of the long
line. Attention! The King!

The battalions got into order. Our hearts were beating;
some approved, others not. Then a group of men on horses
came trotting by. . . . Ah! He who rode in front was not the
King, it was the man with the Hungarian hat and the poncho,
those with him were all red-shirts. The hat pulled down over
his eyes was a sign of trouble. They came and passed, leaving
dismay behind them. Then they turned round at the end of
the avenue and came and went like a whirlwind. Shortly
afterwards the battalions were lined up by sections in column
. . . it looked as though we were to march towards danger and
we were all prepared. . . . Thus we approached the Royal
Palace where we marched past Garibaldi, who stood at the
great gate rigid as though carved in stone. And we knew this
was the last hour of his command. We longed to throw ourselves at his feet crying out: 'General, why do you not lead us
on to death? That is the road to Rome, scatter our bones
along it!' But that meant civil war! And what about France,
our close ally of last year?

The General was paler than we had ever seen him before.
He watched us go by. One could guess that tears were near and
that his heart was sore. I do not know who they were who stood
near him. Only he counted, I saw no one, nothing else. Now I
hear that the General is leaving for Caprera, to live as on
another planet. Here I feel a gale of discord blowing up. I look
at my friends. This wind will catch us all and churn us about

like leaves until each one of us falls at the door of his own home. Oh that we were really leaves, but Sibylline leaves, each bearing a word, and that they could come together again to spell a message of significance to Italy . . . poor sheet of paper . . . stay blank—let us have done.

DATE DUE

MAR 1 8 '64	FEB		
FEB 25 '65	FEB 11 '87		
AUG 4 '65	FEB 26 '87		
AUG 9 '65	28. 8 I ЯАМ		
JUL 28 '66	MAR 1 8 '87		
AUG 4 '66			
AUG 8 '68			
FEB 2 0 67			
MAR 1 3 67			
APR 6 '67			
APR 1 8 '67			
MAR 1 2 '68			
APR 3 '68			
APR 1 7 '69			
OCT 2 69			
APR 24 72			
GAYLORD			PRINTED IN U.S.A.

From words and things, ill sorted and misjoined;
The anarchy of thought, and chaos of the mind.

Hobbes went about in an orderly way to dis-
sect the imagination and ascertain its workings.
"Time and Education begets Experience; Experience
begets Memory; Memory begets Judgement and
Fancy. . . . The Ancients therefore fabled not
absurdly, in making Memory the Mother of the
Muses." There was no mystery here at all. Imagination is a makeshift. If we could keep the whole
world fresh and vivid about us all our days there
would be no call for Fancy in the metaphysics of
true enjoyment. The life of the imagination is a
life of sheer pretense. "Imagination," runs a sentence in Hobbes's *Physics*, "is nothing else but
sense decaying, or weakened, by the absence of the
object." This refusal to credit the imagination
with creative power, this insistence upon reducing
it to its lowest terms and making of it a mechanical
device for reproducing experience as such, is cru-
cial in the history of English poetry. When Bacon
had examined the mental processes of the poet in
the *Advancement of Learning* he had not, to be sure,
come to the conclusion that poets are divine, or
mad; but he had assigned to them a function more
or less creative, which was "to give some shadow of
satisfaction to the mind of man in those points
wherein the nature of things doth deny it, the world
being in proportion inferior to the soul." Now
Hobbes ignored the transforming power in favor of
the recording power. "For Memory is the World
(though not really, yet so as in a looking glass) in

which the Judgment, the severer Sister, busieth herself in a grave and rigid examination of all the parts of Nature, and in registering by letters their order, causes, uses, differences, and resemblances; whereby the Fancy, when any work of Art is to be performed, finding her materials at hand and prepared for use, needs no more than a swift motion over them, that what she wants, and is there to be had, may not lie too long unespied." Which is to say, what is true yet is not the whole truth, that the best poet is he who has the best memory. Ten years before, Milton, in his *Reason of Church Government*, had confided to "any knowing reader" that the great work which he was setting out to do would be a work not "to be obtained by the invocation of Dame Memory and her Siren daughters, but by devout prayer to that eternal Spirit who can enrich with all utterance and knowledge." And twenty-four years after *Gondibert*, Milton's nephew, Edward Phillips, in the preface to his *Theatrum Poetarum*, was to hold a brief for "true native Poetry" as against mere "wit, ingenuity, and learning in verse." But Hobbist psychology was as potent as Hobbist politics, and it was not until a century or more had passed that any really philosophical attack was made upon Dame Memory's position. It was in the wake of such an attack that Blake, in the world of painting, explained all of what he considered had been Sir Joshua Reynolds' critical errors by adducing the one mistaken conception that "originates in the Greeks calling the Muses daughters of Memory." It was in rebuttal of theories like those of Hobbes that Wordsworth wrote: "Imagination has no reference to images that are merely a faithful copy, existing in the mind, of absent external objects; but is a word of higher import, denoting operations of the mind upon those objects, and processes of creation and composition."

All this does not mean that Dryden and others who went to school to Hobbes did not write great, amazing poetry. It only explains why they failed to write poetry of a certain kind. Wonder and brooding reverie were simply not of their world. They transformed nothing; the divine illusion was not for them. They created and composed enduring monuments of art, but not in Wordsworth's way. They were not at all times aware of their limitations. Dryden, as we shall see, struggled a long while to trample them down. He spoke often, in common with his contemporaries, of the *furor poeticus;* he championed poetic license; and he tried to write like Shakespeare. But like his contemporaries he was bound by triple steel. He had to learn to be great in his own way.

Taine, having no reason to doubt the notion current in his time that Dryden had stayed on three years at Cambridge after taking his Bachelor's degree, proceeds: "Here you see the regular habits of an honorable and well-to-do family, the discipline of a connected and solid education, the taste for classical and exact studies. Such circumstances announce and prepare, not an artist, but a man of letters." If to be an artist is to be devoted to an art, and if to be a true artist is to have that devo-

tion not only continue but increase through each
year of a long life, then Dryden was truly an artist,
and Taine is unjust. Dryden's devotion cannot be
called into question. Whether or not the legend be
accurate that he was "too roving and active to confine himself to college life" and that he hastened to
set himself up in London, it is plain that he, like
Ovid, would sooner or later have found it impossible to keep out of poetry. Whenever his career
began, it engrossed him solely and entirely. In
later years he liked to review this career; his conception of it was dramatic, if not theatrical. He
saw himself on a great stage, prominent, almost
alone. He carried with him to London, and always
kept by him there, an "adamantine confidence," as
Dr. Johnson put it, not simply in himself, for he
knew what modesty was, but in the powers which
study and practice had convinced him were his.
Pride of profession, scorn of competitors, devotion
to his trade sustained him. Goldsmith made his
way into the mid-eighteenth century literary world
by a good-humored unconventionality that brought
relief to sufferers from the prevailing gentilities and
rotundities. Dryden, also without violence of blus-
ter, forced himself upon his world through sheer
display of confidence and a large, steady assump-
tion of authority. There was a growing demand
for poetry which could be read and generally discussed. Dryden believed that he could supply the
smoothest and most powerful variety. He was not
long in convincing London that he was right.

It was brought against Dryden by Shadwell, in

The Medal of John Bayes, that he had served as a
hack to Herringman the bookseller during his first
few years in London, writing "prefaces to books for
meat and drink." It is probable that Shadwell exaggerated the meanness of the relation, if it existed
at all. Dryden's private income was not large, and
he must have turned at an early stage to writing for
money, without, indeed, the spiritual support of
Dr. Johnson's avowal that no man except a blockhead ever wrote for anything else. Any connection with Herringman in these years of his appren-
ticeship would have been valuable in that it would
have placed him in one of the main currents of poetic production, Herringman being almost the chief
publisher of poems and plays at the Restoration.
Somewhere, at least, Dryden was learning what was
being written, and coming to feel at home in society;
without which knowledge and feeling he could not
have gone very far.

Personally, Dryden seems never to have prepos-
sessed anyone. His youth had not been precocious,
and his maturity found him more mellow than
splendid. He was genial in his old age, without any
great allowance of spontaneous humor. His mind
always remained warm and strong. Pope told
Spence that he "was not a very genteel man; he was
intimate with none but poetical men." He pretended
to be nothing other than what above all things he
was, a writer. He did not profess to be a hero; he
disliked holding himself rigid. "Stiffness of opinion," he wrote in the dedication of *Don Sebastian,* "is
the effect of pride, and not of philosophy. . . . The

ruggedness of a stoic is only a silly affectation of being a god. . . . True philosophy is certainly of a more
pliant nature, and more accommodated to human
use. . . . A wise man will never attempt an impossi-
bility." Dryden's inconsistencies have generally been
deplored. But it is precisely to his unending powers
of renewal that we owe that serenity and that fresh-
ness in which he never fails us. "As I am a man,"
he told the Earl of Mulgrave in 1676, in the dedication of *Aureng-Zebe*, "I must be changeable; and
sometimes the gravest of us all are so, even upon
ridiculous accidents. Our minds are perpetually
wrought on by the temperament of our bodies;
which makes me suspect they are nearer allied, than
either our philosophers or school-divines will allow
them to be. . . . An ill dream, or a cloudy day, has
power to change this wretched creature, who is so
proud of a reasonable soul, and make him think
what he thought not yesterday."

II

FALSE LIGHTS

Dr. Johnson's brilliant example seems nearly to
have established for all time the procedure of persons who would criticise the poetry of Dryden. The
procedure consists in moving swiftly through his
works, line by line and page by page, noting down
what passages are in shocking taste and what passages are unexceptionable, and at the end qualify-
ing on the basis of the first the praise which ought
naturally to fall to the second. There has been
good reason for this. No critic has felt that he
could afford to commend Dryden in general without proving that he had taken into account the
worst of him in particular. No critic has been willing to go on record as in any way approving the
more flagant stanzas of the *Annus Mirabilis*, the
more impossible speeches of the heroic plays, or the
more meretricious portions of the *Virgil* and other
journey-work. Such caution has been warranted
by the fact that Dryden is more unequal than almost any English poet who has written volumin-
ously. But now it seems worth while to proceed
a little further and ask whether Dryden held any
theories which might have been responsible for the
obvious defects in his product. For it is evident
that the unhappy passages to which exception has

invariably been taken are not passages wherein the
poet's attention seems to have lagged, or his spirits
drooped. They are rather, in fact, his most careful
and ambitious performances; Dryden never dozed.
Nor can they be explained as indiscretions of youth.
They are found everywhere throughout his works,
from first to last. It is plain that Dryden was following false lights when he committed his offenses
against taste. Either he was pursuing ends which
by nature he was unqualified to reach, he was attempting the impossible, he was speaking a language which was not instinctive; or he was reaching ends which were hardly worth reaching, he was
sedulously perfecting a language which though
native was not gauged for sterling utterance. Good
literature is the effect of adequate form applied to
genuine material. The poetry in Dryden which is
not good can be explained by errors which he made
first in choosing his material and second in culti-
vating his form. On the one hand, false lights led
him to employ two kinds of materials which in his
case were spurious: first, the materials of the fancy,
in works like *Annus Mirabilis;* second, the materials of the human passions, in works like the heroic
plays and the tragedies. The results were absurdity and bathos. On the other hand, false lights
led him to give excessive attention to the form of
his verse at times when the matter was of little import, as in the *Virgil.* The results were artificiality
and monotony. The purpose of the present chapter
is to follow Dryden as he pursues his wandering
fires, and to sweep away the rubbish which he leaves

behind him. Only after that is done can we take up in good conscience his genuine performances before the true flame.

When Hobbes and Davenant separated Fancy from Judgment and sent it off to play alone, they condemned it to dull company. Their æsthetics, in setting reason over against imagination, did reason no great service and did imagination real harm. Dryden belonged on the side of the so-called reason. He was not a child of fancy; he never lived what is often too glibly termed the life of the imagination. His true home was the house of Judgment, and his true game was the adult game of common sense. But he was given to experimenting. He was curious, to begin with, to know all that could be known about Fancy, whom Hobbes and Davenant had described as sprightly and fair. "When she seemeth to fly from one Indies to the other," said Hobbes, "and from Heaven to Earth, and to penetrate into the hardest matter and obscurest places, into the future and into herself, and all this in a point of time, the voyage is not very great, herself being all she seeks, and her wonderful celerity consisteth not so much in motion as in copious Imagery discreetly ordered and perfectly registered in the memory." "Wit," said Davenant, meaning Fancy, "is the laborious and the lucky resultances of thought. . . . It is a web consisting of the subtlest threads; and like that of the spider is considerately woven out of our selves. . . . Wit is not only the luck and labour, but also the dexterity of thought, rounding the world, like the Sun, with unimaginable motion, and bringing

swiftly home to the memory universal surveys."
No description could have been more alluring; it is
no wonder that Dryden yielded and followed Fancy
for a time. The two preceptors also conveyed hints
as to the kind of language which the creature spoke.
To write with fancy, said Hobbes, one must "know
much." A sign of knowing much "is novelty of expression, and pleaseth by excitation of the mind; for
novelty causeth admiration, and admiration curiosity, which is a delightful appetite of knowledge." To
write with wit, said Davenant, is to bring truth home
"through unfrequented and new ways, and from the
most remote shades, by representing Nature, though
not in an affected, yet in an unusual dress." That is,
conceits were to be abjured, but dulness was to be
avoided at all costs.

It seems certain that Dryden was thinking of
Davenant's happy phrases when in the preface to
Annus Mirabilis he wrote: "The composition of all
poems is, or ought to be, of wit; and wit in the poet,
or wit writing, (if you will give me leave to use a
School distinction), is no other than the faculty of
imagination in the writer, which, like a nimble spaniel, beats over and ranges through the field of memory, till it springs the quarry it hunted after; or,
without metaphor, which searches over all the memory for the species or ideas of those things which it
designs·to represent." Then, as now, it seems to
have been difficult to speak of the faculties in other
than figurative terms. Dryden here compares wit
to a spaniel; elsewhere he declares that the language of the French "is not strung with sinews like

our English; it has the nimbleness of a greyhound, but not the bulk and body of a mastiff." The dog was not a pretty image, perhaps, but it served Dryden's purpose. Dryden confessed himself captivated by Davenant's own wit. "He was a man of quick and piercing imagination," he said in the preface to the *Tempest*, in the writing of which he had been assisted by Davenant the next year after *Annus Mirabilis*. "In the time I writ with him, I had the opportunity to observe somewhat more nearly of him, than I had formerly done. . . . I found him then of so quick a fancy, that nothing was proposed to him, on which he could not suddenly produce a thought extremely pleasant and surprising. . . . And as his fancy was quick, so likewise were the products of it remote and new . . . his imaginations were such as could not easily enter into any other man." The words "quick," "piercing," and "surprising" should be noted, because they were much in the mode whenever the poetic faculties were being analyzed. Shadwell, when he was still friendly, even used them to describe Dryden.

"Quick" was not the word for Dryden's fancy. Davenant's own adjective, "laborious," fits better. In the early occasional poems there is no surprising facility of phrase or illustration. In no piece did Dryden ever display a happy gift for turning up images. He speaks from time to time of difficulties encountered in curbing a luxuriant fancy. But it is plain that the difficulties were never really great. There are times when, as Dr. Johnson has it, "he seems to look round him for images which he cannot find." His imagination is not bounding, or fertile; he proceeds painfully to scour the surface of life for allusions. His spaniel does not frisk; it must be beaten and driven. To use his own words in another connection, "The fancy, memory, and judgment are . . . extended (like so many limbs) upon the rack; all of them reaching with their utmost stress at nature." The net result is not a pretty or a pleasantly variegated pattern; "'tis like an orange stuck with cloves," to fall back again upon Buckingham in the *Rehearsal*.

Annus Mirabilis, the *locus classicus* of Dryden's "wit-writing," "seems to be the work of a man," says Macaulay, "who could never, by any possibility, write poetry." It is better to call it the work of a man who could never, by any possibility, write a certain kind of poetry—the luxuriant, splendid kind that is studded with significant allusions. No swarm of ideas has beset the imagination of Dryden here. He has had to make an effort for every image, proceeding with an almost childlike seriousness that is oddly accentuated by the halting cadence of his heroic stanza. For most of his happier strokes he has gone to the classics. He is proud to admit in his preface that many of his images are from Virgil, and his notes acknowledge debts not only to Virgil but to Petronius, Tacitus, Pliny, Statius, Horace, and Ovid as well. His notes also furnish scientific explanations for the more obscure allusions in the poem. Wishing in the third stanza to say that the Dutch have had the good fortune to discover jewels in the East Indies, he has written,

For them alone the heavens had kindly heat;
In eastern quarries ripening precious dew.

To this he appends a note: "Precious stones at
first are dew, condensed and hardened by the warmth
of the sun or subterranean fires." His images from
the classics are generally happy. It is when he
draws upon his own resources, or, which is little
better, draws upon Waller, that he proves once and
for all that his career must lie another way. Certain stanzas have been quoted *ad nauseam*. Many
remain.

On high-raised decks the haughty Belgians ride,
Beneath whose shade our humble frigates go:
Such port the elephant bears, and so defied
By the rhinoceros her unequal foe.

By viewing Nature, Nature's handmaid Art
Makes mighty things from small beginnings grow;
Thus fishes first to shipping did impart
Their tale the rudder, and their head the prow.

The gravity with which in these and similar cases
the last two lines of a stanza are made to serve up
an absurd simile for garnishing the first two is the
most lamentable feature of *Annus Mirabilis*. The
attention is drawn down full upon the unfortunate
comparison, and Dryden has no way to conceal his
fundamental weakness. A few figures are excellent;
as when Prince Rupert comes upon the scene,

And his loud guns speak thick like angry men.

The Dutch ships retire, awed by the British cannon:

> So reverently men quit the open air
> When thunder speaks the angry gods abroad.

But Dryden's strenuous efforts have thrown the
balance the other way, and have made it plain, not
that he was incapable of a single happy image, but
that he was incapable of measuring his own success.
Pepys took *Annus Mirabilis* home with him from a
book stall, and found it "a very good poem." It is
a spirited poem, and it is an admirable poem whenever Dryden forgets his spaniel long enough to
speak with the purely metrical rush and emphasis
which were eventually to win him his position in
English verse:

> There was the Plymouth squadron new come in,
>   Which in the Straits last winter was abroad;
> Which twice on Biscay's working bay had been,
>   And on the midland sea the French had awed.
>
> Old expert Allen, loyal all along,
>   Famed for his action on the Smyrna fleet;
> And Holmes, whose name shall live in epic song
>   While music numbers, or while verse has feet;
>
> Now, anchors weighed, the seamen shout so shrill,
>   That heaven, and earth, and the wide ocean rings;
> A breeze from westward waits their sails to fill,
>   And rests in those high beds his downy wings.

Annus Mirabilis is by no means the first or last
poem in which Dryden reveals a fatal want of tact
and subtlety in the use of figures. From his earliest
piece, that on Lord Hastings, through the panegyrics written at the Restoration, through the
Threnodia Augustalis, through the *Britannia Redi-*

viva, through the *Eleonora*, to his last translation from Ovid, he pursues with heavy steps the flashing heels of fancy. In Ovid, it may be remarked, he found a genius who invariably inspired him to excesses. Ovid's inexhaustible fund of grotesque and tasteless yet clear-cut scenes furnished Dryden with dubious riches which he never failed to make the most of, and which he could not have embellished had he tried.

If Dryden should not be expected to compete with other poets on the score of delicacy in simile and metaphor, much less should he be required to display his powers of passionate utterance in drama and narrative. Here he is in competition with Shakespeare and the tragic poets of Greece, and here he fails once again to prove that he possesses discrimination. Not that he lacks assurance. No poet has talked at greater length about the passions, or about "sublimity." Yet no great poet has managed to acquire a firmer reputation as a bungler in these departments. It is another case of a man working with materials which are not gauged for him, and which to a certain extent are irreconcilable with the whole temper of his time.

Dryden lacks that organic conception of man and nature which gives what is called insight. He cannot compress a large amount of emotional experience into a single phrase. He is virtually barren of illuminating comments on human life which move a reader to take new account of himself. His passages on the soul are foolish, treating importantly as they do of something which is not important to him. And

the pessimistic soliloquies which the characters in
his plays deliver on the subjects of fate and decep-
tion are for the most part trash, though not a few of
them have been quoted to prove that Dryden was a
critic of life. The following lines from *Aureng-Zebe*
are compact and bright:

> When I consider life, 'tis all a cheat;
> Yet, fooled with hope, men favor the deceit;
> Trust on, and think tomorrow will repay;
> Tomorrow's falser than the former day;
> Lies worse; and while it says we shall be blest
> With some new joys, cuts off what we possesst.
> Strange cozenage! None would live past years again,
> Yet all hope pleasure in what yet remain;
> And from the dregs of life think to receive
> What the first sprightly running could not give.
> I'm tired with waiting for this chemic gold,
> Which fools us young, and beggars us when old.

Yet there is nothing appalling in their revelation;
and their felicity need disturb no one. They have
done Dryden's reputation in the main more harm
than good by being so often brought forward in a
hopeless cause.

"It requires Philosophy," said Dryden, "as well
as Poetry, to sound the depths of all the passions;
what they are in themselves, and how they are to be
provoked." Dryden did a great deal of experimenting in the depths he speaks of. Having little
or no intuition, and being without discrimination,
he was almost never successful. He had a lasting
curiosity concerning what he called "those enthusiastic parts of poetry" which deal with love and hate,

disaster and death. In the heroic plays, in the tragedies, and in the translations of classical narratives
he labored to render desperate actions in fitting
speech, remembering that the "sublimest subjects
ought to be adorned with the sublimest . . . expressions." The results can rarely be placed to his
credit. In the first part of the *Conquest of Granada*,
the haughty Almanzor, after looking fixedly for a
moment at Almahide's face, which she has just un-
veiled, turns aside and utters this humiliated confession:

> I'm pleased and pained, since first her eyes I saw,
> As I were stung with some tarantula.
> Arms, and the dusty field, I less admire,
> And soften strangely in some new desire;
> Honour burns in me not so fiercely bright,
> But pale as fires when mastered by the light;
> Even while I speak and look, I change yet more,
> And now am nothing that I was before.
> I'm numbed, and fixed, and scarce my eye-balls move;
> I fear it is the lethargy of love!
> 'Tis he; I feel him now in every part;
> Like a new lord he vaunts about my heart;
> Surveys, in state, each corner of my breast,
> While poor fierce I, that was, am dispossessed.

At the end of *Aureng-Zebe*, Nourmahal, distracted
with poison she has swallowed, cries out in the face
of death:

> I burn, I more than burn; I am all fire.
> See how my mouth and nostrils flame expire!
> I'll not come near myself——

Now I'm a burning lake, it rolls and flows;
I'll rush, and pour it all upon my foes.
Pull, pull that reverend piece of timber near;
Throw 't on—'tis dry—'twill burn—
Ha, ha! how my old husband crackles there!
Keep him down, keep him down: turn him about;
I know him; he'll but whizz, and straight go out.
Fan me, you winds; What, not one breath of air?
I burn them all, and yet have flames to spare.
Quench me: Pour on whole rivers. 'Tis in vain;
Morat stands there to drive them back again;
With those huge bellows in his hands he blows
New fire into my head; my brain-pan glows.

These speeches are from the heroic plays, which in
some measure were licensed to rave. Yet, with the
one exception of All for Love, the maturest of the
tragedies, those which are supposed to have been
conceived in better taste under Greek, French, and
Shakespearian influences are everywhere marred
by mortal extravagances. Dorax, in Don Sebastian,
believes he is poisoned:

I'm strangely discomposed;
Quick shootings through my limbs, and pricking pains,
Qualms at my heart, convulsions in my nerves,
Shiverings of cold, and burnings of my entrails,
Within my little world make medley-war,
Lose and regain, beat, and are beaten back,
As momentary victors quit their ground.
Can it be poison!

Cleonidas, in Cleomenes, doubts the immortality of
the soul

Because I find, that, now my body starves,
My soul decays. I think not as I did;
My head goes round; and now you swim before me;
Methinks my soul is like a flame unfed
With oil, that dances up and down the lamp,
But must expire ere long.

And Cleomenes himself, dying, announces:

A rising vapor rumbles in my brains.

Dryden's excuse for every such passage was that "a man in such an occasion is not cool enough, either to reason lightly, or to talk calmly." Yet in his own cooler days, when he had Virgil and Boccaccio for guides, and less fortunately Ovid, he still guided his pen through love and death and regret with clumsy fingers. "With the simple and elemental passions, as they spring separate in the mind," said Dr. Johnson once and for all, "he seems not much acquainted."

Dryden's theory was that if one only entered in with enthusiasm and industrious abandon one could succeed as well as any in striking off brave, fine talk in verse. While occupied with writing heroic plays he was supported by the creed that a heroic poet "is not tied to a bare representation of what is true." Rather he is expected to be reckless.

Poets, like lovers, should be bold, and dare,

runs the prologue to *Tyrannic Love;* and in the preface to the same play scorn is expressed for him who "creeps after plain, dull, common sense." "A solid man is, in plain English, a solid, solemn fool," he was to observe to the Earl of Mulgrave six years later. This rough-and-ready ardor soon found rare support in Longinus, whose treatise *On the Sublime* was translated by Boileau in France in 1674 and almost immediately taken up by Dryden. Horace had insisted that the poet should be more than correct, and the French critics generally had allowed for elevation in style. Thomas Rymer, in his translation of Rapin's *Reflections on Aristotle's Treatise of Poesie*, was writing this sentence in the same year that Boileau's *Longinus* appeared: "Of late some have fallen into another extremity, by a too scrupulous care of purity of language: they have begun to take from Poesie all its nerves, and all its majesty, by a too timorous reservedness, and false modesty." The true poet, says Rymer, will have "flame" as well as "phlegm." It was chiefly from Longinus himself, however, "who was undoubtedly, after Aristotle, the greatest critic among the Greeks," said Dryden, that Dryden derived the substance of his *Apology for Heroic Poetry and Poetic License* in 1677. He quoted Longinus on the meanness of a poet who will shun profuseness and write parsimoniously in order to secure safety from ridicule. And in the light of the famous Greek treatise he formulated a definition of poetic license. But it cannot be granted that he caught all or any of the subtlety of his master in sublimity. Certainly he received no inspiration that served later on to chasten or ripen his manner of dealing with the passions. He was attracted by his teacher's theory of images. "Imaging is, in itself," he wrote, "the very height and life of Poetry. It is, as Longinus describes it, a discourse, which, by a kind of enthusiasm, or extraordinary emotion of the soul, makes it seem to us that we behold those things which the poet paints, so as to be pleased with them, and to admire them." He was referring here to the distinction made by Longinus between poetical and oratorical images. The first, says Longinus, is achieved "when he who is speaking . . . imagines himself to see what he is talking about, and produces a similar illusion in his hearers." The second is merely "designed to give perspicuity, and its chief beauties are its energy and reality." The metaphor which Dryden brings forward from his own works to prove that he has approximated the poetical image of Longinus in unfortunately a typically bad one:

> Seraph and cherub, careless of their charge,
> And wanton, in full ease now live at large;
> Unguarded leave the passes of the sky,
> And all dissolved in hallelujahs lie.

Here if anywhere is final proof that Dryden lacked discrimination in executing and judging figures of speech. He feigns well enough the "enthusiasm, or extraordinary emotion of the soul," but he does not achieve the reality which is after all the end of any writing. He misses the chief point in Longinus, which is that sublimity is not a trick but is a state of mind, is not mere fine writing but is the expression of an important personality. The distinction made by Longinus between true sublimity and "amplification" reflects directly upon Dryden, and scarcely to his credit: "The sublime is often conveyed in a single thought, but amplification can only subsist with a certain prolixity and diffusiveness." Dryden spent energy on both his figures and his heroic declarations; but the effect is one of words rather than things. The words seem stark naked on the page; they throw off no enlarging rings of suggestion or illusion; there is no light behind.

Let Dryden pronounce the final verdict. "To speak justly of this whole matter," he wrote in the preface to *Troilus and Cressida*, " 'tis neither height of thought that is discommended, nor pathetic vehemence, nor any nobleness of expression in its proper place; but 'tis a false measure of all these, something which is like them, and is not them; 'tis the Bristol stone, which appears like a diamond; 'tis an extravagant thought, instead of a sublime one; 'tis roaring madness, instead of vehemence; and a sound of words, instead of sense. If Shakespeare were stripped of all the bombasts in his passions, and dressed in the most vulgar words, we should find the beauties of his thoughts remaining; if his embroideries were burnt down, there would still be silver at the bottom of the melting pot: but I fear (at least let me fear it for myself) that we, who ape his sounding words, have nothing of his thought, but are all outside; there is not so much as a dwarf within our giant's clothes." This handsome recantation was carried still further in the preface to the *Spanish Friar*. But no one should be

deceived. Dryden was an imcomparably better
critic than he was a writer of tragedies. He never
can be said to have "settled his system of propriety,"
as Dr. Johnson would say.

Dryden drew an interesting distinction between
Shakespeare and Fletcher in the preface to *Troilus
and Cressida.* "The excellency of that poet was, as
I have said, in the more manly passions; Fletcher's
in the softer: Shakespeare writ better betwixt man
and man; Fletcher, betwixt man and woman; consequently, one described friendship better; the other
love; . . . the scholar had the softer soul; but the
master had the kinder." Here is offered an approach
to Dryden's own peculiar triumph in the drama.
Failing to distinguish himself in his accounts of love,
he yet succeeded famously in showing friendships
broken and mended. Taking for his model the
quarrel between Brutus and Cassius in Shakespeare's *Julius Cæsar*, he executed four admirable
scenes in as many tragedies. One who would see
him at his best in dialogue should go to the scenes
between Antony and Ventidius in *All for Love*,
Hector and Troilus in *Troilus and Cressida*, Sebastian and Dorax in *Don Sebastian*, and Cleomenes
and Cleanthes in *Cleomenes*. Here he is straightforward, and he writes with his mind on the object.
Here, in the most limited sense of the phrase, he
shows the "manners of men." Almanzor's blunt
direction to Almahide, given before she removes her
veil, is worth all the pages of rant which follow upon
her committing that indiscretion:

Speak quickly, woman: I have much to do.

Dryden was at his best when describing a contest
between two competent minds playing free of sentiment.   It was in his true rôle of sensible observer
that he wrote his quarrel scenes; as it was with his
plainest vision that he watched those two astonishing beasts, the hind and the panther, in their endless game of crafty give and take:

> To this the Panther sharply had replied;
> But, having gained a verdict on her side,
> She wisely gave the loser leave to chide. . . .
> Yet thought it decent something should be said;
> For secret guilt by silence is betrayed.
> So neither granted all, nor much denied,
> But answered with a yawning kind of pride.

It is a commonplace of literary history that the
seventeenth century in Europe saw an almost comi-
cal divergence between poetic theory and poetic
practice, the heroic poem in France being the instance usually given of a type that failed to fulfil its
promise.   In England, as has been seen, the divergence was very wide between Dryden's theory and
Dryden's achievements in so far as they implicated
fancy operating over the face of nature and imagination operating among the human passions under
dramatic strain; one reason beyond all doubt being
that the separation in current doctrine of wit from
judgment, imagination from reason, rendered it
difficult or impossible to discriminate between true
and false expression and sanctioned a certain reck-
lessness which was mistaken for poetic rage.   There

is another group of major defects in the poetry of
Dryden and the Augustans generally wherein form
rather than substance is involved, and wherefrom
has resulted that artificiality of tone which is the
proverbial objection urged by modern critics. Here
again it is possible to find the poets controlled by
theories, and here again promise is hopelessly in
advance of fulfilment owing to the superficial character of the theories and the inadequacy with which
they are applied. The theories are that poetry is
like oratory, that poetry is like painting, and that
poetry is like music.[1] The aim is to achieve the
ends of those three parallel arts as well as the
ends of poetry, and thus enrich poetic expression.
The problem is purely one of expression, or as
was said in the seventeenth century, of elocution.
Art is for the imitation of life. Each separate art
has means whereby it can accomplish direct imitation. If poetry, in addition to its own direct
means, can appropriate the means of other arts and
apply them obliquely to its material, why should not
the eventual product be so much the fuller of beauty
and meaning? Actually the product as we now
regard it is less beautiful rather than more beautiful in consequence of this confusion among the arts.
Instead of deepening its own medium by contact
with oratory, painting, and music, poetry became
shallow; instead of growing more eloquent, more
picturesque, and more harmonious, it only grew
more rhetorical, more vague, and more monoto-

---

[1] "In it are assembled all the Powers of Eloquence, of Musick, and
of Picture." Sir William Temple. *Of Poetry.* 1690.

nous. That is to say, Augustan poetry at its worst
grew rhetorical, vague, and monotonous; at its best
it was something far different. As its worst has often been seized and unduly enlarged upon by contrary critics, and as only the worst of Dryden is
being considered in the present chapter, it seems
necessary to bestow considerable attention at this
point upon these weaknesses which Dryden shared
with all his contemporaries and with most of his
immediate followers.

Tacitus complained in his *Dialogus* that Roman
oratory was being invaded by the dance; orations
were being composed and delivered in dance measures; "orators speak voluptuously," he wrote with
indignation, "and actors dance eloquently." Tacitus was not the first or the last to make objection
to the mingling in spirit and technique of two distinct arts. *Laokoons* were thought, even if they
were not written, long before Lessing. But the
confusion of poetry with eloquence that began to be
current in the Italian Renaissance and persisted
throughout the criticism of all Europe for at least
two centuries aroused no Tacitus and was suffered
to run its own long course unchallenged. The
original invasion of poetry by oratory was no less
gradual and peaceable than the final withdrawal,
if indeed the withdrawal can be said as yet to have
reached a final stage, or can be expected or desired
ever to be complete. The early Renaissance critics in Italy studied poetry and rhetoric together at
a time when neither was flourishing in anything like
perfect health. Both were being made to serve the

purposes of flattery in small despotic courts where a premium was placed on fulness and roundness and ordered pomp of elocution. The Italian critics originated parallels and confusions which were perpetuated by the French Plêiade and the English theorists of Elizabeth's time. These had mainly to do with rules for ornamentation and devices for securing striking effects. The classical critics had confined the application of their rules and devices to prose oratory, all of them agreeing that poetry had a style of its own which could not be taught. Plato had insisted that poets were inexplicably inspired, but he had encouraged men who would be orators to go and study the rules. Aristotle had written separate treatises on rhetoric and poetry, and had treated of artifices in connection with the first which he would have denied could be applied to the second. Cicero, Quintilian, and Tacitus had discussed oratory, not poetry, although Cicero had raised his art both in theory and in practice to an exalted position. In all this body of doctrine there had been gradually developed and clearly explained numerous elaborate methods, not excluding assonance and rhyme, by which prose could be heightened in effect, made more symmetrical, and given a greater appearance of finality. Now when the Italians established their identification between the poet and the orator they were able to offer to the poet handsome if questionable assistance. Poetry in Europe did not become rhetorical over night. In England, for example, the sixteenth century saw eloquence occupying the second place;

Sidney, Webb, and Daniel denied it access to the highest levels. Yet all Elizabethan criticism is curiously concerned with the whole matter of classical figures and decorations so far as they are applicable to the style of poetry; and George Puttenham finds one great difference between prose and poetry to be that poetry is the more "eloquent and rhetorical." "The poets," says Puttenham, "were . . . from the beginning the best persuaders, and their eloquence the first rhetoric of the world." Ben Jonson was thoroughly familiar with the works of the classical and post-classical rhetoricians, and helped to establish a tradition of their sacred efficacy which outlived him a hundred years. It was not until Dryden's time, when the inspiration of the Elizabethans had in a way given out, and the full body of modern classical doctrine was being received in its most systematic form from France, that eloquence came to feel completely at home in poetry. Then it was that sophistication, easy expertness, and obvious perfection of finish became of paramount importance in the manner of verse. A consciously "poetic" style was created. Poets called themselves "virtuosos." The secrets of individuality became obscure, while the conventions became easier each year to follow. It became less and less desirable to state things naïvely; the circumlocution was cherished for its elegance and the antithesis for its effect of completeness and finality even when nothing final was being said. It came to be expected that everything, whether important or not, should be said importantly. There was some-

thing not quite genuine about the poetry which was
the ultimate product of these tendencies. Poetry
at its best leaves the impression that there was
something in the poet's head which must have been
said, whatever the words at hand. The poetry
which first of all was eloquence gave no such impression. "Modern poetry," complained Coleridge
in 1805, "is characterized by the poets' anxiety
to be always striking. . . . Every line, nay, every
word, stops, looks full in your face, and asks and
begs for praise! . . . There are no distances, no perspectives, but all is in the foreground; and this is
nothing but vanity. . . . The desire of carrying
things to a greater height of pleasure and admiration
than . . . they are susceptible of, is one great cause
of the corruption of poetry."

Dryden was peculiarly fitted to lead the rhetorical grand march in English poetry. Possessing all
of Ovid's fondness for exhortation and pleading, he
possessed in addition unexampled powers of classi-
fying and dividing his thoughts, hitting upon happy
generalities, thumping out bold, new epithets, and
accumulating great stores of rhetorical energy as he
proceeded to build his resounding rhyme. He carried eloquence as high as it can go in poetry, which
is not the highest, since eloquence is committed to
dealing with effects rather than forces, with novel-
ties and ardors rather than with convictions. Not
always sympathetic in theory with what he once
condemned as "Ciceronian, copious, florid, and
figurative," he yet was inclined by nature and by
precept towards those very qualities. He was in-

clined to favor a diction that was even and dignified at the expense perhaps of piquancy. "Our
language is noble, full, and significant;" says Neander towards the end of the *Essay of Dramatic Poesy*,
"and I know not why he who is master of it may
not clothe ordinary things in it as decently as the
Latin, if he use the same diligence in his choice of
words. *Delectus verborum origo est eloquentiæ*. . . .
One would think, *unlock the door*, was a thing as
vulgar as could be spoken; and yet Seneca could make
it sound high and lofty in his Latin:

> *Reserate clusos regii postes laris.*
> Set wide the palace gates."

Dryden was also inclined to fall into an exalted antithetical tone of formal address which frequently
suited his needs admirably but which in many cases
has rendered him unattractive in the eyes of later
generations. That tone was indispensable in the
heroic plays, which were supposed by no one to be
real. It was of enormous advantage in *Absalom and
Achitophel*, where it erected great public personages
to their proper height and gave to satire a strange
epic importance; as may best be seen in Achitophel's
address to Absalom beginning:

> Auspicious prince! at whose nativity
> Some royal planet ruled the southern sky,
> Thy longing country's darling and desire,
> Their cloudy pillar, and their guardian fire,
> Their second Moses, whose extended wand
> Divides the seas and shows the promised land,
> Whose dawning day in every distant age
> Has exercised the sacred prophet's rage,

The people's prayer, the glad diviner's theme,
The young men's vision, and the old men's dream,
Thee, Saviour, thee the nation's vows confess,
And, never satisfied with seeing, bless.

It is not in the heroic plays or in the poems on public affairs that Dryden's rhetorical vein has failed to meet with approval; it is rather in those narrative poems where nothing short of exquisite variety and delicacy are demanded by the theme. Here Dryden, instead of proving himself sensitive to the demands made by the successive turns of his story and the altered dispositions of his characters, continues to speak in the cadence of the pulpit or the bar. It is this rigidity of manner which has estranged fastidious readers from the *Virgil* and the *Fables*. The plasticity of Virgil and Chaucer is not Dryden's. Arcite's dying speech to Emily is one of Chaucer's directest and most intimate passages:

Naught may the woful spirit in myn herte
Declare o point of alle my sorwes smerte
To yow, my lady, that I love most;
But I bequethe the service of my gost
To yow aboven every creature,
Sin that my lyf may no lenger dure.
Allas, the wo! allas, the peynes stronge,
That I for yow have suffred, and so longe!
Allas, the deeth! Allas, myn Emelye!
Allas, departing of our companye!
Allas, myn hertes quene! allas, my wyf!
Myn hertes lady, endere of my lyf!
What is this world? What asketh men to have?
Now with his love, now in his colde grave

Allone, withouten any companye.
Far-wel, my swete fo! myn Emelye!
And softe tak me in your armes tweye,
For love of God, and herkneth what I seye.

Dryden's Arcite speaks as follows:

No language can express the smallest part
Of what I feel, and suffer in my heart,
For you, whom best I love and value most;
But to your service I bequeath my ghost;
Which from this mortal body when untied,
Unseen, unheard, shall hover at your side;
Nor fright you waking, nor your sleep offend,
But wait officious, and your steps attend.
How I have loved, excuse my faltering tongue,
My spirit's feeble, and my pains are strong:
This I may say, I only grieve to die,
Because I lose my charming Emily:
To die, when Heaven had put you in my power,
Fate could not choose a more malicious hour!
What greater curse could envious Fortune give,
Than just to die, when I began to live!
Vain men, how vanishing a bliss we crave,
Now warm in love, now withering in the grave!
Never, O never more to see the sun!
Still dark, in a damp vault, and still alone!
This fate is common; but I lose my breath
Near bliss, and yet not blest before my death.
Farewell; but take me dying in your arms,
'Tis all I can enjoy of all your charms;
This hand I cannot but in death resign;
Ah, could I live! but while I live 'tis mine.
I feel my end approach, and thus embraced,
Am pleased to die; but hear me speak my last.

Dryden has no equal in prayers, objurgations, politic addresses, and speeches of defiance; he wears the robes that he has borrowed from the orator with a splended assurance; his accents, although they too are borrowed, ring true. But in poetic narrative his limits are firmly fixed. When the shades of the Forum cannot be beckoned to help him rise, he does not rise. He has always the appearance of being strong, but as Lowell has pointed out, there is stiffness, and there is coldness, in his strength. Taking him altogether, stiffness must be accounted one of his shortcomings.

Under Charles I, secular painting and music had come to England to stay. Van Dyck and Henry Lawes, to name no others, had won the enduring favor of courtiers and poets; and the technique of each of their arts had rapidly become familiar to persons of culture or acquaintance. Interest in those arts from the technical side continued to increase after the Restoration and through the age of Dryden. It became a commonplace of æsthetics that poetry, painting, and music are allied. Congreve said "Poetry includes Painting and Music." English and French writers throughout the eighteenth century carried forward the double parallel, so that when Friedrich Schlegel wrote in 1798 "Die Poesie ist Musik für das innere Ohr, und Malerei für das innere Auge," although he implied something that had not been implied a hundred years before, he yet was dealing with what might have been called an axiom. This axiom was to bear new and strange fruit in nineteenth-century literature. Upon Au-

gustan verse its influence had been purely formal; it
had established a diction and a scheme of numbers.

The single parallel between poetry and painting
was already venerable in Dryden's day. It had
first been drawn in Aristotle's *Poetics;* Horace and
Plutarch had given it momentum; and it had been
sanctioned by virtually every European critic during the sixteenth and seventeenth centuries. In
England the Elizabethan theorists had touched upon
it, and it had been ratified in turn by Ben Jonson,
Cowley, Davenant, and Hobbes. It was cherished
during the Restoration and the early eighteenth
century, but it eventually lost its meaning, so that
when Lessing attacked it in 1766, employing some
of the weapons which Du Bos had used half a century earlier, he was attacking something which
could offer only partial resistance. The parallel had
not borne along any constant body of dogma. Aristotle had merely remarked that the poet, being an
imitator, is therefore like a painter or any artist;
and it had occurred to him to compare the characters and plot of a tragedy to the colors and outline
of a painting. Horace had suggested that poems
and pictures are alike with respect to the circumstances under which spectators should judge them;
some appear better at a distance than when closely
observed, some require more lighting than others,
some should be seen many times to be appreciated
at their full value. Plutarch had called painting
dumb poetry, and poetry a speaking picture.
Lessing objected to the whole theory on the ground
that it had led to a freezing of the drama; in striv-

ing to remove ugliness and suffering from the surface of their art so as to render it capable of comparison with the still surfaces of other arts, dramatists
had thrown away their pity and their terror, and
nothing was left. A stoic hero is not interesting
since he cannot suffer. The bearings of the theory
on dramatic construction are of no concern in the
present connection. The parallel is important here
for its bearing on the question of Dryden's diction.

Dryden was thoroughly familiar with the doctrine of the parallel and with its history. He first
quoted the *Ut pictura poesis* of Horace in his *Defence of an Essay of Dramatic Poesy* in 1668. His
works are loaded with references to technical points
in painting, showing that he considered himself acquainted with the practical problems of the art. He
draws the parallel, with applications of his own, no
less than twenty times; and often he extends it. In
the *Life of Plutarch* history is compared with painting. In the preface to *Sylvæ* the shading of cadences in a Pindaric ode is found to be like the shading
of colors in a picture. In the *Discourse Concerning
Satire* a satirical "character" is compared to a portrait on canvas. It is in the *Parallel of Poetry and
Painting*, however, which Dryden prefixed to his
translation of Du Fresnoy's *De Arte Graphica* in
1695, that he elaborates the parallel to its fullest
extent and explains its bearings on poetic diction.
"Expression," he writes, "and all that belongs to
words, is that in a poem which colouring is in a picture. The colours well chosen in their proper places,
together with the lights and shadows which belong

to them, lighten the design, and make it pleasing to
the eye. The words, the expressions, the tropes and
figures, the versification, and all the other elegan-
cies of sound, as cadences, turns of words upon the
thought, and many other things, which are all parts
of expression, perform exactly the same office both
in dramatic and epic poetry. . . . In poetry, the expression is that which charms the reader, and beau-
tifies the design, which is only the outlines of the
fable. . . . Amongst the ancients, Zeuxis was most
famous for his colouring; amongst the moderns, Titian and Correggio. Of the two ancient epic poets,
who have so far excelled all the moderns, the invention and design were the particular talents of Homer
. . . but the *dictio Virgiliana,* the expression of
Virgil, his colouring, was incomparably the better;
and in that I have always endeavoured to copy
him." Expression, elocution, diction, were cardinal
points with Dryden; they absorbed the greater
part of his effort in virtuoso-works like the *Virgil*
and the *Fables.* To be going hand in hand with
Virgil and Titian, the supreme colorists, was a supreme privilege in his eyes. Yet he labored with a
complacency that one does not expect in a conscientious painter. And his results are what one does not
find in a conscientious poet. For the parallel he
drew between diction in poetry and color in painting was superficial. He conceived color in painting as a kind of splendid wash applied after the
drawing is done. It has no more organic function
than that of decoration. It adds to the glamor rather
than to the meaning of a picture. So elocution in

poetry; it is, "in plain English," says Dryden, "the bawd of her sister, the design . . . ; she clothes, she dresses her up, she paints her, she makes her appear more lovely than naturally she is; she pro cures the design, and makes lovers for her." That is, diction in poetry is a splendid wash that is spread over the framework of the plot. Words have no more organic function than the painter's pigments; the imagination is nothing but camel's hair.

The diction of the *Virgil* and the *Fables* is always vigorous and smooth, and at its best it is nothing short of magnificent. But it is always evident that the poet has laid it on from without. At its best it is gilt rather than gold, and at its worst it is tinsel. The tinsel is what modern readers have found difficult to accept in Dryden. Dryden applied his elocution with a hasty hand, and one that rarely showed discrimination. He has been called the Rubens among English poets because of his lavishness and gusto; surely he can deserve the title for no other reason. He has boundless gusto; but he is almost incorrigibly vague. His vagueness is partly the result of a theory, partly the result of defective vision. The theory is the theory of idealized or generalized Nature. He makes much of it in the *Parallel*, where he shows that the poet and the painter alike should form ideas of a perfect nature in which all eccentricities are corrected and all vulgarities pared away. The surface of a poem or a painting should be smooth and beautiful and decorous; no word or phrase should be inserted which it might strain the intelligence of elegant readers or

spectators to understand. Technical diction is
barred for the benefit of "those men and ladies of
the first quality, who have been better bred than to
be too nicely knowing in the terms." Here is the
source of that generalizing frame of mind which
created the poetry and the painting of the next century; that frame of mind which made Sir Joshua
Reynolds most of what he was as artist or as critic,
and which eventually moved Ruskin and Blake
to awful wrath. "To generalize," said Blake, "is
to be an idiot." Dryden generalized. His feeling
for details was not keen, and his interest in them
was nil. He used a broad brush, and painted
swiftly. He did not mind repeating himself. He
would have been pleased had he been called conventional. Virgil had conventionalized Homer. Dryden conventionalized Virgil. In the thirteenth book
of the *Odyssey* Homer describes the harbor in Ithaca
where Odysseus landed:

There is in the land of Ithaca a certain haven of Phorcys,
the ancient one of the sea, and thereby are two headlands
of sheer cliff, which slope to the sea on the haven's side
and break the mighty wave that ill winds roll about, but
within, the decked ships ride unmoored when once they
have reached the place of anchorage. Now at the harbor's
head is a long-leaved olive tree, and hard by is a pleasant
cave and shadowy, sacred to the nymphs, that are called
the Naiads. And therein are mixing bowls and jars of
stone, and there moreover bees do hive. And there are
great looms of stone, wherein the nymphs weave raiment
of purple stain, a marvel to behold, and therein are waters
welling evermore.[1]

[1] Translation of Butcher and Lang. Oxford, 1879.

This is the work of a poet who would always rather insert a detail than leave it out. Virgil's description of the Libyan harbor where Æneas landed (I, 159ff.) is the work of a poet who cares somewhat less for the concrete than he does for the beautiful:

There, in a deep bay, is a roadstead, which an island forms by its jutting sides. On those sides every wave from the deep breaks, then parts into the winding hollows: on this hand and that are vast rocks, and twin cliffs frowning to heaven; and beneath their peaks, far and wide, the peaceful seas are silent. From the height hangs a background of waving forests, and a grove of dim and tangled shadows. Under the fronting crags is a rock-hung cave—haunted by nymphs—and, within it, sweet water and seats from the living rock. [1]

Dryden's account is the work of a man who altogether lacks fondness for particulars:

> Within a long recess there lies a bay;
> An island shades it from the rolling sea,
> And forms a port secure for ships to ride;
> Broke by the jutting land, on either side,
> In double streams the briny waters glide;
> Betwixt two rows of rocks a sylvan scene
> Appears above, and groves forever green:
> A grot is formed beneath, with mossy seats,
> To rest the Nereids, and exclude the heats.
> Down through the crannies of the living walls
> The crystal streams descend in murmuring falls.

In these "briny waters," "sylvan scenes," and

[1] Translation of John Jackson. Oxford. 1908.

"crystal streams" are the beginnings of the stereo-
typed Nature which graced the verse of England
for at least two generations. No one can be held
more strictly accountable for its vogue than Dryden, whose *Virgil* was read by every poet and
served as a storehouse, like Pope's *Homer*, of cultivated phrases. Dryden supplied himself with a
kind of natural furniture with which he could stock
any house of verse that seemed to him bare. He
laid in a fund of phrases with which he could expand
any passage that seemed to him curt. Thus in the
fifth *Æneid*, when Virgil writes

> ferit æthera clamor
> Nauticus, adductis spumant freta versa lacertis,

Dryden goes beyond him and whips the sea into a
more suitable froth:

> With shouts the sailors rend the starry skies;
> Lashed with their oars, the smoky billows rise;
> Sparkles the briny main, and the vexed ocean fries.

One word in Chaucer's *Knight's Tale*, "huntyng,"
becomes four lines in Dryden's *Palamon and Arcite:*

> A sylvan scene with various greens was drawn,
> Shades on the sides, and in the midst a lawn;
> The silver Cynthia, with her nymphs around,
> Pursued the flying deer, the woods with horns resound.

Three words in *The Flower and the Leaf*, "the briddes
songe," become sixteen in Dryden:

> The painted birds, companions of the Spring,
> Hopping from spray to spray, were heard to sing.

Nor did young poets in the time of Queen Anne
need to go further than Dryden for models of periphrasis. The circumlocution, that pale ghost of
the Roman epithet, that false pigment bound to
fade even before its poet-painter could apply it,
was everywhere in the later Dryden. In the *Æneis*,
an arrow is a feathered death; in the *Georgics*,
honey is liquid gold, tenacious wax, ambrosial dew,
gathered glue; and always the fish are finny.

"Music and Poetry have ever been acknowledged Sisters," said Henry Purcell, the greatest
English musician of Dryden's or any other time.
He had the Greeks for his authority, as well as every
Englishman who had ever written either about
music or about poetry. The analogy of the two arts
may be said to have seemed self-evident to the
Elizabethans, Gascoigne, Sidney, Puttenham, Daniel, Campion, and to writers of the seventeenth century. Davenant confessed that he had composed
the cantos of his *Gondibert* with "so much heat . . .
as to presume they might (like the works of *Homer*
ere they were joined together and made a volume by
the Athenian king) be sung at village feasts, though
not to monarchs after victory, nor to armies before
battle. For so (as an inspiration of glory into the
one, and of valour into the other) did *Homer's*
spirit, long after his body's rest, wander in musick
about Greece." Sir William Temple derived music
and poetry from a single source, a certain heat and
agitation of the brain. The parallel had and always will have multitudinous phases, of which the
opera and the song and the ballad suggest the most

obvious. The connection which Dryden and others made between the two arts purported to be a more subtle one than that which is involved in the accompaniment of words by music. It involved the arrangement of words in such a succession that they themselves should produce the effects of music. This is an important theory, which in different guises and in the hands of different men has been productive of genuine poetry; for no one will deny that the most moving poetry has been in some way musical. But it is not a simple theory, and it cannot be applied complacently or mechanically. In so far as Dryden and his followers applied it complacently and mechanically they failed to produce poetry that moves. As in the case of the analogy from painting they failed to perceive that it is only the color of a distinguished mind that can lend distinctive shades of beauty to a poem, so in the case of the analogy from music they were not always aware that it is only the tone of a genuinely composed and vibrant imagination which can give important harmonies to verse. They relied upon a kind of musical attachment, both to furnish them with a constant pitch and to ring occasional changes suited to the sense.

"I do not hesitate to say," wrote Leigh Hunt in the preface to his *Story of Rimini* in 1816, "that Pope and the French school of versification have known the least on the subject of any poets perhaps that ever wrote. They have mistaken mere smoothness for harmony." This is perhaps the most absolute condemnation which the music of Augustan verse has received. But it is by no means the earliest. Hunt was capping a commonplace of criticism with his climax. Milton, in his preface to *Paradise Lost*, had categorically denied the possibility of true music to heroic verse, with its "jingling sound of like endings." Augustan poets and critics themselves had inveighed against "mere harmony." The Earl of Mulgrave, in his *Essay Upon Poetry* of 1682, had observed that

> Number, and Rime, and that harmonious sound
> Which never does the Ear with harshness wound,
> Are necessary, yet but vulgar Arts.

The preface to that remarkable anthology, the *Poems on Affairs of State* (1697), had contained a robust protest against mere regularity: "There are a sort of men, who having little other merit than a happy chime, would fain fix the Excellence of Poetry in the smoothness of the Versification, allowing but little to the more Essential Qualities of a Poet, great Images, good sense, etc. Nay they have so blind a passion for what they excel in, that they will exclude all variety of numbers from English Poetry, when they allow none but Iambics, which must by an identity of Sound bring a very unpleasant satiety upon the Reader." Pope, in his *Essay on Criticism*, had disposed very neatly of

> these tuneful fools. . . .
> Who haunt Parnassus but to please their ear.

And finally, Cowper in *Table Talk* had found Pope wanting because he

> Made poetry a mere mechanic art,
> And every warbler has his tune by heart.

So that from the beginning there had been no lack of consciousness that heroic verse tended towards monotony. Yet in general the claim of the couplet writers that their essential contribution to English poetry was in the way of harmony went without serious challenge for a good hundred years after Waller and Denham first "came out into the world," as the saying was, "forty thousand strong." It was precisely the music of the couplet, easy and continuous rather than intricate and intermittent, that won the couplet its prestige at the start.

> The relish of the Muse consists in rhyme;
> One verse must meet another like a chime.
> Our Saxon shortness hath peculiar grace
> In choice of words fit for the ending place:
> Which leave impression in the mind as well
> As closing sounds of some delightful bell.

So wrote Sir John Beaumont early in Dryden's century, in his *Concerning the True Form of English Poetry*. Not only delightful rhymes but flawless "numbers" as well became the aim of successive generations of versifiers. At the close of the sixteenth century in France, Malherbe, in his commentary on Desportes, had laid down rules for a kind of negative harmony, a mere smoothness, in French verse. The only distinction between prose and verse, said Malherbe, was to be *nombre*. "Numbers" became paramount both in England and in France. "The music of numbers . . .," wrote Cowley, "almost without anything else, makes an excellent poet." The preface [1] to Joshua Poole's *English Parnassus* (1657), an enterprising forerunner of the handbooks on poetry which Byache, Gildon, and others were to issue in the eighteenth century, placed particular emphasis upon the "Symphony and Cadence" of poesy; right accent, "like right time in Music, produces harmony"; rhyme is the "symphony and music of a verse." It became easy, by Pope's time, to write in flawless cadence. Pope himself, despising as he did the tuneful poetasters, tuned his own instrument with great pains. "The great rule of verse," he told Spence, "is to be musical." Within their narrow range, it must be granted, the Augustan poets were able to achieve a much greater variety of tone than it now is the custom to recognize, and it never is necessary to remind a knowing reader that the best of these poets were anything but slaves to numbers. But no one will deny that their range was too narrow, and that their energies were directed too much into the mechanics of their art.

Dryden, who was considered in his own day to be unrivalled anywhere for diversity, and who must always be prized for his really genuine melody, lived also under the spell of numbers, believing in them with his whole mind and communicating his faith with a proselyting zeal. Such monotony and such glibness as he has result from the conviction which he never abandoned that a poet's best powers should go into the perfecting of his verse in-

[1] Signed "J. D."

strument. Aristotle had not denied to the music of
the flute and the lyre the capacity for imitating
life, but he had observed that the medium through
which musical instruments may function in their
imitation of life is restricted to "harmony and
rhythm alone." Dryden, believing always that
"versification and numbers are the greatest pleasures of poetry," tended to cherish heroic verse as a
musical instrument, and to work for "harmony and
rhythm alone." He thought that "well-placing of
words, for the sweetness of pronunciation, was not
known till Mr. Waller introduced it." He never
doubted that English could be rendered more liquid
than it was, so that in time it might even compete with Virgil's Latin and with Tasso's Italian,
"the softest, the sweetest, the most harmonious"
of all tongues, a tongue which seemed to him "to
have been invented for the sake of Poetry and
Music." His desire was always for more "even,
sweet, and flowing" lines. His objection to English
consonants and monosyllables was that they obstructed the flow of verse. His fondness for Latinistic polysyllables arose from the capacity which
they seemed to have for "softening our uncouth
numbers," for suppling the heroic line, and imparting to it an undulating grace. Circumlocutions rec-
ommended themselves to him and to all Augustans
as much for their sound as for their ingenuity.
"Periphrasis," Longinus told them, "tends much to
sublimity. For, as in music the simple air is rendered more pleasing by the addition of harmony, so
in language periphrasis often sounds in concord

with a literal expression, adding much to the beauty of its tone—provided always that it is not inflated and harsh, but agreeably blended. Plato . . . takes . . . words in their naked simplicity and handles them as a musician, investing them with melody,—harmonizing them, as it were,—by the use of periphrasis." Dryden was well aware at all times that it is possible to become smooth at the expense of more important qualities. "I pretend to no dictatorship," he confessed in his dedication of the *Æneis*, "among my fellow poets, since, if I should instruct some of them to make well-running verses, they want genius to give them strength as well as sweetness." Dryden can rarely be said to have had the appearance of weakness, either in his *Virgil* or elsewhere. Yet it was just in his *Æneis* that he surrendered most completely to the tyranny of numbers. His boundless admiration for Virgil's metrical and verbal genius led him to toy with strange devices. Recognizing clearly enough that Virgil's haunting melody was well beyond his reach, he endeavored to compensate the readers of his translation with obvious and rather sensational substitutes. For the effect of fluency and for "softening" his numbers he depended upon polysyllables; not finding a sufficient stock of dissyllabic adjectives in the language, he devised some of his own, as heapy, spiry, sluicy, sweepy, forky, fainty, spumy, barmy, beamy, roofy, flaggy, ropy, dauby, piny, moony, chinky, pory, and hugy. Not finding, either, a sufficient stock of long Latin words in English, he brought many of Virgil's abundant phrases straight over, rendering them for what they appeared rather than for what they meant. It is impossible to quote any one passage from the *Æneis* which will adequately reveal the virtuoso temper in which Dryden composed it. But it is no exaggeration to say that it shows better than any other Augustan poem the effects of musical principles applied mechanically to verse.

Pope, as is well known, had in mind two kinds of tuneful fools when he was writing his *Essay on Criticism.*

> 'Tis not enough no harshness gives offense,
> The sound must seem an echo to the sense.

The second line of his couplet referred to the Dick Minims who insisted that "imitative harmony," or "representative harmony," or "representative versification," as it was variously called, was an indispensable ingredient in poetry. Dionysius of Halicarnassus was perhaps the parent of the creed. Vida had echoed him in his *De Arte Poetica*, and the dogma had settled gradually down through various Italian and Spanish rhetoricians to Cowley, who in a note to his *Davideis* declared that "the disposition of words and numbers should be such, as that out of the order and sound of them, the things themselves may be represented." The Earl of Roscommon, in his *Essay on Translated Verse* (1684), wrote:

> The Delicacy of the nicest Ear
> Finds nothing harsh or out of Order there.

> Sublime or low, unbended or Intense,
> The sound is still an echo to the Sense.

Pope's lines, which derived no doubt from Roscommon's, gave the doctrine especial currency, and to echo sense with sound became a pleasant duty of versifiers. Pope himself told Spence that he "followed the significance of the numbers, and the adapting them to the sense, much more even than Dryden." Later in the eighteenth century there grew up a rather fine distinction between what Dr. Johnson called the imitation of sound and the imitation of motion in verse. Daniel Webb, in his *Observations on the Correspondence between Poetry and Music* (1769), claimed that the use of words to represent sounds was an inferior artifice, not comparable to the important art of communicating emotion through cadences. James Beattie, in his *Essay on Poetry and Music as they Affect the Mind* (1776), followed Webb; and Dr. Johnson, in his lives of Cowley and Pope, enunciated the distinction most forcibly of all. At its highest, imitative harmony cannot be said to have attained the dignity of an art. It was always a cheap and easy artifice not to be associated with that mysterious power, possessed in the greatest abundance by Virgil, Milton, and Wordsworth, which works its mighty will among the emotions purely through combinations of sounds.

"The chief secret," confided Dryden in the preface to *Albion and Albanius*, "is the choice of words; and, by this choice, I do not here mean elegancy of expression, but propriety of sound, to be varied according to the nature of the subject. Perhaps a time may come when I may treat of this more largely out of some observations which I have made from Homer and Virgil, who, amongst all the poets, only understood the art of numbers." Dryden never treated of the matter on the scale he promised here, nor had he done so is it likely that his treatise would have been profound. He was not only intrigued, he was baffled by the solemn harmonies of Virgil, whose verse, he observed in the preface to *Sylvæ*, "is everywhere sounding the very thing in your ears, whose sense it bears." His own *Virgil* is nothing more or less than an extensive proving-ground for imitative harmony. It is a huge temple of sound, not beautiful on the whole, but sturdy and imposing. Dryden attempts in it to represent both noises and movements, if Dr. Johnson's distinction may be employed once more. The first he accomplished without any subtlety at all. He is particularly fond of storms that churn the seas and shake the shores. Our ears grow accustomed to windy caverns echoing thunder. Time and time again

> The impetuous ocean roars,
> And rocks rebellow from the sounding shores.

There are no gradations of violence in Dryden's weather, and there is rarely any more than an obvious and general fitness in Dryden's language. He is much more cunning when he is representing movements of animals or persons. The fifth book of his *Æneis* is particularly noteworthy in this connec-

tion. The serpent which issues from Anchises'
tomb while Æneas is praying before it moves with
a writhing splendor:

> Scarce had he finished, when with speckled pride
> A serpent from the tomb began to glide,
> His hugy bulk on seven high volumes rolled;
> Blue was his breadth of back, but streaked with
>   scaly gold;
> Thus riding on his curls, he seemed to pass
> A rolling fire along, and singe the grass.
> More various colours through his body run
> Than Iris when her bow imbibes the sun.
> Betwixt the rising altars, and around,
> The sacred monster shot along the ground;
> With harmless play amidst the bowls he passed,
> And with his lolling tongue essayed the taste.
> Thus fed with holy food, the wondrous guest
> Within the hollow tomb retired to rest.

The funeral games are presented in plunging,
roughly felicitous cadences. The boxers Dares and
Entellus seem to strike real blows and fall their actual heavy lengths in Dryden's verse; and the
young horsemen perform their evolutions without
a metrical flaw:

> The second signal sounds, the troop divides
> In three distinguished parts, with three distin-
>   guished guides.
> Again they close, and once again disjoin;
> In troop to troop opposed, and line to line.
> They meet; they wheel; they throw their darts afar
> With harmless rage, and well-dissembled war:
> Then in a round the mingled bodies run;
> Flying they follow, and pursuing shun;

> Broken, they break; and, rallying, they renew
> In other forms the military shew.
> At last, in order, undiscerned they join
> And march together in a friendly line.
> And, as the Cretan labyrinth of old,
> With wandering ways and many a winding fold,
> Involved the weary feet, without redress,
> In a round error, which denied recess;
> So fought the Trojan boys in warlike play,
> Turned and returned, and still a different way.

Dryden's *Virgil* served Pope and many other successors as a sample-book wherein both representative cadences and representative words could be found. Pope's famous lines on Camilla in the *Essay on Criticism* come from Dryden's portrait of Camilla at the end of the seventh *Æneid* more directly than from Virgil himself. Dryden's virago

> Outstripped the winds in speed upon the plain,
> Flew o'er the fields, nor hurt the bearded grain;
> She swept the seas, and as she skimmed along,
> Her flying feet unbathed on billows hung.

Pope's *Homer* owes much to the *Virgil* in this as well as in other departments. Gray's *Progress of Poesy* borrows Dryden's most sounding diction, as in the lines

> Now rolling down the steep amain,
> Headlong, impetuous, see it pour;
> The rocks and nodding groves rebellow to the roar.

From Cowley to Dick Minim Dryden was the great example of the imitative versifier, as he was also the great example of most of what the Augus-

tans believed to comprise a poet. It seems never to
have been suspected that Dryden was speaking
with his most communicative cadences in the satires and the epistles. But nothing is more natural
than that his best music should be heard in the
poems which he most meant. It was when he was
most oblivious of the problem of adapting sound to
sense, when he was fullest of the scorn or the admiration which he knew better than any other poet to
express, that he fell into his properest rhythms.
These two utterly contemptuous lines from *Absalom
and Achitophel*,

> A numerous host of dreaming saints succeed,
> Of the true old enthusiastic breed,

are perfectly tuned; the vowels and the consonants,
whether or not they were thoughtfully chosen, are
steeped in disdain. This gracious triplet from the
poem *To the Memory of Mr. Oldham*,

> Thy generous fruits, though gathered ere their prime,
> Still shewed a quickness; and maturing time
> But mellows what we write to the dull sweets of rhyme,

is otherwise attuned, but its attunement too is perfect. The acceleration in the second line speaks
eagerness to praise whatever can be praised; the
long, ripe cadence of the close breathes consolation. Such passages are worth, as poetry, a thousand Camillas and all the rocks that ever were
heard rebellowing to the roar. It is in them that the
true fire of Dryden's genius will be found to burn.

III

THE TRUE FIRE

The only qualities which Wordsworth could find in Dryden deserving to be called poetical were "a certain ardour and impetuosity of mind" and "an excellent ear." Whether or not Wordsworth stopped short of justice in his enumeration, he hit upon two virtues which are cardinal in Dryden, and confined himself with proper prudence to what in Dryden is more important than any other thing, his manner. His manner, embracing both an enthusiastic approach to any work and a technical dexterity in the performance of it, was constant. The channels through which his enthusiasm drove him were not always fitted for his passage, as we have been seeing; nor was his ease of motion always an advantage, inasmuch as his metrical felicity served at times only to accentuate his original error in choice of province. But when his material was congenial, and when he himself was thoroughly at home in his style, he was unexceptionable.

Dryden was most at home when he was making statements. His poetry was the poetry of declaration. At his best he wrote without figures, without transforming passion. When Shakespeare's imagination was kindled his page thronged with images. When Donne was most genuinely possessed by his theme he departed in a passionate search for conceits. When Dryden became fired he only wrote more plainly. The metal of his genius was silver, and the longer it was heated the more silver it grew. Nausicaa fell in love with Odysseus because the goddess Athene had shed a strange grace about his head and shoulders and made him seem more presentable than he was. No one can be impressed by Dryden who sees him in disguise. One must see him as he is: a poet of opinion, a poet of company, a poet of civilization. It is not to be inferred that he was without passion; no man ever had more. But his was not the passion that behaves like ecstasy; he never got outside himself. His passion was the passion of assurance. His great love was the love of speaking fully and with finality; his favorite subjects being personages and books.

Personages he treated from a variety of motives, but always with honest delight. He celebrated public heroes real or supposed, sketched the characters of men in high places and in low, addressed elaborate compliments to benefactors or friends, described minds and actions both in fact and in fable with an endless relish. Books he treated from a single motive, admiration for them and their makers. Dryden was above all things a literary man. His mind could best be energized by contact with other minds; he himself could become preoccupied most easily with other poets. He sat down with indubitable pleasure to write his addresses to Howard, to Roscommon, to Lee, to Motteux, his laments for Oldham and Anne Killigrew, his prologues and epilogues on Shakespeare, Jonson, and the present state of poetry. He was partial to literary history and literary parallels as subjects for poems, and no one in English has done better criticism in meter. In verse as in prose he earned Dr. Johnson's judgment that "the criticism of Dryden is the criticism of a poet." Personalities, actions, ideas, and art were Dryden's best material.

But let it be said again, the story of Dryden's conquest of English poetry for the most part is the story not of his material but of his manner. It is the story of a poet who inherited a medium, perfected it by long manipulation, stamped it with his genius, and handed it on. That medium was heroic couplet verse. The utility of the heroic couplet had been established for all time in England by Chaucer. Spenser, Marlowe, and Shakespeare had made various uses of it at the end of the sixteenth century, as had also the group of satirists which included Hall, Lodge, Marston, and Donne. It had grown more and more in favor during the early years of Dryden's century and had begun to adapt itself to the type of mind which Dryden represents long before he became of age poetically. This adaptation involved a number of characteristics, of which the end-stop, the best known, was only one; the others were a conformation of the sentence-structure to the metrical pattern, a tendency towards polysyllables within the line, a tendency towards emphatic words at the ends of lines, and a frequent use of balance with pronounced cæsura. The end-stop, and the modification of sentence-structure to

suit the length of measure, made for pointedness if
not for brevity, and provided in the couplet a ratiocinative unit which served admirably as the basis
for declarative or argumentative poems. The polysyllables made for speed and flexibility, and encouraged
a Latinized, abstract vocabulary. The insistence
upon important words for the closing of lines meant
that the sense was not likely to trail off or be left
hanging; and the use of balance promoted that air
of spruce finality with which every reader of Augustan
verse has long been familiar.

Just when and in whom the couplet first reached
a stage something like this is a matter that has not
been settled. In France a similar development can
be traced back pretty clearly to Malherbe, whose
formula for perfect rhetorical poetry called, among
other things, for a cæsura which should cut every
verse into two equal parts. "As for the pauses,"
said Dryden in the dedication of the *Æneis*, "Malherbe first brought them into French within this
last century; and we see how they adorn their Alexandrines." No formula like Malherbe's was contrived in England, but the first half of the seventeenth century there saw couplet verse invaded and
conquered by the principles just specified. Credit
for the innovation has been given to a number of
different poets, none of whom can be said to deserve it wholly. Edward Fairfax, the translator of
Tasso's *Godfrey of Bulloigne* (1600), is the earliest
whom Dryden himself named among the reformers
of English versification; in the preface to the *Fables*
Waller is declared the "poetical son" of Fairfax.

The stanzas of the *Tasso* end in couplets which often have the accent of the Augustans, but which more often have it not, tending less towards a monotony of balance than towards a monotony of series or "triplets" of adjectives and nouns. Michael Drayton at various times during his long career wrote couplets which come very near to having Dryden's ring; his *England's Heroical Epistles* (1597) afford the best examples. Drayton was a good Elizabethan, which suggests that there were many Elizabethans who could write Augustan couplets. Spenser did so in his *Mother Hubberd's Tale;* the closing couplets of Shakespeare's sonnets are curiously like Dryden and Pope, as here:

> For we, which now behold these present days,
> Have eyes to wonder, but lack tongues to praise.

The Elizabethan satirists, particularly Joseph Hall, whose *Virgidemiarum* appeared in 1597–8, spoke occasionally in clear tones, though in general their expression was uneven, and such felicity as they permitted themselves to achieve was not contagious. Ben Jonson's influence on seventeenth century poetry was immense, and he was in large part responsible for the new form of heroic verse; but his chief influence was rather upon diction than upon meter. Sir John Beaumont, who died in 1627, wrote his *Bosworth Field* and other poems in couplets which not only for their own time but for any time are models of sweetness and clarity. The *Metamorphoses* of George Sandys (1621–6) was for a hundred years after its publication a landmark to

all who would trace poetical genealogies. Dryden
called Sandys "the best versifier of the former age"
in the preface to the *Fables*, and Pope paired him
with Dryden's Fairfax as a "model to Waller" in
versification. The couplets of his *Ovid* were what
Drayton called them, "smooth-sliding," but they
were neither as uniform nor as brisk as the new
poetry was to require. Milton wrote four of his
Cambridge poems in couplets which are not significant here. The speech of the Genius in *Arcades*
begins like one of Dryden's prologues:

> Stay, gentle swains, for though in this disguise,
> I see bright honour sparkle through your eyes;

but it does not continue in that vein.

It was Waller who the Augustans themselves,
from Dryden on, declared had been the parent of
their line. Francis Atterbury, in his preface to the
1690 edition of Waller's poems, gave a detailed
account of what he believed Waller's innovations
to have been. "Before his time," said Atterbury,
"men rhymed indeed, and that was all; as for the
harmony of measure, and that dance of words which
good ears are so much pleased with, they knew nothing of it. Their poetry then was made up almost entirely of monosyllables; which, when they come together in any cluster, are certainly the most harsh,
untuneable things in the world. . . . Besides, their
verses ran all into one another, and hung together,
throughout a whole copy, like the hooked atoms
that compose a body in Descartes. There was no
distinction of parts, no regular stops, nothing for the

ear to rest upon. . . . Mr. Waller removed all these
faults, brought in more polysyllables, and smoother
measures, bound up his thoughts better, and in a
cadence more agreeable to the nature of the verse
he wrote in; so that wherever the natural stops of
that were, he contrived the little breakings of his
sense so as to fall in with them; and, for that reason,
since the stress of our verse lies commonly upon the
last syllable, you will hardly ever find him using
a word of no force there." Atterbury was very
greatly exaggerating the chaotic state of English verse
before Waller, and he attributed innovations to
Waller that really should be credited to Marlowe,
Sandys, and others; yet he analyzed with particular
delicacy the salient points in which Dryden's versification differs, for instance, from Donne's.

Cowley's *Davideis* was composed in heroic couplets which could teach Dryden nothing after Waller
and Denham. Cowley handled this measure less
felicitously than he handled any other; the *Davideis*
does not chime. Cleveland's political poems, which
Dryden must have read before the Restoration,
were not smooth or sweet, but they had another
quality which was important for Dryden, the quality of momentous directness. Such pauseless lines
as these,

> Encountering with a brother of the cloth,
> Who used to string their teeth upon their belt,
> Religion for their seamstress or their cook,

gave Dryden his metrical cue on more than one occasion.

Dryden wrote altogether, over a period of exactly fifty years, some thirty thousand heroic couplets. The stream of English verse, flowing through him thus for half a century, both sustained him and was sustained by him. His achievement was to make of it a strong yet light vehicle for miscellaneous loads, a medium for the poetry of statement. He learned to say anything in it that he liked, high or low, narrow or broad. Earlier in the century John Selden had written in his *Table Talk:* "'Tis ridiculous to speak, or write, or preach in verse. As 'tis good to learn to dance, a man may learn to leg, learn to go handsomely; but 'tis ridiculous for him to dance when he should go." Dryden showed how one might speak, and write, and preach, and how one might "go" in verse. Verse became for him a natural form of utterance. "Thoughts, such as they are, come crowding in so fast upon me," he wrote in the preface to the *Fables*, "that my only difficulty is to choose or to reject, to run them into verse, or to give them the other harmony of prose; I have so long studied and practiced both, that they are grown into a habit, and become familiar to me."

Dryden's style was a constant delight to his contemporaries because it was unfailingly fresh; new poems by Mr. Dryden meant in all likelihood new cadences, new airs. He was perpetually fresh because he perpetually studied his versification. He perhaps was not a laborious student of metrics; the *Prosodia* for which he said in the dedication of the *Æneis* that he had long ago collected the materials, but which he never published, might have been anything other than exhaustive. Yet there can be no question that he experimented freely and was always sensitive to novel demands that novel subjects might make upon his medium. He generally knew beforehand what effects he should gain; and he had a happy faculty for hitting at once upon rhythms which would secure those effects. His was not, like Doeg's, "a blundering kind of melody." "There is nobody but knows," declared John Oldmixon in 1728, "that it was impossible for Dryden to make an ill verse, or to want an apt and musical word, if he took the least care about it." He was always conscious that rhyme was a handicap, but he accepted it without any prolonged protest; and within the bounds imposed by it he obtained a surprising diversity of accent. He defended rhyming plays against Sir Robert Howard in the dedication of the *Rival Ladies*, in the *Essay of Dramatic Poesy*, and in the *Defence of the Essay*, taking occasion by the way to declare against the inversions and the strained diction into which the exigencies of rhyme tend to force even good poets. But in the prologue to *Aureng-Zebe* he repudiated his "long-loved Mistress"; in both the epistle to Roscommon and the epistle to Sir Godfrey Kneller he damned her as a barbaric fraud foisted upon Europe by the Goths and Vandals; and in the dedication of the *Æneis* he admitted that "Rhyme is certainly a constraint even to the best poets."

Dryden did not always make his principles of versification clear, nor did he ever follow any of them scrupulously. A good case is that of the monosyllables. The Elizabethans had not been moved to inveigh against monosyllables. "The more . . . that you use," said Gascoigne, "the truer Englishman you shall seem." But the new versifiers found them clogging, and spoke against them with great frequency. Dryden was especially resentful of "our old Teuton monosyllables." Yet he employed the "low words," as Pope called them, time and again with excellent effect. He began his *Æneis* with ten of them:

> Arms and the man I sing, who, forced by fate;

and some of his most telling passages have twenty in succession. He told the young poet Walsh that he was often guilty of them "through haste." It should be understood that his quarrel was only with monosyllabic lines that are heavy with consonants, like this from Creech's *Lucretius:*

> Thee, who hast light from midst thick darkness
> brought,

or this from Ben Jonson's poem to Camden,

> Men scarce can make that doubt, but thou canst
> teach.

He gladly allowed such open, liquid lines as this from the same poem of Jonson's:

> All that I am in arts, all that I know.

Of course, both easy polysyllabic and difficult monosyllabic lines can be effective in ways of their own; no more compendious example of which could be cited than these two from Hamlet's last speech,

> Absent thee from felicity awhile,
> And in this harsh world draw thy breath in pain,

where both serve by means exactly opposite to express the pain of dying. Dryden was probably not always aware of the extent to which he relied upon mechanical devices. Alliteration seems to have been instinctive with him, as indeed it is with most rapid and powerful English writers. It played an integral part in his versification, assisting both sense and sound. Scarcely ten consecutive lines can be found in him wherein alliteration is not conspicuous. It serves a variety of purposes. In satire it is either corrosive in its contemptuousness:

> In *f*riendship *f*alse, implacable in hate,
> *R*esolved to *r*uin or to *r*ule the state;

or simply derisive and pelting:

> And *p*ricks up his *p*redestinating ears,
>
> And *p*opularly *p*rosecutes the *p*lot.

In ratiocination it quietly weaves phrases into a firm texture of thought:

> This general worship is to *p*raise and *p*ray,
> One *p*art to *b*orrow *b*lessings, one to *p*ay;
> And when *f*rail nature slides into of*f*ense,
> The sa*cr*ifice for *cr*imes is penitence.
> Yet, since the ef*f*ects of providence, we *f*ind,
> Are variously dispensed to humankind;
> That *v*ice triumphs, and *v*irtue suffers here,
> (A *b*rand that sovereign justice cannot *b*ear;)
> Our reason prompts us to a future state,
> The last appeal *f*rom *f*ortune and *f*rom *f*ate.

In narrative it lends luxuriance and momentum where it does not lend speed:

Down fell the beauteous youth; the gaping wound
Gushed out a crimson *s*tream, and *s*tained the ground.
His *n*odding *n*eck reclines on his white breast,
Like a *f*air *f*lower, in *f*urrowed *f*ields oppressed
By the keen share; or *p*oppy on the *p*lain,
Whose *h*eavy *h*ead is overcharged with rain.
Dis*d*ain, *d*espair, and *d*eadly *v*engeance *v*owed,
Drove Nisus *h*eadlong on the *h*ostile crowd.

Dryden's gift for adapting his rhythmical emphasis to his meaning amounted to genius. Alliteration, effective rhyme, antithesis, and the use of polysyllables were only auxiliaries to that. It was that which gave him rapidity without the appearance of haste and flexibility without the loss of strength. Bound by the laws of a syllabic system of versification and condemned to a narrow metrical range, he succeeded in manipulating his measures so that he could speak directly and easily yet with dignity. He was more than a believer in mere variety of accent, though he stressed that too as early as the *Essay of Dramatic Poesy*, where Neander observed, "Nothing that does *Perpetuo tenore fluere*, run in the same channel, can please always. 'Tis like the murmuring of a stream, which not varying in the fall, causes at first attention, at last drowsiness. Variety of cadences is the best rule." Dryden was a believer in significant variety of accent. Pope, in a letter to his friend Henry Cromwell, recognized three places within the heroic line where pauses might come: after the fourth, after the fifth, and after the sixth syllables. Dryden knew no limits of the kind. The freedom of blank verse seems to have been in his thoughts. His pauses come anywhere; and often they do not come at all, as in these lines:

> Drawn to the dregs of a democracy,
> Of the true old enthusiastic breed,
> To the next headlong steep of anarchy,
> But baffled by an arbitrary crowd.

He kept himself free to distribute his emphasis where the sense demanded it. The result was what might be called a speaking voice in poetry. Some one seems actually to be reciting *Absalom and Achitophel*:

> Others thought kings an useless heavy load,
> Who cost too much, and did too little good;
> They were for laying honest David by,
> On principles of pure good husbandry.

And the voice of a physical Prologue is plainly heard here:

> Lord, how reformed and quiet are we grown,
> Since all our braves and all our wits are gone! . . .
> France, and the fleet, have swept the town so clear
> That we can act in peace, and you can hear. . . .
> 'Twas a sad sight, before they marched from home,
> To see our warriors in red waistcoats come,
> With hair tucked up, into our tiring-room.
> But 'twas more sad to hear their last adieu:

The women sobbed, and swore they would be true;
And so they were, as long as e'er they could,
But powerful guinea cannot be withstood,
And they were made of playhouse flesh and blood.

Everywhere Dryden's personal presence can be felt. Pope lurks behind his poetry; Dryden stands well forward, flush with his page and speaking with an honest voice if not an honest heart.

The most speaking lines in the last passage quoted are the two which close their respective triplets. Dryden's triplets and Alexandrines have been sources of worry to critics and sources of satisfaction to enemies. Inheriting the triplet from Chapman and Waller, the Alexandrine from Spenser and Hall, and the two in combination from Cowley, he took these devices to himself and made them into important metrical instruments. He did not always succeed in working them into his medium, in rendering them organic within his verse structure; often they were excrescences. The Earl of Rochester was thinking of this when he spoke of Dryden's "loose slattern muse," and Tom Brown, that excellent fooler, made fine fun of the laureate's long lines. Swift was angered at the currency which Dryden had given to triplets and Alexandrines, and Dr. Johnson condemned such of them as were not justified by the general tenor of the passages in which they occurred. Macaulay disposed of them as "sluttish." Dryden put them to various uses. Sometimes his Alexandrines and fourteeners served little or no purpose, being most likely unconscious echoes of the French heroic line. At other times they contributed a sweep of burlesque grandeur, as in the epistle to John Driden of Chesterton:

> But Maurus sweeps whole parishes, and peoples
> every grave.

Elsewhere, and particularly in the translations, they were calculated to yield an effect of splendor. Dryden counted on them, when he was putting Lucretius into English, to represent what he called "the perpetual torrent of his verse." A passage in the dedication of the *Æneis* described how they were used in that work: "Spenser has . . . given me the boldness to make use sometimes of his Alexandrine line. . . . It adds a certain majesty to the verse, when it is used with judgment, and stops the sense from overflowing into another line. . . . I take another license in my verses: for I frequently make use of triplet rhymes, and for the same reason, because they bound the sense. And therefore I generally join the two licenses together, and make the last verse of the triplet a Pindaric; for, besides the majesty which it gives, it confines the sense within the barriers of three lines, which would languish if it were lengthened into four. Spenser is my example for both these privileges of English verses; and Chapman has followed him in his translation of Homer. Mr. Cowley has given into them after both; and all succeeding writers after him. I regard them now as the *Magna Charta* of heroic poetry, and am too much an Englishman to lose what my ancestors have gained for me. Let the French and Italians value themselves on their regularity; strength and elevation are our standard." They were not always used with judgment in the *Virgil*, their frequency being a root of weakness rather than of strength. At certain junctures, in the *Virgil* and elsewhere, they discharged Dryden's accumulated poetic energy in passages that partook of the nature of the ode.[1] In the present connection there remains to be pointed out a function of theirs which is different from the rest and which has not been emphasized before. It is a function that may have been discerned in the prologue from which the last quotation was made; it operates everywhere in the occasional poems; it consists in the supplying of a colloquial, first-hand note. The third line of a triplet in Dryden frequently represents a lowering of the voice to the level of parenthesis or innuendo, as in the *Epilogue Spoken at the Opening of the New House, March 26, 1674:*

> A country lip may have the velvet touch;
> Tho' she's no lady, you may think her such;
> A strong imagination may do much;

or in the prologue to *Troilus and Cressida:*

> And that insipid stuff which here you hate,
> Might somewhere else be called a grave debate;
> Dulness is decent in the Church and State;

or in the prologue to *Love Triumphant:*

> The fable has a moral, too, if sought;
> But let that go; for, upon second thought,
> He fears but few come hither to be taught.

[1] See Chapter VI.

Triplets closing with Alexandrines frequently succeed in imparting a compendiousness to compliment, as in the epistle to Congreve:

> Firm Doric pillars found your solid base;
> The fair Corinthian crowns the higher space;
> Thus all below is strength, and all above is grace.

> In him all beauties of this age we see,
> Etherege his courtship, Southerne's purity,
> The satire, wit, and strength of Manly Wycherley.

> This is your portion; this your native store;
> Heaven, that but once was prodigal before,
> To Shakespeare gave as much; she could not give him
>   more.

Lines like these represent Dryden's metrical license
at its safest and best; he could not always be trusted
to employ it sanely when describing storms of Nature or of passion in Virgil and Lucretius; when he
used it to stamp a statement of his own, as here, he
was well within his province and could not go wrong.

A triplet-and-fourteener which appears in the
Cymon and Iphigenia leads the way to another met-
rical device of which Dryden pretended to be fond.
The triplet runs:

> The fanning wind upon her bosom blows,
> To meet the fanning wind the bosom rose;
> The fanning wind and purling streams continue her
>   repose.

This is one of those "turns" which Dryden in the
Discourse Concerning Satire said that he had been

led by Sir George Mackenzie twenty years before to
study in Waller, Denham, Spenser, Tasso, Virgil,
and Ovid. A "turn" involved the musical repetition of a phrase with variations of meaning. Dryden had a good deal to say about "turns" from time
to time, but in general he thought them below his
dignity, and worthy of no greater geniuses than
those of Ovid and the French, or of such minor
versifiers of the day as pleased themselves with translating Virgil's fourth Georgic and wringing all the
possible echoes out of the name Eurydice. The
sleeping Iphigenia occurred to him as a pretty
enough subject upon which to try one of the metrical toys. He tried few others, though in general
he was perhaps too fond of playing with words for
their own sake, so that he exposed himself to the
censure of Luke Milbourne, to name an enemy, and
John Oldmixon, to name an admirer, for "turning
the Epick style into Elegiack." Virgil's turn in the
seventh Eclogue,

> Fraxinus in silvis pulcherrima, pinus in hortis,
> Populus in fluviis, abies in montibus altis;
> Sæpius at si me, Lycida formose, revisas,
> Fraxinus in silvis cedat tibi, pinus in hortis,

he rendered thus:

> The towering ash is fairest in the woods;
> In gardens pines, and poplars by the floods;
> But, if my Lycidas will ease my pains,
> And after visit our forsaken plains,
> To him the towering ash shall yield in woods,
> In gardens pines, and poplars by the floods.

"He was an improving writer to the last," said Congreve. What Dryden improved in most steadily was the texture of his verse. The difference in respect of texture between the poem on the death of Hastings and *The Hind and the Panther*, to go no further, is enormous; that the author of one should have grown out of the author of the other seems now a kind of miracle. The transformation, which was gradual, involved the discovery and the exploitation of a fundamental rhythm, and it progressed with the adaptation of that rhythm, through modification or enrichment, to widely varying themes. Dryden's metrical evolution began with his earliest verses and proceeded through the plays, through the poems on public affairs, and through the translations.

He scored no decisive technical triumph before the period of the heroic plays. The early poems, distinguished as they are in spots, and approaching Dryden's best manner as they do at times, cannot be supposed to have encouraged the poet to believe that he had caught his stride. The first one, the elegy on Hastings (1649), was done, it must be remembered, before he was eighteen. Metrically it was chaos. Gray remarked to Mason that it seemed the work of a man who had no ear and might never have any. Gray probably had in mind such lines as those addressed to Hastings' "virgin-widow":

> Transcribe the original in new copies; give
> Hastings o' th' better part; so shall he live
> In's nobler half; and the great grandsire be
> Of an heroic divine progeny.

There is nothing of the future Dryden there.   But
in the outburst against old age that precedes there is
a Juvenalian enthusiasm which warms the verse to a
species of transparency; and certain other lines have
a readiness and a bound:

> But hasty winter, with one blast, hath brought
> The hopes of autumn, summer, spring, to naught.
> Thus fades the oak i' th' sprig, i' th' blade the corn;
> Thus without young, this Phœnix dies, new-born.

The *Heroic Stanzas* appeared ten years later, after
what must have been a period of frequent experiments in more than one kind of meter.   The poems
to John Hoddesdon (1650) and to Honor Dryden
(1655) had not told of any advance.   But in this
poem, as in the *Annus Mirabilis* eight years later
still, Dryden wielded with positive assurance a
mighty line which was very much his own.   Spenser in *Colin Clout*, Sir John Davies, Donne, and Ben
Jonson had written heroic stanzas before Davenant;
and Davenant, wishing to adapt his utterance "to a
plain and stately composing of music," had inter-
woven his long-falling, leaden-stepping lines to
form what Dryden and Soame called "the stiff
formal style of *Gondibert*."   But no elegaic quatrains before 1659 had contained verses more emancipated or more confident than these on Cromwell:

> His grandeur he derived from Heaven alone;
> For he was great ere fortune made him so:
> And wars, like mists that rise against the sun,
> Made him but greater seem, not greater grow.

By his command we boldly crossed the line,
  And bravely fought where southern stars arise;
We traced the far-fetched gold into the mine,
  And that which bribed our fathers made our prize.

His ashes in a peaceful urn shall rest;
  His name a great example stands to show,
How strangely high endeavors may be blessed,
  Where piety and valour jointly go.

Each quatrain developed a proposition of its own, and generally, as in the first two which have been quoted, a distinction was stated. It is interesting to see Dryden's earliest fluency coming to him in the exercise of ratiocination. The heroic stanza with its leisurely authority continued to fascinate him even when he resorted to other forms. His next poem, *Astræa Redux* (1660), started off with twenty-eight lines sharply divided into groups of four and developing seven distinct propositions. The brief series of complimentary poems which began with the *Astræa* were quickened and sweetened by the influence of Waller, although Dryden in them did not attain to his eventual flow. The heroic stanza motif was quickly silenced, but no other motif was as yet distinguishable. The close of the *Astræa* had what must have seemed a new sort of drive; and passages like the following from the poem *To His Sacred Majesty, a Panegyric on His Coronation* (1661), must have struck the ears even of Waller's readers as novel because of their swift, smooth rapture:

The grateful choir their harmony employ,
Not to make greater, but more solemn joy;
Wrapped soft and warm your name is sent on high,
As flames do on the wings of incense fly;
Music herself is lost, in vain she brings
Her choicest notes to praise the best of kings;
Her melting strains in you a tomb have found,
And lie like bees in their own sweetness drowned.
He that brought peace, and discord could atone,
His name is music of itself alone.

In the poem *To My Lord Chancellor* (1662) there
were lines somewhat similar on the subject of
Charles I, "our setting sun." Dryden in them is
seen to be at least partially a master of his medium;
his voice is becoming a more important instrument
than his pen. The poem *To The Lady Castlemaine,
Upon Her Incouraging His First Play* (c. 1663) both
began and ended with skilfully modulated tones
and happily emphatic stresses; the *Verses to Her
Highness the Duchess* (1665), prefixed to the first
edition of *Annus Mirabilis*, rode pleasantly on the
wings of Waller:

> While, from afar, we heard the cannon play,
> Like distant thunder on a shiny day.

Certain of the stanzas in *Annus Mirabilis*, as has
been said, struggled not unsuccessfully to surmount
the rubbish that lay about them:

> The moon shone clear on the becalmèd flood,
>   Where, while her beams like glittering silver play,
> Upon the deck our careful General stood,
>   And deeply mused on the succeeding day.

That happy sun, said he, will rise again,
  Who twice victorious did our navy see;
And I alone must view him rise in vain,
  Without one ray of all his star for me.

Yet like an English general will I die,
  And all the ocean make my spacious grave;
Women and cowards on the land may die,
  The sea's a tomb that's proper for the brave.

Restless he passed the remnants of the night,
  Till the fresh air proclaimed the morning nigh;
And burning ships, the martyrs of the fight,
  With paler fires beheld the eastern sky.

"The composition and fate of eight-and-twenty dramas include too much of a poetical life to be omitted," remarked Dr. Johnson. The dramas which Dryden wrote in verse were of the first importance in his metrical development; for it was in them that he became fully aware of the energy which is latent in the heroic couplet, and it was in them that he cut the rhythmical pattern which was to serve him during the remainder of his career. He recognized that a writer of verse plays had first of all to write swiftly; for "all that is said is supposed to be the effect of sudden thought; which . . . admits . . . not anything that shows remoteness of thought, or labor in the writer." He learned to adjust his load while the load was light. Some of his plays were largely dependent for their success upon the quality of their meter, or perhaps the quantity. Writing them with a flesh-and-blood audience, an actually hearing audience in mind, he could not be inattentive to the claims of the ear. His dramatic triumph, such as it was, was a triumph chiefly of the ear. He won his way to fame through sheer metrical genius, this metrical genius first manifesting itself in the heroic plays.

> You in the people's ears began to chime,
> And please the Town with your successful Rime,

grudgingly admitted Shadwell in the *Medal of John Bayes*. The heroic plays, generally speaking, were of manifold origin; they derived from English tragicomedy, from French romance, and from French tragedy. Their verse too derived from more than a single source, perhaps; but Corneille stands forth as a great progenitor of English heroic versifiers for the stage. Dryden adduced "the example of Corneille and some French poets" when in the essay *Of Heroic Plays* he was explaining the pieces which Davenant had produced under the Commonwealth; and Dryden himself knew a good deal about the French dramatist, both as critic and as poet. He found in Corneille a vein of oratory which was effective as poetry no less than as drama; like Corneille he had a fondness for stage argument and for stoic declamation, and from him he learned the value of an obvious, unbroken melody. Dryden was fascinated at an early point by rhymed argumentation. He spoke in the *Essay of Dramatic Poesy* of "the quick and poynant brevity" of repartee; "and this," he said, "joined with the cadency and sweetness of the rhyme, leaves nothing in the soul of the hearer to desire." He employed the

give-and-take of rhymed repartee chiefly in the
heroic plays, but strains of it also appeared amidst
his blank verse and his prose, at such times as he
could not resist the temptation to chime. Dryden
was fascinated again by the possibilities of mere
rhyme, possibilities which are naturally very great
in English. The heroic plays were staged with an
elaborate musical accompaniment, and it is certain
that the audiences accepted the verse as only a portion of a greater *ensemble*. As the authors of *The
Censure of the Rota* less charitably put it, "An heroic
poem never sounded so nobly, as when it was heightened with shouts, and clashing of swords; . . . drums
and trumpets gained an absolute dominion over the
mind of the audience (the ladies, and female spirits);
. . . Mr. Dryden would never have had the courage
to have ventured on a Conquest had he not writ with
the sound of drum and trumpet." *The Indian Emperor* (1665) made the first great impact upon English ears. *The Wild Gallant* (1663), in prose, and
The Rival Ladies (1664), in glib Fletcherian blank
verse, had contained only a few perfunctory couplets;
and *The Indian Queen* (1664), almost entirely the
work of Sir Robert Howard, had lacked rhythmical
plunge although it was composed throughout in
couplets or quatrains. *The Indian Emperor* must
have sounded suddenly and loudly like a gong.
Dryden broke forth in it with consummate rhetoric,
consummate bluff, and consummate rhyme. The
secret of the spell which it cast lay in its pound-
ing regularity of cadence and its unfailing emphasis
upon the rhyme even at the expense of sense and

natural word order. Whether a scene is being sketched from Nature after the manner of some Latin poet or whether a nervous argument is being thrummed out of Dryden's own vocabulary, the cadences never cease to pound or the rhymes to ring. Montezuma demands of his son Guyomar:

> I sent thee to the frontiers; quickly tell
> The cause of thy return; are all things well?

Guyomar describes the appearance of the Spanish vessels:

> I went, in order, sir, to your command,
> To view the utmost limits of the land;
> To that sea-shore where no more world is found;
> But foaming billows breaking on the ground;
> Where, for a while, my eyes no object met,
> But distant skies that in the ocean set;
> And low-hung clouds that dipt themselves in rain.
> To shake their fleeces on the earth again.
> At last, as far as I could cast my eyes
> Upon the sea, somewhat methought did rise,
> Like blueish mists, which still appearing more,
> Took dreadful shapes, and moved towards the shore.

There is not a single departure here from the iambic norm; the diversity which Dryden had already achieved in the early complimentary poems is thrown away. But we are compensated by a more powerful ground-rhythm than has been heard before. It was this metrical bound which was the discovery and glory of the heroic plays. It was exactly this which was to give spring to Augustan heroic verse. The theological disputation between Montezuma and the Christian priests in Act V is a good example of Dryden's controversial chime; and the second scene of the first act sees Cydaria and Cortez falling in love in heroic quatrains:

> *Cydaria.*　My father's gone, and yet I cannot go;
> 　　　　　Sure I have something lost or left behind!
> 　　　　　　　　　　*(Aside)*
> *Cortez.*　Like travellers who wander in the snow,
> 　　　　　I on her beauty gaze 'till I am blind.
> 　　　　　　　　　　*(Aside)*

The Maiden Queen (1667), in excellent prose and decent blank verse, admitted a few rhymes which were out of place and in no way impressive. *Tyrannic Love* (1669) brought back the old rage. In the preface to the printed version of 1670 Dryden described the effect which he believed his verse to have: "By the harmony of words we elevate the mind to a sense of devotion, as our solemn music, which is inarticulate poesy, does in churches." In the second act there is a doctrinal war between St. Catherine and Maximin the Tyrant, and in general there is a vast deal of splendid absurdity. The two parts of *The Conquest of Granada* (1670), which drew Dryden out to his fullest length, are justly famous. They are *The Indian Emperor* in full and double bloom. It is unnecessary to quote more than a dozen lines: four to show the hero and the heroine in give-and-take:

> *Almahide:*　My light will sure discover those who talk—
> 　　　　　Who dares to interrupt my private walk?

Almanzor: He, who dares love, and for that love must
                   die,
                    And, knowing this, dares yet love on, am I;

and eight to illustrate a new cumulative energy in
Dryden which demands *enjambement* and elevates
the verse to another level of music: Almanzor replies to Lyndaraxa, who has made advances,

> Fair though you are
> As summer mornings, and your eyes more bright
> Than stars that twinkle in a winter's night;
> Though you have eloquence to warm and move
> Cold age, and praying hermits, into love;
> Though Almahide with scorn rewards my care;
> Yet, than to change, 'tis nobler to despair.
> My love's my soul; and that from fate is free;
> 'Tis that unchanged and deathless part of me.

There is a rise here, with no corresponding fall,
that denotes new technical powers. The next rhyming play, or "opera," as it was called, the *State of
Innocence*, carried on further experiments in archi-
tectural verse.[1] Triplets and Alexandrines added
embroidery to the old pattern, which perhaps now
seemed a little plain. Raphael tells Adam of the
home he is to find in Paradise:

> A mansion is provided thee, more fair
> Than this, and worthy Heaven's peculiar care;
> Not framed of common earth, nor fruits, nor flowers
> Of vulgar growth, but like celestial bowers;
> The soil luxuriant, and the fruit divine,
> Where golden apples on green branches shine,
> And purple grapes dissolve into immortal wine;

[1] See Chapter VI.

For noon-day's heat are closer arbours made,
And for fresh evening air the opener glade.
Ascend; and, as we go,
More wonders thou shalt know.

The well-known prologue to *Aureng-Zebe* (1675),
Dryden's last heroic tragedy, struck off the fetters
of rhyme in drama, and thereafter no more rhyme
was used, except for a few tail-speeches in *Œdipus*
(1679) and *The Duke of Guise* (1682), until the last
three plays of all, *Amphitryon* (1690), *Cleomenes*
(1692), and *Love Triumphant* (1694), into each of
which a few rocking scenes were allowed to enter.
"According to the opinion of Harte," said Dr.
Johnson, "who had studied his works with great
attention, he settled his principles of versification in
the . . . play of *Aureng-Zebe*." What this means is
not clear; nor is it true to the extent that it can be
used to explain the versification of a poem like *The
Hind and the Panther*. *Aureng-Zebe* still comes short
of the political poems in pliability. Yet advances
have been made over *The Indian Emperor*. Under
the influence of Shakespeare's blank verse, and following up the various licenses with which he had
distinguished the *State of Innocence*, Dryden has
arrived in *Aureng-Zebe* at a limper, more natural
texture of rhyme than he had achieved before in any
play. Nourmahal tells the hero:

I saw with what a brow you braved your fate;
Yet with what mildness bore your father's hate.
My virtue, like a string wound up by art
To the same sound, when yours was touched, took part,
At distance shook, and trembled at my heart.

The rhymed plays alone did not bring Dryden to his metrical maturity. The prologues and epilogues which he wrote to accompany them contributed an important, racy, vocal note which their dialogue never contained. And blank verse, though the connection between it and Dryden's rhyme is not easy to make, was also a valuable school for style. His earlier blank verse is not significant, being easy and banal in the late Elizabethan way, so that the printer was as likely as not to set it up for prose; verse of this sort may be found in *The Rival Ladies*, *The Maiden Queen*, *The Tempest* (1667), *An Evening's Love* (1668), *Marriage à la Mode* (1672), *The Assignation* (1672), *and Amboyna* (1673). It was not until *All for Love* (1678), and the ensuing pair of tragedies composed in the light of French ideals, *Œdipus* and *Troilus and Cressida* (1679), that Dryden attained to any remarkable justice or roundness in his blank verse. The style of *All for Love* is virtually impeccable; it has made the play. It is richly and closely woven, but it is absolutely clear, and it bears no traces of complacency in composition. *The Spanish Friar* (1681) sought again the Fletcherian levels of conversation, as did *Amphitryon* in 1690. In *Don Sebastian* (1690) and *Cleomenes* (1692) Dryden reverted to what he believed to be an Elizabethan "roughness of the numbers and cadences," even departing here and there into a veritable Marstonian crabbedness. In general, all that can be said of his blank verse is that it gave him ample training in the manipulation of phrases. It made no direct contribution to what is after all of most consequence in him, his fund of knowledge about the heroic couplet.

It is not a simple matter to calculate the influence of France on Dryden's style after about 1675, but one may be sure that the influence was of no small account. French characteristics in English manners and English expression throughout the last three-quarters of the seventeenth century have often been exaggerated by historians, yet their significance cannot be brought in question. Under Charles I, after his marriage to Henrietta Maria of France, there had bloomed faintly but truly the précieuse spirit of the Hotel de Rambouillet, with its dilettante elegance. During the Commonwealth the Royalist exiles to France had seen a good deal of the best refinement which the continent possessed. And with the Restoration there had flooded back across the Channel a strong tide of Gallic modernism, involving new fashions of costume, carriage, conduct, cooking, new ideas of medicine, painting, architecture, music, dancing, new accents in cultivated speech, and a new impatience with heavy learning and staid chivalry. Most of what was impossible in the new fashions soon disappeared from English life under the pressure of ridicule. The best remained; and beginning about 1675 a really solid set of improvements were made in taste and speech under the triple guidance of the French formal criticism of men like Le Bossu, the French good sense of Rapin and Boileau, and the French "taste" of which Longinus had been found to be the best expression. As far back as 1668 Dryden had shown

himself in the *Essay of Dramatic Poesy* to be familiar with the critical works of Sarrasin, Le Mes-
nardière, Chapelain, and Corneille; and it is to be
supposed that subsequently he had kept well abreast
of the literary developments in France, for he
was one of the first Englishmen during the following decade to acclaim Rapin and Boileau.
Rapin sems to have found at all times a ready audience in England. His *Reflections upon the Use of the
Eloquence of these Times* appeared at Oxford in 1672,
his *Comparison of Plato and Aristotle* at London in
1673, and his *Reflections on Aristotle's Treatise of
Poesie* at London in 1674, the same year that it was
published in Paris. Dryden drew upon the last
work for the famous definition of wit with which he
closed his *Apology for Heroic Poetry and Poetic License* in 1677, "a propriety of thoughts and words."
Thomas Rymer was Rapin's translator; the Frenchman and the Englishman between them gradually
led Dryden to give a classical turn to tragedy and to
renounce his pristine "bladdered greatness." The
year 1674 was remarkable in France for the publication of five new works by Boileau: the second and
third Epistles, the first four books of the *Lutrin*, the
Art Poétique, and the translation of Longinus. Dryden became acquainted with at least the fourth and
fifth of these almost immediately upon their appearance. He was powerfully moved by the *Longinus*,
which it seems he had not known in John Hall's
English translation of 1652; and the *Art Poétique*
never ceased to appeal to him as a magazine of max-
ims. Dryden was in an important degree responsi-

ble for Boileau's vogue in England through his collaboration with Sir William Soame in 1680–1 upon a translation of the *Art of Poetry*. Up to that time Boileau's effect had been felt chiefly in satire; Etherege, Buckingham, Rochester, Butler, and Oldham in turn had imitated him in that department. Now it was Boileau's whole outlook which was transferred to England. Now it was that the accepted meanings of "wit" and "sense" and "nature" and "the classics" began to draw together; now it was that English speech and English writing in all their parts began to seem nearly civilized. The Earl of Mulgrave's *Essay Upon Poetry* (1682) and the Earl of Roscommon's *Essay on Translated Verse* (1684), two sensible poems in the manner of Horace and Boileau, stamped aristocratic approval upon the Frenchman's creeds at the same time that they spoke his language and breathed his spirit. Almost the first of English verse-essays, they set the standard of decency and urbanity to which Augustans were continually returning over the next three or four decades. St. Evremond, the French exile who spent the greater part of his life in London, was another Gallic influence on Dryden. In 1683, in the *Life of Plutarch*, Dryden remarked that he had been "casually casting [his] eye on the works of a French gentleman, deservedly famous for wit and criticism." This was St. Evremond, who began in 1685 to make his appearance in English print. St. Evremond was not a profound gentleman, but he was a believer in conversation, and his emphasis upon the choicer phases of intercourse went not with-

out its effect on Dryden, who, it will be remembered,
"was not a very genteel man."

Dryden's best style, then, the style of the 1680's,
the style of *Absalom and Achitophel*, the *Religio
Laici*, and *The Hind and the Panther*, owed a good
deal to France. The debt was to French criticism
and to French ideals exquisitely expressed rather
than to any French poetry that Dryden read. The
thinking which he was led by Rapin and Boileau and
Longinus to do, and the conviction which they
forced upon him that adequacy of expression is the
first and last rule of writing, bore fruit, if only directly, in the great satires and ratiocinative poems.
But French poetry itself never had Dryden's respect. "Impartially speaking," he wrote in the
dedication of the *Æneis*, "the French are as much
better critics than the English as they are worse
poets." His habit of depreciation he had con-
tracted in the *Essay of Dramatic Poesy*, where the
regularity of the French had been declared too thin
for English blood. A number of prologues in the
next decade cordially damned French farce and
opera. Doralice, in *Marriage à la Mode*, says to
Palamede: "You are an admirer of the dull French
poetry, which is so thin, that it is the very leaf-gold
of wit, the very wafers and whipped cream of sense,
for which a man opens his mouth and gapes, to
swallow nothing; and to be an admirer of such profound dulness, one must be endowed with a great
perfection of impudence and ignorance." In the
Argument to his Sixth Juvenal Dryden compared
the French affectations of his England with the

Greek affectations of the early Roman empire. In the dedication of the *Æneis* he made the comparison between the French greyhound and the English mastiff which already has been quoted.[1] "The affected purity of the French has unsinewed their heroic verse," he declared. He was by no means alone in this dislike. The distaste for French "thinness" was common. Oldham condemned it in his poem on Ben Jonson, and Roscommon wrote in his *Essay:*

> But who did ever in French authors see
> The comprehensive English Energy?
> The weighty Bullion of one Sterling Line,
> Drawn to French Wire, would thro' whole Pages shine.

The French themselves were ready to admit a distinction. Rymer's translation of Rapin's *Reflections* in 1674 contained a confession, taken literally from Rapin, that the "beauty" of "number and harmony" is "unknown to the French tongue, where all the syllables are counted in the verses, and where there is no diversity of cadence." Englishmen have always been proud of the difference between French verse and their own, a difference which has been used at various times to point various morals; in Dryden's time it was the last refuge of those who, like Dryden himself, leaned upon the tradition of English magnificence and steadfastly refused to recognize a thinning in the contemporary product.

Two-thirds of Dryden's non-dramatic verse consisted of translations from the classics. It is not to

[1] See page 43.

be supposed that so much labor was without important results. The sheer experience involved in composing some twenty thousand couplets was bound either to intrench him in whatever ground of style he already occupied or to draw him forward onto new surfaces of expression. It did both things; but more often it did the first. More often than not Dryden failed to learn anything by his translating. Doing most of it under pressure from the printers, he missed that margin of leisure which allows reflection and experimentation. As a rule Dryden performed well under pressure; but there are limits, which in Dryden's case meant that he was reduced to turning out a great number of stale and undistinguished lines. Yet in a respectable number of instances he did unquestionably enlarge himself through his identification with ancient masters, so that in translating them he produced what cannot be considered other than great original poems. Domestication of Greek and Roman writers was the order of the day in England. A society whose cultivated members lived exclusively, without warm vision and without much concern for problems that pressed, was pleased to feed on echoes of past grandeur and to take frequent account of that "stock of life," as St. Evremond affectionately called it, which the classics furnished in circumscribed and compendious form. Thomas Creech's *Lucretius*, *Horace*, and *Theocritus* in 1682 and 1684 were marks of the rising tide in translation which was to sweep Dryden and Jacob Tonson on to their great successes. Dryden believed that a translator was bound in all honor to enter generously into the spirit of his original and present him fairly as the individual which he once had been. His prefaces abound in distinctions nicely maintained between Homer and Virgil, Juvenal and Persius, Juvenal and Horace, Virgil and Ovid, and so on. He had a true translator's conscience, and liked to think that for the time being he and his masters were "congenial souls." But he seldom succeeded in bestowing individuality anywhere; his translations read very much alike; only his Juvenal and his Lucretius are really living men. Altogether he turned his hand to eight of the ancients: Ovid, Theocritus, Lucretius, Horace, Juvenal, Persius, Virgil, and Homer.

He began with Ovid in 1680, when he contributed three pieces to a volume of *Translations from Ovid's Epistles*. He was always an admirer of Ovid's fertility, and of his faculty for "continually varying the same sense an hundred ways," but his admiration in general was tempered by a conviction that the author of the *Metamorphoses* was a cheaper man then Virgil. He lacked taste; "he never knew how to give over, when he had done well." Only rarely did Dryden translate him with distinction. The three Epistles of 1680 were loose and Latinistic. A brisker piece, the nineteenth elegy of the second book of the *Amores*, appeared in Tonson's first *Miscellany* in 1684. The third *Miscellany*, called *Examen Poeticum*, which was published in 1693, contained Dryden's version of the entire first book of the *Metamorphoses* and the "fables" of *Iphis and*

Ianthe and *Acis, Polyphemus and Galatea,* from the
ninth and thirteenth books respectively. From
only one passage in the three poems does genius
emerge; the impassioned speech of Polyphemus to
Galatea is in Dryden's best vein of suasion. The
Art of Love and the first and fourth elegies of the
first book of the *Amores* were done by Dryden
while he was occupied with his Virgil; they were
not printed during his lifetime. The *Fables* found him
in better form, yet even in that venerable volume
the Ovidian poems are the least engaging. Dryden
learned speed and audacity from Ovid, but nothing
richer. It has been Ovid's narrative materials rather
than his personal qualities that have fired the modern poets; his stories are inexhaustible, but his exterior too often glitters and leaves one cold.

Dryden's four Idylls from Theocritus, the third,
the eighteenth, the twenty-third, and the twenty-
seventh, printed in the first and second *Miscellanies*
of 1684 and 1685, professed to speak in the "Doric
dialect" which Dryden thought had "an incomparable sweetness in its clownishness, like a fair shepherdess in her country russet, talking in a York-
shire tone." The dialect is difficult to distinguish
from Dryden's customary language. When Theocritus writes simply, "O dark eye-browed maiden
mine," Dryden writes,

O Nymph, . . .
Whose radiant eyes your ebon brows adorn,
Like midnight those and these like break of morn.

This is handsome, but its sound is that of a trumpet

rather than that of a shepherd's pipe. Dryden never can be said to have expanded his poetic personality so as to include the rare Sicilian.

Dryden's Lucretius is another story. What he tried to reproduce in Lucretius was a certain "noble pride, and positive assertion of his opinions." His success was signal in at least two out of the five selections which he chose to translate for the second *Miscellany* in 1685. His passages from the second and third books of the *De Rerum Natura* must be numbered among the most convincing specimens of ratiocinative poetry in any language. The spirit of the Roman has invaded and actually moved the Englishman; for a time he is another person. These lines on the fear of death are executed with a new delicacy and a new precision:

We, who are dead and gone, shall bear no part
In all the pleasures, nor shall feel the smart
Which to that other mortal shall accrue,
Whom of our matter time shall mold anew.
For backward if you look on that long space
Of ages past, and view the changing face
Of matter, tossed and variously combined
In sundry shapes, 'tis easy for the mind
From thence t' infer, that seeds of things have been
In the same order as they now are seen;
Which yet our dark remembrance cannot trace,
Because a pause of life, a gaping space,
Has come betwixt, where memory lies dead,
And all the wandering motions from the sense are fled.
For whosc'er shall in misfortunes live,
Must be, when those misfortunes shall arrive;
And since the man who is not, feels not woe,

(For death exempts him, and wards off the blow,
Which we, the living, only feel and bear,)
What is there left for us in death to fear?
When once that pause of life has come between,
'Tis just the same as we had never been.

The skill with which the movement of the verse is
made to correspond to the progress and the outline
of the idea can quite reasonably be called inspired.
Dryden has learned much from Lucretius. This
poem on the fear of death is Dryden's own.

It is rather to be regretted that Dryden never
imitated the satires of Horace as Pope did. He
touched only three odes and an epode, versions of
which appeared under his name in the second *Miscellany* of 1685. The pieces are of no consequence
in connection with the present inquiry. Dryden
could not possibly succeed in miniatures. The
twenty-ninth ode of the third book he made one of
his masterpieces, but only by transforming it into a
Pindaric ode and so egregiously distending it.[1] He
required more space than Horace ever would allow.

The five satires of Juvenal which Dryden published in 1693 along with the whole of Persius are a
triumph quite comparable to the *Lucretius*. In the
Discourse with which he prefaced the volume he
analyzed what he had found to be the distinction of
Juvenal, his impetuosity. The five satires as he
gave them are not only impetuous; they are close
and powerful. A full weight of brutal wrath bears
down upon the antitheses and the rhymes. There is
no tender *enjambement;* the couplets thump and

[1] See Chapter VI.

crackle.   The sixth, against women, is one of the
most terrible poems in English.   It cannot be quoted
where quotation would most score; the opening gives
only a taste of that which follows:

In Saturn's reign, at Nature's early birth,
There was that thing called Chastity on earth;
When in a narrow cave, their common shade,
The sheep, the shepherds, and their gods were laid;
When reeds, and leaves, and hides of beasts were spread
By mountain huswifes for their homely bed,
And mossy pillows raised, for the rude husband's head.
Unlike the niceness of our modern dames,
(Affected nymphs with new affected names,)
The Cynthias and the Lesbias of our years,
Who for a sparrow's death dissolve in tears;
Those first unpolished matrons, big and bold,
Gave suck to infants of gigantic mold;
Rough as their savage lords who ranged the wood,
And fat with acorns belched their windy food.

The largeness of these lines is not specious.   Dryden has developed another voice while in the company of Juvenal.

   Dryden began to work with Virgil as early as the
first *Miscellany* in 1684, when he contributed to
that volume translations of the fourth and ninth
Pastorals.   The fourth Pastoral as he allowed it to
be printed was extremely licentious metrically, and
an unworthy performance.   The ninth was full of
a fresh melody which at once cast a shade over
John Ogilby's *Virgil*, a respectable and often sump-
tuously printed work which had appeared first in
1649 and which up until Dryden's folio was not

superseded. Ogilby had been stingy and literal. Where Virgil's Moeris says regretfully:

Omnia fert ætas, animum quoque; sæpe ego longos
Cantando puerum memini me condere soles:
Nunc oblita mihi tot carmina, vox quoque Moerim
Iam fugit ipsa; lupi Moerim videre priores,

Ogilby's says:

Age all things wastes, and spends our lively heat.
I but a boy, could singing set the sun.
Now all those notes are lost, and my voice gone;
A wolf saw Moeris first;

while Dryden's shepherd sings:

The rest I have forgot; for cares and time
Change all things, and untune my soul to rhyme.
I could have once sung down a summer's sun;
But now the chime of poetry is done;
My voice grows hoarse; I feel the notes decay,
As if the wolves had seen me first today.

Dryden seems keenly to have relished his occupation with the pastorals of Virgil, and it was by no means seldom that he achieved therein a sweet and shining clarity. In the second eclogue his Corydon thus runs over the favors which the nymphs will bestow upon Alexis:

White lilies in full canisters they bring,
With all the glories of the purple spring.
The daughters of the flood have searched the mead
For violets pale, and cropped the poppy's head,
The short narcissus and fair daffodil,
Pansies to please the sight, and cassia sweet to smell;

And set soft hyacinths with iron-blue,
To shade marsh marigolds of shining hue;
Some bound in order, others loosely strewed,
To dress thy bower, and trim thy new abode.
Myself will search our planted grounds at home,
For downy peaches and the glossy plum;
And thrash the chestnuts in the neighbouring grove,
Such as my Amaryllis used to love;
The laurel and the myrtle sweets agree;
And both in nosegays shall be bound for thee.

The second *Miscellany* in 1685 contained versions by Dryden of three episodes from the *Æneid:* the episode of Nisus and Euryalus, from the fifth and ninth books, the episode of Mezentius and Lausus from the tenth, and the speech of Venus to Vulcan from the eighth. The third Georgic was inserted in the fourth *Miscellany* of 1694; and three years later the complete folio itself issued from Jacob Tonson's shop with all the pomp of a state event. Dryden had come very near to despair more than once while he was engaged with Virgil. "Some of our countrymen," he explained to the Earl of Mulgrave, "have translated episodes and other parts of Virgil, with great success; . . . I say nothing of Sir John Denham, Mr. Waller, and Mr. Cowley; 'tis the utmost of my ambition to be thought their equal . . . but 'tis one thing to take pains on a fragment, and translate it perfectly; and another thing to have the weight of a whole author on my shoulders." "I do not find myself capable of translating so great an author," he wrote to Tonson; and in the dedication of the *Æneis* he admitted that he had done "great wrong to Virgil in the whole translation," offering as reasons "want of time, the inferiority of our language, the inconvenience of rhyme." By his own confession, he kept the manuscript of the Earl of Lauderdale's translation by him and "consulted it as often as I doubted of my author's sense," or as often, more likely, as he felt pressed for time. Some two hundred lines of that nobleman's version he appropriated without any alteration at all, and some eight hundred came over only slightly recast. The readiness of the Earl to place his work at the poet's disposal may be accounted for by the fact that he himself had made free with the translations of the episodes of Nisus and Euryalus and Mezentius and Lausus as they had stood under Dryden's name since the *Miscellany* of 1685. There is a tradition that Dryden regretted before he was through that he had not chosen blank verse for his medium. An *Æneid* in the style of *All for Love* might be a truly superb performance. He had been advised to make the attempt. Thomas Fletcher, in the preface to his *Poems* of 1692, had repeated Roscommon's condemnation of rhyme, and had suggested that "If a Dryden (a master of our Language and Poetry) would undertake to translate Virgil in blank Verse, we might hope to read him with as great pleasure in our Language as his own." But it is likely that Dryden on the whole was satisfied with his couplets. He had reasons for dissatisfaction with the poem on other grounds. It is vastly imperfect. The Cyclops, the funeral games, and the gathering of the clans in the *Æneis* are handled in a manner worthy of the best heroic tradition, and every page without exception bristles with energy. Yet in the main the texture of the verse is coarse; Dryden has made no advance in subtlety of speech, he is only applying standard formulas and securing standard results. Virgil has eluded him as Lucretius and Juvenal did not.

Dryden was "fixing his thoughts" on Homer in his last years and halfway projecting a new folio which should stand as a companion to the *Virgil*. He had a notion that Homer was more suited to his genius than Virgil, since he was more "violent, impetuous, and full of fire." He had done into English *The Last Parting of Hector and Andromache* for the third *Miscellany* in 1693, and he included in the *Fables* a complete version of the first book of the *Iliad*. He got no further with Homer, which is to be regretted; for although the two specimens he left behind are neither violent, impetuous, nor full of fire in a preternatural degree, they are honest and various as few translations are.

It is not to be supposed that Dryden had been without his English masters all along. Shakespeare, Spenser, and Milton were constantly enriching him, if not with direct gifts then with less tangible inspirations. His unqualified admiration for Shakespeare scarcely needs to be cited; the tributes to him which Dryden paid in the *Essay of Dramatic Poesy*, the dedication of the *Rival Ladies*, the prologue to the *Tempest*, and the prologue to *Troilus and Cressida* are *loci classici* of criticism. He knew the text of Shakespeare's major dramas as well as he knew his own works; his plays are reminiscent, often only trivially, in word and phrase of *Hamlet, King Lear, Macbeth,* and *Julius Caeser.* Imitation of Shakespeare on a significant scale was out of the question, as it must be always; and it must be confessed that had Shakespeare never written Dryden might never have ranted; yet it is not unreasonable to derive the greatest of the Augustans in a fairly straight line from the greatest of the Elizabethans. The differences are huge, but the line that joins them does not need to be broken. Spenser offered gifts of style which were easier to accept and put in use. "I must acknowledge," wrote Dryden in the dedication of the *Æneis,* discussing the general problem of "numbers," "that Virgil in Latin, and Spenser in English, have been my masters." Spenser he considered in a degree the creator of English harmony, and Spenser's fluency seemed to him to the last a glorious marvel. Fluency as such is a quality which cannot be fingered over by a follower of influences; hence its passage from Spenser into Dryden can be better announced than proved. The passage did occur, Spenser's broad current eventually enveloping the little stream of Waller that flowed to Dryden. Dryden seems to have been thoroughly versed in the *Faerie Queene.* Occasional lines clearly recall its sensitive author, as these two from the Episode of Nisus and Euryalus:

> Black was the brake, and thick with oak it stood,
> With fern all horrid, and perplexing thorn.

The accounts of the fairies at the beginning of *The*

Wife of Bath, Her Tale and in *The Flower and the Leaf*, in the *Fables*, are Chaucer plus Spenser plus Shakespeare. And Thomas Warton pointed out that the sleeping Iphigenia in *Cymon and Iphigenia* owes certain of her beauties to the Elizabethan who best of all could paint enchanting forms.

Milton's impact upon Dryden was not sudden, nor was his influence of a permeating kind. The two poets were worlds apart. Yet Dryden was among the first Englishmen who conferred important honors upon Milton dead; and his works reflect careful reading not only of *Paradise Lost* but of the minor poems, the prose, and *Samson Agonistes* as well. Milton's *Ode on the Morning of Christ's Nativity*, as has been remarked, is probably responsible for Dryden's thirty-fifth stanza on Cromwell.[1] Stanza 232 of *Annus Mirabilis*, which Settle declared was stolen from Cowley, vaguely recalls *Lycidas* as well as the *Davideis*,

> Old Father Thames raised up his reverend head,
>   But feared the fate of Simœis would return;
> Deep in his ooze he sought his sedgy bed,
>   And shrunk his waters back into his urn,

and stanza 293 certainly suggests the *Areopagitica:*

> Methinks already, from this chymick flame,
>   I see a city of more precious mold;
> Rich as the town which gives the Indies name,
>   With silver paved, and all divine with gold.

That the *State of Innocence* is a tagged *Paradise Lost* needs no mention; though the proverbial

[1] See page 3.

corollary that it is a wretched poem calls for emphatic denial. Langbaine pointed out a borrowing in *Aureng-Zebe* from *Samson Agonistes.* "Now give me leave," he asked in his *Account of the English Dramatick Poets* (1691), "to give you one Instance . . . of his borrowing from Mr. Milton's *Sampson Agonistes:*

Dal.   I see thou art implacable, more deaf
          To Prayers than winds and seas; yet winds to seas
          Are reconcil'd at length, and sea to shore;
          Thy anger unappeasable still rages,
          Eternal Tempest never to be calm'd.
Emp.   *Unmov'd she stood, and deaf to all my prayers,*
          As Seas and Winds to sinking Mariners;
          But Seas grow calm, and Winds are reconcil'd;
          Her Tyrant Beauty never grows more mild."

A still more interesting levy on Milton's tragedy was made by Dryden in the first act of *Œdipus.* The blind Tiresias comes upon the stage led by his daughter Manto and addressing her as follows:

              A little farther; yet a little farther,
              Thou wretched daughter of a dark old man,
              Conduct my weary steps. . . . Now stay;
              Methinks I draw more open, vital air.
              Where are we?
Manto: Under covert of a wall;
              The most frequented once, and noisy part
              Of Thebes; now midnight silence reigns even
                  here,
              And grass untrodden springs beneath our feet.
Tiresias: If there be nigh this place a sunny bank,
              There let me rest awhile.

Dryden may have had in mind here at least five
different scenes in classical tragedy. The spectacle
of a blind old man being led upon the stage was
familiar to Greek audiences. In the *Œdipus Tyran-
nus* of Sophocles Tiresias appears hand in hand
with a boy; in the *Œdipus Coloneus* Œdipus follows
after Antigone, whom he pities as "the wretched
child of a blind old man," and who conducts him to
a rocky seat. In the *Phœnissæ* of Euripides Tiresias is conducted upon the scene by Manto, "the eye
of his feet." Seneca begins his *Phœnissæ* with Antigone leading Œdipus, and in his *Œdipus* Manto
guides Tiresias along. Dryden may have had any
of these scenes vividly in his memory. Yet the
opening of *Samson Agonistes* must have furnished
him with certain of his words, and must have
suggested two details for his tableau which neither
the Greeks nor Seneca had provided: the sunny
bank and the draughts of fresh air. Milton's lines
run thus:

Samson: *A little onward* lend thy guiding hand
             To these dark steps, *a little further on;*
             For yonder bank hath choice of sun or shade.
             There I am wont to sit, when any chance
             Relieves me from my task of servile toil,
             Daily in the common prison else enjoined me,
             Where I, a prisoner chained, *scarce freely draw*
             The air imprisoned also, close and damp,
             Unwholesome draught; but here I feel amends,
             The breath of Heav'n fresh blowing, pure and
                  sweet,
             With day-spring born.

The parallel is of interest only as showing that Dryden really knew Milton. The poems on public affairs drew heavily upon *Paradise Lost* for epic machinery and accent. The speeches in *Absulom and Achitophel* are Satanic or Godlike much in Milton's way, and the account in *The Hind and the Panther* (II., 499–514) of Christ's accepting in Heaven the burden of man's sin follows Milton's recital in his third book with remarkable fidelity. Instances might be multiplied without establishing further types of obligation. The obligation was never spiritual; it was rarely that Dryden was moved by anything other than the diction of a great poet. Shakespeare, Spenser, Milton remain on the other side of the world from Dryden; but he visits them and takes from them whatever he can carry away.

By dint of manifold experience, then, and manifold discipleship, Dryden rolled and beat into shape the poetic medium which had descended to him. But he did more than make that medium perfectly clear and strong. He stamped it peculiarly with himself. His genius was for grouping; his passion was for form. He had above most poets "that energy," as Dr. Johnson put it, "which collects, combines, amplifies, and animates." He had a mind; he had grasp; he could follow a subject home. His poems lived. He loved to see things take shape. At the beginning of his dedication of the *Rival Ladies* he told the Earl of Orrery in words which later haunted the imagination of Lord Byron that his play had once been "only a confused mass of thoughts, tumbling over one another in the dark;

when the fancy was yet in its first work, moving the sleeping images of things towards the light." As many as a dozen times throughout his works he played with the notion of a world of scattered atoms, rejecting it for the image of a world composed with care. He wrote to Sir Robert Howard in 1660,

> This is a piece too fair
> To be the child of chance, and not of care;
> No atoms casually together hurled
> Could e'er produce so beautiful a world.

He insisted that a good play could not be a heap of "huddled atoms;" an epic could never succeed if "writ on the Epicurean principles." This genius of his took effect in two ways. It made him a master in the art of grouping and throwing swiftly together statements, reasons, instances, implications; it made him the most irresistible discursive and ratiocinative poet in English. And it supplied him with a powerful rhythmical pulse; it set his verse rolling and welling, leaping and bounding; it established the paragraph, the passage, as his unit of metrical advance, not the line or the couplet; it made him a mighty metrist. Such was Dryden's best manner. Dryden's best material, it has been said, lay in personalities, actions, ideas, art. The two in conjunction brought forth his best poetry, occasional, journalistic, lyric, or narrative.

IV

THE OCCASIONAL POET

There is a sense in which every poem that Dryden wrote was occasional. Not sudden convictions, or happy perceptions of identities in the world of nature and man, but circumstances were required to draw him out on paper. Births, deaths, literary events, political incidents tapped in him the richest commenting mind that English poetry has known. He is the celebrant, the signalizer *par excellence*. He succeeded Ben Jonson, the other great occasional poet of the seventeenth century, in a kind of writing that was peculiarly Augustan. Jonson had created the kind in England, clearing off a broad field for it and practicing it with rare compactness and rightness. He had planted every variety of it which was to have a successful growth: the official panegyric, the complimentary epistle, the epigram, the epitaph, the elegy, the prologue, the epilogue. The growth had been rapid before Dryden. The temper of the century had swiftly become suited to a sort of expression aiming "rather at aptitude than altitude," as Thomas Jordan put it in the dedication of his *Poems and Songs* in 1664. It had become more and more agreeable to read and write verses that suavely wreathed themselves around plain, social facts. The main line of descent from Jonson to Dryden

had been through men like Cartwright and Waller.
Most of Milton's sonnets had been occasional poems
of another order, instinct with the passions of ambition, anger, or worship. True Augustan verse was
to be impersonal, containing no bursts that might
embarrass. Even Milton had approximated the
type in his sonnets to Lawes, to Lawrence, and to
Cyriack Skinner. The type was to be first of all
civil. Every year of the world will see occasional
poetry; but fashions vary, and only at intervals is
hard civility the mode. Poets since Dryden have
been softer, and have expressed themselves upon more
precious occasions; upon receiving a mother's picture,
upon turning up a field mouse with a plow, upon
hearing a lass sing at her reaping, upon spying a
primrose by a river's brim or a violet by a mossy
stone, upon seeing a peasant bent hopelessly over
his hoe, upon looking into the eyes of a harlot, upon
dreaming weird dreams, upon thinking fine-spun
thoughts. The Augustans kept such experiences, if
they had them, to themselves. Their subjects were
prescribed and classified. Their minds were formal, stored with categories and proprieties. Writing upon a subject meant turning it over casually in
the mind and exposing it to preconceptions. The
aim was not at revelation or surprise but at the satisfaction which comes from a topic perfectly covered.

Dryden was a great occasional poet because he
was more than merely that. He was more than
equal to his occasions, few of which moved him. He
condescended to them, brought to them richer

stores of thought and melody than were adequate.
He operated with self-control, he was generally discreet and right; yet there are overtones to be distinguished in all his pieces. He was a large poet
writing largely about medium things. His genius
for grouping and shaping was of extraordinary consequence here. More easily than any other English
poet he could assemble ripe clusters of apposite
ideas, rounding them off by the pressure of his
swift, disciplined mind and welding them into their
true proportions with rhythm.

If we disregard for a moment the satires and the
ratiocinative poems, which can better be considered
by themselves in connection with a study of Dryden
as a journalist in verse, it appears that Dryden's
occasional pieces fall into four divisions: the panegyrics, celebrating public events and compliment-
ing public characters; the epistles and personal addresses; the epigrams, epitaphs and elegies; and the
prologues and epilogues.

The ten years between 1660 and 1670 saw in England a flowering of panegyric that necessarily recalls certain other rather distant periods in the
world's literature. Greeks and Italians have a well-
known capacity for voluble laudation; the classics
are replete with praise. "The inimitable Pindar"
needs only to be mentioned. Isocrates and Demos-
thenes in ancient Greece and Cicero in ancient
Rome wrote in a golden age of panegyrical prose.
Rome saw a silver age in the famous twelve *Pane-
gyrici Veteres* of later days, among whom was
Pliny the Younger; Pliny's oration on Trajan Dry-

den knew and quoted in *Annus Mirabilis*. The last great Roman poet, Claudian, was a professional panegyrist; his verses in praise of Honorius and Stilicho at the end of the fourth century look forward to the poetry of Dryden in respect of their fertility, ingenuity, and general temper. The fifteenth century in Italy was a century of adulation. A dark period of Latinity that interposed itself between the brilliant times of Dante, Petrarch, and Boccaccio and the brilliant times of Ariosto and Tasso, it witnessed the reigns of petty despots who called themselves descendants of the Roman Emperors and thirsted for a Roman kind of praise. The praise was forthcoming, in prose and in verse; the great Poliziano expended as much effort upon Lorenzo de Medici as he did upon the Greek and Roman poets whom he so intensely admired. In England, Queen Elizabeth received at least her meed of formal flattery, and Prince Henry's death in 1612 was the occasion for a veritable Augustan abundance of eulogy. Upon the occasions of visits by James I to the universities, the learned outdid themselves in hyperbole of welcome. Cromwell had his Marvell as well as his Dryden. But it was only with the return of Charles II from France and the setting up of what was believed would be a permanent little social court that literary England came for a while to be something like literary Rome in the fourth century or like literary Italy in the fifteenth. The conditions of such a becoming include a certain pettiness, a certain exclusiveness, a certain blindness, and a certain pretentious unreality in the official psychology. England during the first decade after the Restoration supplied all these conditions. London was intoxicated with peace, and with what it greeted as an established order. Not until after Clarendon's fall, not until after confidence in Charles began to be less general, were larger perspectives opened up. Not that panegyrics ever stopped altogether. Southey and Byron were still to have their turns with George the Third. But this particular Stuart decade must remain unique in English history.

Dryden never ceased to exercise his panegyrical vein while Charles and James were in power. But what may more specifically be called his panegyrical period extended only from 1660 to 1666. The model of all then, including Dryden, was Waller.

> He best can turn, enforce, and soften things,
> To praise great Conquerors or to flatter Kings,

wrote Rochester in his *Allusion to Horace;* and when Dryden inserted his English names in Soame's Boileau he substituted "Waller" for "Malherbe" in the line,

> Malherbe, d'un héros peut vanter les exploits.

> Waller a hero's mighty acts extol.

Waller could be rapt and smooth and fatuous in pleasant proportions. Dryden added other qualities to those three. His official praise rings with a round Roman grandeur. He writes as if he lived to praise, not praised to live. His lines speak contempt for all things small—small passions, small

deeds, small wit. He is warm yet decorous; he
is effectual because of his great confidence and
his unremitting eloquence. And his resources are
infinite. "He appears never to have impoverished
his mint of flattery by his expenses, however
lavish," says Dr. Johnson. "He had all the forms
of excellence, intellectual and moral, combined
in his mind, with endless variation . . . and brings
praise rather as a tribute than a gift, more delighted with the fertility of his invention than mortified by the prostitution of his judgment." The
Heroic Stanzas would seem to have been written
in an age rather remote from the *Astræa Redux*,
although only a year separated them. The difference in quality is the difference between Marvell
and Waller, or better yet, the difference between
Cromwell and Charles. The one has symmetry and
sinewy calm, the other slips along with a kind
of tepid abandon. The *Astræa* is somewhat more
shapeless and profuse than Dryden usually is in
his occasional poetry; he has not yet learned his
grouping. Yet the peroration is well gathered up.
The poem *To His Sacred Majesty, a Panegyric on
His Coronation*, composed about a year after the
Astræa, is an improvement with respect to form.
The ideas are fewer, but each in its turn is rounded
out. The poem climbs in a series of flights, with intervals or landings between, the melody mounting
continuously and tending to be cumulative within
the flights. The poem *To My Lord Chancellor,
Presented on New Year's Day* (1662) is profuse and
tepid again except for one nobly concentrated pas-

sage on Charles I and Clarendon. The *Annus Mirabilis*, published in 1667, is Dryden's most ambitious official compliment, being dedicated "to the Metropolis of Great Britain," and celebrating both a naval war and a great fire. The prophecy with which it ends continues the central motif of his occasional work in that it is collected and sustained. The last twelve stanzas pile themselves up like the Theban stones that obeyed Amphion's lyre. Dryden's panegyrical period now came to a close. The Stuart spell was broken, Clarendon fled to France, and Marvell, bitterly loyal to the best interests of England, answered the vapid flatteries of Waller and his train with exposures which made such men as Pepys weep because they were so true. Nearly twenty years passed before Dryden performed again on his official pipes. This was at the death of Charles II when he wrote his *Threnodia Augustalis*, a "Funeral-Pindaric" which will be considered more fully elsewhere, along with the other Pindarics.[1] The poem lies loosely about for want of any sincere motive that can knit it together. The best constructed passage is that which summons up Dryden's happiest memories, his memories of peace:

> For all those joys thy happy restoration brought,
> For all the miracles it wrought,
>   For all the healing balm thy mercy poured
> Into the nation's bleeding wound,
> And care that after kept it sound,
>   For numerous blessings yearly showered,
> And property with plenty crowned;

[1] See Chapter VI.

> For freedom still maintained alive,
> Freedom, which in no other land will thrive,
> Freedom, an English subject's sole prerogative,
> Without whose charms even peace would be
> But a dull quiet slavery:
>   For these, and more, accept our pious praise.

Britannia Rediviva (1688), on the birth of an heir to James II, is a dull conclusion to the least distinguished division of Dryden's occasional poetry. Like the *Threnodia* it lacks that sanguineness which alone had justified the pieces of the 1660's and which had given them a metrical structure interesting enough to study now. These last two poems lack what it is fatal for Dryden ever to lack, drive.

Dryden's personal epistles and complimentary addresses bring us into a different world. Here he is at home, for here he is speaking to private persons and he is praising books. Three kinds of poetical epistles gained currency during the seventeenth century. The Horatian or didactic kind began with Daniel, Drayton, Donne, and Jonson, and culminated in Pope. The Ovidian or "voluptuous" kind got a start in volumes like Drayton's *Heroical Epistles* and ran on to Pope's *Eloisa and Abelard*. The third kind, the complimentary, was more peculiarly modern and local. Rooted in Jonson, it flowered in Dryden, who practiced virtually no other sort. Having to praise both men and books, he was never in want of excellent models. Jonson's epistles to the owner of Penshurst and to Elizabeth, Countess of Rutland, Drayton's to Sandys and Reynolds, and Waller's to Falkland had established a distinguished line of personal compliment. Waller's verses to the young Viscount as he left for war are among the most genuine which he composed, one indication of which may be found in their radical *enjambement*, as in this passage:

Ah, noble friend! with what impatience all
That know thy worth, and know how prodigal
Of thy great soul thou art (longing to twist
Bays with that ivy which so early kissed
Thy youthful temples), with what horror we
Think on the blind events of war and thee!
To fate exposing that all-knowing breast
Among the throng, as cheaply as the rest;
Where oaks and brambles (if the copse be burned)
Confounded lie, to the same ashes turned.

The line of literary compliment which descended to Dryden was more distinguished still. The more firmly literary standards became fixed the readier were men to praise whatever writing they liked, and the more copious too became critical vocabularies. In the seventeenth century praise of books might be either interested or disinterested. It might be motivated by actual enthusiasm; but it also might be motivated by personal friendship, by hope of patronage, by party feeling, by the fee of a printer, or by something more canny yet, the expectation that the author commended would reciprocate when next he published a volume. Authors, at the instigation of publishers, traded compliments as freely as boys trade marbles, and a book was very poor which could not appear prefaced by at least two poetical

puffs. Whatever the motives, the practice itself produced some of the best occasional poetry of the century; and there is surely something logical about
the predilection of a critical age for critical verse.
The line, to resume, came down through such poems
as Jonson's to Shakespeare and Sir Henry Savile,
through the *Jonsonus Virbius* of 1638, and through
Waller's and Cowley's prefaces to *Gondibert*. Running into Dryden it found itself in the control of a
great man who was fond of bestowing judgments
and who was possessed of unexampled gifts in casual criticism.

Shortly after Dryden entered Trinity College,
Cambridge, in 1650, he contributed some commen-
datory verses to a volume of "divine Epigrams"
published by his friend John Hoddesdon. The
verses have a Puritan tinge and are clumsy in their
approbation. Ten years later he opened a freer
vein of compliment in the piece which he prefixed to a volume of Sir Robert Howard's poems
published by Henry Herringman. Probably the
applause he gave to Howard, who after another
three years was to become his brother-in-law, was
not disinterested; possibly Herringman engaged
him to deliver it. At any rate, he wrote the lines
with real relish, achieving in a slight measure the
felicity, the fluency, and the plenitude of praise
which marked his maturest compliments. He also
indulged in a little general criticism, incidentally an-
nouncing some literary ideals of his own. He de-
nounced conceits, for instance, and informed Howard that

To carry weight, and run so lightly too,
Is what alone your Pegasus can do.

So firm a strength, and yet withal so sweet,
Did never but in Samson's riddle meet.

In 1663 he furnished an epistle to Dr. Charleton
for insertion in his treatise on Stonehenge, which
Herringman was publishing. The epistle was the
first of Dryden's that set out to discuss a literary or
philosophical point. It is virtually an essay on the
conquest of Aristotelianism by experimental science.
The address to Lady Castlemaine which Dryden
probably made soon after the failure of his first
play in 1663 shows him fairly emancipated from the
pedantry and miscellaneity of the poems which preceded it. It runs straight on, swiftly and sweetly,
quickened into life by the sun of gallantry which
shines upon it.

What further fear of danger can there be?
Beauty, which captives all things, sets me free.
Posterity will judge by my success,
I had the Grecian poet's happiness,
Who, waiving plots, found out a better way;
Some god descended, and preserved the play.
When first the triumphs of your sex were sung
By those old poets, Beauty was but young,
And few admired the native red and white,
Till poets dressed them up to charm the sight;
So Beauty took on trust, and did engage
For sums of praises till she came of age.
But this long-growing debt to poetry
You justly, Madam, have discharged to me,

> When your applause and favor did infuse
> New life to my condemned and dying Muse.

It will be observed that no accent here is in the smallest degree misplaced. Another epistle did not appear until 1677, when Dryden supplied a puff for Lee, to go in front of his printed play, *The Death of Alexander the Great.* The epistle begins with an interesting reference to the practice of poetical log-rolling which already has been described. Lee had puffed Dryden's *State of Innocence.* Now, begins Dryden,

> The blast of common censure could I fear,
> Before your play my name should not appear;
> For 'twill be thought, and with some color too,
> I pay the bribe I first received from you;
> That mutual vouchers for our fame we stand,
> And play the game into each other's hand;

but he proceeds to disclaim any other than the purest motives in praising Lee's tragedy. He ends with a defense of Lee's mad way of writing which in seven sharply distinct couplets proves that Dryden has mastered Ovid's art of "varying the same sense an hundred ways":

> They only think you animate your theme
> With too much fire, who are themselves all phle'me.
> Prizes would be for lags of slowest pace,
> Were cripples made the judges of the race.
> Despise those drones, who praise while they accuse
> The two much vigour of your youthful muse.
> That humble style which they their virtue make,
> Is in your power; you need but stoop and take.

Your beauteous images must be allowed
By all, but some vile poets of the crowd.
But how should any signpost dauber know
The worth of Titian or of Angelo?
Hard features every bungler can command;
To draw true beauty shows a master's hand.

The Earl of Roscommon prefixed a complimentary
poem to a new issue of the *Religio Laici* in 1683.
Dryden came back the next year with some lines
applauding Roscommon's *Essay on Translated Verse*.
The opening furnishes the most handsome example
in all Dryden of a piece of versified literary history.
The progress of rhyme from ancient Athens to
modern London is represented by a metrical progression which must have been the despair of all
living poets:

Whether the fruitful Nile, or Tyrian shore,
The seeds of arts and infant science bore,
'Tis sure the noble plant translated, first
Advanced its head in Grecian gardens nursed.
The Grecians added verse; their tuneful tongue
Made nature first and nature's God their song.
Nor stopped translation here; for conquering Rome
With Grecian spoils brought Grecian numbers home,
Enriched by those Athenian Muses more
Than all the vanquished world could yield before;
Till barbarous nations, and more barbarous times,
Debased the majesty of verse to rhymes;
Those rude at first: a kind of hobbling prose,
That limped along, and tinkled in the close.
But Italy, reviving from the trance
Of Vandal, Goth, and monkish ignorance,
With pauses, cadence, and well-vowelled words,

And all the graces a good ear affords,
Made rhyme an art, and Dante's polished page
Restored a silver, not a golden age.
Then Petrarch followed, and in him we see
What rhyme improved in all its height can be;
At best a pleasing sound, and fair barbarity.
The French pursued their steps; and Britain, last,
In manly sweetness all the rest surpassed.
The wit of Greece, the gravity of Rome,
Appear exalted in the British loom;
The Muses' empire is restored again,
In Charles his reign, and by Roscommon's pen.

Roscommon here, however much as an anticlimax he may come to a modern reader, comes at least metrically as a truly stately climax. The manner if not the matter of this sketch, which Dryden enjoyed doing if he ever enjoyed doing anything at all, is without flaw. The next epistle, *To My Friend, Mr. J. Northleigh, Author of the Parallel, On His Triumph of the British Monarchy* (1685) is short and of no account. A year or two after this Dryden wrote for the Earl of Middleton a letter in octosyllabic couplets to Sir George Etherege, who had sent a similar piece to Middleton from Ratisbon. It was for Dryden a *tour de force*. He was not fond of the octosyllabic measure, nor was he temperamentally equipped for a species of verse which seemed to fall somewhere between Butler and Prior. His epistle *To My Ingenious Friend, Henry Higden, Esq., on His Translation of the Tenth Satire of Juvenal* (1687) contained like the poem to Roscommon a literary discussion, this time on the subject of ancient and

modern satire. In 1692 he consoled Southerne for
the failure of his comedy called *The Wives' Excuse*
with an epistle that closed on a note of sage and
compendious counsel. The famous lines to Congreve on his *Double-dealer* (1694), and those to Sir
Godfrey Kneller of the same year, probably in ac-
knowledgment of a portrait of Shakespeare which
Kneller had given him, represent a more reflective
stage in the progress of Dryden's epistolary manner.
They do not charge upon their subjects with the
breathless speed of the early addresses; their discourse, which in one case is upon the dramatic
poetry of the last age and in the other case is upon
the history of painting, seems packed and ripe. The
poem to Congreve opens on a theme which Dryden
had often discussed in prose and which he once had
covered in an epilogue, the superiority of Restoration wit to Jacobean humor. The handling here is
marked by rare composure; the edifice of modern
wit rises steadily and surely:

> Well then, the promised hour is come at last;
> The present age of wit obscures the past:
> Strong were our sires, and as they fought they writ,
> Conquering with force of arms and dint of wit;
> Theirs was the giant race before the flood;
> And thus, when Charles returned, our empire stood.
> Like Janus he the stubborn soil manured,
> With rules of husbandry the rankness cured;
> Tamed us to manners, when the stage was rude,
> And boisterous English wit with art indued.
> Our age was cultivated thus at length,
> But what we gained in skill we lost in strength.

> Our builders were with want of genius curst;
> The second temple was not like the first:
> Till you, the best Vitruvius, come at length,
> Our beauties equal, but excel our strength.
> Firm Doric pillars found our solid base,
> The fair Corinthian crowns the higher space;
> Thus all below is strength, and all above is grace.

The poem ends with a touching last will and testament which has never had to beg for praise, but which borders, it must be admitted, upon the maudlin. In the epistles to Granville and Motteux in 1698 Dryden returned more or less to the glibness of poems like the *Roscommon*. The verses to Motteux the Frenchman, affixed to his tragedy called *Beauty in Distress*, begin with a reply to the newly arisen moral censor of the stage, Jeremy Collier, and end with a tribute to Motteux's powers which affords another example of Dryden's facility in turning over an idea and extracting from it all that could be extracted:

> Let thy own Gauls condemn thee, if they dare;
> Contented to be thinly regular.
> Born there, but not for them, our fruitful soil
> With more increase rewards thy happy toil.
> Their tongue, infeebled, is refined so much,
> That, like pure gold, it bends at every touch;
> Our sturdy Teuton yet will art obey,
> More fit for manly thought, and strengthened with
>   allay.
> But whence art thou inspired, and thou alone,
> To flourish in an idiom not thy own?
> It moves our wonder, that a foreign guest
> Should overmatch the most, and match the best.

In underpraising thy deserts, I wrong;
Here, find the first deficience of our tongue;
Words, once my stock, are wanting to commend
So great a poet and so good a friend.

The last two epistles of all appeared with considerable pomp in Dryden's last volume, the *Fables*. The *Palamon and Arcite* was preceded by a dedicatory poem to the Duchess of Ormond and was followed by a piece upon which Dryden expended a great deal of effort and of which he was justly proud: *To My Honored Kinsman, John Driden, of Chesterton, in the County of Huntingdon, Esquire*. The lines to "illustrious Ormond," though tawdry in a few places, are suffused with a fine old man's gallantry; the medieval lustre of the *Fables* has lent them a new light. Their rapture has all the old pulse, but it is chastened and poised:

O daughter of the rose, whose cheeks unite
The differing titles of the red and white;
Who heaven's alternate beauty well display,
The blush of morning, and the milky way;
Whose face is paradise, but fenced from sin:
For God in either eye has placed a cherubin.
All is your lord's alone; e'en absent, he
Employs the care of chaste Penelope.
For him you waste in tears your widowed hours,
For him your curious needle paints the flowers;
Such works of old imperial dames were taught;
Such, for Ascanius, fair Elisa wrought.

Only the most frigid reader would take exception to the cherubim which God has stationed in the Duchess' eyes. The poem to John Driden of Chesterton

is the most Horatian of all the epistles.   It is a eulogy of country life in general and a commendation
of the kinsman's own rural regimen in particular,
with digressions more or less sardonic upon marriage, medicine, and the present state of Europe.
The closing paragraph is mathematically final:

> O true descendant of a patriot line,
> Who, while thou shar'st their luster, lend'st 'em thine,
> Vouchsafe this picture of thy soul to see;
> 'Tis so far good as it resembles thee.
> The beauties to the original I owe;
> Which when I miss, my own defects I show;
> Nor think the kindred Muses thy disgrace;
> A poet is not born in every race.
> Two of a house few ages can afford;
> One to perform, the other to record.
> Praiseworthy actions are by thee embraced;
> And 'tis my praise, to make thy praises last.
> For ev'n when death dissolves our human frame,
> The soul returns to heaven, from whence it came;
> Earth keeps the body, verse preserves the fame.

Dryden paraded a distaste for epigrams which
was consonant with the contemporary worship of
epic poetry; for from Bacon to Temple the heroic
poem crowded out of the general estimation all
forms that were less pretentious.   "From Homer to
the *Anthologia*, from Virgil to Martial and Owen's
Epigrams, and from Spenser to Fleckno; that is,
from the top to the bottom of all poetry," wrote
Dryden in the *Discourse of Satire*.   Yet he proved
upon a few occasions to have an epigrammatic turn
of some distinction.   His epigram on Milton, which

appeared in Tonson's 1688 folio edition of *Paradise Lost*, is neatly put together. Its shape alone has given it currency. Few have observed that it seems to say more than it does. "Loftinco of thought" and "majesty" seem to make a better antithesis than in truth they do. DeQuincey, in a shrewd essay on this poem, which he calls "the very finest epigram in the English language," marvels at the perfection of form which could intrigue a whole century of readers into accepting as profound a half dozen lines which really say nothing. Dryden was probably drawn to the Greek Anthology long before 1683, when he closed his *Life of Plutarch* with this translation of the epigram by Agathias:

Cheronean Plutarch, to thy deathless praise
Does martial Rome this grateful statue raise;
Because both Greece and she thy fame have shared,
(Their heroes written, and their lives compared;)
But thou thyself couldst never write thy own;
Their lives have parallels, but thine hast none.

Dryden's eight epitaphs all derive a certain pointedness and sufficiency from the shining *Anthology*, although in the main their author tends to weave a heavier burial cloth than that which was woven by Antipater, Leonidas, and Simonides. He stiffens his texture by means of conceits and antitheses, with the result that his effect is likely to be one of rectangularity. His epitaphs by no means lack that seventeenth-century largeness which the next few generations could not muster, and the absence of which in contemporary burial verses Dr. Johnson wrote an essay to lament. Dryden shows best in his lines on John Graham of Claverhouse, Viscount Dundee, and those on the Marquis of Winchester. Both poems celebrate the lives and deaths of loyalists who supported lost causes. The Marquis of Winchester had faught for Charles I, and the great Graham of Claverhouse had been killed at Killiecrankie in 1689. The epitaph on Winchester begins with four couplets which draw or imply four distinctions:

> He who in impious times undaunted stood,
> And midst rebellion durst be just and good;
> Whose arms asserted, and whose sufferings more
> Confirmed the cause for which he fought before,
> Rests here, rewarded by an heavenly prince,
> For what his earthly could not recompense.
> Pray, reader, that such times no more appear;
> Or, if they happen, learn true honour here.

The epitaph on Dundee is a translation from a Latin poem by Dr. Archibald Pitcairne. It follows its original closely enough, but at the end it makes a characteristic departure towards a greater profuseness in antithesis:

> O last and best of Scots! who didst maintain
> Thy country's freedom from a foreign reign;
> New people fill the land now thou art gone,
> New gods the temples, and new kings the throne.
> Scotland and thee did each in other live;
> Thou wouldst not her, nor could she thee survive.
> Farewell, who living didst support the State,
> And couldst not fall but with thy country's fate.

The epitaphs on Lady Whitmore, on "A Fair Maiden Lady who Died at Bath," on "Young Mr. Rogers of Gloucestershire," on Mrs. Margaret Paston, on Sir Palmes Fairborne (in Westminster Abbey), and on Erasmus Lawton have no especial significance.

"We have been all born; we have most of us been married; and so many have died before us, that our deaths can supply but few materials for a poet," wrote Dr. Johnson; and Goldsmith thought there was nothing new to be said upon the death of a friend after the standard classical elegies. Dryden's temper seems anything but elegiac if in connection with elegiac we think of Theocritus Bion, Moschus, Ovid, Dante, Petrarch, Spenser, and Donne. The more mystical of the Elizabethan sonnets on the subject of death, and the exquisite dirges in Shakespeare, Beaumont and Fletcher and Webster were keyed above, or at least keyed in another sphere of poetry than his. He is not a prober among mysteries; he is not exquisite. He is sober and symmetrical, and pays his tribute to the dead with plain, manly melodies. His elegies and Donne's are poles apart. His demand to be read aloud, there being no reason why the music in them should be subdued. Donne's take effect only upon an inner ear and eye, back behind the curtain of the senses, where they stage their dark, fierce little dramas with Love and Hate and Fear and Jealousy and Death in the leading rôles.

Dryden's first elegy happens to be his worst poem. It is scarcely necessary to say that when writing the *Hastings* he was not much concerned

either about the young departed lord or about the
idea of death in general. His next elegy might well
be called his best poem. If one is not pleased by
the lines *To the Memory of Mr. Oldham* one will not
be pleased by anything in Dryden; they are his
touchstone. They appeared in 1684 among several
laments which prefaced a volume of Oldham's
remains. That wrathful young satirist had died
the previous year at the age of thirty. Dryden had
owed him no trifling literary debts. He discharged
them posthumously as follows:

Farewell, too little and too lately known,
Whom I began to think and call my own:
For sure our souls were near allied, and thine
Cast in the same poetic mold with mine.
One common note on either lyre did strike,
And knaves and fools we both abhorred alike.
To the same goal did both our studies drive;
The last set out the soonest did arrive.
Thus Nisus fell upon the slippery place,
Whilst his young friend performed and won the race.
O early ripe! to thy abundant store
What could advancing age have added more?
It might (what nature never gives the young)
Have taught the numbers of thy native tongue.
But satire needs not those, and wit will shine
Through the harsh cadence of a rugged line:
A noble error, and but seldom made,
When poets are by too much force betrayed.
Thy generous fruits, tho' gathered ere their prime,
Still shewed a quickness; and maturing time
But mellows what we write to the dull sweets of rhyme.
Once more, hail and farewell; farewell, thou young,

But ah too short, Marcellus of our tongue;
Thy brows with ivy and with laurels bound;
But fate and gloomy night encompass thee around.

The poem is artificial, perhaps (like *Lycidas*); it
is full of echoes; and its subject is literary. But
the melody is round and sure; every couplet sounds
"like a great bronze ring thrown down on marble;"
and the ideas erect themselves without commotion
into a perfectly proportioned frame of farewell.
There is not an original word in the poem. It is a
classical mosaic, pieces of which Dryden had had by
him for a long time. It is precisely as a mosaic, as a
composition, that it is triumphant. The passionate farewell, the *ave atque vale*, had been a favorite
motif in Greek and Latin elegy. Dryden begins
with a line that savors of Juliet's bewildered outburst when she discovers Romeo's full identity at
the ball:

My only love, sprung from my only hate!
Too early seen unknown, and known too late!

Virgil had been fond of celebrating two souls that
were "near allied"; and Persius in the fifth Satire
had drawn a parallel between himself and his tutor
Cornutus of which Dryden's third and fourth lines
are reminiscent. The story of Nisus seems never to
have been out of Dryden's mind. As early as *The
Indian Emperor* he had made Guyomar declare to
Odmar, his rival for Alibech:

It seems my soul then moved the quicker pace;
Yours first set out, mine reached her in the race.

And very recently he had been translating the episode of Nisus and Euryalus from Virgil for the second *Miscellany*, which was to appear in a few months. He had written then for Virgil,

> One was their care, and their delight was one;
> One common hazard in the war they shared.

And he had spoken for Ascanius to Euryalus thus:

> But thou, whose years are more to mine allied. . . .
> One faith, one fame, one fate, shall both attend.

"Young Marcellus" was the dead nephew of Augustus whom Virgil had mourned in the sixth Æneid. Dryden had inserted a similar lament for the Duke of Ormond's (Barzillai's) son in *Absalom and Achitophel* (ll. 830–855). The ivy, the laurel, the fate, and the gloomy night encompassing around were venerable adornments which could scarcely be avoided. Additional parallels can be of no consequence; these in themselves are enough to show how Dryden was able to pour his memories out upon an occasion. Nothing except his genius can explain the precision with which he grouped those memories in this case, or the harmony with which his passion suffused them. He never succeeded so well in elegy again. The ode in memory of Anne Killigrew is more interesting as an ode than as an elegy, and is reserved for consideration as such.[1] *Eleonora* (1692), composed for a fat fee in honor of the late Countess of Abingdon, whom Dryden had never seen, was declared by Sir Walter Scott, the gentlest

[1] See Chapter VI.

critic whom the poet has had, to be "totally deficient in interest." It is a catalogue of female Christian virtues, virtues which Dryden was not much moved by. It suffers from a threadbare piety everywhere except at the end, in what Dryden calls the "Epiphonema, or close of the poem." Here, as usual, he quickens his pulse and gathers his powers. He is probably inspired in this case by Ben Jonson, who began an epigram to the Earl of Pembroke with the lines,

> I do but name thee, Pembroke, and I find
> It is an epigram on all mankind.

Dryden writes:

> Let this suffice: nor thou, great saint, refuse
> This humble tribute of no vulgar muse;
> Who, not by cares, or wants, or age depressed,
> Stems a wild deluge with a dauntless breast;
> And dares to sing thy praises in a clime
> Where vice triumphs, and virtue is a crime;
> Where ev'n to draw the picture of thy mind
> Is satire on the most of humankind;
> Take it, while yet 'tis praise; before my rage,
> Unsafely just, break loose on this bad age;
> So bad, that thou thyself hadst no defense
> From vice, but barely by departing hence.
> Be what, and where thou art; to wish thy place
> Were, in the best, presumption more than grace.
> Thy relics (such thy works of mercy are)
> Have, in this poem, been my holy care;
> As earth thy body keeps, thy soul the sky,
> So shall this verse preserve thy memory;
> For thou shalt make it live, because it sings of thee.

An elegy of uncertain date *On the Death of a Very Young Gentleman* is even less interesting than *Eleonora*. The account may close with Dryden's only attempt at a pastoral elegy, a poem *On the Death of Amyntas*, also undated. It is a dialogue between Damon and Menalcas. It opens with a fine rush of melody:

> 'Twas on a joyless and a gloomy morn,
> Wet was the grass, and hung with pearls the thorn;
> When Damon, who designed to pass the day
> With hounds and horns, and chase the flying prey,
> Rose early from his bed; but soon he found
> The welkin pitched with sullen clouds around,
> An eastern wind, and dew upon the ground.
> Thus while he stood, and sighing did survey
> The fields, and cursed th' ill omens of the day,
> He saw Menalcas come with heavy pace;
> Wet were his eyes, and cheerless was his face;
> He wrung his hands, distracted with his care,
> And sent his voice before him from afar.

But it soon ceases to give out sound, proceeding through some of the flattest moralizing in Dryden and ending with a very inferior conceit.

As a class, the prologues and epilogues of Dryden are the richest and best body of his occasional verse. There is no surer way to become convinced of his superbly off-hand genius than to read the ninety-five pieces which he is known to have composed for delivery from the front of the Restoration stage. They give, more adequately than any other division of his work, a notion of his various powers: his speed, his precision, his weight, his melody, his tact. He seems to have been braced in writing them by his consciousness that they would be heard by acute and critical ears in actual playhouses; for he has purged himself of conceits, bombast, and mannered elegance. They are his most speaking poems; they have the warmth of flesh and blood. He has written some of them as much for fun as for money, and consciously or unconsciously he has revealed himself in them all to an important extent. They are a running commentary on forty years of his life, as well as a living mirror in which the tiny theatrical world of Charles and James is shrewdly reflected.

Dryden is the master of the prologue and epilogue in English. His peculiar authority was felt in his own day before even a dozen of his supple, terse addresses had been delivered by members of the King's Company; and eventually he was acknowledged to be without any rival in the art of presenting new dramas to old audiences. It came to be understood that a prologue by Mr. Dryden might mean the making of a green playwright or the saving of an unprepossessing play. Spectators relished his confidences and his innuendoes; often there was more real meat in his forty lines of introduction than the whole ensuing tragedy or comedy could furnish forth. The secret of his success lay in the intimacy yet dignity of his harangue. He was both easy and important; he was fluent, but he was also condensed. There was something peculiarly satisfying in his form; he rounded off his little speeches as though they were clay and his brain was a potter's wheel.

The final impression was one of many riches casually summoned but faultlessly disposed.

There is nothing exactly like these pieces of Dryden's in any literature. The classical drama approximated them nowhere except in the *parabeses* of Aristophanes, when the Chorus came forward for the author and delivered torrents of audacious remarks to the audience. Greek tragedies might be prefaced with prologues, but they were more or less integral in the action, and were not personal. Plautus and Terence used prologues mainly to explain the events which were to follow, though Terence in his conducted mild literary quarrels around charges of plagiarism; their epilogues were only perfunctory bids for applause. The French drama never developed either form extensively; the English drama began at an early stage to cultivate both, scarcely, however, in the direction of Dryden. Marlowe introduced his *Tamburlaine* with high astounding terms. Shakespeare preserved a chaste anonymity in the playhouse; his Prologue in *Henry V* is strictly necessary; only in the epilogue to *As You Like It* and in the prologue and epilogue to *Henry VIII* does he take his audience into his confidence, and even there he has his reserves. Ben Jonson opened a vein which was followed along by none of his contemporaries or immediate successors. He was the first English playwright to harangue the pit; he was the father of the militant prologue. He first showed how literary criticism could be run serially, preceding plays; his prologue to *Every Man in his Humour* sounds like Dryden. Dekker and Heywood were more modest; Beaumont and Fletcher did much to discourage altogether the bold, direct address to the audience. The Restoration brought in a new mode. Theater-goers were now more sophisticated and belonged more to a single class; being somewhat familiar as well with the fashionable literary canons, they liked an occasional dash of criticism from a poet not too pedantic to be interesting or even saucy. As time went on, more intimate relations came to be established among dramatists, players, and spectators within the four walls of the theaters; the fortunes of both authors and actors became of real concern to a now well-seasoned public; a greater body of common knowledge took shape; it became possible for audiences to be addressed on certain fairly specialized subjects. Prologues and epilogues were now poems that could stand alone; often it made very little difference at what play or in what order they were spoken. "Now, gentlemen," says Bayes in the *Rehearsal*, "I would fain ask your opinion of one thing. I have made a Prologue and an Epilogue, which may both serve for either; that is, the prologue for the epilogue, or the epilogue for the prologue; (do you mark?) nay, they may both serve too, 'egad for any other play as well as this." Bayes was right; prologues and epilogues had become social events. Etherege helped to set the tone of Restoration performances in this kind, with his pungent reflections on the tastes of the pit and his cavalier trick of speaking of his Muse as his mistress; but Etherege wrote little at the most.

Outside of Dryden the best Restoration performers were Lee, Mrs. Behn, Otway, and Congreve, with their varying degrees of sprightliness and authority. Dryden could stand against them all; they could please, but he could take by storm. The Restoration saw the prologue and the epilogue at their height. The revolutions in taste which introduced the new age of Steele and Cibber and Lillo brought more heterogeneous crowds to the theaters, and it seemed less important to hear what the author, whoever he might be, had to say each day. Yet so old a habit could not be broken at once, and many excellent sets of verses continued to precede and follow plays, particularly farces, throughout the eighteenth century. Pope, Thomson, Goldsmith, and Johnson wrote respectable pieces; but the masters in this century were Fielding and Garrick. Fielding had all of Dryden's energy and wickedness, if not his richness and his form. He pretended to write prologues under protest,

> As something must be spoke, no matter what;
> No friends are now by prologues lost or got. . . .
> I wish with all my heart, the stage and town
> Would both agree to cry all prologues down,
> That we, no more obliged to say or sing,
> Might drop this useless, necessary thing.

Garrick has more of the useless things to his credit than has any other Englishman; he is always dexterous, but he does not carry any considerable weight.

It is likely that Dryden began to write prologues

and epilogues perfunctorily, without any notion of their possibilities; and to the end he maintained a certain nonchalance with reference to them that he could not easily muster for other forms. He felt free in them, for instance, to indulge in feminine rhymes, which elsewhere he renounced as too familiar. Yet he came early to see that some of these poems were almost his best writing. He arranged for the first *Miscellany* in 1684 to include eighteen of the riper specimens; and his relish for the exercise in general steadily increased. He was under no obligations in this form; he could damn the small critics of the pit and he could pour no end of ridicule upon the general taste. Yet he could exercise his gifts of compliment too if he liked. Tom Brown affected to believe that Dryden's flattery of Oxford was very gross, and Dryden himself wrote to Rochester remarking, "how easy 'tis to pass any thing upon an university, and how gross flattery the learned will endure." He took increasing pains to render himself effective, and to make it clear to all that he excelled. He compared the prologue in his hands to a church-bell in the hands of the sexton:

> Prologues, like bells to churches, toll you in
> With chiming verse, till the dull plays begin;
> With this sad difference, tho', of pit and pew,
> You damn the poet, but the priest damns you; [1]

or to a military assault conducted on a large and fierce scale. He compared the epilogue to a benediction:

[1] Prologue to *The Assignation*.

As country vicars, when the sermon's done,
Run huddling to the benediction;
Well knowing, tho' the better sort may stay,
The vulgar rout will run unblest away;
So we, when once our play is done, make haste
With a short epilogue to close your taste. [1]

He selected the most intelligent and vivacious
players as his spokesmen, and adapted his lines to
their known dispositions: Nell Gwynn could do the
surprising, saucy things; Mrs. Bracegirdle, Mrs.
Mountfort, and Mrs. Marshall could deliver more
scurrilous and scandalous messages; Mr. Betterton
could be infinitely grave, as when he impersonated
the ghost of Shakespeare; and Mr. Hart could be
choice and elegant, for the prologues at Oxford.
Nell Gwynn was twice called upon to succeed by
sensational means: in the prologue to the first part
of the *Conquest of Granada*, which she recited
wearing a hat as broad as a coach-wheel, and in the
epilogue to *Tyrannic Love*, which she spoke only
after resisting the efforts of the bearers to convey
her dead body off the stage:

(*To the Bearer*):   Hold, are you mad, you damned con-
                         founded dog,
               I am to rise, and speak the epilogue.
(*To the Audience*):   I come, kind gentlemen, strange news
                         to tell ye,
               I am the ghost of poor departed
                         Nelly.

Dryden came also more and more to pack his pieces
with criticism and allusion. His serried dialectic

[1] Epilogue to *Sir Martin Mar-All*.

flattered the audience which was expected to follow it; though the following was made somewhat easier by the practice of circulating folio copies of the prologue and epilogue before the play began, so that the hearers were likely to be familiar with the lines when it came time for them to be recited. If Dryden wrote his first prologues and epilogues perfunctorily, it is plain that he wrote his later ones both with instinctive delight and with due attention to the precautions necessary for insuring their success.

For his measure he has confined himself almost wholly to the heroic couplet; though the prologues to his *Wild Gallant* and to Joseph Harris' *Mistakes* are in part prose dialogues; and the prologue to the *Maiden Queen*, the epilogue to the *Tempest*, the prologue to *Limberham*, and the prologue to the King and Queen (1682) are in triplets, the effect of which is often slily jovial:

Old men shall have good old plays to delight 'em;
And you, fair ladies and gallants, that slight 'em,
We'll treat with good new plays; if our new wits can
    write 'em.

He is fond of leading off with a simile or metaphor and elaborating it throughout the length of the piece; as witness the prologue to the *Wild Gallant, Revived*, where the author's dramatic muse is compared to a raw young squire who has come up to London bent on making an impression swiftly. He falls at times, for the sake of emphasis, into aphorism, as here in the prologue to *All for Love:*

> Errors, like straws, upon the surface flow;
> He who would search for pearls must dive below;

or here in the epilogue to Lee's *Mithridates:*

> Love is no more a violent desire;
> 'Tis a mere metaphor, a painted fire. . . .
> Let honour and preferment go for gold,
> But glorious beauty is not to be sold.

Only in the satires is his pen as pointed; and indeed it was largely from the sixty-five prologues and epilogues which he had written by 1681 that the author of *Absalom and Achitophel* had learned to wield irresistible satiric cadences. Scorn for French farces and for Whig reformers had been sharpening Dryden's claws during the late 1670's. He had learned the accents of mockery in such lines as these from the prologue to Carlell's *Arviragus:*

> If all these ills could not undo us quite,
> A brisk French troop is grown your dear delight,
> Who with broad bloody bills call you each day
> To laugh and break your buttons at their play;
> Or see some serious piece, which we presume
> Is fallen from some incomparable plume.

He had taken his turn at the Popish Plot in the prologues to Lee's *Cæsar Borgia* and Tate's *Loyal General.* Always there had been his audience at which he could rail.

> The most compendious method is to rail;
> Which you so like, you think yourselves ill used
> When in smart prologues you are not abused.
> A civil prologue is approved by no man;
> You hate it as you do a civil woman,

he had declared as early as 1667, in the epilogue to
the *Maiden Queen*. The fun he was to have with Og
and Doeg was very much like the fun he had had
with the yawning faces in the stalls at *Cæsar Borgia:*

> You sleep o'er wit, and by my troth you may;
> Most of your talents lie another way.
> You love to hear of some prodigious tale,
> The bell that tolled alone, or Irish whale.

Roughly speaking, there are nine subjects treated
in Dryden's prologues and epilogues, or nine reasons
for their being. These will not serve as the basis for
an exact classification, because certain pieces turn on
more than one point; but an enumeration of those prologues and epilogues which play notably on each of
the nine strings may stand as a guide through this
most miscellaneous department of Dryden's poetry.

First, there are those which celebrate theatrical
occasions, such as the "Prologue Spoken on the First
Day of the King's House Acting after the Fire," the
"Prologue for the Women when they Acted at the
Old Theater in Lincoln's Inn Fields," the prologue
and epilogue to "The Maiden Queen, when Acted
by the Women Only," and the prologues and epilogue
"Spoken at the Opening of the New House" in 1674.

Second, there are those which compliment distinguished spectators or flatter special audiences,
like the prologues and epilogues spoken at Oxford,
the prologue and epilogue for *The Unhappy Favourite*
"Spoken to the King and the Queen at their Coming
to the House," the "Prologue to his Royal Highness
[the Duke of York], Upon His First Appearance at

the Duke's Theater Since His Return from Scotland,"
the "Prologue to the Duchess [of York] on Her Return from Scotland," and the prologue and epilogue
"To the King and Queen at the Opening of their
Theater upon the Union of the Two Companies in
1682." Of all these the prologues spoken at Oxford
are deservedly the best known, containing as they
do some of Dryden's most genial verse. One, which
is seldom quoted, shows him in a particularly merry
humor. It is the prologue spoken at the University
during the Duke of York's residence in Scotland in
1681. Certain members of the company, it seems,
had followed the Duke up to Holyrood House:

> Our brethern are from Thames to Tweed departed,
> And of our sisters all the kinder-hearted
> To Edenborough gone, or coached, or carted.
> With bonny bluecap there they act all night
> For Scotch half-crown, in English threepence hight.
> One nymph, to whom fat Sir John Falstaff's lean,
> There with her single person fills the scene;
> Another, with long use and age decayed,
> Dived here old woman, and rose there a maid.
> Our trusty doorkeepers of former time
> There strut and swagger in heroic rhyme.
> Tack but a copper lace to drugget suit,
> And there's a hero made without dispute;
> And that which was a capon's tail before
> Becomes a plume for Indian Emperor.

Mrs. Marshall took this pretty farewell of the learned
in 1674:

> Such ancient hospitality there rests
> In yours, as dwelt in the first Grecian breasts,

Whose kindness was religion to their guests.
Such modesty did to our sex appear,
As had there been no laws we need not fear,
Since each of you was our protector here.
Converse so chaste, and so strict virtue shown,
As might Apollo with the Muses own.
Till our return, we must despair to find
Judges so just, so knowing, and so kind.

Third, there are those which deal in literary criticism, such as the first prologue to the *Maiden Queen*, on the French and English rules, the epilogue to *The Wild Gallant, Revived*, on the difficulties of writing comedy, the prologue to the *Tempest*, on Shakespeare, the prologue to *Albumazar*, on plagiarism, the prologue to *Tyrannic Love*, on poetic license, the epilogue to the second part of the *Conquest of Granada*, on Elizabethan and modern wit, the famous prologue to *Aureng-Zebe*, on rhyming plays, the prologue and epilogue to *Œdipus*, on anglicizing Greek tragedy, the prologue to *Troilus and Cressida*, on Shakespeare again, and the prologue to *Amphitryon*, on the subject of contemporary satire. The epilogue to the second part of the *Conquest of Granada* is as a whole the most perfect of these poems. The contrast between Jonson's humor and King Charles's wit is developed with economy and precision and yet with a staggering copiousness. The subject is turned every possible way; the seventeen couplets lay on seventeen different pieces of fuel to brighten the fire. Dryden exhausts the subject without exhausting the reader. He varies one sense seventeen ways, but each of the ways is fresh and contributive.

Fourth, there are those which introduce young playwrights, such as the prologue to *Circe*, introducing Charles Davenant, the epilogue to *Tamerlane*, commending Charles Saunders, the prologue and epilogue to the *Loyal Brother*, introducing Thomas Southerne, and the epilogue to *The Husband his Own Cuckold*, introducing Dryden's own son John.

Fifth, there are those which berate the audience for its low taste, for its preferring French farce to English comedy, and for the fools and critics that largely compose it. These railing prologues and epilogues are legion. The general taste is lamented the most reproachfully in the prologue to the *Rival Ladies*, the epilogue to *Aureng-Zebe*, the prologue to *Limberham*, the prologue to *Cæsar Borgia*, the prologue to the *Loyal General*, the prologue to *King Arthur*, and the prologue to *Cleomenes*. The weakness for French literary goods is hit the best blows in the epilogue to *An Evening's Love*, the prologue to *Arviragus*, the epilogue to the *Man of Mode*, the prologue to the *Spanish Friar*, and the prologue to *Albion and Albanius*. Critics and fools are both abhorred alike in the prologue to the *Rival Ladies*, the epilogue to the *Indian Emperor*, the second prologue to the *Maiden Queen*, the prologue to the second part of the *Conquest of Granada*, the prologue to *All for Love*, and the epilogue to the *Man of Mode*.

Sixth, there are those which play with contemporary manners in the town and in the theaters; like the prologues written for the women only, the prologue to *Marriage à la Mode*, which makes out a pitiful case for "poor pensive punk" now that the braves are all gone off to war, the prologue to *The True Widow*, on certain familiar vices, the prologue to the *Spanish Friar*, the prologue to the *Princess of Cleves*, the epilogue to the King and Queen, and the prologue to Southerne's *Disappointment*.

Seventh, there are those which seem to have been calculated to please through sheer brutal innuendo. These are unquotable but superb; they are incontestably expert at the game they play. They are the exercises of an adroit and tireless imagination which hesitated at nothing. The prologues and epilogues for the women only, the prologue to *The Wild Gallant, Revived*, the prologue to *An Evening's Love*, the epilogue to the *Assignation*, the epilogue to *Limberham*, the prologue and epilogue to the *Princess of Cleves*, the prologue to the *Disappointment*, the epilogue to *Constantine the Great*, the epilogue to *Don Sebastian*, the epilogue to *Amphitryon*, the epilogue to *Cleomenes*, the epilogue to Bancroft's *Henry II*, and in fact almost every prologue or epilogue thereafter, must be dispatched to this category.

Eighth, there are the political prologues and epilogues. "A Lenten Prologue" of 1683, probably by Shadwell, pointed the way to the new type:

> Our prologue wit grows flat; the nap's worn off,
> And howsoe'er we turn and trim the stuff,
> The gloss is gone that looked at first so gaudy;
> 'Tis now no jest to hear young girls talk bawdy,
> But plots and parties give new matters birth,
> And state distractions serve you here for mirth.

Shadwell, if Shadwell it was, referred to Dryden's

and Lee's *Duke of Guise* (1682). A prologue at Oxford in 1680 had compared critics in the theater to Whigs in the state. During the ten years that followed, almost every prologue or epilogue of Dryden's bore more or less directly upon the constitutional conflict of that decade; the series closing in 1690 with the prologue to Fletcher's *Prophetess*, which contained covert sneers at the Revolution and presented King William's Irish campaign in a ludicrous light.

Ninth, there are those which are personal or controversial, and take the audience into the poet's confidence. The epilogue to *Marriage à la Mode* is an apology for a chaste play. The epilogue to Fletcher's *Pilgrim* (1700) is a none too sober moral recantation following the attacks of Collier and others upon the manners of the stage. The prologue to *Don Sebastian*, Dryden's last play after the Revolution, asks that civil grudges be forgotten, and begs forgiveness for supposed political sins. The prologue to *Love Triumphant*, Dryden's last play of all, is a will and testament bequeathing his various dramatic gifts to the critics and the beaux. It is a sly, ripe piece of raillery, a portion of which should be fitting as a tailpiece to a chapter which has aimed to convey a sense of Dryden's occasional riches. The lines were spoken by Mr. Betterton:

> So now, this poet, who forsakes the stage,
> Intends to gratify the present age.
> One warrant shall be signed for every man.
> All shall be wits that will, and beaux that can. . . .
> He dies, at least to us, and to the stage,
> And what he has he leaves this noble age.

He leaves you first, all plays of his inditing,
The whole estate which he has got by writing.
The beaux may think this nothing but vain praise;
They'll find it something, the testator says;
For half their love is made from scraps of plays.
To his worst foes he leaves his honesty,
That they may thrive upon't as much as he.
He leaves his manners to the roaring boys,
Who come in drunk, and fill the house with noise.
He leaves to the dire critics of his wit
His silence and contempt of all they writ.
To Shakespeare's critic, he bequeaths the curse,
To find his faults, and yet himself make worse. . . .
Last, for the fair, he wishes you may be,
From your dull critics, the lampooners, free.
Tho' he pretends no legacy to leave you,
An old man may at least good wishes give you.

V

THE JOURNALIST IN VERSE

"Is it not great pity to see a man, in the flower of his romantic conceptions, in the full vigour of his studies on love and honour, to fall into such a distraction, as to walk through the thorns and briers of controversy?" So Tom Brown, in his *Reflections on the Hind and Panther*, pretended to lament Dryden's defection from the theaters in the 1680's and his alliance with the new powers of politics and religion. The change, as is well known, meant relief to Dryden from modes of expression which were not altogether adapted to his disposition and by his subjection to which over a period of approximately twenty years he had been somewhat bored. There were a number of reasons, as a matter of fact, for the new departure. Not all of the plays had been successful. "I gad," Bayes had said in the *Rehearsal*, "the Town has used me as scurvily, as the Players have done. . . . Since they will not admit of my Plays, they shall know what a Satyrist I am. And so farewell to this stage forever, I gad." In the dedication of *Aureng-Zebe* to Lord Mulgrave in 1676, Dryden had confessed to his patron that he was weary of play-writing and had asked that the King be sounded on the question of an epic, for which leisure and hence a pension would be required. In

1690, in the preface to *Don Sebastian*, he recalled further reasons why he had deserted the stage ten years before. "Having been longer acquainted with the stage than any poet now living, and having observed how difficult it was to please; that the humours of comedy were almost spent; that love and honour (the mistaken topics of tragedy) were quite worn out; that the theaters could not support their charges; that the audience forsook them; that young men without learning set up for judges, and that they talked loudest who understood the least; all these discouragements had not only weaned me from the stage, but had also given me a loathing of it." Still another set of circumstances must have been impressing themselves upon him during the half dozen years that preceded *Absalom and Achitophel*. The Court, which had served as a setting and a justification for the heroic drama and which in its self-sufficiency had tended to cramp the imagination and restrict the field of literary enterprise, had begun to lose somewhat in significance; politics had grown more complicated; the formation of parties was imminent; and journalism promised new rewards to men who could comment with effect upon topics absorbing the general attention. The Popish Plot injected new fevers into the general blood; violent ups and downs in public fortunes came again, as during the Civil War, to seem matters of course; dramatic reversals of position like those of Titus Oates, who was in glory in 1679, was flogged almost to death in 1685, but was set up with a pension in 1689, were now quite regularly to be looked for. The climax of Dryden's career was coincident with these new crises. The poems on public affairs which he wrote during the six years between *Absalom and Achitophel* in 1681 and the *Hind and the Panther* in 1687 furnished him as a class with his best opportunities and must always, as a class, deserve to be the best known of his work.

Throughout the closing years of his main dramatic period Dryden had been wont to express a strong dislike for those "abominable scribblers," the pamphleteers. It was not only that the pamphleteers of the country party in particular offended his sense of political propriety; pamphleteering in general offended his sense of the dignity of literature and poetry. Meanwhile he was developing a public voice of his own. The prologues and epilogues, the controversial prefaces, and both the rhymed tragedies and the prose comedies in so far as they involved exercise in repartee, had trained his powers of attack, had taught him the damage that might be done with cool, insulting analysis and loaded innuendo. All the while, as it has been seen, he had been discovering important new resources of the heroic couplet, and he had been suppling his medium so that a great variety of materials could be run through it. The new materials were to make severe demands upon his verse, but he came equipped to meet any. He came with unexampled stores of energy and with an incorruptible literary conscience that precluded his writing anything trivial or feeble. "If a poem have genius," he remarked in the preface to *Absalom and Achitophel*, "it will force its own reception in the world." Dr. Johnson's father, the bookseller, has attested the reception which *Absalom and Achitophel* forced in its world; genius paid in that one case at least. Dryden came also with an abiding sense of his superiority; he arrived on a high level from which he looked down not only upon other controversialists but even upon the events which he was to treat; he maintained that elevation and that composure which are never found except in the company of an artistic confidence. He came finally with his most valuable gift of all, his gift of shaping thoughts and composing full, round pictures of men and principles.

He came, it must be admitted at once, without conspicuous principles of his own concerning Church or State. Bishop Burnet denied him religious convictions of any complexion whatsoever, and his name has always been synonymous with "turn-coat" in politics. First of all, as he himself said, he was "naturally inclined to scepticism;" it is not to be believed that he was converted to Catholicism by the works of Bossuet at the age of fifty-four in the same sense that Gibbon was converted at the age of sixteen, though Gibbon thought he was following in Dryden's tracks; nor is it to be believed that he ever possessed a set of nicely distinguished, carefully pondered political ideas. In the second place, he was not as much convinced that principles were necessary as it is generally assumed he should have been; he was not a prophet or a hero, but a party writer, writing at a time when a comparatively neutral field of public opinion had not as yet been cleared. In the third place, such principles as he did possess were not so much principles as prejudices, all of which can be summed up by saying that he hated and feared disturbance of any kind. By temperament a firm believer in order, he learned from Hobbes to set a peculiar value on "peaceable, social and comfortable living" even at the expense of justice and the general health. He was absorbed in the *status quo*, and his instinct was to strike desperately at whatever new thing threatened a dissipation of authority.

> All other errors but disturb a state,
> But innovation is the blow of fate,

he wrote in *Absalom and Achitophel*. He had all of Hobbes' distrust of the multitude, "that numerous piece of monstrosity," as Sir Thomas Browne put it, "which, taken asunder, seem men, and reasonable creatures of God; but, confused together, make but one great beast." He declined to believe that the crowd knew what it wanted.

> The tampering world is subject to this curse,
> To physic their disease into a worse.

What it needed, he said, was "common quiet," and common quiet could only be imposed by a single authority, the King. He had no superstitions about the divine right, but he had no faith in democracy. "Both my nature, as I am an Englishman, and my reason, as I am a man, have bred in me a loathing to that specious name of a Republick," he told the Earl of Danby in the dedication of *All for Love* three years before the appearance of *Absalom and Achitophel:* "that mock-appearance of a liberty, where all who have not part in the government are slaves; and slaves they are of a viler note than such as are subjects to an absolute dominion." Where power already was, there were his sympathies. Any priest or any politician who questioned that power or offered to repair the machinery of state was an enemy of mankind. Dryden's dread of change was neither reasonable nor noble, but it was consistent.

Given a consistent outlook, it was not required that a seventeenth century journalist in verse be a subtle scholar. When journalism becomes subtle, it must go over into prose. It being desirable in that day to work in plain blacks and whites rather than in shades of gray, a type of expression such as Dryden was master of could not fail to be effectual. Both in satire and in ratiocination he wrote with a pulse that could be distinctly felt. His political poems and his religious poems beat against whatever consciousness there was with a regular and powerful rhythm.

Testimony is varied as to Dryden's satirical temper. "Posterity is absolutely mistaken as to that great man," ran an octogenarian's letter in the *Gentleman's Magazine* in 1745; "tho' forced to be a satirist, he was the mildest creature breathing. . . . He was in company the modestest man that ever conversed." It is recorded that latterly at least he was short, fat, florid, had "a down look," and could be "easily discountenanced." He spoke in the preface to the second *Miscellany* of his "natural diffidence," and

in the dedication of *Troilus and Cressida* he said,
no doubt facetiously in part, "I never could shake
off the rustic bashfulness which hangs upon my nature." It was notorious that he could not read his
own lines aloud without hesitation and embarrass-
ment. "He had something in his nature," asserted
Congreve, "that abhorred intrusion into any society
whatsoever . . . and, consequently, his character
might become liable both to misapprehensions and
misrepresentations." George Granville, Lord Lans-
downe, defended him thus against Bishop Burnet's
charge that he had been "a monster of immodesty":
"modesty in too great a degree was his failing. He
hurt his fortune by it; he was sensible of it; he complained of it, and never could overcome it." All
this does not consort with the notion one is likely to
have entertained that Dryden was personally formidable, even overbearing. The scourge of Shaftesbury, Buckingham, Shadwell, and Settle by rights
should have been towering and scowling; the man who
is said to have sent a messenger to Tonson with a
scathing triplet and with the words, "Tell the dog
that he who wrote these lines can write more," should
have been fearful in some physical aspect or other.
Yet the only remark which has come down from his
time which even indirectly connects satire with him
personally is a remark which Aubrey inserted in
his life of Milton: "He pronounced the letter R
(littera canina) very hard—a certaine signe of a
Satyricall Witt—from Jo. Dreyden." Dryden's
power seems to have issued solely from his words.
He had mastered the satirical kind of expression as

he had mastered other kinds before, and what he was like behind his mask of phrases remained of no consequence. He bitterly hated few persons, perhaps none, but he was capable of a sublime contempt, and it was contempt that he knew perfectly how to put into meter. At Shadwell he never did anything but laugh. He was never stupefied with rage as the average man is stupefied in the face of idiocy or infamy. He never forgot that he would be effective only as he remembered to be an artist. "There is a pride of doing more than is expected from us," he said, "and more than others would have done." "There's a sweetness in good verse," ran the preface to *Absalom and Achitophel*, "which tickles even while it hurts, and no man can be heartily angry with him who pleases him against his will."

Tradition distinguishes between satirists who are mild and well-mannered, like Varro, Horace, and Cowper, and those who are angry and rough, like Lucilius, Juvenal, Persius, Hall, Marston, and Churchill. Dryden belongs with Juvenal, but not in the sense that he is angry or rough. His animus is controlled, and his satirical surface is as smooth as worn stone. What he has in common with Juvenal is a huge thoroughness, a quality which he himself attributes to the Roman in the *Discourse of Satire:* "He fully satisfies my expectation, he treats his subject home . . . he drives his reader along with him. . . . When he gives over, it is a sign the subject is exhausted." This largeness and this completeness have seldom come together in a satirical poet.

Juvenal alone among the Romans had the combination in a notable degree. Medieval satire lacked
distinction if it had thoroughness. The so-called
classical satirists at the end of Elizabeth's reign in
England were angry and rough, but they were neither exalted nor exhaustive. Cleveland, Denham,
and Marvell, the first English party satirists, were
at best ragged and hasty, however earnest. Butler
cannot be compared with anyone, least of all with
Dryden, whose laughter never went off into chuckles.
John Oldham gave the most promise before Dryden
of becoming the English Juvenal. With "satire in
his very eye," as a contemporary put it, he went to
Boileau for form and appropriated current passions
for material. His *Satires Upon the Jesuits*, written
in 1679, first in England treated specific contemporary affairs with dramatic grandeur and swelling dignity. The Elizabethans had not been specific; Cleveland, Denham, and Marvell had not been
grand. Oldham, who still seems fresh, must have
struck his first readers with remarkable force. His
solid, angry lines gave warning of an original and
impetuous spirit. Dryden, as the poem which he
wrote in 1684 certifies, was vividly impressed by his
junior. It was from the *Satires Upon the Jesuits*,
particularly from Loyola's speech in the third part,
as well as from *Paradise Lost* that he drew the state-
liness of *Absalom and Achitophel*. He added humor
to Oldham's preponderating gloom, he modified
Oldham's abruptness to directness, and he avoided
the infelicities of rhyme and meter with which Oldham had thought to approximate the fervor of Ju-

venal. But the great original force of the man Dryden did not pretend or wish to modulate. Oldham on his own side had learned much from the elder poet, as numerous passages in his works discover. It is a question whether a couplet that appears in Oldham's *Letter from the Country to a Friend in Town* (1678),

> That, like a powerful cordial, did infuse
> New life into his speechless, gaping Muse,

can be a paraphrase of the conclusion of Dryden's epistle to Lady Castlemaine; [1] Dryden's poem seems never to have been printed before the third *Miscellany* in 1693, and it is possible that in preparing it for that volume Dryden borrowed the couplet from Oldham to reinforce his ending. But there are sixteen lines near the end of the *Letter* which certainly "transverse," as the saying then was, the opening of the dedication of the *Rival Ladies*, published fourteen years before: [2]

> 'Tis endless, Sir, to tell the many ways
> Wherein my poor deluded self I please:
> How, when the Fancy lab'ring for a birth,
> With unfelt throes brings its rude issue forth:
> How after, when imperfect shapeless thought
> Is by the judgment into fashion wrought;
> When at first search I traverse o'er my mind,
> None but a dark and empty void I find;
> Some little hints at length, like sparks, break thence,
> And glimm'ring thoughts just dawning into sense;
> Confused awhile the mixt ideas lie,
> With naught of mark to be discovered by,

[1] See page 147.
[2] See page 135.

> Like colours undistinguished in the night,
> Till the dusk Images, moved to the light,
> Teach the discerning faculty to choose
> Which it had best adopt, and which refuse.

What might be called the satirical accent in Dryden is noticeable from the beginning. The Juvenalian portions of the *Hastings* have already been remarked. Shadwell, in his *Medal of John Bayes*, with what foundation is unknown, declares:

> At Cambridge first your scurrilous vein began,
> When saucily you traduced a nobleman.

The *Astræa Redux* is not without strains of sarcasm, as here:

> Thus banished David spent abroad his time,
> When to be God's anointed was his crime.

The *Annus Mirabilis* comes perilously near to disrespect of Charles when it says of him that he

> Outweeps an hermit, and out-prays a saint.

And so on through the prologues and epilogues, Dryden all the while adding steadily to his stock of satirical devices. He learns that Alexandrines are of little value in a form where the motion must be swift and regular; his major satires have seven altogether. He learns that the medial pause is the most telling in the long run; he perfects himself in antithesis and balance. He discovers that alliteration gives emphasis and helps to set the meter rocking. He sees that pyrrhic feet give speed and assist in making the transitions natural. He finds that

the stressing of penultimates stamps out lines which
are unforgettable:

> He curses God, but God before *cursed him.*

> The midwife laid her hand on his *thick skull*
> With this prophetic blessing: Be *thou dull.*

> I will not rake the dung-hill of *thy crimes,*
> For who would read thy life that reads *thy rhymes?*

> To talk like Do-eg and to write *like thee.*

And gradually he secures full possession of the secret
which is to aid him in becoming the most famous of
English satirists, the secret of the contemptuous
"character."

"Characters" are as old as literature, as old as
human life itself. The summing up of traits was
an instinct before it was an art. With Theophras-
tus it was a moral exercise. As a branch of the
satiric art it was elaborated first by Horace and
Juvenal, who by this and other means gave tones
to satire which at all its high points it has never
lacked. The two Romans went about in different
ways, of course, to sketch personalities. Horace
worked with a smile, delighting most in scraps of
action and dialogue which revealed the fools he knew
in Rome. The bore who joined him along the Via
Sacra (Sat. I, 9) and Tigellius the Sardinian singer
(Sat. I, 3) were laughably real. Tigellius was like
Dryden's Zimri:

This man never did anything of a piece. One while he
would run as if he were flying from an enemy; at other
times he would walk with as solemn a pace as he who

carries a sacrifice to Juno. Sometimes he had two hundred servants, sometimes only ten. Now he would talk of kings and tetrarchs, and everything great; now he would say, I desire no more than a three-footed table, a little clean salt, and a gown (I do not care how coarse), to defend me from the cold. Had you given this fine manager a thousand sesterces, who was as well satisfied with a few, in five days his pockets would be empty. He would frequently sit up all night, to the very morning, and would snore in bed all day. There never was anything so inconsistent with itself.

Dryden knew this Tigellius; and once he took occasion to praise the Rupilius and the Persius who are presented by Horace in a somewhat different manner in the seventh satire of the first book. They too are shown in action, but Rupilius is introduced by a series of epithets which anticipates Juvenal.

> Durus homo, atque odio qui posset vincere Regem;
> Confidens, tumidusque; adeo sermonis amari,
> Sisennos, Barros ut equis præcurrerct albis.

Juvenal invented the chain of scornful epithets and was partial to it in his satiric practice. If he resorted to action at all he made it swift and savage, like that of Messalina going to the stews. His fourth satire is a gallery of portraits, in the manner of *Absalom and Achitophel;* the various councillors who come to advise the emperor what he shall do with his monstrous turbot are seized by a firm hand and dressed in sinister new robes. The Greek parasite described in the third satire is even more of a Zimri than Tigellius was:

Ingenium velox, audacia perdita, sermo
Promptus et Isæo torrentior. Ede quid illum
Eoce putes, Quemvis hominem secum attulit ad nos:
Grammaticus rhetor geometres pictor aliptes
Augur schœnobates medicus magus, omnia novit
Græculus esuriens.

Dryden has translated the passage thus:

> Quick-witted, brazen-faced, with fluent tongues,
> Patient of labours, and dissembling wrongs.
> Riddle me this, and guess him if you can,
> Who bears a nation in a single man?
> A cook, a conjurer, a rhetorician,
> A painter, pedant, a geometrician,
> A dancer on the ropes, and a physician.
> All things the hungry Greek exactly knows.

The Middle Ages and the Renaissance were rich in "characters" of types and individuals. Clerics and laymen, allegorists and chroniclers were busy at portraiture. No one has disposed of individuals in more cursory, stinging phrases than those which Dante used; no one has drawn types better than Chaucer. Barclay's Ship of Fools was full to sinking. Awdeley's *Fraternity of Vagabonds* (1565) was a populous gallery of English rogues. In Elizabeth's reign men like Greene and Nash brought forward other rascals to the light; and formal satirists like Hall and Donne gave a general flaying to the London coxcombs. Donne was a fourth-dimensional Horace; the fop who adorns his first satire deserves to be one of the most famous of all literary effigies.

The seventeenth century, in England and elsewhere, saw an extraordinary development in the art of portraying personages both generalized and real. The abstract Theophrastian "character" is now a well-known form of Jacobean and Caroline prose. The "humours" of Ben Jonson were almost its starting-point; Sir Thomas Overbury, Joseph Hall, John Stevens, John Earle, Nicholas Breton, Geoffrey Minshull, Wye Saltonstall, Donald Lupton, Richard Flecknoe, and Samuel Butler handed it along, enriching it all the time with observation and humor, until Addison and Steele, who also knew LaBruyère and the French type, appropriated it for their Sir Roger de Coverley papers, and Fielding grafted on its stem his own Squire Western. Dryden was well acquainted with this body of prose. But his especial contribution was to be made in the field of personal portraiture, a field which began to be cultivated in prose and in verse somewhat later than the other. The Civil War had created a new public interest in public men, and during the Restoration it had rapidly become profitable for political writers to indulge at considerable length in personalities. The Theophrastian essay modified itself to suit this tendency, admitting each year a more direct observation and a greater proportion of particular and satiric details. But the tendency was best served by another form of prose "character" altogether, the historical-biographical, a form which was evolved simultaneously in France and in England. The models were furnished by the classical historians, chiefly Plutarch, Tacitus, and Suetonius, and by such modern writers of history as the Italian Davila, who treated the Civil Wars of France. In France the development proceeded through the historians, the writers of *Mémoires* like Richelieu and Cardinal de Retz, the romancers like Madeleine de Scudéry, and the composers of *portraits* like Mademoiselle de Montpensier. In England the Earl of Clarendon was the master of the historical "character," with a not very close second in Bishop Burnet. George Savile, Marquis of Halifax, wrote brilliant political estimates of Charles II and others; Walton, Aubrey, and Sprat made some of the earliest attempts at careful biographical delineation; and in many cases remarkable traits were observed by keen eyes and set down on paper from no other motive than pure private delight. The first Earl of Shaftesbury, Dryden's Achitophel, and therefore an important name in the history of caricature, has left in his fragmentary Autobiography a portrait which for richness and clarity of detail ought to have a place among the best known passages of seventeenth century prose. It is given here in full because it illustrates better than any Theophrastian piece or any historian's draft the gift possessed by Dryden's contemporaries of representing flesh and blood in graphic sentences. The subject is his neighbor Henry Hastings, of Woodlands, Dorsetshire, a country gentleman of the old school who was born in 1551 and who died in 1650.

Mr. Hastings, by his quality, being the son, brother and uncle to the Earls of Huntingdon, and his way of living, had the first place amongst us. He was peradventure an original in our age, or rather the copy of our nobility in ancient days in hunting and not warlike times: he was low, very strong and very active, of a reddish flaxen hair, his clothes always green cloth, and never all worth when new five pounds. His house was perfectly of the old fashion, in the midst of a large park well stocked with deer, and near the house rabbits to serve his kitchen, many fishponds, and great store of wood and timber; a bowlinggreen in it, long but narrow, full of high ridges, it being never levelled since it was ploughed; they used round sand bowls, and it had a banqueting-house like a stand, a large one built in a tree. He kept all manner of sport-hounds that ran buck, fox, hare, otter, and badger, and hawks long and short winged; he had all sorts of nets for fishing; he had a walk in the New Forest and the manor of Christ Church. This last supplied him with red deer, sea and river fish; and indeed all his neighbours' grounds and royalties were free to him, who bestowed all his time in such sports, but what he borrowed to caress his neighbours' wives and daughters, there being not a woman in all his walks of the degree of a yeoman's wife or under, and under the age of forty, but it was extremely her fault if he were not intimately acquainted with her. This made him very popular, always speaking kindly to the husband, brother, or father, who was to boot very welcome to his house whenever he came; there he found beef pudding and small beer in great plenty, a house not so neatly kept as to shame him or his dirty shoes, the great hall strewed with marrow bones, full of hawks' perches, hounds, spaniels, and terriers, the upper sides of the hall hung with the fox-skins of this and the last year's skinning, here and there a polecat intermixed, guns and keepers' and huntsmen's poles in abundance. The parlour was a large long room, as properly furnished; in a great hearth paved with brick lay some terriers and the choicest hounds and spaniels; seldom but two of the great chairs had litters of young cats in them, which were not to be disturbed, he having always three or four attending him at dinner, and a little white round stick of fourteen inches long lying by his trencher that he might defend such meat as he had no mind to part with to them. The windows, which were very large, served for places to lay his arrows, crossbows, stonebows, and other such like accoutrements; the corners of the room full of the best chose hunting and hawking poles; an oyster-table at the lower end, which was of constant use twice a day all the year round, for he never failed to eat oysters before dinner and supper through all seasons: the neighbouring town of Poole supplied him with them. The upper part of this room had two small tables and a desk, on the one side of which was a church Bible, on the other the Book of Martyrs; on the tables were hawks' hoods, bells, and such like, two or three old green hats with their crowns thrust in so as to hold ten or a dozen eggs, which were of a pheasant kind of poultry he took much care of and fed himself; tables, dice, cards, and boxes were not wanting. In the hole of the desk were store of tobacco-pipes that had been used. On one side of this end of the room was the door of a closet, wherein stood the strong beer and the wine, which never came thence but in single glasses, that being the rule of the house exactly observed, for he never exceeded in drink or permitted it. On the other side was a door into an old chapel not used for devotion; the pulpit, as the safest place, was never wanting of a cold chine of beef, pasty of venison, gammon of bacon, or great apple-pie with thick crust extremely baked. His table cost him not much, though it was very good to eat at, his sports supplying all but beef and mutton, except Friday, when he had the best sea-fish he could get, and was the day that his neighbours of best quality most visited him. He never wanted a London pudding, and always sung it in with "my part lies therein-a." He drank a glass of wine or two at meals, very often syrrup of gilliflower in his sack, and had always a tun glass without feet stood by him holding a pint of small beer, which he often stirred with a great sprig of rosemary. He was well natured, but soon angry, calling his servants bastard and cuckoldy knaves, in one of which he often spoke truth to his own knowledge, and sometimes in both, though of the same man. He lived to a hundred, never lost his eyesight, but always writ and read without spectacles, and got to horse without help. Until past fourscore he rode to the death of a stag as well as any. [1]

Defoe or Fielding or Scott might have done a series of novels on Achitophel's Henry Hastings; the seventeenth century, so prodigal of its human material, used him neither for that nor for any other purpose.

The type of verse "character" which Dryden found at hand in 1681 was already of a good many years' standing. In the course of its evolution it had drawn upon each of the prose types, the abstract and the individual, for certain of its qualities. From the Theophrastian sketch it had derived a Euphuistic, antithetical niceness of phrasing which tended to resolve it into a pleasant dance of categories. From the historical or biographical or political sketch it had derived its allusiveness, its concreteness, and its pungency. Ever since the days of the Short Parliament there had been Clevelands, Marvells, and nameless writers who had achieved concreteness and pungency, but rarely or never had a note of niceness

---

[1] A full length portrait of Mr. Hastings is reproduced in John Hutchin's *History and Antiquities of the County of Dorset*, 3d ed., London, 1868, vol. III, p. 155.

been heard. Satirists had balanced their epithets, but only roughly; the movement of their verse had been spasmodic rather than fleet. The Earl of Mulgrave's *Essay upon Satire*, which was circulated in manuscript in 1679 and 1680 and thought by many, because of its slashing directness, to be Dryden's, had showed great improvement in the form of its "characters;" that of Tropos (Lord Chief Justice Scroggs),

> At bar abusive, on the bench unable,
> Knave on the woolsack, fop at council table,

and that of Rochester, for which Dryden was beaten in Rose Street, Covent Garden,

> Mean in each action, lewd in every limb,
> Manners themselves are mischievous in him,

had been powerful and swift of dispatch. Now Dryden came with his contribution, which to begin with was a metrical contribution. His Achitophel and his Zimri captivated the town first of all by virtue of their felicity and finish. Without being in the least labored they were felt at once to be important; they had the accent of authority. The "characters" of Arod and Malchus in the anonymous Roman Catholic poem, *Naboth's Vineyard*, which had been printed in 1679 as a protest against the condemnation of Lord Strafford under cover of the Popish Plot, and which more than any other verse pamphlet, by virtue of its epic solemnity, its Biblical tissue, and its general plan, gave Dryden the cue for his own masterpiece, had failed to make a great impression, possibly because Oldham's more striking *Satires* had circulated the same year. In *Naboth's Vineyard*, Jezabel, King Achab's malicious queen and counsellor, had leagued herself with Arod, a kind of Achitophel:

> She summons then her chosen instruments,
> Always prepared to serve her black intents;
> The chief was Arod, whose corrupted youth
> Had made his soul an enemy to truth;
> But nature furnished him with parts and wit,
> For bold attempts, and deep intriguing fit.
> Small was his learning; and his eloquence
> Did please the rabble, nauseate men of sense.
> Bold was his spirit, nimble and loud his tongue,
> Which more than law, or reason, takes the throng.

Arod, in turn, had had for his tool a kind of Oates:

> Malchus, a puny Levite, void of sense,
> And grace, but stuffed with voice and impudence,
> Was his prime tool; so venomous a brute,
> That every place he lived in spued him out;
> Lies in his mouth, and malice in his heart,
> By nature grew, and were improved by art.
> Mischief his pleasure was; and all his joy
> To see his thriving calumny destroy
> Those, whom his double heart and forkéd tongue
> Surer than vipers' teeth to death had stung.

Arod had been invoked at another point in the poem exactly as Zimri was to be introduced on Dryden's stage:

> In the first rank of Levites Arod stood,
> Court-favour placed him there, not worth or blood.

The "characters" in *Naboth's Vineyard* had been interesting, but they had not been felt to be important, they had made no hit; whereas Achitophel and Zimri, who derived directly from them, within the first month after their appearance were known to all the men about town.

> Of these the false Achitophel was first,
> A name to all succeeding ages curst:
> For close designs and crooked counsels fit,
> Sagacious, bold, and turbulent of wit.
> Restless, unfixed in principles and place;
> In power unpleased, impatient of disgrace:
> A fiery soul, which, working out its way,
> Fretted the pigmy body to decay,
> And o'er-informed the tenement of clay.
> A daring pilot in extremity;
> Pleased with the danger, when the waves went high
> He sought the storms; but, for a calm unfit,
> Would steer too nigh the sands to boast his wit.
> Great wits are sure to madness near allied,
> And thin partitions do their bounds divide;
> Else why should he, with wealth and honour blest,
> Refuse his age the needful hours of rest?
> Punish a body which he could not please;
> Bankrupt of life, yet prodigal of ease?
> And all to leave what with his toil he won,
> To that unfeathered two-legg'd thing, a son;
> Got, while his soul did huddled notions try;
> And born a shapeless lump, like anarchy.
> In friendship false, implacable in hate;
> Resolved to ruin or to rule the State.
> To compass this the triple bond he broke;
> The pillars of the public safety shook,

And fitted Israel for a foreign yoke:
Then seized with fear, yet still affecting fame,
Usurped a patriot's all-atoning name.
So easy still it proves in factious times,
With public zeal to cancel private crimes.
How safe is treason and how sacred ill,
When none can sin against the people's will!
Where crowds can wink, and no offense be known,
Since in another's guilt they find their own.
Yet fame deserved no enemy can grudge;
The statesman we abhor, but praise the judge.
In Israel's courts ne'er sat an Abbethdin
With more discerning eyes, or hands more clean;
Unbribed, unsought, the wretched to redress;
Swift of dispatch, and easy of access.

Some of their chiefs were princes of the land;
In the first rank of these did Zimri stand;
A man so various that he seemed to be
Not one, but all mankind's epitome:
Stiff in opinions, always in the wrong,
Was everything by starts, and nothing long;
But, in the course of one revolving moon,
Was chymist, fiddler, statesman, and buffoon:
Then all for women, painting, rhyming, drinking,
Besides ten thousand freaks that died in thinking.
Blest madman, who could every hour employ,
With something new to wish, or to enjoy!
Railing and praising were his usual themes;
And both (to shew his judgment) in extremes:
So over-violent, or over-civil,
That every man, with him, was God or Devil.
In squandering wealth was his peculiar art;
Nothing went unrewarded but desert.
Beggared by fools, whom still he found too late,

He had his jest, and they had his estate.
He laughed himself from court; then sought relief
By forming parties, but could ne'er be chief;
For, spite of him, the weight of business fell
On Absalom amd wise Achitophel.
Thus, wicked but in will, of means bereft,
He left not faction, but of that was left.

Dryden continued throughout his career to exercise a dictatorship in the world of "characters." Often he seemed to be saying the last word about a man when actually he was saying almost nothing; he seemed to weave a close garment about his subject when in truth he only latticed him over with antitheses. He became the acknowledged master of the cadenced epithet. Yet it would be absurd to imply that his success was merely technical. His authority was that of a knowing and a smiling man as well as that of a virtuoso; humor, imagination, wisdom, and thoroughly competent cynicism were also his contributions. He testified in the *Discourse of Satire* that the fine etching of characters was not a simple trick. " 'Tis not reading, 'tis not imitation of an author, which can produce this fineness; it must be inborn; it must proceed from a genius, and particular way of thinking, which is not to be taught. . . . How easy is it to call rogue and villain, and that wittily! But how hard to make a man appear a fool, a blockhead, or a knave, without using any of those opprobrious terms! . . . there is still a vast difference betwixt the slovenly butchering of a man, and the fineness of a stroke that separates the head from the body, and leaves it standing in its place. . . .

The character of Zimri in my *Absalom* is, in my opinion, worth the whole poem: it is not bloody, but it is ridiculous enough; and he, for whom it was intended, was too witty to resent it as an injury.   If I had railed, I might have suffered for it justly; but I managed my own work more happily, perhaps more dexterously.   I avoided the mention of great crimes, and applied myself to the representing of blindsides, and little extravagancies; to which, the wittier a man is, he is generally the more obnoxious.   It succeeded as I wished; the jest went round, and he was laughed at in his turn who began the frolic."   No one will deny that Dryden's pictures of men and parties between the Exclusion Bill and the Declaration of Indulgence are works of genius.   Competent historians agree that his comments, if not always fair, still throw a brighter light upon those six years than do all other contemporary records combined; subsequent research has only increased their respect for the man who left his studies on love and honor and fell into such a distraction as to walk through the thorns and briars of controversy.   Nor can anyone fail to pay tribute to a mind so various that it could proceed from Achitophel and Zimri to Jotham, from Jotham to the rollicking Og and Doeg, from them to the sects in *The Hind and the Panther*, and from the sects to Bishop Burnet, the Buzzard.   Only Pope in the next generation, with his Atticus, his Sporus, and his Wharton, succeeded in carving images as rare as Dryden's.   The Queen Anne poetasters as a rule lacked the necessary intellectual resources. As the author of *Uzziah and Jotham* had rather mournfully remarked in his preface in 1690, "*Ab-salom and Achitophel* was a masterpiece" beyond which none might expect to go. But the cadences of the Drydenian "character," if nothing more, sounded distinctly and constantly through all Augustan verse. The poems that answered the *Absalom* fell into its rhythms, and there were complete copyists like Duke in his *Review* or Mainwaring in his *Tarquin and Tullia* and his *Suum Cuisque*. After Pope the cadences were less plainly heard. Churchill went out of his way to recall them; but neither Goldsmith in his *Retaliation* nor Cowper in his *Conversation* found them indispensable.

Dryden's experience before *Absalom and Achitophel* gave him many contacts with the stuff of human nature. The writing of twenty plays, for instance, afforded him an acquaintance with postures, figures, and mental complexions. He was not brilliant in dramatic characterization; his men and women are seldom easy to visualize; but he grew adept in the specification of traits, he mastered the phraseology of personal description. His great example was Shakespeare, whom he approached in gusto though not in penetration. He has a number of energetic Beatrices, although he has said of none of them,

Disdain and Scorn ride sparkling in her eyes.

The heroic plays abound in creatures who are garnished with symmetrical, balanced hyperbole but who have no significance as human beings. The comedies are much happier. In the writing of his prose comedies Dryden touched upon such stock types as the spendthrift, the rake, the witty mistress, the scold, the affected woman, the swashbuckler. English dramatists from Jonson on had left him a rich legacy of language with which to treat such figures, and he managed his inheritance with some dexterity. The French comic writers, particularly Molière, furnished him at the same time with admirable models for *portraits précieuses*. The outcome was that he acquired a turn for hitting off the blindsides and extravagancies of his people not so much through action, though he does that brilliantly in *Marriage à la Mode*, as through elaborate comments by other participants in the scene. His Sir Martin Mar-All, originally a creation of Molière's, becomes in his hands a really integral clown. "I never laughed so in all my life," said Pepys, who went to see him. The writing of critical essays and prefaces gave Dryden another kind of acquaintance with the outlines of character. His estimates in the *Essay of Dramatic Poesy* of authors past and present, of Wild, Cleveland, Shakespeare, Jonson, Beaumont and Fletcher, together with the frequent contrasts and parallels which he drew between famous poets, taught him discrimination in praise and opprobrium; the critical prologues and epilogues encouraged pertinency and concentration. The writing of complimentary prose and verse did not make for discrimination in the distribution of excellences, but it added to Dryden's stock of attributes and it involved important exercise in the grouping of them.

The specialized "character-cadences" which jolted Achitophel and Zimri into fame were by no means new to Dryden in 1681, although they had not been exactly prominent in his verse before. They had appeared as early as the *Annus Mirabilis*, when it was said of the "Belgian" admirals,

> Designing, subtile, diligent, and close,
> They knew to manage war with wise delay.

They had been heard in the *State of Innocence*, when Adam declared against woman,

> Add that she's proud, fantastic, apt to change,
> Fond without art, and kind without deceit.

Often, as in the *Spanish Friar*, blank verse characters had been sketched in the later Elizabethan cadences rather than in those which were to become known as Dryden's and Pope's. Pedro had spoken thus of Dominick:

> I met a reverend, fat, old gouty friar,—
> With a paunch swoll'n so high, his double chin
> Might rest upon it; a true son of the church;
> Fresh-coloured, and well thriven on his trade,—
> Come puffing with his greasy bald-pate choir,
> And fumbling o'er his beads in such an agony,
> He told them false, for fear. About his neck
> There hung a wench, the label of his function,
> Whom he shook off, i' faith, methought, unkindly.
> It seems the holy stallion durst not score
> Another sin, before he left the world.

Restoration blank verse, it will be seen, encouraged a boundless extravagance in portraiture rather than a Gallic justness, or appearance of justness.

Absalom and Achitophel, then, like Waller's poetry, came out forty thousand strong before the wits were aware. Its impression on Dryden himself was fully as remarkable as its impression on its readers or on the other poets of London. Dryden realized at once that he had woven patches of verse which would wear like iron, and proceeded to acquaint himself with all the varieties of texture which the new weave would admit. From 1681 to 1700 he wrote scarcely a poem which he did not enrich with "characters" or the cadences of "characters." *The Medal* was one long likeness of Shaftesbury, with a few concentrated passages like the following, which showed that gifted Whig sitting for the engraver:

> Five days he sate for every cast and look;
> Four more than God to finish Adam took.
> But who can tell what essence angels are,
> Or how long Heaven was making Lucifer?
> O could the style that copied every grace,
> And plowed such furrows for an eunuch face,
> Could it have formed his ever-changing will,
> The various piece had tired the graver's skill!
> A martial hero first, with early care
> Blown, like a pigmy by the winds, to war.
> A beardless chief, a rebel, ere a man.
> (So young his hatred to his prince began.)
> Next this, (how wildly will ambition steer!)
> A vermin wriggling in the usurper's ear.
> Bartering his venal wit for sums of gold,
> He cast himself into the saintlike mold;
> Groaned, sighed, and prayed, while godliness was gain,
> The loudest bagpipe of the squeaking train.

Mac Flecknoe, whenever it may have been composed, began with a "character" which for sheer cumulative destructiveness has no equal in satire.   Says Flecknoe:

> Shadwell alone my perfect image bears,
> Mature in dulness from his tender years;
> Shadwell alone of all my sons is he
> Who stands confirmed in full stupidity.
> The rest to some faint meaning make pretense,
> But Shadwell never deviates into sense.
> Some beams of wit on other souls may fall,
> Strike through and make a lucid interval;
> But Shadwell's genuine night admits no ray,
> His rising fogs prevail upon the day.
> Besides, his goodly fabrick fills the eye
> And seems designed for thoughtless majesty:
> Thoughtless as monarch oaks that shade the plain,
> And, spread in solemn state, supinely reign.

The second part of *Absalom and Achitophel*, with its Ben-Jochanan, its Og and its Doeg, opened a new world of broad comedy; for once Dryden frolicked like Rabelais. Doeg, or Settle, and Og, or Shadwell, are irresistible. Merriment elbows resentment aside in lines like these:

> Doeg, though without knowing how or why,
> Made still a blundering kind of melody;
> Spurred boldly on, and dashed through thick and thin,
> Through sense and nonsense, never out nor in;
> Free from all meaning, whether good or bad,
> And in one word, heroically mad;
> He was too warm on picking-work to dwell,
> But fagotted his notions as they fell,

And if they rhymed and rattled, all was well.
Spiteful he is not, though he wrote a Satyr,
For still there goes some thinking to ill-nature;
He needs no more than birds and beasts to think,
All his occasions are to eat and drink.
If he call rogue and rascal from a garret,
He means you no more mischief than a parrot;
The words for friend and foe alike were made,
To fetter 'em in verse is all his trade.

Now stop your noses, readers, all and some,
For here's a tun of midnight work to come,
Og from a treason tavern rolling home.
Round as a globe, and liquored every chink,
Goodly and great he sails behind his link;
With all his bulk there's nothing lost in Og,
For every inch that is not fool is rogue:
A monstrous mass of foul corrupted matter,
As all the Devils had spewed to make the batter.
When wine has given him courage to blaspheme,
He curses God, but God before cursed him;
And if man could have reason, none has more,
That made his paunch so rich and him so poor. . . .
But though Heaven made him poor, (with reverence
    speaking,)
He never was a poet of God's making;
The midwife laid her hand on his thick skull,
With this prophetic blessing—Be thou dull;
Drink, swear and roar, forbear no lewd delight,
Fit for thy bulk, do anything but write.
Thou art of lasting make, like thoughtless men,
A strong nativity—but for the pen;
Eat opium, mingle arsenick in thy drink,
Still thou mayst live, avoiding pen and ink.
I see, I see, 'tis counsel given in vain,

For treason botched in rhyme will be thy bane;
Rhyme is the rock on which thou art to wreck,
'Tis fatal to thy fame and to thy neck.
Why should thy meter good King David blast?
A psalm of his will surely be thy last.
Dar'st thou presume in verse to meet thy foes,
Thou whom the penny pamphlet foiled in prose?
Doeg, whom God for mankind's mirth has made,
O'ertops thy talent in thy very trade;
Doeg to thee, thy paintings are so coarse,
A poet is, though he's the poet's horse.
A double noose thou on thy neck does pull,
For writing treason and for writing dull;
To die for faction is a common evil,
But to be hanged for nonsense is the Devil.
Hadst thou the glories of thy king expressed,
Thy praises had been satire at the best;
But thou in clumsy verse, unlicked, unpointed,
Hast shamefully defiled the Lord's anointed:
I will not rake the dung-hill of thy crimes,
For who would read thy life that reads thy rhymes?
But of King David's foes be this the doom,
May all be like the young man Absalom;
And for my foes may this their blessing be,
To talk like Doeg and to write like thee.

Dryden had not stopped laughing a year later when
in *The Vindication of the Duke of Guise* he answered
three pamphleteering adversaries, one of whom he
believed to be Shadwell. "Og may write against
the King if he pleases, so long as he drinks for him,"
he observed; "and his writings will never do the
Government so much harm, as his drinking does it
good; for true subjects will not be much perverted

by his libels, but the wine duties rise considerably
by his claret. He has often called me an atheist in
print; I would believe more charitably of him, and
that he only goes the broad way because the other
is too narrow for him. He may see by this, I do
not delight to meddle with his course of life, and
his immoralities, though I have a long bead-roll of
them. I have hitherto contented myself with the
ridiculous part of him, which is enough in all conscience to employ one man: even without the story
of his late fall at the Old Devil, where he broke no
ribs, because the hardness of the stairs could reach no
bones; and for my part, I do not wonder how he
came to fall, for I have always known him heavy;
the miracle is, how he got up again. . . . But to
leave him, who is not worth any further consideration, now I have done laughing at him. Would every
man knew his own talent, and that they who are only
born for drinking, would let both poetry and prose
alone." So cheerfully it was that Mr. Bayes shed
the venom of his assailants. The *Religio Laici* indulged in a more subdued kind of caricature when
it summed up the accomplishments of the private
spirit in theology. *The Hind and the Panther* was
crowded with mature and calm though none the
less vivid pictures of persons and sects: the Roman
Catholic milk-white Hind herself (I, 1–8); the Inde-
pendents, the Quakers, the Freethinkers, the Ana-
baptists, and the Arians (I, 35–61); the Presbyte-
rians (I, 160–189); the Brownists (I, 310–326); the
noble Anglican Panther (I, 327–510); the mind of
the Anglican establishment (III, 70–79):

> Disdain, with gnawing envy, fell despite,
> And cankered malice stood in open sight;
> Ambition, interest, pride without control,
> And jealousy, the jaundice of the soul;
> Revenge, the bloody minister of ill,
> With all the lean tormentors of the will;

the Latitudinarians (III, 160–172); the Huguenot exiles (III, 173–190); the Anglican tradition (III, 400–409):

> Add long prescription of established laws,
> And pique of honour to maintain a cause,
> And shame of change, and fear of future ill,
> And zeal, the blind conductor of the will;
> And chief among the still-mistaking crowd,
> The fame of teachers obstinate and proud,
> And, more than all, the private judge allowed;
> Disdain of Fathers which the dance began,
> And last, uncertain whose the narrower span,
> The clown unread, and half-read gentleman;

the Martin, or Father Petre (III, 461–468); James II, "a plain good man" (III, 906–937); the Anglican clergy (III, 944–954); and finally the Buzzard, or Bishop Burnet (III, 1141–1191):

> More learn'd than honest, more a wit than learn'd. . . .
> Prompt to assail, and careless of defense,
> Invulnerable in his impudence,
> He dares the world and, eager of a name,
> He thrusts about and justles into fame.
> Frontless and satire-proof, he scours the streets,
> And runs an Indian muck at all he meets.

> So fond of loud report, that not to miss
> Of being known, (his last and utmost bliss,)
> He rather would be known for what he is.

The blank verse tragedies which Dryden wrote after the Revolution were gorgeously hung with portraits. Shakespearean cadences prevailed in them; yet now and then the old lilt would insist upon a hearing, as in the second act of *Don Sebastian:*

> What honour is there in a woman's death!
> Wronged, as she says, but helpless to revenge,
> Strong in her passion, impotent of reason,
> Too weak to hurt, too fair to be destroyed.
> Mark her majestic fabric; she's a temple
> Sacred by birth, and built by hands divine;

or in the third act of the same play:

> The genius of your Moors is mutiny;
> They scarcely want a guide to move their madness;
> Prompt to rebel on every weak pretense;
> Blustering when courted, crouching when oppressed;
> Wise to themselves, and fools to all the world;
> Restless in change, and perjured to a proverb.
> They love religion sweetened to the sense;
> A good, luxurious, palatable faith.

The *Juvenal* and the *Persius*, as might be expected, contain a number of ruthlessly consummate delineations; the Vectidius of Persius (IV, 50–73) is one of Dryden's most mocking. As Dryden proceeded with his translations and his narratives he came more and more to rely upon the antithetical paragraph as a device for introductions, transitions, and summaries. It proved useful not only for analyzing the natures of men but for sketching scenes and stating situations. Almost every page of the *Virgil* and the *Fables* rang with the familiar cadences. Chaucer himself had not been without his rocking rhythms; so when Dryden found lines in the *Canterbury Tales* that were suited to his purpose he brought them straight over. Such a line as this in the Knight's Tale,

> Blak was his berd, and manly was his face,

was no way altered except in spelling. More of Chaucer yet would have been appropriated without change had his syllabication possessed utility for Dryden. The "Character of a Good Parson" in the *Fables*, elaborated from Chaucer's Prologue at the request of Samuel Pepys, was like most of Dryden's Christian poems, tame. The last "character" of all was one of the best. The ten lines on the Rhodian militia in *Cymon and Iphigenia* have as much satiric meat in them as have any ten lines in Dryden or in English. Their cadences, which are well under the poet's control, express burly, amused contempt:

> The country rings around with loud alarms,
> And raw in fields the rude militia swarms;
> Mouths without hands; maintained at vast expense;
> In peace a charge, in war a weak defence;
> Stout once a month they march, a blustering band,
> And ever, but in times of need, at hand.
> This was the morn when, issuing on the guard,

Drawn up in rank and file they stood prepared
Of seeming arms to make a short essay,
Then hasten to be drunk, the business of the day.

Dryden's ratiocinative pulse beats with a longer, slower stroke, but it is never feeble. "Reasoning!" exclaimed Bayes in the *Rehearsal*, "I gad; I love reasoning in verse." Tom Brown, offering once to explain who Dryden was at all, said "He is that accomplished person, who loves reasoning so much in verse, and hath got a knack of writing it smoothly." "The favourite exercise of his mind was ratiocination," thought Dr. Johnson. "When once he had engaged himself in disputation, thoughts flowed in on either side; he was now no longer at a loss; he had always objections and solutions at command." That is to say, Dr. Johnson implied, Dryden may often have looked about him for images which he could not find, but he never needed to scour for reasons or inferences. "They cannot be good poets," said Dryden himself, "who are not accustomed to argue well." Dryden was fascinated by the technical problems involved in making rhyme and reason lie down together. He was a versifier of propositions rather than a philosopher resorting to poetry, or even a poet speculating. No mind mastered him as Epicurus mastered Lucretius, or even, to come much farther down, as Bolingbroke mastered Pope. His imagination did not deeply explore as Dante's and Milton's explored. He was not curious, and absorbed, and quaintly condensed, like Sir John Davies, nor had he a trace of Cowper's neighborly discursiveness. His two chief ratiocinative poems dealt with the most transitory of topics, creeds and ecclesiastical expedients. The *Religio Laici* and *The Hind and the Panther* never have been and never will be read by many persons. The first attracted only slight attention even when it was timely; the second was never timely, for it had its thunder stolen by James's Declaration of Indulgence before it was printed, and within a year it was nullified in most respects by the Revolution. Here, as elsewhere in Dryden, it is not his ideas but his way of thinking that is important. From such a point of view the *Religio Laici* is a truly engaging poem; *The Hind and the Panther* is a great representative work; and Gray's "thoughts that breathe and words that burn" is not an impossible phrase.

It is hardly worth while to become exercised over the question whether Dryden's ratiocinative poems are really poems. It has been categorically denied that argument has any place in poetry. Whatever the truth may be *in vacuo*, it remains that Dryden has achieved an effect of his own which has been achieved by no other writer, in prose or in verse. Congreve was off the scent when he wrote: "Take his verses and divest them of their rhyme, disjoint them in their numbers, transpose their expressions, make what arrangement and disposition you please of his words, yet shall there eternally be poetry, and something which will be found incapable of being resolved into absolute prose." Horace's test is not to be applied to Dryden. It is precisely in his rhymes, his numbers, his expressions, his arrangements, and his dispositions that Dryden has been an artist. The triumph is a fragile one; the spell would be broken by translation; *The Hind and the Panther* in French would almost certainly be dull; but while the spell lasts it is real. Dryden's devices were numerous, his ratiocinative technique was complex. Tom Brown thought arguing in verse to be a simple matter. "To do this," he said, "there is no need of brain, 'tis but scanning right; the labor is in the finger, not in the head." Brown, quite naturally, was not interested in the subtleties which labor of this kind involves. It may not be too fantastic to say that Dryden's brains were in his fingers, that he thought in meter. Alliteration in him binds words, phrases, lines, couplets, paragraphs together. Rhyme, by holding the reader's mind, as Taine says, "on the stretch," gives to the poet's statements a strange factitious potency, so that they satisfy the curiosity of the ear rather than that of the mind. Alexandrines close discussions as if forever. *Enjambement* allows the imagination leisure to thread its way through meditative passages. Series of well-chosen adjectives advance a proposition with steady strides:

> Not that tradition's parts are useless here,
> When general, old, disinterested and clear.

Metaphors unobtrusively employed clinch a point before the reader is aware of the advantage which is being taken of him:

> This was the fruit the private spirit brought,
> Occasioned by great zeal and little thought.
> While crowds unlearned, with rude devotion warm,
> About the sacred viands buzz and swarm.

Exclamations draw many meanings briskly together. Queries serve for transitions. Catchwords and connectives like "then," "granting that," "True, but—," "thus far," "'tis true," keep the game of ratiocination animated and going. Aphorisms set off arguments. Repetition and refrain speak proselyting sincerity or else confessional ecstasy. Abrupt apostrophes seem to denote overwhelming convictions suddenly arrived at. Passages of limpid and beautiful statement appear the issues of a serenely composed conscience. Angry, headlong digressions subside into mellow confessions of faith.

Neither the *Religio Laici* nor *The Hind and the Panther* can be exhibited with any success in fragments. The strength of the two lies in what De Quincey called their "sequaciousness." They must be known in all their ins and outs before they can begin to impress a stranger with the variety yet continuity of their pattern. If some passage must be quoted, one should be lifted from a section lying somewhere between those extremes which are "nearest prose" and those which are most impassioned. This extract from the Hind's address to the Panther on the subject of the Apostolic Succession contains a fair share of Dryden's ratiocinative accents:

> 'Tis said with ease, but never can be proved,
> The Church her old foundations has removed,
> And built new doctrines on unstable sands:
> Judge that, ye winds and rains; you proved her,
>   yet she stands.
> Those ancient doctrines, charged on her for new,
> Shew when, and how, and from what hands they grew.

We claim no power, when heresies grow bold,
To coin new faith, but still declare the old.
How else could that obscene disease be purged,
When controverted texts are vainly urged?
To prove tradition new, there's somewhat more
Required than saying: " 'Twas not used before."
Those monumental arms are never stirred,
Till schism or heresy call down Goliah's sword.

Thus what you call corruptions are in truth
The first plantations of the gospel's youth;
Old standard faith; but cast your eyes again,
And view those errors which new sects maintain,
Or which of old disturbed the Church's peaceful reign:
And we can point each period of the time,
When they began, and who begot the crime;
Can calculate how long the eclipse endured,
Who interposed, what digits were obscured:
Of all which are already passed away,
We know the rise, the progress and decay.

Despair at our foundations then to strike,
Till you can prove your faith apostolic;
A limpid stream drawn from the native source;
Succession lawful in a lineal course.
Prove any Church, opposed to this our head,
So one, so pure, so unconfinedly spread,
Under one chief of the spiritual State,
The members all combined, and all subordinate.
Shew such a seamless coat, from schism so free,
In no communion joined with heresy.
If such a one you find, let truth prevail;
Till when, your weights will in the balance fail;
A Church unprincipled kicks up the scale.

VI

THE LYRIC POET

Dryden owes his excellence as a lyric poet to his abounding metrical energy. The impetuous mind and the scrupulous ear which Wordsworth admired nourished a singing voice that always was powerful and sometimes was mellow or sweet. The songs, the operas, and the odes of Dryden are remarkable first of all for their *élan*.

The seventeenth century was an age of song. Composers like John Dowland, Thomas Campion, William and Henry Lawes, Nicholas Laniere, John Wilson, Charles Coleman, William Webb, John Gamble, and the Purcells, together with publishers like John and Henry Playford, to mingle great with small, maintained a long and beautiful tradition of "ayres;" miscellanies and "drolleries," with their fondness for reckless, rollicking tavern tunes, urged on a swelling stream of popular melody; while poets, from Ben Jonson to Tom D'Urfey, never left off trifling with measured catches high or low. But there were changes from generation to generation. The poets of the Restoration sang in a different key from that of the Jacobeans; and it was generally believed that there had been a falling off.

"Soft words, with nothing in them, make a song," wrote Waller to Creech. It was charged that France had corrupted English song with her Damons and Strephons, her "Chlorisses and Phylisses," and that the dances with which she was supposed to have vulgarized the drama and the opera had introduced notes of triviality and irresponsibility into all lyric poetry.   Dryden for one was fond of dances, and ran them into his plays whenever there was an excuse.   In *Marriage à la Mode* Melantha and Palamede quote two pieces from Molière's ballet in *Le Bourgeois Gentilhomme*.   Voiture's airy nothings also had their day in England.   The second song in Dryden's *Sir Martin Mar-All*, beginning,

> Blind love, to this hour,
> Had never, like me, a slave under his power.
> Then blest be the dart
> That he threw at my heart,
> For nothing can prove
> A joy so great as to be wounded with love,

was adapted from Voiture:

> L'Amour sous sa loy
> N'a jamais eu d'amant plus heureux que moy;
> Benit soit son flambeau,
> Son carquois, son bandeau,
> Je suis amoreux,
> Et le ciel ne voit point d'amant plus heureux.

But the most serious charge against France was brought against her music.

Music had an important place in the education of gentlemen and poets throughout the Europe of the sixteenth and seventeenth centuries.   A larger pro-

portion of trained minds than before or since then
claimed fairly intimate acquaintance with musical
technique. The studies of philosophers as well as
poets included ecclesiastical and secular song, the
uses made of it being various, of course. Hobbes,
says Aubrey, "had alwayes bookes of prick-song
lyeing on his Table:—e. g. of H. Lawes &c. *Songs*—
which at night, when he was abed, and the dores
made fast, & was sure nobody heard him, he sang
aloud, (not that he had a very good voice) but to
cleare his pipes: he did beleeve it did his Lunges good,
and conduced much to prolong his life." Poets drew
much of their best knowledge and inspiration from
musicians, so that any alteration in musical modes
was certain to affect the styles of verse. The seventeenth century in England was a century of seculari-
zation, first under Italian and then under French influences. In former times, when music had been
bound to the service of the church, clear-cut rhythms
had been avoided as recalling too much the motions of the body in the dance, and composers of madrigals had been confined to the learned contrivances of
counterpoint. John Dowland, the Oxford and Cambridge lutanist, Thomas Campion, magical both as
poet and as composer, and Henry Lawes, the friend
of all good versifiers, three seventeenth century native geniuses who were also disciples of Italy, introduced in succession new and individual song rhythms
which were so compelling that by the time of the
Restoration there had come into being an excellent
body of sweet and simple secular airs with just
enough strains of the older, more intricate harmonies

lingering in them to remind of the golden age. Even
in church and chamber music there had been a tendency to substitute songs for madrigals and dance-
tunes for choral measures. The Restoration saw
complete and rapid changes. Charles II, who insisted on easy rhythms at his devotions to which he
could beat time with his hand, sent his choir-boys
to France to school, and encouraged his musicians
to replace the lute and the viol with the guitar and
the violin. The violin or fiddle, which John Playford
called "a cheerful and sprightly instrument," was
as old as the Anglo-Saxons, but it had been used
before only for dancing, not in the church or the
chamber. It was the rhythm of the dance that now
pervaded theater and chapel and all the world of
lyric poetry. There was hearty objection to the new
mode. Playford began the preface to his *Musick's
Delight on the Cithera* (1666) with the remark: "It
is observed that of late years all solemn and grave
musick is much laid aside, being esteemed too heavy
and dull for the light heels and brains of this nimble
and wanton age." The preface to the sixth edition
of the same author's *Skill of Musick* in 1672 continued
the complaint: "Musick in this age . . . is in low
esteem with the generality of people. Our late and
solemn Musick, both Vocal and Instrumental, is now
justled out of Esteem by the new Corants and Jigs
of Foreigners, to the Grief of all sober and judicious
understanders of that formerly solid and good Musick." John Norris of Bemerton, in the preface to
his *Poems* (1687), declared that music like poetry
had degenerated "from grave, majestic, solemn

strains . . . where beauty and strength go hand in hand. 'Tis now for the most part dwindled down to light, frothy stuff." Henry Purcell objected on the whole with greater effect than the others against what he called "the levity and balladry of our neighbours;" for his attack upon French opera in favor of Italian opera was in the end entirely successful. Yet even Purcell was well aware that French music had "somewhat more of gayety and Fashion" than any other, and he was not so insensible to current demands as to compose songs for the stage that were lacking in Gallic vivacity. Dryden, who had secured the services of a French musician, Grabut, for his opera *Albion and Albanius* in 1685, was considered in 1690 a convert to "the English school" when in the dedication of *Amphitryon* he wrote of "Mr. Purcell, in whose person we have at length found an Englishman, equal with the best abroad. At least my opinion of him has been such, since his happy and judicious performances in the late opera (*The Prophetess*), and the experience I have had of him in the setting my three songs for this 'Amphitryon.'" Before Purcell died in 1695 he had not only written the accompaniment for an opera of Dryden's, *King Arthur*, but he had set to music the songs from *Cleomenes, The Indian Emperor*, an adaptation of the *Indian Queen, Aureng-Zebe, Œdipus, The Spanish Friar, Tyrannic Love*, and *The Tempest;* so that Dryden had the full advantage of an association with this powerful composer who, as Motteux put it in the first number of his *Gentleman's Journal* in 1692, joined "to the delicacy and beauty of the Italian way, the graces and gayety of the French."

It is doubtful whether the potency of the musical personalities of Purcell and contemporary composers was in general a good or a bad influence on Restoration lyric style. It is at least thinkable that as the new rhythms asserted themselves more powerfully the writers who supplied words for songs were somehow the losers in independence and originality. There was complaint at the end of the century that the obvious, almost jingling music from France had won the field and was domineering over poetry. Charles Gildon in his *Laws of Poetry* (1721) pointed to a degeneration in song, attributing it to "the slavish care or complaisance of the writers, to make their words to the goust of the composer, or musician: being obliged often to sacrifice their sense to certain sounding words, and feminine rhymes, and the like; because they seem most adapted to furnish the composer with such cadences which most easily slide into their modern way of composition." Others besides Gildon felt with justice that genius was being ironed out of lyric verse; song was becoming singsong. Relations between poets and composers were now the reverse of what they had been in the time of Henry Lawes. Lawes had been content to subordinate his music to the words; for him the poetry was the thing. If it seemed difficult at the first glance to adapt a given passage to music, the difficulty was after all the composer's, and the blame for infelicities must accrue to him. "Our English seems a little clogged with consonants," he wrote in the preface to the first book of *Ayres and Dialogues* (1653), "but that's much the composer's fault, who, by judicious setting, and right tuning the words, may make it smooth enough." Milton was acknowledging the generous, pliant technique of his friend in the sonnet of 1646:

> Harry, whose tuneful and well-measured song
> First taught our English music how to span
> Words with just note and accent, not to scan
> With Midas' ears, committing short and long;
> Thy worth and skill exempts thee from the throng,
> With praise enough for Envy to look wan;
> To after age thou shalt be writ the man
> That with smooth air could humour best our tongue.

It was the delicacy and justness of Lawes that won him the affection of the most gifted lyrists of the mid-century; it will always be remembered of him that he loved poetry too well to profane the intricate tendernesses of songs like Herrick's to the daffodils.

Whatever conditions imposed themselves upon English song in the Restoration, Dryden for his own part was inclined to welcome swift, simple, straight-on rhythms, and he was destined to become master of the lyric field solely by virtue of his speed. His range of vowels was narrow; his voice was seldom round or deep, limiting itself somewhat monotonously to thin soprano sounds. Nor was the scope of his sympathies wide; a number of contemporaries sang more human songs. Rochester's drinking-pieces, like that which begins,

> Vulcan, contrive me such a cup
> As Nestor used of old,

Sedley's love-lines,

> Not, Celia, that I juster am,
> Or better than the rest,

And Dorset's playful flatteries,

> To all you ladies now at land,
> We men at sea indite,

are likely to touch nerves which Dryden leaves quiet.
Congreve's diamond-bright cynicism and Prior's
ultimate social grace exist in worlds farremoved from
his own. It was sheer lyrical gusto and momentum
that carried Dryden forward, that drew to him the
attention of the Playfords as they published their
new collections, that made the editor of the *Westminster Drolleries* of 1671 and 1672 hasten to include
his six best songs to date in those "choice" volumes.

Dryden's first song had something of the older
Caroline manner in that its stanzas were inclined to
be tangled and reflective. It was sung in the *Indian
Emperor*, and began:

> Ah fading joy, how quickly art thou past!
> Yet we thy ruin haste.
> As if the cares of human life were few,
> We seek out new:
> And follow fate that does too fast pursue.

Dryden passed swiftly from this to a more modern,
more breathless world of song, a world where he fell
at once, in *An Evening's Love*, into the dactylic swing
that was to win him his way into the irrepressible
Drolleries:

After the pangs of a desperate lover,
    When day and night I have sighed all in vain,
Ah what a pleasure it is to discover,
    In her eyes pity, who causes my pain.

Another song in *An Evening's Love* ran more lightly yet; it was marked by the anapestic lilt which on the whole is Dryden's happiest discovery:

Calm was the even, and clear was the sky,
    And the new-budding flowers did spring,
When all alone went Amyntas and I
    To hear the sweet nightingale sing.
I sate, and he laid him down by me,
    But scarcely his breath he could draw;
For when with a fear, he began to draw near,
    He was dashed with "A ha ha ha ha!"

This lilt is heard in Dryden as many as fifteen times, being at its best in *Marriage à la Mode:*

Why should a foolish marriage vow,
    Which long ago was made,
Oblige us to each other now,
    When passion is decayed?
We loved, and we loved, as long as we could,
    Till our love was loved out in us both;
But our marriage is dead, when the pleasure is fled;
    'Twas pleasure first made it an oath.

If I have pleasures for a friend,
    And farther love in store,
What wrong has he whose joys did end,
    And who could give no more?
'Tis a madness that he should be jealous of me,
    Or that I should bar him of another;

> For all we can gain is to give ourselves pain,
>   When neither can hinder the other;

in *Amphitryon*, where Dryden for once is very much like Prior:

> Fair Iris I love, and hourly I die,
> But not for a lip nor a languishing eye:
> She's fickle and false, and there we agree,
> For I am as false and as fickle as she.
> We neither believe what either can say;
> And, neither believing, we neither betray.
>
> 'Tis civil to swear, and say things of course;
> We mean not the taking for better or worse.
> When present, we love; when absent, agree;
> I think not of Iris, nor Iris of me.
> The legend of love no couple can find,
> So easy to part, or so equally joined;

and in *The Lady's Song*, a piece of Jacobite propaganda which represents Dryden's long, loping jingle in its most gracious and mellow aspects:

> A choir of bright beauties in spring did appear,
> To choose a May-lady to govern the year;
> All the nymphs were in white, and the shepherds in
>   green;
> The garland was given, and Phyllis was queen;
> But Phyllis refused it, and sighing did say:
> " I 'll not wear a garland while Pan is away."
>
> While Pan and fair Syrinx are fled from our shore,
> The Graces are banished, and Love is no more;
> The soft god of pleasure, that warmed our desires,
> Has broken his bow, and extinguished his fires;

And vows that himself and his mother will mourn,
Till Pan and fair Syrinx in triumph return.

Forbear your addresses, and court us no more,
For we will perform what the deity swore;
But if you dare think of deserving our charms,
Away with your sheephooks, and take to your arms:
Then laurels and myrtles your brows shall adorn,
When Pan, and his son, and fair Syrinx return.

The Lady's Song calls to mind two iambic pieces of a graver sort. The song from the *Maiden Queen* is subdued to a plane of elegy which Dryden seldom visited:

I feed a flame within, which so torments me,
That it both pains my heart, and yet contents me;
'Tis such a pleasing smart, and I so love it,
That I had rather die than once remove it.

Yet he for whom I grieve shall never know it;
My tongue does not betray, nor my eyes show it:
Not a sigh, nor a tear, my pain discloses,
But they fall silently, like dew on roses.

Thus to prevent my love from being cruel,
My heart's the sacrifice, as 'tis the fuel;
And while I suffer this, to give him quiet,
My faith rewards my love, tho' he deny it.

On his eyes will I gaze, and there delight me;
Where I conceal my love, no frown can fright me;
To be more happy, I dare not aspire;
Nor can I fall more low, mounting no higher.

The "Zambra Dance" from the first part of the *Conquest of Granada* begins with two stately stanzas that shed a soft Pindaric splendor:

Beneath a myrtle shade,
Which love for none but happy lovers made,
I slept; and straight my love before me brought
Phyllis, the object of my waking thought.
Undressed she came my flames to meet,
While love strewed flowers beneath her feet;
Flowers which, so pressed by her, became more sweet.

From the bright vision's head
A careless veil of lawn was loosely spread:
From her white temples fell her shaded hair,
Like cloudy sunshine, not too brown nor fair;
Her hands, her lips, did love inspire;
Her every grace my heart did fire;
But most her eyes, which languished with desire.

Dryden has used the iambic measure only slightly more often than the anapestic, but he has used it more variously. The two poems just quoted are far removed from the Cavalier conciseness of these lines in *An Evening's Love:*

You charmed me not with that fair face,
Tho' it was all divine:
To be another's is the grace
That makes me wish you mine;

or from the lively languor of these in the *Spanish Friar:*

Farewell, ungrateful traitor!
Farewell, my perjured swain!
Let never injured creature
Believe a man again.

> The pleasure of possessing
> Surpasses all expressing,
> But 'tis too short a blessing,
> And love too long a pain;

or from a pretty, rocking conceit like this in the *Song to a Fair Young Lady Going Out of Town in the Spring:*

> Ask not the cause, why sullen Spring
> So long delays her flowers to bear;
> Why warbling birds forget to sing,
> And winter storms invert the year.
> Chloris is gone, and fate provides
> To make it Spring where she resides.

The trochaic pieces, such as that in *Tyrannic Love*,

> Ah how sweet it is to love!
> Ah how gay is young desire!

and that in *King Arthur*, sung in honor of Britannia,

> Fairest isle, all isles excelling,
> Seat of pleasures and of loves;
> Venus here will choose her dwelling,
> And forsake her Cyprian groves,

attack the ear with characteristic spirit.

The songs of Dryden never go deeper than the painted fires of conventional Petrarchan love, but in a few cases they go wider. The "Sea-Fight" from *Amboyna*, the incantation of Tiresias in the third act of *Œdipus*, the Song of Triumph of the Britons and the Harvest Song from *King Arthur* are robust departures in theme from the pains and desires of Alexis and Damon. The incantation from

Œdipus brings substantial relief, promising cool retreats:

> Choose the darkest part o' the grove,
> Such as ghosts at noon-day love.
> Dig a trench, and dig it nigh
> Where the bones of Laius lie.

The one hymn known to be Dryden's, the translation of *Veni, Creator Spiritus* which appeared under his name in the third *Miscellany* of 1693, is in a certain sense a rounder and deeper utterance than any of the songs. The vowels are more varied and the melody has a more solid core to it; the bass of a cathedral organ rushes and rumbles under the rhythms. Scott printed two other hymns as Dryden's, the *Te Deum* and what he incorrectly called the *Hymn for St. John's Eve;* and it cannot be positively denied that most or all of the hundred and twenty hymns which made up the Catholic *Primer* of 1706 had been translated from the Latin by the great convert sometime between 1685 and 1700. The question of authorship is of no importance to poetry in connection with such of the doubtful pieces as are commonplace, like the vast majority of English hymns; but it is an important fact that real Drydenian overtones can frequently be distinguished, as here at the beginning of the *Te Deum:*

> Thee, Sovereign God, our grateful accents praise;
> We own thee Lord, and bless thy wondrous ways;
> To thee, Eternal Father, earth's whole frame,
> With loudest trumpets, sounds immortal fame.

Lord God of Hosts! for thee the heavenly powers
With sounding anthems fill the vaulted towers.
Thy cherubims thrice, Holy, Holy, Holy cry;
Thrice, Holy, all the Seraphims reply,
And thrice returning echoes endless songs supply.

Dryden was a born writer of hymns, though the hymns he wrote were seldom labelled as such. Praise with him was as instintcive as satire; he delighted as much in glorious openings and surging, upgathered invocations as in contemptuous "characters." The King's prayer in *Annus Mirabilis*, Achitophel's first words to Absalom, the beginning of the *Lucretius*, the beginning of the *Georgics*, and the prayers in *Palamon and Arcite* are his most godlike pleas. "Landor once said to me," wrote Henry Crabb Robinson in his *Diary* for January 6, 1842, "Nothing was ever written in hymn equal to the beginning of Dryden's *Religio Laici*,—the first eleven lines."

Dim as the borrowed beams of moon and stars
To lonely, weary, wandering travellers,
Is Reason to the soul; and, as on high
Those rolling fires discover but the sky,
Not light us here, so Reason's glimmering ray
Was lent, not to assure our doubtful way,
But guide us upward to a better day.
And as those nightly tapers disappear
When day's bright lord ascends our hemisphere;
So pale grows Reason at Religion's sight;
So dies, and so dissolves in supernatural light.

Dryden's operas, as poetry, are unfortunate. Here for once, partly from apathy towards a form of

writing which the prologues and epilogues show did
not command his respect, partly from a sense of
obligation or dependence, he capitulated to the composer; thinking to produce new musical effects with
his pen, he succeeded in bringing forth what was
neither poetry nor music. The result in each of
two cases, at least, was what St. Evremond defined
any opera to be, "an odd medley of poetry and
music wherein the poet and the musician, equally
confined one by the other, take a world of pain to
compose a wretched performance." The *State of Innocence*, which was never performed but which was
first published as "an opera" probably in 1677, is
not one of the two cases. It is an independent poem
of some originality and splendor. *Albion and Albanius* (1685), however, and its sequel *King Arthur*
(1691) deserve a fair share of St. Evremond's disdain. Dryden has taken the trouble in connection
with them to describe his labors as a poet-musician.
In the preface to *Albion and Albanius* he says he
has been at pains to "make words so smooth, and
numbers so harmonious, that they shall almost set
themselves." In writing an opera a poet must have
so sensitive an ear "that the discord of sounds in
words shall as much offend him as a seventh in
music would a good composer." "The chief secret
is the choice of words"; the words are "to be varied
according to the nature of the subject." The "song-
ish part" and the chorus call for "harmonious sweetness," with "softness and variety of numbers," but
the recitative demands "a more masculine beauty."
The superiority of Italian over French or English

as a musical language is heavily stressed; and it is
plain that throughout the opera Dryden has aimed
at an Italian "softness" through the use of feminine
rhymes and disyllabic coinages similar to those which
were to mark the *Virgil*. The work as a whole is
inane, and often it is doggerel; it is at best a welter
of jingling trimeters and tetrameters, tail-rhyme
stanzas, heroic couplets, and tawdry Pindaric passages. One song by the Nereids in Act III begins
better than it ends:

> From the low palace of old father Ocean,
> Come we in pity your cares to deplore;
> Sea-racing dolphins are trained for our motion,
> Moony tides swelling to roll us ashore.
>
> Every nymph of the flood, her tresses rending,
> Throws off her armlet of pearl in the main;
> Neptune in anguish his charge unattending,
> Vessels are foundering, and vows are in vain.

King Arthur is in blank verse, with many departures
into song and dance. The dedication praises Purcell and admits that the verse has in certain cases
been allowed to suffer for the composer's sake. "My
art on this occasion," says Dryden, "ought to be
subservient to his." "A judicious audience will
easily distinguish betwixt the songs wherein I have
complied with him, and those in which I have followed the rules of poetry, in the sound and cadence
of the words." The "freezing scene" in the third
act does neither the poet nor the composer any
credit; the effect of shivering, even if legitimate, is
not exactly happy. The best songs are those in

which, as Dryden says, he has "followed the rules
of poetry": those like "Fairest isle, all isles excel-
ling," the "Harvest Home," and the song of the
nymphs before Arthur:

> In vain are our graces,
>   In vain are our eyes,
>   If love you despise;
> When age furrows faces,
>   'Tis time to be wise.
> Then use the short blessing,
> That flies in possessing:
> No joys are above
>   The pleasures of love.

The short "Secular Masque" which Dryden wrote
for a revival of Fletcher's *Pilgrim* in 1700 is the least
objectionable of the pieces which he designed to accompany stage music. The masque celebrates the
opening of a new century. Janus, Chronos, and
Momus hold a sprightly review of the century just
past and come to the conclusion that the times
have been bad. Diana, representing the court of
James I, is the first to pass in review, singing as she
goes a hunting song which long remained popular:

> With horns and with hounds I waken the day,
> And hie to my woodland walks away;
> I tuck up my robe, and am buskined soon,
> And tie to my forehead a wexing moon.
> I course the fleet stag, unkennel the fox,
> And chase the wild goats o'er summits of rocks;
> With shouting and hooting we pierce thro' the sky,
> And Echo turns hunter, and doubles the cry.

The three gods agree with her of the silver bow that

> Then our age was in its prime,
> Free from rage, and free from crime;
> A very merry, dancing, drinking,
> Laughing, quaffing, and unthinking time.

Mars next thunders in and recalls the wars of Charles I. But Momus is a pacifist:

> Thy sword within the scabbard keep,
>   And let mankind agree;
> Better the world were fast asleep,
>   Than kept awake by thee.
> The fools are only thinner,
>   With all our cost and care;
> But neither side a winner,
>   For things are as they were.

Venus now appears to celebrate the softer conquests of Charles II and James II. But she also is found wanting, and so Dryden's poem ends with a sweeping dismissal of three Stuart generations:

> All, all of a piece throughout;
> Thy chase had a beast in view;
> Thy wars brought nothing about;
> Thy lovers were all untrue.
> 'Tis well an old age is out,
> And time to begin a new.

The force which drove Dryden forward through the somewhat foreign waters of song plunged him into a native ocean in the ode. His greatest lyrics are odes. He was constitutionally adapted to a form of exalted utterance which progressed by the alternate accumu-

lating and discharging of metrical energy. The study
of his utterances in this kind begins not with his
first formal ode, but with the first appearance of
swells in the stream of his heroic verse. That first appearance, as has been suggested before, is in the heroic
plays, where the thump and rattle of the couplets
is relieved from time to time by towering speeches
like that of Almanzor to Lyndaraxa.[1] The *State of
Innocence* is virtually one protracted ode. Partly
in consequence of a new and close acquaintance with
Milton's blank verse, partly as the fruit of his experience among rhythms, Dryden here has swollen
his stream and learned to compose with a powerful,
steady pulse. Milton's paragraphing, whether or
not it has been an important inspiration, is after all
Dryden's greatest example in this instance, though
Milton's metrical progression is little like that of his
junior. Milton relies chiefly upon *enjambement* to
give roll to his verse; as can best be seen for the
present purpose in the *Vacation Exercise* of 1628,
which is in heroic couplets. The bond of the couplets
is broken only once, and then by drawing the sense
variously from one line into another. The poet is
addressing his native language:

> Yet I had rather, if I were to choose,
> Thy service in some graver subject use,
> Such as may make thee search thy coffers round,
> Before thou clothe my fancy in fit sound.
> Such where the deep transported mind may soar
> Above the wheeling poles, and at Heaven's door
> Look in, and see each blissful Deity

[1] See page 113.

How he before the thunderous throne doth lie,
Listening to what unshorn Apollo sings
To the touch of golden wires, while Hebe brings
Immortal nectar to her kingly sire;
Then, passing through the spheres of watchful fire,
And misty regions of wide air next under,
And hills of snow and lofts of piléd thunder,
May tell at length how green-eyed Neptune raves,
In heaven's defiance mustering all his waves;
Then sing of secret things that came to pass
When beldam Nature in her cradle was;
And last of Kings and Queens and Heroes old,
Such as the wise Demodocus once told
In solemn songs at King Alcinous' feast,
While sad Ulysses' soul and all the rest
Are held, with his melodious harmony
In willing chains and sweet captivity.

Dryden relies less on *enjambement*, though occasionally he relies on that too, than on sheer rhythmical
enthusiasm, an enthusiasm that expresses itself first
through a series of rapidly advancing couplets and
last in a flourish of triplets or Alexandrines. One
example has been given from the *State of Innocence*.[1]
Another is the speech of Lucifer at the end of the
first scene:

On this foundation I erect my throne;
Through brazen gates, vast chaos, and old night,
I'll force my way, and upwards steer my flight;
Discover this new world, and newer Man;
Make him my footstep to mount heaven again:
Then in the clemency of upward air,
We'll scour our spots, and the dire thunder scar,

[1] See page 113.

> With all the remnants of the unlucky war,
> And once again grow bright, and once again grow fair.

Eve's account of Paradise in the third act is more
elaborately heaped:

>   Above our shady bowers
> The creeping jessamin thrusts her fragrant flowers;
> The myrtle, orange, and the blushing rose,
> With bending heaps so nigh their blooms disclose,
> Each seems to swell the flavor which the other blows;
> By these the peach, the guava and the pine,
> And, creeping 'twixt them all, the mantling vine
> Does round their trunks her purple clusters twine.

The *State of Innocence* was only a beginning. Dryden's proclivity towards the ode grew stronger each
year. His addresses, his invocations, his hymns were
only odes imbedded in heroic verse. Even a prologue might end with a lyrical rush, as for instance
that "To the Duchess on Her Return from Scotland" (1682):

> Distempered Zeal, Sedition, cankered Hate,
> No more shall vex the Church, and tear the State:
> No more shall Faction civil discords move,
> Or only discords of too tender love;
> Discord like that of Music's various parts;
> Discord that makes the harmony of hearts;
> Discord that only this dispute shall bring,
> Who best shall love the Duke and serve the King.

It is perhaps a question whether the poem on Oldham
is an elegy or is an ode. The "epiphonema" of the
Eleonora is surely an ode of a kind; and the *Virgil*
is one long Pindaric narrative.

Dryden's habit of dilating his heroic verse with Alexandrines not only grew upon him so that he indulged in flourishes when flourishes were not required, but it became contagious. Poetasters like John Hughes who lacked the impetus of Dryden learned his tricks and abused his liberties. There was something tawdry, in fact, about all but the very best of even Dryden's enthusiastic rhythms. It seemed necessary at least to Edward Bysshe in 1702, when he was compiling some "Rules for making English Verse" for his *Art of English Poetry*, to warn against license and to place restrictions on the use of long lines, allowing them only in the following cases:

1. "When they conclude an episode in an Heroic poem."
2. "When they conclude a triplet and full sense together."
3. "When they conclude the stanzas of Lyrick or Pindaric odes; Examples of which are frequently seen in Dryden and others."

Regardless of form, there always have been two distinct modes of utterance in the ode, two prevailing tempers. The Horatian temper is Attic, choice, perhaps didactic, and is stimulated by observation of human nature. The Pindaric temper is impassioned and superlative, and is inspired by the spectacle of human glory. In English poetry the Horatians have been Ben Jonson, Thomas Randolph, Marvell, Collins, Akenside, Cowper, Landor, and Wordsworth in the *Ode to Duty;* the Pindars have been Spenser,

Milton, Cowley, Dryden, Gray, Wordsworth in the *Intimations*, Coleridge, Byron, Shelley, Keats, Tennyson, and Swinburne. Cowley is included among Pindaric writers of odes more by courtesy than from desert, for he was mortally deficient in afflatus; his importance is that of a preceptor and experimentalist, not that of a creator. His *Pindaric Odes* of 1656, with the preface and the explanatory notes that accompanied them, constituted a kind of charter for a whole century of English *vers librists* who sought in the name of Pindar to become grand and free. A parallel movement in France involved a gradual departure from the rigors of Malherbe and implicated such men as Corneille, La Fontaine, Molière, and Racine; Boileau making himself the spokesman in 1693 when in his *Discours sur L'Ode* he defended Pindar against the current charges of extravagance and declared for the principle of enthusiasm in lyric poetry. Cowley considered that he was restoring one of the "lost inventions of antiquity," restoring, that is, what he believed was Pindar's art of infinitely varying his meter to correspond to the involutions of his theme. It was his notion that Pindar had been lawless in his splendor, or at the most only a law to himself; that he had proceeded without a method, now swelling, now subsiding according as his verse was moved to embrace great things or small. Cowley's *Praise of Pindar* began:

> Pindar is imitable by none,
>   The Phœnix Pindar is a vast species alone;
> Whoe'er but Dædalus with waxen wings could fly
> And neither sink too low, nor soar too high?

What could he who followed claim,
But of vain boldness the unhappy fame,
    And by his fall a sea to name?
Pindar's unnavigable song
Like a swoln flood from some steep mountain pours
    along;
The ocean meets with such a voice
From his enlargéd mouth, as drowns the ocean's noise.

So Pindar does new words and figures roll
Down his impetuous dithyrambic tide,
    Which in no channel deigns to abide,
    Which neither banks nor dykes control;
Whether the immortal gods he sings
    In a no less immortal strain,
Or the great acts of God-descended kings,
Who in his numbers still survive and reign;
    Each rich embroidered line
    Which their triumphant brows around
    By his sacred hand is bound,
Does all their starry diadems outshine.

Cowley had an interesting theory that the Hebrew
poets were sharers with Pindar of the great secret.
In his preface he remarked: "The Psalms of David
(which I believe to have been in their original, to
the Hebrews of his time . . . the most exalted pieces
of poesy) are a great example of what I have said."
And one of his *Pindaric Odes* was a version of
Isaiah xxxiv. "The manner of the Prophets' writing," he observed in a note, "especially of Isaiah,
seems to me very like that of Pindar; they pass from
one thing to another with almost Invisible con-

nections, and are full of words and expressions of the highest and boldest flights of Poetry." Gildon followed Cowley in his *Laws of Poetry* (1721) when he cited among the great odes of the world the psalm that begins, "By the waters of Babylon we sat down and wept, when we remembered thee, O Sion."

Congreve wrote a *Discourse on the Pindarique Ode* in 1706 to prove that Cowley had violated the first law of Pindar when he discarded shape; he explained the rigid strophic structure of the Greek ode and deplored the "rumbling and grating" papers of verses with which Cowley's loose example had loaded the England of the past half century. He was not the first to make this point; Edward Phillips in the preface to his *Theatrum Poetarum* (1675) had observed that English Pindaric writers seemed ignorant of the strophe, antistrophe, and epode, and that their work seemed rather on the order of the choruses of Æschylus; while Ben Jonson had left in his ode on Cary and Morison a perfect specimen of Pindar's form. But Congreve was the first conspicuous critic of Cowleian *vers libre*, and it was not until after him that Akenside and Gray and Gilbert West demonstrated on a fairly extensive scale what could be done with strophe and antistrophe in a Northern tongue. Yet the difference between Cowley and Gray was far more than the difference between lawless verse and strophic verse. Cowley's crime had been not so much against Pindar as against poetry; he had written and taught others to write what metrically was nonsense. The alternation of long with short lines in itself does not of necessity

make for grandeur; often, as Scott suggests, the effect
of a Restoration ode was no different rhythmically
from that of the inscription on a tombstone. Cowley
was out of his depth in the company of Pindar; he was
constituted for wit, for "the familiar and the festive,"
as Dr. Johnson said, but not for magnificence. The
passage which has been quoted from the *Praise of
Pindar* is not equalled by him elsewhere; most of
the time he is writing like this, at the conclusion of
The Muse:

> And sure we may
> The same too of the present say,
> If past and future times do thee obey.
> Thou stop'st this current, and does make
> This running river settle like a lake;
> Thy certain hand holds fast this slippery snake;
> The fruit which does so quickly waste,
> Man scarce can see it, much less taste,
> Thou comfitest in sweets to make it last.
> This shining piece of ice,
> Which melts so soon away
> With the sun's ray,
> Thy verse does solidate and crystallize,
> Till it a lasting mirror be!
> Nay, thy immortal rhyme
> Makes this one short point of time
> To fill up half the orb of round eternity.

The trouble here is simply that there are no "numbers"; the stanza is not organic metrically; there are
no involutions which the ear follows with the kind of
suspense with which it follows, for instance, an intricate passage in music. Cowley has thought to fore-

stall such an objection in the general preface to his folio of 1656. "The numbers are various and irregular," he says, "and sometimes (especially some of the long ones) seem harsh and uncouth, if the just measures and cadences be not observed in the pronunciation. So that almost all their sweetness and numerosity (which is to be found, if I mistake not, in the roughest, if rightly repeated) lies in a manner wholly at the mercy of the reader." But the most merciful and best of readers must fail to make certain of the odes of Cowley sound like poetry. Cowley had not a dependable ear.

It was Dryden's "excellent ear" which saved the Pindaric ode for Gray. Dryden diagnosed the ills of contemporary Pindarism with lofty precision in the preface to *Sylvæ* in 1685. "Somewhat of the purity of English, somewhat of more equal thoughts, somewhat of sweetness in the numbers, in one word, somewhat of a finer turn and more lyrical verse is yet wanting. . . . In imitating [Pindar] our numbers should, for the most part, be lyrical . . . the ear must preside, and direct the judgment to the choice of numbers: without the nicety of this, the harmony of Pindaric verse can never be complete; the cadency of one line must be a rule to that of the next; and the sound of the former must slide gently into that which follows, without leaping from one extreme into another. It must be done like the shadowings of a picture, which fall by degrees into a darker colour." This is by far his most significant statement on the ode; it is not only an accurate analysis of the errors of others; it is an intimation of his own ideal, and incidentally it embodied a forecast of his best accomplishment. For his peculiar contribution was none other than the shading and the "finer turn" of which he speaks here. He let his ear preside; he let his cadences rule and determine one another in the interests of an integral harmony. He placed his words where they would neither jar nor remain inert, but flow. His best Pindaric passages are streams of words delicately and musically disposed.

The earliest example of all, the "Zambra Dance" [1] from the *Conquest of Granada*, is fine but slight. The first ambitious effort is the translation of the twenty-ninth ode of the third book of Horace in *Sylvæ*. "One ode," explains Dryden in the preface, "which infinitely pleased me in the reading, I have attempted to translate in Pindaric verse. . . . I have taken some pains to make it my master-piece in English: for which reason I took this kind of verse, which allows more latitude than any other." The combination of Horatian felicity with Pindaric latitude is the happier for Dryden's excellent understanding of the bearings of each. Creech's *Horace*, published the previous year with a dedication to Dryden, had shown, as certain pieces from Horace in the first *Miscellany* (1684) had shown, what might be done in the way of running the Stoic odes into elaborate stanzaic molds; but Creech was most of the time perilously near prose. His version of the present poem, not particularly spirited but solid and just, may have suggested further possibilities to Dryden, who indeed did appropriate his predecessor's best

[1] See page 230.

phrases. As for the language of Horace, says Dryden, "there is nothing so delicately turned in all the Roman language. There appears in every part of his diction . . . a kind of noble and bold purity. . . . There is a secret happiness which attends his choice, which in Petronius is called *curiosa felicitas*." As for his own versification, which of course is anarchy compared with Horace, he hopes that it will help to convey the Roman's "briskness, his jollity, and his good humour." The result is as nice as anything in Dryden. The ear has presided, and the shading is almost without flaw. Only five lines disappoint; four of these are Alexandrines (lines 33, 38, 59, 64) and one is a fourteener (line 39). Dryden has not learned as yet in this least rigid of all forms to dispose his long lines so well that none of them will halt the movement and kill the stanza; in the present instance it is significant that all of the five dead lines are attempts at reproducing effects of Nature. The first, second, third, fourth, sixth, eighth, ninth, and tenth stanzas are unexceptionable. The poem begins with a passage of remarkable carrying power; something somewhere seems to be beating excellent time:

> Descended of an ancient line,
>   That long the Tuscan scepter swayed,
> Make haste to meet the generous wine,
>   Whose piercing is for thee delayed:
> The rosy wreath is ready made,
>   And artful hands prepare
> The fragrant Syrian oil, that shall perfume thy hair.

The eighth stanza is in a way the most distinct and final writing that Dryden did:

Happy the man, and happy he alone,
  He, who can call today his own;
  He who, secure within, can say:
"Tomorrow, do thy worst, for I have lived today.
  Be fair, or foul, or rain, or shine,
The joys I have possessed, in spite of fate, are mine.
  Not Heav'n itself upon the past has power;
But what has been has been, and I have had my hour."

This is brisk yet liquid. The current of the stream
widens and accelerates swiftly, but there is no leaping or foaming. The "cadency" of each line noiselessly transmits energy to the next. Alliteration
helps to preserve an equable flow, while varied vowels heighten the murmur. And the monosyllables
now have their revenge; for fifty-nine words of the
sixty-eight are monosyllables. The next Pindaric
ode of Dryden's, the *Threnodia Augustalis*, is rambling and arbitrary in its rhythms; there is little or
no momentum. A few passages, however, shine in
isolation. At the news that Charles had rallied and
might live, says Dryden,

Men met each other with erected look,
The steps were higher that they took,
Friends to congratulate their friends made haste,
And long-inveterate foes saluted as they passed.

There is a pride of pace in these lines that suits the
sense. When Charles was restored from France,
continues Dryden,

The officious Muses came along,
A gay harmonious choir, like angels ever young;
(The Muse that mourns him now his happy triumph sung.)

Even they could thrive in his auspicious reign;
    And such a plenteous crop they bore
Of purest and well-winnowed grain
    As Britain never knew before.
Though little was their hire, and light their gain,
Yet somewhat to their share he threw;
Fed from his hand, they sung and flew,
Like birds of Paradise, that lived on morning dew.

The ode *To the Pious Memory of the Accomplished Young Lady, Mrs. Anne Killigrew*, written in the same year with the *Horace* and the *Threnodia*, while it is sadly uneven is yet the most triumphant of the three. For although its second, third, fifth, sixth, seventh, eighth, and ninth stanzas are equal at the most only to Cowley and are indeed a good deal like him, the first, fourth, and tenth are emancipated and impetuous. The first stanza, which Dr. Johnson considered the highest point in English lyric poetry, rolls its majestic length without discord or hitch; its music is the profoundest and longest-sustained in Dryden, and its grammar is regal. The fourth stanza hurls itself with violent alliteration down the steep channel which it describes:

O gracious God! how far have we
Profaned thy heavenly gift of poesy!
Made prostitute and profligate the Muse,
Debased to each obscene and impious use,
Whose harmony was first ordained above
For tongues of angels and for hymns of love!
O wretched we! why were we hurried down
    This lubric and adulterate age,

(Nay, added fat pollutions of our own,)
   To increase the steaming ordures of the stage?
What can we say to excuse our second fall?
Let this thy vestal, Heaven, atone for all.
Her Arethusian stream remains unsoiled,
Unmixed with foreign filth, and undefiled;
Her wit was more than man, her innocence a child!

The last stanza is a musical and grammatical triumph like the first, but one of a lesser magnitude. The triplet in the middle of it is something of an obstruction, and three near-conceits give the effect of a melody scraped thin. The *Ode on the Death of Mr. Henry Purcell* (1696) also suffers from conceits, being nowhere remarkable save perhaps in the first stanza, which aims at prettiness:

Mark how the lark and linnet sing;
         With rival notes
   They strain their warbling throats
      To welcome in the spring.
      But in the close of night,
When Philomel begins her heavenly lay,
      They cease their mutual spite,
      Drink in her music with delight,
And listening and silent, and silent and listening, and
      listening and silent obey.

It seems now to have been almost inevitable that there should grow up at the end of the seventeenth century a custom of celebrating St. Cecilia's Day with poems set to music; so close were poets and musicians together, and so worshipful of music in that age were men as different from one another as Milton, Cowley, Waller, Marvell, and Dryden. Dur-

ing half a century before 1683, when the first Feast
was celebrated, Orpheus and Amphion had been
among the mythological personages most affectionately cultivated in English verse; and a whole splendid
language had been constructed for the praise of the
powers of harmony. Dryden's *Song for St. Cecilia's
Day* in 1687 and his *Alexander's Feast* in 1697 were
the most distinguished performances of the century,
each making fashionable a new and sensational
method. There was something sensational and monstrous, it must be admitted, about the whole series
of music odes from Fishburn, Tate, Fletcher, and
Oldham before Dryden to Bonnell Thornton in the
eighteenth century, whose burlesque ode called into
service of sound and fury such implements as salt-
boxes, marrow-bones, and hurdy-gurdies. There was
very little excellent poetry on the whole laid at the
feet of St. Cecilia, and there was a deal of cheap
program-music offered to her ears, even by Purcell
and Händel. But the music had always a saving
vigor; sixty voices and twenty-five instruments, including violins, trumpets, drums, hautboys, flutes,
and bassoons, could make amends of a kind for the
paltriest verse. Dryden's odes, if artificial and
sensational, were the last thing from paltry; they are
among the most amazing *tours de force* in English
poetry.

The *Song* of 1687 established a new kind of imitative harmony in which verse became for practical
purposes an orchestra, the poet drawing upon his
vowels and his cadences as a conductor draws upon
his players. Dryden had toyed with somewhat

similar devices before. The song from the *Indian Emperor* had ended with the noise, he thought, of gently falling water:

> Hark, hark, the waters fall, fall, fall
> And with a murmuring sound
> Dash, dash upon the ground,
>   To gentle slumbers call.

Oldham in his Cecilia Ode of 1684 had employed some such scheme as Dryden was soon to make famous. And of course it had been almost a century since Spenser had performed his miracles of sound with verse. But Dryden now was the first to declare a wholly orchestral purpose and to rely upon a purely instrumental technique. The first stanza is a rapid overture which by a deft, tumbling kind of repetition summons and subdues to the poet's hand all the wide powers of harmony. The second stanza slips through liquid cadences and dissolves among the sweet sounds of a harp:

> What passion cannot Music raise and quell!
>   When Jubal struck the corded shell,
>   His listening brethern stood around,
>   And, wondering, on their faces fell
>   To worship that celestial sound.
> Less than a god they thought there could not dwell
>   Within the hollow of that shell
>   That spoke so sweetly and so well.
>   What passion cannot Music raise and quell!

A suggestion for this may have come from Marvell's *Music's Empire:*

> Jubal first made the wilder notes agree
> And Jubal tunéd Music's Jubilee;
> He called the echoes from their sullen cell,
> And built the organ's city, where they dwell;

although Marvell has only hinted of the possibilities that lie in the figure of Jubal and in the "-ell" rhymes; while Dryden has extracted the utmost, whether of drama or of sound, from both. The third, fourth, and fifth stanzas secure by obvious but admirable means the effects of trumpets, drums, flutes, and violins. From the sixth there ascend the smooth, softly rushing notes of the organ. The "Grand Chorus" which closes the poem is cosmically pitched:

> As from the power of sacred lays
>   The spheres began to move
> And sung the great Creator's praise
>   To all the blest above;
> So, when the last and dreadful hour
> This crumbling pageant shall devour,
> The Trumpet shall be heard on high,
> The dead shall live, the living die,
> And Music shall untune the sky.

Dryden seems always to have been moved by the idea of universal dissolution. The Hebrew notion of the Day of Judgment had reached him through the Bible and Joshua Sylvester. The Lucretian theory of disintegration had fascinated him when he was at the university if not before. He must have long been acquainted with Lucan's rehearsal of the final crumbling in the first book of the *Pharsalia*.

His concern was with the physics rather than the metaphysics of a disappearing world. Milton's *Solemn Musick* and *Comus* spoke of a mortal mould which original sin had cursed with discord but which on the last day would melt into the great harmony of the invisible spheres. Dryden is not theological; his finale is the blare of a trumpet, and his last glimpse is of painted scenery crashing down on a darkened stage. His ode on Anne Killigrew and his *Song* of 1687 end hugely and picturesquely, like Cowley's ode on *The Resurrection*, where Dryden had read:

> Till all gentle Notes be drowned
> *In the last Trumpet's dreadful sound*
> That to the spheres themselves shall silence bring,
> *Untune* the universal string. . . .
> Then shall the scattered atoms crowding come
> Back to their ancient Home.

On the third of September, 1697, Dryden informed his sons at Rome: "I am writing a song for St. Cecilia's Feast, who, you know, is the patroness of music. This is troublesome, and no way beneficial; but I could not deny the stewards of the feast, who came in a body to me to desire that kindness." There is a tradition that he became agitated during the composition of this song, which was to be the *Alexander's Feast*, and that Henry St. John, afterwards Lord Bolingbroke, found him one morning in a great tremble over it. It is likely that he worked coolly enough at all times; yet he may well have exulted when the idea for this most famous of his lyrics first took shape in his mind. The idea of casting a music ode into narrative or dramatic form was itself a new and happy one. The materials for the story of Alexander probably came harder and were only gradually pieced together in Dryden's imagination. It had been a commonplace among classical, post-classical, and Renaissance writers that ancient Greek music, especially "the lost symphonies," had strangely affected the spirits of men; Pythagoras had cured distempers and passions by the application of appropriate harmonies. Longinus had written (xxxiv): "Do not we observe that the sound of wind-instruments moves the souls of those that hear them, throws them into an ecstasy, and hurries them sometimes into a kind of fury?" Athenæus had cited Clitarchus as authority for the statement that Thais was the cause of the burning of the palace in Persepolis. Suidas, quoted by John Playford in his *Skill of Musick*, had related that Timotheus moved Alexander to arms. "But the story of Ericus musician," added Playford, "passes all, who had given forth, that by his musick he could drive men into what affections he listed; being required by Bonus King of Denmark to put his skill in practice, he with his harp or polycord lyra expressed such effectual melody and harmony in the variety of changes in several keyes, and in such excellent Fugg's and sprightly ayres, that his auditors began first to be moved with some strange passions, but ending his excellent voluntary with some choice fancy upon this Phrygian mood, the king's passions were altered, and excited to that height, that he fell

upon his most trusty friends which were near him,
and slew some of them with his fist for lack of another weapon; which our musician perceiving, ended
with the sober Dorick; the King came to himself,
and much lamented what he had done." Burton,
after Cardan the mathematician, had said in the
Anatomy of Melancholy that "Timotheus the musician compelled Alexander to skip up and down and
leave his dinner." Cowley's thirty-second note to
the first book of the *Davideis*, a veritable discourse
on the powers of harmony, had contained the remark:
"Timotheus by Musick enflamed and appeased Alexander to what degrees he pleased." Tom D'Urfey's
ode for St. Cecilia's Day in 1691 had run merrily
on through change after change of tempo, somewhat
in the manner which Dryden was to employ:

> And first the trumpet's part
> Inflames the hero's heart; . . .
> And now he thinks he's in the field,
> And now he makes the foe to yield, . . .
> The battle done, all loud alarms do cease,
> Hark, how the charming flutes conclude the peace . . .
> Excesses of pleasure now crowd on apace.
> How sweetly the violins sound to each bass,
> The ravishing trebles delight every ear,
> And mirth in a scene of true joy does appear. . . .
> Now beauty's power inflames my breast again,
> I sigh and languish with a pleasing pain.
> The notes so soft, so sweet the air,
> The soul of love must sure be there,
> That mine in rapture charms, and drives away despair.

In Motteux's *Gentleman's Journal* for January,

1691–2 was written: "That admirable musician, who could raise a noble fury in Alexander, and lay it as easily, and make him put on the Hero, or the Lover, when he pleased, is too great an Instance of the power of Music to be forgotten." And only three months before Dryden was writing to his sons at Rome, Jeremy Collier, who is seldom thought to have been a benefactor of Restoration poets, had published in the second part of his *Essays upon Several Moral Subjects* an essay *Of Musick* wherein it was told how "Timotheus, a Grecian, was so great a Master, that he could make a man storm and swagger like a Tempest, and then, by altering the Notes, and the Time, he would take him down again, and sweeten his humour in a trice. One time, when Alexander was at Dinner, this Man played him a Phrygian Air: the Prince immediately rises, snatches up his Lance, and puts himself into a Posture of Fighting. And the Retreat was no sooner sounded by the Change of Harmony, but his Arms were Grounded, and his Fire extinct; and he sate down as orderly as if he had come from one of Aristotle's Lectures." Such were the scraps that lay at Dryden's hand in September of 1697.

"I am glad to hear from all hands," he wrote to Tonson in December, "that my Ode is esteemed the best of all my poetry, by all the town: I thought so myself when I writ it; but being old I mistrusted my own judgment." It is a question whether *Absalom and Achitophel* and the *Oldham* are not better poetry than *Alexander's Feast*, which perhaps is only immortal ragtime. Some of the cadences are disappointing; lines 128, 139, 140, and 145 puzzle and lower the voice of the reader. Yet few poems of equal length anywhere have been brought to a finish on so consistently proud a level and in such bounding spirits. Here is brilliant panorama; here are responsive, ringing cadences; here is good-nature on the grand scale.

> And thrice he routed all his foes, and thrice he
> slew the slain.

The enormous vitality of this ode not only has insured its own long life; for a century it inspired ambitious imitators and nameless parodists. John Wilkes in 1774 [1] and the Prince of Wales in 1795 [2] found themselves hoisted in mockery to the highest throne that pamphleteers could conceive, the imperial throne of Philip's warlike son.

[1] W——s's Feast, or Dryden Travesti: A Mock Pindaric Inscribed to His Most Incorruptible Highness Prince Patriotism. London. 1774.

[2] Marriage Ode Royal After the Manner of Dryden. 1795.

VII

THE NARRATIVE POET

That the greatest of all poems have been narrative does not prove that the highest function of poetry is to tell a story. It may merely have happened to be in connection with accounts of human actions that poets could perform to the best advantage. The conquest which prose fiction has made in the world of story since the day of Dryden may or may not signify that poetry is beaten; whether the withdrawal by poets into special corners where they cultivate fine static temperaments rather than copious narrative sympathies denotes that the poetry of the future will not be important like the poetry of the past, only time will tell. Certain it is that the idea of narration in verse is often now discredited. At any time in the seventeenth century this would have been heresy. Among theorists at least, occasional, journalistic, or lyrical verse was seldom if ever taken seriously; the epic was undisputed king. Yet out of the quantities of narrative verse which that age produced little had much or any meaning. The decay of the heroic tradition was already well-nigh complete. Even Milton's triumph, to modern secular minds, is one chiefly of style and mood; his supreme moments are moments of gorgeous reminiscence, when in his imagination the regions and the deeds made famous centuries before *illustrium poetarum fabulis* come sweeping by.

There is no reason to feel sorry with Scott that Dryden never got round to writing his projected epic on Arthur or the Black Prince. It would most likely have been a disappointment; much as Dryden revered the institution of the heroic poem, he had not the power to illuminate and interpret heroic motives. His contribution was critical. His *Essay of Heroic Plays*, his *Apology for Heroic Poetry*, his *Discourse of Satire* and the dedication of his *Æneis* summed up contemporary tastes and theories in this department as no other group of essays did; he was the sponsor but not the chief performer. His tributes to the epic, "the most noble, the most pleasant, and the most instructive way of writing in verse," as well as "the greatest work of human nature," were many and resounding. His requirements for the writer of an epic, as set forth in the *Discourse of Satire*, were many and rigorous; a heroic poet, he said, is one "who, to his natural endowments, of a large invention, a ripe judgment, and a strong memory, has joined the knowledge of the liberal arts and sciences, and particularly moral philosophy, the mathematics, geography, and history, and with all these qualifications is born a poet; knows, and can practice the variety of numbers, and is master of the language in which he writes." Dryden's narrative sphere was a slighter one than this; it was the sphere of the episode or the tale. He is even said to have been capable of being intrigued by humble ballads. Addison wrote in the eighty-fifth *Spectator*,

"I have heard that the late Lord Dorset . . . had a numerous collection of old English ballads, and took a particular pleasure in the reading of them. I can affirm the same of Mr. Dryden;" and Gildon, in *A New Rehearsal* (1714), declared his victim Rowe another Mr. Bayes in "his admiration of some odd books, as 'Reynard the Fox,' and the old ballads of 'Jane Shore.'" Dryden's specialty was the short story; he belongs in the company not of Homer, Virgil, Dante, Spenser, and Milton, but of Ovid, Chaucer, Crabbe, Scott, Macaulay, Byron, Keats, Tennyson, Longfellow, Arnold, Morris, and Masefield.

Dryden was neither an original nor a skilful weaver of plots. He did not tell a story particularly well. Yet he always had the air of telling a story well; he was master of a swift, plausible manner. He was not adept in psychological research, or refined, or especially true; he was often slovenly and gross; but he was never limp or lame. His verse was as strong as the English mastiff and as fleet as the Frenchman's greyhound; and like a good hound it never tired. "I must confess," said Daniel in his *Defense of Rime*, "that to mine own ear those continual cadences of couplets used in long and continued poems are very tiresome and unpleasing, by reason that still methinks they run on with a sound of one nature, and a kind of certainty which stuffs the delight rather than entertains it." Dryden was not without monotony and stiffness; yet the last analysis must find him fresh and various as few other poets have been. Spiritually, there was always his capacious cynicism to keep him sensible; technically, there was always his speed to dissolve his blemishes and lend a vividness to his materials good and bad. "The wheels take fire from the mere rapidity of their motion," observed Coleridge in the *Biographia Litteraria*. Dryden paused only to gather momentum. There was pulse in his narrative medium as there had been pulse in his occasional, satirical, and lyrical mediums; his settings, his addresses, his descriptions of persons, his expositions of emotional cause and effect, were never dead; they were magazines of narrative energy. There can hardly be said to exist in English a perfect verse instrument for narrative; continuous couplets give too little pause, while stanzas halt too often. Dryden has come as near as any poet to a durable compromise. He can run straight on as far as he likes; then when he likes he can bring himself up sharply, and go on by leisurely stages. He can hesitate and exclaim, he can stop and wonder, he can meditate and meander.

Dryden's first narrative poem was not a tale but a chronicle. The *Annus Mirabilis* was almost the last echo of Lucan in English. Warner, Daniel, and Drayton had been the Elizabethan "historians in verse"; Dryden in 1666 constituted himself the chronicler of Charles's war with the Dutch and of the Great Fire of London. He was hardly geared, like old Nestor in Shakespeare's *Troilus and Cressida*, for walking hand in hand with Time; his gait was better suited to breathless, bizarre romance. His heroic stanzas stalk along with a quaint, spectral dignity, while no great amount of history gets told, though more perhaps than got told in the elaborately embroidered stanzas of the Elizabethans. The couplet, not the quatrain, was to be his vehicle.

The writing of plays gave Dryden's hand valuable practice in the quick sketching of action. There was an audience in this case which needed to know briefly what had happened off the stage. The necessity was for being straightforward, not for wandering among rare similes and precious allusions. A fair example is the speech of the Duke of Arcos to King Ferdinand in the second part of the *Conquest of Granada*, recounting the death of the master of Alcantara:

> Our soldiers marched together on the plain;
> We two rode on, and left them far behind,
> Till coming where we found the valley wind,
> We saw these Moors; who, swiftly as they could,
> Ran on to gain the covert of a wood.
> This we observed; and, having crossed their way,
> The lady, out of breath, was forced to stay;
> The man then stood, and straight his faulchion drew;
> Then told us, we in vain did those pursue,
> Whom their ill fortune to despair did drive,
> And yet, whom we should never take alive.
> Neglecting this, the master straight spurred on;
> But the active Moor his horse's shock did shun,
> And, ere his rider from his reach could go,
> Finished the combat with one deadly blow.
> I, to revenge my friend, prepared to fight;
> But now our foremost men were come in sight,
> Who soon would have dispatched him on the place,
> Had I not saved him from a death so base,
> And brought him to attend your royal doom.

This is far from Dryden's maturest narrative writing; the inversions are stilted, and the movement in general is somewhat mechanical. Its only significance lies in its directness and its clarity. The rhymes are less relied on to accentuate the movement than is usually to be the case hereafter. Dryden at his best did not smother his rhymes, but propelled himself by them and by the steady forward stroke of the end-stopped couplet.

Three of the satires gained by being cast in a narrative mould. *Absalom and Achitophel*, which took its tone from *Paradise Lost* and Cowley's *Davideis*, was an epic situation overlaid with humor and huge scorn. *Mac Flecknoe* was a full-blown mock-heroic incident. *The Hind and the Panther* began and ended on a note that was neither heroic nor familiar, but was well adjusted to Dryden's complicated motive. Near the close of the second part there is a passage that positively invites:

By this the Hind had reached her lonely cell,
And vapours rose, and dews unwholesome fell.
When she, by frequent observation wise,
As one who long on Heaven had fixed her eyes,
Discerned a change of weather in the skies.
The western borders were with crimson spread,
The moon descending looked all flaming red;
She thought good manners bound her to invite
The stranger dame to be her guest that night.
'Tis true, coarse diet, and a short repast,
(She said,) were weak inducements to the taste
Of one so nicely bred, and so unused to fast;
But what plain fare her cottage could afford,

> A hearty welcome at a homely board,
> Was freely hers; and, to supply the rest,
> An honest meaning, and an open breast.

No portion of the poem is more charged with irony; almost every line here fires a political shot. At the same time Dryden has capitulated to the genius of story-telling. He has fallen into his most engaging narrative style purely for the pleasure of doing so. The two fables of the swallows and the doves in the third part are justly famous. The emphasis there is on situation rather than on action, as befits the poet's satiric and didactic purpose; yet flourishes are added from time to time that evince real relish in the tale that is being told. In the fable of the swallows, for instance, there is a triplet that Dryden remembered twelve years later when he was giving his account of Iphigenia asleep:

> Night came, but unattended with repose;
> Alone she came, no sleep their eyes to close;
> Alone and black she came; no friendly stars arose.

The great bulk of Dryden's narrative verse consists of episodes translated or adapted from other poets. The habit of versifying events out of Ovid and Virgil was an old one at the Restoration, but it grew upon English poets rather more rapidly after 1660, leaving its deepest mark on the *Miscellanies* which Dryden himself began to edit in 1684. Dryden's first examples are the *Nisus and Euryalus* and the *Mezentius and Lausus* which he brought over from Virgil for the second *Miscellany* in 1685 and which he incorporated with slight changes in the folio of 1697.[1] He was particularly fond of the Nisus stories, as the poem on Oldham shows and as is even more clearly seen in a letter to Tonson concerning the make-up of the volume in which they first appeared: "I care not who translates them besides me, for let him be friend or foe, I will please myself, and not give off in consideration of any man." The poems, both as they were then printed and as they now stand, are marred by hasty lines and Latinisms, but taken as wholes they are manly narratives, rich, passionate, flushed with friendly warmth and reinforced by strong intelligence. They are profusely colored throughout and in places they are highly spiced with alliteration. They glorify a reckless personal loyalty and a shouting defiance of fate, the qualities which Dryden in his less critical moments delighted most to treat, the qualities which moved Byron at nineteen to try his own hand with Nisus and Euryalus. The deaths of Nisus and his friend in Dryden are brutish but effective. *Enjambement* is used to smooth transitions, as here:

Thus armed they went. The noble Trojans wait
Their issuing forth, and follow to the gate
With prayers and vows. Above the rest appears
Ascanius, manly far beyond his years.

But at the more critical stages of the action and in the speeches the couplets are conventionally definitive. Mezentius addresses his horse before he mounts to ride to his death:

[1] See his *Æneis,,* V, 373–475 and IX, 221–600, for the first episode, and X, 1071–1313 for the second.

O Rhœbus, we have lived too long for me,
(If life and long were terms that could agree).
This day thou either shalt bring back the head
And bloody trophies of the Trojan dead;
This day thou either shalt revenge my woe,
For murdered Lausus, on his cruel foe;
Or, if inexorable fate deny
Our conquest, with thy conquered master die.
For, after such a lord, I rest secure,
Thou wilt no foreign reins, or Trojan load endure.

The episodes from Ovid and Homer in the third *Miscellany* of 1693 are not remarkable, in spite of Dryden's statement in the preface that those from Ovid "appear to me the best of all my endeavours in this kind. Perhaps this poet is more easy to be translated than some others whom I have lately attempted; perhaps, too, he was more according to my genius. . . . I have attempted to restore Ovid to his native sweetness, easiness, and smoothness; and to give my poetry a kind of cadence, and, as we call it, a run of verse, as like the original, as the English can come up to the Latin." The first book of the *Metamorphoses* as here given is swift and smooth, and the other pieces are picturesque and copious, but it must always be clear to anyone that Dryden was more at home among the warriors of the *Æneid*. Ovid was attractive mainly because of his enamelled extravagrance; he wrote with license yet with elegance; poetically he was a finished rogue.

Dryden's career ended as it began, in a triumph of the spirit. His resolution at twenty-three to proceed to London and become a poet is matched only

by the fire and the perseverance which drove him
at the end of his life through pain and sickness to
the conclusion of his *Fables*. An old man divorced
from the Court and vilely lampooned by Whigs each
year that he lived, he might have raged or snarled
or complained or degenerated. He settled down
instead to the telling of excellent stories. "The
tattling quality of age," he had written in the *Discourse of Satire*, "as Sir William Davenant says, is
always narrative." He kept his gracious grand-
niece, Mrs. Steward of Cotterstock Hall, well informed concerning the progress of his volume. "Between my intervals of physic," he wrote to her on
Candlemas-Day, 1698, "I am still drudging on: always a poet, and never a good one. I pass my time
sometimes with Ovid, and sometimes with our old
English poet Chaucer; translating such stories as
best please my fancy; and intend besides them to add
somewhat of my own; so that it is not impossible,
but ere the summer be passed, I may come down
to you with a volume in my hand, like a dog out of
the water, with a duck in his mouth." On the fourth
of March he continued: "I am still drudging at a
book of Miscellanies, which I hope will be well
enough; if otherwise, threescore and seven may be
pardoned." Twenty days before his death, on the
eleventh of April, 1700, he could write her with some
pride: "The ladies of the town . . . are all of your
opinion, and like my last book of Poems better than
anything they have formerly seen of mine." The
work was certainly drudgery, and it was done as
rapidly as possible for money; but it is clear that

Dryden grew fonder of his occupation as he proceeded. The golden *Preface* describes his delighted progress from Homer to Ovid, from Ovid to Chaucer, and from Chaucer to Boccaccio, the volume constantly swelling in his hands; "I have built a house," he concludes, "where I intended but a lodge." If he had thought of the lodge as a green retreat for a fading muse, he found the house a bustling hall built for the entertainment of his ripest powers; there had been no fading. At no time after the Revolution did he need to say like Virgil's Mœris:

> Cares and time
> Change all things, and untune my soul to rhyme.
> I could have once sung down a summer's sun,
> But now the chime of poetry is done.
> My voice grows hoarse.

The chime of Dryden's verse was never done.

There is no fine bloom of romance about the *Fables*. The generation for which they were produced was not possessed of tender ideals; Spenser's vision of the virtues of man was as remote as Wordsworth's vision of the quiet powers of Nature. "Dryden had neither a tender heart, nor a lofty sense of moral dignity," wrote Wordsworth to Scott in 1805. "Whenever his language is poetically impassioned, it is mostly upon unpleasing subjects, such as the follies, vices, and crimes of classes of men, or of individuals." The *Fables*, with certain notable exceptions, catered to a jaded taste that craved the strong meat of romance, incest, murder, flowing blood, cruel and sensual unrealities, or else the biting acid of satire. Dryden's search for materials was far and wide. He did not confine himself to what Cowley in 1656 had contemptuously dismissed as "the obsolete threadbare tales of Thebes and Troy." He plundered medieval as well as ancient story; he went to the greatest tellers of tales wherever they were, whether they were Greek, Roman, Italian, or English. In a different sense from Walt Whitman's he decided:

Come, Muse, migrate from Greece and Ionia.
Cross out, please, those immensely overpaid accounts;
That matter of Troy and Achilles' wrath, and Æneas',
    Odysseus' wanderings. . . .
For know a better, fresher, busier sphere, a wider, untried
    domain awaits and demands you.

Whatever the reason, Homer and Ovid do not show quite so well in the *Fables* as do Chaucer and Boccaccio. "That matter of Troy" and those "confused antiquated dreams of senseless . . . Metamorphoses," to quote Cowley once again, only occasionally here ring familiar and true. *The First Book of Homer's Ilias*, in translating which Dryden did not use the original Greek, is striking only in its passages of invocation and abuse. The closing scene with Vulcan is grandiosely convivial:

At Vulcan's homely mirth his mother smiled,
And smiling took the cup the clown had filled.
The reconciler bowl went round the board,
Which, emptied, the rude skinker still restored.
Loud fits of laughter seized the guests, to see
The limping god so deft at his new ministry.

> The feast continued till declining light;
> They drank, they laughed, they loved, and then
>   'twas night.
> Nor wanted tuneful harp, nor vocal choir;
> The muses sung; Apollo touched the lyre.
> Drunken at last, and drowsy they depart,
> Each to his house, adorned with labored art
> Of the lame architect.

Pope's rendering of the same scene is not half so lively; the laughter of his gods is imitation laughter, this is real. It is thinkable that a complete *Iliad* by the author of these lines would be, even now, the most Homeric thing in English. From Homer, says Dryden, "I proceeded to the translation of the Twelfth Book of Ovid's *Metamorphoses*, because it contains, among other things, the causes, the beginning, and ending, of the Trojan war. Here I ought in reason to have stopped." But he went on, so that almost a third of the *Fables* derives from the *Metamorphoses*. The *Meleager and Atalanta* from the eighth book is a hectic recital of a bloody boar-hunt and a triple murder. Ovid has been lavish and audacious enough, but Dryden goes him one better; he is facetious when Ovid is sober, and he plays with words when Ovid speaks plainly. Ovid's Althea, when the corpses of her brothers are brought in, cries out merely and goes into mourning. In Dryden it is written:

> Pale at the sudden sight, she changed her cheer,
> And with her cheer her robes.

Ovid's Meleager, as soon as his image has been

thrown to the fire by his mother, writhes and laments
the bloodless death that he must die. Dryden says:

> Just then the hero cast a doleful cry,
> And in those absent flames began to fry;
> The blind contagion raged within his veins,
> But he with manly patience bore his pains;
> He feared not fate, but only grieved to die
> Without an honest wound, and by a death so dry.

Dryden has a pretty "turn" where Ovid has none;
it occurs in the account of the grief of the sisters of
the Calydonian hero:

> Had I a hundred tongues, a wit so large
> As could their hundred offices discharge;
> Had Phœbus all his Helicon bestowed,
> In all the streams inspiring all the god;
> Those tongues, that wit, those streams, that god in vain
> Would offer to describe his sisters' pain.

The *Baucis and Philemon* from the eighth book is
by far the best of the Ovidian pieces. Dryden
praises this "good-natured story" in the *Preface*.
"I see Baucis and Philemon as perfectly before me,"
he declares, "as if some ancient painter had drawn
them." It had always pleased him to write of homely
hospitality and rustic honesty. In the prologue to
All for Love he had remarked how those in high
places liked at times to descend among the low and

> Drink hearty draughts of ale from plain brown bowls,
> And snatch the homely rasher from the coals.

The household cheer of his Hind had been of this

sort, as has been seen. Some of his most genial letters were those he wrote in old age to Mrs. Steward thanking her for gifts of venison and marrow pudding. "As for the rarities you promise," he protested on one occasion, "if beggars might be choosers, a part of a chine of honest bacon would please my appetite more than all the marrow puddings; for I like them better plain; having a very vulgar stomach." He revelled among Ovid's details and added others of his own, stirring all in to make his poem rich. Jove and Hermes fared like this:

High o'er the hearth a chine of bacon hung;
Good old Philemon seized it with a prong,
And from the sooty rafter drew it down;
Then cut a slice, but scarce enough for one;
Yet a large portion of a little store,
Which for their sakes alone he wished were more;
This in the pot he plunged without delay,
To tame the flesh and drain the salt away.
The time between, before the fire they sat,
And shortened the delay with pleasing chat. . . .
Pallas began the feast, where first were seen
The party-colored olive, black and green;
Autumnal cornels next in order served,
In lees of wine well pickled and preserved;
A garden salad was the third supply,
Of endive, radishes, and succory;
Then curds and cream, the flower of country fare,
And new-laid eggs, which Baucis' busy care
Turned by a gentle fire and roasted rare. . . .
The wine itself was suiting to the rest,
Still working in the must, and lately pressed.
The second course succeeds like that before;

Plums, apples, nuts, and, of their wintry store,
Dry figs and grapes, and wrinkled dates were set
In canisters.

There is no padding here, no clutter of circumlocutions. Dryden feels at home, which means that he
is rapid, vivid, and concrete, and therefore for once
a good story-teller. *Pygmalion and the Statue*, from
the tenth book, had a good Restoration theme which
lent itself to vulgarization; it was so treated by
Dryden, who could rarely be trusted with lovers.
The *Cinyras and Myrrha*, from the same book, a
tale of incest, was likewise handled without restraint.
The *Ceyx and Alcyone*, from the eleventh book, the
history of a shipwreck, a drowning, and a body
washed ashore, is extremely fantastic in Ovid; in
Dryden, who now is plainly tired, it is grotesque and
literal. Ovid's two lines on King Ceyx in the water,

Dum natet, absentem, quotiens sinit hiscere fluctus,
Nominat Alcyonen ipsisque inmurmurat undis,

become four in the *Fables:*

As oft as he can catch a gulp of air,
And peep above the seas, he names the fair;
And even when plunged beneath, on her he raves,
Murmuring Alcyone below the waves.

The twelfth book, which is "wholly translated," re-
counts the famous fight in the cave, Dryden being
fully as graphic and gory as the original. *The
Speeches of Ajax and Ulysses*, from the thirteenth
book, find him once more in his element. A forensic
contest is on between brain and brawn, and the

translator of Lucretius is in his best argumentative trim. The verse is strong, intelligent and swift. Ulysses concludes, speaking to Ajax:

> Brawn without brain is thine; my prudent care
> Foresees, provides, administers the war.
> Thy province is to fight; but when shall be
> The time to fight, the king consults with me.
> No dram of judgment with thy force is joined.
> Thy body is of profit, and my mind.
> By how much more the ship her safety owes
> To him who steers, than him that only rows;
> By how much more the captain merits praise
> Than he who fights, and fighting but obeys;
> By so much greater is my worth than thine,
> Who canst but execute what I design.

When Dryden in the preface to his *Fables* elaborately declared the superiority of Chaucer to Ovid in sanity and truth to nature he revived the sunken reputation of one of the greatest of English poets much as in the *Essay of Dramatic Poesy* he had established for all Augustan generations the tone of evaluation of the greatest, and he reared himself head and shoulders above contemporary levels of criticism. Perhaps the most saving thing about him as a poet is the fact that he championed and gave vogue to the *Canterbury Tales*. The reputation of Chaucer was lower in the seventeenth century than it had been before or has been since. No edition of his works was issued between the two reprints of Speght in 1602 and 1687. He was seldom read, though he was often mentioned as a difficult old author who had a remarkable but obscure vein of gayety. Spenser's tribute was forgotten, and Milton's went unobserved. "Mr. Cowley despised him," according to Dryden, and Addison, in the *Account of the Best Known English Poets* which he contributed to the fourth *Miscellany* in 1694, pronounced what seemed a final benediction over the skeleton of his fame:

> In vain he jests in his unpolished strain
> And tries to make his readers laugh in vain. . . .
> But now the mystic tale that pleased of yore
> Can charm an understanding age no more.

Now Dryden, in an age when "nature" was more talked about than explored, took pains to deny that Chaucer was "a dry, old-fashioned wit, not worth reviving," proving rather that he had "followed Nature everywhere," and had written for all time. "We have our forefathers and great-grand-dames all before us, as they were in Chaucer's days; their general characters are still remaining in mankind, and even in England, though they are called by other names . . . for mankind is ever the same, and nothing lost out of Nature, though everything is altered." The humanity of Chaucer had its effect on the *Fables*, where *The Cock and the Fox*, for instance, is bubbling and droll like nothing else in Dryden. It is keenly a pleasure to behold the old poet who has dealt so exclusively throughout his career in the styles and accidents of utterance expand and ripen under the influence of a richly human personality. "In sum, I seriously protest," he concluded, "that no man ever had, or can have, a greater veneration for Chaucer than myself. I have translated some part of his works, only that I might perpetuate his memory, or at least refresh it, amongst my country-men."

In modernizing Chaucer Dryden had to overcome two current prejudices concerning his language. On the one hand there was a majority who considered that language too stale to be worth restoring; on the other there was a minority consisting of certain "old Saxon friends" like the late Earl of Leicester who supposed, according to Dryden, "that it is little less than profanation and sacrilege to alter it. They are farther of opinion, that somewhat of his good sense will suffer in this transfusion, and much of the beauty of his thoughts will infallibly be lost, which appear with more grace in the old habit." His an-swer to the first was that now they might see for themselves whether Chaucer was worth knowing, and his answer to the second was that he worked in the interest not of scholars but of those "who under-stand sense and poetry as well as they, when that poetry and sense is put into words which they under-stand." A more serious problem that had to be met in the process of modernization was the problem of versification. Dryden's dilemma at this point has not been sufficiently appreciated. He has been smiled at, to begin with, for his ignorance of Chau-cer's metrical scheme; and by those who do not mind that, he has been condemned for his obliteration of Chaucer's exquisite metrical personality. His ig-norance, which was real, he shared with most of his contemporaries; and he cannot be altogether blamed

when it is considered that the text which he used was
so wretchedly mangled that no uniform meter
emerged. It was literally true for him that not all
lines had the full ten syllables; Speght had not
guarded his final *e*'s as must a modern editor. The
passage in which Dryden surveys the field is too important not to be quoted: "The verse of Chaucer, I
confess, is not harmonious to us; . . . they who
lived with him, and some time after him, thought it
musical; and it continues so, even in our judgment,
if compared with the numbers of Lidgate and Gower,
his contemporaries: there is the rude sweetness of a
Scotch tune in it, which is natural and pleasing,
though not perfect. 'Tis true, I cannot go so far
as he who published the last edition of him; for he
would make us believe the fault is in our ears, and
that there were really ten syllables in a verse where
we find but nine: but this opinion is not worth con-
futing; 'tis so gross and obvious an error, that common sense (which is a rule in everything but matters
of Faith and Revelation) must convince the reader,
that equality of numbers, in every verse which we
call heroic, was either not known, or not always
practiced, in Chaucer's age. It were an easy matter
to produce some thousands of his verses, which are
lame for want of half a foot, and sometimes a whole
one, and which no pronunciation can make otherwise." But even if Dryden had known all that was
to be known about the verse of Chaucer, it still
would have been impossible for him, as it must be
always for anyone, to modernize that verse and preserve its flavor. To use Dryden's own word, its

most precious qualities "evaporate" when exposed to another air. The crux is in the weak final syllables, which have a caressing sound never heard in the necessarily brisker poetry of modern times. Since it seemed especially important in Dryden's day to throw the full weight of each line into the last syllable or the last word, and since Dryden himself had a dislike for feminine rhymes and indecisive endings, it is not to be wondered that he sharpened and hardened his fourteenth-century master.

"I have not tied myself to a literal translation," he says in the *Preface:* "but have often omitted what I judged unnecessary, or not of dignity enough to appear in the company of better thoughts. I have presumed further, in some places, and added somewhat of my own where I thought my author was deficient, and had not given his thoughts their true lustre, for want of words in the beginning of our language." That is to say, his aim has been to round out Chaucer and give him an even, enamelled surface; he has wished to remove all traces of the Gothic. He has had in mind a kind of fourth "unity," the unity of effect, to secure which it has been necessary to employ different means in different poems.

In *Palamon and Arcite* he has applied the seventeenth-century heroic formulas to Chaucer's Knight's Tale, which he says he prefers "far above all his other stories" because of its epic possibilities. The result is a sometimes stilted poem, one of the least interesting for its length in the *Fables*. Surrendering to the Restoration heroic tradition, Dryden has drawn

the sting of Chaucer's tender colloquialism and injected with a blunt needle the false dignity of Almanzor and Aureng-Zebe. Neither the jovial satire
nor the purple melodrama of the other tales is here.
Epithets, circumlocutions, Latinisms, grave conceits, and standard allusions are run profusely in to
thicken but not ennoble the original texture. The
verse is uniform and handsome, but the psychology
is almost everywhere gross. For Chaucer's lines,

> The quene anon, for verray wommanhede,
> Gan for to wepe, and so did Emeleye,
> And alle the ladies in the companye,

Dryden has substituted:

> The queen, above the rest, by nature good,
> (The pattern formed of perfect womanhood,)
> For tender pity wept: when she began,
> Through the bright choir the infectious virtue ran.
> All dropped their tears, even the contended maid.

And Chaucer's simile,

> As wilde bores gonne they to smyte,
> That frothen whyte as foom for ire wood,

becomes:

> Or, as two boars whom love to battle draws,
> With rising bristles, and with frothy jaws,
> Their adverse breasts with tusks oblique they wound;
> With grunts and groans the forest rings around.

The poem is partially redeemed on one side by the
regal "characters" of Lycurgus and Emetrius, the
prayers of Palamon, Emily, and Arcite to Venus,

Cynthia, and Mars, the splendid settings which are given for martial actions, and on the other side by occasional couplets in which Dryden's mind has slashed with a shining malice through the tissue of knightly palaver. As usual, his cynicism is not ugly, not smart. He never looks greedily out of the corner of his eye to see how you take it; it is too native with him for him to be concerned about that, and he himself is too humane. At the end of Ægeus' consolatory speech on the death of Arcite, Dryden, not Chaucer, observes somewhat enigmatically:

> With words like these the crowd was satisfied,
> And so they would have been, had Theseus died.

Both poets like to describe groups of men conversing; but when Chaucer was only amused, Dryden became contemptuous. Chaucer's delicious account in the Squire's tale of the loquacious courtiers who gathered around the steed of brass that stood before the throne of Cambinskan and speculated upon its origin is perhaps matched here in the Knight's Tale by a few lines hitting off the throng that forecast the outcome of to-morrow's tournament:

> The paleys ful of peples up and doun,
> Heer three, ther ten, holding hir questioun,
> Divyninge of thise Theban knightes two.
> Somme seyden thus, somme seyde it shal be so;
> Somme helden with him with the blake berd,
> Somme with the balled, somme with the thikke-berd;
> Somme seyde, he looked grim and he wolde fighte;
> He hath a sparth of twenty pound of wighte.

Thus was the halle ful of divyninge,
Longe after that the sonne gan to springe.

Dryden is more graphic in this case, and more caustic:

In knots they stand, or in a rank they walk,
Serious in aspect, earnest in their talk;
Factious, and favoring this or t'other side,
As their strong fancies and weak reason guide.
Their wagers back their wishes; numbers hold
With the fair freckled king, and beard of gold;
So vigorous are his eyes, such rays they cast,
So prominent his eagle's beak is placed.
But most their looks on the black monarch bend,
His rising muscles and his brawn commend;
His double-biting ax, and beamy spear,
Each asking a gigantic force to rear.
All spoke as partial favor moved the mind;
And, safe themselves, at others' cost divined.

The Cock and the Fox is another story; it is one of the best and most original of the *Fables*. It must be sheer affectation to insist that Chaucer's Nun Priest's Tale has greatly suffered in the hands of Dryden. Chaucer's poem is surpassingly human, concrete, and sly; but Dryden's is no less so, though its pitch is somewhat altered. The opening account of the poor old widow in her cottage and of the amorous Chanticleer among his dames is superior comedy; Dryden has tactfully elaborated such facetious hints as are given from time to time by the original. The disputation between Dane Partlet and the Cock on the subject of dreams offers an opportu-

nity which is both welcome and improved.   Parte-
lote's simple gibe,

> I sette not a straw by thy dreminges,
> For swevenes been but vanitees and japes.
> Men dreme al-day of owles or of apes,
> And eke of many a mase therewithal;
> Men dreme of thing that nevere was ne shal,

becomes in Partlet's mouth a piece of Lucretian
exposition:

> Dreams are but interludes which fancy makes;
> When monarch Reason sleeps, this mimic wakes;
> Compounds a medley of disjointed things,
> A court of cobblers, and a mob of kings.
> Light fumes are merry, grosser fumes are sad;
> Both are the reasonable soul run mad:
> And many monstrous forms in sleep we see,
> That neither were, nor are, nor e'er can be.
> Sometimes forgotten things long cast behind
> Rush forward in the brain, and come to mind.
> The muse's legends are for truth received,
> And the man dreams but what the boy believed.
> Sometimes we but rehearse a former play;
> The night restores our actions done by day,
> As hounds in sleep will open for their prey.
> In short the farce of dreams is of a piece,
> Chimeras all.

The episode of the brother murdered at the inn is
excellently and swiftly told.   The digression on
freewill gives Dryden a ratiocinative cue which he
takes half in the spirit of *Religio Laici* and half in
the spirit of the Nun Priest's Tale itself.

The Flower and the Leaf and *The Wife of Bath,
her Tale* are extraordinary in Dryden for their
luxuriant, spirited representation of fairy worlds.
The Flower and the Leaf, a poem not by Chaucer,
is a singularly pure and magical piece of pageantry
in rhyme-royal. Dryden has flushed and accelerated
it; its wheels have caught fire, and glowing masses
of fresh detail are swept into the race. The splendor
is mostly genuine; few of Dryden's descriptions are
less prolix. The genius of Spenser has rushed to
reinforce the old Augustan in this couplet on the
nightingale:

> So sweet, so shrill, so variously she sung,
> That the grove echoed, and the valleys rung.

And in the passage on the jousting knights Dryden
has remembered the metrical pattern which he used
some years before to describe the Trojan boys as
they wheeled and met in warlike play on the plains
of Sicily: [1]

> Thus marching to the trumpets' lofty sound,
> Drawn in two lines adverse they wheeled around,
> And in the middle meadow took their ground.
> Among themselves the turney they divide,
> In equal squadrons ranged on either side;
> Then turned their horses' heads, and man to man,
> And steed to steed opposed, the justs began,
> They lightly set their lances in the rest,
> And, at the sign, against each other pressed;
> They met; I sitting at my ease beheld
> The mixed events, and fortunes of the field.

[1] See page 83.

> Some broke their spears, some tumbled horse and man,
> And round the field the lightened coursers ran.
> An hour and more, like tides, in equal sway
> They rushed, and won by turns and lost the day.

The twenty-five lines with which Chaucer began
the story of the Wife of Bath have grown into forty-
five in the *Fables*. Dryden has drawn upon Shakespeare's *Romeo and Juliet* and *Midsummer Night's
Dream*, Spenser's *Faerie Queene*, and Milton's
L'Allegro to enrich the text of the *Canterbury Tales*:

> I speak of ancient times, for now the swain
> Returning late may pass the woods in vain,
> And never hope to see the nightly train;
> In vain the dairy now with mints is dressed,
> The dairymaid expects no fairy guest,
> To skim the bowls, and after pay the feast.
> She sighs, and shakes her empty shoes in vain,
> No silver penny to reward her pain;
> For priests with prayers, and other godly gear,
> Have made the merry goblins disappear;
> And where they played their merry pranks before,
> Have sprinkled holy water on the floor. . . .
> The maids and women need no danger fear
> To walk by night, and sanctity so near;
> For by some haycock, or some shady thorn,
> He bids his beads both even song and morn.
> It so befell in this King Arthur's reign,
> A lusty knight was pricking o'er the plain. . . .

An open attack on the court follows soon after, commencing:

> Then courts of kings were held in high renown,
> Ere made the common brothels of the town.

The tale proceeds without especial distinction; the long speech at the end by the loathly lady is expanded from Chaucer with the aid of Lucretius.

"I think his translations from Boccaccio are the best, at least the most poetical, of his poems," wrote Wordsworth to Scott. They are among the best known of the *Fables;* and they are the most successful of all Dryden's poems as narratives. It must be admitted that in general his stories in verse are interesting not so much for their action as for something by the way: the meter, the speeches, the settings, the "characters," the satiric interpolations, the semblance of action. With the exception perhaps of *Palamon and Arcite*, none of the pieces from Chaucer or Ovid is remembered wholly for what happens in it; as the outer dome of St. Paul's cathedral is beautiful but not necessary, so Dryden's narrative surface is animated but not moving. But in those from Boccaccio the story is everything; these poems burn with narrative energy. It was not for nothing that Dryden turned at last to the prince of story tellers and went in frankly for melodrama. *Sigismonda and Guiscardo* is a blazing tale of lovers' lust and murder. We see a secret bride and groom somewhat brutally enjoy each other until the father discovers them and orders the husband put to death. Wordsworth's criticism can hardly be improved upon. "It is many years since I saw Boccaccio," he said, "but I remember that Sigismunda is not married by him to Guiscard. . . . I think Dryden has much injured the story by the marriage, and degraded Sigismunda's character by it. He has also, to the best of my remembrance, degraded her still more, by making her love absolute sensuality and appetite; Dryden had no other notion of the passion. With all these defects, and they are very gross ones, it is a noble poem." The poem on the whole is swift, though there are some wide wastes of verbiage. Sigismonda's address to Tancred defending Guiscardo and vindicating virtuous poverty is sound oratory but it is too long and too formal. Dryden in the *Preface* invites comparison between it and the speech of the hag at the end of *The Wife of Bath*. Neither speech as it is written belongs exactly where it is placed. *Theodore and Honoria* is a haunting tale of terror, long popular and the only one of Dryden's narratives with an atmosphere that is organic and sustained. The forests of old Ravenna cast a deep romantic shade over the knights and ladies, real and visionary, who play their grisly parts. Dryden has opened both eyes wide upon a dark fantastic world; and his ear was never fitter. The poem makes a rousing start:

> Of all the cities in Romanian lands,
> The chief, and most renowned, Ravenna stands,
> Adorned in ancient times with arms and arts,
> And rich inhabitants, with generous hearts.
> But Theodore the brave, above the rest,
> With gifts of fortune and of nature blest,
> The foremost place for wealth and honour held,
> And all in feats of chivalry excelled.
>   This noble youth to madness loved a dame,
> Of high degree, Honoria was her name;

Fair as the fairest, but of haughty mind,
And fiercer than became so soft a kind.

The setting for the apparition of the hunted maid
owes its success to a group of ominous cadences
which reproduce the terror and suspense of Nature
herself:

It happed one morning, as his fancy led,
Before his usual hour he left his bed,
To walk within a lonely lawn, that stood
On every side surrounded by the wood.
Alone he walked, to please his pensive mind,
And sought the deepest solitude to find. . . .
While listening to the murmuring leaves he stood,
More than a mile immersed within the wood,
At once the wind was laid; the whispering sound
Was dumb; a rising earthquake rocked the ground;
With deeper brown the grove was overspread:
A sudden horror seized his giddy head,
And his ears tinkled, and his color fled.
Nature was in alarm; some danger nigh
Seemed threatened, though unseen to mortal eye.
Unused to fear, he summoned all his soul,
And stood collected in himself, and whole;
Not long: for soon a whirlwind rose around,
And from afar he heard a screaming sound,
As of a dame distressed, who cried for aid,
And filled with loud laments the secret shade.

The story whirls on without an interruption or a
couplet out of place. The effect is single; Dryden
nowhere stops merely to heap up words or to paint
an impossible, unnecessary scene. *Cymon and Iphigenia*, the last of all the *Fables*, is less of a piece

than the *Theodore*. It is famous not for its plot but for its by-play. No one remembers the last two-thirds of the poem; but the first hundred and fifty-seven lines are classic. Dryden has conceived simple Cymon and the most desirable Iphigenia with infinite zest. The hero is removed by his father to the farm:

> Thus to the wilds the sturdy Cymon went,
> A squire among the swains, and pleased with banishment.
> His corn and cattle were his only care,
> And his supreme delight a country fair.
>   It happened on a summer's holiday,
> That to the greenwood shade he took his way;
> For Cymon shunned the church, and used not much to pray.
> His quarterstaff, which he could ne'er forsake,
> Hung half before, and half behind his back.
> He trudged along, unknowing what he sought,
> And whistled as he went, for want of thought.

He comes upon Iphigenia asleep much as Thomson's Damon in *Summer* comes upon Musidora, and after a spell of staring he is inspired to analyze his first love's charms:

> Thus our man-beast, advancing by degrees,
> First likes the whole, then separates by degrees,
> On several parts a several praise bestows,
> The ruby lips, the well-proportioned nose,
> The snowy skin, the raven-glossy hair,
> The dimpled cheek, the forehead rising fair,
> And even in sleep itself a smiling air.

This is romance, but romance sunned and dried

in the smiling mind of a massive old satirist. Here
in this legend of two preposterous lovers and afterwards in the "character" of the raw militia swarming on the fields of Rhodes are exhibited most of
the traits of Dryden. One will observe the absence
of wonder, and the powerful presence of hard, substantial laughter.

VIII

REPUTATION: CONCLUSION

The reputation of Dryden as a poet has not been international. Where English is not spoken his name is likely to be respected, but his poetry seldom is read. A man who has had so little to say to his countrymen has had no claim at all on the ears of foreigners. It is only a few poets who can be or need be translated. Dryden, in whom style was paramount, and whose manner proved generally incommunicable even to native successors, can hardly have expected to appear to advantage in other languages. Thackeray asserted in his essay on Congreve and Addison that Dryden died "the marked man of all Europe," but that is an exaggeration. Naturally enough, he was heard more of in France than elsewhere on the continent; yet he was never famous there. At no time before 1700 were the French much interested in England's *belles lettres;* it did not much matter to Boileau whether Dryden or Blackmore was best among the poets across the Channel. Boileau, indeed, when told of Dryden's death is said to have affected never to have heard his name. Rapin, on the other hand, may have learned English merely to read him. At all events, it was not until the next century, when everything English suddenly became of enormous concern to

Frenchmen, that Voltaire celebrated and gave some
little vogue to "l'inégal et impétueux Dryden,"
"un très-grand génic," as he called him in the dedication of *Zaïre* in 1736. He had introduced the
author of *Aureng-Zebe* to the French public in 1734,
in his letter on English tragedy: "C'est Dryden
Poëte du tems de Charles second, Auteur plus fécond
que judicieux, qui aurait une réputation sans mé-
lange, s'il n'avait fait que la dixième partie de ses
Ouvrages, et dont le grand deffaut est d'avoir voulu
être universel." In 1752, in the thirty-fourth chapter of his *Siècle de Louis XIV*, he announced of
Dryden's works that they were "pleins de détails
naturels à la fois et brillants, animés, vigoureux,
hardis, passionés, mérite qu'aucun ancien n'a sur-
passé." He drew upon *The Wife of Bath* in 1764 for
the idea of his tale in verse, *Ce Que Plait Aux Dames.*
Alexander's Feast was always for him a *point de re-
père* in English poetry. In his article on Enthusiasm
in the Dictionary he showed an excellent understanding of the conventional English judgments upon
it: "De toutes les odes modernes, celle où il règne
le plus grand enthousiasme qui ne s'affaiblit jamais,
et qui ne tombe ni dans le faux ni dans l'ampulé,
est le *Timothèe*, ou la fête d'Alexandre, par Dryden;
elle est encore regardée en Angleterre comme un chef-
d'oeuvre inimitable, dont Pope n'a pu approcher
quand il a voulu s'exercer dans le même genre.
Cette ode fut chantée; et si on avait eu un musicien
digne du poëte, ce serait le chef-d'oeuvre de la poésic
lyrique." To M. de Chabanon, who had just published a translation of Pindar with an essay on the

Pindaric *genre*, he wrote from Ferney on the 9th of March, 1772: "Vous appelez Cowley le Pindare anglais . . . c'était un poète sans harmonie. . . . Le vrai Pindare est Dryden, auteur de cette belle ode intitulée *la Fête d'Alexandre, ou Alexandre et Timothèe*. Cette ode . . . passe en Angleterre pour le chef-d'oeuvre de la poésie la plus sublime et la plus variée; et je vous avoue que, comme je sais meux l'anglais que le grec, j'aime cent fois mieux cette ode que tout Pindare." Boswell told Johnson "that Voltaire, in a conversation with me, had distinguished Pope and Dryden thus: 'Pope drives a handsome chariot, with a couple of neat trim nags; Dryden a coach, and six stately horses.'" It will be seen that Voltaire had not listened for nothing to the wits and savants of London. And he must have known that he was safer in extolling *Alexander's Feast* than he would have been on any other ground. Dryden's last ode has penetrated where none of the other poems will ever go. Händel's music kept it long familiar to Germans who had no taste for the other lyrics. Henry Crabb Robinson wrote in his diary in 1803, after a visit to Voss, the German translator of Homer: "I was quite unable to make him see the beauty of Dryden's translations from Horace,—such as the 'Ode on Fortune.'" A. W. Schlegel was at a loss to understand what he considered the inflated reputation at home of the plays, the translations, and the "political allegories." It is in England, and incidentally in America, that one must remain if he would find what fame the name of Dryden has enjoyed.

"I loved Mr. Dryden," said Congreve with a simplicity that was rare with him and his generation. The stout old poet with his cherry cheeks, his heavy eyes, his long grey hair, and his snuff-soiled waistcoat was not in want of affectionate as well as valuable friends after the Revolution. He kept company not only with poets, but with important laymen. He was a believer in conversation, though he may not have been an adept himself. "Great contemporaries whet and cultivate each other," he wrote in 1693 in the *Discourse of Satire*. Back in the time of Charles he had been intimate with the wits and poets of the court. "We have . . . our genial nights," he reminded Sedley in the dedication of *The Assignation* in 1673, "where our discourse is neither too serious nor too light, but always pleasant, and, for the most part, instructive; the raillery neither too sharp upon the present, nor too censorious on the absent; and the cups only such as will raise the conversation of the night, without disturbing the business of the morrow." In his last decade he was welcome in the houses of his relations, Mrs. Steward of Cotterstock Hall, near Oundle, Northamptonshire, and John Driden of Chesterton, in Huntingdonshire, and in that of the really noble Duke of Ormonde. Thomas Carte, who wrote a life of the Duke in 1736, said that "once in a quarter of a year he used to have the Marquis of Halifax, the earls of Mulgrave, Dorset, and Danby, Mr. Dryden, and others of that set of men at supper, and then they were merry and drank hard." [1]

[1] John Caryll of Lady Holt, Sussex, who formed the amiable habit late in the century of inviting celebrities to his house and accompanying

His position among the poets of that decade is too well known to require an elaborate account. Pope told Spence that "Dryden employed his mornings in writing; dined, *en famille;* and then went to Will's." His coffee-house dictatorship has long been proverbial in English literary history; "the great patriarch of Parnassus" who ruled by the fire in winter and out on the balcony in summer is the most striking figure between the blind Milton and the rolling Dr. Johnson. His prologues and epilogues, and later his satires, made him respected, feared, and sought as a judge of verse. There has come down from about 1682 a decision which he wrote for an unknown company concerning a disputed passage in Creech's *Lucretius.* The dispute was as to whether the passage made sense. Dryden reported: "I have con-

---

his invitations with gifts of venison, transcribed for Pope or himself about 1729 a letter from Dryden, dated July 21, 1698, sent in answer to one of his hospitable notes. The copy may be found among the Additional MSS. at the British Museum (28, 618, f. 84). It runs as follows:

Sir

'T is the part of an honest Man to be as good as his Word, butt you have been better: I expected but halfe of what I had, and that halfe, not halfe so Good. Your Vaneson had three of the best Qualities, for it was both fatt, large & sweet. To add to this you have been pleased to invite me to Ladyholt, and if I could promise myself a year's Life, I might hope to be happy in so sweet a Place, & in the Enjoyment of your good Company. How God will dispose of me, I know not: but I am apt to flatter myself with the thoughts of itt, because I very much desire itt, and am Sr with all manner of Acknowledgement,

Yr most Obliged and most
faith full Servant

July 21, 1698.   John Dryden.

sidered the verses, and find the author of them to have notoriously bungled; that he has placed the words as confusedly as if he had studied to do so." He proceeded to analyze the error and to suggest an amendment of it, concluding: "The company having done me so great an honour as to make me their judge, I desire . . . the favour of making my acknowledgments to them; and should be proud to hear . . . whether they rest satisfied in my opinion." By 1685 his authority at Will's already was established, if Spence's story of how young Lockier won his approbation there may be trusted. Robert Wolseley the same year, in his preface to Rochester's play *Valentinian*, referred a quarrel with Mulgrave in all confidence to "Mr. Dryden, . . . whose judgment in anything that relates to Poetry, I suppose, he will not dispute." There was little disposition among the younger followers of literature like Walsh and Dennis to contest a definition or a preference of Mr. Dryden's. Nor was there serious doubt in the minds of beginning poets as to what was the best in matter, form, and style; Dryden had stamped an image of himself on every world of verse, and few could refrain from falling in some measure into the cadences of his prologues, his epistles, his satires, his discourses, his songs, his odes, his narratives. Publicly also it was understood that Dryden represented the taste of the nation in poetry. The man who once had subsisted by panegyrizing the Crown, by propitiating the coxcombs of the theaters, and later by being a partisan in verse, was now more honorably engaged in selling his verses to the readers

of England generally. The two folios of 1697 and
1700, the *Virgil* and the *Fables*, are memorials not
only of an aged poet's power but of an awakening
audience's temper. The book-seller with his sub-
scription editions was now in a position to guarantee
a kind of independence and professional prosperity
to men of gifts; there was coming into existence a
reading public. Long before the first of the two
folios appeared it was a prevailing wish that Dryden
might build an English monument in meter. "We
hope that Mr. Dryden will undertake to give us a
Translation of Virgil," wrote Motteux in his "News
of Learning from Several Parts" in the *Gentleman's
Journal* for March, 1694; "'tis indeed a most difficult work, but if anyone can assure himself of success in attempting so bold a task, 'tis doubtless the
Virgil of our age, for whose noble Pen that best of
Latin Poets seems reserved." The *Virgil* and the
Fables seem today to stand astride of the interval
between *Paradise Lost* and Pope's *Homer*. For a
generation at least anyone who pretended to be a
reader read them, as one who expected to be a poet
studied them. Dryden himself, complacently enough,
was the first to admit his own supremacy; knowing
that no man wrote better poetry, he said as much,
and so infuriated for a new reason such rivals in
trade as grudged him his eminence, such enemies in
politics as still remembered his ill-timed conversion
to Roman Catholicism, and such desperate wits as
subsisted at the fringe of literary society by making
sport of the famous. "More libels have been written
against me, than almost any man now living," he

could say in 1693. He suffered both the advantages
and the disadvantages of having no real rival to
draw a portion of the fire.

An investigator of the reputation of a poet seeks
to answer three questions. As for his vogue, what
poems have continued to be read? As for his standing, how has he been criticised and where has he
been ranked? And as for his influence, what poets
have been governed or at any rate touched by his
technique and personality? It seems advisable in
the case of Dryden to pursue each of these inquiries
through three periods since his death: the eighteenth
century, or such portions of it as preserved fairly
uniform Augustan standards; the late eighteenth and
early nineteenth centuries, when there was a more
or less abrupt break with those standards; and all
subsequent time.

Dryden's vogue as a poet in any one period cannot be determined with exactness on the basis of
collected editions. Taken in proportion to the whole
of the literary public the readers of Dryden's poems
in the nineteenth century were scarcely one-fourth
as numerous as they had been in the eighteenth;
yet the nineteenth century saw four times as many
editons. Tonson printed a very imperfect folio in
1701 consisting chiefly of *Poems on Various Occasions
and Translations from Several Authors* extracted
from the *Miscellanies,* binding it with two volumes
of the plays and the 1700 issue of the *Fables.* No
other collection appeared until forty-two years
later, when the house of Tonson and the Rev.
Thomas Broughton brought out in two compact

volumes the "Occasional Poems and Translations;" although Congreve's edition of the plays in six volumes in 1717 was popular, furnishing the material for new editions in 1725, 1735, 1760, and 1762. Two volumes of *Poems and Fables* appeared in Dublin in 1741 and 1753, while Glasgow supported two volumes of *Original Poems* in 1756, 1770, 1773, 1775, and 1776, the last time in company with the *Fables*. Samuel Derrick in 1760 and 1767 produced for the Tonsons again what he claimed was a complete set of the miscellaneous poems and translations in four beautiful octavo volumes, adding an ambitious *Life* and some elaborate notes, the first of their kind upon the subject. This work probably forestalled a somewhat more bulky edition of both the prose and the verse projected by James Ralph in 1758. Two volumes of *Original Poems and Translations* (1777) were followed in rapid succession during the next three-quarters of a century by the famous series of reprints of British poets, a series more bought than read. The collections of Bell in 1777 and 1782, those called Johnson's in 1779, 1790, and 1822, and those of Anderson in 1793, Park in 1806 and 1808, Chalmers in 1810, Sandford in 1819, the Aldine Poets in 1832–33, 1834, 1843, 1844, 1852, 1854, 1865, 1866, 1871, and 1891, the Cabinet Poets in 1851, Routledge in 1853, Robert Bell in 1854, 1862, and 1870, and Gilfillan in 1855, 1874, and 1894, to name no others, did not succeed in bringing great bodies of eager new readers to Dryden. Scott's exhaustive edition of 1808, reissued in 1821 and revised by Professor Saintbury in 1882–1893, was unfortunately as well as fortunately a monument; it never has lent itself to familiar handling. The four volumes edited from the notes of the Wartons in 1811, intended to complement Malone's four volumes of the prose (1800), were printed again in 1851 and 1861. W. D. Christie's Globe *Dryden* of 1870, since republished many times, has furnished the model for editions of the poems in a single volume. Its successors have made the poet easily accessible and in matters of textual accuracy and bibliography have done him justice. The Cambridge *Dryden* is an American masterpiece. Most of these many editions have indicated little more than that the English-reading world has expanded and that new libraries have called for new sets of standard works. It is elsewhere that one must go to find what poems of Dryden in particular and in truth have lived to please.

The eighteenth century, being interested mostly in Dryden's style, was much devoted to his translations, in which it was considered, not very accurately, that his style showed fullest and best. The *Virgil* was reprinted in 1698, 1709, 1716, 1721, 1730, 1748, 1763, 1769, 1772, 1773, 1782, 1792, and 1793, the exceptional interval between 1730 and 1763 being partly explainable by the appearance of Christopher Pitt's translation of the *Æneid* in 1740. Pitt was a better scholar than Dryden, and for a time he stood more in favor. But Dr. Johnson was of the opinion "that Pitt pleases the critic, and Dryden the people; that Pitt is quoted, and Dryden read." Neither is read often or carefully now, but it is plain that if Dryden lost by departing from Virgil, Pitt gained nothing by staying close. The *Juvenal* and *Persius* were published in 1697, 1702, 1711, 1713, 1726, 1732, and 1735. Various portions of the Ovid appeared in 1701, 1705, 1709, and 1712. Sir Samuel Garth's composite *Metamorphoses* gave due prominence to Dryden's pieces both in the first edition of 1717 and in the later editions of 1751 and 1794; but these came out separately again in 1719, 1720, 1725, 1729, 1735, 1761, 1776, 1782, 1791, and 1795. The *Fables* were well known to the writers of the *Spectator* and *Tatler*, and even Swift permitted himself to quote them. They were freshly issued in 1713, 1721, 1734, 1737, 1741, 1742, 1745, 1755, 1771, 1773, 1774, and with sumptuous engravings in 1797. "It is to his Fables," predicted Joseph Warton in the *Essay on Pope*, "that Dryden will owe his immortality." The most famous single poem of Dryden's throughout the century seems to have been the *Alexander's Feast*. Performed by musicians, quoted by æstheticians and essayists, printed in anthologies, translated into Greek and Latin, and parodied, it had every reason to be known; published for the second time by Tonson in the *Fables* of 1700, it was republished in other forms in 1738, 1740, 1743, 1751, 1756, 1758, 1760, 1773, 1778, 1779, and 1780. The *Song for St. Ceclia's Day* (1687) was less in vogue, but it found its way into type in 1754, 1760, 1764, and 1778. The ode on Anne Killigrew seems never to have commanded serious attention until Dr. Johnson's bold praise of it in the *Life*, praise which shocked certain readers of the *Gentleman's Magazine* into sober protest. In general the miscellaneous

non-dramatic verse had to live by anthologies
and pirations. As has been observed before, Tonson's imperfect edition of 1701 had no successor until
1743; and neither Broughton's volumes then nor
those of Derrick later were notably popular. Yet
during the interval between Tonson and Broughton
it was never difficult to become acquainted with
Dryden the occasional and lyric poet. The earlier
editions of *Poems on Affairs of State* virtually exclu-
ded him on the ground of his politics, but into the
later volumes of that series and into most other
repositories he had easy entry. From the *Westminster Drolleries* in 1671-2 to Tom Durfey's *Pills
to Purge Melancholy* in 1719-20, and longer, no
collection of English songs omitted the most rousing of those from Dryden's plays, while broadsides
flung them into rougher company. Handbooks like
those of Bysshe and Gildon drew heavily upon him
for examples of good verse. More than half of
Bysshe's "Collection of the most Natural, Agreeable and Noble Thoughts . . . that are to be found
in the best English Poets" hails from Dryden. But
Dryden's *Miscellany* itself gave him the most currency. The four *Miscellany* volumes which he had
engineered for Tonson in 1684, 1685, 1693, and 1694,
and which had been by no means the least sign of
his leadership while he lived, were followed after
his death by a fifth part in 1704 and a sixth part in
1709. In 1716 and again in 1727 all six were collected and reissued with new material, Dryden
being honored by the inclusion of ninety-six of his
pieces. The first volume opened with *Mac Flecknoe*,

as it had at the beginning of the series, in 1684; and here or there all the public poems found place: that is to say, the two parts of *Absalom and Achitophel*, the *Heroic Stanzas*, *Astræa Redux*, *To His Sacred Majesty*, *To My Lord Chancellor*, *The Medal*, *Annus Mirabilis*, *Threnodia Augustalis*, *The Hind and the Panther*, *Britannia Rediviva*, and *Religio Laici*. The occasional verse was represented by nineteen of the prologues and eleven of the epilogues, by the epistles to Etherege, Kneller, Howard, Lady Castlemaine, Charleton, Higden, the Duchess of York, Congreve and Roscommon and by the elegies, epitaphs and epigrams on Hastings, "Amyntas," "A Very Young Gentleman," Dundee, "Young Mr. Rogers," Lady Whitmore, Sir Palmes Fairborne, "Eleonora," Anne Killigrew, and Milton. There were six songs and the *Veni Creator;* there was the *Art of Poetry;* and there were the translations from Theocritus, Lucretius, and Horace, with the *Hector and Andromache* from Homer, and the fourth and ninth Eclogues together with the episodes of Nisus, Mezentius, and Vulcan from Virgil. Here was the body, certainly, of Dryden's verse. Yet it is a question whether he gained by being shuffled so recklessly between Tonson's covers among dozens of other poets living and dead, good and indifferent, like and unlike him. It was Broughton's aim, at least, in 1743, to separate him from the mass and give him the dignity of two pleasant duodecimo volumes that could be set alongside the small editions already current of the *Fables*, the *Virgil*, the *Juvenal*, and the dramatic works. The collectors throughout the century of fugitive and minor poetry, like Dodsley, Pearch, and Nichols, were inclined to pass Dryden by as already standard. A. F. Griffith's *Collection . . . of English Prologues and Epilogues Commencing with Shakespeare and Concluding with Garrick*, in four volumes, 1779, the completest thing of its kind in the language, gave him the first place with eighty prologues and epilogues. It may safely be concluded of Dryden in the eighteenth century that although he was never contagious except as a songster, or much on the lips of society, he yet was respectably current. Lady Mary Wortley Montagu carried his best couplets in her mind to Constantinople. Upon the occasion of Thornhill's first visit to the Vicar of Wakefield's daughters, music was proposed and "a favourite song of Dryden's" was sung. For the most part Dryden continued to keep the company of literary men. The *Spectator* and *Tatler* made frequent use of the translations and of the "characters" from the satires; Dr. Johnson, virtually every page of whose Dictionary gleamed with lines from Dryden as well as with lines from Pope and Shakespeare, was fond of quoting him in his own letters; Gibbon, who said he had grown up on the *Virgil* and Pope's *Homer*, knew the *Fables* and the satires particularly well; and Burke and Charles James Fox were deeply indebted to the prose.

As the eighteenth century wore away it was increasingly difficult to be interested in much of Dryden's political and occasional verse or in many of his translations from the classics. Editions of the *Juvenal and Persius* in 1810, 1813, and 1822, of the

Virgil in 1802, 1803, 1806, 1807, 1811, 1812, 1813, 1819, 1820, 1822, 1823, 1824, 1825, and 1830, and of the *Ovid* in 1804, 1807, 1812, 1815, 1824, 1826, 1833, and 1850, to come no further down, signified ambition in publishers or the survival of old-fashioned tastes in readers, rather than any real vogue. Scott's efforts in behalf of a Dryden tradition included an attractive picture of "Glorious John" in the fourteenth chapter of *The Pirate*, a picture which appealed at least to antiquarian and tory minds. "I wish I could believe," wrote Lockhart in the *Life*, "that Scott's labours had been sufficient to recall Dryden to his rightful station, not in the opinion of those who make literature the business or chief solace of their lives—for with them he had never forfeited it—but in the general favour of the intelligent public. That such has been the case, however, the not rapid sale of two editions, aided as they were by the greatest of living names, can be no proof; nor have I observed among the numberless recent publication of the English booksellers a single reprint of even those tales, satires and critical essays, not to be familiar with which would, in the last age, have been considered as disgraceful in any one making the least pretension to letters." Lockhart was perhaps too pessimistic. The *Fables* had found publishers in 1806 and 1822; the anthologists of the time were paying due attention both to them and to the satires, the best of the occasional poems, and the odes. Campbell's *Specimens of the British Poets* (1819) included the "characters" of Achitophel, Zimri, Og, and Doeg, the *Killigrew*, the descriptions of Lycurgus and Emetrius and of the preparation for the tournament in *Palamon and Arcite*, all of *Cymon and Iphigenia*, and *The Flower and the Leaf*. Hazlitt's *Select British Poets* (1824) offered *Absalom and Achitophel*, *Mac Flecknoe*, *Religio Laici*, and *The Hind and the Panther*, the epistles to Congreve, Kneller, and Driden of Chesterton, the elegy on Oldham, *Alexander's Feast* and the *Secular Masque*, *The Cock and the Fox*, *Sigismonda and Guiscardo*, *Theodore and Honoria*, *Cymon and Iphigenia*, and *Baucis and Philemon*.

The trend of the nineteenth century away from Dryden aroused a number of genuine but ineffectual protests from professional literary men. The editor of a volume of *Selections* in 1852 began his preface thus: "The merits of Dryden are not sufficiently acknowledged at present. Our zeal for the poets who preceded the civil wars, like most reactions, is become too exclusive." The reviewer of Bell's edition of 1854 in the *Edinburgh* for July, 1855, enumerated four reasons for "the oblivion into which the works of Dryden have so singularly fallen": inability to distinguish between Dryden and his unworthy imitators; failure to see that Dryden himself was not another Pope; "monstrous" ignorance on the part of Wordsworth, Keats, and the new schools; and a heretical notion generally that Dryden and Pope were not poets. There were other and better reasons. But whatever the whole cause, it was and is true regarding the bulk of Dryden's work that, as Lowell declared, "few writers are more thoroughly buried in that great cemetery of the 'British Poets.'"

He has not become absorbed into English speech like Pope, nor are his longer poems read with enthusiasm as wholes. He lies about in splendid fragments: the four "characters" of Shaftesbury, Buckingham, Burnet, and Settle, and the two of Shadwell; the beginning of *Religio Laici* and the passage there on tradition; the first eighty lines of *The Hind and the Panther* and the eulogy of the Roman Catholic Church in the second part; the translations of Lucretius on death and Horace on contempt of Fortune; the epigram on Milton; the elegy on Oldham; the prologues at Oxford and before *Aureng-Zebe;* the epistles to Congreve and John Driden; the odes on Anne Killigrew and St. Cecilia's Day; and half a dozen of the songs. *Alexander's Feast* has probably never been rivalled in popularity by another of the poems. The two Cecilia Odes were all of Dryden that Palgrave printed in his *Golden Treasury*, and no anthologist since has neglected them. On the whole it may be said that Dryden's odes, "those surprising masterpieces," Robert Louis Stevenson wrote to Mr. Edmund Gosse on the sixth of December, 1880, "where there is more sustained eloquence and harmony of English numbers than in all that has been written since," seem the most indestructible portions of his verse.

No important detailed criticism of Dryden appeared in the eighteenth century outside of Dr. Johnson's *Life*, which in itself covered all the ground then visible. Remarks were made, eulogies were delivered, commonplaces were handed along, but little was said that penetrated. Swift was always contemptuous, though never long or elaborately so. Spence quotes Tonson as saying: "Addison was so eager to be the first name, that he and his friend Sir Richard Steele used to run down even Dryden's character as far as they could. Pope and Congreve used to support it." A publisher of a man's works may be pardoned some jealousy of his reputation, but it is probable that Tonson exaggerated the feuds that were waged even in the Augustan temple of fame. Addison showed himself early and late to be closely acquainted with Dryden's poetry, and usually he was judicious in his observations upon it. In his poem *To Mr. Dryden* (1693) and his *Account of the Greatest English Poets* (1694) he gave the old poet warm if vague praise. In the *Tatler*, the *Spectator*, and the *Guardian* he discounted Dryden's tragic style as bombastic, revised his definition of wit, praised his satires at the same time that he predicted short life for them because of the temporary character of their allusions, and pointed out defects in his otherwise admirable translations. Whatever may have been Addison's attempts to injure Dryden in conversation, in writing he was a fair and indeed a salutary critic. At one time it was believed of Pope that, far from coming to Dryden's aid, he was conspiring against his remains. John Dennis, who had been born in 1657 and who consequently had been brought up on Dryden in another generation than Pope's, was moved in 1715 to defend the great poet of his choice against what he understood to be a determined conspiracy. A letter to Tonson on the fourth of June expressed his sentiments: "When I

had the good fortune to meet you in the city, it was
with concern that I heard from you of the attempt
to lessen the reputation of Mr. Dryden; and 'tis
with indignation that I have since learnt that that
attempt has chiefly been carried on by small
poets. . . . But when I heard that this . . . was
done in favour of little Pope, that diminutive of
Parnassus and of humanity, 'tis impossible to
express to what a height my indignation and disdain were raised. Good God!" And he goes on to
justify his "zeal for the Reputation of my departed
Friend, whom I infinitely esteemed when living for
the Solidity of his Thought, for the Spring, the
Warmth, and the beautiful Turn of it; for the Power,
and Variety, and Fullness of his Harmony; for the
Purity, the Perspicuity, the Energy of his Expression; and (whenever the following great Qualities
were required) for the Pomp and Solemnity, and
Majesty of his Style." As a matter of fact, nothing
is more familiar than the veneration of little Pope
for Dennis's hero. Congreve's preface to Tonson's
edition of the dramatic works in 1717 pursued a
lofty vein of eulogy, as did a passage in Garth's preface to the *Metamorphoses* the same year. Thereafter, Dryden was discussed almost exclusively as
a man with a style. John Oldmixon blamed Pope
for this turn of affairs. "Mr. Dryden's genius," he
observed in his *Essay on Criticism* (1728), "did not
appear [according to Pope] in anything more than
his Versification; and whether the critics will have
it ennobled for that versification only, is a question.
The Translator [of Homer] seems to make a good

genius and a good ear to be the same thing. Dryden
himself was more sensible of the difference between
them, and when it was in debate at Will's Coffee-
house, what character he would have with posterity,
he said, with a sullen modesty, 'I believe they will
allow me to be a good versifier.'" But the process of
ennobling Dryden for his versification only went on.
It has been seen that Dennis drew or implied a distinction between Dryden and Pope on the score of
wealth and fire of expression. This survived and
became hackneyed; men repeated it who had no
other notion of it than that it justified a noble negligence in the older poet. Dryden's name seems to
have been destined to come down jointly with
Pope's; if not to support a distinction, as in the
eighteenth century, at least to imply an identity,
as in the nineteenth. Pope himself, convinced as
he was that Dryden had wanted "the greatest art—
the art to blot," struck the note that was to rever-
berate through all the criticism of his master for a
century:

> Waller was smooth; but Dryden taught to join
> The varying verse, the full resounding line,
> The long majestic march, and energy divine.

It occurred to some to couple Dryden with Milton
rather than with Pope. Gildon did so, on the score
of harmony in versification, in his *Laws of Poetry*
(1721). Gray seemed at least to do so when in *The
Progress of Poesy* he followed praise of Milton's epic
with praise of Dryden's odes, but did not go on to
Pope:

Behold, where Dryden's less presumptuous car,
Wide o'er the fields of glory bear
Two Coursers of ethereal race,
With necks in thunder clothed, and long-resounding pace.

James Beattie, in a long footnote to his *Essay on Poetry and Music as they Affect the Mind* (1776), objected to any identification of Pope with Dryden: "Critics have often stated a comparison between Dryden and Pope, as poets of the same order, and who differed only in degree of merit. But, in my opinion, the merit of the one differs considerably in kind from that of the other;" that is to say, Dryden is more original, various, and harmonious though less correct. Dr. Johnson in the *Life of Pope* gave the palm for genius "with some hesitation" to Dryden. His answer to Boswell when Boswell quoted Voltaire's *mot* concerning Pope's "neat nags" and Dryden's "stately horses" was characteristic: "Why, Sir, the truth is, they both drive coaches and six: but Dryden's horses are either galloping or stumbling: Pope's go at a steady even trot." A passage in the *Life of Pope* again is perhaps the classical statement of the contrast: "Dryden's page is a natural field, rising into inequalities, and diversified by the varied exuberance of abundant vegetation; Pope's is a velvet lawn, shaven by the scythe, and levelled by the roller." The distinction thrived long after it ceased to be of critical value. In 1788 Joseph Weston translated a Latin poem on archery, *Philotoxi Ardenæ*, by John Morfitt, into couplets "attempted in the manner of Dryden," and wrote an enthusiastic preface to demonstrate "the Superiority

of Dryden's Versification over that of Pope and of
the Moderns." "I cannot help thinking," he confessed, "that English Rhyme was brought by that
Wonderful Man to the Acme of Perfection; and that
it has been, for many years, gradually declining from
good to indifferent—and from indifferent to bad."
He anticipated Wordsworth's attack on "Poetic
Diction," appealing in Dryden to vague, romantic
powers of speech and music. Anna Seward, defending Pope, debated with Weston at great length in
the *Gentleman's Magazine* during 1789 and 1790.
Half a dozen others were drawn into the controversy, which ended only when a neutral reader protested to the editor against so many stale irrelevan-
cies. The subject was never completely dismissed.
When Mrs. Barbauld edited Collins in 1797 she
could still speak of "Dryden, who had a musical
ear, and Pope who had none." The insistence by
amateur critics upon a comparison of the two poets
had even furnished material for burlesque. Dick
Minim had said all that needed to be said in the
sixtieth *Idler* in 1759. George Canning's critique of
"The Knave of Hearts" in the *Microcosm* for February 12, 1787, did not lack a sober pronouncement that
"Ovid had more genius but less judgment than Virgil;
Dryden more imagination but less correctness than
Pope."

In whatever relation he was kept to Pope, Dryden's position on the scale of English poets at the
end of the eighteenth century was very different
from that which he had enjoyed in 1700. During
the first half of the eighteenth century, roughly

speaking, it was customary to mention him without shame among the most famous of all poets, to set him a little lower perhaps than Shakespeare and Milton and Spenser but at least to leave him secure in their company. The "poetical scale" which Goldsmith drew up for the *Literary Magazine* in January, 1758, was standard mid-century criticism:

	Genius	Judgment	Learning	Versification
Chaucer	16	12	10	14
Spenser	18	12	14	18
Shakespeare	19	14	14	19
Jonson	16	18	17	8
Cowley	17	17	15	17
Waller	12	12	10	16
Milton	18	16	17	18
Dryden	18	16	17	18
Addison	16	18	17	17
Prior	16	16	15	17
Pope	18	18	15	19

Men like Joseph Warton changed all that. His sentimental but potent essay on Pope in 1756 placed the Elizabethans on another level from the Augustans, and refused Dryden and Pope admittance on any poetical basis to the society of Shakespeare and Spenser and Milton. Among what he called "the second class" of poets, the panegyrical, occasional, and didactic poets, he found the author of *Windsor Forest*, *The Rape of the Lock*, and *Eloisa to Abelard* first because of his perfection; but the author of *Alexander's Feast* crowded a close second by virtue of the "genius" he had shown in that "divine" poem. Dryden's ode was called on more than once to save the face of Augustan verse. "Goldsmith asserted, that there was no poetry produced in this age," wrote Boswell, referring to a conversation in 1776. "Dodsley appealed to his own *Collection*, and maintained, that though you could not find a palace like Dryden's *Ode on St. Cecilia's Day*, you had villages composed of very pretty houses. . . . *Johnson* . . . 'You may find wit and humour in verse, and yet no poetry.'" Warton's main thesis outlasted any of its qualifications. Dryden and Pope were buried by him where it seemed less and less important each year to decide which had more or any genius. The glance of the new century fell on the standard poets of England from new and dizzy altitudes. Even now, when "orders" and "classes" of poetry mean nothing, Dryden is likely to be discounted before he is read.

"He has not written one line that is pathetic, and very few that can be considered as sublime," decided Jeffreys in his review of Ford's plays for the *Edinburgh Review* in 1811. Add of Dryden that it was generally believed he had written little that was ineffably beautiful, and the central position of early nineteenth century Dryden criticism is established. Criticism of poetry at that time usually meant the invoking and imposing of categories rather than the first-hand studying of men; the preoccupation of critics was mostly with "kinds" of writing. There were dogmas then as there had been dogmas at the beginning of the last century. New conceptions of the creative function of the imagination had led

to a deep distrust of Hobbes's psychology and the
poetry of the "empirical school." Admiration of
Dryden had to be expressed in terms of opposition
to the new creeds or in terms of Pope. A few Tories
in taste fell back on the old-fashioned glories. To
the editor Scott, Dryden was "our immortal bard,"
second only to Milton and Shakespeare; "Glorious
John," even when he had said nothing, had written
imperishably noble verse; *Alexander's Feast* was
the best of English lyrics. George Ellis, writing
to Scott about the edition he had fathered, admitted
that "I ought to have considered that whatever
Dryden wrote must, for some reason or other, be
worth reading;" and he professed himself in particular a passaionate admirer of the *Fables*, "the noblest
specimen of versification . . . that is to be found in
any modern language;" *Theodore and Honoria*, he
said, should have "a place on the very top-most
shelf of English poetry." George Canning, writing
on July 26th, 1811, spoke to Scott of "the majestic
march of Dryden (to my ear the perfection of harmony)." Henry Hallam's review of the *Dryden* in
the *Edinburgh* deplored Scott's occupation with the
rubbish of the minor works, but agreed, while finding fault with the *Fables*, that at the best Dryden's
animation and variety were hardly surpassable. The
most important criticism of Dryden in this period,
however, ranged itself along the question whether
he and Pope had been poets. "It is the cant of our
day—above all, of its poetasters," said Lockhart,
"that Johnson was no poet. To be sure, they say
the same of Pope—and hint it occasionally even of

Dryden." It was more than "said" of Pope, and
it was more than "hinted" of Dryden; it was solemnly asseverated of both, one of the results being an intermittent controversy between Bowles,
Wordsworth, Keats, Southey, Coleridge, and the like
on the one hand and Byron, Campbell, Crabbe,
Rogers, Gifford, and the like on the other. The controversy started over Pope. Bowles' edition of Pope
in 1806 contained some strictures on his character
as a man and as a poet. Byron was careful to ridicule Bowles for this, among other things, in his *English Bards* of 1809. To Campbell's championship
of Pope in the preface to his *Specimens* in 1819
Bowles replied in the same year with a paper on the
Invariable Principles of Poetry. In Wordsworth's
Essay Supplementary to the Preface (1815) had appeared a few remarks derogating Dryden's treatment
of Nature. Byron broke out in the third canto of
Don Juan:

"Pedlars" and "Boats" and "Waggons!" Oh! Ye shades
  Of Pope and Dryden, are we come to this?
The "little boatman" and his Peter Bell
  Can sneer at him who drew "Achitophel"!

And in 1821 he published a *Letter . . . on the Rev.
William L. Bowles' Strictures on the Life and Writings of Pope*. A letter written from Ravenna on
March 15th, 1820, in reply to an article in *Black-
wood's* on *Don Juan*, was devoted in the second half
to a passionate defense of Pope. Byron attributed
what he found to be a decline in English poetry to
the fact that poets could no longer appreciate the

little Queen Anne master. "Dilettanti lecturers" and reviewers were following in the wake of the poetasters, and only a handful of men remained in England—Crabbe, Rogers, Gifford, Campbell, and himself—with liberal perspectives. As for himself he declared: "I have ever loved and honored Pope's poetry with my whole soul, and hope to do so till my dying day." Nothing was being produced now, he swore, to match Pope's *Essay on Man, Eloisa to Abelard, The Rape of the Lock,* and "Sporus," or Dryden's *Fables,* odes, and *Absalom.* Bowles had preferred Dryden to Pope on musical grounds. Byron himself had written in the *English Bards,* after some lines on Pope:

> Like him great Dryden poured the tide of song,
> In stream less smooth, indeed, yet doubly strong.

But in general he was inclined to call Pope a better because a more perfect poet. The tradition of Dryden's "genius" survived in one form or another throughout the discussion. Coleridge decided that "if Pope was a poet, as Lord Byron swears, then Dryden . . . was a very great poet." Hazlitt, in his essay on Dryden and Pope, was no more inclined than Coleridge to credit either with essentially poetic powers, though as he surveyed them within their class he found Pope to be a more consummate artificer; Dryden seemed largely tinsel, his odes wholly mechanical and meretricious. Yet it mortified Hazlitt, who knew that the Augustans, if they had not been great poets, had been at least great writers of some sort, to hear Wordsworth disparage Pope and

Dryden, "whom, because they have been supposed to have all the possible excellences of poetry, he will allow to have none." Wordsworth's position is well known. His letter to Scott in 1805 contained all the praise that he could honestly give, which was that Dryden possessed "a certain ardour and impetuosity of mind, with an excellent ear;" while his various prefaces sternly denied both to Dryden and to Pope the highest imaginative gifts. Henry Crabb Robinson, in his diary for January 6th, 1842, recorded a walk with Wordsworth: "Today he talked of poetry. He held Pope to be a greater poet than Dryden; but Dryden to have most talent, and the strongest understanding." Landor was moderately an admirer of the great satirist of the Exclusion Bill.

> None ever crost our mystic sea
> More richly stored with thought than he;
> Though never tender nor sublime,
> He wrestles with and conquers Time,

he wrote to Wordsworth. In the second Imaginary Conversation with Southey he confined his praise to Dryden's couplet-verse, dismissing the Pindarics as vulgar. "*Alexander's Feast* smells of gin at second-hand, with true Briton fiddlers full of native *talent* in the orchestra." Its author, he answered for Southey, must be content with credit for "a facility rather than a fidelity of expression."

If Dryden's reputation left the romantic battleground somewhat battered, it has pursued a fairly smooth course down the nineteenth century highway. Historians of English literature have been busy establishing Dryden's importance as a representative figure and giving him his due as an innovator; æstheticians have contributed their notions of the points wherein he is entitled to please; and great cosmopolitan critics have brought to him a learning and a taste ripened through contact with many other literatures. He emerges without his old glory, perhaps, but with a respectable group of virtues which seem to be his now for all time. Discussion of him has inclined to be general, and writers, often casuistically, have tended to grant him vaguely defined powers which they themselves have not always understood; yet a limited body of readers has continued to know him intimately and soundly. A steady succession of articles in the Tory periodicals, notably in the *Quarterly Review*, perhaps the mainstay of his reputation, has kept his personality reasonably fresh, while from time to time new emphasis has been laid upon the obscurer portions of his work. Robert Bell's *Life* in 1854, as well as reviews of it in *Fraser's Magazine* and elsewhere, singled out the prologues and the epilogues for applause. Tennyson, Fitzgerald, Professor Conington, and others have insisted upon the original and enduring qualities of the *Virgil*, which Wordsworth gave up trying to surpass, and which still has more vitality than any other translation. The *Juvenal* and the *Lucretius* maintain a solid place among versions of the classics, both for their strength and for their beauty. Latterly there has been a tendency to emphasize the lyrics, especially the songs, those from the plays having been reprinted in the last

two editions of the poems in a more complete form
than that in which the Warton volumes presented
them in 1811. Macaulay's brilliant but doctrinaire
essay of 1828 has made it seem necessary to most
subsequent critics to discuss the character of Dryden. While Dryden the turncoat, Dryden the
flatterer, Dryden the writer of indecent plays and
poems has been scrupulously damned by men like
Christie, numerous editors and reviewers have
stepped to his defense bringing elaborate excuses.
The better view seems latterly to be that there is
little reason to be sorrowful over the behavior of a
canny man of letters who never at any time pretended to be equipped with principles worth dying
or becoming a pauper for. As a poet his personality
has often been sketched. Lowell, whose respect for
Dryden was permanent and wholesome, and whose
essay of 1868 contains what is still, except for that
of Dr. Johnson, the most conscientious criticism of
the poet in English, found, after making all the
necessary deductions from his character and his
fame, that something indefinably large yet remained. "You feel," he said, "that the whole of
him is better than any random specimens, though
of his best, seem to prove." "There is a singular
unanimity in allowing him a certain claim to *greatness* which would be denied to men as famous and
more read,—to Pope or Swift, for example." "He
is a curious example of what we often remark of the
living, but rarely of the dead,—that they get credit
for what they might be as much as for what they
are,—and posterity has applied to him one of his

own rules of criticism, judging him by the best rather than the average of his achievement, a thing posterity is seldom wont to do." These were shrewd remarks; yet they were not followed by an account equally shrewd of Dryden's rhythmical genius and intellectual gathering-power, it being there that his largeness, indefinable or not, resides. Emerson, blandly wild, threw all of Dryden overboard in the essay on *Poetry and Imagination* which he cast into final shape in 1872. "Turnpike is one thing and blue sky another. Let the poet, of all men, stop with his inspiration. The inexorable rule in the Muses' court, either inspiration or silence, compels the bard to report only his supreme moments. . . . Much that we call poetry is but polite verse." "A little more or less skill in whistling is of no account. See those weary pentameter tales of Dryden and others." Matthew Arnold, warring against provincialism in the study of literature and bringing "touchstones" from the ends of the earth wherewith to test the poets of his own country, found, as he reported in the Introduction to Ward's *English Poets* (1880), that Dryden and Pope had been the inaugurators of an immensely important "age of prose and reason" but that they were insignificant as poets, perhaps not poets at all. In the essay on Gray he explained his position in greater detail, saying, "The difference between genuine poetry and the poetry of Dryden, Pope and all their school, is briefly this: their poetry is conceived and composed in their wits, genuine poetry is conceived and composed in the soul." This proposition sounds at least broad enough; yet in Arnold it was susceptible of and received a somewhat narrow handling. "Soul" in Arnold suggests stoicism; stoicism suggests philosophic melancholy; philosophic melancholy suggests sentiment; a poem "conceived in the soul" suggests a poem conceived in spiritual pain. Arnold's touchstones, if not sentimental, did deal in pain, sad old memories, and death, an atmosphere which Dryden could hardly expect to survive. If there were to be no touchstones ringing with malice, disdain, or merriment, Dryden could lay no claim to a soul. He had not written his verse to "console" or "sustain" a bewildered generation of *fin de siècle* scholars. He had written to please hard-headed men of the world; he had labored to satisfy critics of poetry, not critics of souls. He had written genuine poetry, but he was not a Dante. In the *Introduction* again Arnold thought he detected a truer note in a passage of Dryden's prose which, if the truth be known, is the least expressive possible of the indomitable Augustan: "What Virgil wrote in the vigour of his age, in plenty and at ease, I have undertaken to translate in my declining years; struggling with wants, oppressed with sickness, curbed in my genius, liable to be misconstrued in all I wrote." Arnold felt tenderly towards this; Swift had simply roared. Arnold was distinctly unjust to the odes. In the essay on Gray he placed the most miserable stanza of the *Killigrew* alongside of the best three lines in Pindar and observed that Pindar killed Dryden. It may be true that Pindar will kill Dryden under any circumstances; in the present instance Dryden died without even a fighting chance. Pater agreed with Arnold that Dryden's prose was more beautiful than his verse. "Dryden," he wrote in 1888 in *Style*, "with the characteristic instinct of his age, loved to emphasize the distinction between poetry and prose, the protest against their confusion coming with somewhat diminished effect from one whose poetry was so prosaic." The influence of Arnold has been very great. In an age whose infinitely flexible prose has captured the throne of the imagination and promises to hold it while the language lasts, he has taught nine readers out of ten that Dryden is a prosaic poet. He is dogmatic and wrong; but protests are irrelevant till the whole wheel of fashion turns another round.

Dryden is nothing if not a poets' poet, which Lowell denied he was. He is not for philosophers, plainly, or for laymen; he does not move the minds of the few or the hearts of the many. He has tempered not spirits but pens; Lowell notwithstanding, he is as much as Spenser a poet for poets. Not only in his own generation, or in the next, but in all that have succeeded he has stood on the shelves of writers and offered the stimulus of a style that is both musical and stout. Poets of widely varying complexions have made important use of him, never exactly reproducing him, for that is impossible even if desirable, but drawing from him the strength or the beauty they have seemed to need.

In the eighteenth century he shared with Milton and Pope the distinction, enviable or not, of inspiring the "poetic diction" which Wordsworth later

on was to receive so coldly.   Milton in blank verse
and Dryden and Pope in the heroic couplet were,
if Spenser and his stanza be for the moment disregarded, the great models of versification under Queen
Anne and the first two Georges.   On the side of the
heroic couplet Dryden exercised two varieties of influence according as he was identified with Pope or
distinguished from him.   In a certain sense he had
identified himself with Pope when he had created
him; for if Dryden had not written, it is a question
what Pope would be.   "I learned versification wholly
from Dryden's works," Pope told Spence; he has
echoed Dryden everywhere, not only cadence for
cadence but sometimes word for word and line for
line.   Zimri and Og begat Wharton and Sporus;
Mac Flecknoe begat the *Dunciad;* the *Religio Laici*
and *The Hind and the Panther* begat the *Moral
Essays;* the *Cecilia* of 1687 begat the *Cecilia* of 1708;
the *Virgil* begat the *Homer;* and the *Fables* begat the
Paraphrases from Chaucer.   Yet in another sense
Pope derived not from Dryden at all, but from the
smooth, equable tradition of Sandys and Waller.
Poets who knew this, and who set Dryden's "genius"
over against Pope's correctness, thought to capture
the secret of that "genius."   In the first place, they
remarked, Dryden, for an Augustan, was bewilder-
ing in his variety.   A passage of only eight lines
from *Tyrannic Love,* for instance, combined three
styles as far apart from one another as those of
Shakespeare's *Julius Cæsar,* Pope's *Pastorals,* and
Beattie's *Minstrel:*

Him have I seen (on Ister's banks he stood,
Where last we wintered) bind the headlong flood
In sudden ice; and, where most swift it flows,
In crystal nets the wondering fishes close.
Then, with a moment's thaw, the streams enlarge,
And from the mesh the twinkling guests discharge.
In a deep vale or near some ruined wall,
He would the ghosts of slaughtered soldiers call.

In the second place he was impetuous, and when
need was, negligent. The negligence was easy to approximate, the impetuosity not so easy. Gildon inveighed against versifiers who aped Dryden's man-
nerisms without reviving his spirit, John Hughes
and Walter Harte being conspicuous among those
who affected triplets and Alexandrines so as to become like the author of the *State of Innocence*. Harte
introduced his *Vision of Death* in 1767 with a tribute
which might have done for a contemporary Dryden
creed:

Who but thyself the mind and ear can please,
With strength and softness, energy and ease;
Various of numbers, new in every strain;
Diffused, yet terse, poetical, though plain;
Diversified midst unison of chime;
Freer than air, yet manacled with rhyme,
Thou mak'st each quarry which thou seek'st thy prize,
The reigning eagle of Parnassian skies. . . .
Thy thoughts and music change with every line;
No sameness of a prattling stream is thine. . . .
Infinite descant, sweetly wild and true.
Still shifting, still improving, and still new! . . .
To Spenser much, to Milton much is due;
But in great Dryden we preserve the two.

Dryden's essential energy went by no means unobserved. Akenside's *Epistle to Curio* of 1744 was a
more powerful poem than it might have been if its
author had never studied *Absalom and Achitophel*.
Gray told James Beattie, according to Mason, that
he had learned all he knew about versification from
the long-resounding Dryden; "Remember Dryden,"
he wrote to Beattie in 1765, "and be blind to all
his faults." "By him," concluded Dr. Johnson,
"we were taught *sapere et fari*, to think naturally
and express forcibly." More obstreperous disciples
rushed to him because they were tired of Pope and
thirsty for poetic license. Goldsmith, in the dedication of his *Traveller* in 1764, remarked without tenderness upon the "blank verse, and Pindaric Odes,
choruses, anapests and iambics, alliterative care
and happy negligence" with which poets were amus-
ing themselves though not their readers; a man like
Churchill the satirist, he intimated, was receiving
credit that scarcely was due him; "his turbulence is
said to be force, and his frenzy fire." Churchill fled
Pope for Dryden and Shakespeare. He complained
in the *Apology* that contemporary verse had degenerated into

> A happy tuneful vacancy of sense.

He wished to restore "Great Dryden" to his own,
and to cultivate

> The generous roughness of a nervous line.

He succeeded in striking up a fresh but not a lasting

tune.   Cowper reviewed his achievement in *Table Talk:*

> Churchill, himself unconscious of his powers,
> In penury consumed his idle hours,
> And, like a scattered seed at random sown,
> Was left to spring by vigour of his own. . . .
> Surly and slovenly, and bold and coarse,
> Too proud for art, and trusting in mere force,
> Spendthrift alike of money and of wit,
> Always at speed, and never drawing bit,
> He struck the lyre in such a careless mood,
> And so disdained the rules he understood,
> The laurel seemed to wait on his command,
> He snatched it rudely from the Muse's hand.

Cowper himself had not been ignorant of Dryden. The lines in the *Task*,

> There is a pleasure in poetic pains
> Which only poets know,

harked back to the *Spanish Friar:*

> There is a pleasure sure
> In being mad which none but madmen know.

And the "characters" in *Conversation* and other poems recalled Dryden as much as Pope. But now it was fairly rare that either Dryden or Pope was called upon as tutor to an English poet. Cowper, and later Crabbe, wrote for another world than either of theirs had been; Gifford's *Juvenal* only echoed, not recalled the past; the chime of Augustan verse was done, and thenceforth one who went to Dryden for aid went because he recognized an intrinsic gift, not because Dryden was the mode.

Wordsworth, inhospitable to his predecessors as he was, knew many thousand lines of Dryden and Pope by heart, and was never insensible to the effects that Dryden had gained by virtue of his "excellent ear." Tom Moore, said Leigh Hunt in the *Autobiography*, "contemplated the fine, easy-playing, muscular style of Dryden with a sort of perilous pleasure. I remember his quoting with delight a couplet of Dryden's which came with a particular grace from his lips:—

> Let honour and preferment go for gold;
> But glorious beauty is not to be sold."

Hunt himself was one of the first of the Cockney School to succumb to that "stream of sound" which Hazlitt called the *Fables*. His *Story of Rimini* derived from Dante in plot, in style from Dryden. As he explains in the *Autobiography*, "Dryden, at that time, in spite of my sense of Milton's superiority, and my early love of Spenser, was the most delightful name to me in English poetry. I had found in him more vigour, and music too, than in Pope, who had been my closest poetical acquaintance; and I could not rest till I had played on his instrument. . . My versification was far from being so vigorous as his. There were many weak lines in it. It succeeded best in catching the variety of his cadences; at least so far as they broke up the monotony of Pope." The *Story of Rimini* is liberally Alexandrined after the manner of the *Fables*, but it signally fails to achieve much or any of Dryden's strong-backed vigor. It has a Cockney limpness and pertness, but there is nothing that is significant in its metrical variety. What Hunt did not do Keats in some measure did in his *Lamia*, which according to Charles Armitage Brown he wrote "with great care after much study of Dryden's versification." In "Sleep and Poetry," in the *Poems* of 1817, he had taken pains to address a most unscholarly rebuke to Dryden and Pope:

> Why were ye not awake? But ye were dead
> To things ye knew not of,—were closely wed
> To musty laws lined out with wretched rule
> And compass vile; so that ye taught a school
> Of dolts to smooth, inlay, and clip, and fit,
> Till, like the certain wands of Jacob's wit,
> Their verses tallied.

The *Endymion* had shown not even the slightest acquaintance with the secrets of Dryden's meter. But now in *Lamia*, Keats,

> Whom Dryden's force and Spenser's fays
> Have heart and soul possessed,

as Landor wrote to Joseph Ablett, not only stiffened and brightened his verse, cleaned and sharpened his pen, improved and simplified his narrative procedure; but he indulged in all the tricks of Dryden, the Alexandrine, the triplet, the triplet-Alexandrine, the antithesis, the inversion, the stopped couplet; and he took to harmonizing his sentence-structure with his verse form.

From vale to vale, from wood to wood, he flew,
Breathing upon the flowers his passion new,
And wound with many a river to its head,
To find where this sweet nymph prepared her secret bed.

She was a gordian shape of dazzling hue,
Vermilion-spotted, golden, green, and blue;
Striped like a zebra, freckled like a pard,
Eyed like a peacock, and all crimson barred. . . .
She seemed, at once, some penanced lady elf,
Some demon's mistress, or the demon's self.

He even ventured into graceful cynicism; his heroine
was canny in her behavior towards Lycius the lover,

> So threw the goddess off, and won his heart
> More pleasantly by playing woman's part,
> With no more awe than what her beauty gave,
> That, while it smote, still guaranteed to save.

He seldom caught the accent exactly, or caught it
for long at a time, nor did his new cloak always fit
him; to be caustic was hardly his rôle. It was as if
a gardener had suddenly called for a two-handed
sword to trim stray petals from his gentlest rose.
But his ambition to become another man than himself is everywhere apparent. Not that Keats wished
to be Dryden; he only wished to extend his metrical
bounds. Only once did he help himself to an idea
of Dryden's for its own sake. The third stanza of
Annus Mirabilis,

> For them alone the Heavens had kindly heat,
> In Eastern Quarries ripening precious Dew;
> For them the Idumæan Balm did sweat,
> And in hot Ceilon spicy Forrests grew,

became the fifteenth stanza of *Isabella:*

> For them the Ceylon diver held his breath,
>   And went all naked to the hungry shark;
> For them his ears gushed blood; for them in death
>   The seal on the cold ice with piteous bark
> Lay full of darts; for them alone did seethe
>   A thousand men in troubles wide and dark;
> Half-ignorant, they turned an easy wheel
> That set sharp racks at work, to pinch and peel.

Byron's imagination seems to have been saturated with the *Fables,* particularly with *Theodore and Honoria.* Ravenna to him meant deep romantic woods and a lady pursued by hounds, as it had meant them to Gibbon before. His letters from that place were full of Dryden's story, and in the third canto of *Don Juan* he apostrophized the scene of Honoria's punishment:

> Evergreen forest! which Boccaccio's lore
> And Dryden's lay made haunted ground to me.

Later in the century poets as different from Dryden and from one another as Tennyson, Poe, and Francis Thompson drew upon him for musical effects. Tennyson studied his meters, both in the couplet-poems and in the songs, admiring, even envying, the force of both. "'What a difference,' he would add," writes Hallam Tennyson, apropos of translating Homer, "between Pope's little poisonous barbs, and Dryden's strong invective! And how much more real poetic force there is in Dryden! Look at Pope:

> He said, observant of the blue-eyed maid,
> Then in the sheath returned the shining blade,

then at Dryden:

> He said; with surly faith believed her word,
> And in the sheath, reluctant, plunged the sword."

It is difficult to believe that Poe did not have in mind the superb second stanza of the *Song for St. Cecilia's Day* (1687) [1] when he began his *Israfel* thus:

> In Heaven a spirit doth dwell
>   "Whose heart-strings are a lute";
> None sing so wildly well
> As the angel Israfel,
> And the giddy stars (so legends tell)
> Ceasing their hymns, attend the spell
>   Of his voice, all mute.

Francis Thompson, a Roman Catholic mystic, a writer of rapturous odes, a lover of strange cadences, was intoxicated with Dryden's verse, and proposed an essay upon it. His ambition as a poet was that he might endure as long as Dryden, Milton, and Keats. His poem *To My Godchild Francis M. W. M.* goes directly back to the world of Dryden and Congreve:

> The Assisian, who kept plighted faith to three,
> To Song, to Sanctitude, and Poverty,
> (In two alone of whom most singers prove
> A fatal faithfulness of during love!);

[1] See page 253.

He the sweet Sales, of whom we scarcely ken
How God he could love more, he so loved men;
The crown and crowned of Laura and Italy;
And Fletcher's fellow—from these, and not from me,
Take you your name, and take your legacy!

Or, if a right successive you declare
When worms, for ivies, intertwine my hair,
Take but this Poesy that now followeth
My clayey hest with sullen servile breath,
Made then your happy freedman by testating death.
My song I do but hold for you in trust,
I ask you but to blossom from my dust.
When you have compassed all weak I began,
Diviner poet, and ah! diviner man;
The man at feud with the perduring child
In you before song's altar nobly reconciled;
From the wise heavens I half shall smile to see
How little a world, which owned you, needed me.
If, while you keep the vigils of the night,
For your wild tears make darkness all too bright,
Some lone orb through your lonely window peeps,
As it played lover over your sweet sleeps,
Think it a golden crevice in the sky,
Which I have pierced but to behold you by!

And when, immortal mortal, droops your head,
And you, the child of deathless song, are dead,
Then, as you search with unaccustomed glance
The ranks of Paradise for my countenance,
Turn not your tread along the Uranian sod
Among the bearded counsellors of God;
For, if in Eden as on earth are we,
I sure shall keep a younger company:
Pass where beneath their rangéd gonfalons

The starry cohorts shake their shielded suns,
The dreadful mass of their enridgéd spears;
Pass where majestical the eternal peers,
The stately choice of the great Saintdom, meet—
A silvern segregation, globed complete
In sandalled shadow of the Triune feet;
Pass by where wait, young poet-wayfarer,
Your cousined clusters, emulous to share
With you the roseal lightnings burning 'mid their hair;
Pass the crystalline sea, the Lampads seven;—
Look for me in the nurseries of Heaven.

In almost all respects, this still is very far from the
world of Dryden's *Congreve*. It is only an approach
along the avenue of meter. Thompson has returned
to the poet who spiritually is as little like him as
any past poet, to learn the secret of full and level
music, of generous but sober ratiocinative procedure
through couplets, triplets, antitheses, and needful
Alexandrines. Here is godfatherly tenderness on an
unearthly scale; the tenderness and the unearthliness
are Thompson's, the scale is Dryden's. Thompson's *Heard on the Mountain* applies the license of
the triplet-Alexandrine to a basic meter of fourteeners. And his hoarse choral odes break now and then,
though rarely, into the opening strains of the hymn
to Anne Killigrew. So the story goes on. Dryden
the satirist, the journalist, the celebrant, the reasoner
in verse will continue to show the way to those who
would deal in frost and iron; Dryden the manifold
metrician will continue to reveal new melodies to
those who would deal in bronze or in gold.

Good poets long dead have a way of defying

changes in taste and of belying reasons why they should not be read. It may be urged against Dryden that he was the too unctuous spokesman of a decaying order; that, clear as he may have seemed to a smaller, more literary world, for the purposes of modern life he is hard and opaque; that he handles not images but facts, that by naming he destroys and by failing to suggest he fails to create, that he elaborates and disguises rather than foreshortens and intensifies experience; that he is more journalist than artist, more orator than seer. But even while this is urged, warning may issue from other quarters that foreshortening implies bad perspective and intensification a heat that withers as well as inspirits. If there was something fatuous about the opulence of the Augustans there is often something desperate about the simplicity of the moderns. If an aristocratic society fattens and sleeks the poets of its choice, democracy grinds many of its sons to powder. A man who composes verse too exclusively out of his faculties can hardly be judged by men who write too much with their nerves; the imagination, the umpire of art, might acknowledge neither. Dryden lives not as one who went out to rear great frames of thought and feeling, or as one who waited within himself and caught fine, fugitive details of sensation, but as one who elastically paced the limits of a dry though well-packed mind. He braces those who listen to his music; he will be found refreshing if, answering his own invitation,

When tired with following nature, you think fit,
To seek repose in the cool shades of wit.

APPENDIX

APPENDIX

The Authorship of *Mac Flecknoe*

Recent investigations [1] having overcast *Mac Flecknoe* with curious uncertainties concerning the authenticity of its first publication, the date of its composition, and the identity of its author, it becomes necessary to summarize both what is known and what can be reasonably conjectured about a poem which it has not been unusual to consider Dryden's masterpiece.

There seems to be no doubt that the edition of 1682, recognized now as the first, was a pirated one. The publisher was not Dryden's Jacob Tonson, as would be expected, but D. Green, who not only was obscure but desired to remain so, since he printed no address other than London adjacent to his name on the title page. The publication of the pamphlet could hardly have proceeded under the supervision of its author. There was no preface, strangely enough at least for Dryden, and the text was one of which an intelligent man would have been permanently ashamed; as witness line 82,

> Amidst this monument of *varnisht* minds,

or line 92,

> Humorists and Hypocrites *his pen* should produce,

[1] Babington, Percy L. Dryden not the Author of Mac Flecknoe. *Modern Language Review. January*, 1918. Thorn-Drury, G. Dryden's Mac Flecknoe. A Vindication. *Ibid.* July, 1918. Belden, H. M. The Authorship of Mac Flecknoe. *Modern Language Notes.* December, 1918.

metrically impossible, or lines 135–6,

> And from his brows damps of oblivion shed,
> Full *of* the filial dulness,

where the only conceivable point is lost, or line 167,

> But write thy best, *on th' top;* and in each line—

which means nothing.

Had the poem been brand new in 1682, as has been supposed by those who have believed it an almost *extempore* reply to Shadwell's *Medal of John Bayes*, it is difficult to see why it should have escaped so completely from the author's hands; since surely he would lose no time himself in getting it to a printer. The fate of *Mac Flecknoe* was a fate not uncommonly visited upon works for some time existent and circulating in manuscript. That *Mac Flecknoe* was such a work is far from impossible. It is possible, for instance, that it had been composed upon the occasion of Flecknoe's death (1678?), an event somewhat ambiguously referred to by Dryden in the dedication of *Limberham* in 1680. As a satire on Shadwell it would have been as timely in 1676 as it was in 1682. It alludes to no play published by Shadwell later than 1676. It makes no capital out of Shadwell's politics, which were conspicuously Whiggish after the Popish Plot and which would naturally draw Dryden's fire after *Absalom and Achitophel*, *The Medal*, and particularly *The Medal of John Bayes*. The epithet applied to Shadwell on the title page, "True-Blew-Protestant," may only have been D. Green's; it was not repeated in later editions. The occupation of the poem is wholly with personalities and literary principles; chastisement is administered not to a Whig, or even to a drunken treason-monger, as in the second part of *Absalom and Achitophel*, but simply to a fat dull poet who deals too much in "humours." Furthermore, there is incontrovertible evidence that the verses were in existence, either in manuscript or in pamphlet form, eight months before the date traditionally assigned to them on the strength of a note by Narcissus Luttrell and considerably before Shadwell's *Medal of John Bayes*. Luttrell's date was October 4, 1682. But the following passage has been cited from an attack on Shadwell in *The Loyal Protestant and Domestic Intelligence* for February 9, 1681-2: "he would send him his Recantation next morning, with a *Mac Flecknoe*, and a brace of Lobsters for his Breakfast."

That *Mac Flecknoe* was not the work of Dryden has been argued from evidences of varying worth. D. Green's attribution of the poem to "the author of Absalom and Achitophel" has been dismissed on the grounds that that gentleman, being a liar no less than a pirate, knew he could sell ten times more copies under such auspices than he could sell under any other. It cannot be shown that Dryden was particularly at outs with Shadwell during the later '70's. The two men had combined against Settle in 1674, in the *Remarks on the Empress of Morocco*, and in 1678 Dryden had furnished Shadwell a prologue to be spoken before his *True Widow*. In Tonson's *Miscellany* of 1684, a volume more or less edited by Dryden, *Mac Flecknoe* occupied first place, being followed by *Absalom and Achitophel* and *The Medal;* but it had no title page, and it was not assigned, as *The Medal* was, to "the author of Absalom and Achitophel." A legend dating from the next year has been taken as proof that Dryden was strangely unfamiliar with the general class of mock-heroic material which the satire represents. One of Spence's anecdotes relates that Dean Lockier went when a boy to Will's Coffee-House and heard Dryden claiming a complete originality for the poem. Upon the boy's interposing that Boileau's *Lutrin* and Tassoni's *Secchia*

Rapita were obvious models, Dryden, the story goes, turned and said, " 'Tis true, I had forgot them." Shadwell insinuated a doubt as to Dryden's right to the poem in 1687, in the dedication of his Tenth Juvenal: "It is hard to believe that the supposed author of *Mac Flecknoe* is the real one, because when I taxed him with it, he denyed it with all the Execrations he could think of." Tom Brown gleefully quoted this passage in the preface to his *Reasons for Mr. Bayes Changing his Religion* in 1688. Dryden did not openly claim the poem until a year after Shadwell's death (1692), when in his *Discourse of Satire* (1693) he spoke of "my own, the poems of *Absalom* and *Mac Flecknoe*." He had omitted it altogether from a list of his works which he appended to *Amphitryon* in 1690.

A more arresting piece of evidence against Dryden's authorship is a late seventeenth century manuscript volume in the Bodleian Library at Oxford (Rawlinson Poetry 123) containing most of John Oldham's works transcribed by a single hand, as if for the printer, under the title "*Poems on Several Occasions.*" Three items in this volume, *A Satyr upon Man*, *A Letter from Artemisia in the Town to Chloe in the Country*, and *Upon the Author of a Play called Sodom*, are generally believed to be the work of Rochester, "that incomparable person," according to Oldham in his *Preface* of 1681, "of whom nothing can be said, or thought, so choice and curious, which his Deserts do not surmount." They are entered without comment; but more than half of the pieces are dated and placed in this manner: "July, 1676, at Croydon;" "October 22–76, at Bedington;" "Written at Croydon Anno $167^7/_8$;" "Writ Feb 1680 at Rygate;" "March 18th, $167^7/_8$;" "Aug 5, 1677;" "Written in May 82;" "Wrote the last day of the year 1675." In the three cases where comparison is possible between these dates and those

printed under the titles of poems in Oldham's volumes of
1681 and 1683, the agreement is perfect.   On pages 232,
233, 234, 235, and 214 is found:

Anno 1678.   *Mac Fleckno*
A Satyr.

Four pages, or lines 49–150, are missing; the rest is written
smoothly, without interlineations or erasures, but hastily,
with here a word omitted and there a word varied from
the accepted text.   On no account may 1678 be taken
as the date of transcription, since it is plain that the volume as a whole was drawn up later than 1680, either by
Oldham himself during the last two years of his life or
by another person after his death.   Whether 1678 stands
for the date of composition, and whether Oldham is the
author, are questions of a more perplexing sort.   The
affirmative in each case is supported by certain coincidences that cannot be ignored.

Oldham, no less than Dryden, though perhaps in common with all his contemporaries, understood the name
Flecknoe to be synonymous with the name of bad poet;
so that the idea for the satire which, as it happens, has
immortalizd that name, might more or less easily have
occurred to him.   In his imitation of Horace's *Art of
Poetry* he opposed Flecknoe as the worst of poets to
Cowley as the best:

> Who'er will please, must please us to the height.
> He must a Cowley, or a Flecknoe be;
> For there's no second rate, in poetry.

The idea, furthermore, of giving bad poetry and Flecknoe
a mock-heroic send-off is one he is even more likely than
Dryden to have come readily by in 1678, the date, not
impossibly, of Flecknoe's death.   It will be remembered
that Dryden had forgotten by 1685, or had pretended to

forget, *Mac Flecknoe's* debt to the mock-heroic tradition in general and to Boileau's *Lutrin* in particular. Boileau was certainly no stranger to Dryden in 1678 or 1679; and it was in 1680 that he revised Soame's translation of the *Art Poétique*. But Oldham was still more significantly involved with the Frenchman. He "imitated" the eighth Satire and "translated" the fifth; and if the Bodleian Manuscript is to be believed, he translated the entire first Canto of the *Lutrin* itself, "Anno 1678." It would appear that he was trying out his mock-heroic vein that year, at first as the disciple of a foreigner and later as an independent artist with a native theme. Not only that; there are specific parallels between passages in works known to be his and passages in *Mac Flecknoe*. In his *Imitation of Horace, Book I, Satire IX*, which does not appear in the Bodleian Manuscript but which, according to the *Poems and Translations* published by him in 1683, was "written in June, 1681," occurs a line,

> St. André never moved with such a grace,

that is unmistakably akin to line 53 of *Mac Flecknoe*:

> St. André's feet ne'er kept more equal time.

A Satyr against Poetry, dated in the manuscript 1678, printed first in 1683 without remark, and reprinted as a pamphlet in 1709 in company with *Mac Flecknoe* (whether as the result of a resemblance only then observed between the two poems or on the strength of authentic evidence concerning their original relation is not known), is considerably like *Mac Flecknoe* 100–103, which runs,

> From dusty shops neglected authors come,
> Martyrs of pies and relics of the bum.
> Much *Heywood*, *Shirley*, *Ogleby* there lay,
> But loads of *Shadwell* almost choked the way,

in the following passage:

How many poems writ in ancient time,
Which thy Fore-Fathers had in great esteem. . . .
Have grown contemptible, and slighted since,
As *Pordage*, *Fleckno*, or the *British Prince* ?
Quarles, *Chapman*, *Heywood*, *Withers* had applause,
And *Wild*, and *Ogilby* in former days.
But now are damned to wrapping drugs and wares,
And curst by all their broken stationers.
And so mayst thou perchance pass up and down,
And please a while th' admiring Court, and Town,
Who after shalt in Duck-Lane shops be thrown,
To mould with *Sylvester* and *Shirley* there,
And truck for pots of ale next Sturbridge Fair.

A number of deductions can be arrived at from these parallels: (1) the coincidences are only coincidences; or (2), if a manuscript *Mac Flecknoe* was circulating in 1678, it was Dryden's, and Oldham drew upon it while writing his *Horace* and his *Satyr against Poetry*, or (3) it was Oldham's, and Dryden knew nothing of it until it was published as by him in 1682; (4) if a manuscript *Mac Flecknoe* did not exist before 1682, neither did the Bodleian text of Oldham's poems. In support of (2), it will be remembered that Oldham was borrowing from *The Rival Ladies* in 1678, [1] so that his interest in Dryden, no doubt always great, can be supposed to have been especially keen that year, even to the extent of his occupying himself with a Dryden manuscript. If (3) is true, it must also be true that Dryden, having Oldham's manuscript by him in 1684, several months after the young satirist's death, followed it scrupulously as he corrected the 1682 *Mac Flecknoe* for Tonson's 1684 *Miscellany*. Tonson's text contains 33 variants from D. Green's. The Bodleian text differs considerably from both, but of its 15 variants from either alone, only 3 are in favor of Green, while

[1] See page 187.

12 are in favor of Tonson. [1] Now it is improbable that the 1684 *Mac Flecknoe* derives from the Bodleian manuscript or from any manuscript of Oldham's. It is more probable that the Bodleian manuscript derives from the 1684 *Mac Flecknoe*, which would mean, what is more probable still, that (4) is the safest deduction—that the whole of the volume at Oxford was transcribed after Oldham's death by an admirer, perhaps a literary executor, who, having both of the editions of *Mac Flecknoe* at hand, transcribed that poem too because he liked it, as Oldham before him had liked it.

Whatever the date of *Mac Flecknoe*, and 1678 deserves consideration, Dryden's right to the poem still is and must be always, except as definite evidence to the contrary come to light, undeniable. It is not true that he ever seriously disclaimed responsibility for it. The edition of 1684 was equivalent to a full confession of authorship. The execrations with which he reassured Shadwell could have reassured only Shadwell, who seems to have been devoid of humor in personal and controversial relations. He omitted to list *Mac Flecknoe* with his other works in 1690; but so did he omit to list the *Heroic Stanzas*, *The Hind and the Panther*, and *Britannia Rediviva*. The Lockier anecdote proves that Dryden carried affairs with a high

---

[1] Another seventeenth century manuscript of *Mac Flecknoe* in the Lambeth Palace Library (vol. 711, no. 8), palpably from the hand of a copyist, contains, among many variants that are uninteresting, 6 that coincide with 6 otherwise unique readings in the Bodleian manuscript:

> line 11: And pondering which of all his sons *were* fit.
> line 12: To reign, and wage immortal *wars* with wit.
> line 29: Heywood and Shirley were but types *to* thee.
> line 178: *Or* rail at arts he did not understand.
> line 185: But so *transfuse* as oils on waters flow.
> line 196: But sure *thou art* a kilderkin of wit.

hand at Will's, and was not accustomed to interruption
or emendation by his juniors; but this has been a proverb
for two centuries. It is not difficult to believe him incapable of treating Oldham so badly as to steal from him
a poem worth five times all his others put together; "there
being nothing so base," according to his preface to the
Tempest (1670), where he was thinking of Davenant, "as
to rob the dead of his reputation." Oldham had ample
opportunity to reclaim *Mac Flecknoe* while he was yet
alive; one wonders why, if the poem were his, he failed
to include it in the volume of *Poems and Translations*
which he published in 1683. It is not known in the first
place that he had ever had an occasion for writing a satire
on Shadwell; he had had no quarrel with that indefatigable disciple of Ben Jonson. On the other hand, it is
well known of Dryden that from the beginning of his
career he was subject to irritation by Shadwell; and it is
to be supposed that the differences between the two were
personal as early as they were literary. His contempt
no doubt was intermittent, but it must have been easy
to excite; that he wrote a prologue for Shadwell early
in 1678 does not mean that *Mac Flecknoe* was impossible
for him the same year or the next. It has been remarked
that *Mac Flecknoe* was in large part an attack on Shadwell's theory and practice of "humours" in comedy. It is
significant that Dryden had for an even decade before
1678 been Shadwell's chief decrier on these points. The
Restoration battle between Wit and Humour during
those years had almost been fought by Dryden and Shadwell alone. Dryden's *Essay of Dramatic Poesy* and
Defense of the Essay (1668), his preface to *An Evening's
Love* (1671), his epilogue to the second part of the *Conquest of Granada* and his *Defense of the Epilogue* (1672)
had been answered by Shadwell's prefaces to *The Sullen*

Lovers (1668), *The Royal Shepherdess* (1669) and *The Humourists* (1671), and by the dedication of *The Virtuoso* (1676). Dryden, then, rather than Oldham or anyone else, was likely to be familiar enough with Shadwell's critical utterances to hit upon a parody, in lines 189–192 of *Mac Flecknoe,*

> This is that boasted bias of thy mind,
> By which one way to dulness 'tis inclined,
> Which makes thy writings lean on one side still,
> And in all changes, that way bends thy will,

of these four lines in the epilogue to *The Humourists:*

> A humour is the bias of the mind
> By which with violence 'tis one way inclined.
> It makes our actions lean on one side still,
> And in all changes that way bend our will.

If there are passages in Oldham's miscellaneous works that suggest an interesting affinity between their author and the author of *Mac Flecknoe*, there are passages in Dryden that are more than interesting, that in fact are convincing. There are coincidences that seem better than coincidences. No one would have been readier, for example, than Dryden, considering his close acquaintance with Davenant's *Gondibert*, to borrow from that poem the line (Canto V, stanza 36)

> And called the monument of vanished minds

for *Mac Flecknoe:*

> Amidst this monument of vanisht minds.

It has been pointed out [1] that *Mac Flecknoe* parodies a line in Cowley's *Davideis,*

> Where their vast courts the mother-waters keep,

a line that could not have been strange to Dryden in 1678,

[1] See page 27.

since he had quoted it as recently as 1677 in his *Apology for Heroic Poetry*. Nor was Flecknoe out of his mind during these years. In the dedication of *Limberham* (played 1678, printed 1680) he was writing: "You may please to take notice how natural the connection of thought is betwixt a bad poet and Flecknoe." He even was turning Flecknoe's pages and reading them, though it may have been somewhat later than this that he did so. One of the happiest images in his "character" of Doeg,

> He was too warm on picking-work to dwell,
> But fagotted his notions as they fell,
> And if they rhymed and rattled, all was well,

seems to be borrowed from Flecknoe's *Enigmatical Character* of a schoolboy: "For his learning, 'tis all capping verses, and fagoting poets' loose lines, which fall from him as disorderly as fagot-sticks, when the band is broke." The poet who made merry with Shadwell's bulk in *Mac Flecknoe* was at least very nearly related to the poet who made merry with that same bulk in the second part of *Absalom and Achitophel*. Whatever the relation, if it was not identity, the creator of Og can be said to have had *Mac Flecknoe* by heart. So had the author of *The Medal* when he sketched

> Whole droves of blockheads choking up his way

in remembrance of the line

> But loads of Shadwell almost choked the way;

so had the author of the *Vindication of the Duke of Guise* when he called Shadwell "the Northern Dedicator" in remembrance of the line

> And does thy Northern Dedications fill;

so perhaps had the author of the ode on Anne Killigrew when he wrote of

A lambent flame which played about her breast

in remembrance of the line

And lambent dulness played around his face.

In addition to all this, there is the fact that no other man living and writing in 1678 or 1680 or 1682 had the genius for *Mac Flecknoe*. Every fresh reading either of Dryden or of his contemporaries proves this fact yet more a fact. Certain Persons of Honour were clever enough to have conceived the poem and to have done a line of it, or a paragraph; but in none of them was there energy enough to carry him triumphantly through with it as Dryden came through. Oldham had carrying power and staying power, but he had not this much humor; his canto of the *Lutrin* approaches the *Satyrs upon the Jesuits* as a limit, not *The Rape of the Lock*. The verse also was well and away beyond his reach. Professor Belden has demonstrated that he never elsewhere wrote this many perfect rhymes in succession. A simple appeal to the ear will convince an experienced reader of Augustan poetry that here is meter twice happier than Oldham's happiest. The poem, in short, is almost better than Dryden himself. But that is for Dryden to explain.

INDEX

Abingdon, Countess of, 160.
Ablett, Joseph, 330.
Absalom and Achitophel, 62, 85, 98, 119, 135, 160, 170, 179–186, 190, 202–3, 206, 233, 258, 265, 304, 306, 307, 318, 327, 340–2, 349.
Absalom and Achitophel, Part II., 207–9, 340, 349.
Achitophel, character of, 197–200, 202, 307.
Addison, Joseph, 11, 13, 192, 277, 292, 309, 314.
Æschylus, 244.
Agathias, 155.
Akenside, Mark, 241, 244, 327.
Albion and Albanius, 81, 223, 234–5.
Alexander's Feast, 252, 255–9, 293–4, 302, 307, 308, 314, 315, 316, 319.
Alexandrines, 99–102.
All for Love, 50, 55, 115, 129, 182.
Alliteration, 96–97.
Amboyna, 115, 231.
Amphitryon, 114, 115, 223, 228, 342.
Amyntas, On the Death of, 162, 304.
Annus Mirabilis, 3, 12, 19, 29, 39, 40, 42–6, 105–8, 132, 140, 143, 188, 205, 233, 263, 304, 331.
Anthology, Greek, 154–5.
Antipater, 155.

Apology for Heroic Poetry and Poetic License, 52, 117, 261, 349.
Aristophanes, 164.
Aristotle, 15, 17, 19, 23, 26, 52, 59, 66, 78, 147.
Arnold, Matthew, 262, 322–4.
Art of Painting, 67.
Art of Poetry, 28, 118, 304.
Ashmole, Elias, 18.
Assignation, The, 9, 115, 295.
Astræa Redux, 16, 22, 106, 142, 188, 304.
Athenæus, 256.
Atterbury, Francis, 91–2.
Aubrey, John, 8, 184, 193, 221.
Aureng-Zebe, 38, 48, 49, 114, 132, 178, 223, 293.
Awdeley, John, 191.

Babington, Percy L., 339.
Bacon, Francis, 15, 17, 19, 33, 154.
Barbauld, Mrs., 313.
Barclay, John, 191.
Barker, G. F. R., 7n.
Baucis and Philemon, 273–5, 307.
Beattie, James, 81, 312, 325, 327.
Beaumont, Sir John, 25, 76, 90.
Beaumont and Fletcher, 157, 165, 204.
Behn, Mrs. Aphra, 166.
Belden, H. M., 339, 350.
Bell, Robert, 320.
Bellarmine, Roberto, 16.
Benlowes, Edward, 3.

Redwood Library

SELECTIONS FROM THE RULES

1. Three volumes may be taken at a time and only three on one share. Two unbound numbers of a monthly and three numbers of a weekly publication are counted as a volume.

2. Books other than 7-day and 14-day ones may be kept out 28 days. **Books cannot be renewed or transferred.**

3. Books overdue are subject to a fine of one cent a day for fourteen days, **and five cents a day for each day thereafter.**

4. Neglect to pay the fine will debar from the use of the Library.

5. No book is to be lent out of the house of the person to whom it is charged.

6. Any person who shall soil (deface) or damage or lose a book belonging to the Library shall be liable to such fine as the Directors may impose; or shall pay the value of the book or of the set, if it be a part of a set, as the Directors may elect. All scribbling or any marking or writing whatever, folding or turning down the leaves, as well as cutting or tearing any matter from a book belonging to the Library, will be considered defacement and damage.